SECRET SINS

SECRET SINS

JoAnn Ross

ST. MARTIN'S PRESS
New York

Design by Judy Dannecker

Library of Congress Cataloging-in-Publication Data

Ross, JoAnn.
    Secret sins / JoAnn Ross.
      p. cm.
    ISBN 0-312-04145-4
    I. Title.
    PS3568.0843485S4 1990   89-77822
  813'.54—dc20   CIP

First Edition
10 9 8 7 6 5 4 3 2 1

To Jay and Patrick—for all that you are, and all that you've given me. With all my love.

ACKNOWLEDGMENTS

No novel can be written without help, and I am fortunate to have been on the receiving end of an overwhelming amount of it. My heartfelt thanks to:

My agent, Maria Carvainis, who believed in this story from conception and guided me with sensitivity and insight through every draft.

Toni Lopopolo, whose astute editorial talents helped make *Secret Sins* the best it could be.

Cherry Wilkinson, Richard Willford, and Robin Lester, for their enthusiasm and support.

Karen and Thomas Grover, for being there when I needed them.

And finally, Bill Heywood, because I owe him one.

Hollywood
1981

Flashbulbs popped like gunfire the moment they entered the room. Along with all three major television networks, WBC had also sent a camera crew. The upstart network's investigative reporter, Peter Bradshaw, had broken the story, setting off the chain reaction that brought them all here today.

Jockeying for position with the network crews were jean-clad, T-shirted cameramen and -women from local television stations. Beside them stood the field reporters—the men bronze, blond, and handsome, the women tawny, blond, and beautiful. Behind these uniformly attractive golden individuals, notebooks in hand, were the print journalists, delegated, as always, to the back of the room.

Posted on either side of the doorway were two Brinks guards, their eyes alert, continually sweeping the crowded room. Only moments earlier the uniformed men had delivered a million dollars in newly minted thousand-dollar bills to

Leigh Baron. They had remained to ensure that none of those crisp green portraits of Grover Cleveland fell into the wrong hands.

Leigh was not surprised by the turnout. Viewed by many to be Hollywood's reigning royalty, she and Matthew had lived in glass houses for years. As heir to Baron Studios, she had grown up in the unrelenting glow of the spotlight, and while Matthew had a compelling background and had built himself a remarkably successful career, Leigh had the feeling he would have drawn attention to himself whatever he'd chosen to do. Put the two of them together and they were bound to make news.

She spoke first, enjoying the buzz of excitement her words caused. Excitement rippled through the crowd like a shot of adrenaline and it was obvious that the reporters were dying to dash out of the room and file the Story of the Year. But they wouldn't. Not until they'd heard from the man standing next to her.

Matthew St. James.

For much of the last decade the name had appeared on movie screens in darkened theaters all over the world: SCREENPLAY BY MATTHEW ST. JAMES. DIRECTED BY MATTHEW ST. JAMES. A MATTHEW ST. JAMES PRODUCTION. Once he had been the bane of Joshua Baron's existence. Today Matthew St. James was the ace of Baron Studios. In Hollywood vernacular, he had the world by the balls.

Her performance completed precisely as she'd rehearsed it, Leigh stepped aside to watch Matthew weave his seductive spell over his audience. In a town where blond was the norm, where men and women alike strove to achieve the image of sunny beaches and Mercedes convertibles with the tops down, Matthew St. James stood out like a blizzard in July. His thick, wavy hair was as dark as anthracite coal and thick brows jutted over eyes the color of smooth, aged whiskey. Those intriguing eyes could turn dangerously dark at a moment's notice or flame amber with unequaled passion. Leigh had experienced both in their years together.

He was a natural-born actor, she thought, not for the first time, as she watched him play his audience with an innate talent that could never be taught. Bogie had had it. Gable had had it. So did Newman and Redford. Matthew St. James had it in spades. One by one the reporters tumbled into his hands, professional detachment disintegrating like morning sea mist under a bright Malibu sun. Leigh had seen it too many times not to know exactly what was happening.

The women were all imagining what it would be like to be in bed with Matthew St. James.

The men were all imagining what it would be like to *be* Matthew St. James.

And Leigh? She was remembering.

Those early intoxicating, passionate days. The barren, in-between years of separation. The sun-filled glory days of their marriage. And then . . .

Betrayal.

Divorce.

Regret.

Her gaze drifted slowly over the rapt crowd, returning momentarily to a man standing at the front of the room, his eyes unblinkingly riveted on Matthew. The lack of a camera revealed that he wasn't a photographer. And he wasn't carrying one of those long, slender notebooks favored by reporters the world over. Nor did he have a portable recorder in the hand that was visible. His other hand, she noted with slow-building apprehension, was tucked away in the pocket of his faded denim jacket.

A moment later she saw it. The gun. Pointed directly at Matthew.

Events seemed to slow to the agonizing pace of ten frames per minute. She grabbed the bronze bust of her father, Joshua Baron, from its marble pedestal beside her and hurled it at the gunman. Then she screamed.

The sudden sound of the shot ricocheted around the room like the snap of a firecracker. The riveting explosion was immediately followed by another. Then a third.

After what seemed an eternity, the reporters began to react, shouting and shoving violently, trying to force their way to the front of the room. A blood red haze covered Leigh's eyes; someone a long distance away was calling for an ambulance.

A cold, dark mist enveloped her, and Leigh wondered if she was dying.

Instinctively she reached out for Matthew. Just as their fingers touched, Leigh surrendered to the darkness.

BOOK ONE

Los Angeles
1972

I t was a Friday afternoon in late July—dog
days—and the City of Angels was caught in
the grips of the worst heat wave in fifty years. Hot shimmering
waves rose from the asphalt freeways, radiated off the mirrored surfaces of downtown buildings, and made everyone
miserable. The unrelenting record-breaking temperatures
were a great equalizer, proving that everyone—from the privileged glitterati of Beverly Hills to the teenage hookers roaming Sunset Boulevard on their impossibly high platform
sandals—sweat.

Those who could escape work early streamed down to the
beaches like lemmings. On Zuma Beach, golden girls in
minuscule crocheted bikinis played volleyball with boys
whose classic physiques resembled statues of young Greek
gods. At Venice's famed Muscle Beach, bodybuilders worked
to surpass perfection, while nearby, thousands of tanned,
stunningly fit, half-naked people were stretched out on

gleaming yellow acres of sand like prime meat sizzling on a gigantic grill.

At Malibu's Surfriders State Beach, the surfer was undisputed king. Young men, along with those few women daring enough to invade what had always been a male-dominated realm, sported sun-bleached hair and swaggering attitudes. They welded their bodies to floatable Fiberglas and waited for the perfect wave.

While the surfers bobbed on the sun-silvered swells, beach bunnies rubbed Coppertone into one another's already bronzed backs, preened, and planned their weekend parties. Don McLean's "American Pie" and cuts from the Rolling Stones' *Hot Rocks* album blared defiantly from portable radios.

To these archetypes of California's sun-filled myths, the beach was not only home. It was Endless Summer personified.

Matthew St. James had been out on the water since noon. He'd come to the beach today to exorcise a deep, familiar feeling that had seethed inside him for as long as he could remember—a low, rumbling virulence, like a volcano on the brink of erupting. In his younger days, this anger had resulted in frequent fistfights; wiser now at twenty-eight, he chose to purge the demon with demanding and often dangerous physical activity. Challenging the vast power of the sea fit this criterion perfectly.

After five hours his arms and legs ached, his body was covered with sea salt, and he had a small cut over his left eye where he'd been hit by his board after being caught by a riptide that had engulfed him in tons of churning water and sand. Matthew hadn't been afraid; he had survived two tours of duty in Vietnam; he felt strangely invincible. Once he'd surfaced, he'd retrieved his board and rode the very next wave all the way to shore.

Now, when more and more surfers had paddled out to join him on the turquoise swells, Matthew decided to call it a day. He'd never identified with these purely recreational surfers. Besides, he had to work this evening, and it wouldn't do to show up in Beverly Hills with sand in his shorts.

He waded toward shore with a lazy, hip-swaying stride. Unlike the baggy Hawaiian jams favored by most surfers,

Matthew was wearing a pair of black Speedos that left little to the imagination, even as they made girls yearn for more.

Nubile young nymphets, looking like Southern California travel posters, thrust out their oiled breasts, extended long, gleaming legs, licked Vaseline-coated lips. Those who had managed to learn his name (which wasn't easy, the word was out that this guy was definitely a loner) called out to him, receiving only a vague wave in return. Matthew St. James was not into beach bunnies.

"Damn, dude, but you are fuckin' A," a muscular young man wearing blue swim trunks and a faded gray Sex Wax T-shirt exclaimed. Matthew dropped his board and sank down onto the hot sand. "Where'd you learn to ride a wave like that?"

" 'Nam." He took the beer Jeff Martin offered and, tilting his dark head back, poured it down his throat.

"Almost makes me wish I'd gone to war."

"No, you don't. It's a rotten war; you're lucky to have gotten out of it." A high draft number, along with three juvenile marijuana busts, had successfully kept Jeff from obligatory military service.

"I suppose so," Jeff said, thinking fondly of all those Thai sticks. "Still, any country whose major industry is drugs can't be all that bad."

Leaning back on his elbows, he watched a blonde a few feet away roll over onto her back. When her unfastened bikini top fell away, he got a glimpse of a pair of bouncy tits he rated as high 8s on his personal scale of 1 to 10.

"Contrary to popular belief, Vietnam isn't all surfing, drugs, and bar girls." Matthew crushed the empty Coors can in his hand, tossed it into a nearby green barrel with a high, looping toss, and immediately reached into the cooler for another one.

If it hadn't been for the Marines, promising to pay his college tuition when—and if—he returned from Vietnam, he sure as hell wouldn't have volunteered. Not that he could have kept from going. Matthew's own less than pristine juvenile record had included fights, truancy, and running away with almost monotonous regularity. Nothing to make the military turn him away. And he certainly hadn't been one of those fortunate rich kids with powerful fathers who knew whose palms to grease, what strings to pull.

Matthew St. James had never known his father. Or his mother. In true Hollywood melodrama, he'd been left in a cardboard box on the steps of St. James's Catholic Church when he was three months old. Pinned to his blue receiving blanket was a note that read:

> *I can no longer take care of my son. Please find him a home with people who will love him. Thank you and God bless you. P.S. His name is Matthew.*

Since no last name was given, social workers named the infant Matthew St. James and placed him in the Sacred Heart Boys' Home where, unadoptable without his mother's signature on a multitude of official forms, he lived for the next seven years.

Innately unable or unwilling to accept life without questioning the status quo, Matthew came to dread Saturdays, when he would enter the dark, velvet-draped confessional and recite his childish sins to a rigid, moralistic priest who would sentence him to a long afternoon of penance. While the other boys would be outside enjoying the California sunshine, Matthew would be on his knees in the chapel, reciting a litany of Hail Marys and Our Fathers.

The single bright spot in his life was Sister Jude, a young nun who had taken a special interest in Matthew from his first day at Sacred Heart. She rocked him to sleep, dried his tears, smuggled in Fig Newtons from the kitchen for secret, late-night snacks. It was Sister Jude who taught him to read, to pluck out a few simple chords on the guitar, and to play baseball, her heavy black skirts flying wildly around her ankles as she ran the bases.

Most important, it was Sister Jude who taught Matthew about the power of love. Every night, when she bent down, brushed his dark hair off his forehead, and kissed him tenderly, he inhaled the crisp, clean scent of Ivory soap and felt his heart expand in his chest. To Matthew, Sister Jude was Love itself.

Unfortunately he learned at a very early age that love was fleeting. When a fire gutted the interior of the red brick orphanage shortly after Matthew's seventh birthday, the State of California decreed that the boys of Sacred Heart would be better off residing in "normal family settings."

That decision led to Matthew's placement in the revolving door of the California foster care system, and he was shuffled from home to home, school to school. During the 1950s, when television defined the nuclear American family, Matthew was an obvious outsider. He quickly became a target of the other kids and it was Jimmy Collins, a porky fourth-grade bully with mean, squinty eyes, who first called him a bastard. The taunt, immediately picked up by Collins's loyal admirers, followed Matthew for years, fueling his smoldering inner anger.

In Beverly Hills, Joshua Baron's French Regency mansion was hidden behind high stone walls. In the center of the wall were a pair of heavy iron gates, ten feet tall, with spikes at the top. In the center of each gate was an elaborate filigreed crown positioned above curlicued letters that spelled out *Baron.* Black-and-white signs posted on either side of the electronically controlled gates warned that intruders would encounter killer guard dogs and an armed response. The signs, de rigueur in this neighborhood, were Beverly Hills' answer to the welcome mat.

Behind the gates Japanese gardeners clipped away at a lush emerald lawn that could have doubled as a putting green. Workers, clad in blue coveralls with orange lettering on the back, were erecting an enormous yellow-and-white-striped tent over the garden while the pool man skimmed rose petals from the shimmering blue surface of the water.

Inside the mansion Leigh Baron calmly faced down a hysterical florist. "David, you have to get a hold on yourself. This is simply not the catastrophe you're making it out to be."

David Thomas dragged his sensitive, manicured fingers through his thinning hair. His heart was pounding a million miles an hour—Christ, what he wouldn't give for a Valium right now—and he could envision his entire career going right down the toilet.

"What an optimist you are, Leigh darling," he said, gesturing toward a table where two dozen matching Baccarat vases sat empty. Empty! "Perhaps you didn't hear me, dreamheart. The refrigeration on the truck broke down; all my lovely Sterling Silver roses have died! They're gone. Kaput. Finished!"

He slumped into a spindly gilt chair. "Just like me. Finished. What am I going to do? My reputation will be absolutely destroyed. I'll have to move to Burbank. Or, God forbid, Encino!"

Leigh cast a glance at her watch; there wasn't time for David's theatrics. Joshua Baron insisted on perfection and Leigh had always done her best not to fail him.

She had been serving as her father's hostess for the elaborate parties the head of Baron Studios liked to throw since her sixteenth birthday, only days after her mother's death. Since her parents' marriage had been merely one of economic and social convenience, the untimely crash of the Mercedes sports car that took Signe Baron's life on the winding road to their Malibu Colony beach house hadn't been reason enough to call off a party months in the making, Joshua had argued.

However, the lack of a proper hostess had been annoying—until he gave Leigh another long look. Fortunately, his firstborn daughter possessed an air of poise not acquired by many individuals in a lifetime. Drafted into service, Leigh filled the role so well that nine years later she continued to add the perfect woman's touch Joshua considered vital to his social occasions.

"David." Leigh put her hand on the sleeve of the distraught florist's mauve linen jacket. "This isn't the end of the world."

He looked up at her with bleak, sorrowful eyes. "Leigh, dearheart, have you ever *seen* Encino? Restaurants there actually put plastic flowers on the tables." He shuddered dramatically at the horrible thought.

Leigh thought fondly of her favorite Italian restaurant with its cozy decor: a mural of the Coliseum, candles in Chianti bottles, and artificial grape leaves twined around white trellises. "You're not going to end up in Encino, David dear. You're entirely too important. Why, none of us would know what to do without you."

"Really?"

"Really. Now, about this little setback—"

"Setback? How can you call nearly three hundred dead roses a setback?"

"It might be a problem for someone else," she admitted. "Someone without your special talents. But I know you can do it. You'll simply have to replace the roses with something else."

"Replace twenty-four dozen roses? In the next two hours? With what?" He wasn't entirely convinced, but Leigh thought she could hear the wheels beginning to turn in his blond head.

"We still have the caspia," she coaxed prettily. "And the baby's breath. Surely that's a start. What else can we round up?"

David rubbed his bearded chin as he seemed to be considering her question. "I could probably locate some lily of the valley."

"I love lily of the valley."

"And wild daisies are plentiful this time of year."

"My very favorite."

"If I get on the phone right away, I suppose I could track down a few dozen tiger lilies."

"Perfect; the arrangements will look like spring."

"They should be carefree, even whimsical." His eyes brightened with a creative light. "Like a fresh April breeze, ideal for these stultifying days. Why, by tomorrow morning every florist in town will be dying to copy the look."

Leigh knew her problems were over when he kissed her warmly on both cheeks. "Dreamheart, you are an absolute genius!"

"Not me." Leigh's smile was echoed in her calm gray eyes. "You're the genius, David."

"I know," he bubbled, scurrying off to make his calls.

Another catastrophe averted. Leigh was just congratulating herself when a strident clash of pots suddenly shattered the momentary calm, followed by shouting and a string of heated curses strong enough to turn the refrigerated air blue. Stifling a sigh, she headed in the direction of the kitchen.

"Earth to Matt. Hey, man," Jeff complained, waving his hand in front of Matthew's face, "what planet are you on, anyway?"

Matthew refocused his thoughts on the present. "Sorry. I was thinking about something."

"From the look on your face, it must've been a bummer."

He shrugged. Matthew had never shared his past with anyone, and he wasn't about to begin with this beach bum–aspiring actor. And full-time hustler. If there was a buck to be made anywhere in town, Jeff would probably try to horn in on the deal. Matthew had known guys like him in Vietnam; most of them had returned to the States with a bundle made on the black market and a profitable East Asian drug connection.

"Hey, if you don't wanna talk about it, that's cool. I just wanted to let you know that I wouldn't be riding with you tonight. Nothin' against your wheels, dude, but I'm arriving at that party in style." He grinned. "Wait till you see how good yours truly looks in a stretch limo. Just like Redford. Hell, better."

They'd been hired to tend bar at a party in Beverly Hills. The money wasn't bad, but neither was it anything to get excited about. "What did you do, work out a commission deal for the liquor you pour?"

"I guess I forgot to tell you, I'm not working the bar to-night. I hooked on to another job. One that pays a helluva lot better than mixing martinis for a bunch of Hollywood pho-nies."

"Doing what? Pushing dope?"

"Nah, you know I'm not into that scene anymore," Jeff lied unconvincingly. "I'm working for an escort service."

Stud service was more like it. Matthew had admittedly been down and out in his day. Being male and human and not looking for any long-term involvements, he'd even suc-cumbed to temptation and gone to bed with some of the tanned, eager, and oh-so-lonely Beverly Hills wives who hired him to work their parties. But he'd never considered hustling lonely old ladies for a buck.

"For chrissakes, what're you doing that for?"

"Lighten up, willya? The way I figure it, I'm gonna be screwing anyway, so I might as well get paid. Jesus, Matt, get with it. Half the guys in my acting class work for Patsy."

Matthew took another long pull on his beer. He was getting tired of hearing how out of it he was. Perhaps if Jeff had spent some time in the jungle, he'd be out of it too. "So who's Patsy?"

"Patsy Judd. She works out of a place on Wilshire. Nice thing about Patsy is that she only deals in first-class clientele. You get to go to all the groovy parties and the tips are a helluva lot better than what you'd make in a month of pouring booze." Jeff gave Matthew's hard, bronze body a brief, professional appraisal. "Shit, the chicks all creamed their bikini bottoms when you came strolling out of the surf. You could really clean up working for Patsy. How about I introduce you and—"

"I think I'll pass. But thanks for the offer." Matthew stood up and brushed the sand off his legs. "I'd better get moving. I still have to get today's scene written before the party."

"Hey, man, summer's supposed to be time for the three Ss—Surfin', Sunnin', and Screwin'," Jeff said. "And you know as well as I do that the Writers Guild is practically a closed shop. Those hotshots running the show aren't about to share any real power with an outsider. So how come you keep working so hard?"

Matthew tossed the second empty can into the barrel and picked up his white Fiberglas board. "I'm in a hurry."

Tina Marshall was in a hurry.

She had spent the entire day cruising the Golden Triangle—Bel Air, Beverly Hills, Brentwood—with an absolute gorgon of a woman who wouldn't know a decent house if it bit her on her surgically corrected nose. The air conditioner in the Rolls was excellent, keeping the interior of the car at an optimum seventy-four degrees. But since you couldn't sell a house from inside a Rolls-Royce, Tina was forced to brave the blistering heat while she listened to a litany of complaints.

The silent movie star's estate in Bel Air—a steal at two million—was too old. And it lacked a tennis court. Privately, Tina didn't believe the obese woman physically capable of dragging herself around a court without inviting a massive heart attack, but she wisely kept her thoughts to herself as they trudged back to the car. The exquisite, two-story English manor, surrounded by nearly three acres of parklike grounds in Beverly Hills, was too small; the Spanish-style hacienda in Brentwood too far from the Polo Lounge.

For five hours, including the obligatory lunch at La Scala during which time the woman whined nonstop about the lack of movie stars in attendance, Tina had been forced to inhale clouds of Youth Dew, listen to disparaging remarks about California from the native Texan whose husband had recently purchased a number of California oil wells, and try to control the impulse to wring the woman's fat neck.

They'd finally given up for the day, agreeing to meet again in the morning. Now Tina had exactly thirty minutes to shower, do something with her wilted hair, put on her makeup, dress, and make it to Joshua Baron's party before all the good gossip had been exchanged.

Could she do it?

You bet.

Tina Marshall was an expert at overcoming seemingly unbeatable odds.

Matthew balanced the case of Tattinger Rose champagne on his shoulder and cursed under his breath as he looked around for the Mexican woman who'd opened the kitchen door only a moment earlier. After reluctantly allowing him entrance to the house, she'd disappeared, leaving him without any idea where Joshua Baron wanted the bar set up.

He was just about to start shouting—not that anyone could hear him over the cacophonous sound of the rock band warming up nearby—when a young woman entered the kitchen with long, purposeful strides. Her tailored silk business suit was unrelieved by any jewelry, her blond hair twisted into a practical knot at the back of her neck, and an oversize pair of tortoiseshell-frame glasses rested on the slender bridge of her nose. From the notebook she was holding in her hand, Matthew took her to be one of Joshua Baron's legion of secretaries.

"It's about time someone showed up," he said. "You wouldn't happen to know where Baron wants the bar set up, would you?"

Leigh's swift, judicious inventory was as much force of professional habit as personal interest. His face was dark and lean, with angular planes and shadows; jet black hair flowed to the top of his collar. He was astonishingly handsome, but she had grown up on the back lot of Baron Studios, where handsome men were the rule rather than the exception, and Leigh had long been immune to masculine good looks.

She glanced past him. "There were supposed to be two bartenders."

"There will be. The other guy ditched at the last minute. Jesse told me to tell Mr. Baron that he's looking for a replacement and will send someone over as soon as possible. Meanwhile, I'm it."

Leigh hoped that Jesse Martinez, owner of Martinez Temporary Personnel, located a second bartender before her father arrived home from Baron Studios. "I suppose we'd better put you out by the pool," she decided, turning to show him the way. "When the second bartender arrives, we'll put him in the music room."

Matthew followed her through a series of rooms that possessed all the ambiance of a baronial manor. Gilt-framed paintings hung on silk-draped walls; satin-upholstered French period furniture rested on Sarouk carpets. "I sure hope Baron's paying you a bundle, sweetheart. Because you're obviously worth every penny."

"I'll keep that in mind the next time I ask for a raise," she murmured.

"You do that." Matthew nodded his satisfaction. "It's important to realize your worth."

Curious at his quietly deliberate tone, Leigh glanced back over her shoulder. "Spoken like a man who knows his own."

His compelling amber eyes met hers. "I do."

Marissa Baron hummed along with the rock music blasting from her bedroom stereo. She was intent on scrutinizing her reflection in the dressing table mirror. The mirror was surrounded by round white bulbs that made Marissa feel like a movie star. Determined to look like one as well, she had been diligently working with the colorful pots, sable brushes, and gold tubes for the past hour.

"Lookin' good," she murmured with an admiring smile, smudging a wide swath of kohl eyeliner with her little finger.

Her fingernails, painted a vivid, daring scarlet, had been bitten to the quick. Taking a drag from the joint she'd left burning in a Waterford ring holder, Marissa drew the hot, acrid smoke deep into her lungs, holding it there while she stood back and examined her handiwork.

Above the ebony liner her lids glittered with metallic gold shadow; she'd applied two pairs of false eyelashes, one above, the other below. Her cheekbones, which she'd always considered too round—what she wouldn't give for Leigh's perfectly chiseled bones—were expertly highlighted with varicolored shading pencils and gleamed with a frosted amber blush. Her lips glistened with a rosy gloss. The face smiling back at her, surrounded by shaggy copper hair, was admittedly striking, but this was Los Angeles, movie capital of the world, where equally striking faces were a dime a dozen. What was unusual about this one was that it belonged to a girl not yet out of her teens.

Her makeup finally completed to her satisfaction, Marissa took the dress out of its hiding place in the back of the closet. She'd just tugged the sparkling gold lamé over her hips when there was a knock on her bedroom door.

"Marissa? Are you in there?"

"Just a sec." Marissa ground out the joint, tossed the ring holder into a dressing table drawer, and sprayed the air with perfume in an attempt to hide the sweetly scented smoke. A dense cloud of Opium wafted over the room when she opened the door.

"Lemon Cokes," Leigh said, holding up twin glasses filled with dark liquid over ice. "Just like the old days."

Leigh took in her younger sister's outré makeup and skin-tight dress and wondered why it was that Marissa seemed unable to believe that she was a naturally beautiful girl. The gold lamé hugged Marissa's ample breasts, girdled her hips, strained against her thighs. Leigh had to stop herself from suggesting that her sister dispense with at least one pair of false eyelashes.

Lemon Cokes. Marissa couldn't believe it. "Whatever happened to champagne?"

"You know Daddy would ban me from this house if I encouraged you to drink. Especially after the accident."

"So I dented the fender of his precious Porsche," she said with a defiant toss of her tawny head. "It was only a teensy-weensy dent. There wasn't any reason for him to behave as if I'd totaled it."

Crossing the room, she twisted the volume dial on the stereo, defiantly flooding the room with Neil Young's "Heart of Gold." Marissa identified with the rock superstar because he wrote about the frustrations of not being able to achieve what you want—a feeling she knew well.

All her life Marissa had lived in Leigh's luminous shadow, waiting for a single word, a touch, a smile from her father. After seventeen years she was still waiting, while her older sister had not only been elevated to Queen of the Manor, but was reputed to be Baron Studios' Wonder Woman as well. The jealousy eating away at Marissa's heart had become a habit. A type of bondage that got her through the lonely days.

"He wasn't upset about the car, Mar," Leigh said, not quite truthfully. At the time Joshua had certainly appeared more concerned about the indentation in the gleaming black paint than Marissa, who had required two stitches over her right eyebrow to close the wound made when her forehead hit the steering wheel. She'd been too stubborn to buckle her seat belt.

Leigh knew that Marissa's psychologist—the third one this year—had warned Joshua that his younger daughter's accident may have been an attempted suicide. Or at the very least a dramatic cry for help.

"Perhaps he's right," Leigh had answered carefully, when her father had informed her of the psychologist's opinion.

"Bull," Joshua had countered. "Marissa's only problem is that she's spoiled rotten. She just needs a firm hand." He scowled as he held out his glass for a refill. Leigh immediately obliged, filling the glass with Scotch—a Glenfiddich single malt—from a nearby Baccarat decanter. "The girl's incorrigible; I'm tempted to wash my hands of her."

"That would be a terrible mistake. You know Marissa's incapable of taking care of herself."

"If she wants to remain in this house, she can damn well straighten up and obey the rules." Joshua frowned into his glass. "Otherwise, she's out of here. The choice is hers."

That conversation had been two weeks ago and, as far as Leigh could tell, her younger sister had been behaving herself. For the time being. The trouble with Marissa was that she was like a lit fuse on a keg of dynamite. The question was not *if* she was going to explode, but *when*. Although Leigh yearned for a home of her own, she dutifully remained under her father's roof in an ongoing attempt to keep Marissa and Joshua from one another's throats.

"He really was concerned about you," she said now.

"Sure. Tell me another fairy tale, why don't you?" Marissa turned back toward the dressing table mirror, busying herself unnecessarily with sable brush and powder.

The flippant words were spoken with bravado, but Leigh could hear the pain behind them. The two sisters' images, reflected in the pane of silver-backed glass, were a study in contrast. Leigh was tall and willowy, her Nordic coloring—light gray eyes, porcelain complexion, and sleek, pale hair inherited from her mother—bringing to mind jagged mountain peaks cloaked in ripples of sequined snow, iridescent glaciers, and ice blue winter light.

If Leigh was ice, Marissa was fire. Her thick copper hair blazed like wildfire, her skin gleamed a deep, tawny gold, and her bright green eyes glittered with emotions that continuously teetered on the brink of control. Her body was lush, voluptuous, inviting erotic fantasies from the most sober-minded of men.

"Honey, driving after you'd been drinking was a foolish, dangerous thing to do," Leigh said.

"So I shared a couple of six-packs with the pool guy. Big fucking deal."

"You could have been hurt. Even killed."

"And give the old man the pleasure of having me out of his life for good?" Marissa's petulant expression turned speculative as she gnawed on a ragged fingernail and observed her sister with renewed interest. "Speaking of our beloved pater, have you had a chance to ask him again about my screen test?"

Marissa's desire to become an actress was no secret. After having been steadfastly refused work at the family studios, she'd tried to finagle a screen test with the competition. Unfortunately, the word was out that the head of Baron Studios did not want his daughter working in films and, everywhere she went, Marissa found doors closed. Ever since graduating from Beverly Hills High School two months ago, she had adopted a more circuitous route, asking her sister to intercede for her. Leigh, as always, had agreed to help.

"Not this week," Leigh said. Marissa's answering oath was short and rude. "But he's been in Las Vegas," Leigh added quickly. "I thought we'd have a better chance if I waited and asked him again in person."

"The bastard will just say no, like he always does."

"You don't know that for certain." Leigh wished that her words held more conviction; in truth, she was afraid that Joshua would reject her renewed pleas on behalf of her sister. Something she could not—would not—allow to happen. Because she had her own reasons for wanting her father to test Marissa.

"That's my big sister, always the optimist. But I suppose it's not so surprising, since you've had our dear daddy wrapped around your little finger all your life." Marissa took a long swallow of the iced cola drink, then grimaced. "This stuff sucks; I'm going downstairs for some champagne."

"You used to like lemon Cokes."

"I used to be a kid."

Despite the way the conversation had turned yet again to the discomforting subject of her favored status in the family, Leigh couldn't resist a slight smile. "Seventeen is so old?"

Marissa's gleaming lips curved in a caustic smile. "Old enough."

Her sister's words, carelessly tossed back over her shoulder, stirred a long forgotten memory inside Leigh's head.

"She's damn well old enough to be here."

Joshua Baron's eyes had flashed with silent warning as they circled the room, daring any other foolhardy studio department head to complain about his nine-year-old daughter's presence. Although Leigh had practically been weaned on the movie business, accompanying her father to the studio since her third birthday, this was the first time Joshua had allowed her to sit in on an executive meeting. She'd been so excited when they left Beverly Hills this morning; never had she expected to be met by such a group of unsmiling, stern faces.

Now, as she sank down into the too large leather chair her father held out for her—significantly at his right hand—Leigh's legs were shaking.

Across the vast expanse of the polished ebony conference table, the dour man who had initially objected to Leigh's presence, Richard Steiner, head of distribution and marketing operations, leaned back in his chair, lit a cigar, and scowled.

Unreasonably nervous, Leigh crossed her legs, squeezing off a sudden, insistent need to go to the bathroom. Her fingers brushed at nonexistent wrinkles on the daisy-sprigged cotton skirt of her favorite Kate Greenaway dress. Her hair, tied back with a navy ribbon, cascaded down her back, Alice-in-Wonderland–style. Her feet, clad in white anklets with lace trim and gleaming black patent-leather Mary Janes, did not reach the floor, and it took a major effort to keep them from swinging back and forth.

Surprised by the vivid detail of this sixteen-year-old memory, Leigh wandered over to the French windows and stared out over the formal gardens. But she was not seeing the elaborate party preparations taking place on the grounds of the vast estate; instead her view turned inward, her attention riveted on the scene playing in her head.

The business meeting had been acrimonious, even by Baron Studios' trenchant standards, the department heads vocally divided upon discovering that their upcoming musical, *The Playboy Prince*, had been penned under a pseudonym to hide the fact that the author of the screenplay was actually a writer who'd been blacklisted after refusing to name his "pinko" friends before HUAC—the House Un-American Activities Committee.

"Why the hell didn't anyone catch this?" Joshua growled. "How come nobody noticed that this Robert Ransom guy was actually Richard Reinhart?"

"Ransom was always kind of a phantom," Ira Katzenbaum, in charge of production, explained. "The script came through Corbett Marshall over at William Morris. Marshall's always been your pal. Who'd suspect him of sneaking a Red past the studio gate?"

"You know, now that you mention it, that guy never has

been much of a flag waver," Steiner pointed out. "If he's not careful, he's going to end up in the Bible." He held up a dog-eared copy of *Red Channels*, that infamous, mimeographed pulp manual of blacklisted artists. Leigh knew that the list, published by former FBI agents and conservative businessmen who'd organized into a group calling itself AWARE, was updated weekly, sometimes even daily. Only last week she'd gone downtown to buy a birthday present for her mother and had had to push her way past the crowd at the newsstand at Hollywood and Vine, lined up for the latest edition. "I say we put the damn thing on the shelf and try to slip it into a few backwater theaters sometime in February or March."

"You got some kind of death wish?" Katzenbaum argued. "Sneaking it out like that'd kill it for sure."

"This movie's got Oscar potential," Norman Levy countered. "If it wins and Hedda Hopper gets wind of who wrote it, we might as well shut down the studio." Levy's complaint showed him to be firmly in Steiner's camp. "Hell, Reinhart wouldn't be the first commie to have his career torpedoed by that broad. Why let him take the studio down with him?"

"Fuck Hopper, McCarthy, and the horse they rode in on," Katzenbaum spat out with unaccustomed anger. He glanced over at Leigh. "Whoops! Sorry for the bad language, darling."

Leigh nodded, understanding that one of the reasons the men hadn't wanted her at their meeting was the feeling that they wouldn't be able to curse with her in the room. As if she hadn't heard far worse during her father's frequent tirades.

The argument continued. As the hours wore on, Leigh never once wiggled in her chair or fidgeted. Instead, she sat upright, her hands folded in her lap, watching the proceedings with fascination.

She knew about the blacklist, of course. She'd watched in shock when the newsreels had shown the Hollywood Ten being taken off to prison for refusing to say whether or not they were communists and refusing to name others. She knew those people; they'd been guests at her parents' home, they'd brought her birthday presents, and every time Richard Reinhart visited, he brought along a new magic trick to show her.

Only last month, he'd made a silver dollar disappear behind her ear. Then he made it come back and gave it to her for a kiss. If they could go to jail, who was safe?

Somehow, when no one was looking, terror had become a Hollywood watchword. Even now, fear welled up in Leigh's young heart at the idea that Senator McCarthy might send her father to jail. A bleak, dangerous jail, the composite of every prison movie she'd ever seen.

When it looked as if they'd reached an impasse, Steiner, frustrated by his inability to sway the opposition, suddenly turned to Leigh. "So what do you think?" he growled around the stump of his black cigar.

Surprised to have her presence suddenly acknowledged, Leigh blinked owlishly. "Me?"

"If you're old enough to be here, you're old enough to have an opinion." He glanced at the others, the first humor he'd revealed thus far flashing in his eyes.

"Leigh is merely here as an observer," Joshua broke in.

"Hell, Josh," Steiner argued, "if the kid's actually gonna run this place someday, you may as well let her get her feet wet."

Joshua gave her a long look. "Okay, princess," he decided. "Why don't you share with these gentlemen what you told me on the drive into the studio this morning?"

It was one thing to talk business with her father, alone in the car, another thing entirely to voice her opinion to this group of grownups who were eyeing her with a mixture of good-natured condescension and out-and-out scorn. She rubbed her palms on her crisp skirt, wondering how ice-cold skin could be so sweaty.

"*The Playboy Prince* is a wonderful film," she began falteringly, glancing toward her father for confirmation. Joshua nodded his encouragement. "It's got everything audiences love—a marvelous score, a romantic setting, adventure, romance . . ."

"You tell 'em, darling," Katzenbaum said in a big, booming voice that revealed his Brooklyn roots. He grinned at Leigh and winked broadly.

At the outward show of support, Leigh blushed. "I think it would be a mistake to bury it."

"You got something against your old man, little girl?" Steiner asked. "You want to see him end up in the slammer?"

The horrid man was talking like a character from a James Cagney movie. Leigh hated him. "Of course not," she said with a coolness that the others would later learn to recognize as controlled anger.

"Well, you sure as hell could've fooled me." Steiner shook his bald head with ill-concealed disdain. "Why don't we just agree to dump the thing in a few small-town theaters in February and see how much we can recoup?"

"Wait just a minute." Josh Miller, in charge of foreign acquisitions, had remained silent during the heated meeting. "Why don't we let the little girl explain her reasoning?" His blue eyes were kind as they met hers.

Leigh took a deep breath. Giant butterflies were flapping their wings inside her stomach and her legs were shaking so badly that she knew she'd never be able to stand. She pressed her hands tightly together beneath the tabletop and reminded herself that her father had honestly seemed to like her ideas this morning.

"Baron Studios has made a lot of money making films about the good guys against the bad guys." She echoed the words she'd heard her father say time and again with a high, clear voice that only trembled slightly. "In all our movies the good guy always wins and when he does, all the people cheer," Leigh said. She was beginning to pick up steam. "I've seen it happen lots of time. Just last week, even, at Grauman's. And since Senator McCarthy is meaner than any villain in any of our movies, maybe if we stand up to him, people will decide that Baron Studios is one of the good guys." She glanced tentatively around the table. The sight of heads nodding gave her a much needed burst of confidence.

There was a long moment of thoughtful silence. "You know," Norman Levy murmured, "that's not an entirely off-the-wall idea."

"Whose side are you on, anyway?" Steiner spat out, irritated by one of his supporters suddenly shifting allegiance.

"The studio's side," Levy answered. "And what the little lady says makes sense. So what if the word does get out about Ransom's true identity? Maybe the folks in Topeka and Peoria are as sick to death of McCarthy as we are. Maybe they'll see Baron Studios as a bastion of truth and light in a dark sea of innuendo and intimidation."

"We could take a real bath," Steiner insisted. "Hell, a stunt like this could get all of us called before the Committee."

"My grandfather and father always said that Baron Studios doesn't run with the pack." Her opinion succinctly stated, Leigh sat back and watched, flushed with an infectious feeling of stimulation as the arguments hit new levels of acrimony. She was nine years old, and she'd just experienced her first taste of power. She loved it.

An hour later, when the smoke had cleared, Baron Studios' five department heads had voted 4 to 1 to adopt the "little lady's" suggestions.

The Playboy Prince went on to win an Oscar, as predicted. Hedda Hopper, ever vigilant in her search for communists lurking behind the silver screens of Tinseltown, eventually managed to uncover the true identity of the author and the charade became front-page news until it was replaced by a story about a black woman in Montgomery, Alabama, who had refused to give up her seat on a bus to a white man.

If Americans were confused and divided about what was happening in the South, they seemed to be of one mind when it came to Baron Studios' refusal to buckle under to the infamous blacklist. They showed their approval at the box office, giving Baron an unprecedented fourth-quarter profit.

And in a town where geniuses were as common as starlets, Leigh Baron's reputation as a Hollywood prodigy became legend.

But Leigh hadn't known what the future would bring that long-ago afternoon. She'd only known that her father was proud of her. As a reward for her sterling performance, he'd taken her to the Santa Monica Pier, where they rode the carousel. Astride a gleaming white horse, embellished with fanciful medieval armor, Leigh leaned back against Joshua's chest, reveling in the raucous music of the calliope, the salty ocean breeze, and the strong, reassuring feel of her father's arms around her.

"How about some ice cream for my princess?" Joshua asked after they'd ridden three times.

"Nanny doesn't let me have ice cream after five o'clock. She says it spoils my dinner."

"Screw Nanny." Joshua lifted a giggling Leigh atop his shoulders and marched over to the vendor who'd set up shop under a bright red-and-white umbrella.

Funny, the things you remember, Leigh considered now as she watched David Thomas overseeing the arrangement of his flowers beneath the garden tent. More and more lately, these images of her childhood had come unbidden into her mind, like scenes from some forgotten movie. Some were clear, others misty. But all had remained hidden in her mind until this summer.

"Daddy had vanilla," she murmured. "And I had strawberry. And we shared licks. And then we laughed, and Daddy hugged me and told me how proud he was of me and then we went . . . where?" The vivid image faded, veiled by the shadows of time.

Try as she might, Leigh could not recapture the memory.

But for some reason she could not discern, on the hottest day of the year, Leigh began to shiver.

3

Joshua Baron was not in a party mood.

His flight from Las Vegas had been delayed due to a malfunctioning fuel gauge on the studio jet. He'd arrived back in L.A. in time to get stuck in afternoon traffic on the drive to the studio, and no sooner had he finally reached his office when Corbett Marshall had phoned with a new list of demands from one of Hollywood's hot new stars. And on top of that, the rep from the damned WGA had the nerve to threaten him with a strike.

"The bastards are trying to bring me to my knees," Joshua muttered as he marched out to the Porsche parked in its reserved space. Leigh's adjacent parking space was empty, revealing that she'd gone home early to prepare for the party. Joshua hoped she had everything under control; he didn't know how many more problems his stomach could handle for one day.

"They know damn well that a strike could shut the studio

down," he continued talking to himself. "And then where would all those fucking prima donna writers be?" Joshua Baron considered screenwriters to be in the same devil's league as actors and agents. He hated the whole greedy lot.

When the security guard called out a cheery good night as he drove through the gates, Joshua managed only an absent wave in return. He was piloting the Porsche west on Sunset Boulevard when he remembered Leigh's instructions to offer birthday greetings to the elderly man. It had been only this morning that she'd phoned him at his hotel to remind him of Harry Potter's sixty-fifth birthday.

Sixty-five years old. Only five years his senior. Christ, was he going to look that ancient and grizzled?

Stopping for a red light at the intersection of Sunset Boulevard and La Cienega, where one can, on a clear day, see one of the most panoramic views L.A. has to offer, Joshua took a judicious survey of his reflection in the rearview mirror. His thick white hair was expertly styled by his personal barber, who came to his office every Thursday afternoon. His complexion was the requisite Hollywood bronze, acquired from afternoons spent on the tennis courts or golf course at the Hillcrest Country Club. Although a faint network of lines surrounded eyes shaded by Ferrari sunglasses, women always assured him that the lines added character rather than age to his features. An admittedly vain man, Joshua chose to believe them. Still, he'd had the puffy bags under his eyes removed last year by the most expensive plastics man in Beverly Hills. The exorbitant cost of the surgery had been worth every penny; it took ten years off his looks.

In this gold rush industry of moviemaking, in a place boasting of at least one plastic surgeon every four-and-a-half blocks, it was imperative that people on both sides of the camera look young. Vital. Joshua was all too aware that Hollywood was built on fantasy and illusion. Image was everything; a healthy appearance equaled a successful business.

Business. An unseen hand twisted his gut. Reaching into the pocket of his white-on-white silk shirt, Joshua pulled out a pack of Rolaids and popped two antacids into his mouth. As he crunched down on the chalky tablets, he contemplated that if things didn't turn around pretty soon, he'd have to begin buying the damn things by the case.

He wondered if Harry Potter had ulcers and decided he probably didn't. How much stress could there be in sitting in an air-conditioned booth, checking names off a list, and watching Dodger games on a portable TV? Potter, hired by Walter Baron, Joshua's father, had come to work at Baron Studios forty-five years ago, a decade after Walter had founded the studio.

Using tactics usually attributed to Eastern Seaboard robber barons, Walter had single-handedly wrested power from a loosely connected group of silent filmmakers and turned the new enterprise into the largest, most profitable movie studio in America. In the world.

It had not always been easy, Joshua mused. As he headed up into the green hills overlooking Los Angeles, Joshua thought back to those dark days of the 1940s. The studio had lost most of its leading men to the armed forces, and although they'd continued to make War Bond films, union troublemakers had begun eating into their profits. Then, as if they hadn't had enough problems, in 1946 a British film—Olivier's *Henry V*—was nominated for the Oscar, making British acting, costumes, cinematography, and accents all the vogue. The floodgates had been opened. Soon the Academy began nominating French and Italian films, along with the British. When foreign films won four Oscars in 1947, American studios nearly had a collective coronary.

The subsequent influx of foreign films proved such a menace that in 1948, the heads of all six major Hollywood studios—Warner Bros., Paramount, MGM, 20th Century–Fox, RKO, and Baron Studios—banded together for the first time since the labor crises of the 1930s and voted to withdraw their sponsorship of the Academy Awards.

It was during those unsettled times that Walter had come up with his latest scheme to keep the studio afloat. He instructed his son to court the daughter of Jens Eldring, a Norwegian-born, San Francisco–bred shipping magnate and financier. Joshua, who had been enjoying a lusty existence as playboy heir to the Baron Studios throne, was not eager to settle down. And even if he were, Signe Eldring would not have been his first choice for a wife.

Still unmarried at the age of thirty, Signe was tall and painfully thin, with a waspish tongue that had discouraged more than one potential suitor over the years. But Joshua was not your usual, easily rebuffed young Romeo; he was a man on a mission. Save Baron Studios, whatever the cost.

Two weeks after their first date, Joshua proposed, flashing a ten-carat emerald-cut diamond set in platinum from Cartier. The money for the extravagant piece of carbonized stone came from Baron Studios' advertising budget.

As it turned out, Walter and Joshua needn't have bothered risking their valuable capital. Signe, always the pragmatist, realized that the man sitting across the candlelit table was her last chance to escape a lifetime of playing maiden aunt to her numerous nieces and nephews. After making him wait until the following morning, she accepted Joshua's proposal.

When Joshua Baron exchanged vows with his stoic, Dior-clad bride twelve weeks later, the majority of guests invited to the elaborate ceremony understood that what they were witnessing was more merger than marriage. At the extravagant reception dinner held in the gold-leaf splendor of the Biltmore Hotel's ballroom, Jens Eldring, relieved to have his daughter finally married off, handed his new son-in-law a check in excess of ten million dollars, effectively yanking Baron Studios from the ravenous jaws of bankruptcy.

As he pulled the sports car into the curving driveway of his Canyon Drive estate nearly thirty years later, Joshua found himself wishing that the answer to his current financial dilemma could be solved with similar expediency.

4

Baccarat glittered, Limoges gleamed. Perfumes—floral, spicy, oriental, as exotic and individual as the women who wore them—mingled with blue clouds of tobacco smoke and the sweet scent of lily of the valley. The yard, illuminated with softly glowing lanterns, was abloom: magenta bougainvillaea blossoms competed with orange Cape honeysuckle for claim to the most colorful, while creamy hibiscus added a quiet sophistication to the displays of riotous color. Beneath the gaily striped garden tent, flamboyant bouquets of spring flowers in crystal vases garnered appropriate *oohs* and *aahs* as everyone agreed that this time David Thomas had outdone himself.

Damask—yards and yards of it—was adorned with ornately patterned trays fashioned of gleaming silver. Thin, long-stemmed crystal glasses captured the light and split it into a thousand shimmering rainbows. The draped table held the weight of a vast assortment of dishes beautifully presented with the formal arrangement of a still life.

Rosy slices of lamb sprigged with watercress rested on gold-rimmed Royal Copenhagen porcelain. The ubiquitous chèvre lay on a bed of crisp, dark green spinach leaves. There were tiny circlets of smoked eel on brioche, squares of dark pink salmon dabbed with glossy black Iranian caviar, and peppery paté lavishly spread on circles of toasted Italian bread.

At the far end of the table were sweet temptations—puff pastry wrapped around cognac-flavored pastry cream and a hazelnut torte, the meringue layers sandwiched together with butter cream and topped with Swiss chocolate curls. The champagne flowed freely, the guests' tulip glasses continually replenished by tanned young men clad in dark formal wear.

In the lush, silk-draped sanctuary of the music room, the complex strains of baroque music, performed by a string quartet hired from the Hollywood Symphony, accompanied the steady drone of conversation, while outside a driving rock beat pounded unrelentingly on the fragrant night air.

The guests, like the atmosphere and the food, possessed a distinctive California flair. The men were casually, albeit expensively dressed, the women dressed equally as pricey, but more flamboyantly, in gowns by Norell, Halston, Yves Saint Laurent, and Givenchy. Conversation, as always, centered solely on the industry.

Those Americans unfortunate enough to reside outside the movie colony were currently caught up in rumors that the CIA had orchestrated last month's break-in at Democratic headquarters in Washington's Watergate Hotel; Martha Mitchell's sanity (or lack of it) provided juicy cocktail party speculation and everyone from Seattle to Sarasota waited to see how long it would take George McGovern to drop Thomas Eagleton from the ticket, now that news had been leaked to the press revealing his hospitalization for psychiatric care (complete with electroshock treatment!). The long hot summer of 1972 had more than its share of gossipy intrigues, but in this close-knit, secular society, movie deals were all that mattered. With the right vehicle you could burst forth like a blazing comet to become the brightest star in the Hollywood firmament. One wrong move and casting agents would forget your name, the maître d' at Chasen's would suddenly find new bodies to seat at your table, and producers who only weeks ago had been crawling all over themselves to package a deal with you were too busy to come to the phone.

It was nothing if not an intensely competitive atmosphere. Power was the game. And parties like this were the playing field.

"Believe me, sweetheart, one look and you're gonna be begging to cast him in your new project. He's a blond Al Pacino . . ."

". . . a brunette Carol Lynley."

". . . a young Peter O'Toole."

". . . a taller Shirley MacLaine."

". . . a shorter Rock Hudson."

Over the years the names had changed, but the game always remained the same.

Matthew had been working the poolside bar for about thirty minutes when he saw her. Actually, he heard her first. The band, Suicide Express, had taken a break, and her laughter rang out in the sudden silence. Searching out the owner of the musical sound, he saw her standing between two actors, obviously enjoying something one of the men had just said.

For a moment Matthew didn't recognize the vision in the white silk Grecian-style gown with the rippling, spun-silver hair. But then her soft gray eyes met his and he realized that this siren with the face of a Botticelli angel was a long way from the secretary he'd initially taken her to be. His eyebrows rose only a fraction as he acknowledged his error. Leigh's response was a faint, enigmatic smile.

A tuxedoed waiter arrived with an empty tray and an order for drinks; Matthew turned his attention to mixing a pitcher of frozen margaritas. The next time he looked up, she was gone.

Tina was seated beside her husband in his gold Rolls-Royce Corniche with the vanity plates spelling out DEALS. They were in a long line of limousines snaking their way up the curving drive.

"Have I told you that you look gorgeous tonight?" Corbett Marshall asked.

"You have, but that certainly shouldn't stop you from saying it again," Tina answered with an appreciative grin. Knowing that bright colors complemented her light olive
complexion, she'd dressed for the party in a swirling silk hot
pink and violet Pucci sheath. Plum stockings displayed her
legs to advantage, as did the strappy purple sandals with their
skyscraper heels.

For a woman who barely topped five-foot-one, Tina possessed surprisingly long legs. Her husband had often been
heard to profess that Tina's body consisted mainly of legs and
tits. Which seemed to please Corbett immensely. The tall,
handsome, graying-at-the-temples agent was an anomaly in
Hollywood—one of the few husbands who didn't play around.

"Oh, God, I don't believe it," Tina groaned.

Corbett put his right hand on Tina's firm thigh. God, how
he loved this woman's legs! He loved looking at them, touching them, tasting them, and he especially loved the way they
felt wrapped around his hips.

"What?" he asked somewhat distractedly as he felt his body
stiffen in response to his sensual thoughts. Fifteen years and
she could still make him hard. The woman must be a miracle
worker. Or a witch.

"See the woman who just got out of that limo four cars in
front of us?"

Corbett took in the enormous individual clad in a voluminous beaded red-and-gold caftan. Diamonds dripped from
her ears, throat, wrists, and fingers. Climbing out of the
stretch white limousine behind her was a man young enough
to be her grandson, wearing a nubby, cream silk leisure suit.
His tight pants were widely flared, his lavender paisley shirt
was unbuttoned to the waist.

"The one who looks like Moby Dick in drag?"

"That's her," Tina agreed grimly. "Mrs. Edith Halladay, of
the zillionaire Dallas Halladays."

Corbett lifted a dark eyebrow. "She's the shrew who ran
you all over town today?"

"In the flesh." And so much flesh too. Acres and acres of
it.

"Small town," he murmured thoughtfully. "I take it that's
not Mr. Halladay."

"Hardly. Old man Halladay's in his seventies, bald as a billiard ball under his two-hundred-dollar Stetson, and reeks of cigar smoke." Tina's wide brown eyes, framed by sleek dark hair styled in a trendy Vidal Sassoon geometric cut, turned thoughtful. "They've only been in California a few days; I wonder how she managed to wangle an invitation to this party."

"Maybe her tycoon husband is tired of oil wells and wants to buy a movie studio."

"Well, if that's the case, and I doubt it, he's wasting his time on Baron Studios. Joshua would never sell."

"Money tends to be a mighty powerful motivator."

"Spoken like a true agent. Josh has more money than God. Besides, everyone knows he's grooming Leigh to take over."

"Let's hope all his efforts aren't in vain."

"I know she's young, but she's incredibly bright. And she has a natural flair for the business. By the time Josh is willing to relinquish control, Leigh will be more than capable of carrying on the family tradition."

Corbett was not surprised by the unflagging support of Joshua's older daughter evident in Tina's tone. Leigh had been a child the first time he'd taken his new bride to the Baron mansion. Ten years old, with wide, sober gray eyes and a grave manner that Tina later told him had made her want to hug the little girl right on the spot. Instead, Tina had simply shaken the small outstretched hand and stated her desire to be friends. Something she had the feeling that Leigh Baron had needed. A lot.

During Leigh's adolescence, Tina served as a kind of surrogate mother, offering the love and support that the glacial Signe Baron seemed incapable—or unwilling—to give. After Signe's death, the bond between the quiet young heiress and the outspoken real estate broker became even stronger.

"I've no doubt she'll be able to fill her father's—and her grandfather's—illustrious shoes when the time comes," he acknowledged. "I just hope there's a studio left for her to run."

"Then the rumors are true? About Baron Studios' financial difficulties?"

"According to Joshua, they've experienced a rough year,

but all he needs is one really strong vehicle to get them back on the fast track." He paused. "One like *Dangerous*."

Dangerous was a compelling novel written by one of Corbett's lesser-known clients. The story of a charismatic terrorist cult leader who kidnapped an heiress, only to fall in love with her, and she with him, was so compelling that Tina had devoured it in one reading. Although a far cry from the epics that had long been the signature of Baron Studios, Joshua had taken an option on the work, immediately turning the project over to Leigh, who had lobbied unceasingly for the acquisition in the first place. That had been three years ago. Thus far, she had been unable to bring the project to the screen.

"If any one movie could turn a studio around, *Dangerous* is the one to do it," Tina agreed. "It's a marvelous novel."

"I know. The problem is that the money men in this town don't read anything except *Variety* and audit sheets. They're only interested in the bottom line. They also tend to get nervous when you try to pitch a project without stars."

"I take it Leigh's still insisting that the two key roles be played by new faces."

"Of course. You know as well as I do that Leigh rivals her grandfather when it comes to that damnable Baron intransigence," he answered with a frustrated grimace. "She's tested everyone in town for the parts of Marilyn Cornell and Ryder Long—I should know because I sent most of them to her—and she still hasn't come up with either character."

Tina had lived with her husband long enough to know when he had something on his mind. Something he wasn't saying. "And?"

"I'm thinking of suggesting Josh test Marissa."

"You are kidding."

"Not at all. You saw how she stole the show last month with her performance in *Bus Stop*."

"Darling, that's a great role; it would make any fairly competent actress look good. Also, may I point out that we're talking about a high school production."

"A lot of stars have come out of Beverly Hills High School. And for the record, Leigh just happens to like the idea of Marissa in the role."

"Really?"

"Well, it took a while for the idea to sink in," he admitted reluctantly. "But she called me this morning to tell me that after having reread the novel—twice, as a matter of fact—she believes I may have hit on something."

Realizing that her husband was serious, Tina considered his surprising statement. The role of the pampered heiress-turned-terrorist for love would be a good one. It could even win an Oscar for the young woman fortunate enough to be given the part. But even more important, it could mean instant stardom. Tina knew all about Marissa's acting ambitions. Just last week Corbett had come home with a remarkable story about the girl showing up at his office, wearing nothing but a pair of high heels, a bold, dangerous smile, and a white mink coat. He had no sooner risen to greet the teenage daughter of his oldest friend when Marissa had shrugged out of the coat, flung it dramatically down onto the Aubusson carpet, and said, "What's the matter, Uncle Corbett? Haven't you ever fucked on a mink before?"

Still shaken from the encounter hours later, Corbett had assured Tina that he'd somehow convinced Marissa to put the coat back on and hurried her out of his office. Although Tina was furious at the sexually charged teenager for having attempted to seduce her husband, she was not particularly surprised by Corbett's story. After all, Marissa was determined to succeed in a town where tales of beautiful young starlets rising to the top on their backs were legion; unfortunately, there continued to be enough success stories, even these days, to make the idea attractive to a woman willing to sell her body for a part.

"Josh would never permit it," Tina predicted. "Everyone knows he's dead set against Marissa becoming an actress."

"I know," Corbett said on a reluctant sigh as they reached the parking valet. "But I'd love to have that girl as a client. With ten percent of her potential earnings, we could buy that island in the Caribbean you're always talking about retiring to."

Tina didn't answer. There was no need. One of the few things she and Corbett had in common was the fact that they were both incurable workaholics.

The parking valet, wearing a royal blue T-shirt bearing the

crown logo of Baron Studios, was obviously an out-of-work actor. His wavy blond hair had been professionally sun-streaked, his toothpaste-commercial teeth were capped, and Tina had no doubt that he had the obligatory all-over Holly-wood tan. He was undeniably gorgeous. He also looked like every other guy his age in town; throw a stick on a Malibu beach and you'd hit a dozen of them.

Not for the first time, Tina Marshall—nee Theresa Salerno—was grateful that her youthful dream of becoming an actress had failed to come true.

Jeff Martin was in his element. Expensive booze, bitchin' food, and the best-looking chicks in town. Everything would have been perfect had it not been for the nonstop whining of the great white whale hanging on his arm. From the moment he'd picked Edith Halladay up at the flamingo pink Beverly Hills Hotel, the evening had been one long gripe session.

The champagne stocked by the limousine company was domestic, the limo itself wasn't long enough, they had to wait in line to gain admittance to the party, how come he wasn't introducing her to all the movie stars, why didn't he get her a drink, some food, dance with her? On and on until he was tempted to push the fat bitch into the pool and watch her sink to the bottom and stay there.

Relief came when they entered the music room. Recogniz-ing the bartender immediately, Jeff left the diamond-draped monster expertly boring a producer from Warner Brothers with tales of her futile search for a suitable house while he made his way to the portable bar.

Jeff waited impatiently for an over-the-hill matinee idol and his obviously hired-for-the-evening blond bombshell to make up their mind between vodka martinis or Manhattans. Finally they left, martinis in hand.

"Hey, man," he said, "I am in desperate need of some downers. You got any Nembutal or 'ludes?"

The bartender glanced around. "Sorry, man, but you know as well as I do that parties like this usually go for coke or grass."

"Shit." Jeff scowled as he glanced back at the whale.

"Come to think of it," the bartender said, "I do have a

Noctec that I was savin' for a special occasion." Noctec was a brand-name form of the sedative chloral hydrate; the combination of chloral hydrate and alcohol was notorious as the Mickey Finn. "I could let you have it for a ten spot."

The price was highway robbery, but Jeff was in too much of a hurry to waste precious time bartering. "Sold."

He handed over some of the expense money Patsy had given him this afternoon in exchange for the orange capsule. No one noticed as he surreptitiously dissolved the capsule into the frothy pink strawberry margarita.

As he crossed the room, doctored drink in hand, Jeff Martin was smiling.

ina Marshall was the undisputed queen of the Hollywood game of musical houses. In a town infamous for conspicuous consumption, the forty-five-year-old real estate maven traded pieces of property like a wily Las Vegas dealer shuffling through a deck of cards in search of an ace.

Gossip invariably played a key role in her success; whenever Tina heard that an actress had signed for a blockbuster movie, she sent a bottle of Dom Perignon along with a little note stating that she had "just the perfect house" for the actress's important new image.

A series cancellation earned an invitation to a home-cooked dinner. Since the movie community was a very superstitious place, failure was perceived as contagious, which caused the hapless former star to be treated like a pariah. By everyone but Tina Marshall.

Over a casual, friendly meal of linguini, avocado salad, and a crisp Napa Valley Chardonnay, she would mention that she'd just listed the most darling bungalow in Beverly Hills, whose anxious owner was desperate to sell. Before dessert was served, the out-of-work actor had convinced himself that he was actually trading up by moving to a smaller, more manageable place.

While the capriciousness of the film industry provided constant up-and-down movement, divorce was the mother lode of her real-estate business. Every night, as she climbed between her silk Pratesi sheets, Tina thanked God for California's community property laws. Always careful not to take sides, she would commiserate with the angry wife over lunch at The Bistro Garden, patiently listen to the husband's complaints during Sunday brunch at the Polo Lounge, and inevitably end up with another listing and two new sales.

By the time she'd been at the party an hour, she'd chatted with a recent Academy Award–winning director, a rock star whose latest album had just gone platinum, and the castoff third wife of a hot talk-show host, all of whom expressed interest in changing residences. Tina, naturally, knew just the house for each of them. She was also approached by Brendan Farraday, one of the few actors left in town who could qualify as an old-fashioned movie star.

Back from one of his star-studded Vietnam excursions, Farraday was in the market for a small house in the Valley. For a friend. Since the San Fernando Valley was conveniently separated from his vast Bel Air estate—and his wife—by the Santa Monica Mountains, Tina had a good idea exactly what type of friend the actor was talking about. Murmuring something about being too busy to take on any new clients, she plucked his wandering hand off her hip and walked out to the pool in search of a stiff drink. She'd gotten enough work done for one evening.

It was then that she first saw Matthew. Standing behind the bar, mixing a pitcher of frozen daiquiris. Tina couldn't believe her luck.

"You are just the man I've been looking for."

"Looks as if you've found me," Matthew said agreeably. "What can I get for you?"

"The question, you impossibly sexy young man, is what can *I* do for *you?*"

Matthew took a long look at the woman standing before him. Her smile was open, her dark eyes vivacious and unabashedly friendly. She didn't look the type to pick up strange men at parties, but experience had taught him that looks were deceiving.

"Have we met?"

"I'm Tina Marshall," she said with a bold, infectious grin. "The fairy godmother who is about to change your life."

"You've outdone yourself, princess," a deep voice offered in Leigh's ear.

Leigh turned and greeted her father with a faint smile. "I'm glad you approve."

"You know I approve of everything you do. Speaking of parental approval, have you seen your sister's dress?"

"It's not that bad," she hedged with careful loyalty.

"She looks like a slut."

"I suppose you told her that?"

"Of course."

Of course, Leigh echoed silently. And by doing so, her father had merely validated Marissa's rebellious behavior.

"Have you given any more thought to letting her test?" she had to ask carefully. After Corbett's unexpected suggestion, Leigh had reread the novel with Marissa in mind and discovered a striking similarity between the temperamental, love-starved young heiress and her sister.

Joshua scowled. "I've already told you, it's out of the question."

"But she's incredibly talented. If you'd only come to her senior play last month—"

"You know I had to go out of town that night."

Leigh didn't believe Joshua's alleged need to rush off to New York, and she knew Marissa hadn't bought the flimsy excuse either. She'd always tried to calm the choppy waters between her father and younger sister, but the chances of the two strong-minded individuals ever getting along seemed to grow more impossible with each passing day. Leigh wished that she could do something, anything, to bridge the widening gulf between them.

"Have you talked with Corbett?" she asked, seeming to change the subject. Leigh was counting on Corbett's practiced, persuasive ways to succeed where she'd failed.

"Not since this afternoon when he called to inform me that Johnny Banning wanted six points of *High Country Riders*.

Johnny Banning had proven one of last year's few success stories when he'd appeared in a low-budget Western. The enormously handsome former bull rider had made the genre popular again, thanks to all the women who sat in the theaters and fantasized about playing saloon hall queen to Johnny Banning's sexy gunfighter. What none of them suspected was that during the filming of the movie, the macho actor had spent his nights being handcuffed by the movie's equally handsome sheriff.

"What did you tell him?"

"That there was no way I was going to agree to Banning's demands. Then I reminded him about the morals clause in that faggot's contract."

Her father would never enact that clause while Banning was still on top; it would be killing the goose that gave the golden egg. "Meaning that you're willing to give three points?"

His eyes gleamed with parental pride. "Three and a half. Am I that obvious, or do you know your old man so well?" As he put his arm around her shoulder, Leigh experienced a vague stirring of misgiving that was as familiar as it was undefinable.

"We know each other," she murmured.

The princess was locked in a tall stone tower. When she heard her name called, the princess obediently lowered her long blond hair out the window. As she felt the familiar weight on her golden tresses, the princess grew afraid.

Strangely shaken by the childhood fairy-tale image that flashed through her mind, Leigh was relieved to hear someone calling her name. Glancing around, she saw a tall, dark-haired man standing on the other side of the pool, enthusiastically beckoning to her.

"I'd better see what Jimmy wants," she said with a great deal more aplomb than she was feeling. "Did you know he's up for Marlon Brando's role in Olympus Studio's remake of *On the Waterfront*?"

"I believe Corbett mentioned something about it."

"Oh, that reminds me, Corbett's looking for you." She tossed the words back over her shoulder, as if they were a mere afterthought. "Something about *Dangerous*."

Leigh's words caught Joshua's instant attention, expunging the jealousy he'd felt when his daughter had flashed her bewitching smile at that muscle-bound actor.

Although initially he hadn't been enthusiastic about the story, after a great deal of nonstop lobbying (in her own calm way, his daughter could wear away a stone) Leigh had managed to convince him that the intense, electrifying drama possessed Academy Award potential.

Those were the magic words. In recent years, an Oscar had begun to demonstrate an astonishing—or frightening, depending on your point of view—power at the box office, and it didn't take a Wall Street banker to realize that the little statuette had turned from gold to platinum. An Academy Award–winning film guaranteed massive money harvests—as much as five million dollars to the picture's gross income. If a movie won several important Oscars, the payoff was easily doubled.

Joshua rubbed his hands together with anticipation. All he needed to do was get *Dangerous* into production to surpass his father's exalted place in Hollywood history.

When he'd first taken over the studio after his father's death, the consensus was that Walter Baron's philandering, free-spending son would run Baron Studios into the ground within two years. But he'd proven them all wrong. Out from under his father's shadow, he broke new ground by expanding into foreign markets, creating films for the lucrative television market, and traveling to remote, exotic locations earlier producers had eschewed as too expensive. Studio coffers had swelled; his detractors had been silenced.

The Rolodex in Joshua's head was filled with names—Wall Street's top bankers, power brokers, politicians, agents, newspaper publishers in Los Angeles, New York, London, Paris, and Rome. His face was immediately recognizable at all the Beverly Hills bistros; there wasn't a maître d' or parking attendant who didn't know that Joshua Baron expected his table and his car to be waiting. The guest lists of his Sunday brunches read like a *Who's Who* of the industry and tales of Hollywood's most respected citizens battling with the ferocity of pit bulls to win an invitation to his acclaimed Academy Award extravaganzas were legion.

For the past twenty years, Joshua Baron had reigned over Tinseltown from the loftiest peak of Hollywood's Valhalla.

Then things began to unravel. Like every other Hollywood studio, Baron Studios had undergone a period of change, no longer making a hundred movies a year. Instead, they were producing less than a dozen, and since all but one of last year's releases had proven financial failures, the wolves had begun to gather hungrily at the door.

Lord, how he hated the new, murky financial conglomerates that were threatening to take over the movie business. What he wouldn't give for the good old days, when the studios produced, the directors directed, the actors played their parts, and long lines extended outside huge, elaborate theaters. When dollars seemed to come from a gigantic money-making machine, stimulated by the steady stream of successful, profit-producing movies. These days all his time seemed to be spent deciding who was going to get what percentage of the profits before the damn screenplay even rolled from the typewriter.

Somehow, when he wasn't looking, Baron Studios' profit-and-loss statement had begun to hang like a sword of Damocles over his head, and his life had declined into a shitawful mess.

Except for Leigh. Beautiful, steadfastly loyal Leigh.

Plucking an icy martini from a passing waiter's tray, Joshua forged his way through the ebullient crowd, searching out Corbett Marshall.

Marissa was seething. She stood in the shadows, chewing on a bloody cuticle as she watched the hunk behind the bar watch Leigh. As if he thought the high and mighty Miss Studio Executive would even look at a common bartender. And even if Leigh did deign to diddle the hired help, Joshua would have the guy in question run out of town on the nearest rail.

The thought of her father reminded her of his furious expression when he'd seen her new dress. The memory caused a small, mean flame of satisfaction to glow inside her. The dress had proven every bit as effective as she'd planned; it had garnered a reaction. If the mean-spirited bastard thought that was something, Marissa considered, smiling, wait until he got the bill. She could hardly wait for the upcoming explosion.

She had achieved her goal of aggravating her father. Now Marissa spent twenty minutes walking back and forth in front of Matthew, during which time he remained frustratingly oblivious to her presence. When Tina began flirting with him, Marissa decided the time had come to take the bull by the horns. Running her hands over her gold lamé–clad hips, she tugged the clinging bodice even lower and made a beeline for the bar.

Brendan Farraday downed a martini—his fifth of the evening—and watched Tina come on to that oversexed bartender. Who the hell did she think she was, walking away from him? He was Brendan Farraday. A star. While she was nothing but a failed actress turned real-estate agent. And an aging one to boot. Despite her long legs and sensational knockers, she had to be at least forty. Probably older than that. She ought to be damned grateful he'd given her a second glance.

As a rule, Farraday preferred his woman young. The younger the better. But there was something intriguing about Tina Marshall. Something almost primitive; her polished skin exuded a mysterious melange of oriental perfume, musk, and sex.

That's why, when he saw her looking and smelling like the star of every man's favorite wet dream, he had come up with the idea of having her locate a suitable love nest for his latest mistress. Of course he and Tina would have to try the place out first, just to make sure the vibes were right. So what did the bitch do when he brought up the idea? Told him she was too busy to take on any new clients, then walked away.

A red-hot anger boiling in Farraday's blood, he marched toward the poolside bar. No over-the-hill cunt was going to turn him down and get away with it. Tina Marshall had a lesson to learn. And he was just the guy to teach it to her.

* * *

"I'll have a champagne cocktail," Marissa ordered imperiously. So what if the hunk and Tina were engrossed in their private conversation? He was hired to mix drinks, not hustle the guests.

Irritation flashed in Tina's eyes, but she banked it as she turned to Joshua Baron's younger daughter. Good heavens, she thought. That dress is remarkable. If the girl so much as sneezes, she'll provide some unexpected entertainment.

"Hello, dear. What a stunning gown." Eyeing the scrap of glittering fabric, she decided that Marissa appeared to have been dipped in a vat of metallic paint.

Marissa laughed, tossing her hair back over one shoulder with a practiced gesture that Rita Hayworth had perfected in *Gilda*. "That's not exactly the word Daddy used."

"I can imagine," Tina murmured.

"Poor Daddy can't get used to the idea that I'm a grown woman. Capable of making my own choices." Marissa picked up the glass Matthew had silently placed in front of her, took an appreciative sip, and eyed Tina over the crystal rim. "Did Corbett tell you that I'm going to be an actress?"

"I believe my husband mentioned that you were interviewing agents." Tina felt guilty for playing games with a child. But this particular child had the voluptuous body of a woman. A body she'd attempted to use to seduce a married man. Tina's man. "Tell me, dear, have you found someone to represent you yet? Or are you still going door to door with your—uh—portfolio?"

The attack was like a stiletto sheathed in silk. Marissa's bright green eyes narrowed as she tried to decide what Tina had been told about the incident. Her mane of flaming hair fanned out combatively as she tossed her head back, polishing off her drink.

"Why should I be talking to other agents when Corbett was absolutely wonderful?" Marissa's wide, kohl-rimmed eyes turned blissfully reminiscent. "And so very encouraging." Her voice was lush with sexual undertones. "Why, after how close we've become, I can't imagine anyone else ever representing me."

Tina assured herself that this underdressed, overendowed teenager was lying. If anything had happened between them,

Corbett never would have told her about Marissa's seduction attempt in the first place. Unless he was trying to establish an alibi, a niggling little voice in a back pocket of her mind pointed out. *For chrissakes, look at this girl,* the voice insisted. *How many men do you think could resist taking her to bed? Or, in Marissa's case, to mink.*

The tableau—a silent, watchful Matthew, an uncertain Tina, a vindictive Marissa—appeared to have been captured on freeze frame. Nearby the rock band's female vocalist—yet another Cher clone—broke into what Matthew decided was an appropriate chorus of "Gypsys, Tramps and Thieves."

The charged moment was broken by Farraday's arrival. "Damnit, Tina," he said, slurring his words, "since when do you turn down a chance for a fuckin' commission?" His fingers curved around her arm with a force Tina knew would leave bruises; his booming voice garnered instant attention from nearby guests, including a columnist from the *Hollywood Reporter.*

As the columnist fluffed her cotton-candy hair and looked inclined to join them, Tina's worried gaze went from Marissa to Farraday, then back to Marissa, as she attempted to decide which troublemaker to deal with first. Finally she glanced over at Matthew, deciding that he probably wasn't going anywhere.

"Don't you dare leave without talking with me," she instructed.

"I wouldn't think of it."

Tina turned to Farraday. "Come on, Brendan, let's get you out of here before you blow your chances of making SAG president." She didn't give a damn about the upcoming Screen Actors Guild election, but she did care a great deal about their hostess, and wasn't about to let this bastard ruin Leigh's party. Taking hold of his arm, she practically dragged him away.

"Leigh, dear, it's an absolutely marvelous party." Richard Steiner flashed Leigh a patently false smile. "You never cease to amaze me."

Leigh forced a polite smile of her own. "Thank you, Richard. I'm so pleased that you're enjoying yourself."

As she exchanged brief party pleasantries with the recently retired head of distribution and marketing operations, Leigh thought back to that summer after her graduation from college, when Joshua had assigned her to Steiner's department.

Steiner, intent on sabotaging Leigh's fledgling career, put her in charge of a merchandising campaign for a time-travel movie that was over budget and behind schedule. Undaunted, Leigh traveled to toy conventions and merchandise trade fairs, where she pitched the movie unceasingly. Living out of a suitcase, she rinsed out her underwear and stockings in hotel room sinks each night as she shook the trees, finding money in locations that Steiner, on his most imaginative days, had never thought of.

While her unflagging enthusiasm created undeniable interest, she still had one immense hurdle to overcome. With the movie behind schedule, Leigh had no film to show potential licensees. And without the film, it was difficult, if not impossible, to entice any astute businessmen into signing on the dotted line.

Although Leigh knew that Richard Steiner was secretly waiting for her to fall flat on her face, she refused to give her adversary the pleasure of reporting failure to her father. Just when it looked as if she was going to run out of time, in a stroke of genius, she leased Disneyland for one memorable night. The magnificent presentations she staged in each of the fanciful venues succeeded in setting the standard for future industry promotions.

To the delight of onlookers in Fantasyland, a stuntman double for the adventurous time traveler suddenly appeared in the midst of a dazzling fireworks display, drifting to the ground in front of Sleeping Beauty's castle beneath a silver parachute.

Another stuntman wrestled with live alligators on Adventureland's famed jungle ride, while in Frontierland, a buckskin-clad actor exchanged gunfire with a trio of desperadoes who'd just robbed the Disneyland train.

But the pièce de résistance was what Leigh had arranged for Tomorrowland. There, on an elaborately designed sound stage built specifically for this party, guests sat on the bridge of a starship and battled alien spaceships on a three-dimensional screen that made the special effects appear dazzlingly realistic.

The party was an unqualified success. Months before the

film's release, *Time After Time* T-shirts, ashtrays, key rings, bumper stickers, and plastic action figures appeared in all the stores—along with a colorful board game that took the nation by storm. McDonald's featured *Time After Time* characters on their cups and hamburger containers; Pepsi ran TV commercials featuring the picture's intrepid hero carrying the familiar red, white, and blue can on his journeys through time.

Utilizing a surfeit of superlatives, *Variety* proclaimed that Baron Studios' marketing department had never known an energy vortex like Leigh Baron. She was talented, creative, ingenious. She was indefatigable. Brilliant. And best of all, she was beautiful.

Media gushing aside, Leigh proved very good at her job. Enough so that when she left the marketing department six months later, Richard Steiner—who'd resented her presence at Baron Studios since that long-ago afternoon when he'd made the mistake of crossing swords with a nine-year-old girl—was almost sorry to see her go.

"Pushy old cow." A blistering scowl marred Marissa's carefully made-up face as she watched Tina and Farraday leave. The scowl was instantly replaced by a dazzling smile. She handed Matthew her empty glass for a refill. "You're very good," she purred, watching him mix the drink.

"And you're a brat." He placed the champagne cocktail in front of her.

His derogatory words were not what she'd been expecting. She lifted her chin. "Do you know who I am?"

Matthew shrugged. "Nope." His tone indicated that he also didn't care.

"I'm Marissa Baron."

"Congratulations."

"My father owns this house."

"Nice place," Matthew said pleasantly.

"This is his party." When he didn't answer, she leaned forward, offering him an unrestricted view of her perfumed breasts spilling over the top of the gold dress. "Which makes you his employee."

"So?"

"So he can fire you."

"Since it'd leave him a bartender short, I doubt if he'd do that. Besides, from what I can tell, it's your sister who's in charge around here."

Leigh again. It was always Leigh. "You mix a lousy drink." She slammed her glass down on the top of the bar with such force that the delicate stem shattered.

Matthew watched the exaggerated swing of Marissa's hips as she flounced away. The idea that such disparate individuals could be sisters proved that Mother Nature was more than a little fond of practical jokes.

Cleaning up the broken glass, Matthew wondered what Tina Marshall could possibly want with him. Other than the obvious, of course. Despite a lambent sexuality that clung to Tina like a particularly stimulating scent, Matthew didn't have the impression that she was looking for a quick roll in the hay. No, instinct told him that she had something else in mind.

Something more serious.

Something she insisted would change his life.

So what the hell was it?

He poured a Chivas on the rocks for an aging character actor and mixed a Harvey Wallbanger for the actor's young wife. Matthew decided that it was going to be a very long night.

"What the hell is this? A goddamn conspiracy?"

Joshua's stomach clenched; he popped an antacid into his mouth and chased it with a long swallow of Scotch and milk. "First Leigh tries to talk me into giving Marissa a screen test. Then you come up with the insane idea of having her test for *Dangerous*. Christ, that'd be like casting Mae West to play the leading role in *The Nun's Story*."

Corbett had suggested they go into the library, where they could talk in private. He had hoped he could convince the studio head that the answer to his casting dilemma was living right under his nose.

"Look, I know Marissa's unconventional—"

"That's a new word for tramp."

An image of a dangerously seductive seventeen-year-old, nude save for a pair of high heels, flashed into Corbett's mind. He'd known Marissa Baron from the day she was born; his

feelings for her had always been paternal. Except for that one
fleeting moment of temptation when his traitorous body had
responded to her allure like a lecherous old man.

"You're too hard on the girl, Josh. Underneath that sexpot
glamour, Marissa possesses a deep-seated insecurity that
would make an audience believe that she'd do anything—
even kill—to win Ryder Long's love."

Joshua slammed his glass down onto the antique mahogany
bar. Liquid splashed over the top and went unnoticed. "Now
you're sounding just like her shrink."

"Perhaps all those psychologists are right. When was the
last time you actually sat down and talked with her?"

Joshua Baron's glare could have cut diamonds. "None of
your damn business. Besides, I don't have to talk to her to
know that she's entirely wrong for the part."

Corbett had negotiated enough contracts with Joshua to
know when he'd hit the brick wall of the movie executive's
intransigence. "Hey, she's your kid," he said with a shrug.

Busy refilling his glass from the heavy crystal decanter,
Joshua failed to answer.

Tina dragged Farraday through the throng of guests to the
front driveway, where she instructed the parking valet to call
a cab for the inebriated actor. Not that she'd mind the bastard
killing himself in that new Lamborghini he'd been bragging
about all evening; she just didn't want him taking any innocent drivers who might happen to be on the road tonight
along with him.

"Your place or mine?" Farraday slurred, reaching behind
her to grab a handful of Pucci-covered ass.

"In your dreams." Tina yanked his groping hand off her
body.

"Anyone ever tell you that you're too friggin' old to play
coy?"

"Go to hell," she said, turning away.

He pulled her roughly around by the arm, holding her
against him. "You know you like it."

Tina's dark eyes blazed with hatred. Even as drunk as he
was, Farraday read their blistering message and quickly released her before taking an unsteady step backward.

"You listen to me, Brendan Farraday," she said, thrusting a plum-tinted nail into his chest. "And listen good. If you ever so much as look at me crosswise again, let alone try to touch, I'll get a gun and blow your fucking balls off. Is that clear?"

Sweat beads formed on his brow as Farraday tried to remember that he was a major star. And stars didn't take shit from nobodies. "I can break you, bitch. A few words from me and you won't be able to get a job pushing tract homes in Compton."

"Give it your best shot. But lay one finger on me and you're a dead man." With that she spun around and marched away, her four-inch-high heels tapping brisk staccatos on the flagstone.

"Uh . . . excuse me, but your cab's here, Mr. Farraday," the valet offered with an encouraging smile.

The first thing the rookie actor had learned upon arriving in Hollywood eighteen months ago from Denver was to humor all the old farts. Although the balance of power was beginning to shift to a new generation, some of these guys still wielded a helluva lot of power. Brendan Farraday more than most. "By the way, Mr. Farraday, your performance in *The Star Seekers* was brilliant."

His unpleasant altercation with Tina Marshall was instantly forgotten as Farraday turned his attention to the young man with the wavy blond hair and hard, muscular body. Christ, he thought, the competition was getting younger every day. At least this one knew a bona fide star when he saw one. Although it took a major effort, he pulled himself up to his full height of six-foot-four-inches tall.

"You an actor?"

His sudden interest earned a flash of white teeth. "Yes, sir, Mr. Farraday."

"What's your name?"

"Royal Harmon."

"Belong to SAG, do you?"

"Yessir. And you've definitely got my vote for president."

Brendan nodded as he pressed a crisp green bill into the young man's hand. "Well, hang in there, Royal Harmon," he advised expansively. "Thanks for your support. And tell all your friends to vote." Having gotten his pitch in, he allowed the valet to help him into the backseat of the cab.

As soon as the taxi's amber taillights returned back down the curving drive, Royal checked out the tip. As a rule, drunks tended to be generous. Especially ones running in the upcoming Screen Actors Guild elections.

The valet's oath was harsh and succinct as he viewed the one-dollar bill. Brendan Farraday's opponent had just won Royal Harmon's vote by default.

Marissa's arms were wrapped around Jeff Martin's tanned neck and her body clung to his as they swayed to the music. "Did you come here with someone?" she asked, moving her pelvis sinuously against his erection.

Jeff hadn't seen the whale lately. He hoped she'd passed out in some quiet corner where he could retrieve her later. Much later.

"No one important." He slid his knee between her legs. Marissa sighed happily.

"I'm glad. I'm don't like to share."

The way the chick was rubbing her crotch against his leg, Jeff half expected her to have an orgasm any moment. "Don't knock it till you've tried it," he suggested, cupping her buttocks and lifting her more firmly against him. "You know what they say."

"What?"

"Double your pleasure." His teeth nipped at her neck; Marissa went weak from the knees down. "Double your fun."

Marissa was not inexperienced; she'd willingly surrendered her virginity shortly after her thirteenth birthday to one of the estate's gardeners. She'd found the experience painful, messy, and not nearly as thrilling as described in the banned books she kept hidden beneath her mattress.

But she couldn't deny that the look in the old man's eyes— raw lust—had excited her. It was the same way her father looked at Leigh when he thought no one was nearby.

"Hey, sweetcakes." Jeff's tongue played wetly in her ear. "How about you and me ditch this dull old crowd and go somewhere we can make our own party."

His penis was pushing demandingly against her dress; dewy moisture gathered between her legs. "The pool house is being remodeled." She gasped when his dark hand slid between them to press against her heat. "It's empty."

Jeff grinned. "Darlin', I thought you'd never ask."

Matthew was frowning. He mixed a pitcher of martinis. Tina Marshall had returned, as promised, with a proposition that was as surprising as it was impossible.

"Let me get this straight," he said slowly, a hint of suspicion underscoring his words. "You're offering me—a guy you've never seen before—a role in Baron Studios' new picture."

"I'm offering you a chance to test," Tina corrected. She plucked an olive from the bowl in front of her and popped it into her mouth. "But believe me, you're a shoe-in for the role."

"But you're a real-estate agent."

"You've found me out."

"It'd be difficult to miss your signs; they're on all the best lawns in the city."

"More prevalent than crab grass," she agreed cheerfully. "But my husband is Corbett Marshall—"

"The agent."

She bobbed her sleek dark head. "That's him. And he's the one who'll arrange the test. You see, Corbett and I are a team. When I'm not pushing overpriced real estate, I freelance as his scout, just like all those retired jocks who travel around the country discovering new talent for the Dodgers."

Matthew remained unconvinced. "Corbett Marshall only handles stars."

"That's true, but—"

"I'm not a star."

Tina's grin was immensely confident. "Trust me, kiddo, you will be."

A faint line etched its way between his dark brows. From the looks of Tina Marshall, Matthew would have expected the woman to be more imaginative. "Nice line. Not terribly original, but I've been told it's effective. On some people."

Tina decided not to be offended by his accusation. She was certain a man as good looking as this one must have a constant stream of women throwing themselves at his feet. Or some other more vital part of his anatomy. "But not you."

"No." The long, level look he gave her was calm. Assured. "Not me."

The waiter returned for the martinis, interrupting their conversation. Once they were alone again, Tina smiled to ease the suspicion she viewed in his eyes. "I'm afraid I haven't made myself clear. As sexy as you admittedly are, my interest in you is strictly professional. Besides, I love my husband. I'd never screw around on him."

Watching the way her wide brown eyes had turned earnest when she mentioned her husband, Matthew wondered if Corbett Marshall realized that he was a very lucky man.

"Look," he said, his tone gentler now that he'd determined she was telling the truth, "I appreciate your interest, but I'm not an actor. I'm also one of the few people in this town with no dreams of stardom."

"Am I supposed to believe that bartending is your life?"

Matthew smiled, realizing he fit into her stereotype more closely than he'd thought. Was there anyone in Hollywood not playing a role? he wondered. "Okay, you've got me. But I'm not an actor."

"So what are you? A singer?"

"A writer."

He saw no need to mention the nightmares that began occurring with increasing frequency during his second tour of duty in Vietnam. Instead of turning to drugs as so many others had, on the advice of a sympathetic nurse he'd begun to write down the nightmares in a small notebook he always carried with him. For some reason, putting the horrifying images down on paper seemed to sap their strength, enabling him to get on with the day-to-day business of living. And killing. He had returned home with notebooks filled with stories. Stories he intended to tell to the world.

"Novels or screenplays?"

"Screenplays."

She leaned her elbow on the bar, rested her chin in her palm, and observed him thoughtfully. "Are you any good?"

"Yes. I am."

Tina liked the way he answered simply, without embellishing. If he was going to make it in this business, a steely self-confidence was vital. On the other hand, nothing could do a person in quicker than an overinflated ego. She'd watched more than one career founder on the shoals of swollen vanity. "You'd make it a lot faster if you could devote all your time to your writing."

She wasn't telling him anything Matthew hadn't told himself hundreds of times. After getting out of the Marines, he'd taken advantage of his GI benefits and enrolled at USC. For the next three years, he'd attended classes in the morning, parked cars at the Beverly Hills Hotel in the afternoons, and tended bar at night. He eventually gave up the hotel job when it became too much of a hassle to explain to a seemingly continuous parade of sexually liberated females why he had no desire to while away his few free hours with them in the hotel's bungalows.

"Believe me," Tina insisted, "you are perfect for the starring role in *Dangerous* because you're every parent's worst nightmare. You ooze sex appeal and, best of all, you're totally unknown, which is exactly what Josh Baron's looking for."

"I'm not sure I appreciate that part about being every parent's nightmare."

"It sure as hell didn't hurt James Dean's career," Tina shot back. "Look, with the money you'd make from *Dangerous*, you could quit these part-time jobs and concentrate on your real work."

Matthew couldn't deny the idea of ample funds had merit. But an actor? "I'll give it some thought," he agreed finally as he realized Tina was waiting for an answer.

She nodded, satisfied for now. Twenty years of selling real estate had taught her when not to push. She'd seen his reluctant look of interest when she'd mentioned giving up his part-time jobs. It was enough. For now.

"You do that," she said agreeably. Reaching into her plum satin evening bag, she pulled out one of the business cards she was never without. "Here's my husband's card. Give him a call when you're ready to talk, okay?"

Matthew shrugged. "I'm not promising anything," he warned. "Except to think about it."

"That's all I'm asking." She flashed him a parting smile, more brilliant than any he'd witnessed from her thus far, and turned away. She'd only gone a few steps when something occurred to her. "What's your name?"

Matthew wasn't surprised that she hadn't bothered to ask before. He was an unknown. And in this town, that translated to a nobody. "Matthew. Matthew St. James."

"Matthew St. James." She repeated his name slowly, as if savoring the taste and feel of it on her tongue. "I like it." She nodded in satisfaction. "I can't wait to see it up on that big silver screen in Westwood."

With that she was gone, leaving Matthew holding the gray business card and wondering why in the hell he was even considering Tina Marshall's outlandish proposal.

Jeff Martin was ruled by his cock.

He went through life pistol hot, his sexual radar honing in on a target with the speed and accuracy of a Minuteman missile. And it didn't take a rocket scientist to figure out that Marissa Baron was one hot piece of ass.

"Take off your clothes," he said, the moment they entered the deserted pool house.

Marissa, eager to oblige, lowered the zipper at the back of the dress. She wasn't wearing underwear and as she wiggled out of the clinging gold lamé, his predatory gaze settled on each newly exposed piece of flesh—on her high round breasts, her rosy nipples surrounded by dark brown areolas, the curve of her waist, the fiery nest of hair nestled between firm gold thighs. The sharp scent of chlorine assailing the night air was rapidly being replaced by a warm, musky aroma emanating from Marissa's skin.

"Turn around."

Hot desire rose higher and higher as she turned her back, exposing her round buttocks to his silent appraisal. Marissa knew that if he didn't take her soon, she'd come from the force of those intense blue eyes.

"Okay, you can turn around again." His voice was steady. Impersonal. As if they were two strangers sharing idle conversation while waiting for a bus. But as she watched him take off his own clothes and viewed his swollen sex, Marissa knew that he was not as unaffected by her naked body as he was pretending to be. Such knowledge made her inner fires burn even hotter.

When she started toward him, he held up his hand. "Not yet."

"But I want you."

"Don't worry, you'll have me," he said. "All in good time." He reached out and traced her lips with a fingertip; Marissa, eager for some physical contact, drew the finger inside her mouth and sucked it. "God, you are a greedy little thing, aren't you," he said on a low laugh, retrieving his finger and trailing it wetly across the top of her breasts. "Just like a bitch in heat."

Marissa did not like being laughed at. "I thought you wanted me," she pouted.

"I do. But I can wait." He surveyed the room, his gaze settling on a white wicker lounge chair. "Sit down over there." Marissa sank gladly onto the wicker seat, ignoring the piece of broken cane that dug into her naked buttocks. His eyes held a cruel note of amusement. "Touch yourself, baby. Let me see you play with your tits."

There was something about his dangerously authoritative tone that Marissa found impossible to resist. She cupped her hands over her breasts, pinched the hardened buds, and felt a respondent tug between her legs.

"Good girl. Lift your legs up over the arms of the chair." When she obliged, he nodded. "Now fuck yourself."

She'd never masturbated in front of a man, but now, as her fingers caressed the tender pink folds exposed to his unrelenting gaze, Marissa found the experience a definite turnon. Cream flowed heavily over her hand as she twisted her fingers together and pushed them deep into her moist warmth. Her hips tilted up involuntarily, her head rolled back as a jolt of electricity burst forth from her vagina, catapulting her into the throes of climax. When it was over, she lay wantonly sprawled, dampness glistening in the russet curls between her outstretched legs.

"Feeling better?" Jeff asked in that same casual tone.

Her eyelids fluttered open. He was standing over her, looking at her with a smug satisfaction she found hateful. "You're a bastard."

"And you loved every minute of it."

She couldn't deny it. But that didn't mean she had to like him acting like such a cocksure son of a bitch. "I could make you crawl."

His mouth quirked. "Next time."

The lounge chair groaned in protest as he forced her thighs even farther apart and moved inside her with one hard thrust that made her scream. He was so big. Before her body had a chance to adjust to the enormous phallus throbbing inside her, he began to move, pulling away and reentering her with a force that created pain pulsating through her entire body.

His fingers dug deeply into her soft, yielding flesh, his teeth left purple marks on her perfumed breasts. He pounded into her like a jackhammer for what seemed like hours and, when he finally came, he seized fistfuls of her tangled hair and yanked them hard enough to bring tears to her eyes. But before she could cry out, he crushed an ampule of amyl nitrite under her nose and as the incredible, intense rush exploded between Marissa's parted legs, she forgot all about the pain.

Tina heard it the moment she entered the gilt and mirrored powder room. A low, whimpering moan. Looking around, she saw the woman in the corner of the plush gold carpet, slumped against the wall.

"Mrs. Halladay?"

Edith Halladay's beady, pink-veined eyes pleaded with Tina from folds of pale green flesh. "I'm sick. You have to take me back to my hotel."

Kneeling down beside the woman, Tina took hold of her fleshy wrist and felt for a pulse. Edith Halladay's skin felt clammy, but her heartbeat, when Tina found it, was steady. "Can you stand up?"

The woman made a feeble attempt that failed. As she folded back to the floor, the voluminous red-and-gold beaded caftan settled around her body like a collapsed hot-air balloon.

"I'll never be able to get you out to the car by myself," Tina complained. "You'll have to wait here while I find my husband."

She hurried back down the winding staircase, thinking that tonight had definitely been one of contrasts. Marissa, Farraday, and Edith Halladay all represented the down side. Matthew St. James, on the other hand, was proof that even the gloomiest cloud possessed a silver lining.

The house was quiet. The guests had departed, the caterer had taken his pots and pans away, Joshua had retired to his den, and Marissa had disappeared to God only knew where.

Leigh was in the kitchen, watching Matthew count the partially filled bottles of liquor. "You did a terrific job tonight," she said.

Matthew's only response was a muffled "Yeah." He was making notations in a small wirebound notebook.

"I received several compliments on the margaritas."

"The trick is to use fresh limes."

"Oh. I'll remember that."

Silence.

She decided to try again. "Are you an actor?"

"No."

"But I saw Tina give you one of Corbett's cards."

Matthew cursed under his breath. He had lost count of the Wild Turkey bottles. "Look, Jesse's charging you by the hour. So do you want me to talk or work?"

"Can't you do both?"

Not when her damn perfume was infiltrating his senses like an inhaled drug, Matthew could have answered. "Apparently not."

She appeared to consider that for a moment. "Then I believe I'd like to talk," she decided. "If you don't mind."

Matthew shrugged. "It's your money." Leaning against the counter, he crossed his arms over his chest and gave her a long, appraising look.

Leigh wondered why she was even bothering to attempt conversation with such an impolite, brusque man. Then she remembered that time, midway through the party, when their eyes had met and held. In that suspended moment Leigh had imagined that she heard the clash of cymbals.

"If you're not an actor, why did you take Corbett's card?" she asked, genuinely curious.

"I hadn't realized my behavior was being so carefully monitored."

"A good hostess keeps a close eye on everything."

"And you're a good hostess."

"One of the best."

"And modest, too," he said dryly.

"Someone once told me that it's important to know your worth."

Matthew suppressed a smile. "That's good advice."

"I know. So, if you're not an actor, what are you?"

"A writer."

For some reason Leigh did not want to take time to discern, she was pleased that he wasn't just another handsome face hoping to make a fortune by cashing in on his good looks. And he was incredibly good looking, she admitted. In a disturbing sort of way.

"Baron Studios is always looking for writers. Are you any good?" she asked, echoing Tina Marshall's earlier question.

"I suppose that would depend on personal taste."

His eyes locked onto hers, and Leigh felt a strange tightening in her stomach. She willed herself to look away, but couldn't and felt herself drowning in those smooth amber depths, like a swimmer caught in an undertow.

Christ. What the hell did he think he was doing, standing here in Leigh Baron's Beverly Hills kitchen, wondering what, if anything, she was wearing under that virginal white dress. Would her skin feel as soft as it looked? Matthew wondered. Would it taste as good as it smelled?

Matthew was no stranger to the purely physical need that suddenly flared between them. He had willingly given up his virginity during his sophomore year of high school to a horny, big-breasted foster mother who seduced him on the steps of the family swimming pool while her husband was fishing with the guys at Lake Arrowhead. At first Matthew found sex for two a decided improvement over jerking off in the shower, but then the woman grew increasingly possessive—entering his room without knocking, sneaking into his bed at night while her husband snored unconcernedly in the next room, squeezing his groin under the table during Sunday dinner.

And although Matthew had never been fond of his hatchet-faced social worker, when she showed up with the news that it was time for him to move on to a new family, he could have kissed the woman on her grim, orange-painted lips. Having learned at an early age to avoid commitment, over the years Matthew had settled for one-night stands with an occasional brief affair. He'd given his body in those short-lived relationships, but never his heart.

But now, as he became lost in Leigh Baron's wide gray eyes—eyes that brimmed over with reluctant desire and something else that looked strangely like fear—all his instincts told him that this woman was a siren who could lure him into dangerous, uncharted waters.

"I'd better go," he said abruptly. "It's late."

"It's not that late," Leigh protested, wishing that she hadn't sounded so damned eager. "I haven't had a moment to relax all night; I'd love some company while I unwind. Besides, I've already agreed to pay Mr. Martinez for your time."

Matthew wondered if Leigh Baron always got everything she wanted and decided that she probably did. The woman had been born with a silver spoon in one hand and a fistful of credit cards in the other. It was only sheer luck that she was born into Hollywood royalty, mere good fortune that she was being groomed to succeed her father as head of Baron Studios instead of having to struggle like everyone else. Ancient resentments came swirling up from deep inside him.

He gave her a slow, assessing glance. "I never would have taken you to be the type of woman who'd have to pay for company, Ms. Baron."

His contempt hung heavily on the refrigerated air. The only sign of her distress were the bright splotches of scarlet that appeared high on her cheekbones. Leigh tilted her chin and looked into his uncivilized eyes.

"You're right." Her tone was glacial. "It *is* time for you to go." She handed him an embossed envelope. Inside was the generous tip she had decided on before his insulting remark.

"I'll tell Mr. Martinez that your performance was exemplary."

After six years in the military, Matthew could recognize a command when he heard it. "It's always gratifying to hear a woman has found my performance exemplary."

Lifting the box with the remaining bottles onto his shoulder, he gave her a brief salute, which she took like a slap in the face, and turned sharply on his heel. He was out the door, swallowed up by the darkness, before Leigh noticed that he'd left the envelope behind on the counter.

The princess was trapped in a dark, damp dungeon. The dank odor in the dungeon emanated from a monster with flaming eyes and dragon's breath. Ignoring her desperate pleas for mercy, the monster chained her wrists and ankles to the algae-covered stone wall, then began ripping at her flesh with his razor-sharp talons, again and again.

Leigh's terrified screams woke her, rescuing her from the monster's brutal savagery.

Venice, California, was a theater of the absurd. Although Mack Sennett's bathing beauties no longer cavorted on the beach and the days of Sarah Bernhardt, Charlie Chaplin, and Mary Pickford performing in the city of canals had faded into memory, the exotic beachfront town still maintained its share of entertainers.

Magicians, musicians, and white-faced mimes made the streets their stage while bicyclists and roller skaters raced along Ocean Front Walk. Although the energetic scene provided a continual delight to the senses, on this particular July evening Matthew remained oblivious to the action swirling past him.

He was sitting on the porch of his rented Venice home, nursing a beer and gazing out over the vast expanse of Pacific Ocean. The tide was coming in, the water tinted brilliant shades of crimson, lemon, and amethyst by the setting sun. On the horizon a catamaran rode at anchor and Matthew imagined he could hear the water faintly slapping at the boat's sides.

Under normal conditions, the ever-changing panorama of the Pacific soothed him, cleared his mind and calmed his senses. But not tonight. Matthew was unreasonably edgy. He'd been like this since Joshua Baron's party two days earlier. It was more than Tina Marshall's surprising proposition that had him feeling so uptight, and if he were to be perfectly honest with himself, he'd have to admit that the money she had promised sounded better with each passing day.

Matthew would enjoy the freedom that such money would bring, but he found it almost impossible to imagine himself as an actor. He was a writer, he reminded himself. Still, if playing one role in one film allowed him to work full time at his craft, wouldn't he be a fool to pass up what so many struggling would-be actors would consider a golden opportunity?

Temptation warred with a deep-seated pragmatism. Matthew's mind tossed the problem around, like a fallen leaf in a whirlpool, circling and circling, attempting to work free. Frustrated by his atypical vacillation, he turned his thoughts to another problem. Leigh Baron.

He'd rerun their brief conversation in his mind and was forced to admit that perhaps he'd come across too surly. Thinking back on it, nothing she'd said indicated that she was looking down on him. It was only his own frustration—and that dark, castrating fear of failure, which had attacked without warning—that had caused him to treat her so brusquely.

It was common knowledge that Leigh was being groomed to replace her father. Joshua Baron was a dying breed: the last of the Titans, those legendary studio heads who wielded unchallenged power. They were brutal men and Joshua, like his father before him, was no exception. Matthew wondered idly if Leigh—who reputedly possessed her father's intelligence—had also inherited Baron's ruthless streak.

"Hey, Matty," a bright feminine voice called out, shattering his introspection.

He turned his attention toward the woman waving energetically at him from the porch next door, her waist-length chestnut hair backlit by the setting sun. She was wearing her usual outdated flower-child costume—an ankle-length peasant skirt, a scoop-neck blouse that allowed an enticing, shadowy hint of nipple through the thin gauze material, and bare feet. Dressed as she was, no one would ever guess the attractive young hippy's income came from a hefty portfolio of blue chip stocks inherited from her maternal grandmother.

"Hi, Lana," Matthew greeted her without enthusiasm.

Lana Parker, daughter of San Francisco stockbroker Leland Parker, had one credo: to enjoy life to the fullest. She hated seeing anyone unhappy. Especially Matthew St. James. Although nothing had ever come of the brief fling they'd had when she first moved to Venice, she still thought he was one of the sexiest—and here was the surprise, *nicest*—men she'd ever slept with.

"You look a little down."

Matthew shrugged.

Lana had grown used to her neighbor's enigmatic silences and, while she knew they might intimidate a lesser woman, she believed that keeping your feelings bottled up led to bad karma. "So, how's the screenplay coming along?"

"Okay, I guess."

"I'd love to read it."

He tilted the beer bottle to his lips and took another drink before answering. "Maybe. When I'm done."

"I can't wait. I know it's going to be wonderful."

Matthew's only response was a shrug.

"Are you working tonight?"

"No."

"Then why don't you come over? I just got back from Acapulco with some primo grass that'll blow your mind, and if I've ever seen a man in desperate need of some serious partying, Matthew, it's you."

Matthew wondered what it would be like to have all the money you'd ever need at your fingertips and all the time in the world in which to spend it. When he'd first expressed surprise that someone as wealthy as Lana was living in such a modest place, she had answered simply that people in Venice knew how to party. It was only later that he learned her family owned the entire block of rental houses, his included.

Rich women. He was certainly meeting his share of them

lately. Yet, other than their wealth, Matthew decided that Leigh Baron and Lana Parker had very little in common. As far as he knew, Lana had never worked. After dropping out of Berkeley three years ago, she'd drifted aimlessly from town to town, man to man, enjoying life to the hilt. While Leigh was reputed to be a workaholic.

"Sorry," he said, "but since I've got a rare free evening, I'd better take advantage of it and pound the typewriter keys."

"A girl could get jealous of that horrible old mechanical rival," Lana pouted prettily. Then she shrugged her tawny shoulders. "Well, if you change your mind, the door's always open."

"I'll keep that in mind."

"You do that." She flashed him an appealing grin, then turned around and went back into the house. A moment later, the scratchy sound of Bob Dylan's "Blowin' in the Wind" drifted out onto the sea air, as it did every night about this time, making Matthew wonder why, with all her dough, Lana couldn't at least spring for a new record.

Leaning back in the chair, he twisted the dial on the portable radio beside him. As Vin Scully announced the second game of a Dodgers-Giants twinight doubleheader, Matthew sipped his beer and allowed his thoughts to drift.

To Tina Marshall.

And Leigh Baron.

And what getting involved with either one of those attractive, powerful women could mean to his life.

It was nearly eleven o'clock at night. The studio was quiet, everyone having gone home hours ago. Everyone but Leigh.

She was seated at her desk, reading glasses perched on the end of her nose, her stocking-clad feet curled up under her on the leather chair, reading a novel. It had been a week since the party and for the last four of those seven days Joshua had been in Las Vegas, seeking funding for *Dangerous*. During that time she'd struggled to do not only her own work, but his as well, along with reading the myriad novels Baron Studios had optioned. Over the past few days, she'd begun to feel as if she were searching for a single brilliant diamond in an ever-expanding sea of zircons.

Tonight's novel was a dark and depressing story of a back-
woods Kentucky child repeatedly and horrifyingly raped by
her stepfather. For seven years the girl bore her abuse in stoic
silence, until she became pregnant. It was then that something inside the girl finally snapped. Picking up her father's
squirrel gun after a particularly brutal attack, she shot him.
Again and again. Until the rough-hewn walls of the rustic
cabin were covered in blood and ragged bits of human flesh.

The story, especially the horrifying ending, was riveting.
"But too depressing," Leigh murmured, taking off her
glasses. The headache teasing behind her right eye for the
final three chapters had arrived full blown, threatening to
escalate into a migraine. "It'd die at the box office within a
week."

Reaching into her center drawer, she took out a bottle of
aspirin, poured two into her palm, and swallowed them with
a glass of mineral water. Then she leaned back in her chair
and closed her eyes.

The princess stared at the gilt doorknob. She watched it rattle, her
wide gray eyes pale with terror. The hands were coming again; nothing
would stop them, not even a locked door. The princess hated the hands.
She hated the way they smelled: of hair tonic and aftershave, tobacco
and brandy. She hated the way they made her feel: frightened and dirty,
guilty and ashamed. Trembling, she reached beneath her satin pillow,
feeling for the dagger she'd hidden there. Her fingers curled tightly
around the jeweled hilt. Someday she would kill the hands. She would
stab them with the dagger. Again and again, until they were dead. Then
she would finally be safe.

Clouds of sweetly scented smoke hung over the bedroom.
The slow, sultry fire of Roberta Flack's voice throbbed from
the stereo.

"That's it, baby," Jeff crooned. "Give me some of that
sizzling sex you're so good at."

Marissa, nude save for the milky string of pearls Joshua had
given Leigh for her twenty-first birthday, leaned back against
the black polyester, satinlike pillows and smiled enticingly at
the camera lens.

Jeff eyed her appraisingly. "Almost, but not quite." He

arranged her hair over one naked shoulder. "Think heat."

Marissa thought about her father. And how he'd react if he ever got a glimpse of these photos.

"That's it," Jeff murmured encouragingly, misunderstanding the restless pleasure that flooded into her eyes. "Now think about how it feels when I kiss you." He covered her softly parted lips with his, forcing his tongue deep into the inner recesses of her mouth. "When I touch you here." When his hand cupped her breasts, causing her nipples to tighten, Marissa wondered if Jeff's film would correctly depict their warm, rosy hue.

Since that first night in the pool house, Marissa had continued to enjoy the outrageous sex Jeff offered while deftly manipulating the affair so that he believed himself to be in control. He even thought this photo session was his idea. She spread her legs, imagining her father's reaction when he received the photographs. She'd overheard Leigh fussing over his diet, fretting about his high blood pressure. Wouldn't it be wild if he had a stroke? Or a heart attack? If the stone-hearted old bastard actually croaked, she wouldn't have to worry about him giving her a part in one of his lousy pictures; she'd inherit half of Baron Studios. She'd have real power, the kind spelled with a capital P.

Power. God, how she loved that word!

Unaware of her thoughts, but pleased with the way Marissa was practically setting the sheets on fire, Jeff lifted the camera once again. She was caught there, like a quarry in the cross hairs of a scope. "Imagine me fucking you, baby. Think about my cock inside you, how good it feels."

Rather than contemplate Jeff's mental image, Marissa instead imagined the unblinking lens to be the steely gaze of her father and licked her lips lasciviously. When her hand fluttered to her engorged clitoris, the camera shutter opened and closed.

The thought of how much dough he was going to get for this batch of photos stimulated the most magnificent erection in Jeff's recent memory. "That's enough for today," he said, tossing the camera aside. When he stripped off his jeans and approached the bed, Marissa arched her hips off the slick ebony sheets.

Ignoring her silent invitation, he flipped her over onto her stomach and spread the cheeks of her plump round ass. She gave a short surprised gasp when his teeth sunk into her flesh, but then he was inside her and there was only his pounding, relentless energy and heat. When she came, it was a violent series of convulsive spasms.

Later, lying beside Jeff on the musky, sex-rumpled sheets, sharing the joint he passed her, Marissa couldn't remember being happier.

After a restless night's sleep, Leigh was back at work, feeling as if she'd gone fifteen rounds with Muhammad Ali. She had just completed a meeting with a group of SAG representatives when she found herself picking up the novel she'd finished late last night. Rereading selective sections, she found it every bit as mesmerizing as she remembered. It was also entirely unsuitable for the big screen. Audiences wanted happy endings in return for the price of their tickets; if they wanted grim reality, they could stay home and turn on the evening news.

A deep voice broke into her introspection. "So how's my right-hand girl?"

Leigh glanced up to see her father standing in the doorway. So he'd finally returned from Las Vegas. It was about time. "Myopic. This is the fifth novel I've read this week. I'm beginning to wonder why we bothered to option any of them." She took off the dark-rimmed glasses, revealing the fatigue in her eyes.

"To keep anyone else from bringing them to the screen, of course." He consulted the diamond-studded Rolex on his wrist. "How about going out to lunch with your old man?"

She smiled apologetically. Her hand swept over a stack of hardcover novels taking up a good portion of her desk. "I'd planned to send down to the commissary for a salad. But thanks just the same."

Joshua frowned. "I thought we should catch up on what happened while I was away."

"Fine." Leigh reached for the phone. "Want me to order two salads?"

"I made reservations at Musso and Frank's."

It was an order. Couched in silk, but an order just the same. Rising immediately from her dove-gray leather chair, Leigh tucked a few errant blond hairs back into the twist at the nape of her neck. "Give me two minutes to freshen up and I'll be right with you."

"Take five minutes," he allowed expansively. "And have Meredith clear your calendar for the rest of the afternoon."

"But I have a meeting with Pamela Winter at three. She's designing the costumes for *Kaleidoscope* and has some sketches she wants me to approve."

"*Kaleidoscope* isn't even going to begin shooting until October. Instruct Meredith to reschedule Pamela. You and I are celebrating."

"Celebrating?" She belatedly realized that her father's eyes were actually twinkling. How long had it been since she'd seen him looking so pleased with himself? Too long.

"I'll tell you all about it over lunch," he promised, shooing her from the room. "Now hurry and get ready; you know I hate to be late."

Leigh didn't budge. "And you know how I hate secrets."

Joshua's exaggerated sigh resembled a deflating blowfish. "Stubborn," he muttered, "just like her grandfather. All right, I'll give you one hint: it's about *Dangerous*."

Her heart leaped into her throat. "Tell me it's good news."

"The best."

It was all she needed to hear. As she hurried from the room, Leigh felt as if she'd just been given a shot of adrenaline.

Corbett Marshall had never considered himself to be a superstitious man. Still, he had noticed that his most profitable deals had been made over the sauerbraten at the Musso & Frank Grill. Not one to tamper with success, when Matthew telephoned one week after Joshua Baron's party, Corbett suggested that they meet for lunch.

The Musso & Frank Grill was a bastion of L.A. nostalgia. It opened its door in 1919, making it the oldest restaurant in Hollywood. Its clientele consisted mostly of writers, directors, and actors who came to bask in the lingering ambiance of Faulkner and Fitzgerald. Corbett hoped that as an aspiring writer, Matthew St. James would find the atmosphere intoxicating. If he was as perfect for the part of Ryder Long as Tina professed—and he'd never known his wife to be wrong—the man could solve a great many problems. And make them all richer in the bargain.

As soon as Matthew arrived, the maître d' led him to the high-backed, red-leather booth. Even seated, Corbett Marshall gave off an impression of tremendous strength and power. Not just physical power, but the steely self-determination of a man used to getting his own way. The agent's silent, judicial study made Matthew feel like a side of beef on display.

"Perhaps this was a mistake," Matthew said.

Corbett blinked, then shook his head. "I'm sorry," he said. "I'm afraid that once every decade I'm guilty of professional bad manners."

Although he'd learned long ago to trust Tina's judgment, Corbett hadn't honestly expected to meet Ryder Long in the flesh. Christ, he thought, wait until Leigh saw this one. He felt like shouting out *eureka*. Now if Matthew St. James only talked half as good as he looked . . .

He held out his hand, his easy smile belying his earlier impersonal behavior. "I'm pleased to meet you, Matthew. My wife has talked of little else since Josh's party last week."

Matthew shook the older man's hand before taking a seat in the red booth. "It's good to meet you too, Mr. Marshall, but—"

"The name's Corbett," he corrected amiably. "Whenever anyone calls me Mr. Marshall, I'm tempted to look over my shoulder for my father."

"Was your father an agent?"

"An attorney. Actually, he represented the greats: Selznick, Theda Bara, Doug Fairbanks. My grandfather was one of D. W. Griffith's personal bankers."

"That's very interesting." Matthew wondered what the hell he was doing sitting here in a landmark Hollywood restaurant with one of the most powerful people in town.

"Yes, my family's been involved with the movie business in one way or another for as long as there's *been* a Hollywood," Corbett said. "In fact, when my grandfather got involved in the industry, it was still based in New Jersey. The talent was all working in New York theaters at the time and the actors would sneak across the river to earn the money the movie producers were paying."

"Sneak?"

"They didn't want their names attached to anything they considered a bastard industry," Corbett explained. He paused briefly when the waiter arrived to take their drink orders. That out of the way, he picked up his story where he'd left off. "They made a helluva lot of movies in those early years. Griffith, during one five-year stretch, directed over five hundred movies. Some theaters changed entire shows every day." His eyes took on a faraway, reminiscent glow, as if he were imagining working during such a boom time. "All those pictures resulted in the birth of Hollywood."

Matthew leaned forward, intrigued. Although he liked to believe that he'd remained unaffected by the glitter of Hollywood, in his more honest, introspective moments he wondered if anyone could live in Los Angeles without fantasizing about those early glory days.

"Most people think the weather was the underlying reason behind the move west," Corbett continued, enjoying the opportunity to impart his vast knowledge of the business. "And granted, our bright California sunshine was a major factor. But the initial reason was that the studios had to pay Thomas Edison a fee for each and every film. The motion picture was his invention, you know."

Matthew nodded as he took a drink from the frosted mug of dark German beer. "Moving three thousand miles from New York made it easier for pirate studios to steal," he guessed.

"Exactly." Corbett plucked an olive from the glass the waiter had delivered with his martini. The glass of extra olives was routinely bestowed upon the regulars by the management, a perk Corbett had never questioned. As a lifelong Hollywood insider, he was accustomed to being treated with the type of reverence reserved elsewhere for visiting royalty. "Some things never change," he pointed out reflectively. "Which is why agents exist. To protect actors' interests from greedy studios."

Matthew had decided that he owed it to Corbett Marshall to be up front about his lack of acting ambition. "I have to be honest with you," he began carefully.

Corbett waved an impatient hand. "One important lesson my father taught me was never to discuss business on an empty stomach." He motioned for the waiter, who appeared instantly with their menus.

"You can't go wrong with the homemade chicken pot pie," Corbett suggested, not bothering to open his own menu. "Although personally, I'd recommend the sauerbraten."

Although Matthew had vowed never to play Hollywood games, neither was he a complete fool. "The sauerbraten sounds great."

Even as he reminded himself that he was not a superstitious man, Corbett couldn't hide his satisfaction.

"Well?" Leigh asked, picking at her zucchini Florentine. It was delicious, but anticipation had dulled her appetite.

Joshua eyed her mildly. "Well, what?"

He was so damn smug. It could only mean good news, Leigh considered. So why didn't he just come out with it? She waved a breadstick threateningly at him. "You realize, of course, that you could be accused of mental cruelty."

Joshua chuckled. "First things first," he said, taking a small, gift-wrapped package from his jacket pocket.

Leigh recognized the robin's-egg blue wrapping instantly. Tiffany was one of Joshua's favorite haunts; her father had always believed in going first class. She shook her head as she slipped off the white satin ribbon. "You spoil me."

"Nonsense." He touched a fond finger to her cheek. "It's impossible to spoil a princess."

Leigh drew her head back slightly, breaking the delicate physical contact. She had come to the conclusion a long time ago that the world was divided into two groups of people— the touchers and the nontouchers. Tina Marshall, for instance, seemed unable to keep her hands to herself. Like graceful birds, they continually fluttered, caressingly, reassuringly. It was not any attempt to invade personal space; it was simply Tina's way. Marissa was also a toucher. As was Joshua.

Leigh was not.

"Oh." She stared in awe at the peacock-hued black pearl earrings. The perfectly matched pearls were so large it was almost impossible to believe they were real. But of course they were.

Joshua frowned. "You don't like them."

Unable to resist their iridescent luster, Leigh ran her finger over the gleaming surface of the gemstones. "How could I not?" she murmured. "They're lovely. But surely they were also horribly expensive?"

Joshua shrugged. "Don't worry about it; I had a run of luck at the baccarat tables. Besides," he said, covering her hand with his, "you've grown into a beautiful woman, Leigh. And beautiful women deserve pearls. Of all the gems in the world, pearls are the most feminine. And romantic."

As she avoided his eyes, Leigh felt the color rise in her cheeks and wished that her father wouldn't talk to her this way. Oh, she knew that underneath his brusque, impatient exterior dwelt the heart of a true romantic—why else would he be so drawn to the film industry? Still, his continually flattering statements always embarrassed her.

"Really, Daddy," she protested on a quiet, not-so-steady laugh, "how you do carry on. I hate to think what would happen if people discovered what a soft touch you are."

Leaning back in the booth, Joshua chuckled as he sipped his Scotch. "Probably ruin me," he said agreeably.

Casting one last fond glance at the pearls, Leigh slid the box into her Gucci alligator bag and folded her hands on the table. "Don't you think it's time you told me what, exactly, it is we're celebrating?"

"We've got the funding for *Dangerous*."

She'd been hoping that was the case. But there had been too many times during the past three years when she'd allowed herself to get her hopes up before, only to have them subsequently dashed. "Who?"

"It's not exactly a who, but a what. I've been promised all the money we need from a land development company that wants to branch out into new areas. Fortunately for us, they liked the idea of investing in your movie."

"Who are the principals in this land company? And why, out of all the scripts floating around today, did they choose *Dangerous*?"

"Really, Leigh, the answer to your second question should be obvious. After all, you're the one who's been insisting that *Dangerous* has Academy Award–winning potential. Besides," he pointed out gruffly, his annoyance evident, "your old man just happens to be one helluva salesman."

"I'm well aware of your vast talents," she said. "But you still haven't told me who, exactly, these generous, farsighted people are."

Joshua was not accustomed to finding himself on the defensive. He bristled. "No one you'd know. Does it really matter? We've got the money, Leigh. That's the important thing."

Leigh could not understand why her father was being so evasive. Knowing better than to push him into a corner, she opted for a more circumspect tack. "I'll want to meet with them," she warned.

"Of course," he answered curtly. His features were rigidly set. "Now, if you don't mind, I believe I'll order dessert. Unless my daughter would rather drag me down to the Beverly Hills police station and submit me to a polygraph test?"

Leigh stifled a weary sigh. For a man who wielded such extensive power, her father could certainly take things personally. "Don't be so dramatic," she said mildly, "I was only trying to get a grasp on the details of the deal."

"Details are for lawyers. The important thing is that you've got your funding."

"But—"

He cut her off with an almost imperceptible narrowing of his eyes. It was a warning gesture she'd come to respect. "I believe I'll have the cheesecake," he said to the waiter, who had appeared beside the table instantaneously, as if pulled out of one of Joshua Baron's bag of tricks. "Leigh?"

Leigh bit back a curse, knowing that to create a scene with her father in public would not only set tongues wagging all over town, but start rumors about even more problems at Baron Studios. "I believe I'll pass on dessert," she said with a great deal more equanimity than she felt. "I'd better be getting back to the studio; I still have a lot of work to do."

Although he'd been the one to insist that she clear her calendar for the remainder of the afternoon, Joshua seemed disinclined to continue their conversation. "Fine. I'll see you at home."

As she rose from the table, Leigh viewed the flash of disappointment in her father's eyes. She knew it hurt him when they argued, and although their working so closely together was bound to generate conflict, Leigh was always left feeling guilty. Giving in, she bent down and gave him a quick peck on his tanned cheek.

"Thank you for the earrings," she said, feeling genuine warmth. "They're absolutely beautiful."

Their earlier dispute forgotten, Joshua beamed. "Not as beautiful as my girl."

While Corbett pitched the same line Tina had at the party, Matthew's gaze wandered across the room to Leigh Baron. She was, he admitted, beautiful: a slim, chisel-featured blonde in the finest Scandinavian tradition. She was also not his type.

"What makes you think I can act?" he asked, returning his attention to the conversation.

Corbett shrugged. "To paraphrase Spencer Tracy, all there is to acting is learning your lines, showing up on time, and trying not to bump into the furniture."

Matthew remained unconvinced. "I'll admit that the money you're offering is attractive," he said slowly. "But I still can't believe what you're suggesting is even possible. I wasn't one of those kids who took drama courses in school; hell, I never even played a tree in any grade-school plays." He didn't men-

tion that attending eight different grammar schools had precluded such youthful opportunity.

"Let's just take things one step at a time," Corbett said with
careful casualness. He was trying to hide his building enthusiasm.

During the leisurely lunch, Matthew St. James had proven
himself to be an intelligent, level-headed, albeit intensely restrained, individual. Under normal circumstances, such a reserved attitude might work against an actor, making him seem
shallow, or even worse, dull—a cardinal sin in this town.

Yet there was something different about Matthew; he possessed an unnerving aura of explosive energy lurking just
beneath his steely, controlled surface. And, as Tina had been
pointing out for days, the guy was gorgeous. In a dark, unsettling kind of way. Matthew St. James, Corbett mused, like
Ryder Long, was definitely not the type of man a girl would
want to take home to Daddy.

He did not trust easily, nor was he a man who took anything
at face value. The deep-seated personality trait would serve
him well, Corbett considered, if he intended to work in this
town where ethics were often skin deep. He also was an expert
at keeping his emotions to himself. Matthew St. James would
not be here today if he wasn't at least moderately intrigued
with the idea of acting in a major motion picture. But his face
had given nothing away.

Almost nothing. There had been that one time, when his
eyes had drifted over to Leigh and Joshua Baron, and a fleeting interest had flickered in those tawny depths. It had come
and gone so quickly that if Corbett hadn't been watching
Matthew closely, he would have missed it.

"You'll need photos."

"Photos?" Matthew asked unenthusiastically.

"A portfolio to send over to Baron Studios. To pique their
interest."

"I can't afford a professional photographic session."

Corbett brushed the problem aside, as if it were a pesky fly.
"No problem, I'll advance you the funds—"

"I don't borrow money."

Corbett could respect Matthew's stubbornness, since he
possessed a fair share of that trait himself. But enough was

enough. "Don't be so damnably hard-headed; you'll pay me back after Baron signs you to star in *Dangerous*." He took out a gold Waterman fountain pen and scribbled a telephone number down on the back of one of his gray business cards. "Jill Cocheran's the best in the business," he said, handing Matthew the card. "When Jill's finished, Leigh Baron will be on her knees, begging for you."

Matthew couldn't resist a smile at that particular mental image. "Where do I sign?"

Corbett didn't hesitate. "Right here," he said, penning the brief agreement on a paper cocktail napkin.

Matthew perused it quickly, took the pen Corbett offered, and signed his name in a bold, spiky script.

"Now that our business is concluded," Corbett said, "we should order champagne."

Matthew shook his head. "Thanks, but since I'm working tonight, I have to go by the warehouse and pick up the liquor."

The agent looked inclined to argue, but quickly changed his mind. "I've always admired a man who knows how to put work before pleasure. It's a rare trait in this town." He rose, extending his hand once again. "We'll have the champagne after the pictures are finished."

"After I get the part," Matthew corrected firmly, a statement with which the older man immediately concurred.

Matthew had just reached the door when he came face to face with Leigh. Experiencing an immediate—and disturbing—sexual tug, he frowned and nodded brusquely as he stepped aside to let her pass.

Leigh recognized him immediately. This was not the type of man a woman would meet and easily forget. Recalling their last encounter and the unpleasant way it had ended, she was no more eager than he to engage in a feigned polite conversation.

Lifting her chin, she preceded him out the door without a backward glance. Once outside the stone-and-glass block restaurant, Matthew headed in one direction, Leigh in the other. Neither had said a word.

Yet as she drove her racing green Jaguar sedan back down Hollywood Boulevard toward the arched Spanish gates of

Baron Studios, Leigh recalled the instantaneous flash of anger in the look he'd given her and wondered at the cause.

Later that afternoon, in a warehouse across town, Matthew shoved a dime into the slot of a pay phone. He was not surprised when the woman on the other end of the line assured him that she'd love to have him drop by after he got off work tonight.

As he replaced the receiver in its wall cradle, Matthew tried to convince himself that Lana Parker had been his first choice all along.

"Are you sure you want to do this?"

Leigh sat on the edge of Marissa's bed, watching her sister haphazardly throwing things into the Louis Vuitton cases.

Marissa held up two bikinis for consideration—one consisting of little more than two pieces of yellow yarn, the other crocheted from black string. After a moment's hesitation, she tossed both into the suitcase.

"I've never been so sure of anything in my life."

"But it's only been what, ten days? How can you be ready to live together?"

"I've been going with Jeff for two weeks. Which is thirteen more days than I needed to make up my mind." She chewed on a ragged coral thumbnail and observed the clothing strewn over the pink-satin spread. "God, I need some new threads. Jeff's taking me to a party and this junk is so ancient."

Leigh didn't point out that, less than two months ago,

Marissa had spent a king's ransom practically buying out Neiman-Marcus's entire junior department in search of a suitable wardrobe for the Beverly Hills High School's senior trip to Maui.

"Where's the party?"

"I don't know." Marissa was purposefully vague. "Somewhere in West Hollywood or Malibu. I forget . . . I know!" Her expression brightened as she turned to Leigh. "How about letting me borrow your black dress?"

It was a Bill Blass, simply fashioned of black crepe, beautifully draped and ridiculously expensive. Leigh had fallen in love with it at first glance while shopping for a new suit at Bonwit Teller last week and had managed to justify the exorbitant price tag by assuring herself that its classic lines would allow her to wear it forever. "But it's brand-new. I haven't even had a chance to wear it yet."

"So? I'm not going to go surfing in it or anything. God, sometimes you sound just like Daddy. No wonder you're his favorite; you're turning into a damn Joshua Baron clone."

Years of acrimony hung heavily on the air as the two sisters faced each other across the bed, cool gray eyes dueling with gleaming green. Marissa blinked first, managing to look almost contrite.

"I'm sorry." Her soft voice begged absolution, her lips trembled. "You know what a bitch I am right before my period."

Even as Leigh admired Marissa's performance, she wanted to believe her sincerity. "Don't worry about it; we've all been under a lot of stress lately."

"Tell me about it! Can you keep a secret?"

"Of course."

"Cross your heart and hope to die?"

Leigh smiled. "Cross my heart."

"It doesn't count unless you actually do the motions."

Marissa looked just like a little girl again, reminding Leigh of the years she'd mothered her, made allowances for her, defended her rebellious behavior to their father.

Leigh crisscrossed her index finger over her left breast. "Cross my heart."

"And hope to die."

"And hope to die."

Marissa nodded, satisfied. "This party is really important, Leigh. I haven't said anything because I was afraid nothing would come of it, but Jeff took some pictures of me last week and showed them to a producer, who wants to meet me."

"Really? Who?"

"Jeff didn't tell me his name; he said he wanted it to be a surprise. But he's the one throwing the party, and Jeff thinks I've got a great chance for a part in the picture he's casting."

Although Leigh hadn't seen a great deal of Marissa these past two weeks, she had noticed that every other sentence her sister uttered began with "Jeff says" or "Jeff thinks." She'd seen the man in question only twice, and then only briefly. A little over six feet tall, he was tan, athletic-looking, and hand-some, in a California beachboy sort of way. His sun-bleached hair had hung well over his collar and a trio of gold chains had filled in the open neck of his shirt. Actually, Leigh had consid-ered at the time, Jeff appeared to be a male version of Marissa.

"Do you know what picture?" As much as Leigh wanted to believe that her sister was being offered a legitimate part in an actual motion picture, she couldn't help wondering if there was a producer left in town their father hadn't gotten to in his effort to keep Marissa from becoming an actress.

"Jeff didn't say. But he promised it was a good part. And the producer liked my still shots a lot."

"You know, honey," Leigh cautioned, "there are a great many unscrupulous people in this town. And you are awfully young."

Marissa's face hardened. "I'm old enough to know the ropes. You're not the only one who grew up around a movie studio, you know." As if immediately regretting her harsh tone, she flashed Leigh her sweetest smile. "But the thing is, all my clothes look like kids' stuff. I need something really sophisticated."

"Like my black dress." Leigh could feel herself weakening.

"Exactly." Marissa's smile turned positively angelic. "Please, Leigh? I promise not to eat or drink anything all night, so I won't spill on it. And I swear I'll take it to the dry cleaners before I return it."

Leigh relented, as she'd known all along she would. "Wait

here," she said on a sigh. "I'll go get it."

Marissa clapped her hands together in childish delight. "You are an absolute lifesaver!" She came around the end of the bed and impulsively kissed Leigh's cheek. "When I'm a big star, I'm going to tell everyone that I owed my first break to my wonderful, beautiful big sister."

Leigh sighed. "Just try to bring the dress back in one piece."

For Matthew, who had expected a cold, intimidating photography studio, Jill Cocheran's loft proved a revelation. The cavernous interior was cluttered with furniture, books, ancient props, and photographic equipment. Bright sunshine poured through a skylight, flooding the room with soft yellow light. An enormous orange cat lounged on an overstuffed sofa, basking in the warmth of the sunbeam. When Matthew entered the studio, the cat opened one eye and studied him with an attitude of feline superiority.

Photographic prints covered the walls: expected photos of movie stars and rock performers shared space with candid shots of heads of states, farmers, factory workers, captains of industry, miners, and migrant workers.

At five-feet-ten-inches tall in her bare feet, Jill possessed just enough curves to prevent her from appearing angular. Her expressive face, framed by a tangled mane of sun-streaked honey hair, possessed a firm chin and cheekbones any cover girl would kill for, and her eyes were a remarkable china blue. Tanned legs, clad in a pair of brief white shorts, went on forever. Her only flaw, if it could be considered a flaw, was her overly full, unpainted lips. Deciding that they added a ripely sexual appeal to her idealized, American girl-next-door looks, Matthew was surprised that with all she had going for herself in the looks department, Jill Cocheran had opted for the business end of the camera.

"My daddy gave me a camera for my eighth birthday," she explained when he offered his opinion midway through their photo shoot. Matthew had been uncomfortable when he had first arrived at the loft, but Jill's open personality and comfy, down-home West Texas drawl gradually eased his discomfort.

Over coffee served in earthenware mugs, she explained that she never approached a shoot as just another job. They were here to do something together. To establish a rapport. Eventually he almost managed to forgot the unblinking lens. Almost. But not quite.

"It was just a little ole Kodak," she said as she moved a light stanchion. Studying her hand-held light meter, she frowned because the reading disallowed his face to be in sharp focus. "But Ah was hooked before Ah finished my first roll of film. All ducks."

"Ducks?"

She adjusted the silver Mylar fill. "You know, sugah, those fluffy white things that float on ponds and eat standing on their heads with their flat orange feet in the air. Ducks."

"Sounds as if you started out to be a wildlife photographer."

"Not at all." She began to click the remote camera switch. A bare bulb flashed from behind a sheet of blue background paper. "We lived next door to a golf course water hazard. Since Ah wanted to use up all the film and get it developed before my daddy left town again, the ducks proved the handiest subjects."

Pleased with how the arrangement of the lights added additional sparkle to his intriguing amber eyes, Jill decided that the time had come to add a little beefcake to the portfolio.

"You can take off your shirt now."

"Why?"

She wasn't surprised when he balked. Just as she'd instructed when setting the appointment, Matthew was wearing a faded blue chambray shirt and a pair of jeans worn white at the stress points. Aware that this was a man unaccustomed to displaying his body for an audience, she softened her tone. "Because you're going to need a torso shot in your portfolio."

Matthew folded his arms across his chest. "If getting the role depends on how I look without my shirt, I think I'll pass. This is a ridiculous idea, anyway."

When he looked inclined to leave, Jill suffered a momentary sense of panic. Although she wouldn't know for certain until she developed the film, all afternoon she'd been getting a sense of something special evolving. She couldn't let Matthew get away.

"Look here, sugah," she coaxed, coming from behind the bank of lights to place her hand lightly on his arm. Beneath her fingers his muscles were tensed hard as boulders. "Ah promise not to take any shots that might come back to haunt you. Or embarrass you. But hell, honey, beefcake—uh, torso shots—are part of this business." Her Texas twang had thickened to the consistency of maple syrup and her guileless smile offered reassurance. "Casting directors jus' want to be sure that y'all don't have some tattoo of a naked lady etched across your pecs."

Matthew smiled as she'd hoped he would. "I really hate this."

Jill nodded. "Ah know." Her bright blue eyes held sympathy. And resolve. "And Ah truly do promise to make it as painless as possible."

Matthew weighed his options and decided that since he'd already come this far, he may as well see this farce out. "How about making it as fast as possible?"

"It's a deal." She managed to avoid looking too triumphant. "Ah thought we'd put you by the window," she suggested, moving across the room. Matthew noticed that once she'd gotten her way, her drawl grew less pronounced. "The natural light's fantastic and the block wall and unpainted windowsill will add a rustic charm."

She turned around and was momentarily stunned into silence. Lordy, Jill considered, with a body like that, she wouldn't be at all surprised if the guy was hung like one of her Grandpappy Cocheran's Texas Longhorns.

"No tattoos," she said finally.

"Nary a one," Matthew agreed.

There was a moment of shared silence. "Well," she said, "let's get this here show on the road."

The remainder of the afternoon flew. She had read the novel Corbett messengered over to her, and knew from the beginning what she wanted to achieve from the session. And now, when everything clicked into place, it was like a shot of electricity shooting through her. A high-energy person, she was able to draw the best from a subject. And Matthew St.

James, she mused, as she took a few final parting shots, had more than most.

"How about dinner?" she asked as she went around the loft, turning off the bright lights. "Ah make a mean chiliburger. If you're not afraid to try genuine West Texas chili, that is."

Matthew realized that they'd worked straight through lunch. "A chiliburger sounds great."

The brilliance of her smile rivaled the sunset streaming through the windows. "Y'all are a risk taker, Matthew St. James," she decided. "Ah've always liked that in a man."

Later that evening, they were sitting on her overstuffed couch, listening to James Taylor and sipping brandy. Matthew was pleasantly surprised to discover that this afternoon's energy-driven dynamo could also be quietly companionable. A pleasant silence settled down around them and, as Matthew's gaze swept the room, he noticed a group of riveting photographs he'd missed the first time.

"Did you take those Vietnam shots?"

"Uh-uh. Those are my daddy's."

Matthew left the comfort of the sofa to study them in greater detail. All the photographs were of soldiers, the young, dirt-streaked faces achingly familiar. "They're damn good. But I suppose that's to be expected."

"Daddy was the best. He was an AP photographer who was—"

"Wounded during a firefight at Chu Lai in '69. His death ten days later was officially attributed to peritonitis and pneumonia resulting from his wounds."

Jill stared at him. "How on earth did you know that?"

Matthew shrugged. "I knew Bill Cocheran. He was a great guy. And the only man I ever met who could say 'Don't shoot, I'm a journalist' in eight different languages. There was this one time . . ." His voice trailed off as he belatedly realized he should be more circumspect. After all, Wild Bill Cocheran had been this woman's father.

Jill was curled up in the corner of the couch, her long legs tucked under her. "Y'all don't have to watch your words on my account, Matthew. I'd like to hear something about those days."

Matthew sat down beside her, cradling his glass in his palms. Jill waited as he stared into the brandy, collecting his thoughts.

"It was shortly before all hell broke loose during the Tet Offensive. This guy in my unit had just gotten word he was a father—a girl, seven pounds, three ounces. Funny the things you remember," he mused out loud. "Anyway, your dad decided that we should take him to Cholon to celebrate."

"Cholon?"

"The Chinese section of Saigon. Somehow—don't ask me how—Bill had gotten hold of this case of Seagram's. After all the homemade hootch and Saigon Tea, that damned colored water the bar girls were always pushing," he explained at her questioning glance, "that premium booze was cause in itself for a celebration. We ordered grilled chicken, boiled shrimp, and plates piled high with what sure as hell tasted like real beef, all paid for by your father with the beneficence of his Associated Press expense account."

"Daddy always was a generous man," Jill agreed matter-of-factly. "Particularly when he was spending some Yankee's money."

"So I discovered. Wild Bill Cocheran's expense account sheets will probably go down in literary history as some of the Vietnam era's most creative writing. Anyway, after dinner we all sat around drinking and smoking cigars and talking about kids and families—all that homey stuff."

Then Matthew's expression changed. He recalled the envy he'd felt, listening to the others reminisce about loved ones waiting for them back home. Jill took note of the fleeting frown and decided not to comment on it. She'd already determined that Matthew was an intensely private man.

"This pretty little whore, dressed in one of those shiny, paper-thin silk dresses so many of the bar girls wore, had obviously figured out which of us had the dough. She climbed up on your dad's lap and began biting his ear and running her fingers through his hair. We were all going crazy, watching this, but Bill didn't seem to notice. Instead, he kept on talking about his daughter who—and this is a quote—had more talent in her pinky than he had in his entire body."

A warm feeling flooded through her. Warmth and a nostalgic longing that she'd learned to live with. "Daddy said that?"

"He sure as hell did. I remember because about that point the girl got tired of being ignored and assured your father that she had more talent in *her* pinky than any American baby-san."

"Baby-san?"

"Virgin."

"Oh." Jill had to ask. "What happened next?"

Matthew shrugged. "I can't remember. It was probably about that time we all passed out."

Jill had the distinct impression that he was being deliberately circumspect on her account and appreciated his concern for her feelings. "Thank you for sharing that with me," she said quietly. "Ah never knew my father very well. My parents were divorced when Ah was still a baby and Daddy was always off chasing his photo stories—Selma, Birmingham, Vietnam." She shivered, remembering the scenes of the dogs, the fire hoses, those terrifying crosses blazing in the night, the death and destruction of war.

Matthew didn't say a word. He simply reached over and put his arm around her. Jill put her head on his shoulder.

"Whenever he'd come visit, he'd scoop me up and hold me against his chest. He was so big and strong that Ah let myself believe no one could ever hurt him."

She turned her head upward, gazing directly at his lips. Lowering his head, Matthew tasted the softness of her mouth. He kissed her once, lightly. Then again. Slowly, artfully, hungrily.

After a long, pleasurable time, Jill tilted her head back. "Do you want to make love to me, Matthew?"

Matthew had always believed in being straightforward. "Yes."

She stood up, extending her hand. "Well, then, what are we waiting for?"

They undressed each other, hands lingering over warming skin, lips caressing newly freed flesh. When they lay facing each other on the bed, Jill's hands skimmed the planes and hollows of Matthew's body, her fingers tracing long, corded muscles that contracted under her exploring touch. In turn, Matthew moved his hands over her slender curves, drawing out a slow, smoldering need that had her aching for release.

He stopped only long enough to put on the condom he was never without—no bastard kids for Matthew St. James—and then his tongue slid into her, creating explosions of mind-blinding pleasure. Unable to remain passive while he was driving her mad, Jill's touch grew greedy. She dragged him up to lie full length on her, drawled dirty words in his ear as she wrapped her long, tanned legs around his hips and guided his penis home. The fluffy comforter slid unnoticed onto the floor; the sheets became hot and tangled.

Control disintegrated as the power swept them away, their bodies fused, moving in unison until they climaxed together in a hot flood of release. When it was finally over, they lay beside each other on the rumpled bed.

"That was," Matthew said, still breathing heavily, "one of the most intense sexual encounters of my life."

"Sugah," she said, on a low, throaty chuckle, "you ain't seen nothin' yet." She was smiling as she bent her head and took him deeply into her mouth.

When his half-limp penis rose to her intimate demands, Matthew decided that truer words had never been spoken.

Much later, while Matthew slept, Jill crept from the bed and disappeared into the darkroom. After developing the day's work, she sat in the eerie glow of the red light and studied the contact sheets for a long, silent time. Then she began dialing the telephone she'd taken into the room with her.

"Ah'm glad Ah caught you home," she said when the male voice on the other end of the line answered. "What? No, Ah most certainly have not been drinking. As a matter of fact, Ah've been working. How the hell should Ah know what time it is?"

Again that gruff voice.

"Really? Four A.M.?" She paused, allowing the man to give her a few choice suggestions as to what she could do with both her camera and the telephone. Finally, she broke into his heated monologue. "Don't you dare hang up on me, Corbett Marshall," she insisted. "Not until you hear my news about your new client, Matthew sexy-as-all-get-out St. James."

That got his attention. Jill had known it would. "Tell you

what, sugah. Y'all get Baron Studios to give me an exclusive on all his still work and Ah'll comp you a set of publicity shots that'll knock your socks off.''

Satisfied with Corbett's response, she belatedly apologized for waking him up, hung up the phone, and went back to work.

Watching the eight-by-ten image of Matthew slowly appear beneath the developing fluid, Jill experienced a satisfied burst of pleasure at the idea of having made love to Hollywood's new sex symbol. And hot damn, she'd found him first.

Baron Studios brought to mind a California mission. Entrance to the hallowed grounds was through a pair of tall white arches; the buildings were gleaming white stucco topped with rust-red Spanish tile. Looking at the architecture from the visitors' parking lot, Matthew expected to see a flock of swallows swooping down on the towering belfry.

If the exterior of the studio was reminiscent of long-ago settlers, the interior blended old-time Hollywood opulence with modern California chic. The walls were covered in soft suede the color of sand, bark brown leather chairs with curved brass arms rested beside ebony end tables inlaid with ivory. The ornate gold-and-crystal chandeliers could have come from the prop room of an early Cecil B. De Mille epic; the paintings with their heavy gilt frames could been taken directly from the walls of Selznick's Tara; and the enormous glass display case filled with Oscars—the little gold statuettes standing in rows by movie and by year—was evidence of the longevity of Baron Studios' success.

A receptionist attractive enough to be one of the studio's starlets examined Matthew with interest as he approached her desk. "I'm Matthew St. James. I have an appointment with Mr. Baron at four o'clock." It was one minute to four.

Lines furrowed the young woman's brow. "I'm sorry, Mr. Baron's out of town. Perhaps you mean Ms. Baron," she suggested helpfully.

She ran a carmine-tinted nail down the page of the appointment book. Matthew's heart thudded in his chest. If he had been uncomfortable talking with Leigh Baron in the kitchen of the Baron mansion, the idea of reading for her was abhorrent.

"Here it is," she said happily. "I was right; your appointment is with Ms. Baron at four o'clock." She picked up the phone and announced Matthew. "Ms. Baron's secretary will be with you in a moment."

Only pride kept Matthew from leaving. That and his unflagging ambition. He'd come this far, there wasn't any point in turning back now. When a striking young redhead stepped into the reception area, Matthew wondered if good looks were a requirement for working at Baron Studios.

"Good afternoon, Mr. St. James," she greeted him with a welcoming smile. "I'm Meredith Ward, Ms. Baron's secretary. I'm so sorry for the misunderstanding; someone should have informed you that Ms. Baron is conducting all the reading auditions for *Dangerous*."

"So I just discovered."

She seemed surprised by his grim tone. "Do you have a problem with reading for Ms. Baron?"

A problem? That had to be the understatement of the century. "Not at all."

She nodded. "I'm glad. Ms. Baron will see you now." Matthew followed her down the hall. The suede-covered walls of the hallway were lined with framed black-and-white glossies of the galaxy of Baron Studios stars. The faces, covering four decades, were so immediately recognizable that Matthew wondered what the hell he was doing here.

"By the way, Mr. St. James," Meredith Ward offered sotto

voce, when they reached the ornately carved set of double doors at the end of the hallway, "I thought you might like to know that you're the sexiest man to read for the part of Ryder Long yet." Her smile was brimming with feminine invitation.

Matthew wiped his sweaty hands on his slacks and managed a weak smile of his own. "Thanks."

Leigh Baron was seated behind a lovingly tended burr walnut desk that gleamed with the patina of age. He walked across the plush beige carpeting, and she rose to greet him.

"Hello, Mr. St. James. It's a pleasure to meet you." Her smile remained distant and displayed no warmth.

Matthew wondered on whose account she'd decided to forget their first two meetings. His? Or hers? She was wearing a slate-gray suit, severely cut, and a trim white blouse. Her hair was back in its tight twist at the nape of her neck and as her cool gray eyes observed him through her glasses, Matthew had no doubt that her entire look had been carefully chosen to make her appear remote and forbidding. Unlike the highly agreeable Meredith Ward, who settled into a chair across the room, crossed her legs, and continued to show her warm, Cheshire-cat smile.

"It's a pleasure to meet you, Ms. Baron," he said evenly and shook her outstretched hand. Some perverse masculine instinct made him rub his thumb lightly against the soft skin of her palm; Matthew was rewarded when her eyes, shielded behind the oversize lenses, revealed a mild shock of female awareness.

She recovered quickly. "Please have a seat." Retrieving her hand, she gestured toward an Eames chair on the other side of the desk.

Leigh sat back down, somewhat relieved to put the expanse of polished walnut between herself and Matthew. He'd come to the audition in a black shirt and lean black slacks that made her think of pirates, radiating a dangerous unpredictability she found as intriguing as it was unnerving.

"Have you had any acting experience, Mr. St. James?" she asked with a glacial politeness. It was important—vital—that she establish control. Having learned at her father's knee that Hollywood was filled with people looking for signs of weakness, Leigh was adept at hiding her feelings.

Bitch. Matthew knew that Corbett had sent his résumé over with his photos. She knew he didn't have any previous acting experience. She only wanted to make certain both of them knew exactly who had the upper hand. "No."

She folded her hands atop the desk. Her fingernails were buffed to a glossy sheen. No rings, Matthew noticed. No bracelets. Her only jewelry consisted of a slim, gold-banded watch with Roman numerals and a pair of perfectly matched black pearl earrings. He'd spent enough time in the East to know that the pearls were genuine and wondered if the earrings had been a gift from a lover.

"*Dangerous* has the potential to be an important film, Mr. St. James. I can't risk casting it with unqualified individuals." Her gray eyes flicked over him, submitting him to a long, impersonal examination. Then she opened a manila file, taking out what Matthew recognized to be the studio shots Jill Cocheran had taken. Leigh remained silent for a long, nerve-racking time. She appeared to be comparing the original with the photos. "No matter how attractive any of those individuals might be," she finished up finally.

For an executive at a studio that had made a fortune on the appearance of its stars, she made good looks sound like a dirty word. Matthew rubbed his jaw thoughtfully. A day's growth of beard cast a dark shadow on his chiseled features. "I'm certainly glad to hear that, Ms. Baron. Since I've never considered myself to be particularly good-looking."

Perfectly shaped blond brows rose above the dark frames. "Oh? Yet Ryder Long is a very handsome man."

Matthew leaned back in his chair and locked his hands behind his head. The muscles in his upper arms swelled against his black shirtsleeves. "Far be it for me to argue with you, Ms. Baron, but you're wrong. Actually, Ryder Long isn't at all handsome. At least not in the conventional sense."

Leigh could feel the beginning twinges of a headache in her right temple. "Don't tell me that you've gotten hold of a screenplay. All of the copies are supposed to have been kept under lock and key."

"I read the book."

"Really." Her acid tone was laced with blatant disbelief.

"Really. I've always enjoyed reading. And you're right

about *Dangerous* being an extremely compelling story."

Leigh was momentarily nonplussed. Although she had spent her life surrounded by professional storytellers, she knew very few individuals who actually read for pleasure.

"Yes, it is," she said at length. "Well . . ." She glanced significantly at her watch. "I'd hoped to have someone else here, but since she seems to be late, I suppose we may as well get started." She handed him a sheaf of papers. "Will you need time to prepare?"

Before he could answer, the door to the office burst open and a whirlwind wearing tight black jeans and a bright red silk T-shirt studded with emerald rhinestones dashed into the room. "Christ, the traffic in this town just gets worse and worse," she complained, throwing her petite body into the chocolate brown chair next to Matthew. "I swear, one of these days the entire place is going to come to a screeching halt." Combing her fingers through her long, sleek black hair, she turned to Matthew. Although her quick study was just as professional as Leigh's had been, her brown eyes immediately brightened with feminine admiration. "Where in the hell did Leigh find you?"

"In her kitchen."

"That does it," the woman muttered. "I'm going to learn to cook if it kills me."

"First you'd have to locate your kitchen," Leigh countered with the first flash of humor Matthew had witnessed. "Mr. St. James, Kim Yamamoto. Mr. St. James is reading for Ryder," she added unnecessarily. To Matthew she said, "Kim has agreed to edit *Dangerous*."

Matthew gave her a rare, genuine smile. "I can't think of a better person for the job," he said. "Your work on *Street Smarts* was brilliant."

Kim's almond eyes narrowed as she studied him with renewed interest, obviously surprised that he'd mentioned one of her lesser-known projects. "Thanks, but in case you've forgotten, that little gem bombed at the box office."

"Only because marketing blew their job by promoting what was obviously a coming-of-age story as just another action film."

Kim preened visibly. "That's how I always viewed it."

"It was the only way possible." He looked at her curiously. "Isn't it unusual for an editor to come onto a project this early?"

"Most editors."

"But you're not most editors."

"No. I like to come onto a film in the beginning, so I can be involved through the evolution of a story—through all the various scripts—so that by the time the director begins shooting I have a firm grip on the story. Contrary to popular belief, editing isn't about taking out. It's about putting all these random scenes filmed from a hundred different angles into a workable, believable story. And I can't do that until I know what I'm doing and why I'm doing it."

"Sounds a lot like writing."

Kim bobbed her ebony head eagerly. "Exactly! Good looks and brains too," she enthused on a tone of exaggerated disbelief. "How would you like to get married?"

They could have been the only two people in the room. Deciding that the meeting of the Matthew St. James–Kim Yamamoto mutual admiration society had gone on long enough, Leigh cleared her throat.

"Excuse me for interrupting, but Mr. St. James was just about to begin reading," she said with clipped deliberation.

The spirited editor grinned. "Sorry, Leigh. But it was all this marvelous man's fault for getting me started." She nodded toward Matthew. "Please carry on; I promise not to open my mouth."

The friendly exchange with Kim Yamamoto had managed to banish his early tension. Matthew skimmed the pages, noting that Leigh had chosen the scene where Ryder Long explains his behavior to his terrified yet unwillingly fascinated hostage.

Once he began, the words came remarkably easily. Having reread the novel several times in preparation for this audition, Matthew discovered that not only did he empathize with the kidnapper, but he also shared many of the antihero's feelings of anger, isolation, and frustration.

"I believe that it all comes down to power," he said as the lengthy monologue came to a close. His quiet voice was more deadly than the harshest shout. "Power's the key thing. I was just a kid when I discovered I have it in my personality. I used to be afraid of it."

"But you're not any longer?" Leigh asked, prompting him from her own copy of the script.

"No." As his eyes met hers and held, she felt vaguely like a mongoose hypnotized by the unblinking, painted eye of the cobra. "I'm not." Beneath the steely outward arrogance, Leigh could see the tangled undergrowth of Ryder Long's— or was it Matthew St. James's?—dark soul. She shivered imperceptibly.

The room was hushed; everyone in attendance appeared stunned by Matthew's performance. Out of the corner of his eye, he viewed Meredith Ward applauding silently. Next to him, Kim flashed a thumbs-up sign. Only Leigh appeared unmoved.

"Thank you, Mr. St. James," she said, her tone as cool and polite as it had been when he first walked through the door. "Your interpretation was very interesting. And I'd like to discuss it further, but unfortunately, I have some pressing business to attend to first. If you'll just allow Meredith to direct you to the commissary, I'll join you there as soon as possible."

Matthew felt drained. As if he'd taken a knife and poured his guts out all over the impeccable surface of Leigh Baron's antique desk. The fact that the haughty bitch had encased herself in enough ice to cover Jupiter did nothing to improve his mood.

"I'll be happy to wait," he said, rising abruptly from the leather chair. "For ten minutes."

"Ten minutes?"

This time, as he met her disbelieving gaze, Matthew's eyes held a direct challenge. "That's right. Ten minutes. If you haven't completed your business by then, I'll have to leave. You see, Ms. Baron, I have a few pressing matters to attend to myself this evening."

"Another bartending engagement, I presume?" The words were no sooner out of her mouth than she regretted the catty put-down.

"No," Matthew corrected. "I'm having dinner with friends. I believe you know them."

"Oh?" Leigh's tone suggested that the possibility of their having mutual acquaintances was slim to none.

"Corbett and Tina Marshall."

His look reduced her to six inches tall. Before she could respond he was gone, leaving Meredith Ward to hurry after him.

Leigh realized that this was the second time Matthew St. James had walked out on her with the last word. One thing was certain: if he came to work for Baron Studios, that was going to change.

"Well?" Kim asked as soon as she and Leigh were alone.

"Well, what?"

"What are you going to do about that gorgeous guy?"

"I don't know. How are you coming along with the trailer for *Scattershot*?"

Kim shrugged. "Shit, Leigh, that movie is overflowing with sex and violence. If I can't edit a trailer out of it, I can't edit a trailer. And you're begging the question."

"I know."

Seeking something, anything to do, Leigh began straightening the few items on her desk. Both women knew the sudden display of tidiness was unnecessary. The crystal paperweight, the only sign of femininity Leigh permitted herself in her office, was precisely where it always was, three inches to the left of the leather-bound appointment book. The gold pen-and-pencil set was in its assigned place six inches from the front of the desk; memo pad, Rolodex, and brass paper-clip container right beside it.

"He *is* gorgeous," Kim offered.

"I know."

"And he's without question the best so far."

"I know."

"In fact, in a lot of ways, the guy actually seems to *be* Ryder Long."

Leigh sighed. "I know. And that's precisely what has me so worried."

"And intrigued?"

She and Kim Yamamoto had met when Joshua assigned the editor to Leigh's first feature-length movie four years ago. The film, a controversial World War II story about a young

Nisei newspaper reporter and the married navy captain who fell in love with her, had garnered rave reviews. From their very first meeting, it had been as if the two women had known each other all their lives. Leigh knew better than to try and keep a secret from her best friend.

"This town is filled with so many shallow people that a complex person is bound to be a bit intriguing," she argued.

Kim crossed her arms across the front of her rhinestone-studded shirt. "Don't pull that Ice Maiden routine with me, Leigh Baron," she warned. "We go back too far." Kim appraised her frankly. "Contrary to what those nuns at parochial school taught you, lust isn't really a mortal sin. If it were, ninety-nine percent of this town's population would have been turned into blocks of salt years ago."

"How did we get started in on lust?" Leigh began twisting a paper clip into figure 8s.

She did not want to think about how she'd been held spellbound during Matthew's reading; she did not want to remember how she'd looked at his hands holding that script and wondered what they would feel like on her body. Such thoughts—such sensual feelings—were dangerous, threatening to undermine what she'd worked so hard to become.

"If Matthew St. James didn't start your juices flowing, you are in desperate need of sexual rehabilitation," Kim said. "Why, when he started in on that power bit, it was all I could do to keep myself from jumping his manly bones."

"You've got a dirty mind."

"Guilty. And thank God. The way you've kept me working my tail off the past six months, fantasizing about screwing is as close as I've gotten to the real thing." She smiled. "So how many projects are you working on now?"

"Ten," Leigh answered promptly, relieved that the conversation had returned to work. "Most are in the early development stage; *Scattershot*, as you know only too well, is in final editing; *Frenzy* hits the theaters Friday. We begin shooting *Kaleidoscope* in October and *Dangerous* ..." She shook her head again, this time in frustration. "And *Dangerous* is, as usual, up in the air."

"Which brings us back to that guy you've kept waiting in the commissary for six"—Kim glanced down at her wide-banded diver's watch—"make that seven minutes. And counting."

"I know."

"So are you going to have him test?"

Leigh hesitated. "I haven't decided," she admitted as she tossed away the mangled paper clip. "I'll make up my mind on the way to the commissary."

Leigh changed her mind at least a dozen times on her way to the commissary. Entering the elaborately appointed dining room, she weaved her way past two uniformed motorcycle cops, a trio of doctors clad in green scrubs, and an exuberant group of extraterrestrials who were playing liar's poker with dollar bills.

From his vantage point at the back of the room beside a towering potted palm, Matthew watched as Leigh approached, stopping to exchange a few words, a smile, a casual hug. He noticed that despite her outwardly friendly behavior, she stiffened almost imperceptibly at each occasion of physical contact.

"Thank you for waiting," Leigh said as she sat down across the table from him.

"No problem." Twelve minutes had elapsed since he'd walked out of her office. Since she had entered the commissary precisely on time, he decided to be generous and give her the extra two minutes.

Leigh waved away the waiter who approached with a sterling silver coffeepot. Her nervous system was already horribly agitated; she didn't need any caffeine to make things worse. "I thought you were a writer," she said abruptly, dispensing with small talk and getting right down to business.

"I am."

"Yet here you are, reading for a part in a movie. Why?"

"Perhaps I didn't have anything better to do this afternoon."

Damn the man for baiting her. "Have you had any theatrical training?"

"None at all."

"Your performance was very interesting."

"So you said."

"Kim Yamamoto was quite impressed."

"Thank you. Given the quality of her work, I'll take that as a compliment."

Leigh folded her hands together atop the table. The deeptoned claret and forest green tablecloths echoed the colors of the trompe l'oeil woodland scenes on the far wall. The scenes had been copied from a 1930s Baron Studios' Robin Hood movie. "That was Kim's opinion, you understand."

She sure as hell wasn't going to make it easy on him. Wondering if she was the type of little girl who had pulled the wings off butterflies, Matthew refrained from answering immediately. Instead, he took a long sip of his coffee. "Oh, I believe I understand, Ms. Baron." He looked directly at her over the rim of the Spode cup. "Perhaps more than you think."

Leigh didn't appreciate his insinuation that she was taking their earlier encounter personally. "I like to believe that my reputation for being a fair businesswoman is deserved, Mr. St. James. If you're implying that I'd hold your previous behavior against you, you're mistaken."

"Ah," he said. "I was wondering how long you planned to continue that little charade."

"Charade?"

"Pretending that we'd never met."

"I thought you'd appreciate the others not knowing the circumstances of that meeting," she said, not quite truthfully.

"I'm not afraid of honest work, Ms. Baron," Matthew countered. Although his voice was calm, his eyes were not. "And unless memory fails me, I seem to recall some mention of bartending during our brief conversation."

Color darkened her cheeks as Leigh looked down at the table. When she lifted her gaze to Matthew's, her eyes expressed genuine regret. "I'm sorry about that."

He waved away her apology with a lazy flick of his wrist. "Don't worry about it."

There was a slight pause. "Obviously you weren't exaggerating about having read *Dangerous*." Matthew was accustomed to having women gaze at him with blatant feminine admiration. Leigh's grave gaze seemed to be measuring him. "You seem to have very strong feelings about Ryder Long."

"You could say that."

She knew Matthew was waiting for her decision and wondered what he'd say if he knew she still hadn't made up her mind. She fell silent once again as she studied him for a long, drawn-out moment. His face, while impossibly handsome, was chiseled and full of character. Lines fanned out from deep-set eyes the color of dark amber; at close glance, his nose appeared to have been broken, and a thin white scar cut across a square jaw. It was the face of a man used to living life on his own terms, even if those terms at times included violence and danger. But was it, she wondered, the face of a man she could trust?

"Do you identify with the character?"

Her wary implication hung heavily on the refrigerated air. Matthew decided that there was no way he was going to admit that in order to prepare for today's reading, he'd had to open some very personal doors and venture down some dark cellar steps.

"What's the matter, Ms. Baron, are you afraid of being kidnapped?" There was something new in his voice. A cold, precise anger that could have come from Ryder Long himself.

Leigh repressed a shiver. "Certainly not." She tugged her slim gray skirt over her knees as she crossed her legs. "I was merely wondering how you managed to hit upon precisely the right note. Especially since you've had no formal training."

"Perhaps I'm a natural."

"Perhaps."

As she looked into his uncivilized eyes, Leigh was suddenly reminded of her recent rash of nightmares. She'd experienced the bad dreams off and on since childhood, but lately, ever since Matthew St. James had entered her life, stirring emotions that were better left untapped, they'd begun tormenting her with increasing regularity.

Viewing the distant panic that flashed into her eyes, Matthew was struck with the realization that he'd seen that look from too many of the villagers in Vietnam not to recognize it. The unappealing truth of the matter was that on some basic level Leigh Baron was afraid of him.

"Whatever else you may think of me, Ms. Baron," he said quietly, "I'm not a sociopath like Ryder Long."

Leigh was beginning to realize that she was dealing with a very complex man. She had no doubt that Matthew had experienced his share of violence. Those rigid lines bracketing his mouth and fanning out from his eyes were proof of that. At the same time, however, instinct assured her that he'd never harm a woman.

"I'm pleased to hear that, Mr. St. James." She managed a faint smile that only wavered slightly. "We already have all the sociopaths we need in Baron Studios' legal department."

Matthew nodded his satisfaction with having gotten that little matter clarified. "So," he said, "where do we stand now?"

"I'd like to arrange a screen test." A voice in the far reaches of her mind screamed out *What are you doing?* Leigh ignored it. "Are you free tomorrow afternoon?"

"I'll make it a point to be."

"Fine. I'll make an appointment for you in makeup at one-thirty; your test will be at two. If that intensity you portrayed in your reading today translates to the screen, you may just turn out to be an actor after all." She glanced down at her watch. The pointed gesture was not lost on Matthew. Brushing a palm frond out of the way, he stood up.

"I'll try not to disappoint you," he said agreeably, extending a hand that, as much as she wanted to, Leigh knew she could not ignore.

It was only a hand, she told herself. Like any other. But when his fingers closed around hers, she was dismayed by the thrill that rocketed through her. Desire and something else. Fear? Shame? Whatever it was, Leigh knew that this was neither the time nor the place to dwell on it.

"Just don't get your hopes up," she warned. "Frankly, Mr. St. James, the odds aren't in your favor."

The smile he gave her was tinged with irony. "Don't worry, Ms. Baron. I'm used to that."

Leigh watched him walked away with a lazy, arrogant gait that fit the outlaw Ryder Long to a T. Her palm still tingled. It was not, she decided, the most propitious of omens.

Leigh had spent a lifetime suppressing her feelings; some instinct had warned her since childhood that emotions had a way of making you vulnerable, causing life to veer out of control just when you least expected it. She'd never met a man capable of triggering such a volatile sense of sexual awareness. With a single look, a mere touch, Matthew St. James had proven himself capable of arousing passions she'd been unaware of possessing.

She found herself saying a silent prayer that tomorrow's screen test would be a dismal failure. Once Matthew St. James proved unsuitable for the role, he'd be out of her life. Out of her thoughts.

It was a scene from the lowest circle of Dante's hell. VC, dressed in black pajamas, bandoleers strung across their chests, hand grenades on their belts, AK-47 assault rifles in their hands, streamed into Khe Sanh village. There were hordes of them—hundreds, thousands, tens of thousands. Incoming artillery screamed out of the sky, the hill was ablaze with napalm, the mortaring and rocketing went on and on, growing louder and louder until the earth shook.

Matthew fired, but his rifle jammed after only forty rounds. All around him living, breathing men and women were reduced to nothing more than lumps of red clay. The fighting continued while Matthew stood in the center of the chaos, alone and impotent. When it was finally over and silence settled over the village, the heavy, sweet smell of death flooded his nostrils. Mangled bodies littered the landscape, sprawled in pools of dark blood. The only sign of life was the rats that had come out of hiding.

It was then that he heard the baby. Lying beside its dead

mother, the child was screaming his lungs out. Matthew approached. Then stopped in his tracks when he saw the Russian pineapple grenade tied around the infant's neck. Another person staggered into the center of the village. Matthew instantly recognized the stunned soldier as one of the cherries who had joined up with K Company the previous day. The kid was headed toward the baby, obviously intent on salvaging some semblance of humanity from a ridiculously inhumane war.

Matthew tried to shout out a warning, but the words were stuck in his throat. He tried to move, but his feet were mired in the concretelike mud. He could only watch in horror as the teenage soldier gently picked up the crying baby. The world exploded.

Jerked out of his tortured sleep, Matthew pushed himself up to a sitting position and wearily leaned his head back against the wall. He was alone and shaken and drenched with sweat. The nightmare was not unfamiliar; having begun during the seventy-seven-day Siege of Khe Sanh—the longest battle of the war, where eighteen hundred Marines were killed and wounded—it continued to invade his sleep whenever he found himself in a situation out of his control.

It had been nearly six months since he last had the nightmare. Which was, Matthew reminded himself, a distinct improvement. When he first arrived stateside, the visions had tortured him on a nightly basis.

Getting out of bed, he went into the kitchen and made a cup of instant coffee. While he sat in the predawn darkness, drinking coffee and waiting for morning, Matthew was forced to admit just how badly he wanted the part he was testing for that afternoon. It wasn't good to want anything so badly. It smacked of weakness. And Matthew had never considered himself a weak man.

He didn't want to win the part in order to become a star; if he thought such a thing was even remotely possible, Matthew never would have walked into Leigh Baron's office in the first place. No, what he wanted was freedom. The freedom that could be bought with the money the role offered. Freedom that would enable him to direct all his energies toward his goal of becoming a screenwriter.

Although Matthew would be the last person to describe

himself as a mystic, over the years he'd come to believe that movies marked lives. He could remember exactly where he was—and who he was—the first time he saw *High Noon*. *Citizen Kane*. *Rebel Without a Cause*. From the time the neighborhood theater had first given season passes to the residents of the Sacred Heart Boys' Home, he'd been hooked on movies.

The summer of 1950 had been hot. Hot enough to break records all over the country. By July most Californians had taken to the mountain lakes or the beaches. Others, seven-year-old Matthew St. James included, escaped to the air-conditioned sanctuary of movie theaters.

In the third row of the balcony of a theater in Glendale, Matthew sat alone. Coming from behind him, a bright white beam cut through the darkness and lit up the giant silver screen. First the newsreel—fighting on the 38th Parallel in North Korea; Joseph McCarthy brandishing an FBI report he claimed exposed communists in the State Department; the New York Yankees leading the American League pennant race; previews of fall fashions in Paris revealing women's skirts rising to mid-calf. A narrated short showed off the new Fords, which boasted a new, revolutionary power-steering system. An advertisement pushed buttered popcorn and ice cold Coca-Cola available at the snack bar. The cartoon: Bugs Bunny foiling a befuddled Elmer Fudd. And then (finally!) the feature film—Walt Disney's *Treasure Island*.

The movie was like a magic carpet, whisking him away to a land of fantasy and adventure. No longer Matthew St. James, an unwanted bastard shuffled from foster home to foster home, he'd become Jim Hawkins, boy-hero, outwitting the villains on a hair-raising search for buried treasure. When the door behind him opened, emitting a brief flare of light, Matthew prayed that the beam of the usher's flashlight would continue down the aisle.

Up on the screen, Jim hid in a barrel of apples and listened as Long John Silver told the story of blind Pew. In the theater, Matthew slumped lower in the red velvet seat and held his breath as the usher drew nearer.

"There you are," a harsh, feminine voice crowed triumphantly. His social worker, the grim, relentless Miss Tomlin, had found him. Again. As she jerked him to his feet, a light-ning sharp pain shot through his arm. His latest guardian, Helen McCrea, had caught him drinking out of the milk bottle this morning. Screaming incoherently about germs, she'd twisted his arm behind his back and tossed him out the kitchen door, where he'd fallen headlong down the rickety wooden stairs and sprawled on the parched yellow grass.

"Do you have any idea how much trouble you've caused, young man?" Miss Tomlin huffed as she dragged him out of the theater into the bright California afternoon. Although he couldn't help blinking at the sudden harsh sunlight, Matthew refused to flinch, despite the pain that felt like fire shooting up his arm. He remained silent, his hands curled into fists in the pockets of his faded jeans.

"Do you think that I have nothing better to do than spend all my time in movie theaters, tracking down some runaway kid who doesn't appreciate the effort people have gone to to give him a home? I've a good mind to take you right down to the Hall of Detention, since that's undoubtedly where you're going to end up, anyway," Miss Tomlin predicted. "With all the other juvenile delinquents."

Her tirade continued nonstop all the way back to the house. Matthew didn't bother to listen; he'd heard it all before. He wondered idly if Helen would be passed out when he got back to the house. Her husband, a traveling salesman, was out on the road this week, which meant a constant string of men coming and going. He knew from bitter experience that some of those men would get drunk and try to knock him around. Still, he reasoned, with a pragmatism that had become second nature, if Helen stayed smashed, she might not discover the fifty cents he'd stolen from her purse for movie tickets.

They were passing Beverly Hills. As he looked out the car window at the palatial estates and imagined the perfect, pam-pered lives of those lucky enough to have been born to wealth and privilege, a sense of injustice and angry rebellion rose up inside him. The social worker's words were like wasps, buzz-ing noisily in his ears. Matthew returned his mutinous gaze to his ragged sneakers and imagined Long John Silver cutting Miss Tomlin's head off with his cutlass.

* * *

August 1965 had been hot and steamy. The monsoons had arrived and the afternoon rain came down in torrents. The constant mist in the air made the red, white, and green flares over Pleiku look soft and hazy, like falling stars. At the 71st Evacuation Hospital, the still air was pregnant with moisture, rendering the rusty paddle-blade fan next to useless as it creaked slowly overhead.

But the wounded men in the hospital ward were oblivious to the stifling humidity, their attention riveted on the World War II movie being screened on a sheet nailed to the wall.

"Go get 'em, Duke," a grunt sitting in a wheelchair beside Matthew shouted out as John Wayne's battleship chased down the Tokyo Express. "Splash those fuckin' Zeros," an SP/4 hollered. The soldier's head was bandaged, tubes coming out of his mouth and nose, and he could only see out of the corner of his left eye through a ragged hole cut in the bloody tape. Yet his enthusiasm was no less than if he'd been on that battleship himself. Other battle-weary and wounded soldiers, caught up in the story, yelled similar encouragement.

It was amazing, Matthew considered. Only an hour ago, the ward had been filled with moaning, screaming wounded. Kids, mostly, missing arms and legs, their heads smashed in and pieced together, their eyes lost and their hearts broken. Yet somehow, this uncomplicated, ninety-minute film had managed to transport its audience to a better place, a less complicated time.

Although the suspension of reality lasted no longer than the movie, Matthew wondered what it would feel like to have such an impact on people's lives.

By the time his second tour of duty was over, the idea of becoming a screenwriter had become fixed in Matthew's mind. These days his goal remained the driving force in his life, and although he knew it was a long shot, Matthew also knew that he wouldn't fail. He wouldn't allow himself to fail.

Now if only he could make it through Leigh Baron's damn screen test.

Matthew needn't have worried. His test was riveting, the electricity from his perform-ance arcing through the air. As she viewed the film with her father in Baron Studios' screening room, Leigh knew that they'd found their Ryder Long.

"Do you have any idea what you've done?" Joshua asked slowly as the lights came back on.

Leigh's palms were damp. Matthew—or Ryder, she couldn't quite tell where one left off and the other began—had seemed so blatantly masculine, with his mesmerizing eyes and strong hands. No. She didn't want to think about him that way. There was too much living etched onto his angular face; a woman would be insane—or a masochist—to let a man like Matthew St. James into her life.

Shaking off her thoughts, she brushed her palms against her slim navy skirt. "What have I done?"

"You've discovered the life raft that's going to save this

studio from drowning in red ink. Women will show up at theaters in droves to see Matthew St. James, while their husbands and lovers will sit beside them and fantasize having so much power over a woman she'd be willing to kill for you." He looked at Leigh with unbridled admiration. "That bartender is going to prove to be the find of the century. And the way you found him, working one of our parties, is going to be a gold mine of publicity."

"I didn't really discover him at the party," Leigh felt obliged to point out. "Tina was the one who recognized his potential."

Joshua shrugged as he pulled a cigar out of his pocket. "Lana Turner wasn't really discovered sitting at the counter of Schwab's Drugstore either," he reminded her over the flame of the gold lighter. "But who the hell remembers? Or cares?"

He frowned in concentration as he lit the cigar. "So, you've got the funding. And your protagonist. Now all you have to do is come up with your heiress and your project will definitely be a go. Have you thought about my suggestion?"

"About using an established actress to play Marilyn?"

"I still think it's a good idea."

"Both Ryder and Marilyn need to be played by unknowns," Leigh said mildly. It was not the first time she'd stated her position on the matter; Leigh doubted that it would be the last. "If we use someone whose image is familiar, it will only distract the audience from what I want this film to convey."

"If you want to send a message, use Western Union," Joshua quoted the memorable Goldwynism. "Besides, unknowns are a box office risk; casting a star would guarantee a hedge against disaster. Get yourself the right name and even if the movie turns out to be a turkey, it'll still open."

Although Leigh hated the practice, she was all too aware that a key way of judging a picture was by the opening weekend box office receipts. It was an industry conclusion that star appeal would cause people to flock to the theater. If the public stayed away, word immediately got out that the movie "didn't open." Which, in movie parlance, was a death knell.

"It's not going to be a turkey."

Joshua eyed her through a veil of blue smoke. Even as he

found her steely intransigence frustrating, he couldn't help admiring her strength. Holding the cigar out in front of him, he studied the glowing end for a long, thoughtful time. "How about we cut a deal?"

"What type of deal?" she asked cautiously. When her father suddenly turned agreeable was when he was the most dangerous.

"I convince our backers that you're right about using unknowns in the major roles and you agree to sign a name for the part of Dirk Young."

The role of Dirk Young, the obsessed FBI agent determined to track the pair down, was a pivotal part of the movie. But it had been written in a way that kept it from diminishing the main conflict between the protagonists.

"All right. You've got yourself a deal."

Joshua knew that Leigh never began a day without a detailed list of things she wished to accomplish, never entered into any venture without a distinct goal. She was also not a woman to make snap decisions.

"You knew all along what I was going to propose and were already prepared to concede on that point, weren't you?"

She couldn't resist a slight smile. "I don't know what you're talking about."

Joshua leaned over and squeezed her fingers with parental affection. "You're damned good at bluffing, sweetheart. But don't ever try an out-and-out lie," he advised good-naturedly. Matthew St. James's electrifying screen test had left him feeling more optimistic than he had in months. "Your face gives you away. Every time."

Leigh slipped her hand from his. "I'll keep that in mind."

"You do that," he agreed easily, leaning back in the plush seat. "So, what are you going to do about your sexy new star?"

"I'll call Corbett in the morning and get negotiations started."

"Fine, fine." He puffed thoughtfully on the cigar, clouds of smoke rising to the ceiling. "I also think you should telephone this St. James fellow. Invite him to lunch. Or better yet, dinner. An intimate dinner with wine and candlelight would probably be in order."

In all the years she'd been coming to the studio, her father had never—not once—suggested that she spend personal time with an actor. In fact, there had even been an unpleasant incident when she was fourteen and had a crush on the twenty-two-year-old star of Baron Studios' popular teenage surfer movies, Chance Murdock. Joshua had caught the two exchanging a kiss behind the sound stage one summer afternoon. The resulting fireworks had practically set the studio ablaze.

Two days later, Chance was discovered in a Santa Monica motel room with a fifteen-year-old girl. The girl's mother had no qualms about telling her story to the press; the hapless actor was charged with statutory rape and, although his attorney managed to get him off with probation, Chance Murdock's career as a teen idol came to a screeching halt. Rumors had persisted around Hollywood that Joshua Baron had set his young star up. A rumor Joshua denied.

"Why on earth would I want to have dinner with Matthew St. James?"

"Matthew St. James is the answer to our current financial difficulties. It's important to keep him happy." His eyes turned hard. Calculating. "Never underestimate the insecurity of an actor, Leigh, especially one destined to be a star. Being revered is a dual-edged sword—although fans' adoration brings stars fame and fortune, it also gives them that much farther to fall. Which most of them do. But while they are on top, my dear, they can make a studio one helluva lot of money."

Joshua placed the cigar in the ashtray located in the chair's arm and turned toward Leigh, shaping her tense shoulders with his palms. "It's not like I'm asking you to marry this St. James fellow," he assured her, thinking back on that fateful day when his father had instructed him to court Jens Eldring's frigid daughter. "Just take the man under your wing. Have dinner with him. Use your feminine wiles to keep him contented."

"Are you asking me to go to bed with him?"

"Of course not. You're a big girl, Leigh. Surely you can flirt a little with a man without having it get out of hand. All I'm asking you to do is see that St. James doesn't get away before we've got him safely signed, sealed, and delivered." His hands moved up and down her arms, coaxing acquiescence. "You'll do it, won't you, princess? For the studio?"

Bull's-eye, Leigh considered bleakly. To her, Baron Studios was more than a three-generational business. It was her roots as well as her future. Joshua often claimed that if his daughter were Scarlett O'Hara, the studio would be her Tara. Which was, Leigh considered now, an incisively accurate assessment.

She loved Baron Studios. And she'd do anything to save it. Including being nice to a man she didn't like. A man who made her too aware of being a woman.

"All right. I'll do it."

Pleased, Joshua rubbed his hands together as if he'd never expected any other outcome. Which indeed, he hadn't. Marissa might continually question his authority, but not Leigh. Never Leigh. "That's my girl."

Leigh was proud of her work at Baron Studios. Despite the fact that it had taken three long and frustrating years to get *Dangerous* to this point, she had no qualms about her ability to bring the film to the screen. She was confident enough to believe she could handle any situation that might arise.

But Matthew St. James was turning out to be another story altogether. Because Leigh had the uneasy feeling that the man was going to prove inordinately more challenging, radically more dangerous, than his fictional counterpart.

It was a classic morning at the beach. A clean swell was angling in out of the west at six to eight feet, the wind was calm, and long, hollow waves peeled off left and right. Although conditions were near perfect, the lineup was almost empty of surfers, due to the great white shark scare.

The rumor mill was well greased this time. Only one day after the initial sighting, the shark was reported to be twenty-five feet long and sixty feet off Manhattan Beach, fifteen feet long and two hundred yards off Redondo Beach, caught and killed off Topanga, responsible for the disappearance of a UCLA student off Zuma Beach. In the last alleged incident, all that the lifeguards were reportedly able to recover of the hapless surfer was an egg-shaped Bonzer board with an enormous bite taken out of it.

Stalking the border between supreme confidence and absolute disregard for life and limb, Matthew was not about to retreat and leave the surf to whatever shark may or may not have been lurking in the murky early-morning waters. Besides, he considered after cracking a wave all the way to shore, as angry as he was, any shark that even tried to attack him would be shit out of luck.

Whenever he thought about Leigh Baron, that icy rich bitch who had grasped control of his life, it was all he could do not to drive to Baron Studios, march into her sterile office, and wring her neck. Forced to admit that he was the one who had handed the reins over to her by testing for her goddamn movie, Matthew was thoroughly disgusted with himself and the situation he'd gotten himself into.

"Hey, man," Jeff Martin called out from his perch on the wet morning sand, "you look super-bummed."

"That's an understatement." Matthew picked up the Fiberglas board, intending to wade back out into the surf when he spotted the broken fin. "Shit."

"Just as well," Jeff said pragmatically. "Go back out there again and you could end up shark bait."

"The way my life is going lately, that could only be an improvement."

"Well, dude, your luck is about to change."

"Oh, yeah?"

"Yeah. I've been looking all over for you." Jeff's attention wandered as a tall platinum blonde strolled by walking a magnificent matched pair of Harlequin Great Danes. "Jesus Christ, would you look at that ass."

Matthew cast an appraising glance at the impressive rear end clad in a pair of skintight hot pants. "Not bad."

"Not bad?" Jeff leered, looking inclined to go after her. "What I wouldn't give for just one bite."

"If I were you, I'd try to control my appetite." Matthew nodded toward the two men trailing a short distance behind the woman. Dressed incongruously in dark business suits, they scowled at the wet sand clinging to their alligator shoes.

"Sal Licata and Dominic Alioto, two of Rocco Minetti's soldati," Jeff observed with respect.

Matthew was not particularly surprised that Jeff recognized

the Las Vegas gangster's henchmen; everyone in town knew that the Mafia controlled the porno racket in California, bringing in more than a hundred million dollars a year.

"So why were you looking for me?"

Jeff cast one last covetous look at the curvaceous blonde in the ass-clinging shorts as she continued down the beach. Some guys had all the luck. Not only did Minetti own the Lucky Nugget Hotel and Casino in Las Vegas, his trucking, real estate, and restaurant-supply businesses raked in enough bread to fill Fort Knox. And that was just the legal stuff.

"Because, dude, this is your lucky day." Jeff held out the joint he was smoking, offering a hit. When Matthew declined with a brief shake of his head, he simply shrugged. "It's goddamn true, you know."

"What's true?"

"That it's not what you know, but *who* you know. And you just happen to know a guy who can open all the right doors."

"I'm still not interested in working as a gigolo."

"I've graduated from that gig, man. Yessir, old Jeffy has moved on to bigger and better things. I'm into art films these days."

"Stag films, you mean."

"Hey, man, how long has it been since you've seen a really good adult film? The genre has grown up. We're using Technicolor and soundtracks, fog lens, flashbacks, all sorts of artsy stuff. We're even putting plots in the stories."

"Look, the world might not be beating a path to my door in order to buy my screenplays. But that doesn't mean that I'd ever succumb to writing trash like *Bambi Blows Baltimore.*"

"The money's bitchin', the work's a fuckin' breeze, and the side benefits are not to be believed." Jeff grinned, remembering last night's marathon. For a chick brought up in the rarefied atmosphere of Beverly Hills, Marissa Baron sucked cock like a natural-born whore. "In fact, there's this tender young fox that I have big plans for. All I need is the right script."

"Which is where I come in, right?"

"I told Minetti all about you, really gave you a big buildup. So big, in fact, he's willin' to look at anything you've written."

Matthew scowled. "Forget it."

"Look, you want to write for movies, right? So everyone's

gotta start somewhere. Don't forget, Monroe posed for that girlie calendar and Joan Crawford, back when she was still Lucille LeSuer, is rumored to have starred in that unforgettable stag classic, *Velvet Lips*. Hell, even Clara Bow—"

"I get the point," Matthew said.

"All you have to do is come up with seven to ten scenes, six of them hard-core, throw in some lesbian pussy eating, and a couple of threesomes. How fucking hard can that be?"

Matthew was only half listening. He was thinking back to the time when he and Jeff were both sixteen and hanging out at the beach together, drinking beer, trying to score with girls, smoking (tobacco in those days), and acting tough.

A helluva lot can change in twelve years, Matthew decided, grateful that his life hadn't taken Jeff Martin's dubious path. He'd felt the energy in that room when he'd read Ryder Long's lines and, although Leigh Baron refused to admit it, he knew she wasn't going to find anyone else better for that part.

Despite the damn waiting game Miss Studio Executive was making him play, Matthew knew that what Tina and Corbett had predicted was going to come true. He was definitely on his way up—while his old high school buddy was on a fast slide down a very slippery slope.

"Thanks for thinking of me," he said, turning to leave. "But I'm still not interested."

"Damnit, Matt," Jeff complained. "I promised Minetti I could get him the hottest damn script ever written. But artistic, you know, which is what he's really stoked about, since it's a big step up from the shit he's been getting from his regular writers. If you cop out on me, what am I gonna do?"

"You'll think of something," Matthew shot back over his shoulder as he walked toward the parking lot. "You always do."

Marissa had prepared carefully for the party at the Malibu beach house. She had applied her makeup with an unusually light hand; her hair was tamed and flowed over her shoulders like a flame cascade. She looked, she thought with satisfaction, almost like Leigh.

Her camouflage did not fool anyone. Her voluptuous body did things to the simply draped dress that Bill Blass had never dreamed of. The black silk caressed her lush breasts and hugged her ass in a way that shouted out sex. With a capital S.

Basking in the pointed looks from the other party guests—blatant lust from the men, glittering envy from the women—Marissa made her way across the room to where her host was holding court. A six-foot-tall, impossibly stacked blonde clad in a clinging emerald green minidress and a pair of thigh-hugging, high-heeled black boots hung on his arm. A show girl, Marissa decided. Some bimbo he'd brought with him from Vegas. Nearby, guests were helping themselves to the cocaine offered on a large Baccarat tray tastefully surrounded by white cattleya orchids flown in from Hawaii.

"Mr. Minetti," she purred, interrupting Brendan Farraday, who'd been telling everyone who'd listen about his latest role in Baron Studios' new picture. "I wanted to tell you that I'm having a delightful time. Thank you for inviting me."

Rocco Minetti was a tall, lean man with the type of muscular body that came from a lifetime of working out. He was wearing a red silk shirt, tight white linen pants, loafers and no socks. His hair was dark, streaked at the temples with silver, his eyes as unreadable as a pair of hard black marbles.

"Those photos Jeffy took piqued my interest," he said. "When I saw them, I said to myself, Rocco, here is a girl we can make into a star."

"Do you really mean that?"

He shrugged. "Rocco Minetti never says anything he doesn't mean. Hell, if I could make a truckdriver into a household name, doing the same thing for a pretty young thing with knockers like yours should be a cinch, right, Bren?"

"Sure, Rocco," Farraday said unenthusiastically. Talking about the old days was not his favorite way to pass the time.

"Tell me, sweetheart," Rocco said, "don't you like to party?"

"Of course I do."

His eyes took a cold, judicious tour of Marissa, from the top of her fiery head down to her tasteful black silk Maud Frizon high heels. "So how come you're dressed for a funeral?"

She ran her hands nervously over her hips. "I wanted you to see that I have a lot of different looks. It's important for an actress to have range," she said, repeating the words of her Beverly Hills High drama teacher.

"Range, smange." Minetti exchanged an amused look with his minions, who immediately laughed on cue. "Look, sweetheart," he said, "you gotta understand, the kind of flicks I make, all that's required is that you be legal age, have the kind of body that makes men walk into walls, and like to fuck like a rabbit."

Marissa felt a flash of red-hot anger when everyone laughed again. They might see her as a source of amusement now, but one of these days, she vowed, she was going to get the last laugh.

She flicked her hair back over one shoulder and met his sardonic gaze with a patently seductive one of her own. "I'm eighteen." It wasn't really a lie; her birthday was in two short months. "I think my body speaks for itself." She ran her palms seductively down her sides from her full breasts to her thighs, successfully capturing the attention of every male present. "As for the last, I can supply references."

The show girl obviously decided that a poacher had wandered into her hunting ground. "Rocco, I want to dance."

Rocco's dark eyes didn't move from Marissa's. "Sure, babe. Bren, be a good boy and take my lady out for a spin."

It was an order. Softly couched, but carved in stone. Although neither Farraday nor the blonde looked all that eager, both wisely took to the crowded dance floor.

"So," Rocco said, "I guess the next order of business is to schedule a screen test." He pulled a card out of the pocket of his slacks. "Call my casting director Monday; he'll take care of everything."

Take risks, be bold, her father was always saying. Hesitate and you're lost. "Why wait until Monday when I can audition for you tonight?" She managed a manufactured smile and thrust her breasts toward him.

"Why not?" he said, shrugging. "Come into my office and we'll see what you've got."

They'd no sooner entered the book-lined room when Minetti told her to turn around, put her hands on the desk, and lift her skirt. "You got a nice ass," he commented conversationally as he yanked down her black bikini panties. "Not too skinny, like so many broads these days. Spread your legs."

Marissa liked sex; she enjoyed the high, the feeling of control. But this was different. As Minetti positioned himself between her rounded cheeks, she felt like a piece of meat.

Take risks.

Be bold.

Marissa closed her eyes and repeated her father's words over and over in her mind while Rocco Minetti pounded into her. It could have been a minute, an hour, an eternity, but finally he erupted and it was over.

"You're okay, kid," he said as he wiped off his limp penis with a white linen handkerchief. Marissa could now see he hadn't even bothered to take off his pants.

"Gee, thanks," she muttered and pulled her underpants back up, noting that he didn't offer the handkerchief so she could wipe the sticky semen off her buttocks. She felt dirty and used and was regretting her decision to come here in the first place. His next words instantly changed her mind.

"By the way, you got the part."

Warmth coursed through her. It was the chance she'd been waiting for. This time her answering smile was genuine. "Thank you, Mr. Minetti. I promise you won't regret it."

Marissa experienced an almost sexual tremor of anticipation when she considered that soon—very soon—her father would realize that she was more like him than his precious Leigh would ever be.

Joshua Baron sat alone in the library, nursing a tall glass of Scotch. The view from the arched ceiling-to-floor windows was spectacular; as the purple shadows of dusk gave way to night, the lights of Los Angeles looked like fallen stars. And the city certainly had its share of those, he mused, thinking of all the performers who had passed through Baron Studios' gates in the fifty-five years of the studio's existence.

They came and, if they were lucky enough to be in the right place at the right time, they could make themselves, and more important, the studio a lot of money. As soon as their name on a marquee ceased to bring in profits they were gone, back to the unemployment line, cattle calls, and these days, that most remote of all outbacks, television.

Fifty-five years. During that time ten men had served as Chief Executive of the United States; only two men had claimed the executive office of Baron Studios. And Leigh would be the first woman. Everyone else came and went, only the family lasted forever.

As his mind drifted to his elder daughter, Joshua thought about her remarkable new discovery and considered how ironic it was that once again the fate of Baron Studios had fallen on the shoulders of a single individual. And an outsider, at that.

This time the key to the studio's survival was Matthew St. James. Last time it was Signe.

Joshua remembered his wedding day and the disastrous wedding night that followed. He was not particularly surprised to discover that his bride was sexually inexperienced; after all, men hadn't exactly been beating a path to her door. What he hadn't counted on, however, was that she would behave like some goddamn sacrificial vestal virgin.

"My God, you're beautiful," he'd said in amazement when he viewed Signe, clad in a long white satin nightgown.

Her white blond hair, freed from its usual tight bun at the back of her neck, cascaded down her back. The plunging neckline of the clinging gown displayed high, firm breasts, and although she was thinner than the women he usually preferred, her wasplike waist allowed for an inviting curve of hip. Her face, free of makeup, appeared years younger and a great deal more appealing. It crossed Joshua's mind that perhaps this marriage wouldn't be such a sacrifice, after all.

When he would have drawn her into his arms, Signe held up her hands. "I know why you married me," she said stiffly.

The twin shadows of her nipples were visible though the gleaming satin. Joshua's body hardened. "I married you because I love you," he lied.

"No." When she shook her head, her silken hair settled over her breasts. Joshua wondered what that hair would feel like draped across his chest. "You married me so that my father would save your father's precious studio."

"That's ridiculous." He cupped her shoulders with his palms. Her perfumed skin was as smooth as porcelain. And every bit as cold. "You're a wonderful woman," he said, caressing her in an attempt to soothe, to warm. "Intelligent, beautiful." He nuzzled her neck. "Sexy. Christ, baby, any man would want you." Damn if it wasn't turning out to be the truth. As his lips moved slowly downward toward the swell of her breasts, Joshua couldn't remember ever feeling so horny.

Signe remained rigid in his arms. "Our marriage is one of economic convenience," she insisted, her slightly accented voice revealing her Scandinavian roots. "But I understand that men have certain biological needs." At that idea, her face twisted in distaste. "I will attempt to live up to my part of the bargain by being a proper wife in all respects."

Joshua's hard-on began to sag. "I appreciate your willingness to do your part to make our marriage work," he said, his
own tone matching her formality. "And I promise to make our
lovemaking as enjoyable for you as I know it's going to be for
me."

Drawing her into his arms, he kissed her cold lips, stroked
her hair, her shoulders, her arms. Although she didn't instantly respond, Joshua took heart in the fact that neither did
she protest as he lowered her to the turned down double bed.

Joshua had never had to coax a woman into having sex. The
women of his acquaintance were not afraid to admit that a
female's body was every bit as capable of enjoying pleasure
as a male's. His new bride, however, was proving to be the
exception. When he touched her, she flinched. When he
stroked, she trembled, but not in passion. And when his lips
moved over her body in a futile attempt to warm her flesh, she
turned as cold as a block of ice.

Tenderness gave way to frustration, frustration to irritation, irritation to anger. Although Signe remained unrelentingly unresponsive, his own body, stirred by his continued
attempts to rouse her to passion, ached for relief. Finally,
unable to hold back any longer, he surged into her unwelcom-
ing dryness, slowed momentarily by the taut, forbidding barrier of her virginity.

He came almost instantly. His penis had no sooner collapsed than Signe slid out from under him and rushed from
the bed. A moment later Joshua heard the shower running in
the adjoining bathroom.

When twenty minutes had passed and she still hadn't come
out, he cursed, put his clothes back on, and went downstairs
to the Biltmore Hotel's bar, where he proceeded to get royally
drunk.

That first night set the tone for their marriage. For years
Signe remained a coldly fastidious block of ice, submitting to
sex only when he insisted. Although sexual satisfaction was
easily found elsewhere, his father kept pointing out that it was
necessary that Joshua's wife give birth to an heir in order to
ensure the future of Baron Studios. The day Signe finally,

petulantly, announced that she was pregnant, Joshua ceased going to her bedroom.

"It's just too damn bad the kid isn't a boy," Walter Baron had grumbled eight months later as he and Joshua stood beside the white wicker bassinet and looked down at the infant who bore a remarkable resemblance to her mother.

As if on cue, Leigh reached up and grabbed her father's finger with a strong grip that surprised him. When her somber gray eyes met his, Joshua sensed that those tiny pink hands would someday be capable of controlling an empire.

"Just wait," he promised his father. "This little girl will top us all."

Determined to give her a proper start in the business, Joshua began taking Leigh to the studio shortly after her third birthday, initiating her into the society of moviemaking. She proved to be a prodigy, surprising everyone but her father. He'd seen her potential from the beginning.

And now, as he sipped his Scotch and thought about Leigh's strength and dedication to the family business, Joshua only wished that her grandfather had lived long enough to see how well she'd lived up to the name of Baron.

When the phone rang the following morning, Matthew forced himself to let it ring once, twice, three times. It wouldn't do to look too eager.

"So when are we going to get together for that champagne?" Corbett asked without preamble.

"I got the part." Matthew was unaware of holding his breath until he heard the quick, relieved exhalation of air.

"Didn't I tell you that you would? We still have the details to hash out, but I'll take care of all that."

Although his tone was couched to reassure, Matthew could hear the repressed excitement in Corbett's voice. He knew that although Corbett, the man, appeared to be genuinely interested in his welfare, the agent's primary interest was in the deal.

Matthew recalled a joke he'd heard while tending bar at a party in Laurel Canyon. The way the story went, Corbett was on a cruise ship bound for La Paz when he fell overboard.

When an enormous shark came swimming circles around the agent, the passengers standing at the ship's railing began to shout and scream. Just when it looked as if Corbett was going to end up as brunch, the shark turned and swam away.

"My God," one of the passengers gasped, "it's a miracle."

"Not a miracle," another passenger corrected cynically. "Just professional courtesy."

Thinking of the story now, Matthew grinned. "I don't know how to thank you."

"Hey, it's my job. Just be free when Tina calls you for a celebratory dinner, okay?"

"Any time," Matthew confirmed. They talked for a few more minutes, during which Corbett outlined his plan of attack. When Matthew mentioned that a few of the items on the agent's agenda sounded overly optimistic, Corbett assured him that Leigh Baron was desperate enough to agree to just about anything.

As the conversation progressed, Matthew found it difficult to concentrate on details. All he could think of was that now, finally, he was free to write. Corbett assured him that it would be weeks before the movie went into production; plenty of time to finish the first draft of his screenplay.

After thanking the agent again, Matthew hung up. A minute later, he was making two more telephone calls. One to Jesse Martinez, quitting his job, the other to Beverly Hills Floral Creations, instructing the florist to send a dozen long-stemmed American Beauty roses to Tina Marshall. Those items of business out of the way, he went to the refrigerator, pulled out a can of Coors, and went out onto his porch.

Looking out over the vast expanse of cerulean water, Matthew realized that Corbett Marshall's phone call had inexorably changed his life.

Returning from lunch at The Bistro Garden with Kim Yamamoto, Leigh stopped in front of Meredith's desk. "Would you get Matthew St. James on the phone for me?" she asked her secretary.

"Are you going to sign him to play Ryder?"

"If we can reach an agreement with his agent."

"You will," Meredith said, flipping through her Rolodex.

"The guy was magnificent. God, I'd love to have him kidnap me."

"Let's hope that millions of other women feel the same way," Leigh said dryly.

She wasn't about to admit that she'd dreamed a disturbingly similar scenario just last night. She'd been sipping a piña colada on some scenic tropical beach, surrounded by a trio of attentive, sophisticated men who lived only to satisfy her every whim, when a pirate, clad all in black, suddenly appeared in the their midst and carried her off to his ship, where they sailed the high seas in search of dazzling treasures . . . Flash forward . . . Giddy with the richness of their bounty, Leigh allowed the pirate to drape her in heavy ropes of diamonds, rubies, emeralds, and pearls. His eyes gleamed with a primitive purpose as they took a slow, sensuous tour of her body, nude save for the dazzling plunder. She whispered not a word of protest when his firm lips captured her softly parted ones. He slowly, deliberately lowered his body over hers, then Leigh's clock radio switched on and the overly cheery voice of the morning DJ shattered the erotic image, leaving her feeling both ashamed and aroused at the same time.

"You're making the right decision," Kim said, once they were alone in Leigh's office.

"I know."

"Then why are you looking so down in the mouth?"

Leigh shrugged. "He's not an actor."

"So? The hunk's a natural."

"We don't even know if he can memorize lines."

"If that's all you're worried about, I'll volunteer to hang around the set and cue him."

"You just want to sleep with him."

"Of course I do." Kim's grin was one of friendly female lust. "Although sleeping wasn't exactly what I had in mind. After all, Leigh, how could any woman with blood stirring in her veins not want to go to bed with a man who's a dead ringer for Heathcliffe?"

Leigh wasn't about to touch that one. She was saved from answering by a short buzz on her intercom, signaling that Meredith had Matthew holding on the line. Was it her imagination, or was the blinking of the orange light actually beating with the same runaway rhythm of her heart?

Taking a deep breath that was meant to calm, but didn't, she picked up the receiver. "Hello, Mr. St. James. I assume Corbett has informed you of our offer."

"He's given me the bare bones." Matthew wondered if she actually thought him stupid enough to enter into negotiations himself.

His tone was every bit as remote and unfriendly as Leigh remembered. She had a good mind to hang up, when her father's instructions flashed through her mind. Matthew St. James was an unknown quantity, she reminded herself. He was also seemingly independent-minded enough to walk away before she could close the deal. And where would that leave Baron Studios?

"Are you calling for any special reason, Ms. Baron?"

"Well, yes, now that you mention it, I was. Actually, I called to invite you to have a drink with me."

"A drink?"

"That's right. Perhaps early this evening, around six? At the Polo Lounge?"

Would wonders never cease. "I don't know if that's such a good idea, Ms. Baron. If you want to discuss my contract, I'd suggest you call my agent."

Leigh wondered if the insufferable man was going to make her beg. "I promise not to discuss a word of business. This would be a purely social drink."

A social drink with Leigh Baron. Things were getting curiouser and curiouser. Matthew was reminded of the White Queen, who believed six impossible things could happen before breakfast.

"Are we talking about a date?"

"Oh, no, not a date," she said quickly. Too quickly, Leigh realized. "Our last two meetings haven't exactly been overly cordial," she reminded him unnecessarily. "Since we'll be working quite closely on this project, I thought it might be easier on everyone involved if you and I got to know one another a bit better."

"I suppose that couldn't hurt," Matthew decided after a slight pause. "Six o'clock, did you say?"

"That's right. If the time is convenient with you."

He'd promised to take Jill Cocheran out for Chinese to celebrate his contract. "I guess I could do some shuffling."

"I appreciate your fitting me into your busy schedule," she ground out between clenched teeth.

"No problem. I'll see you later."

"Later," Leigh agreed, returning the receiver to its cradle with more force than necessary.

"I knew it." Kim grinned devilishly. "You do have the hots for the guy."

"Don't be ridiculous."

"I can see it all now: drinks at the Polo Lounge, a long leisurely drive up the Coast Highway, dinner in some romantic, candlelit, out-of-the-way spot, a moonlight stroll along the beach. And before you know it, Ms. Leigh Baron, Baron Studios' renowned workaholic and professional celibate is smack-dab in the middle of a mad, passionate romance with her studio's newest star."

"That's ridiculous. Despite what I said, my meeting with the man is strictly business."

"Sure," Kim returned. "That's what Scarlett said when she rode off wearing the family drapes to talk Rhett into giving her the money to save Tara."

Deciding that such a ridiculous comparison didn't deserve a response, Leigh turned the conversation back to what they'd been discussing at lunch, Kim's work on *Dangerous*.

Across town, Jill looked up at Matthew's grim expression and wondered at the cause. The man had just been offered the hottest role in town. What on earth could have happened to cause him to scowl so? "Leigh Baron actually called you herself?"

"Her secretary placed the call. But, yeah, that was her. She wants me to have a drink with her."

"When?"

"This evening at six. At the Polo Lounge."

Jill whistled under her breath. "You really are on the fast track, aren't you?"

The unexpected telephone call had left him feeling both let-down and uneasy. What the hell was she up to? "Seems like it," he said on a shrug. "I guess we're going to have to go out to dinner later than we'd planned."

"Sure. Ah certainly wouldn't want to interfere with your chance to become rich and famous."

Matthew, looking for some sign of sarcasm, found none. "You really don't mind?"

"Matthew, Ah have told you Ah don't believe in messin' up a good thing with unnecessary obligations. Ah don't have any strings on you, sugah."

If only the rest of his life was as uncomplicated as his relationship with Jill. "You know," he said, drawing her to him, "you are one helluva woman, Jill Cocheran."

When she lifted her arms to link her hands around his neck, the rumpled sheet, which still carried the redolent scent of their recent lovemaking, fell away. "And you, Matthew St. James," she said, "are one helluva man."

Marissa lay on her back in the center of the round bed, trying to remember to groan on cue as two women—one white, the other black—made love to her. The glaring klieg lights hit the bed at hard angles, emphasizing every glistening pore.

"For chrissakes, put a little feeling into it, willya," the director complained, not for the first time. "We don't have all day."

"I'm trying"

Closing her eyes, Marissa willed her body to respond to the women's sensual ministrations. But it was impossible. The barren warehouse where the film was being shot was unbearably hot, she was sweating like a pig, and although she'd always fantasized about doing it in front of an audience, the disinterested attitude of the crew was not at all encouraging.

"Cut," the director shouted in disgust. "Okay, Martin," he said to Jeff, "you've got exactly five minutes to turn this broad around or we get ourselves another girl."

Jeff wiped the sweat off his brow. "Don't worry, Mr. B, I'll take care of everything."

"You'd better," Joe Bompensiero warned, chomping the stump of a fat black cigar. "Because every minute we sit around on our asses waiting for the chick to get it in gear is another bundle down the toilet. And Mr. Minetti don't like to see his money wasted. Capisce?"

"Yessir." Jeff grabbed a red satin kimono and threw it around Marissa's shoulders. He pulled her off the bed and behind a tower of boxes containing hijacked color TVs.

"What's the matter, kid?" His friendly tone didn't reveal that he was on the verge of knocking her ass across the damn warehouse.

"You try fucking in front of that bunch of Neanderthals," she complained. "And that blonde reeks of garlic. Every time she kisses me I feel like I'm going to throw up."

"It's just stage fright." He stroked her shoulders under the kimono. "All performers get it, even the big ones. But you don't have to worry, sweetheart, old Dr. Jeff has just the medicine to make everything all right." He reached into his shirt pocket and took out a small glassine envelope. Marissa watched as he shook some of the fine white powder out onto his palm.

"I don't do coke." Cocaine had scared her ever since a boyfriend—a drummer in a rock band—had died of a heart attack after snorting one too many lines at a party.

"Then you're missing the ultimate high, sweetheart." He dipped his little finger into the powder, then sucked it up one nostril, then the other. "Now it's your turn."

Marissa hesitated. She knew that this was her last chance. If she couldn't pull off this scene, Bompensiero would dump her and she'd never break into the business.

At first she had to press her finger against her nose to stifle a sneeze, but then suddenly, without warning, the cocaine swept to her brain like a trail of glittering diamond dust. Her body became unbearably sensitive and when she returned to the bed, her erect nipples tingled and her thighs quaked with excitement. Dark hands stroked her belly, glossy wet lips suckled at her breasts, sharp white teeth nipped at her buttocks. Fingers probed, explored, tormented the hidden niches of Marissa's body until she was writhing on the sheets. Out of the corner of her eye, she caught a glimpse of the crew watching with uncensored lust and, when release came, the applause magnified her climax.

It was six-twenty. After having spent the last agonizing twenty minutes trying to carry on a conversation with Matthew St. James, Leigh had come to the conclusion that she would have had better luck attempting to communicate with the Sphinx.

"Your résumé stated that you served in Vietnam. That must have been rough."

Matthew shrugged. He didn't believe that anyone who hadn't been there could begin to understand. "It wasn't a picnic."

"Corbett tells me that you're working on a screenplay about those days. I assume he's also warned you that the war is not a very popular subject."

"Not at the moment. But it's bound to end soon. And after a period of national denial, people will want to know the truth."

"And you intend to be the one who provides it?"

"Someone's going to write about it. It might as well be someone who was there, instead of a draft dodger who studied English literature at some nice, safe Canadian college."

"Point taken," she said. "But the way feelings are running right now, I think you're going to have a very long wait until the country's ready to look at this war without prejudice."

"Probably." He shrugged. "I'm used to waiting for what I want."

"But you don't necessarily like it."

"No." His eyes met hers and held. "Neither do you."

Touché. At this moment, it was a simple matter to imagine Matthew as a pirate, enjoying his stolen plunder and his women with the same lusty pleasure. Deciding it was time to change the subject, Leigh leaned back in the booth and observed him thoughtfully.

"Your résumé also said you're one of a rare breed—a California native."

"I was born in L.A." Matthew had always assumed he was born in the city, although his mother could have given birth to him anywhere before dumping him on the steps of St. James's.

His tone was less than encouraging, but Leigh had come here determined to get to know the man a little better and she wasn't going to let his sullen, uncooperative behavior stop her. "Do you have family here?"

"No." His abrupt tone did not encourage elaboration.

"None at all?"

"I never knew my family. I spent the first seven years at the Sacred Heart Boys' Home, the next nine in foster homes."

"I'm sorry," she murmured, wishing she hadn't brought the subject up.

"Don't be. From what I've seen, families aren't all they're cracked up to be."

"Sometimes they can certainly complicate your life," she agreed. "I realize that if my grandfather hadn't created Baron Studios, I could still be knocking my head against the wall, trying to prove that a woman can succeed on the business end of a camera. But on the other hand, there are times that I find myself giving in to my father; if he were any another boss, I'd probably be a little tougher."

She smiled, inviting a response. Matthew remained mute.

Frustrated by his continued silence, Leigh began talking about her work. Describing how she had been involved with the studio since childhood, her current duties, her lofty plans for the future, her every word underlined the difference between her privileged upbringing and Matthew's humble beginnings. And although Leigh realized that she was making him uncomfortable, she didn't care. He'd been unpleasant from the beginning.

Matthew wasn't really listening to her lengthy monologue. Instead he was wondering why the hell he had agreed to have a drink with this pampered bitch when he could be back home having a good time with the uncomplicated, agreeable Jill.

Joshua settled into in his customary power booth, facing the door. A quick glance around the Polo Lounge revealed that Leigh had followed his instructions concerning Matthew St.

James. He watched with interest, noting that although Leigh was chatting amiably and smiling right on cue, St. James was definitely not cooperating. Knowing firsthand his daughter's considerable charms, Joshua wondered if the guy was gay and made a mental note never to cast him in a film with Johnny Banning, just in case. He'd had enough trouble keeping the actor's sexual proclivities under wraps during the shooting of that damn Western last year, and although stories about love affairs between co-stars provided a big boost at the box office, as a general rule fans preferred their sex symbols to be heterosexual.

Of course if he was queer, Joshua decided, opting to look at the bright side, he sure as hell wouldn't have to worry about the guy trying to get into Leigh's silk panties. Not that he'd have a rat's chance of succeeding. Leigh was too smart a girl to get involved with a man who was so obviously from the wrong side of the tracks. When she did marry—and he assumed eventually she'd have to, if only to provide a fourth generation to run Baron Studios—she'd choose a mate who'd prove useful to the business. As he had done. Not that there was any hurry, Joshua assured himself. She was only twenty-five. There were still years to go before he'd be forced to share her with another man.

At that unwelcome idea, Joshua scowled.

The arrival of Brendan Farraday shattered his unpleasant introspection. "Sorry I'm late," Brendan said, sliding into the booth. "But I was at the club and the game ran a little longer than I'd planned."

"Golf or tennis?"

Farraday grinned. "Neither. These days I'm more into indoor sports."

Joshua was not surprised. Farraday's sexual appetites were well known. The only surprise was that he hadn't been shot in the ass by some jealous husband years ago. Joshua had often wondered if Sylvia Farraday kept a few discreet men on the side, or if she simply put up with her husband's affairs because being the wife of a star paid damn well. "Anyone I know?"

Farraday ordered a Scotch, rocks, before answering. "Would you believe Margie Wentworth?"

Margie Wentworth was the granddaughter of Giles Wentworth, one of Hollywood's biggest stars back in the golden
days of the 1930s. She'd been acting since appearing in an
Ivory Snow commercial when she was six months old. Recent
rumors had her hitting the bottle with increasing frequency.

"Christ, Brendan, talk about your jail bait. That kid can't be
more than sixteen."

"She turned fifteen last month," Farraday revealed, not
bothering to acknowledge the waiter who'd placed his drink
on the table, along with a second for Joshua. "But you'd never
know it. The kid's got moves even I couldn't believe."

"You're the one who was so hot for a part in *Dangerous*. If
you get your ass thrown in jail for statutory rape, Leigh'll
replace you before your lawyer shows up with the bail
money."

"Never happen." Farraday leaned back in the booth, appearing unconcerned, sipping the Scotch. "You're the boss of
the studio. She's just your kid."

"It's her project."

Farraday's eyes hardened. "Do I have to remind you where
the funding for this project is coming from?" His gaze moved
across the room to where Leigh was still struggling to carry
on a congenial conversation with Matthew. "Perhaps, if it's
really Leigh's baby, we ought to fill her in on a few of the more
critical details of the deal."

A hot flush rose from beneath Joshua's white silk collar. "I
told you before. We're keeping her out of this."

Farraday's answering smile didn't quite reach his eyes.
"Sure, Josh. Whatever you say."

So long as you play the game our way. The words were left
unstated, but they hovered threateningly in the air between
them. Joshua tossed back his Scotch, then stood up. "It's
getting late. And I've got that damn charity thing to get ready
for tonight."

"Sure. Sylvia and I will see you there. Oh, Josh, aren't you
forgetting something?"

"What?"

Farraday reached in the pocket of his pale cream linen
blazer and pulled out a plain white envelope. "Mr. Minetti
sends his best wishes for a successful film."

Christ, how he hated that smug look on Farraday's once handsome face. Looking as if the envelope was something that had crawled out from under a particularly slimy rock, Joshua took it, slipped it into his own pocket, and walked out of the restaurant.

Alone in the Polo Lounge, Farraday contemplated exactly how far he'd come. Who would have thought that he'd ever have a powerful man like Joshua Baron in his pocket? Like so many others who'd trekked to Hollywood in search of fame and fortune, Farraday, the former Arnie Stoller of Elko, Nevada, came from humble beginnings. Arnie's mother had been a seamstress who also took in ironing in order to make ends meet while his drunken father routinely drank up what little money Mary Stoller managed to earn. When Arnie was twelve years old, Mary packed her bags and disappeared on a Greyhound bus for parts unknown, leaving her son alone with an increasingly brutal father.

Arnie put up with the drinking and the beatings until his sixteenth birthday, when he greeted his father's arrival home from a drinking binge with an Ithica 12-gauge shotgun. Afterward, he walked out the door, never bothering to look back.

The sixteen-year-old changed his name to the ordinary-sounding John Brown, got a job driving a truck between Reno and Las Vegas, made some contacts at the casinos, and within eighteen months had turned to the more lucrative business of hauling contraband liquor and cigarettes. It was Rocco Minetti, owner of the Lucky Nugget Hotel and Casino, who first recognized the potential in the young truckdriver's all-American good looks.

Rocco changed Arnie's name again—this time to Brendan Farraday—and introduced him to Joshua Baron, a regular high roller at the casino. When Joshua, never known for his luck at cards, was offered an opportunity to cash out his markers in exchange for signing Farraday at Baron Studios, he didn't think twice before accepting the deal. He also, at Minetti's request, introduced Farraday to Corbett Marshall, an ambitious young agent at William Morris. Corbett took Farraday on as a client, Joshua signed him to play a hero in a World War II epic, and as they say in Hollywood, a star was born.

Farraday definitely liked being a star. He liked the perks: the fame, the money, the women, the power. And he definitely liked making Joshua Baron grovel.

"How the mighty have fallen," he murmured to himself with a slow, satisfied smile. He sipped his Scotch and took in the silicone-enhanced breasts of the actress in the next booth. Did Joshua realize that this was only the beginning?

Rocco Minetti's booth was in the corner of the Polo Lounge, allowing him to watch the action without drawing undue attention to himself. Sitting beside Marissa, he had seen Joshua Baron's discomfort during the brief conversation with Brendan Farraday. Farraday might be a world-class prick, but the guy was definitely useful. He'd have to tell him to ease up on Baron for a while, though, Rocco thought. Whatever he'd said, the old man had looked like he was going to have a heart attack or a stroke right then and there. Timing, Rocco mused, was everything.

Interesting how Baron had walked out without saying anything to his kid, Rocco considered, his gaze moving from Farraday to Leigh. It wasn't that her father hadn't noticed her; his eyes had kept drifting her way and, from the tight set to his jaw, Rocco determined that whatever Josh had been thinking, it sure as hell wasn't good. Wondering if there was a rift building between father and daughter, he made a mental note to make a few phone calls. If there were any more problems brewing at Baron Studios—problems he hadn't initiated—he damn well wanted to know about them.

The kid sure was a looker. She reminded him a lot of her mother—cool, distant, like a marble statue. But looks were deceiving, Rocco knew, wondering idly if the ever-so-proper Leigh Baron was as hot in the sack as Signe had been.

Marissa was getting sick of the way her sister drew everyone's attention without even trying. It was bad enough that she was having a drink with that hunk bartender from the party (in public, yet!), but their old man hadn't been able to keep his eyes from her the entire time he'd been talking with Brendan Farraday, and now even Rocco was looking at Leigh like he was considering casting her in his next skin flick.

"Hey, baby." She ran her ragged fingernails slowly up his thigh. When she'd reached her goal, she began seductively stroking his groin under the pink tablecloth. "I'm getting bored. Why don't we blow this joint and go back to your place and get it on in the Jacuzzi?"

"Later," Rocco said, pushing her hand away. What the hell was it that had turned this current crop of young chicks into crotch grabbers? Although he liked fucking as much as the next guy—hell, more than most—he was getting damn tired of being assaulted under tablecloths. Must be that damn women's lib, he decided grimly.

"But Rocco—" Marissa pouted prettily.

"I said later." He stood up. "Right now I got a business meeting with a friend of mine."

His eyes were hard. Unyielding, reminding her of the risks of arguing. She watched him walk over to Brendan Farraday's table and Marissa promised herself that once she became a star, she'd have any man she wanted. And one thing was for sure—that scumbag Minetti wasn't going to be one of them.

"Well, as much as I've enjoyed our little chat," Leigh said abruptly, "I do have a dinner engagement."

Matthew rose from the table, not bothering to conceal his relief.

They were standing at the entrance to the hotel, waiting for their cars when Matthew turned to her. "Thanks for the drink."

"You're welcome." Looking up into his dark eyes, Leigh had the feeling that the man was actually going to break down and say something personal, perhaps even profound.

When he continued to look at her for a long time without saying another word, Leigh found herself holding her breath. She was about to ask him if something was wrong when the valet arrived with her Jaguar; once again he disappointed her, leaving her to drive away from the restaurant, wishing she'd never have to see Matthew St. James again.

The club was packed. A blue cloud of smoke hovered over the room, along with the scents of perfume, sweat, and marijuana. The floor was awash with discarded cigarettes and spilled drinks. A driving rock beat accompanied by incomprehensible lyrics blared from monstrous speakers hung on every wall. Strobe lights flashed, adding a surreal feeling to the scene.

Matthew elbowed his way through the teeming sea of humanity, wishing he was anywhere else. Anywhere but wherever Leigh Baron was tonight, he amended as an afterthought. It had been Jill's idea to come here and, since he felt he owed her a good time after the way he'd left her this afternoon to go running off to the Polo Lounge, he was struggling not to let his distaste for the raucous scene show.

"Isn't this fun?" Jill shouted over the music, pulling him by the hand as she tugged him toward the crowded dance floor.

"Loads," he muttered.

"What?"

Her strapless sequined stretch top revealed a generous amount of golden flesh, the taste of which he still carried on his lips. Her hair was a wild tangle of gleaming blond, her eyes eager, her smile bright enough to light up the entire city. Matthew reminded himself that it wasn't her fault that his encounter with Leigh Baron had left him in a rotten mood.

"It's loads of fun," he assured her, grateful when the DJ in the tall booth switched to Neil Diamond's "Song Sung Blue." Although Matthew knew he could be considered a throwback to the dark ages, he had never understood the point in dancing if you couldn't hold the woman in your arms.

"Y'all are a rotten liar, Matthew," Jill accused as she lifted her arms around his neck. "But Ah like you anyway."

The flashing lights turned the dancers vivid shades of crimson, saffron, and purple. Matthew tried to relax, but his unsatisfactory conversation with Leigh kept running through his head, over and over again, like a record with the needle stuck in a groove. An hour later, he had still not managed to put it out of his mind when he heard a familiar voice behind him at the bar.

"Hey, man," Jeff said, "I thought you spent all your time sweating over a typewriter."

"Or mooning over women he won't ever get," a feminine voice added meanly.

Matthew slowly turned around. "I manage to get out from

time to time." His eyes narrowed and focused on Marissa Baron. "As for women, I like the one I'm with just fine."

"That's good, because any man who thinks he can get into my sister's pants is wasting his time." Her eyes were glazed, the shiny black pupils dilated. "Leigh has always had ice between her legs, isn't that right, sweetie?" She looked up at Jeff.

"Whatever you say, babe. So, Matt, what's a Mr. Clean guy like you doin' in a swingin' joint like this?"

"We're celebrating Matthew's contract," Jill said brightly. "Contract?"

"He just got the starring role in Baron Studios' new film." Both Jeff and Marissa stared at Matthew in disbelief.

"You're kidding," Jeff said finally.

"I don't believe it," Marissa echoed. "My father would never hire some bartender to star in one of his movies."

"The details still need to be ironed out, but it looks pretty good," Matthew confirmed.

Emotions washed over Jeff's face. Surprise, envy, anger. "Well, hey, dude, this calls for a celebration. Yo, bartender," he called out, "another round of drinks on the movie star here."

"We were just leaving," Matthew said, taking hold of Jill's elbow and turning her unprotestingly toward the door. He tossed a five-dollar bill onto the bar. "But have a beer on me."

Once in the car, Jill turned toward him. "Are you all right?"

"Sure." He gave her what he hoped was a reassuring smile. "It's just been a long day."

Returning his smile with a dazzling one of her own, she reached out and patted his hand. Matthew was grateful when she remained silent during the drive home.

Jeff was pissed. Here he was, busting his balls on those goddamn dead-end porno films and his old high school buddy just glides into Baron Studios, slicker than snot on a doorknob. It just wasn't fair. He sat in the dark, drinking himself into oblivion. He was alone because Marissa had locked herself in the bedroom after he'd gotten a little mean and knocked her around. Usually the chick liked it rough, but when he split her lip, she'd screamed at him like a banshee and raked her fingernails down his cheek, drawing blood.

Damn bitch. He tipped the bottle of Jack Daniel's back and swallowed deeply. If it wasn't for those pictures he'd taken of her, she'd still be waiting for her big break.

Deciding that she'd pouted long enough, he rose unsteadily from the chair and headed toward the bedroom.

Even as drunk as he was, the flimsy hollow-core door proved no obstacle. When he kicked it in, Marissa scrambled off the bed, clutching the sheet to her breasts. She was wearing the see-through black nightgown with heart-shaped cutouts in provocative places that she'd surreptitiously stuffed into her voluminous shoulder bag after today's filming. "You'd better get out of here."

He was swaying dangerously. "This is my pad, remember?"

She reached into the drawer of the bedside table and took out the gun she'd seen the first night she moved in. "You come one step closer, you son of a bitch, and, so help me God, I'll use this."

He continued toward her, oblivious to the pistol pointed at him. "Come on, baby, quit playing hard to get. It's casting against type."

Marissa backed up until she was pressed against the wall. "I'm not kidding, Jeff."

"It's not loaded."

In one swift gesture he ripped her black nightgown to the waist. When he ground his mouth against hers, Marissa felt a surge of dangerous intensity, but before she could respond, Jeff suddenly went limp and slumped to the floor in an alcohol-sodden lump.

Her own head spinning from too many tequila sunrises, Marissa stared down at him for a long, incoherent time.

16

The waiting was driving him crazy as the pre-production days dragged on. Although Corbett had passed on to him what was promised to be the final draft screenplay of *Dangerous* (the third in the past week), and the director had been signed, the studio was a long way from beginning to shoot. Frustrated by the continual delays, Matthew spent the time learning his lines and writing. So far, moviemaking was about as exciting as watching two guys fish.

"You're what?" Joshua stared at Leigh in disbelief.

"I'm moving out," Leigh said, looking her father straight in the eye.

"The hell you are!" His face flushed, a vein pounding darkly at his temple. "We've been over this before. You have a home. With me. And your sister."

No. She wasn't going to let him do it to her again. She wasn't giving into emotional blackmail of any kind. It was strange how he only treated Marissa like a member of the family when it suited his own purposes. And although she was afraid that this time he'd actually have that stroke his doctors had warned her about, Leigh held her ground.

She was standing across his office from him, her hands resting on the back of one of the leather visitor's chairs. "I need a home of my own," she said calmly. "A place where I can be alone."

"To do what? Screw some ambitious stud who's only using you as an entry to me? To the studio?"

Leigh refused to be insulted. "Because I love you, I'm going to pretend I didn't hear that. And although I am honestly sorry that you're so upset, there's nothing you can say that will change my mind. Now, if you'll excuse me, I'm late for an appointment."

To her surprise and relief, Joshua didn't try to stop her. Thirty minutes later Leigh was standing on the balcony of the two-story house on Santa Monica's Gold Coast, looking past a pair of tall fan palms to the stretch of beach and the ocean beyond.

"Well? What do you think?" Tina asked.

"It's perfect."

"I have to be honest with you," Tina said. "The reason you're getting such a good deal is that after last winter's mud slides, a piece of the Palisades ended up in the owner's backyard. Right after that, he chickened out and bought a place in Brentwood."

"His loss."

"Then there's the traffic. It's gotten terrible. Not to mention the tourists who will park illegally and block your driveway, and drunks who spin out on the highway and land in your living room."

Leigh had heard the story. A few years ago a car had nearly done exactly that, crashing through the fence and landing in the compound of a scion of one of the old-time studios. The crash had been filmed by the owner's security cameras.

"I still love it," she insisted. "It's loaded with history."

Back in ancient times, when films were called moving pictures, it was this particular stretch of beach that was known as the Colony. Indeed, in those days, Malibu, a long haul away on a dusty, unpaved road, was for second stringers and those whose cars had sturdy shocks and rugged axles.

The house had once belonged to a silent film star infamous for his wild parties. She could look down at the beach, and almost imagine F. Scott Fitzgerald and William Randolph Hearst, dressed in white flannels, playing Ping-Pong while Marion Davies and Norma Shearer sipped dry martinis and cheered them on.

"It's also got dry rot," Tina felt obliged to point out.

"The wood can be replaced. I'm not looking for just a house, but something . . . more."

"A way of life." Tina wished she had a dollar for every time she'd heard that one.

Leigh nodded. "Exactly. Imagine waking up every morning to the Pacific Ocean."

"Along with flooding, damp air, salt corrosion, drunks sleeping it off in your front yard—"

"I'll take it."

Leigh needed a retreat. A place where she could escape Joshua and Marissa's constant battling, Baron Studios' ongoing financial difficulties, and her most distracting problem of all, the studio's new star. Although Leigh hated to admit it, lately she'd found herself thinking about Matthew St. James in ways that had nothing to do with business.

Not that there was anything wrong with fantasizing, she'd assured herself only this morning, after a particularly lengthy shower, during which time she'd closed her eyes and imagined the stinging hot water sluicing over her body to be Matthew's hands. After all, to believe *Cosmopolitan* magazine, entertaining sexual fantasies was perfectly normal behavior for modern women in these liberated 1970s.

But now, even as she reassured herself that she had nothing to be ashamed of, Leigh knew she'd feel better if the male starring in her erotic fantasies were any other man.

"Sold." Tina's satisfied voice broke into Leigh's thoughts. "You know," she said, slipping from the role of real estate broker to friend, "your father is not going to be pleased."

"I'm twenty-five. It's past time I had a home of my own."

"Still, it's obvious that Josh would prefer you to stay in

Beverly Hills. And your father has never been one to suffer defeat gracefully."

Leigh's calm gray eyes had a determined look. "Perhaps it's time he learned that he can't always have things his way."

Matthew was fuming as he strode through the hallowed halls of Baron Studios. By the time he reached Meredith's polished desk, smoke was practically coming out of his ears.

"Is she in?"

"Yes, but she's on the phone. Long distance. If you'll just take a seat—"

"I'll wait in her office."

One look at the fire in his dark eyes stopped any objection Leigh's secretary may have been about to raise.

Leigh glanced up as he marched into her office. Only a blond brow rising above the dark frame of her glasses revealed her surprise by his unexpected appearance.

"Peter," she said into the receiver, "something's come up. I'll have to get back to you on that, all right? Terrific. I appreciate all you've done."

"That was Peter Worth," she said as she hung up the phone. "There's talk in Washington of us losing the tax shelter from advertising expenses. If the investors get back their original expense, plus a guaranteed percent, the IRS may consider it a loan and disallow the tax deduction. If that happens, we'll have a more difficult time finding investors, which in turn would limit the number of films we could make each year. Baron Studios pays Mr. Worth a great deal of money to take our case to the appropriate members of Congress. I assume," she continued briskly, "that whatever has you charging in here today is equally important?"

He was already angry enough; Matthew knew if he allowed Leigh's cool, superior attitude to get under his skin, he'd explode. "We need to talk," he said, flinging his body into a chair.

Leigh took off her glasses, leaned back in her leather chair, put her elbows on the padded arms, and studied him over linked fingers. "About what?"

"About that twinkie you've got running the promotion department."

"Janet Bridges? That twinkie happens to have a master's degree in journalism."

"Undoubtedly yellow journalism."

Leigh ignored his sarcasm. "She's also the best in the business. I couldn't count the number of times she's pulled our chestnuts out of the fire."

"So let her handle *your* nuts. Just leave mine out of it."

"Did you come here today to impress me with your prowess of the English language? Or was there another reason?"

"She told *Variety* about the Silver Star I got in 'Nam."

"You got one, didn't you?"

"That's beside the point."

"It's hardly beside the point when Baron Studios' newest star is awarded a medal for gallantry in action."

"Aren't you afraid people will think Baron Studios' newest star is a baby burner?"

"Not after the follow-up story in tomorrow's *Variety* about your Purple Heart. Compassion for your wound should cancel out any antiwar feelings."

"You've got everything all figured out, don't you?"

"It was Janet who came up with the medal strategy. The war is a tricky subject. She decided it would be better to be upfront about your participation than to let some supermarket tabloid break the news."

"I can remember when serving your country could be construed as patriotism," he muttered.

"True. And as much as people would undoubtedly prefer to continue believing that war is like it was portrayed in all those heroic John Wayne movies, the evening news has brought reality home to the dinner table. What other complaints do you have?"

"How about her releasing that picture of me to the L.A. *Times*?"

"The one Jill Cocheran took? I selected that particular shot myself. It was quite good." Better than good. One glance and the image of the tight cords of his neck, the firm sinews of his arms, his powerful chest and washboard stomach, had been fixed on her mind for all time.

"Did you have to choose the only one where I wasn't wearing a shirt?"

"There's an old saying in this business, Matthew: If you've got it, flaunt it. Next?"

Somehow, without raising her smoothly modulated voice, she'd managed to subdue his rage. Matthew found himself admiring her technique. "The premiere tonight."

"Ah yes." She swiveled back and forth in her chair. "Don't tell me; you refuse to wear a tuxedo." She wondered vaguely what would happen if he showed up at the premiere dressed in those faded tight jeans and bare pecs. The women would go crazy; it'd be like throwing him into a bucket of man-eating piranhas.

Matthew saw a faint smile tease at the corners of her lips and wondered at its cause. "I'm not wild about the idea of dressing up like a headwaiter," he admitted. "But I categorically refuse to escort Cindy Raines."

"Cindy is one of our hottest young actresses. The press loves her; the publicity could do you a lot of good."

"She also has the IQ of a toaster."

"You don't have to talk to her, Matthew. You'll be watching a movie."

"Yeah, but I'm starting to get a handle on how you guys operate. All I have to do is show up at the theater with Miss Silicone in tow and the next thing I know your overeducated Janet Bridges will be leaking a blind item to the *Hollywood Reporter* that Cindy and I are having some hot affair."

"So?"

Matthew stared at her. Was he suddenly talking in Swahili? Why the hell couldn't he make her understand? "So I don't want people thinking I'm sleeping with Cindy Raines."

"Any people in particular?" she asked with studied casualness. If she had been worried about her unwilling attraction to Matthew, Leigh was aghast at her reaction to his being seriously involved with some nameless, faceless woman.

"How about everyone in particular? I'm not going, Leigh. Understand?"

Despite their initial lack of rapport, Leigh had met with Matthew several times to arrange carefully selected public appearances and interviews. If everything went as planned, by the time *Dangerous* made it to the screen, the public, enamored with the preproduction hype of Matthew St. James, would be eagerly waiting for the film.

Although their relationship had remained strictly professional, she watched how he worked, and was aware of how focused he was on his goal of becoming a screenwriter. Leigh couldn't help admiring Matthew's drive. She had also discovered that she could only push him so far.

"All right," she said, "I suppose we can arrange for Parker Masterson to escort Cindy. His new comedy is opening next week and, from the looks of the final cut, it's going to need all the help it can get."

"Thanks." Matthew stood up. "Sorry about interrupting your phone call." Now that he'd achieved victory on the most important of his demands, he could afford to be gracious.

"That's all right. Just don't make it a habit." Leigh stood up as well, coming around the desk to walk him to the door. "There is just one little thing."

"What's that?" Matthew asked, instantly suspicious at her casual, offhand tone. He'd already determined that Leigh Baron was never casual about her work.

"You're still going to have to attend that premiere."

"With whom?"

"I don't know. Why don't you call me back later this afternoon after Janet and I have time to work on it?"

"May I make a suggestion?"

Leigh glanced up at him curiously. Thus far, Matthew had displayed no interest in the promotional side of the business. On the contrary, she often felt as if she were using up a lifetime store of patience cajoling him into the few appearances he had agreed to make.

"Of course. Who do you have in mind?"

"You."

The single word ricocheted around them in the sudden stillness of the office. "Me?"

"That's right." He tested the waters a little further. "Got a problem with that, boss lady?"

Leigh studied him warily. Was this some kind of test?

"Not at all. It's just that the idea of you and I . . . of us . . . together . . . it never crossed my mind."

She was obviously uncomfortable with the sudden turn the

conversation had taken. Matthew had already come to the conclusion there were very few things that could fluster the ever-so-proper Ms. Baron. He decided he liked being one of them.

He regarded her with amusement. "What's the matter, Leigh? Does Baron Studios have a rule against the brass frat-ernizing with the talent?"

"Of course not."

"Good." His teeth flashed in a satisfied, wolfish smile. "I'll pick you up at seven-thirty." He turned to leave, then stopped in the doorway. "Wear something sexy. And get rid of that damn bun. I like your hair down."

With that he was gone, leaving Leigh to stare after him. Who the hell did he think he was? For a man who six weeks ago was tending bar and had yet to film his first scene, he had a lot of nerve, telling her how to dress and how to wear her hair.

She'd give him time to get home, then telephone with the news that something urgent had come up and she was going to have to cancel. No. That wasn't the way to handle it. She was Leigh Baron, heir to Baron Studios; she didn't owe the man any explanation. She'd simply tell him that he'd be at-tending the premiere with someone else—the most obnox-ious actress she could find on such short notice.

That's exactly what she'd do, she decided, marching back to her desk. It was high time that Mr. Matthew St. James learned who, exactly, was boss. As Leigh picked up the re-ceiver, a pair of thoughts occurred to her.

The first was that she really was the boss.

The second was that as boss, she could do any damn thing she wanted to.

"Meredith," she said, when her secretary came on the line. "Please clear my calendar for the rest of the afternoon, then call Julio and see if he can squeeze me in for a shampoo and blow-dry."

When Leigh hung up the phone, she realized she was smil-ing.

17

Carole King was singing "It's Too Late" on the car radio when Matthew drove through the studio gates. "You can sure say that again, Carole baby," he muttered, wondering what in the hell had possessed him to ask Leigh to go to the premiere with him.

Wasn't it enough that he spent too much time thinking about her as it was? Hadn't he wasted too many hours that he should have spent writing, staring at the blank piece of white paper and seeing her face materialize on the page?

Matthew knew that if he didn't sort out these feelings he'd been having about Leigh before tonight, he could end up with a helluva lot more trouble than he needed.

She was admittedly lovely, with her wide eyes and blond hair gleaming like silk in the bright California sun. But he knew other women just as lovely. She was intelligent, but no more so than some other women of his acquaintance. She was maddeningly stubborn and ambitious when it came to her work, but despite what he considered an unhealthy obsession with Baron Studios, the more time he spent in her company, the more she intrigued him.

One of the problems, he considered, taking the exit that led off the Hollywood Freeway to the Santa Monica, was that in all their dealings, all Leigh had ever permitted him to see was the tip of the iceberg.

Carole King gave way to James Taylor, and Matthew reminded himself that it was beneath what was the iceberg that had sunk the *Titanic*.

Smiling an apology to the driver she'd just inadvertently cut off, Leigh pulled her Jaguar sedan to a stop between a sporty little red Mercedes 280-SL and a gunmetal gray Rolls-Royce with the windows tinted black.

Leigh had never understood the appeal of Rodeo Drive, where impossibly thin, too rich women with too little to do shopped with a fervor that gave new meaning to conspicuous consumption. Personally, despite her high-image profession, she preferred buying classic styles made from good fabric that she could wear year after year. The idea of buying a spectacular, one-of-a-kind evening dress for a single occasion had always seemed incomprehensible.

"I've just the thing." The ultrachic saleswoman, clad in a black sheath, whisked a scarlet satin strapless dress with a short bell skirt from a nearby rack. "This would look absolutely divine on you, dear."

"Even if I could keep it up, which I doubt, I'd freeze to death before we made it through the first reel," Leigh said.

"Then how about this one? It's such a lovely color, don't you think?"

The emerald silk cocktail dress with a matching beaded jacket was closer to what Leigh had in mind, but the color was all wrong. "Green makes me look sallow."

The clerk switched gears with the deftness of a natural-born saleswoman. "Black is always appropriate."

The black floor-length evening dress was simply cut, with a slender skirt and tight sleeves ending in narrow points at the wrists. But the neckline was also slit to the waist in front, and there was no way she'd have the nerve to greet Matthew at the door wearing anything so blatantly revealing.

"I don't think so." Leigh was beginning to remember why she hated shopping.

"You're certainly slim enough to look marvelous in this," the woman suggested, displaying an abbreviated froth of pastel pink organza ruffles.

"It reminds me of cotton candy." Definitely not the image she wanted to portray to Matthew St. James.

"These are dazzling, don't you think?"

Leigh rejected the gossamer gold-and-flame harem pants and blouse with a firm shake of her head. "I'd feel like a reject from Central Casting. All that's missing are the seven veils."

The saleswoman remained undaunted. "Gracious, I nearly forgot. We received the most gorgeous dress this morning; it's still in the back room. Let me get it for you." She was gone before Leigh could tell her that she'd changed her mind.

"It's you," the woman proclaimed, returning with a triumphant gleam in her eyes.

Even as Leigh opened her mouth to thank the salesclerk for her trouble and explain that she wasn't in the market for a new dress after all, she drew in a quick, sudden breath.

"It's stunning." The dress, an ice blue silk Valentino, with thin silver threads, was the most ravishing thing Leigh had ever seen. "I've never seen a color like it."

"The threads were individually hand-dyed before the fabric was woven in Paris. Edith Head had a similar fabric made for Grace Kelly's 1955 Oscar appearance, but personally, I think this gown is even more divine than the princess's."

"It's beautiful. And undoubtedly ridiculously expensive."

The clerk deftly plucked the coded tag from the hanger. "Why don't you try it on?" she coaxed.

Leigh found the shimmering blue lure impossible to resist. The dress flowed over her like rippling water cascading down a mountain stream. The ice blue silk skimmed her body, hugging her slender curves in all the right places. The off-the-shoulder neckline framed a tantalizing display of creamy flesh, while the slit in the skirt displayed her legs to advantage. But it was when she turned around that the dress revealed its full potential: the neckline, which skimmed the crest of her breasts in front, plunged below her waist in back.

"How is it?" the woman called in to her.

"It's a little snug," Leigh lied, vowing to get out of the dress—and the boutique—before she gave in to temptation.

"Let me see." The saleswoman entered the dressing room without an invitation. "Didn't I tell you it was absolutely perfect? I almost feel sorry for that poor guy."

"Excuse me?" Leigh turned this way and that, studying her reflection, feeling like a little girl playing dress-up for the first time. She was enthralled against her will, amazed at the magic the dress had performed. She looked . . . sexy.

"Whatever man you're buying this dress for. One look at you and he's going to be a goner."

Leigh was stunned by the image in the mirror. Whereas moments before she'd entered the dressing room an attractive, sophisticated woman, now she was seductive.

Leigh surrendered to impulse. "I'll take it."

On some distant level, Leigh knew that she was probably making one of the biggest mistakes of her life. But she couldn't stop staring at the sexy stranger in the mirror.

Westwood was the movie capital of Los Angeles, boasting the most intense concentration of first-run theaters in the world. Surrounded by the posh communities of Beverly Hills, Bel Air, Brentwood, and Holmbly Hills, Westwood possessed a fascinating energy, derived in part from the cosmopolitan mix of students and young people drawn to nearby UCLA.

As they approached the theater, Leigh smiled with satisfaction at the serpentine lines of people curving around the block waiting to buy tickets. There was nothing quite like the enthusiasm of Westwood audiences; they had a way of reminding her what this business was all about.

Magic.

Excitement.

Make-believe.

Although searchlights no longer blazed across the night sky, the frenzied neon energy of the theater marquees created an excitement all their own. On a movie's opening night, the Paparazzi crowded near the entrance, cameras at the ready, and fans lined the sidewalk, hoping to catch a glimpse of a famous star.

Janet Bridges had done her job well. Although the first scene of *Dangerous* had not yet been shot, Matthew's face was becoming familiar. When he and Leigh emerged from the limousine, a clutch of teenage girls clad in stretchy Lurex tube tops and tight jeans excitedly screamed out his name.

"How does it feel to be famous?" Leigh asked. Necks craned to get a glimpse of the couple walking down the red-carpeted aisle.

"I feel like a trained bear in a cage."

"Does that bother you?" she asked as they took their seats.

"Of course. Wouldn't it you?"

"Having grown up in this business, I've learned to live with publicity. Of course, I've never had any interest in acting."

"Don't feel like the Lone Ranger."

"Yet you did end up auditioning for *Dangerous*."

"The dough you're paying me to make this movie will allow me to write full time. That's the only reason I agreed to test for the damn thing in the first place."

"You sound as if you're having second thoughts."

The contract negotiations had not yet been concluded. If Matthew got it into his frustratingly hard head to walk now, Leigh didn't know what she would do. His next words caused a frisson of fear to skim up her spine.

"I suppose I am."

The brief, unsettling conversation was cut short when the lights dimmed, the velvet curtain parted, and the screen filled with the familiar Baron Studios crown. Sitting in the dark, Leigh thought of all those thousands who had gravitated to the city from all over the world to try their luck at the incredible odds of becoming a star. She knew many aspiring actors and actresses would sell their souls for a single shot at the opportunity the man seated beside her had been given.

Two hours later, Leigh had no doubt that the featured film, *Scattershot*, would prove popular; as Kim Yamamoto had succinctly pointed out, the thriller was packed with sex and violence. It also had a complex plot, strong characterization, and fast-moving dialogue. All in all, a studio couldn't ask for anything more.

They got up to leave. "Looks as if you've got yourself a hit," Matthew said.

"I think we do," she agreed, smiling her thanks to the driver who'd opened the door of the limo. "Which just goes to show how much of this business is based on luck," she continued when Matthew joined her in the backseat and the car pulled away from the curb. "That script was turned down by six other studios before it finally ended up with us."

"Why?"

"Because so many different locations made it expensive to shoot, because the love interest is a multiracial couple, because the plot's too complicated; it moves so fast that if you leave your seat to buy popcorn, you'll miss something important. You name it, each studio had a different reason for turning the project down."

"But you bought it."

"I knew it was a movie people would enjoy."

"As simple as that?"

"Unfortunately, nothing is simple any longer," she said on a soft sigh. "These days most studio executives are selected for their business expertise rather than their feel for films. With them, everything is numbers, the bottom line. They just don't love movies."

"And you do."

"I'm passionate about them."

Belatedly realizing that it was the wrong thing to do, Leigh made the mistake of meeting Matthew's suddenly intense gaze.

"That's an intriguing idea."

"What?"

"You. Passion. The two together." He tugged lightly on the ends of her hair that tumbled freely over her bare shoulders.

Julio Mendoza, self-proclaimed hairdresser to the stars, had labored for the better part of two hours with shampoo, conditioner, gel, and spray, defying nature to force Leigh's straight blond hair into a mass of curls atop her head. Realizing that it was useless to argue with a hairdresser in the throes of creating, she had downed Julio's frothy confection under the shower immediately after returning home.

"I like your hair down."

"So you said. Not that I wore it this way for you."

"It makes you look softer. Warmer. More approachable . . .

Did I mention that I like that dress too?"

"I don't believe the subject came up." Her voice was calm; Leigh was not.

He shook his head and ran his fingertip along the neckline. "Damn. I must be losing my touch."

"Matthew—" When his fingers trailed up her neck, Leigh wondered if he could feel the increased beat of her heart.

He could. "Your heart's racing."

"Of course it is. You're making me nervous."

"Personally, I'd call it something more elemental. But I'm willing to settle for nervous. Until one of us comes up with a better word."

She watched, unable to move as his head descended, his intent obvious. Part of her mind told her to back away—both physically and emotionally—before things got out of hand. Another, more sensual part, the part that had succumbed to the seductive vision in the boutique mirror earlier this afternoon, welcomed Matthew's kiss.

His lips, now on hers, were clever, experienced, but that was no surprise. Leigh knew that a man as ruggedly handsome as Matthew would have had plenty of opportunity to perfect his technique. What was a surprise was that such a light touch could create such scintillating heat.

He deepened the kiss, degree by glorious degree. Matthew's broad hand cupped the back of her head. His mouth was firm, persuasive, his lips nibbling at hers, coaxing a response. Desires too long untapped rose to the surface, drawing her into a world of steamy, potent passion. She could get lost in this dark and smoky world, Leigh realized. Too easily.

Matthew knew that the kiss, which had begun as a casual sort of experimentation, was fast turning out to be something more intense. More dangerous. The attraction for Leigh had been there from the beginning, along with a basically sexual male desire he refused to apologize for. But no attraction had ever made him ache this way, and desire had never made him feel as if he were slowly, inexorably sinking into quicksand.

"I knew it," he murmured, lifting his head. Her eyes were filled with a confused desire that tugged at something elemental but unnamed inside of him.

"Knew what?"

"That there was fire under all that ice."

"That shouldn't have happened."

"You're right."

It was not what she'd expected him to say. "I am?"

"You sound surprised that I agree with you."

"I am."

Matthew shrugged. "Look, Leigh, you're a nice woman, when you're not playing that damn Joan Crawford, female-executive role. You're also remarkably intelligent, and as beautiful as any actress in this town. If you were a baseball player, you'd be a triple threat."

"Thanks," she murmured. "I think."

"It was meant as a compliment. And the truth is, if you were any other woman, you'd be spending tonight in my bed."

"You are incredibly arrogant."

"Perhaps. I'm also right. There were sparks there, and they weren't all mine. But I have a rule against sleeping with any woman who already has too much power over my life."

"And I have a rule against sleeping with anyone connected with Baron Studios."

"Fine." Matthew gave her a long, hard look. "Then we shouldn't have any problems, should we?"

"None at all." Her brisk, self-assured tone belonged to the icy studio executive Matthew found so unlikable.

But later, alone in the bedroom of her new home, Leigh pressed her fingertips against her lips, imagining that she could still feel the heat, and wondered.

18

Matthew was irritated when the memory of the kiss he and Leigh had shared lingered in his mind, teasing him with sensual suggestions that proved more frustrating with each passing day. She had infiltrated every corner of his mind, disturbing first his sleep, and then his work. And when he found himself facing an uncharacteristic writer's block for the third day in a row, he became furious at the idea of any woman having such power over him.

Swiftly calculating how long it had been since he'd made love to a beautiful woman, he realized the last time had been with Jill, the day he'd found out he'd won the part. That had been four weeks ago. Too long. That was all that was wrong, Matthew assured himself. He was simply reacting to Leigh because he was in need of a woman; it had nothing to do with her personally. Matthew began to feel better.

"So, what are you doing this weekend?" Kim asked over salads at The Bistro Garden the Friday before Labor Day.

"View some dailies, read some screenplays, walk the floor worrying about when and where I'm going to find someone to play opposite Matthew St. James in *Dangerous*," Leigh answered.

"Joshua is still dead set against Marissa?"

"He insists his feet are set in concrete." She speared an artichoke heart. "I'm still hoping to change his mind."

"Have you brought the subject up with her?"

"I haven't dared get her hopes up."

"How is she, anyway?"

Leigh put down her fork. "I don't really know. I told you she moved in with Jeff Martin."

"The beachboy."

"That's him. She mentioned something a few weeks ago about being up for a part, but I haven't heard anything about it since, and every time I call their apartment, there isn't any answer."

Kim took a sip of Chablis. "I wouldn't waste any time worrying about her. Marissa can take care of herself."

"She's more vulnerable than she looks. Or acts."

"That's probably what they said about Bloody Mary. So, how's the hunk?"

"I assume you're referring to Matthew St. James."

Kim's dark almond-shaped eyes observed her with renewed interest. "Some other good-looking stud you've been dating lately?"

"No. And I haven't been dating Matthew. I'm only seeing him for business reasons."

"That was quite some business suit you were wearing the night of *Scattershot*'s premiere. Don't forget, I was sitting behind the two of you and, believe me, the way that guy was looking at you, if you'd been a Hershey bar, you would've been a goner."

"Your imagination is not to be believed."

"It's the truth."

"It never pays to get involved with an actor," Leigh said, folding her napkin and putting it on the table. "They're all children."

"True. But Matthew isn't really an actor. He's a writer. And he's good, Leigh. Really, really good."

Leigh, who had been reaching into her wallet for her American Express card, looked across the table at her friend with undisguised interest. "You sound as if you've read his work."

Kim, avant-garde as usual, was wearing a kelly green silk-fringed cowboy shirt with mother-of-pearl buttons and a pair of navy blue hot pants with a cartridge belt worn low on her slender hips. Dressed as she was, with her gleaming black hair framing her smiling face, a casual observer would have taken her for a starlet, rather than the newly elected president of the Editors Guild. Leigh had watched the male heads turn when Kim had entered the restaurant. Now she couldn't help wondering if Matthew had also found the glamorous young editor irresistible.

"I was in Venice a couple days ago," Kim answered offhandedly. "And who should I run into but your sexy new star."

"Not unreasonable, since he lives in Venice." She quickly scanned the bill, then handed her card to the waiter.

"So I discovered. Anyway, we got to talking, then it got late, and pretty soon we were in his kitchen and I was reading his screenplay while he made lasagna."

"Sounds cozy." Something that felt too much like jealousy curled through her. Something she couldn't quite keep from her voice.

Kim grinned. "It would have been, if Matthew had cooperated. Unfortunately, he was a perfect gentleman."

"Now that is a surprise," Leigh said dryly. Try as she might, she hadn't been able to get that kiss they'd shared from her mind. She had spent too many sleepless hours since, trying to recall the last time she'd been kissed like that and had come to the reluctant conclusion that she had *never* been kissed like that. "I'm also surprised he let you read his screenplay."

"Well, to tell the truth, he didn't really let me," Kim admitted with an unrepentant grin. "It was on the counter and I couldn't resist glancing through it while he was down at the corner market getting the tomatoes for the sauce." Her smiling eyes turned serious. "It really was damned good, Leigh. Good enough that the guy's crazy if he gives up writing for acting."

"I hope you didn't tell him that."

"Are you kidding? Before I get a chance to edit him in *Dangerous*? The guy could be the next F. Scott Fitzgerald and

I wouldn't open my mouth until the wrap party."

Leigh nodded her satisfaction, added the tip, then signed her name to the charge slip. "Good."

"Oh," Kim said as they rose to leave, "I almost forgot. I'm invited to a cookout tomorrow at Doherty State Beach. How would you like to come along?"

"Don't you have a date?"

"The beach should be swarming with great-looking guys. Why take a bologna sandwich to a banquet? So, what do you say? It should be a lot of fun."

"I really should work."

"You know, you are in grave danger of becoming a drudge. Worse. A spinster drudge."

"Spinster? What Victorian dictionary did you get that out-dated word from? This is 1972, remember? I prefer to think of myself as a dedicated career woman."

"Fine. So what does a dedicated career woman do for sex-ual relief when she gets tired of going to bed with her stacks of scripts and optioned novels?"

Leigh considered herself to be a thoroughly modern woman, but conversations about sex—particularly when they involved her sex life, or lack of it—made her uncomfortable. "I do all right."

"For a Carmelite nun . . . At least give it some thought," Kim advised. "I'll call you later this afternoon."

"I have a meeting this afternoon."

Kim's frustrated sigh ruffled her sleek black bangs. "You are impossible. But I'm not giving up on you, Leigh Baron. Not until you learn to have some fun."

Back at her office, Leigh thought about Kim's words. The talented film editor managed to play every bit as hard as she worked, a talent that had somehow escaped Leigh. She had enough difficulty juggling the demands of the studio and her father and sister, without the added demands of a romantic relationship.

Leigh accepted the stack of phone messages from Mere-dith, and sitting down at her desk, experienced a fleeting wish that she could learn Kim's trick of keeping all the balls in the air.

*   *   *

Matthew had almost been able to convince himself that he was not interested in Leigh Baron. Until he walked into her office the Friday afternoon before Labor Day weekend.

"Good afternoon, Matthew," she greeted him with polite interest. "What can I do for you?"

Wanting her outrageously and cursing her heatedly for creating such heretofore unknown emotional turmoil, he turned inward. "Corbett told me you'd signed Brendan Farraday to play the FBI agent in *Dangerous*."

"That's right. We were lucky to get him; he had almost decided to do a thriller for Warner Brothers, but after he read the screenplay, I was able to persuade him to come over to us."

"Why wasn't I informed?"

"I suppose because I've been busy and the deal was just consummated. Besides, when you come right down to it, signing Brendan really doesn't have anything to do with you."

"The hell it doesn't!"

She tried to discern the reason for his gritty tone and failed. "We signed Brendan for star appeal. You may find this difficult to believe, Matthew, but your name doesn't bring in the big investment dollars."

"Not yet."

"That's right. Not yet."

There was a challenge in his tone that made Leigh worry that Matthew was beginning to believe his own press. Thinking that he was the last man she would have expected to have fallen prey to an inflated vanity, she frowned in annoyance. "There is nothing in your contract about casting approval."

"Common courtesy demanded that you tell me you were planning to cast Farraday."

"Would it have actually made a difference?"

"I never would have signed if I'd known I'd be working with that guy."

Leigh was surprised at Matthew's unprecedented animosity. Granted, Brendan could be pompous. And although he did tend to drink too much between pictures, he was a pro once the cameras began rolling. His recent election as president of the Screen Actors Guild proved that he was popular among his peers. In fact, Leigh considered now, the only person she'd ever met who openly disliked Brendan Farraday was Tina.

"I assume you have a valid reason for your aversion to working with Brendan?"

"Let's just say that after seeing a few of his Vietnam tours, I don't much care for the guy."

It was more than that. Something Matthew wasn't saying, but he'd encased himself in an impenetrable armor Leigh had come to know all too well. She folded her hands on the desk and observed him gravely. "You know, Matthew, military behavior was undoubtedly in order in Vietnam," she said quietly. "But it doesn't serve you very well in Los Angeles."

"What the hell does that mean?"

"It means that you go through life as if it's a journey behind enemy lines. You look at everyone, even those people who want to help you, with suspicion, and you face every day as a continuing series of battles to be won."

She'd hit a little too close for comfort. "I hadn't realized you had a degree in psychology."

"It doesn't take a degree to recognize hostility. I don't know what your problem is, Matthew, but it won't be long before *Dangerous* begins production and it's vital that harmony be established among the cast and crew. This attitude of yours could endanger my project." She gave him a long, warning look. "Which is something I will not, under any circumstance, allow to happen. I'm sorry that you're not happy about working with Brendan Farraday, but the bottom line is that we need his name recognition, so I suggest you just grow up and adjust to the fact that you can't always have things your way."

Her frosty, remote behavior only served to increase his own aggravation. "Doesn't it ever get old?"

"Doesn't what ever get old?"

"The Iron Maiden act. Centering your entire life around Baron Studios."

"Not that it's any of your business, but my entire life is certainly not centered around the studio."

"So what are you going to do this weekend?"

"I haven't decided."

"Let me guess."

Frustrated, Leigh pulled off her dark-frame glasses and sat back in her chair. "Be my guest."

"You're going to work. Like the good, nose-to-the-grindstone little girl your daddy raised you to be."

"Excuse me?"

He wondered what had gone wrong with his mind that he'd wasted so much time thinking about such an icy, unfeeling woman. As difficult as he found talking about his feelings, he'd come here today to admit to his discomfort about working closely for months with a man he detested, yet all she could talk about was business. And the goddamn bottom line.

"When was the last time you actually took time to enjoy yourself?"

"I went to that premiere with you," she reminded him. "Or have you been with so many women since last week that you've already forgotten?"

"I haven't forgotten a thing. Including how you responded when I kissed you. You can say what you want about not sleeping with people you work with, but I could have had you that night, lady. In my bed, crying out, begging me to take you."

The provocative image was too close to Leigh's increasingly frequent fantasies for comfort. "I wish I'd never let you read for that damn part in the first place," she flared uncharacteristically. "You're arrogant, egotistical, insufferable . . ."

"And right," he said when she paused to take a breath. "Don't forget that one, lady studio executive, because it's the most important of the lot. No matter what successful, Ice Queen face you show to the world, inside you're nothing but a confused mess of sexual inhibitions."

The truth stung more than Leigh ever could have imagined. She flung her head back. "You're a bastard."

Her careless words, spoken in anger, hit their mark. He flinched as if she'd hit him, his eyes turning to dark slits. Her cruel words reverberated about her head. Leigh sucked in several deep, calming breaths. What on earth was wrong with her? She never lost her temper. Never shouted. She was Leigh Baron. Cool, composed, dignified. Leigh Baron would never, ever, scream like a fishwife.

"I'm sorry."

"Actually, that one just happens to be the truth. Are you quite finished?"

"Quite," she said. "And you?"

"For now."

"What does that mean?"

"It means that we'll continue this conversation some time when you're more reasonable."

Temper flashed in her eyes until she realized she'd been expertly baited. "We really are going to have to settle this," she warned. "Or we might as well retitle *Dangerous* as *Disastrous*. Because that's how the movie's going to turn out."

"If you find me that difficult to work with, perhaps you ought to find yourself another Ryder Long."

"No." She shook her head. "You really are perfect for the part, Matthew. I also know how hard you've been working and how frustrating all these changes and delays must be."

"It's not having control over my life that's frustrating."

She managed a wry smile at that. "Tell me about it." She held out her hand. "Truce?"

Knowing exactly how Adam must have felt when Eve showed up in the Garden of Eden with that apple, Matthew found her coaxing smile impossible to resist. "Truce," he agreed gruffly.

Marissa was unusually calm sitting at the kitchen table in Jeff's apartment. Be bold. Take risks.

"That's exactly what I'm doing, Daddy dear," she murmured, leafing through the stack of photographs one last time, remembering how psyched she'd been when Jeff had taken them. She'd felt sexy. And sex, she considered, even more than money, was the animating factor in this world.

She slipped the photographs into a padded, oversize brown envelope, then addressed it to her father, care of Baron Studios. Across the bottom of the envelope, she printed PERSONAL in large bold letters, and underlined it three times.

Marissa smiled. She had made her plans. Now it was time to carry them out.

Her concentration shattered by her altercation with Matthew, Leigh finally threw in the towel late that afternoon.

Since she'd sent Meredith home early, in order to allow her secretary to get a start on the holiday weekend, she picked up the telephone and dialed the familiar number herself.

"Hello?"

"Hi, Kim," Leigh said, forcing a breezy tone she was a long way from feeling into her voice. "Did I interrupt anything?"

"Not at all. I was just watching the Olympics. Speaking of which, have you seen the Omar Sharif lookalike who's winning all those swimming medals?"

"Mark Spitz?"

"That's him. God, talk about star potential. If I were you, I'd be on a plane to Munich to sign him up before any other greedy studio gets its hands on him."

"I've already talked with his agent about a possible screen test," Leigh acknowledged. "But, believe it or not, I'm not calling about work."

"No?"

"Actually, I've decided to take you up on your offer."

"Terrific. I'll pick you around ten-thirty tomorrow morning."

"What should I bring?"

"Beer and chips are always good. Oh, and don't forget suntan lotion and your birth control pills."

"My what?"

"Hey, you never know when you're going to get lucky at one of these beach parties. And this former Girl Scout's motto is *Be Prepared.*"

"With an attitude like that, I'm amazed Matthew was able to resist."

"You're amazed?" Kim countered. "I was absolutely flabbergasted. Oh, my God."

"What?"

"You don't think he could be into guys, do you?"

Leigh thought about the heated kiss they'd shared in the backseat of the limo. And the way his eyes had turned dark and intense when his fingers had curled around hers this afternoon. "No. I don't think Matthew's gay."

"I hope you're right. Christ, what a waste that would be."

Hanging up, Leigh decided that, for once, she and Kim were in total agreement.

19

The mood was decidedly festive when Leigh and Kim arrived at Doherty State Beach shortly before noon. Rows of faded green tents lined the pine tree–shaded beach, making it look as if the Marines from nearby Camp Pendleton had chosen this weekend to go on bivouac. Hot dogs roasted over campfires, beer flowed from shiny aluminum kegs, dogs leaped into the air to catch bright plastic Frisbees in their jaws. Impromptu football and volleyball took up much of the sand.

Out on the water, surfers rode the breaking waves. One particular surfer captured Leigh's attention. Tall and muscular, with a physique that backed up any challenge the ocean might dare to make, his style was tautly controlled and precise, unlike so many of the others who were wiping out. She watched, entranced by the unknown surfer's combination of strength and grace riding the white surf all the way to shore. It was then that she recognized him.

"My goodness." She gave Kim an accusing look. "Of all the beaches in the state, what a coincidence that we just happened to show up at the same one as Matthew St. James."

Kim waved merrily at Matthew, who began walking toward them. "Isn't it?"

"Well, have fun."

When Leigh turned away, Kim grabbed her arm. "Where do you think you're going?"

"This is supposed to be my day off, remember? So I'm leaving before Matthew and I get into another argument."

"But you can't leave. Not now."

"Why not? Don't you want to be alone with him?"

"The guy's already turned me down; now it's your turn at bat."

"What are you talking about?"

Kim was forestalled from answering by Matthew's approach. "That was absolutely wonderful," she gushed.

He shrugged. "It's getting glassy; they'll be higher this evening." He glanced over at Leigh. "This is a surprise."

"Isn't it?"

"Well," Kim said quickly, "I see my friends; I'd better get over there before they run out of Fritos. You two have fun; Leigh, maybe I'll see you later." She ran off, leaving them alone.

"Why do I feel like high school?" Leigh asked.

Matthew managed a half smile. "Join the club."

She glanced down at his surfboard. "Don't let me keep you."

"I was ready for a break."

"Oh." Leigh reminded herself that she was an adult, an individual who wielded a great deal of power. So why was she suddenly behaving like a tongue-tied schoolgirl?

A charged silence settled over them while Matthew tried to think of something, anything, to say. "Want a beer?" The sea breeze blew a few strands of blond hair across her cheek; his fingers itched with the urge to brush them away.

Leigh tucked her hair behind her ears. "That would be nice. It was a long drive down here and Kim's Corvette doesn't have air conditioning."

"I've got a cooler back at my tent. It's just around the corner."

"Which means it's out of sight of this beach."

"Does that bother you?"

Her glance moved to Kim, who had joined a group of people Leigh recognized to be fellow editors and cinematographers. All of them were eyeing Leigh and Matthew with undisguised interest. "What do you think?"

Matthew chuckled. "I think that if we disappear, they're going to go crazy wondering what we're doing."

"Serves them right." Cast in the role of a fellow conspirator, she smiled up at him. "Lead the way."

"What took you so long?"

Marissa greeted Jeff at the apartment door wearing a filmy black negligee from Frederick's, matching crotchless panties and a plunge bra.

"Just delivering a few pharmaceuticals, babe." When she handed him a glass of champagne, Jeff dropped the athletic bag to the floor.

"I hope you saved some goodies for me."

"Don't I always? So how come you're not dressed?"

"Don't you like my new outfit?" she asked on a pout.

"It's bitchin'. I just thought we were goin' to the beach."

"I changed my mind. I decided that it would be more fun to stay home and celebrate." She shrugged out of the negligee, letting it drop to the floor.

Jeff's body stiffened at the sight of her nipples, darkly rouged, jutting impertinently through the lacy cutouts of the bra. "Baby," he said, yanking off his gray cotton gym shorts, "you're on."

Later, as they lay panting on the avocado green shag carpeting, Jeff thought to ask, "What the hell are we celebrating?"

"Didn't I tell you?" Marissa refilled their glasses with the Cristal champagne she'd filched from Joshua's wine cellar. "My daddy's going to make me a star."

Matthew's campsite faced the beach. The beer was cold, the sun hot, and the company surprisingly enjoyable. Leigh could see that the sea relaxed him. She sat cross-legged on the sand

and watched the waves roll in to shore. It smoothed off his rough edges, calmed his inner anger, wore away at the parapets that normally kept everyone at arm's length.

While they indulged in obligatory small talk, Matthew found Leigh much more accessible. She'd discarded the severely tailored suits she usually wore like a suit of armor in favor of a sunshine yellow T-shirt and white shorts. With her long blond hair free and blowing in the breeze, she was more natural.

"Mmm," she sighed happily, leaning back on her elbows and stretching her legs out in front of her, "I needed this." She took a deep breath, filling her lungs with the invigorating salt air. "I have this theory that if everyone took thirty minutes a day to walk along the beach, all the psychologists and psychiatrists in L.A. would go out of business in a week."

"The beach is one reason I live in Venice." He took a drink from the long-necked brown bottle. "That and the atmosphere."

More than anything, funky Venice, birthplace of fads, was what had given Los Angeles its reputation as La-La Land. A mixture of quaint and seedy, rich and poor, it had always been a home for dreamers, beginning with Abbot Kinney, whose vision had transformed the sleepy little ocean community into a miniature of its Adriatic namesake, replete with miles of canals, gondolas, and seaside hotels. Today all that remained of the Grand Lagoon was a traffic circle, but the town continued to attract more than its share of individualists.

"You're a dreamer," Leigh suggested softly.

Matthew shrugged. "I suppose, in a way, I am. After all, who else but a dreamer would be crazy enough to think he could actually earn a living telling stories?"

"Kim says you're very talented."

"Kim's a nice lady. And an excellent judge of talent."

Leigh laughed at that, as she was supposed to. Her gaze drifted out toward the lineup of surfers. "You were very good out there."

"Thanks."

"You don't move around as much as the others."

Matthew shrugged. "I believe in a less-is-more approach."

"It was beautiful. Almost elegant, but at the same time,

powerful.'' She turned back toward him. "I don't know much about the logistics of surfing, but I like your style, Mr. St. James.''

"That makes us even. Because I definitely like your style, Ms. Baron.''

"That's not the impression I got yesterday.''

"It's a holiday." He took her hand and linked their fingers comfortably together. Matthew wondered if everything between them would be such a close and perfect fit. "Let's forget about work. Just for today.''

"Just for today,'' she agreed softly.

"Great. Don't go away." He stood up and walked a few yards down the beach to where a couple was locked in a passionate clinch. After exchanging a few words, he returned, carrying a long white surfboard with a likeness of Ann-Margret wearing a shiny black-vinyl bikini laminated onto the back. "Come on, boss lady, we're wasting those waves." He reached out and pulled her to her feet.

"Wasting what waves? Are you talking about surfing?''

"Of course.''

"I don't surf.''

"You're kidding! You grew up in L.A. and you've never surfed?''

"You don't have to make it sound as if I've suffered a misspent childhood,'' she complained. "For your information, I have body surfed. Lots of times.''

"Great. Board surfing is simply the next step.''

When a trio of surfers disappeared under a wall of crashing white water, Leigh dug her heels into the sand. "Matthew, I don't think this is a very good idea.''

"You'll be terrific, trust me.''

"How do I know this isn't some sadistic scheme to pay me back for yesterday?''

"I told you, forget yesterday. That was then. This is now. And the question on the table is whether or not you're willing to trust me not to let anything bad happen to you.''

Leigh looked up into the unrevealing dark lenses of his sunglasses and realized that what had begun as an offhand suggestion had metamorphosed into some sort of a test. A test that could determine the future of Baron Studios. Leigh remembered her promise to humor Matthew.

"All right. But if I break my neck, I'm going to kill you."

"You've got yourself a deal." For a fleeting moment, Matthew's self-satisfied grin reminded Leigh uncomfortably of her father.

"I know I'm going to regret this," she said, reaching for the hem of her T-shirt. She stripped out of her shirt and shorts, revealing a sleek body clad in a white bikini.

"You're going to love it," Matthew insisted, resisting the urge to drag her, caveman-style, into the nearby tent.

The house was quiet; wanting to be alone, Joshua had given the servants the weekend off. He was in the library, drinking Scotch and milk and staring down at the photographs that had arrived this afternoon at the studio, Special Delivery. After he had flicked through the glossy eight-by-tens of Marissa in a series of increasingly sexual scenes, Joshua's mind raced back to the day Signe had announced that she was pregnant again.

There was no way the baby could have been his; he and his wife hadn't slept together since she'd become pregnant with Leigh years earlier. If he'd given the matter any thought, Joshua would have guessed that Signe had remained celibate; to discover that she had had an affair was an unpalatable revelation.

When he suggested that she take her bastard and go live with whoever was responsible, Signe calmly replied that not only was the man in question already married, she had no intention of telling him he was about to be a father.

"You should at least make him pay for the doctor," Joshua advised. "Because I'll be damned if I'm going to spring for the cost of getting rid of some other guy's kid."

"Don't be ridiculous," Signe replied. "In case you've forgotten, Joshua, the one and only thing we have in common is that we were both raised as Catholics. Abortion is out of the question."

"But adultery isn't?" he shot back. "I want you the hell out of here by the time I get back from the studio tonight."

Signe surprised him by laughing. A cold, unpleasant sound that made him want to kill her. "Very good, darling," she said. "Just the right amount of husbandly outrage with a touch of wounded male pride. Perhaps you should have been an actor instead of a studio head."

His hands clenched into fists at his side. "You're a slut."

"And you're a pompous prick." Her smile was brittle ice. "I'd say we belong together." She crossed the room and placed her hand on his arm. Her scarlet fingernails looked like blood against the navy sleeve of his suit jacket. "Don't forget, darling, it was my money that saved your precious studio from bankruptcy. You owe me."

Joshua stared at her. "You actually expect me to stay married to a woman who made a laughingstock out of me?"

"You have no need to worry; I was quite discreet." Her fingers stroked the rigid muscles of his forearm. It was the first time she'd touched him in years. "There isn't anyone—including my child's father—who won't automatically assume this baby is yours. Besides, think of the advantages continuing our marriage would have for you."

"Name one."

"If you get enmeshed in a long, expensive divorce proceeding, Baron Studios could go right down the drain. But what even you should realize, Joshua, is that by remaining a married man, you'll have a ready excuse for not marrying all those young actresses you're always sleeping with."

Joshua reluctantly decided that Signe had a point. "All right," he said. "You can stay."

"And you'll claim my child as yours?" Signe had no intention of having her baby born under the stigma of illegitimacy.

He scowled. "It'll have my name. That's all I'm promising."

She smiled. "That's all I'm asking."

Over the next few months they entered into an uneasy truce. Unfortunately, the idea of some faceless man inflaming the frigid Signe to passion left Joshua feeling strangely inadequate. To his further dismay, he discovered himself to be sexually impotent.

It was then that he sought comfort in the one aspect of his life he could still control: Leigh.

After he crossed society's inviolate moral boundary, Joshua lived in constant fear of detection. Until he began to realize that Leigh had no memory of that night. Of the betrayal that had taken place.

Instead of destroying his life, as he'd feared, a secret bond had been created between father and daughter—a bond that possessed the tensile strength of silk. And although Leigh had no memory of how that silken cord had been woven, Joshua knew that she accepted the reality of its existence. She'd never leave him. He was the only man she could ever love.

He burned the pornographic photos of Marissa and thought of his beautiful, talented daughter.

20

It was not nearly as easy as it looked.

By the time she'd been out on the water for an hour, Leigh's arms and legs ached, her sinus cavities were filled with brine, and a bruise the size of Alaska was forming on her hip where she'd been struck by another surfer's board.

Matthew watched her struggle out of the sucking white foam to climb aboard the surfboard again and again, displaying all the tenacity of a bull terrier. He admired her grit. Most women—hell, most people—would have given up a long time ago.

"Feel like one more try?" he asked. They bobbed together in the gentle swells.

Leigh looked toward the horizon where the monster waves were being born. She had already discovered that what appeared to be small, ridable waves turned into gigantic, roiling mountains as soon as she tried to stand up.

"I'm going to do it this time," she swore, paddling toward

where Matthew said the wave would break. "This one's going to be it."

It had to be. Because she didn't know if she had the strength to climb onto that damned board one more time. Somehow, what had begun as Matthew's test had turned into her own personal challenge. She was no longer trying to prove anything to him; now she was struggling to prove something to herself. Something as powerful as it was unnamed.

She rose unsteadily to her feet, clinging to the rails, the board bucking angrily against the rolling water. Just when she thought she was going to land headfirst in the surf again, a sudden calm came over her, flooding her mind, soothing her senses.

After an hour of fighting it, she'd become one with the dark green sea, riding the curling wave, feeling as if she were flying. Free. Untethered. Her body and mind in pure harmony with the water. It was the most peaceful, yet thrilling, feeling she'd ever experienced.

"That was wonderful!" She grasped Matthew's hand, the surf creaming around their ankles. "Let's go out again."

"Don't you think you've had enough? You're going to be sore as hell tomorrow morning."

"It's a holiday." She pushed her wet hair out of her eyes. "And I fully intend to make the most of it. If I wake up stiff tomorrow, I'll spend the day soaking in the Jacuzzi." She gave him a challenging look. "Well, are you coming or not?"

Matthew shook his head. "Now I know how Dr. Frankenstein felt when his monster ran amuck."

The mellow, late-summer afternoon slowly ripened, then faded all too soon. The sky turned indigo, then ebony, illuminated by the glow of campfires up and down the beach. Rock music from portable radios and laughter filled the night air.

Leigh sat on a blanket on the cooling sand, gazing up at the soft, far-flung stars that seemed just out of reach and wondered if she'd ever experienced a more perfect day.

"Do you realize that we've managed to go all day without an argument?" she asked.

"The thought had crossed my mind." Matthew tossed another piece of driftwood onto the fire, causing a brief flare of orange sparks. "But I didn't want to bring it up for fear of breaking the spell."

Leigh took a sip of the red wine Matthew had produced from the cooler. He was right, she decided. It was as if a magic spell had been cast over them all day. A spell that lingered, even now.

They could have been the only two people on the beach. The moonlight streamed down, making the sand sparkle like diamonds. Music drifted on the salt-tinged air, accompanied by the distant sound of crashing surf. Just beyond the blanket, little wavelets lapped on the glistening sand. It was a night made for romance.

"I had a wonderful day."

"If you'd gone to that party in West Hollywood with Kim and her friends, you'd have eaten a lot better."

"I like hot dogs."

"Sure. Everyone knows that hot dogs and potato chips are the only food to serve with Dom Perignon."

It was the first time today that she'd heard that gritty tone. The old Matthew was back, Leigh realized with a soft sigh. In spades. Her glance moved from his face to his right thigh, where a jagged white line cut across the darkly tanned flesh. She'd seen the scar earlier and had determined it to be a result of the wound that had won Matthew his Purple Heart.

Seeming to ignore his challenging statement, she reached out and gently traced the jagged white line with her fingernail. "Does it hurt?"

"Only on bad days."

Leigh could practically see the NO TRESPASSING signs going up all around him. "I'm sorry you were wounded," she said quietly. "Although to tell you the truth, Matthew, I'm surprised that your shoulder doesn't give you more pain than your leg."

"My shoulder?"

"That's a very large chip you're carrying around. It must get very heavy."

Matthew knew she was right. What surprised him was the hurt he detected in her voice. "You're exaggerating."

"No. I don't think I am. May I make a suggestion?"

Matthew shrugged. "You're the boss."

Determined to avoid another fight, Leigh chose to ignore

his disparaging remark. "I'll stop thinking of you as a rude, overbearing, ill-tempered snob if you stop thinking of me as an unfeeling, spoiled rich bitch."

"I never thought of you as that," he insisted, not quite truthfully. "Pampered, perhaps. And you are bossy, in your own quiet way. But I'd never accuse you of being a bitch." As her words sank in, his eyes narrowed. "A snob? Me?"

"Well, you do have a tendency to put people into nice tight little pigeonholes and you don't seem to like anyone who has any money at all . . . Did you say bossy?"

Their eyes held, each waiting for an apology from the other. Finally, they laughed and the uncomfortable moment passed.

Matthew lay down on the blue-and-black plaid blanket and folded his arms behind his head. He stared up at the vast expanse of sky. "Look at those stars," he murmured. "They look as if you could reach up and touch them."

Leigh murmured an agreement, but she wasn't looking at the sky. Her eyes were drinking in the way his gray USC T-shirt molded the hard lines of his body. Knowing it was a dangerous thing to do, she allowed her surreptitious gaze to travel down his long legs, lingering on his muscled thighs.

"Back in 'Nam there were times when I'd look up at the sky and think that those stars were the same ones that were shining back in the world. I know it probably sounds dumb, but sometimes it helped, remembering that."

It was the first glimpse of his life in Vietnam he'd shared with her. "It's not dumb," she said quietly.

Matthew turned his head toward Leigh just as her gaze returned to his face. She was trembling despite the warmth of the fire. And her eyes were far from calm. Even as he was gratified to see that he possessed some measure of control over her, he had to admit that such success was not one-sided. His own heart was pounding furiously.

"Come here."

She shook her head. "I can't."

"Can't? Or won't?"

Her mouth was so dry. Leigh took a sip of her wine. Then another. Then a gulp. Nothing helped. "I think I'm afraid," she whispered.

The sea breeze ruffled her hair. Matthew sat up and leaned toward her, brushing a few shimmering strands away from her face. The gesture, while outwardly innocent, turned out to be remarkably intimate. He could feel her skin warm under his touch, a heat that had nothing to do with the nearby fire. A heat that was echoed in his own body.

"That makes two of us." Cupping his fingers under her chin, he drew her to him with only that light, enticing touch.

The constant ringing was a litany of failure in his ear. Slamming down the receiver, Joshua resumed pacing the floor. Where the hell was she? He'd called both the studio and that damn beach house she'd insisted on moving into and she wasn't at either place. So what was she doing? And more important, with whom?

The phone rang. Grabbing it up, he barked out, "Leigh?"

There was a moment's silence. "Sorry, Daddy," Marissa said. "Wrong daughter."

"No daughter of mine would allow pornographic pictures to be taken of her."

"Don't hang up," Marissa said, correctly perceiving his intention. "I have a proposition I want to discuss with you."

"You and I have nothing to discuss."

"Oh, really? How would you like to see those pictures on the front page of the *Enquirer*?"

"You're under age; they wouldn't dare print them. And if they tried, I'd slap the fucking publisher with an injunction so fast he'd never know what hit him."

"For your information, Daddy dear, I turned eighteen last week. Aren't you going to wish your baby daughter a happy birthday?"

"If you sell those photos to anyone, I'll cut off your allowance."

Marissa laughed at that. "For what I could get for those photos, I wouldn't need an allowance. But as difficult as this will be for you to accept, this isn't about money."

"Since when does blackmail not involve money?"

"Please, Daddy." Marissa clucked her tongue. "Blackmail is such a nasty word, don't you think?"

He could feel his blood pressure rising. The vein at his temple pounded furiously. "What the hell would you call it?"

"Persuasion."

Joshua refilled his glass and took a long drink. "What do you want?"

"A screen test. That's all. One screen test to prove to you that I'm the answer to all Baron Studios' prayers."

"Nightmares, you mean. And you'll get a screen test over my dead body. Baron Studios doesn't hire sluts."

Instead of sounding offended, Marissa laughed. "What a joke. Not only do you hire sluts, Daddy dearest, you also screw them. In fact, now that you've brought it up, I wonder if the *Enquirer* would like a behind-the-scenes view of the Baron Studios' casting couch? It would make a nice story to go along with the pictures, don't you think?"

"If you dare sell those—"

"Sleep on it," Marissa suggested silkily. "You can give me your answer at ten o'clock Tuesday morning." She gave him an address on Wilshire, repeating it twice to make sure he'd written it down correctly. Then she hung up.

Red with rage, Joshua pushed down the disconnect button and immediately redialed. When he was greeted with that now-familiar ringing tone, he yanked the phone out of the paneled wall and flung it across the library, where it skidded to a stop atop the carpet.

"Where the hell is she?" His roar sounded like a wounded lion as it reverberated through the silent, empty house.

Leigh had never thought of herself as a sexual person. Experimental teenage fumblings in the backseat of cars at drive-in movies left her cold; in college her virginity achieved daunting proportions, making her believe herself to be the only virgin left in California and, although there had been times that she had considered going to bed with a man just to get it over with, she had never met anyone who stirred her interest enough to make the symbolic act worth the effort.

After graduation, she directed her energies into her work and never gave sex a second thought. Until Matthew St. James came into her life and turned her world upside down.

Although they'd kissed before, Leigh was not prepared for the explosion that rocketed through her as his mouth met hers. Gasping at that fiery initial contact, she tried to pull away.

"No," Matthew said. "Not yet."

His eyes reflected the flickering glow of the firelight. When they settled on her lips, Leigh felt her resistance melting away, like the foundation of a sandcastle at high tide. Reading her acceptance, Matthew returned his lips to hers.

The kiss was subtle persuasion—a feathery brushing of lips, a slow stroking of his tongue against Leigh's skin, his teeth nipping at her bottom lip. It was more temptation than proper kiss, more promise than pressure. When a rich, liquefying pleasure flowed through her, Leigh let out a shuddering little breath.

"This is crazy."

"Insane." Matthew abandoned her lips to press kisses along the curve of her jaw. His hands moved up and down her back, caressing her with a confident, practiced touch. When his fingers slipped under her T-shirt, something rippled along her skin, something alien. Exciting. Frightening. "But that doesn't stop me from wanting you."

"Nor me from wanting you."

Rising from the blanket, he pulled her to her feet and kissed her. "You deserve better."

"Better than you?"

"No. Well, that too, probably, but I was talking about the location. You're a woman who deserves silk sheets and candlelight and champagne. Not jug wine and a sleeping bag."

The mellow sounds of "If Loving You Is Wrong, I Don't Want to Be Right" floated by on the sea breeze; Leigh decided that the title was prophetic. "We have music. And hot dogs. And moonlight."

"I do believe that you're a card-carrying romantic, Ms. Baron."

"And we've already determined that you, Mr. St. James, are a dreamer. So where does that leave us?"

He traced her lips with his finger. "A dreamer and a romantic? It's a hopeless combination."

"Or a perfect one."

He gave her a long, considering look. "Perhaps." The fire was dying out, the air cooled. Although she did her best to hide it, Matthew didn't miss Leigh's slight shiver.

"You're getting cold. Want me to get the blanket?"

She shook her head. "I'd rather that you keep me warm."

Matthew needed no further invitation. Gathering her up, he carried her into the tent.

"I'm afraid I haven't had a great deal of experience," she murmured as he laid her on the down-filled sleeping bag.

"Don't worry. I have." He began to undress her, pulling her cotton shirt over her head with an abrupt movement that displayed his impatience. The bikini top followed. When he blazed a trail of kisses over her breasts, Leigh tensed.

"I'm sorry," she said.

He lifted his head. "Don't be. I was rushing things."

"It's not that."

"It's your prerogative to change your mind."

"I'm not going to change my mind." She pressed her palm against his cheek. "I'm afraid the truth is that I haven't had any experience."

The only sign of surprise Matthew allowed was a momentary hesitation that lasted no longer than a heartbeat. "All the more reason to make this last," he said, lying down beside her and drawing her to him. She was as rigid as a bar of cold steel. "I've always loved sleeping outdoors," he murmured, looking up at the star-studded sky through the mesh ceiling of the tent. "Every house should come equipped with a glass roof."

"My house has a skylight."

"Really?"

"Three, actually. One in the living room, another in the bedroom, and a third in the bathroom."

"What decadence." He pressed his lips against hers, lightly, unthreateningly. "Next time we'll make love in your bed. Or your bathtub. Think of it, Leigh, you up to your chin in bubbles, drinking champagne, the moonlight making your flesh gleam like pearls while I wash your back. Or your front." His hands caressed her breasts, his lips recaptured hers in a long, drugging kiss that took her breath away.

Her skin warmed and her blood hummed as Matthew's hands and lips moved over her. Her white shorts seemed to dissolve away and when his fingers slid under the waistband of the bottom half of her bikini, Leigh lifted her hips off the sleeping bag, straining for his touch.

"Not yet." His breath fanned the satin skin of her abdomen, moving down, following the path his fingers had blazed as they rid her of the final barrier. Closing her eyes to his beguiling touch, Leigh moved fluidly under Matthew's stroking hands. Where he led, she followed willingly, letting him bring her to higher and higher planes as he discovered flash points of pleasure that she never knew existed.

When his roving tongue slid up the sensitive skin of her inner thighs, she quivered in response and knew that, if she were capable of speech, she'd be begging him to take her now. Instead, she could only moan his name as his stabbing tongue grew greedy, turning her to quicksilver in his arms. She trembled as passion too long suppressed exploded in a dizzying release.

No longer passive, she moved under him, her hands fretting against his back, his thighs, his buttocks. With one hand never ceasing his caresses, he managed to get rid of his clothing and put the condom on with the other. Free of the barrier of material between them, Leigh gasped at the fiery feel of flesh against flesh. She wrapped her legs around his hips.

"Now," she said achingly.

"Now."

To Leigh's surprise, there was no pain, just momentary surprise as Matthew entered her. Then she was moving with him, instinctively knowing his rhythm as if they'd made love a thousand times before. And then it was coming again, the spiraling pressure stretching her body tighter than ever before, the wetness, the shattering spasm of release.

When he felt the rippling convulsions rip through Leigh's body, Matthew followed her to his own tumultuous climax.

Afterward, they lay in a tangle of arms and legs and Matthew thought about how fully, how freely Leigh had given herself to him. She'd held nothing back, surrendering completely. But who had done the surrendering? And who had emerged the victor?

He propped himself up on one elbow and looked down at her. "I don't think I'll ever get enough of you."

His frown was not that of a man who'd just experienced bliss. "You don't sound very pleased about that."

"It's not having a choice that I'm finding difficult to accept."

Leigh considered that. "You're a man used to your own choices. Making your own way."

"Yes."

"I don't think either of us had a choice, Matthew, from the beginning," she said soberly. "And although I realize that we'll have to talk about it, if you don't mind, I'd rather think about all this tomorrow."

"Tomorrow." Matthew wondered if Leigh realized that she was at her most appealing when she was being earnest. "At Tara."

She smiled at that. "At Tara," she agreed, twining her arms around his neck.

It was all either of them were to say for a long time.

The princess, clad in a jeweled white gown, lay in a glass bier. A forest of thorns had grown up around her, protecting her, shielding her, keeping her hostage. All the knights in the kingdom tried to make their way through the thick brush, but for every thorny branch they cut, a hundred would appear in its place.

A year passed. Ten. A hundred. Then one day the most handsome prince in all the kingdoms came riding by, astride a gleaming white stallion. The prince's magical sword cut a wide swath through the thicket, and soon he was lifting the glass top of the bier, freeing the princess he'd come so far to find. The moment the prince's lips touched hers, the princess awakened, tears of joy and love shining in her eyes. But as he began to lift her from the bier, a dark cloud moved across the sun and the air turned cold and dank. Like the inside of a dungeon.

It was then that the princess realized that there was no escaping the monster. The monster's claws reached out for the prince. She began to scream.

"It's all right . . . Leigh, listen to me. Everything's okay."

Leigh awoke to find herself wrapped in Matthew's arms, his lips pressed against her hair. "It's all right," he repeated, running his hands up and down her icy arms. "You're here. With me. And you're safe."

She clung to him. "I was so afraid," she whispered. She looked up at him, her eyes, illuminated by the silvered moonlight, holding a lingering dread he knew all too well. "Oh God, it always seems so real."

"I know," he said, brushing the tears off her cheeks with extraordinarily gentle hands. "Believe me, Leigh, I know."

he phone was ringing when Leigh walked in her door the following morning. She gave Matthew an apologetic glance and picked up the receiver. "Hello? Oh, hello, Daddy."

Realizing that this could be a lengthy call, Matthew began to idly roam around the room. If he'd expected Leigh's home to give him any insights into her personality, Matthew would have been disappointed. The place mirrored the same perfect, self-controlled image she presented to the world. White predominated—the glazed floor tile was the color of vanilla fudge, the walls were a stark alabaster, the modular sofa and matching chairs were wrapped in shell white cotton. Brass cachepots and candlesticks provided gleaming color but no warmth.

"I've been at the beach," he heard her say.

Unlike his own home, no magazines cluttered the nearby tables, no dirty glasses marred the white marble mantel. There was no clutter, no mess, not a speck of dust. From what he could see, everything was absolutely perfect. Matthew felt something akin to claustrophobia.

"Yes, all night. I went to a party with Kim." When Matthew looked at her, color flooded into her cheeks. The soft blush, blooming under yesterday's sun-brightened skin, drew him like a magnet. Matthew wrapped his arms around her and began wetly nuzzling her neck.

"Really, Daddy, I am twenty-five years old; far too grown up for a curfew."

"Do you have any idea what I want to do to you?" Matthew murmured in her ear.

"Stop that," she hissed when he began to unzip her shorts. "No, Daddy, not you." Kneeling, Matthew pressed his mouth against her.

Leigh gasped. Her head felt light, almost faint; her knees were turning to water, and if Matthew hadn't been holding her so tightly, she wasn't certain she could stand.

"Look, Daddy," she said on a ragged voice nothing like her usual calm one, "it's a holiday. Can we continue this conversation Tuesday at the office?"

Matthew slipped a finger into her and even as her body clutched at it, it wasn't enough. Leigh wanted all of him. Again. Now. "To tell you the truth, at this moment I don't really give a damn what Marissa's done," she said. "Daddy, I have to go. Have a nice weekend; I'll see you Tuesday."

His objections ringing in her ear, she quickly hung up, then immediately lifted the receiver and placed it in the desk drawer. "Now," she said, lifting Matthew's shirt over his head, "where were we?"

Joshua stared down at the telephone, unable to believe what had just happened. Leigh had actually hung up on him. After having spent the entire night on the beach like some tramp. And not with Kim. A woman Leigh's age was too old for slumber parties; she had been with a man.

The idea of his daughter in bed with some faceless, anonymous man made Joshua's gut clench. He popped two Rolaids into his mouth and dialed another number.

"I've got a job for you," he told the man who answered. "But you'll have to start immediately."

The voice on the other end of the line agreed, as Joshua

knew it would. Ever since some damn woman he'd been sleeping with had hit him with a phony paternity suit, he'd learned that it was worth a hefty retainer to keep the private investigator at his beck and call.

After giving the detective Leigh's Santa Monica address, Joshua resumed pacing the floor. First he'd find out who the hell his daughter was sleeping with. And then he'd get rid of the bastard, whoever he was.

By the time the sun streamed in through the skylights early Tuesday morning, there was nothing Matthew didn't know about Leigh's sleek, responsive body. No secrets had been withheld as he'd brought her to repeated orgasms.

In return, he had held nothing back, urging Leigh's tentative, exploring fingers to become more intrepid, learning to read his needs and desires as a blind woman would read Braille.

They knew everything about one another. And they knew nothing.

"I had a marvelous time this weekend," she said softly. They were sitting on her bedroom balcony. Below them, a lone beachcomber gathered shells that were scattered on the shoreline.

Now that Tuesday morning had arrived, reality had come crashing down on Leigh, making her wonder where, exactly, they would go from here. Although her behavior was an anomaly for her, she was certain that Matthew was accustomed to such sexual marathons.

She was dressed in a chic black-and-white suit from Givenchy's fall collection, her hair tucked into the chignon he'd come to hate. The black pearls gleamed at her earlobes. She was every inch the coolly efficient lady executive; looking at her, no one would suspect that she'd spent the better part of the last two days making love.

"So did I." He brushed his knuckles over her cheekbone. "I like it when we use our energy for something besides fighting."

"We're bound to have differences." She sounded cautious.

"I realize that. Don't worry, Leigh, I can keep my personal life separate from my professional one."

The implication was there, that whatever they had shared

would last beyond the weekend. The idea was both thrilling and terrifying at the same time. "That's a great deal more difficult to do when the press gets involved."

"We'll keep them out of it."

"Then we're agreed? That our relationship will remain discreet?"

Matthew had considered relationship to be one of those 1970s female words, right up there with commitment and marriage. It had been a word to be avoided at all costs. Not that he hadn't always been forthright about his lack of commitment; his short-lived affairs had always been based solely on mutual pleasure. In that respect, his personal life had always been satisfactory. If, after passions cooled, Matthew found himself from time to time experiencing disillusionment, or an odd, empty feeling, he would force those thoughts away.

But Leigh was turning out to be an entirely different matter. Because now, as he looked into her soft gray eyes, he found himself wanting to stick around for as long as this lasted.

"As much as I hate the idea of sneaking around, it's probably best."

"Oh, it is." Her relief was obvious. Relief that they'd have more nights together? he wondered. Or relief that he was willing to keep their affair secret. "You know, Matthew, a little intrigue might just add zest to things."

"Add any more zest to what we've got going between us, and I wouldn't have been able to get out of bed this morning. You wore me out, lady."

"I don't believe that's possible." Her lips curved in a soft, reminiscent smile. "In fact, if we could find a way to bottle whatever it is that keeps you going, we could probably make a fortune."

"The answer is simple." His dark eyes held her captive. "It's you."

Although they'd struggled to treat the weekend lightly, their lovemaking had catapulted them into a relationship that neither had been prepared to accept. Leigh knew that they both needed time to sort out their thoughts.

"Dinner tonight?" he asked.

She thought of all the scripts waiting to be read, the correspondence that needed to be answered. Whatever new problems her father was having with Marissa. Her life did not allow time for romantic dalliances, no matter how enticing. "What time?"

"Seven. My place."

Seven o'clock. Only eleven hours away. It seemed an eternity. "I'd love to, but I have a meeting with Christopher Burke at seven. I'd reschedule, but he's returning to Melbourne first thing tomorrow morning." Burke had been signed to direct *Dangerous*, and although the Australian was a genius at his craft, Leigh knew him to be a highly temperamental one.

"Hey, don't worry about it," Matthew said on a shrug. "It was just a thought. No big deal."

She was losing him; Leigh could see Matthew retreating behind those damn barricades again. "Make it eight-thirty." She pressed her lips against his. "And you've got yourself a date."

Joshua's first thought was that he was having a stroke when he entered the warehouse on Wilshire and found Marissa lying nude on the round bed, illuminated by a bank of klieg lights, a biker's head burrowed between her thighs. A vein throbbed wildly in his temple, his blood pounded in his ears.

"Turn those goddamn lights off," he roared.

Heads turned. Expressions ranged from surprise to fear to irritation. Marissa propped herself up on her elbows and observed her father with what appeared to be out-and-out glee.

"Hello, Daddy."

"Daddy?" Joe Bompensiero said, looking back and forth between father and daughter. "Well, shit, who would have suspected the chick was connected?"

Joshua ignored the director. "Get some clothes on. We're leaving."

"In the middle of my big scene?"

"I said, get dressed. Now."

"No."

Jeff appeared from behind the lights with the red kimono. "Come on, baby," he said under his breath. "You got your old man's attention. Let's not blow it, okay?"

"Hey, man," Bompensiero complained, "what gives you the right to come busting in here?"

"I'm Joshua Baron."

"So? I don't go fucking up your movies, why don't you just get the hell out of here and let us get back to work?"

"I'll leave as soon as you give me the film."

The director stared at him. "You gotta be kidding."

Joshua folded his arms over his chest. "I'm not leaving until I get that film."

"Perhaps I didn't make myself clear." Bompensiero made a slight gesture with his left hand; a trio of massive, stone-faced men appeared at his side. Any one of them could have played linebacker for the L.A. Rams; indeed, the largest of the three had played fullback for the Cleveland Browns. Although he'd been too slow to last more than one season in the pros, Clayton "The Crusher" Armstrong had managed to set an NFL record for broken bones inflicted on his opponents in a single season.

Joshua held his ground. "Why don't you go call your boss," he suggested. "Before you make a big mistake." He glanced around the warehouse, eyeing the crates piled nearly to the ceiling. "Interesting inventory you have here. Of course you've got purchase invoices for the electronic equipment."

A muscle began to twitch at the corner of Bompensiero's left eye. "I'll be back."

Joshua nodded. "I'll be waiting."

Less than three minutes later the director returned. "Mr. Minetti wants you to know that he was unaware that this was your daughter. The girl used a phony name. She also came to him of her own free will."

"I've no doubt of that."

"Mr. Minetti also wants you to understand that since she's legally of age, there is nothing preventing her from appearing in this film. However, having a daughter of his own, Mr. Minetti appreciates your feelings," Bompensiero allowed. "He says that the film is yours."

Joshua had never had a single doubt that things would turn out this way. He and Rocco Minetti went back a long way. Too long to let a little slut like Marissa ruin what had always been a congenial working relationship.

"Please extend my appreciation to Mr. Minetti," he said politely. His business concluded, Joshua reluctantly turned toward Marissa. His face twisted in disgust. "I'll see you this evening, at the house. Seven o'clock. Sharp."

After watching the way the tyrant of a director had bowed to her father's demands, Marissa wondered if she'd underestimated her hand. "Why can't we talk now?"

His eyes raked her kimono-clad body. "Because this isn't the place to discuss business, you're not dressed, and I have a lunch meeting with your sister and Corbett Marshall. Seven o'clock," he repeated, turning abruptly on his heel.

Leigh again. Watching her father march out of the warehouse, Marissa coldly reflected on exactly how much she loathed her sister.

Leigh was at lunch with her father and Corbett, sipping a cream soda and wondering how many hours of exercise it would take to work off the enormous sandwich she'd eaten.

"Look who's getting nabbed," Corbett said with undisguised glee. Outside the window a meter maid was citing a white Rolls belonging to Alan Bernstein, a top agent.

"That's the reason you asked for this booth, isn't it?" Leigh accused with a smile. "You enjoy watching your rivals get parking tickets."

"Best seat in the house," Corbett agreed cheerfully.

"I talked with Matthew last Friday," Leigh mentioned offhandedly. "He wasn't very happy."

"Oh?" His carefully schooled expression was one of puzzled interest, but Leigh had the feeling Corbett knew precisely what she was referring to.

"He said that had he known Brendan Farraday was going to be in *Dangerous*, he never would have signed."

Joshua's eyes narrowed. "You never mentioned that to me."

"We haven't had a chance to talk since then," Leigh said, hoping her father would not bring up their abbreviated Sunday morning conversation. "Besides, it's all straightened out."

"You know, Matthew mentioned something along the same lines to me," Corbett admitted. "But I certainly didn't expect him to go to you with his complaints."

"It came as quite a surprise. Do you know why he has such

animosity toward Brendan? It may help me know what to do if we have any problems between them once we begin filming."

"I've absolutely no idea," Corbett said, lifting his hands in a palms-up gesture. "The only other person I've ever known to dislike the guy so intensely is Tina. Did I ever tell you that she refused to marry me until I dropped Farraday from my client list?"

"I told you at the time that was a stupid, female demand," Joshua said.

"It certainly wasn't something I was very eager to do. Brendan Farraday was a very profitable client."

"Tina gets along with almost everyone," Leigh said.

"I know. That's what made her hostility toward Brendan so odd, but when I tried to get her to explain, she refused to talk about it."

"She was probably just smarting over a foiled love affair with the guy," Joshua offered. "Hell, Farraday's screwed just about every woman in town."

Corbett's eyes offered his long-time friend a silent warning. "Not Tina. Anyway, although I know I can be accused of being single-minded when it comes to business, I finally gave in to Tina's demands, rather than lose her."

"At which time Farraday began lining Alan Bernstein's pockets," Joshua said. "All in all, that little maneuver cost you one helluva lot of money."

"Tina was worth every penny."

"What a nice thing to say." Leigh smiled. "I envy you two, sometimes."

Corbett patted her hand paternalistically. "Don't you worry, sweetheart, one of these days you'll meet the man of your dreams and Tina and I will be first in line to dance at your wedding."

The man of her dreams. Although he was far from that, Leigh couldn't stop the image of Matthew's hard, tanned body from coming to the forefront of her mind. As she felt the color flood into her cheeks, she pretended a sudden interest in the scene outside the window in order to avoid her father's suddenly intense gaze.

*　*　*

Leigh sat in her office, stunned by the scene being played out on the television screen. A guerilla group, calling itself Black September, had taken the Israeli Olympic team hostage. As she watched the black–ski-masked terrorists on the hotel balcony in Munich, all Leigh could think was that the world must be going mad.

When her father called, insisting that she join him in the screening room, it was with a sense of relief that she darkened the nineteen-inch screen.

"Well," Joshua demanded, as the lights came back on in the screening room later that afternoon, "what do you think?"

Leigh shook her head in disbelief. Although she'd always considered herself to be a sophisticated adult, the scenes from the pornographic movie had left her momentarily speechless. Had anyone told her that Marissa was making such a film, she supposed she would not have been surprised. If she'd known exactly what such a performance entailed, she would have been stunned.

"The setting was certainly less than luxurious," she managed. "And the lighting was terrible."

"Atrocious," Joshua agreed, lighting a cigar.

"The cinematography will never win any awards."

"It was absolutely uninspired."

"You know," Leigh said cautiously, "the pornography business can be dangerous. If you'd only allow Marissa to work here, we'd be able to keep a closer eye on her activities."

"That's one thought. I told you the little bitch is threatening to blackmail me with those stills."

"I don't believe Marissa would actually carry out that threat. She's simply bluffing to get your attention."

"Well, she certainly succeeded. Aside from the bad lighting, budget set, and horrendous cinematography, what did you think of your sister's performance?"

Leigh took a deep breath and jumped into the dangerous conversational waters. "She was riveting."

"Exactly what I was thinking."

Joshua studied the glowing end of the cigar and considered his options. Only minutes before leaving his office to come to the screening room, he'd received a phone call from the detective, informing him that the man Leigh had spent the weekend with was none other than Matthew St. James. When he'd instructed Leigh to get close to their new discovery, he never expected her to get so damn close.

A very strong part of him wanted to fire Matthew. To utilize one of the loopholes the studio's lawyers always wrote into the contracts. Another, more pragmatic side, realized that Baron Studios needed a blockbuster like *Dangerous*. And like it or not, Matthew St. James was a natural for the role; it was as if the part had been written with him in mind.

There was, Joshua considered, a chance that were he to succumb to Leigh's request that he cast Marissa to play the part of Marilyn Cornell in *Dangerous*, she and Matthew would get sexually involved. He'd been aware of Marissa's sexually permissive behavior for years (just like her slut of a mother) and, according to the report the detective had compiled, St. James sure as hell hadn't spent the years since his return from Vietnam in a monastery.

"You know," he said thoughtfully, "you may be right about your sister."

"In what respect?"

"About her starring opposite St. James in *Dangerous*. Although this porn is unadulterated trash, she does light up a screen. And there's always the chance that she and the guy will strike sparks off one another."

Even as Leigh found that idea particularly unpalatable, she couldn't repress the excitement she felt at the thought of finally having the key roles in her pet project cast.

"I'll call her right away and give her the good news."

"She'll be at the house at seven tonight," he said. "Let's wait until then; it'll do her good to sweat this one out."

"I suppose it wouldn't hurt," Leigh agreed. "After this latest stunt."

"She's always been a handful." Joshua ran his fingers down the side of Leigh's face. "Unlike her big sister. You'd never disappoint me, would you, princess?"

Leigh wondered what her father would say if he knew that she'd spent the weekend making love—no, she corrected firmly, having sex—with Matthew. Disappointed would be putting it mildly.

Before she could answer, Joshua flashed her a smile. "Why
don't you come by the house for dinner tonight? I'd say that
this calls for a family celebration."

She looked at him suspiciously, trying to recall the last time
he'd acted as if he believed the three of them to be a family.
"I'd love to, Dad, but I have other plans."

"What could be more important than toasting the success
of your new picture?"

What indeed? Just the memory of Matthew's lovemaking
sent a thrill of anticipation racing through her. "I'm having
dinner with a friend."

"Anyone I know?"

"Actually," Leigh said with a nervous little laugh, "it's Matthew."

"St. James."

Leigh would have had to have been deaf not to hear the
disapproval in her father's tone. "You're the one who told me
to keep him satisfied." Damn, she'd come off sounding too
defensive.

Joshua merely nodded. "So I did. I have another idea."

"What's that?"

"Bring St. James along to dinner. After all, if he and Marissa
are going to play lovers, it only stands to reason that they'll
be more convincing if they become well acquainted before
you start to shoot." He winked. "Just think of the box office
appeal if the two of them became an item. Probably increase
the gross several hundred thousand dollars."

Even as she secretly agreed with him, Leigh was appalled
to discover how upsetting she found that particular scenario.

"Matthew's already made plans. I don't think he'd be
thrilled with me changing things at the last minute."

Joshua could feel the pressure building up behind his eye.
"Well, you certainly know the man best. So, have we agreed
to give your sister the part?"

"Agreed," Leigh echoed softly.

Matthew and Marissa were a casting director's dream
match—Leigh had no doubt that when Matthew's smoldering
danger collided with Marissa's golden fire, the result would be
explosive on the big screen. So why was she feeling so appre-
hensive?

22

The fall of 1972 saw the reelection of Richard Nixon, which pleased Joshua, who'd given generously to CREEP, and depressed Leigh, who, knowing that she was supporting a losing cause, had voted for George McGovern on principle. The Dow closed above 1,000 for the first time in history (displaying confidence in the continuing administration, Walter Cronkite proclaimed). Dashing hopes that the war in Southeast Asia would soon be over, the Vietnam cease-fire agreement was postponed (yet again!) as North and South Vietnam negotiators continued to bicker.

Back on the homefront, an unprecedented epidemic of teacher strikes disrupted classrooms all over America. Placard-carrying men and women shared the sidewalks with the Jesus Freaks (the latest evolution in the youth movement's never-ending search for new highs) who'd taken to the streets, making parents yearn for the good old days when kids wore love beads and got stoned on pot.

Billie Jean King became a symbol for women everywhere, while Playboy Bunny impostor Gloria Steinem (brains and looks, admirer J. K. Galbraith enthused) was fast emerging as a leading cover girl of women's lib, proving to a legion of dazzled detractors that she was much more than just a pretty face.

At Baron Studios, the single most important event of the year (although David Brinkley failed to mention it on the evening news) was that *Dangerous* was finally scheduled to begin shooting.

And although Leigh knew that she should be thrilled to have achieved her long-awaited goal, she was depressed. Because her time with Matthew was rapidly drawing to a close.

"You're early."

It was four o'clock in the afternoon. The autumn sun was low on the horizon when Leigh stood on the porch of Matthew's small house, her arms filled with brown grocery bags from a nearby Ralph's. "I know. I decided to cook dinner for a change, so I took off work to go shopping."

"Amazing." Matthew took the bags out of her hands. "It's usually like pulling teeth to get you to leave that damn studio before eight or nine. And even then you insist on reading scripts in bed."

There had been times when Matthew had been irritated at being relegated to second place in her life, but not wanting to waste their time together fighting, he'd bitten back his resentment, pushing it further and further into the back of his mind.

"I'm not always reading scripts in bed." She followed him into the home she knew as well as her own.

"Thank God." Tossing the bags onto the ceramic tile counter, he took her into his arms, kissing her on the back of her neck, in a special place he'd discovered that first night she liked to be kissed. "Am I allowed to ask what precipitated this uncharacteristic display of domesticity?"

He was wearing a pair of jeans, zipped, but with the button undone. As she slipped her hands into his back pockets, Leigh reveled in the feeling of his toned, hard body against hers. "I wanted to fix you a farewell dinner."

Two months ago, Matthew had been going crazy, anxious

to begin work. Now, as his fingers expertly plucked the pins out of her hair, releasing the long blond strands, he marveled that their time together had passed so swiftly. Tomorrow he left for Paris to begin filming on *Dangerous*.

"Good-byes can wait. How about giving me a hello kiss first?"

She rubbed her breasts, clad in a silvery gray silk Ralph Lauren blouse, against his bare chest. "I thought you'd never ask."

Joshua lay on his back in a comped suite at the Lucky Nugget Hotel and Casino while a blond whore in her mid-twenties sucked enthusiastically on his limp penis. The woman, whose name was Iris, gave the best head in town. Today, however, his body refused to rise to the occasion.

"You're so tense," Iris murmured, massaging his inner thighs with her hands. "What's the matter, Daddy? You drop a bundle at the tables?"

"I wish to hell my problem was that easy to solve." Grabbing her by her long flaxen hair, he lifted her head. "Let's give it a break, okay? Before I get a blister."

"Sure thing, hon." She reached over to pour herself a glass of champagne from the silver bucket beside the round, king-size waterbed. "Want some bubbly?"

"I think I'll pass."

"Good idea. Alcohol tends to make things worse." As she sipped the icy champagne, her gray eyes lit up with the enthusiasm of yet another idea. "Remember when you got off drinking champagne from my boobs? How about giving that a try?"

At least she was trying to cheer him up. Which was a helluva lot more than his own daughter had been doing lately. Over the past two months he'd noticed a distinct change in Leigh. And although she'd become frustratingly secretive about her activities, he knew exactly who had precipitated this unwelcome change.

Matthew St. James.

Joshua hated his new star more and more with each passing day. There had been too many times lately when Leigh returned to work after a long lunch, flushed with an unmistakable glow that revealed she had been well and thoroughly fucked. By that bastard.

Although he wanted to forbid Leigh to see Matthew, Joshua forced himself to bide his time. One thing he had learned from his father was to choose his battles well. All he could do for now was assign her more and more duties to curtail the amount of time she had to spend with her illegitimate lover.

"The day *Dangerous* finishes filming," he vowed under his breath, "that bastard's balls are going to be mine."

"Well, look at that." Iris grinned lasciviously, discarded her empty glass carelessly onto the plush carpeting and lowered her silvery blond head. "I don't know what got you so turned on, Daddy, but whatever it is, hold that thought."

Leigh had never suspected how large a void Matthew's absence would leave in her life. Although they talked often on the telephone, the long-distance conversations were strained to the point of being forced.

Part of the problem, Leigh mused one night as she tossed and turned on a bed which now seemed unbearably lonely, was that she was never sure exactly how she felt about Matthew. Or if she should even think about it long enough to figure it out.

She only knew that she missed him. Desperately.

Mental images of Matthew and Ryder Long—so alike, yet so different, like opposite sides of a coin—tumbled around in her head like the facets of a kaleidoscope. Constantly changing, whirling, shifting, never leaving her at peace. Finally she surrendered. Getting up from her rumpled bed, she put on a pair of jeans, a heavy sweater, a pair of ski socks, and went out onto the balcony.

The sun was rising over the mountains behind her house, splintering the wisps of high fog with streaks of pink and lavender. By the time the sky was a wide blue bowl overhead, she'd made her decision. Going back into the house, she picked up the phone and placed three calls.

The first was to United Airlines, booking a seat on the first flight to JFK, with a connecting flight to Orly.

The second was to Meredith, instructing her secretary to reschedule her appointments.

The third was to Joshua. Despite her father's outspoken

objection to Leigh's trip, Leigh was smiling as she hung up the receiver.

Rain fell from a slate gray morning sky, drumming on the roof of the barge where Marissa lay on a narrow bunk, clad in tight jeans and a torn silk blouse. Her lover's lips burned a path across her bare shoulders, as the brown waters of the Seine lapped against the side of the barge, making it rock.

"You're mine," he muttered, his teeth nipping at her warming flesh. When he yanked her jeans down her legs, Marissa trembled in a delicious mixture of pain and pleasure.

Without warning, he grabbed her wrists in one hand and held them up over her head. His dark eyes held the untamed gleam of a predatory animal. "Say it, damnit."

"Yours," Marissa whispered.

"Louder." He unfastened his jeans with his free hand.

"I'm yours," she cried out as he crouched over her.

"That's better." When he lowered his body onto her pliant one, Matthew's lips curved into a cruel, sensual smile.

Leigh glanced at her watch as the taxi driver sped recklessly through the confusing maze of Paris traffic, horn blaring. With any luck and barring an accident, she should arrive on location about the time the crew was breaking for lunch. It was a cold gray, foggy day, but as the wipers swished back and forth across the windshield, Leigh's body warmed with anticipation of seeing Matthew again.

"Cut," shouted the director.

"Cut," echoed the assistant director.

Christopher Burke slammed his battered khaki bush hat onto the floor. "We'll have to do it again; the bloody boom operator buggered it." He glared up at the young man perched over the bed, dangling a microphone strapped to the boom. " 'Ow in the bloody hell do you expect us to get this friggin' movie made if you keep sticking the bloody microphone into the picture? Wanna tell me that? Christ, you're movin' around up there worse'n a blue-arsed fly . . . And Marissa looks like she's got the fucking measles. Where the hell are the bloody makeup people?"

Recognizing an impending tirade, Matthew left the bed

without a word and shrugged into his shirt. When a harried-looking makeup woman dashed in and began sponging Light Egyptian body makeup onto Marissa's bare shoulders and breasts, he went out on the deck and stood under a tarpaulin that had been erected to protect the crew from the rain.

Matthew had heard it said that film crews were like families. In this case, it was turning out to be more like a reunion with a bunch of relatives who couldn't stand each other. At the root of the problem was the Australian director's insistence on creating a film-noir look—high contrast and deep shadows. Moody images. Although Matthew would be the first to agree that the script was intense enough for such a treatment, they'd already shot enough film trying to render the proper mood to make three feature-length movies.

Meanwhile, the crew, particularly the camera operators, dolly grips, and boom operator, were forced to try to keep up with Burke's impromptu inspirations. In one memorable instance yesterday, the first assistant cameraman had to manually turn the camera two-hundred-and-eighty degrees from a dolly that cut through the cabin roof. When the barge began to rock dangerously on the rising water, the kid fastened his foot to the camera with C-clamps to keep from being thrown overboard.

Pulling a pack of cigarettes from his pocket, Matthew lit one, allowing his thoughts to drift—as they had on too many occasions lately—to Leigh. He had spent much of the past three weeks cursing himself a fool for letting her get under his skin. He'd wanted her—from the beginning—and he'd had her. Again and again. But each time he touched her, kissed her, felt the tremor of her body next to his, had only left him wanting more.

Their encounter hadn't gone the way it was supposed to. The plan had been to take advantage of what he knew to be their mutual attraction and make love to her. Finally, his curiosity satisfied, his desire sated, he could get on with his life.

That had been his plan. Carefully executed and expertly conceived. But then she'd surprised him with her soft admission of inexperience, something he'd hadn't expected any more than he'd expected to care so damn much for her feelings.

He inhaled, pulling the strong, acrid smoke into his lungs. It tasted lousy. That had been one of the reasons he'd given the habit up shortly after his return from 'Nam with a minimum of effort. Then, just last week, he'd broken down and bought a pack of Gauloise in the hotel gift shop. That he found himself wanting—hell, *needing*—a cigarette after all this time was additional proof that Leigh Baron was nothing but trouble. So why the hell didn't he accept one of the many enticing feminine offers he'd received since arriving in Paris and forget about Leigh? Now, before things became even more complicated. He looked up, as if seeking answers in the gloomy, overcast sky.

"God," Marissa said, joining Matthew under the tarp, scantily clad in her scarlet kimono, "you'd think the guy was Otto Preminger, the way he carries on."

Matthew shrugged.

Marissa was getting fed up with the way Matthew continued to ignore her. She still couldn't figure out how any guy could be rolling around in the sack with her one minute, then turn it off and walk out the door as if she didn't exist. If she hadn't reached down and felt his erection this morning, she would have thought Matthew was queer. "This isn't my first film, you know."

Matthew blew out a stream of smoke and studied the view, which was, in a word, magnificent. The towers of Notre Dame were at his back, the great facade of the Louvre on his right, a frieze of chimney pots on the Left Bank. From the deck of the barge, the snarling combat of traffic sounded like the sigh of wind in treetops.

"Of course the other was more fun to do; we didn't have some power-hungry director screaming 'Cut' just when the sex began to get interesting." He hadn't bothered buttoning his shirt; Marissa pressed her palms against his bare chest. "How about slipping away during lunch for a private rehearsal?"

Matthew plucked her hands off his body. "When are you going to get it through your head that I'm not interested? If you're that eager to screw someone, sweetheart, you've got plenty of candidates to choose from. Practically the entire crew, from the director right on down to the clapper loader has been panting after you since day one. And Farraday's scheduled to arrive in town next week. His reputation as a stud should satisfy even you."

"But I don't want any of them. I want you." She licked her lips suggestively. "And you can deny it all you want, Matthew St. James, but you want me too. Don't forget, I'm the girl whose boobs you just finished playing with. And I'm the one who made your cock hard."

It had been an involuntary physiological reaction, triggered by the unexpected realization that she was wearing the same scent her sister favored. "Don't flatter yourself, it had nothing to do with you."

"Why fight it, Matty? When we both know that I could give you the hottest time you've ever had." Twining her arms around his neck, she went up on her toes and kissed him with a fierce, angry passion.

"Excuse me." Leigh stood on the dock, beneath an umbrella the same dark gray as the sky, her face schooled to a composure she was a long way from feeling.

He stared at her over the top of Marissa's head, feeling surprised and guilty. Marissa resembled a cat who had just swallowed a particularly succulent canary.

"Hi, Leigh," she said breezily, not bothering to take her arms from around Matthew's neck. "What a nice surprise. Matty and I were just rehearsing our big scene."

A tabloid headline she'd seen in the airport flashed through Leigh's mind. Something about Paris and lovers, accompanied by a photo of Matthew and Marissa in a heated embrace, the Eiffel Tower in the background. She'd told herself at the time that the story was only gossip, the photo a composite. But it had done nothing to raise her spirits.

"If that kiss was any indication of what Chris has in the can," she said, "you two are going to burn up movie screens all across the country."

"Believe me, that was only a sample of what we can do when we really get going, huh, Matty?"

Matthew didn't answer. He pulled Marissa's hands away, his eyes fixed on Leigh. "I wasn't expecting you."

"Marissa," Christopher Burke shouted before Leigh could answer, "get your lovely round arse back in here, darling, we need to get a new light reading. Jaysus," he complained loudly, "where the hell does everybody get off to?"

"I'd better get back in there before he goes apeshit again," Marissa said, pressing her hand possessively against Matthew's dark cheek. The smile she turned to her sister was guileless. "It's great to see you, Leigh. Are you going to stick around and watch our big love scene this afternoon?"

"I'll be here for the next three days."

"Terrific. Matty and I are going to have to take you out on the town." With that parting remark, she went strolling back toward the cabin, her hips swinging provocatively beneath the red satin.

Matthew wanted to go to Leigh, but afraid of what she was thinking behind that smooth, polite mask, he remained where he was. "I don't suppose you'd believe me if I told you that there's absolutely nothing—less than nothing—between your sister and me."

She'd known it. But she hadn't expected to feel so relieved to hear him say the words. "I just have one question," she said as she boarded the barge and came to stand in front of him.

"What's that?"

"Have you missed me as badly as I've missed you?"

It had been so long. Three weeks. An eternity. Unable to resist, he reached out and touched her hair. "What the hell do you think?"

She wanted to touch him, to wrap her arms around his hard body and press her lips against his chest. She wanted to open herself to him—her heart, her mind, her body—here, now, before common sense and reason overcame need.

The folly of such temptation was demonstrated by the sudden arrival of Christopher Burke on deck. "Matthew, if you could be so good as to favor us with your illustrious presence—" He stopped in his tracks when he viewed Leigh. "Stone the bloody dingoes, if it isn't the lovely boss lady."

Genius or not, Leigh knew that Burke could be a tyrant on a film, and experience had taught her that he slipped into his native slang when he was at his most dictatorial. "Hello, Chris," she said, holding out her hand. "How are things going?"

He swept his hat off with a flourish. "She's jake, Leigh."

Leigh looked puzzled. "I forget, is that good or bad?"

"Oh, good enough that you don't need to be worrying."

"Yet I hear that you're using a great deal of film."

"It's important to get the right look."

"And you're running a bit behind schedule."

"We've had some hard kack—bad luck," he translated at her sharp glance. "The bloody bureaucrats wouldn't let us bring our props into the country. Said they lost the permits for our guns."

"But I thought that was taken care of the next day."

"Oh, it was. But then this bloody rain started. The beginning of the week the river was so high we couldn't get the barge under the bridges. So we had to wait."

"I see."

"But the forecast is good for next week and we'll be able to make up the lost time then."

"I certainly hope so," Leigh said. "We can't afford to go over budget on this one, Chris."

"And we won't. You have my word on it." Inquisition over, he flashed her a smile the likes of which Matthew, who had been working with the man for three weeks, had never seen. "How long are you planning to grace us with your lovely presence?"

"Three days."

"We hadn't scheduled to shoot over the weekend, but if you don't mind paying overtime, we can move things up."

"Oh, don't change the schedule on my account. As producer of this movie, I thought it might be a good idea to drop in and see how things were going." She smiled. "And being in Paris over the weekend gives me an excuse to do some shopping."

The director's relieved expression was that of a death row inmate who had just received a reprieve from the governor. "Well, you've certainly come to the right place. Are you staying at the hotel?"

"No. I was afraid my presence might put a damper on the crew's leisure time, so I booked a room at the Abbaye Saint-Germain."

"I don't think I know it."

"It's a former seventeenth-century convent not far from

here on the Left Bank. It's small and they don't take credit cards, but it's cozy and there's a lovely garden. And best of all," she said, exchanging a brief, meaningful glance with Matthew, "it's peaceful and private."

"Sounds bloody boring to me," the director decided.

Leigh smiled. "Different strokes."

"Ain't that the bloody truth, luv," Burke said. "Well, we're using up precious light. Not to mention Baron Studios' valuable time and money. You will stay and watch us shoot the next scene, won't you? It's a pivotal one. Where Ryder and Marilyn go to bed for the first time."

Leigh forced a smile. "I'm looking forward to it." Actually, she couldn't think of anything less palatable than watching Matthew in bed with her sister.

"Good. Well, Matthew, are you coming?"

With a quick, apologetic look, Matthew ground the butt of the cigarette into the deck with his heel, then followed the director into the cabin, wondering how the hell he was going to pull off a heated love scene with Leigh watching every move he made.

If there was one thing Joshua hated, it was losing control. It made him angry; when he was angry he paced. He had nearly worn a path in the carpeting of his office when the disembodied voice of his secretary came over the intercom, advising him of Jeff Martin's arrival.

"Send the young man in," he said, taking his place in the tall chair behind the desk.

Believing a good defense to be a strong offense, Jeff walked into the room as if he owned it. "So, Mr. B," he said, flinging his body into a chair without waiting for an invitation. "What gives?"

Unaccustomed to such arrogance from those privileged few who were granted access to his sanctum sanctorum, Joshua experienced a flare of annoyance. One he managed to control. "I understand that you are friends with Matthew St. James."

"Matt and I go all the way back to high school. The two of us are like that," Jeff said, holding up a pair of crossed fingers.

"My sources also tell me that you're an aspiring actor."

"In this town, who isn't?"

Joshua didn't bother to answer. The dossier the detective had gathered on Jeff Martin was remarkably detailed. From what Joshua could determine, there wasn't anything Martin wouldn't do, for a price. "As it happens, I'm in a position to offer you a part."

Jeff couldn't believe his ears. After that little debacle in the warehouse with Marissa, he'd half expected her old man to order a hit on him. And here he was, offering him a job. Something didn't fit.

"Why?"

"One of the actors working on *Dangerous* has suffered an unfortunate attack of appendicitis. He was rushed to a Paris hospital last night for emergency surgery and, although I'm told that he's doing fine, he won't recover in time to return to the set. It's not a large part, but there are a number of good lines. Are you interested?"

"Do bears shit in the woods?"

"I'll take that to be a yes. There's just one slight favor I must ask in return."

"Who do I have to kill?"

"Nothing that drastic, I assure you. I merely want you to see to it that once this picture wraps, Matthew St. James disappears from Los Angeles. Permanently. Needless to say, I will pay for any expenses you incur."

Jeff stared at the studio head for a full minute. The guy had to be kidding. Or else he was crazy to think he'd fuck over his buddy, just for a part. Not any old part, but a part in a major motion picture, he reminded himself, along with the perfect opportunity to fuck Marissa's brains out in Paris. He was wondering about the chances of making it with her on top of the Eiffel Tower when he remembered that picture on the front page of the *Enquirer* of his old pal Matt and Marissa in a clinch.

So much for the buddy system. Once a guy made the big time, he figured the world—and all the chicks in it—was his own private fucking oyster.

Jeff made his decision. "Hey, the minute the flick wraps, the dude's history."

23

Leigh was taking a bath in an ancient, claw-footed tub, thinking about Matthew when she slowly became aware of someone else in the room. Turning her head, she saw him, leaning against the doorjamb, looking sexier than ever in the faded chambray shirt and jeans he'd worn for the filming.

"I knocked, but you didn't answer."

After all they'd shared. After the hours and days and weeks of lovemaking, why did she feel so uncomfortable? "I probably didn't hear you over the running water."

He nodded. "That was undoubtedly the case. The concierge didn't blink twice when I asked her for a duplicate key."

"This is Paris."

"I still don't like knowing that any man can get into your room. Christ, Leigh, I could have been the Parisian strangler."

"Ah, but since I had to go out for a while, I told her I was expecting a very special visitor."

"That makes me feel better. I'd hate to think that just any man can talk his way into your bathroom."

"Not any man." Her lashes swept down and her fingers tightened on the bath sponge. "Only you."

The sight of her, amid all those bubbles, made him ache. But there was an emotional distance between them that kept him where he was. "You left before we had a chance to talk."

Leigh picked up a bar of fragrant soap from the tile holder and began working up a creamy lather between her palms. "By the twenty-third take, I think it was obvious to everyone that you either wanted to prolong the scene as long as possible, or I was making you unreasonably nervous."

"Which do you think it was?"

"Actually," she said in a conversational tone as she worked the lather up her arm, "I was hoping I was the cause."

"You were driving me crazy." He entered the room and squatted down beside her. "The entire time I was kissing your sister, touching her, all I could think about was how I wished that she were you."

The desire that was never far away sprang up between them, so palpable that Leigh felt as if she could put out her hand and touch it. "Marissa's very beautiful. And sexy."

"Flash and trash," Matthew said dismissively, lathering the French milled soap between his hands. When his soapy palms caressed her breasts, tingling vibrations ran from her nipples to her vagina.

"Now you're the one making me crazy."

"Really?" His fingers moved down her rib cage, over her abdomen, tangled in the silken curls at the juncture of her thighs.

When his hand pressed against the throbbing ache between her legs, Leigh leaned her head back against the blue-and-white flowered tile and closed her eyes. "Damn you, Matthew," she complained on a half-laugh, half-moan, when his fingers slipped into her, "I'm going to pay you back for this."

His thumb tantalizingly brushed against her swollen clitoris. "I certainly hope so."

Then he touched her—really touched her—and Leigh crested in a series of shuddering peaks.

*   *   *

"When are you leaving for Paris?" Joshua asked Brendan Farraday over double Scotches at the Polo Lounge.

"Monday. They don't begin shooting my part for another two weeks, but I figured I may as well go over early and enjoy some French pussy before I have to get down to work."

Who the hell did the guy think he was kidding? Work had never put a damper on Farraday's extracurricular fucking before, and Joshua doubted that this time would be any different. Every film Farraday had ever worked on, his expense sheets ended up being astronomical. It didn't take a CPA to realize that the actor was charging something a helluva lot juicier than coffee and croissants onto his room service bill.

"I've always enjoyed Paris," Joshua said. "French women know how to have a good time without feeling the need to put a ring through a man's nose."

"Or his prick."

One thing about Farraday, Joshua considered, the guy had a way with words. "I've got a little problem," he divulged offhandedly.

"Oh?" Farraday matched his casual tone.

"Nothing serious. Just a little cash flow problem."

"How much do you need?" Farraday didn't blink when Joshua mentioned an amount in the high six figures. "The money will be in your account when the bank opens tomorrow," he said. "I assume you'll send the appropriate papers over to my house."

"They'll be there before your morning paper." Rising from the table, Joshua reached into his pocket and pulled out his American Express card.

"I've got it," Farraday said expansively. With what he was going to end up getting in return for a few hundred grand, he could afford to be generous.

After Joshua left the restaurant, Farraday signaled the waiter for a telephone. As he placed the call that would put Joshua Baron more deeply in debt to Minetti, Farraday smiled. One of these days he and Rocco were going to end up the proud owners of Baron Studios.

Three weeks of separation had done nothing to lessen the feelings Matthew had for Leigh. If anything, the attraction was stronger than ever. The mere proximity of her body kept him in a constant state of arousal and for two days the room—the luxurious brass bed—became the center of their universe. He loved keeping her eager and pliant, yielding under his intimate touch; he thrilled at the way her gray eyes widened when he hit the right spot; he reveled in her gasps of pleasure.

She gave herself openly to him, never holding anything back. Matthew had never been with a woman who made him feel as happy and as carefree as he felt when he was making love to Leigh. Admittedly unromantic and cynical, a man who'd slept with more women than he could count, as he dressed for work that Monday morning, Matthew found himself wanting to believe that a life—a love—with one very special person might actually be conceivable.

But at the same time a lifetime of experience had taught him that the obstacles to such a storybook, happily-ever-after ending were unsurmountable.

Weren't they?

As they stood beside the taxi that was waiting to take her to the airport, Matthew couldn't miss the distress in Leigh's soft gray eyes.

"Have a good flight."

"Good luck with today's chase scene."

They laughed uneasily when they both spoke at once. Matthew slowly brushed his knuckles up the side of her face. "It was good seeing you."

"It was good, wasn't it?" Except for the silences, Leigh considered. Those fleeting moments between making love and talk about the picture. Those moments when one of them had seemed on the verge of discussing what was happening between them, only to back away.

"Do you think you'll be able to get back again, anytime soon?" Do you care about us enough to leave your precious studio? he wanted to ask, but didn't. Is this as important to you as it is to me?

"I don't know." Do you want me to come? Do you care? "Fall's such a busy time, what with all the upcoming holiday releases."

"Must be hectic."

"That's one word for it."

They were looking deep into one another's eyes, trying to divine what the other was thinking. "I'll try to clear my calendar so we can spend Christmas together," Leigh said.

"I'll book our room this afternoon."

Wrapping her in his arms, he fused his mouth against hers, his kiss hard and long, laced with a desperation he was unable to put into words. "You'd better go," he said finally. "Before you miss your plane."

"And you're late on the set." She attempted a smile that failed. "As producer of this picture, I have a responsibility to see that you show up on time."

Matthew didn't bother to try and return her smile. "I'll call you in a few days."

Tears stung behind her lids; she resolutely blinked them away. "Yes." Unable to say another word, she shoved her suitcase at the driver and escaped into the backseat of the taxi before she changed her mind and stayed here in Paris. With Matthew.

Matthew remained standing in front of the former convent watching as the driver tore off down the rue Cassette. If Leigh had glanced back out the rear window, she would have seen him watching the departing taxi thoughtfully, his face tense, troubled.

Leigh missed Matthew desperately. She missed his low, rumbling chuckle, the caress of his amber eyes when she returned home at the end of the day. She missed his tautly controlled energy, his powerful body, the melting touch of his hands. She also missed the way sleeping with him had kept her nightmares—which were beginning to return—at bay. Without her realizing it had happened, Matthew had become a crimson thread who had woven his way through the gray fabric of her life. She wondered how she had ever believed herself to be happy or satisfied without him.

Ignoring her father's relentless sulk, she returned to Paris to spend Christmas with Matthew, but the trip turned out to be a disaster. In a blatant disregard for Baron Studios' budget, Christopher Burke had arranged for the entire crew to celebrate the holiday with dinner at the Hotel Ritz. Although she'd hoped to spend a quiet, private day with Matthew, Leigh knew that if she and Matthew disappeared, the resultant gossip could be detrimental to the film. There was already enough acrimony on the set without everyone knowing that their star was sleeping with the executive producer.

The dinner began inauspiciously when Christopher Burke expounded on the superiority of Australian films compared to those coming out of America. "It's true," he pronounced loudly, "American filmmakers are only interested in the almighty fucking dollar. You Yanks," he pointed a finger at Leigh across the table, "are falling into a self-destructive trend of using flashy, shallow stories, while we Aussies still choose substance over superficiality. Art and originality before profits." He stared at her through bleary eyes, daring her to argue.

Partly because he had a point, but mostly because he'd practically emptied the outrageously expensive bottle of Château Mouton-Rothschild 1947, single-handedly, Leigh refused to be drawn into the fray. "Even if that's true," she said, feeling the need to defend her film in front of the crew who'd worked so hard, "surely you'll admit that *Dangerous* is the exception that proves the rule."

"Of course it is, luv," the director said. "Because you had the good sense to hire me to direct it."

Just when Leigh was congratulating herself on avoiding that particular minefield, they drew the ire of a haughty Gallic waiter by forestalling ordering until Marissa and Jeff arrived. They arrived thirty minutes late. Marissa, true to form, was decked out in a low-cut red dress that fit as tightly as a coat of lacquer. She was also high, flirting outrageously with every male at the table, most particularly Matthew.

Jeff, who'd already sampled more than his share of alcoholic holiday cheer, grew increasingly jealous and contentious as the meal dragged on. Before the waiter arrived with the first course of omblé-chevalier, Jeff had threatened to wipe the floor with the best boy, who being twenty and human, could not take his eyes off the lush swell of Marissa's breasts.

From there it was all downhill.

The strain of keeping up appearances during what could only be described as a debacle, followed Leigh from the dining room to the bedroom, where she was forced to spend forty-five minutes soothing Joshua, who had called to complain about being forced to spend Christmas with Tina and Corbett instead of his own flesh and blood.

"I'm sorry," she said, turning back to Matthew, who was lying on the bed, his head pillowed on his arms, staring up at the ceiling.

He'd been strangely withdrawn all day and, although he'd assured her that his attitude had nothing to do with her, Leigh couldn't help worrying. Perhaps he'd grown tired of her. Perhaps he was wishing that she hadn't come.

"It's only natural your father would want to talk to his daughter on Christmas Day."

She rested her head on his shoulder. "This hasn't been a very jolly holiday, has it?"

"Don't worry about it. I've never made a big deal about Christmas, anyway." Truthfully, Matthew had always hated the holiday, which seemed to be created solely for families. Christmas always reminded him that he had no one. That he was an outsider.

"That was quite a story Brendan told about his Vietnam Christmas show getting shelled in Pleiku."

Matthew had spent that particular Christmas in a bunker with sandbags and steel over his head, seated on a green cot that had been white before it had mildewed, listening to the enemy rockets while he ate meatballs and beans in tomato sauce, with juices, out of a can.

"The NVA was a tough audience. It's too bad they had such poor aim."

She glanced at him curiously. "You really don't like Brendan at all, do you?"

"I thought I'd made myself clear on that point."

He had, Leigh remembered. The day before they'd made love for the first time. She found Matthew's inexplicable enmity toward Brendan Farraday as curious now as she did then. "Has working with him been too hard?"

"I don't want to talk about Farraday, Leigh. Not today. And especially not with you."

Secrets. There seemed to be so many secrets between them, Leigh thought sadly. But he was right about today not being any time for serious discussion. Putting the subject away, she kissed his shoulder. Beneath her lips, his muscles were tightly knotted.

"You're too tense," she murmured, moving her mouth slowly down his chest. "What can I do to relax you?"

When her tongue dipped seductively into his navel, Matthew pulled her into his arms. "What you're doing isn't bad. For starters."

"For starters," Leigh agreed. Her low, throaty laugh was part honey, part smoke. When she took his sex in her hands and slipped her mouth over him, the dark shadows of the past disintegrated and there was only now. Only Leigh.

Although Matthew's lovemaking was as ardent and skilled as ever, an unrelenting tension hovered over the bed like a dark presence. When Leigh faked an orgasm for the first time, she had an uneasy, guilty feeling that she wasn't fooling Matthew for a minute.

She wasn't.

Later, as they lay side by side listening to the depressing drizzle of December rain roll down the windowpane, Matthew was the first to break the silence. "It'll get better, Leigh. When we aren't forced to crowd so much into such little pieces of time. After this damn film wraps."

Leigh touched the gold heart hanging from a slender chain around her neck—a Christmas present from Matthew—as if it were a talisman. "After *Dangerous* wraps," she whispered.

It was part promise. Part prayer.

24

March 1973

When *Dangerous* finally finished shooting, twenty-four days late and two million dollars over budget, Leigh was in Toronto, scouting locations for a project still in the development stages.

Peter Ustinov had piqued her interest in the city when he described it as "New York run by the Swiss." During the last few days, she had decided he was right. Toronto bore a remarkable resemblance to New York City. One that would permit her to film less expensively than in Manhattan. Of course, the film crew would have to mess up the gutters and spray-paint rude commands on a few of the buildings— Torontonians appeared to have a deep-seated aversion to graffiti and litter—but on the plus side, she wouldn't have to pay off street gangs to prevent them from disturbing the film set.

After spending the day trudging through slush and snow, ruining a pair of pewter gray Ferragamo boots purchased expressly for this trip, Leigh was not in the best of moods. She was having a solitary dinner in her suite on the eighteenth floor at Sutton's Place Hotel when Matthew called from France. It had been more than two months since Christmas. Sixty-eight lonely days and even lonelier nights.

"How's the sexiest woman in the world?" his deep voice rumbled over the faint hiss of thousands of miles.

Sexy. No man had ever described her that way before. Until Matthew. Leigh clasped the receiver more closely to her ear, as if she could lessen the distance between them. "I'm freezing. The forecast is for snow flurries tomorrow, so I spent the entire day trudging through Chinatown, Cabbagetown, and Kensington Market."

"Too bad I'm not there to warm you up."

"Isn't it?"

"You know, the telephone company lied."

"About what?"

"Long distance is *not* the next best thing to being there."

"I know," she whispered. For some reason she could not discern, talking to Matthew on the telephone had become more painful than pleasurable.

"Hey, the picture wrapped today. I could be in Toronto by tomorrow afternoon. Day after at the latest."

She paused. The idea was so tempting. As much as she had come to look forward to their frequent telephone conversations, the enforced separation had begun to take its toll.

"Oh, Matthew." Her throat was tight; her eyes burned.

"You have to work."

How often had he heard that excuse over these past months? How many times had a planned trip to Paris fallen through at the last minute because of some perceived emergency at the studio? Too many times. Her decision to go to Toronto, just as the filming on *Dangerous* was coming to a close, only added to Matthew's suspicions that Leigh's feelings for him had begun to wane.

"We wouldn't have any time together," she said. "And knowing that you were in the city, but not being able to be with you, would be worse than having you all the way across the Atlantic. You do understand, don't you?"

No. He didn't. Even Leigh couldn't work all night, and from

Matthew's point of view, any time they could have together would be well spent. But knowing the futility of pressing his case long distance—they'd already had too many arguments each time she canceled her plans to join him in Paris—he lied.

"Sure."

"Why don't you take advantage of your free time and new-found wealth and see Europe?" she coaxed. "You've been working so hard, you deserve a vacation."

"Looking at a bunch of crumbling churches isn't my bag. Sightseeing alone sounds even worse. I'll just go back to California and get back to work."

"You can get some surfing in. You must have missed it."

There was a significant pause as Matthew failed to answer.

"Matthew, I really would rather be with you. You do know that, don't you?"

"Sure. Look, Leigh, if I'm going to get a flight home, I'd better call the airline. I'll see you soon, okay?"

"I'll be back in L.A. in two weeks," she promised. "Not a minute more."

"Two weeks."

He hung up first, leaving Leigh to vow that if she ever met Helen Gurley Brown, the first thing she'd do was ask the Cosmo girl's secret of juggling personal and professional lives.

Escondido, Mexico, was a surfer's paradise. Its variety of big barrels provided something for every mood and taste. But when Matthew arrived, the famous Mexican break was suffering from a massive wave drought, the glassy waters of the Pacific giving a convincing imitation of Lake Placid. Even the slightest hint of a swell was greeted with cheers by the surfers lining the sand and promptly assaulted.

"I don't know why the hell I let you talk me into this," Matthew complained. He'd been in Mexico for three days and so far he'd been lucky to catch four mediocre waves.

"Because Mexico's a fucking bash, man," Jeff said, winking lecherously at a comely young señorita who passed by. "And after spending all those weeks with that Nazi asshole of a director, we are in desperate need of some serious party time."

Last night Jeff had arrived back at the bungalow with two willing women and a quart of José Cuervo. When Matthew declined to join in the fun, Jeff had disappeared into the adjoining bedroom with both women. From the way the bed-springs had squeaked all night, Matthew decided that Jeff, at least, was making the most of the trip. The trouble was that Matthew wasn't interested in some anonymous vacation fuck and, since the woman he wanted was still in Toronto, he decided that he might as well get back to work.

"I think I'll go home," he said.

"Hey, man, the weather's gotta change. It'd be a bummer to come all this way, then leave right before the primo waves hit."

As much as he hated to admit it, Jeff had a point. Besides, with Leigh in Toronto, he sure as hell didn't have anyone waiting for him back home. Not that he ever had. Reminding himself that he'd always been content to be a loner, Matthew shrugged and popped the top on another bottle of Corona.

"I suppose I could stick around another day or two."

Jeff grinned his satisfaction. "Now that's the fun-lovin' dude I remember."

The beer flowed like water on the beach that afternoon. Surfers sat and waited and swapped stories of classic swells and monster curls. Exotic locations—Rarotonga, Tasmania, Sri Lanka—were spoken of with wistful longing while other, more popular sites—Ouahu's North Shore and Australia's Warriewood—were breathed with awe.

When night fell on the glassy, moonlit surf, the troop moved indoors. The drinks changed from beer to pitchers of margaritas, but the talk remained the same. Blowouts. Shark scares. Ten-foot tubes. Hot-dogging. The new macramé bikinis.

Hours later, after a surfeit of beer and margaritas, Matthew was in bed when a trio of uniformed Mexican police officers burst into the room, automatic weapons drawn.

"What the hell?"

"You are under arrest," one of the men said. He went straight to Matthew's duffel bag and pulled out a cellophane baggie. "For possession of an illegal drug."

Shaking his head to clear it of sleep and alcohol, Matthew

stared at the marijuana as if he'd never seen it before. Which he hadn't.

"You've got the wrong guy."

"You are Matthew St. James, sí?"

"Sí, but—"

"If you are Matthew St. James, señor, then we have the right man. Put on your pants and come with us, por favor."

Over the next ten days, Matthew quickly discovered the disadvantages of being arrested in a country whose law was premised on the Napoleonic Code—declaring a detainee guilty until he proved himself innocent.

He was interrogated constantly, kept awake day and night. When a lawyer finally did arrive, Matthew was not encouraged to learn that his attorney was the police captain's brother-in-law. Since he'd already decided that this particular group of cops were about as clean as the tap water, he was not surprised when a magistrate declared the evidence sufficient to hold him over for trial.

"So when do we go to trial?" Matthew asked his attorney.

The man shrugged. "The courts are crowded. Since our law allows a suspect to be held for a year without a trial, I would expect that's how long it will be before you have an opportunity to present your case."

His expression was not encouraging. And why should it be? The evidence was overwhelming and, although Matthew had continued to profess his innocence, he knew that even his own attorney had tried him and found him guilty.

"I'm going to be stuck here a year before I even go to trial?"

"Probably. Sí."

"I want to talk with the American consul," Matthew demanded, not for the first time since his incarceration.

"He's been called."

Matthew didn't believe him. There hadn't been a word from the American consulate office. "Then, damnit, I want to make a personal telephone call to the States." Surely Corbett, a lifetime wheeler-dealer, would figure out some way to get him out of this nightmare.

"I'm afraid that is up to the district attorney."

The police captain's uncle. Strike three. "I don't suppose they've found the other guy who came down here with me."

"No. Your friend seems to have disappeared."

No surprise there. Jeff was known for his expert vanishing act whenever there were cops around. "Okay. One more question."

"Sí?"

"If I'm found guilty, what kind of sentence am I looking at?"

"You have to understand, Señor St. James, in my country, possession of narcotics is a felony. It is not inconceivable that you could receive the maximum sentence."

"And that is?"

"Twelve years."

25

"I can't understand it."

"I assume we're talking about St. James again." Joshua leaned back in his chair.

They were sitting in his office and his distaste with the turn the conversation had taken was obvious. Leigh took a sip of her coffee. Since returning to Los Angeles to find Matthew gone, she had been running almost solely on caffeine. Caffeine and frazzled nerves.

"He should have returned from Europe by now."

"Leigh, you've grown up in this business; you know actors . have no sense of responsibility. They're impulsive children, responding to instinct. To whatever brings them pleasure. It's difficult to hold their attention as long as it takes to shoot a picture." He shrugged. "St. James's disappearance, as you insist on calling it, is simply another case of an immature performer taking off on a binge as soon as the picture wraps."

"Matthew's different."

"So you've been saying for the past two weeks." Joshua gave her a piercing look. "If I didn't know you to be an extremely sensible young woman, I'd worry that this actor had turned your head."

"It's nothing like that," Leigh lied unconvincingly. "I'm simply worried about the way he seems to have dropped off the face of the earth. What if he's been hurt? Or worse?"

"Then *Dangerous* would get a great deal of free publicity."

Leigh had always known her father to be cold-hearted, but this time his words struck her heart like a stiletto of ice. "That's disgusting."

"That's business," he countered brusquely. "Don't tell me you've forgotten James Dean. Hell, in the three years after his death, Dean's studio got more mail addressed to him than any of its living stars. If the poor bastard had lived, he'd never have been able to live up to his publicity. . . .

"Beside, it's a moot point. St. James will be back," Joshua predicted. "When he runs out of bucks, booze, and broads."

Matthew wasn't like that. Leigh had been telling herself that ever since she had returned home from Toronto and discovered him missing. After fourteen days, she'd almost managed to convince herself.

Almost.

Marissa was naked, her voluptuous breasts bouncing on the bubbling hot waters of the Jacuzzi, garnering the full attention of the man seated across from her—Barry James, the latest candidate produced by a desperate television network in an attempt to unseat Johnny Carson as king of the night.

James, a former television game show host, had three things in common with the perennial late night television host: boyish good looks, quick wit, and multiple marriages. His current divorce was a messy affair, even for Hollywood, the details hashed out daily in the headlines. Just last week he'd been quoted as saying that after five failed marriages, he'd sworn off women forever. He had no way of knowing that such a statement was like waving a red flag in front of a bull.

Marissa, newly back from Paris, had never been able to resist a challenge. Although Jeff was all for continuing their relationship, now that they had returned to Los Angeles, she'd become bored with the predictability of their affair.

More than one psychiatrist over the years had tried to explain to Joshua that the absence of a loving male figure in her life had made Marissa intolerant of the calmness of long-term relationships. Reasonably quick to feel ignored and hurt, once the veneer of new passion wore off, her childhood pain resurfaced, causing her to rush off to the narcotic of a new love. The moment she'd seen that headline about Barry James, she'd decided to make him her new conquest.

During the three months that Barry had hosted the late night talk show, nearly every actress in town had appeared on his program; several of those had also made a starring appearance in his bedroom. "The Barry James Show" might not be the guaranteed career maker the "Tonight Show" was, but it did validate whatever publicity the studio press corps was churning out. If sleeping with the host was part of the deal, more than one budding young actress merely shrugged and decided that a blow job was a cheap price to pay for instant stardom.

Barry didn't question this obvious perk of his position; it was simply how the game was played. Having hosted innumerable asinine game shows over the years, he felt as if he'd paid his dues; now it was time to reap the rewards. To Barry, sex was a natural, everyday part of life, like eating or sleeping. It was difficult to value something in such abundant supply.

"The taping went well," he said, his gaze arrested by a drop of moisture glistening on her rosy red nipple. All his wives had been model-thin, the better to wear their expensive designer dresses. He couldn't remember when he'd been presented with such an amazing pair of tits. "You're a natural-born star, kid."

"Really?"

"Would I lie? You've got the comedic timing of Monroe with the bawdy lustiness of Mae West. The audience loved you."

"They would have loved me a helluva lot more if your producer hadn't stuck that damn handkerchief down the front of my dress." She'd worn a shimmering black-and-silver metallic dress that appeared to have been poured across her body.

"The network censors would have shut us down if we'd allowed you to go on without it."

"I bought that dress especially for you." Marissa pouted prettily. Relaxing her head along the rim of the tub, she allowed her outstretched legs to float up.

When Barry's cock hardened at the sight of that wet, flame-colored pubis, he conveniently forgot his recent vow of celibacy. "You looked fantastic, baby. Like an intergalactic Barbie doll. I can't believe you're Leigh Baron's sister." Leigh was one of the few women Barry had struck out with over the years, not for any lack of trying.

"Every family has its black sheep. By the time I was born, Leigh had already taken the role of the good sister."

He shifted positions, moving next to her in order to take her taut nipple into his mouth. "Which left you with the part of the bad sister?" he murmured around a mouthful of water-silkened flesh. Taking her hand, he wrapped her fingers around his cock.

She was floating on air. The audience had loved her, and even more important, Barry loved her. Why else would he bump that new young comedian and an over-the-hill *Sports Illustrated* swimsuit model turned actress and devote his entire hour to her?

"Sweetie, I am so bad I'm good."

He was sucking energetically on her breast. Marissa closed her eyes, fantasized becoming the sixth and final Mrs. Barry James, and obediently stroked him to climax.

Matthew watched the guard fondle the breasts of the young woman seated on his fat lap. The woman worked at the cantina; it was her job to bring the two meals a day to the jail. Enchiladas, rice, beans, tortillas, and beer for the guard, beans and water for Matthew.

In the beginning, she had angrily brushed aside the man's clumsy advances, but lately she'd begun flirting with the obese, unshaven man. She'd also taken to wearing low-cut gauze blouses that allowed an enticing view of her full, dusky breasts.

Two nights ago, she hadn't complained when he'd smacked her on her ass as she'd left the jail.

Last night she'd allowed him to kiss her.

Tonight, when the man tilted a beer to his mouth with one dark hand while pushing her blouse off her shoulders with the other, Matthew decided they were actually going to do it, right on that creaky wooden chair.

She was naked to the waist, her full skirt gathered around her thighs. The guard's beefy hand was making its way up under that cotton skirt when his head suddenly lolled. Climbing off him, the woman hitched up her blouse and watched impassively as he slid silently, bonelessly, to the floor. Then she turned toward Matthew and pressed her finger against her lips.

Matthew was not about to say a word.

He watched as she knelt beside the guard, her fingers deftly unfastening the key he wore clipped to his belt. She crossed the room and unlocked the cell door. They both went rigid when the rusty door squeaked with a noise that seemed to rival the roar of a jet airliner, but to Matthew's relief, the guard continued snoring away. The mickey the girl had slipped into the man's *cerveza* seemed to be doing its job.

Making his way quickly past the unconscious man, Matthew had no idea why this woman was helping him escape, but after nine weeks in this dank, rat-infested cellar of a Mexican jail, he decided that there was merit in the old saying about justice delayed being justice denied. And he'd been denied too damn long.

They had just stepped out on the street when a shout shattered the still night air. A moment later a bullet whizzed over Matthew's head. He took the woman's hand and began to run.

They raced through the shadows. Matthew reminded himself that he'd always been a survivor. Hadn't he survived his mother's desertion? And what about when he was twelve and living in his ninth foster home? The owner of the home, a high school wrestling coach, had made the mistake of attempting to share an intimate shower with him. He'd changed his mind when he found himself facing the business end of a switchblade.

In 'Nam the enemy shelled their compound with 120-mm mortars and artillery. During the prolonged assault, Charlie had been jumping around in the bushes, firing AK-47s and tossing grenades around like they were going out of style. Ammo kept exploding all night and, when morning finally came, and the mortars stopped and the VC had disappeared back into the thick brush, the body count was six dead and twenty-nine wounded, including Matthew, who'd taken a carbine round in the thigh.

He was put aboard a chopper and flown to the 71st Evacuation Hospital at Pleiku, where he was stitched and cleaned up just in time for that most thrilling event: the muckety-muck general's arrival (along with the ever present contingent of reporters) to give out Purple Hearts. If he could make it through that damn dog-and-pony show, Matthew considered, he could make it through anything. Even this.

Suddenly his side burned with a flash point of heat.

Matthew kept running.

26

May 1973

Leigh sat beside Kim, with Christopher Burke standing behind her as producer and director watched the editor spin her unique magic on the Moviola. Bits of conversation punctuated the steady whirring and clacking of the reels. In the background, Kim's radio was tuned to the Watergate hearings, which had finally commenced.

"I am a fucking marvelous genius," Burke declared.

"And modest too," Kim said.

"Modesty is for losers."

"Well, that description certainly doesn't fit," Leigh said. When Matthew appeared on the editing screen, Leigh felt her heart clench. "I think you're going to get another Oscar with this one, Chris."

"Of course I am, love. Does that vote of confidence mean that you're no longer angry at me?"

"I wasn't angry. I merely pointed out that you were over budget."

"To give you a masterpiece."

Perhaps not a masterpiece. But the director had succeeded beyond Leigh's wildest hopes. "It is good."

"It'll win Best Picture. Best Director. And," he said, reaching out to ruffle Kim's sleek black hair, "Best Editor."

"Thanks for the bone," Kim muttered, backing the reel up to concentrate on the scene where Ryder Long is killed in a prolonged shootout with the police, Interpol, and the FBI agent, played by Brendan Farraday, who'd tracked the pair to Barcelona.

"Hey, luv, you've done a remarkable job. Of course it helped that I gave you a near perfect film to start with." The alarm on his gold Rolex sounded. "Sorry, ladies, but I must dash. I have an important appointment."

"Appointment, my ass," Kim said after Burke had gone. "I heard him making a date with one of the extras on that space flick they're shooting on stage 17. That man is just one constant fucking machine; I'm amazed he ever gets a movie finished."

"The rumor is that he remains celibate during a shoot in order to save his creative juices for his work."

"No wonder he's a dictator on the set. And as for giving me a perfect movie, with enough miles of film to reach to the moon and back, the guy probably turns over more of a mess than any director in the business. Although I will admit that most of the clips are brilliant." Kim stopped on a scene of Marissa, kneeling over Matthew's supine body, tears flowing copiously from her dazzling green eyes. "Do you believe Burke was actually able to resist this?"

"There *are* men capable of resisting my sister's appeal."

"Name three who aren't either gay or eunuchs."

"I'll name one. Matthew."

"He'll be back, Leigh." Kim was the only one Leigh had told about her affair with Matthew. She was also the only one who knew how much Leigh was hurting.

"I went by his house again last night," she admitted.

"And?"

"His neighbor—this gorgeous, 1960s flower child type—

was sitting out on her porch, so I asked if she'd seen him. She said he'd gone to Mexico the day after he got back from Europe . . . She seemed to know him well."

"Exactly how well?"

"Well enough that we had quite an illuminating conversation about Matthew's unwillingness to commit."

"What you and Matthew had was special, Leigh."

"That's what I thought. But perhaps I was wrong." She sighed. "Lord knows, I'm no expert on affairs, and these days everyone takes sex a lot more casually." Everyone except her, apparently.

"Have you asked Corbett if he's heard from Matthew?"

"Of course. All he knows is that Matthew refused to consider any more acting roles, said that he was going back to work, and would let Corbett know when he had something for him to read. When I told Corbett about Mexico, he suggested that perhaps Matthew just wanted to go away somewhere where he could write without distractions."

Is that what he'd considered her? Leigh wondered. A distraction? Ignoring the familiar pain gripping her heart, she turned her attention back to the screen. "Let's see that one again. This time starting with the dolly shot of Marissa."

"What the fuck do you mean, he got away?" Joshua paced the floor of his office, his red face reflecting his anger.

"Hey, Mr. B," Jeff said, lifting his hands in a gesture of self-protection. "Don't blow a gasket, okay? The cops are looking for him. He won't get within fifty miles of the border."

"You'd better hope to hell he doesn't," Joshua growled.

"Hey, I'll go down and find the dude myself, if you want."

"I want you to stay the hell out of it. You're a fuck-up, Martin." It was bad enough that Leigh had learned about St. James's trip to Mexico and contacted the consular officer; now she was actually considering going to Escondido herself.

"Jesus, it's not my fault the damn greasers let him escape," Jeff complained, wiping at his nose with the back of his hand.

The prick kid was weak. Impotent. All he cared about was getting stoned and getting laid. He'd been a fool to turn over a job this important to a sniveling doper. Joshua's face twisted in disgust. "Just get the hell out of here," he growled. "I've got work to do."

As soon as he was alone, Joshua took a plastic bottle of Maalox out of his desk drawer and poured the contents down his throat. Then he reached for the telephone.

He hadn't gotten to where he was today without learning the importance of always having a backup plan.

Whoosh. Bam. Boom. Incoming artillery screamed from the blood red sky. Monkeys and birds shrieked in trees illuminated by flames; all around him men were screaming in pain. The grunt next to him took shrapnel in the face and Matthew watched in horror as the freckled young features of an Iowa farm boy turned into a mass of red clay.

He was sweating. His clothes were drenched with perspiration; rivers of salt-drenched moisture streamed down his face. Matthew saw a man and a woman arguing heatedly. But something was out of sync. They were speaking Spanish, not Vietnamese. Before Matthew could figure it out, a dark cloud of unconsciousness settled back over him and the nightmare continued. In living color.

Matthew had been gone for three months when Leigh stopped by his house yet again. When she saw the car parked in his driveway, her heart soared. It was a new Thunderbird convertible with Sonoran Mexican plates.

"Sí?" The woman who opened the door was a Mexican in her mid-twenties, her shapely body clad in tight white jeans and a red halter top. Her hair was a mass of dark curls, her eyes the color of freshly brewed coffee. She frowned when she took in the sight of Leigh, crisp and cool-looking in a cream Chanel suit, standing in her doorway.

"I'm here to see Matthew."

"Matthew is not home. Good-bye." She attempted to shut the screen door, but Leigh was quicker, grabbing hold of the edge of the door.

"Wait!"

"I told you, Matthew is not home."

Leigh's first thought was that Matthew had used some of his newfound wealth to hire a maid. But there was something about this woman, the way she was dressed, the possessive way she spoke his name that caused a rising anxiety in her chest.

"But he is in the city?"

"Sí. But he is not home."

"May I come in and wait?"

The woman didn't budge. "What do you want with mi esposo?"

Although Leigh had a working knowledge of Spanish, she was certain she must have misunderstood. "Your what?"

"Matthew is mi esposo. My husband."

No. It couldn't be. "I don't believe it."

"Es verdad." The young woman nodded her head emphatically. "You wait." She disappeared back into the house, leaving Leigh standing on the front porch, her head reeling. Down the beach, a group of exuberant volleyball players shouted out friendly insults to one another; their voices reverberated like a distant echo in her ears. A moment later the woman was back. "This is my husband," she insisted, shoving a photograph into Leigh's hand.

It was as if the moment was frozen in time. A movie moment, Leigh considered, staring down at the couple. The woman was dressed in a frothy confection of a wedding dress, a crown of flowers atop her dark head. Her eyes, looking up at Matthew, were brimming over with love. Beside Matthew was another man, obviously a priest, from his dark shirt and stiff white collar.

Reality came crashing down atop Leigh with the force of a seismic jolt. "I'm sorry to have disturbed you," she managed through lips that had turned to stone. She felt lightheaded. As if she was going to faint. But that was ridiculous. She'd never fainted in her life.

The woman shrugged. "No problema. I will tell my husband you came to see him." Her dark eyes took another long, judicious tour of Leigh. "I do not know your name."

"It doesn't matter," Leigh murmured as she backed down the steps. She felt strangely lost, as if she could no longer recognize Matthew's house and couldn't fathom how she'd gotten there. "Not any longer."

It was only a nightmare, Leigh assured herself in the car.

One of those horrifying nightmares where demons were chasing you in the dark and, just before they grabbed you, you woke up, safe and sound in the comfort of your own bed.

Later that night, as she sat on her balcony, watching the moon-gilded waters lap relentlessly against the sand, Leigh wrapped her arms around herself in a futile attempt to hold the pain and loneliness out and the tears in.

Despite the popularity of glitzy premieres, Leigh preferred sneak previews. She preferred having her films previewed by warm bodies—real people, who paid real money. Slipping into the back row of a theater in Portland, Oregon, Leigh nervously awaited the audience's reactions to *Dangerous*.

When their interest was effectively captured by the first scene, even as the opening credits continued to run, Leigh began to breath a little easier. Their attention remained riveted to the screen and by the time the outlaw Ryder Long and his now willing hostage (wielding a sawed-off shotgun) successfully robbed the Paris branch of the Credit Suisse ninety minutes later, the mood was absolutely electric.

Then came the scene that succeeded in holding an entire theater—Leigh included—spellbound.

"I can't believe we did it!" Marissa / Marilyn exclaimed when she and Ryder entered their compartment on the night train that would take them from Paris to Barcelona. "I can't believe *I* did it. God, it was wonderful! It was the most exciting thing I've ever done!"

Marissa's eyes were as bright as newly polished emeralds, her face flushed, and she was quivering with excitement like a thoroughbred at the starting gate.

Matthew / Ryder was leaning against the wall, arms folded across his chest, watching her dance around the compact compartment. "I thought fucking me was the most exciting thing you've ever done."

"Well, of course," she agreed, unzipping the leather bag as the train pulled out of the station. "That goes without saying. But robbing banks definitely comes in a close second." She turned the bag over and shook it, sending a shower of colorful banknotes streaming over the narrow bunk. "Just look at this,

Ryder," she enthused, sifting the bills through her fingers like grains of sand. "There must be a million dollars worth of francs here. At least." She began sorting through it. "Do you want to divide it now? Or later? After we get to the hotel in Barcelona."

Ryder shrugged. "I'm not so sure we should divide it."

"But you promised! Equal partners, that's what you said."

Again his shoulders, clad in a black fisherman's sweater, lifted and dropped. "I was thinking, perhaps it would add a little spice to things if we wrestled for it."

"Wrestling? Like in arm wrestling?"

"Uh-uh. Real wrestling."

"Good idea." Marilyn laughed, confident he was teasing her. "Mud or mats?"

"Actually I was thinking about the bunk. Or the floor. But I'm open for any other suggestions you might have."

Her eyes widened. Surprise, laced with wary temptation, rose in their vivid green depths. "You're not joking, are you?"

"You should know me well enough by now to know that I never joke," he said calmly. "Especially about money. So, what do you say? One pin. Winner take all."

There was a long, thoughtful moment of silence, punctuated only by the rhythmic clickety-clack of the train's wheels on the rails. "But I don't know how to wrestle." She gave a nervous little laugh. "It wasn't on the class list at Madame Fontaine's Dance Academy."

"Don't worry." He yanked his sweater over his head. "You'll get the hang of it right away. It's a lot like sex. Only in this case, it pays a lot better."

"I still don't think—"

"The only problem is that you're overdressed."

Marilyn stood very still. He quickly, deftly unbuttoned her blouse and pushed it off her shoulders onto the floor. When he reached out, she drew in a quick breath, expecting his touch, but instead his hand shot past her, plucking a crisp bill from the money strewn over the bunk.

"Think of it," he suggested silkily, stoking her throat with the bill. "This can all be yours." He trailed the paper money down the slope of her breasts, along the scalloped edge of her silk camisole. "All you have to do is pin me. Once."

"But you're so much stronger," she complained, trembling with a heady mixture of anticipation and passion. "It wouldn't be a fair fight."

Taking his finger to her shoulder, he pushed aside one of the camisole's straps. "I'll only use one hand."

He was left-handed. She looked up at him, then down at the money. "Make it your right hand and you've got yourself a deal."

His lips brushed aside the other strap; the ivory silk clung tenuously. "You've gotten tough, lady."

Marilyn's breath was audible. "I've had a good teacher."

"Let's see exactly how good." Without warning, he pulled her roughly down onto the bunk, thrust his right hand through her hair, and kissed her deep and long. She appeared on the verge of succumbing to the passion that had been building ever since the wild drive from the bank to the train station, when she suddenly remembered Ryder's challenge.

"No fair distracting me." Pulling away, she pushed as hard as she could against his chest, forcing Ryder onto his back. Hiking her skirt high onto her bare thighs, she straddled him, her palms pressing against his shoulders. "I win," she cried out triumphantly.

"That's what you think." With a move so fluid, so quick that she hadn't seen it coming, Ryder turned, sending her sprawling. Locking her in a scissors hold between his legs, he thrust his hand beneath her skirt, eliciting a soft moan of pleasure. "Lesson number one," he said. "Overconfidence can be a dangerous mistake."

"Ryder, please." She was panting like an animal, while he was not even winded, but Marilyn was not yet prepared to give up the fight. Outside the wide window the French countryside flashed by, ghostly pale in the moonlight. "Just give me a minute to catch my breath," she pleaded prettily.

"Surrender and you'll have all the time you need." He loosened his viselike grip just enough to allow her to slip free.

"Someone once told me that overconfidence can be a dangerous mistake," she panted. "You haven't won, Ryder. Not yet." She was on her knees, her hair a damp, wild tangle around her bare shoulders, her breasts heaving with exertion.

Her skin, slick with sweat, gleamed pearly in the streaming moonlight. Their eyes locked.

A man seated two seats away from Leigh groaned. Behind her a young woman sighed.

Drawing in a deep, ragged breath, Marilyn screamed and flung herself against Ryder like a wildcat. They grappled, rolling across the mattress as if chained together, an agile tangle of arms and legs. Flesh against flesh, passion exuding from every glistening pore. Mouth to mouth, hot, open, hungry. Newly minted bills clung to their skin. Ryder's heavy beard scraped the soft skin at the inside of her thigh; Marilyn's long nails raked crimson trails along his back. Shaking and rocking, listing on curves, the train raced steadily toward the Pyrenees.

For a long, immeasurable time the camera lens never lingered on any one spot. It shifted from Ryder to Marilyn and back again. Long shot. Close-up of Ryder. Close-up of Marilyn. Cut to the hexagon mirror over the sink, reflecting the sinuous movements that were like a dance as the pair twisted, turned, came together, pulled apart, created new shapes, new designs in a blinding kaleidoscope of images and sensations.

And although she'd seen the dailies innumerable times and had sat by while Kim edited the blatantly erotic clips into a dazzlingly sensual scene, Leigh found herself caught up in the audience's mood. It was quiet in the theater. But there was something lingering in the air. A hushed, almost preclimactic tension.

Marilyn was on her hands and knees, swaying with the movement of the railroad car as Ryder crouched over her like some great lion. King of the beasts, Leigh mused, experiencing a familiar painful constriction around her heart.

"I win," he growled. Lowering his warrior body in a reverse one-handed push-up, he pressed her exhausted, prone body into the mattress demanding submission.

"Yes." Struggling to fill her lungs with air, she squirmed under him pleading, cajoling, laughing, and moaning at the same time. "Damn you, Ryder Long, I knew this wasn't going to be a fair contest."

"Say it."

"You win, damnit. All right?"

"All right." It was all he'd been waiting for. Turning her
over, he pinned her hands above her head with his right hand.
With his left hand he scooped up a fistful of crumpled bills
and rained them down on her. His eyes were intense, dark,
dangerous. Then, unzipping her skirt, he began tugging it
down her legs.

As the scene faded to black (something that Christopher
Burke had vehemently protested, but Leigh insisted was necessary to prevent their R rating from slipping to a dreaded X),
the spellbound audience finally released a long, drawn-out
breath.

When she left the theater fifteen minutes later, Leigh knew
that her sister's lifelong dream had come true. Because there
was no longer any doubt about it; when *Dangerous* was released, Marissa Baron was going to be a star.

Two weeks after the sneak preview in Portland, Leigh struggled out of bed like a zombie. It was a typically warm California spring, but she felt colder than she'd ever felt before. Cold
and numb. The nightmares had returned again, more vivid,
more frightening than ever.

"I'm worried about you," Joshua said as she exited her
Jaguar, parked beside his Porsche in the Baron Studios lot.

"Worried about me?" she asked vaguely, realizing that she
could not remember driving into the studio from Santa
Monica.

"You haven't been yourself."

"Nonsense. I've just been a bit distracted."

"That has been only too obvious. I received a call from Ed
Davidson yesterday afternoon."

"Ed? Our insurance man?"

"He said that you've received two speeding tickets in the
past fourteen days."

"Three, counting the one I got last night."

"Three tickets? In two weeks?"

Leigh shrugged. "Everyone in California speeds."

"You never have."

"Perhaps I'm simply making up for lost time," she suggested, not wanting to admit that she'd been surprised each

time the flashing red and blue lights had appeared in her rearview mirror.

It was as if she'd been operating on autopilot, a feeling obviously shared by the officer last night, who'd requested that she take a sobriety test. She'd passed, of course. Leigh didn't need artificial anesthetics; her mind was more than capable of producing its own numbing effects.

Joshua gave her a long look. "Well, the way you've been driving lately, you're going to get your license taken away. Or end up in the morgue. I think you need to get away."

It was the same thing Kim had been telling her for days. "I don't want to take a vacation." She didn't add that work was the only thing keeping her sane.

"Who said anything about a vacation? I was talking about a job."

"What kind of job?"

"I need a location producer for *Arabian Nights*."

Arabian Nights was a film suggested by the story of Aimée Dubucq de Rivery, a convent girl captured by corsairs and thrown into the harem of the Grand Turk. It was one of the old-fashioned costume epics Baron Studios was famous for. They'd been scheduled to film the story in Egypt when the Six Day War broke out, causing the project to sit on the shelf for six years. Until Leigh revived the movie by suggesting they move the filming to the United Arab Emirates, a newly established, oil-rich federation on the Persian Gulf.

"What happened to Peter Fowler?"

"Damn fool had a heart attack."

"That's terrible. I hope it wasn't fatal."

"No. But he'll probably wish it had been when he gets out of the hospital. Turns out that he was romping around the dungeon he and Freda had built in the basement of their Pacific Palisades house with a makeup woman from Paramount. Word around town is that by the time Freda got through with her, the girl didn't have a hair left on her head."

Although she suspected the story of being an exaggeration, Leigh wouldn't want to have been attacked by the robust former actress. Freda Fowler's temper was legendary. As was her collection of bullwhips.

"I really am in a bind, princess. The film's set to begin

shooting in five days and here I am without a location producer."

A location producer was a cross between a line producer,
or production manager, and babysitter, responsible for all the
niggling little problems that popped up during filming. It was
incredibly demanding work, requiring continual attention to
detail. And it was, Leigh decided, exactly what she needed.

"All right, I'll take it."

"You're a lifesaver." Joshua smiled his satisfaction. "I took
the liberty of picking up a token of my appreciation.

"You knew I'd do it, didn't you?"

"I knew you'd never let your old man down."

The blue-wrapped package contained a perfectly round
black pearl ring that matched the earrings her father had
given her last summer. Slipping the ring on her finger, Leigh
didn't bother to answer Joshua's supremely confident statement.

There was no need; it was, after all, the truth.

27

The frantic scene at the Abu Dhabi airport was a cross between a Roman circus and a Chinese fire drill. In the noisy terminal, Leigh looked around for the driver Erin McMurphy, the film's director, had promised would meet her.

"Ms. Baron?"

A deep voice at her elbow captured her attention and Leigh turned around to find herself face to face with one of the most striking men she'd ever seen. He looked to be in his mid- to late-thirties and his dark eyes reminded her of obsidian, without the flinty hardness. His dark face was lean—all planes and hollows—with a strong, slightly hooked nose and firm lips under a black mustache. His stark features made him appear harsh and forbidding, until he flashed a dazzling smile.

"You are Ms. Baron, are you not?"

"I am."

"I am Khalil Al-Tajir." At Leigh's blank look, he elaborated. "Assistant Minister of Culture."

The man who had been assigned by the government to act as liaison between the crew from Baron Studios and the local film crew, Leigh remembered. She knew she was staring, but she couldn't help herself. He was tall, distinguished, with a great presence, yet something about him hinted of the mystic. Something that conjured up fanciful visions of romantic Arabian nights. She found herself imagining him in robes and a burnoose.

Cupping his hand under her elbow, he led her through the crush of people and away from the long lines snaking through the terminal. "If you'll come with me, Ms. Baron, I will attempt to facilitate your passage through Customs." He shepherded her down a long corridor to a narrow door.

Within a matter of minutes she had cleared Health, Security, Immigration, and Customs. When they passed the long lines once again, Leigh noticed that they had not moved forward an inch.

"They'll probably be standing there another two to four hours," Khalil commented. If she'd been grateful for Khalil's intercession earlier, now she was doubly grateful. He snapped his fingers and, as if conjured up from Aladdin's magic lamp, a porter appeared with her luggage. A long black Rolls-Royce limousine was waiting by the curb, air conditioner running. The windows of the limousine were heavily tinted in deference to the heat.

The traffic was heavy, cars bumper to bumper. Drivers seemed determined to use up every inch of available space. Leigh watched a young girl clad in blue jeans and a striped T-shirt roar past the limo on a motorbike, carrying the carcass of a dead goat on the handlebars as she manuevered her way through the crush of Toyota pickups and Land Rovers.

"Erin said she was sending a gofer to meet me."

"That was her initial intention, but since a mere gofer would not have been able to ease your way through Customs, I felt you might appreciate my personal intervention."

"I did. Thank you."

"It was my pleasure."

Khalil had never had any intention of allowing anyone else

to greet the American filmmaker. During his student years at Oxford, he'd seen Leigh's picture in a British magazine. She had been twelve years old at the time and, although his mother had married at exactly the same age, Khalil knew that in America, Leigh would be considered a mere child. That knowledge hadn't stopped him from being intrigued by the secrets he thought he saw residing in her cool gray eyes.

When she'd entered the terminal today, looking fresh and cool in ivory linen slacks and a white silk shirt, he decided that before her time in Abu Dhabi came to an end, he and the lovely Leigh Baron would be lovers.

Abu Dhabi was a beguiling mix of ancient East and modern West. Ancient mosques and minarets were silhouetted against shining glass towers. The sidewalks were as crowded as the streets, lovely young girls in scant Parisian miniskirts waiting at bus stops, side by side with veiled women who moved like shadows under layers of voluminous black cloaks.

"It's incredible," Leigh said.

"Only thirteen years ago, Abu Dhabi was a quiet Gulf village of fishermen. Then revenues skyrocketed and Sheik Zayid began spending millions to create this instant city. I was studying in England when the oil first began to flow; when I returned home, I could hardly recognize the city. There are still times when I drive down a street and see a skyscraper that I've never noticed before, as if it had sprung out of the desert overnight."

He pointed out a Bedouin family living in a goat-hair tent while their government home was being built next door. "So much is changing," he said. His soft tone made Leigh wonder if he disapproved of the instant westernization. "And although the oil reserves may have been the bounty of Allah, we must still work to appreciate what we've built. Inshallah— God willing—we will learn how to utilize our newfound wealth without destroying our society. I only pray that these threads of gold futures weaving their way through the ancient fabric of our past will create a durable tapestry."

"If what you've created this far is any indication, I think it will be more than durable. It will be exquisite."

"The goal is to rival Beirut's seaport glitter; we hope to accomplish that without losing touch with our past."

"Inshallah," Leigh echoed the newly learned term, earning an appreciative glance from Khalil. "Are you from Abu Dhabi, originally?"

"No, I am a Bedouin. Not only was I the first in my family to come to the city, I was also the first to study abroad."

"That must have taken an enormous adjustment."

"It was extremely difficult, in the beginning," he admitted. "When I returned home from reading law at Oxford, I spent three frustrating weeks trying to locate my family." He chuckled at the long-ago memory. "I was afraid all that English rain had destroyed my desert instincts."

"But you eventually found them."

"Of course." Of course, Leigh concurred silently, from what she'd seen thus far, this was a man who would always achieve whatever he'd set out to do.

She stared out the window, like a child who'd just caught her first close-up glimpse of Oz. Donkey carts and motorbikes fought for street space with flatbed trucks loaded with cement and steel, rumbling graders, dump trucks, and busloads of Pakistani construction workers. Turbaned vendors hawked their wares—dates and nuts, copper pots, leather goods, freshly killed plump pigeons—on the same streets frequented by businessmen dressed in dark European suits. It was as if the eighteenth, nineteenth, and twentieth centuries had merged together into some sci-fi time warp. Everything and everyone seemed to coexist in this strange and wonderful place.

"Would you be offended if I admitted that most of my images of your part of the world come from our American movies?"

"I can't imagine being offended by anything you might say. Or do."

His appreciative tone and warm smile encouraged her to open up to him. "When I was eight years old, my third-grade teacher, Sister Luke, asked our class what we wanted to be when we grew up. Everyone responded with the typical answers: doctor, nurse, fireman, policeman, teacher, mommy, movie star—"

"Movie star is a typical American aspiration?"

"It is in Beverly Hills. Anyway, I think I offended Sister's delicate sensibilities when I announced that I intended to be a belly dancer in the Casbah." She felt the color drifting into her cheeks. "Do you know, I've never told that story to anyone."

Khalil chuckled appreciatively. "Then I feel doubly privileged. And as enticing an image as that admittedly is, I feel obliged to point out that despite its new, modern image, Abu Dhabi is a city that can not be taken in with a single glance. It reveals itself slowly, layer by layer. Like its people."

Although his tone remained politely conversational, when his dark eyes met hers and held, Leigh experienced a vague, distant flutter somewhere deep inside her.

"This script is shit. Just like all the others."

Marissa tossed the pages onto the brick decking of the swimming pool. She had bought the Laurel Canyon house with the proceeds from *Dangerous*.

"It's not that bad," Corbett said.

"The hell it isn't. I've already told you, Corbett, I don't want to be just another pair of tits."

As she leaned toward him, her breasts overflowing the yellow crocheted bikini top, Corbett considered that no one could ever consider Marissa's tits as just another pair. "I'd say you locked yourself into that role when you went on 'The Barry James Show.' Hell, Marissa, you looked like you were going to eat that guy alive on national TV."

"The audience loved me."

"And they're going to love you in this."

"It's exploitative."

Corbett wondered why it was that actresses who used their bodies to get roles were so often the first to scream that they were being exploited. He decided against mentioning that her sister had given her an excellent opportunity to avoid typecasting with her role in *Dangerous*. It wasn't Leigh's fault that Marissa had gone on television and thrust her boobs into America's face.

"It's a comedy, a remake of a French farce. You'll be terrific."

She chewed on a ragged nail and looked down at the script. "And you really think the audience will like me in this part?"

When her gaze returned to his face, she suddenly looked like the insecure teenager Corbett knew her to be. That was the main reason he'd taken on Marissa as a client, risking Tina's tacit disapproval. Someone needed to look out for the girl, someone who cared about more than his ten percent.

"They'll love you," he repeated. "And by the time you finish filming this one, *Dangerous* will be out and, who knows, you could be swamped with scripts featuring more serious roles."

"I'd like to do something like *Klute*," she mused.

Last year's Oscar had resulted in moving Jane Fonda from the ranks of just another bimbo and wartime protester to a major force in Hollywood. Personally, Marissa had been betting against Fonda ever escaping *Barbarella*.

"Let's just take one film at a time," Corbett counseled.

"So you think I ought to sign?"

"I think it would be good for you to get back to work." Corbett had noticed that Marissa was rudderless when she wasn't working. The last few times he'd been by the house, he'd been worried about the direction in which the girl was drifting.

"Okay, I'll do it. What about the part for Jeff?"

He glanced over toward the pool, where Jeff Martin was floating nude on an air mattress. After the short-lived fling with Barry James fizzled out, Martin had reappeared. "Your father doesn't want Jeff working for Baron any longer."

"Why not?"

"I don't know," the agent answered honestly. "But he seemed emphatic about not giving him a part."

"Shit." Marissa reached for a striped canvas bag beside the lounge, took out a compact and a small vial of white powder. Ignoring Corbett's disapproving look, she sliced and fluffed the powder onto the mirror, arranged it into two neat lines, and inhaled it. The rush was instant, clearing her mind, allowing her to think clearly enough to outmaneuver her father.

"All right," she said, "we'll do it another way. Put expenses for a second makeup man into the contract, and I'll sign."

"Fine."

Corbett knew exactly who that alleged second makeup man was going to be. Perks were an accepted part of the business.

When creating a budget, it was referred to as "adding in one third for the shit," the shit being the star's entourage. Hell, he'd just finished negotiating a contract with Paramount that included salaries for the female star's private hairdresser, the hairdresser's homosexual lover, two secretaries, her personal fitness trainer, her astrologer, and the bodybuilder-chauffeur who was currently screwing the star. On top of that, the studio had agreed to lease the star's personal trailer and car, at double what it would cost to rent them from a dealer.

That was the way the game was played in the big leagues. Marissa had grown up on the playing field and had learned the subtleties of the game well.

Gathering up his papers, he prepared to leave. "One more thing."

Marissa looked up at him. "Yeah?"

"That stuff is bad news."

"You're my agent, not my keeper." Her beautiful young face turned hard as she took her dark glasses from atop her head and shielded her eyes. "Good-bye, Corbett. I'm sure you can see yourself out."

As he drove back down the winding canyon road, it crossed Corbett's mind that for all her father's denials to the contrary, Marissa was a great deal like Joshua. Both of them could be as hard as stone.

The rich, unmistakable aroma of coffee roused him. Matthew leaned up on his elbows and looked around the room that was both familiar and strange at the same time.

"You're awake." The woman sitting beside his bed smiled.

"I think I am. Unless you're another dream." But his dreams had been nightmares. This young woman was a vision.

"No dream, señor. You have been very ill."

He rubbed his face, flinching at the pain the slight movement caused. "You were shot," she explained at his questioning look.

Matthew lay back against the pillows, trying to think back through the fog of nightmares. "Someone was chasing me. The police?"

"No, an old boyfriend." She gave him an apologetic smile.

"When he gets drunk and sees me with other men, he goes a little loco. Crazy, you know?"

Matthew grimaced as he tried to sit up. It felt as if his entire chest muscle was ripped open. "What the hell did he use? An elephant gun?"

"I do not know, señor."

It was beginning to come back to him. "You're the girl from the cantina. The one who broke me out of jail."

"Sí."

"Why?"

"They are saying at the cantina that you are a movie star."

"I'm not, really."

"But you do work in Hollywood? In the movies?"

"Yeah, I guess I do." Funny how he still didn't think of himself as an actor.

She handed him a stack of drawings. "I am a seamstress and dress designer. My dream is to work in Hollywood, in the movies. Perhaps you know someone who will arrange for my green card?"

"I'm sure we can work something out. Did you know I was arrested for drug dealing?"

"Sí."

"Then you should also know that I'm innocent."

"No es importa." She shrugged. "Mi hermano said that you made someone very angry because the policia were keeping you a secret."

Her brother. Matthew vaguely recalled an argument. "He refused to let you call a doctor because he didn't want to attract the police's attention." He flexed his shoulder, studying the expertly wrapped bandage. "I guess you won the argument."

"No. I am afraid not."

"Then who took out the bullet? Surely not you?"

"No. My cousin is studying medicine at the university. He is the one who removed the bullet and taught me how to care for you." Her wide dark eyes were grave. "You became very ill, señor. You had a fever."

Another memory returned. One of a woman—an angel—bathing his heated flesh with cooling cloths. Matthew was suddenly all too aware of his unclothed state.

"What's your name?"

"Rosaria, señor," she said softly. "Rosaria Ramirez."

"Well, Rosaria, I appreciate all you've done," he said. He wrapped the top sheet around himself toga-style and walked away from the bed. "And I promise to repay you for all your troubles, as soon as I get back home." He was about to ask what had happened to his clothes, when a man entered the room. In his hand was a .38 magnum revolver, pointing at Matthew.

"As much as I would like my sister to receive a reward for her generous good deeds, I am afraid I cannot let you leave, señor."

28

*Z*apata Canyon, fifteen miles south of San Diego, was a gravelly, garbage-strewn frontier. The forbidding canyon was the largest single route of illegal entry into the United States. Los Angeles, Matthew's destination, was one hundred and forty miles and another world away.

Despite the sagging Third World shacks that leaned against the steel fence, a fiesta atmosphere existed in the dusty canyon. Food stalls proliferated, along with tables selling denim jackets as protection against the cold Pacific Coast nights. A young boy, no older than eleven, sold maps obviously stolen from a Chevron gas station. San Diego. Los Angeles. Orange County. Sacramento. Fresno. Modesto. Lands of opportunity for those willing to do the hard, physical work norteamericanos didn't want to do.

It had been more than five months since Matthew's arrest. Five long and frustrating months. Patience had never been his strong suit; now, when he could see his country on the other side of that damn fence, he just wanted to be back home.

In the beginning, Jesus Ramirez, Rosaria's brother, had not wanted anything to do with Matthew. A professional smuggler, he earned a comfortable living bringing workers and Acapulco Gold into the United States from Mexico while moving Chevys back across the border the other way. Although he willingly paid off the local authorities, he was careful not to attract undue interest from the federales. Harboring an American fugitive under his roof would do exactly that.

But then Matthew's wound became infected and Rosaria, displaying the same stubbornness that had discouraged any of the village men from proposing to her, refused to allow him to leave until he was strong enough to travel. By that time Matthew had been staying at the house long enough to involve Jesus if he was captured, so the smuggler reluctantly decided that it was in his own best interests to get the gringo back to Los Angeles. And if that weren't motivation enough, a thousand American dollars wired from Corbett Marshall had clinched the deal.

"So what do we do now?" Matthew asked.

"Wait." Jesus stopped in front of a battered blue pickup truck with TACOS VARIOS painted on the sides of the bed. After a brief discussion with the vendor, Jesus purchased two bean burritos and a bottle of beer.

"Wait for what?"

"Night. What else?" Jesus asked around a mouthful of burrito. "When we can slip past la migra."

It wasn't Immigration that Matthew was afraid of, but the Mexican police. If there was a warrant out for his arrest, he could disappear back into the slow-grinding Mexican judicial system for years. "What about the police?"

Jesus shrugged. "The policia are no problem," he said in an offhanded way that added credence to the claim that several members of the police force worked for the coyotes, or people smugglers. Also supposedly in league with the coyotes were the bandits who lurked in the dark, attacking and robbing any illegal foolish enough to try to cross the border unescorted. It was, Matthew considered, the perfect protection racket.

More than two hundred immigrants—mostly men, with the occasional woman or child—lined the fence, watching. Waiting. As they had for years. Because he'd had grown up in Southern California, Matthew was aware of the illegal's game of playing catch-me-if-you-can with the U.S. border patrol. But now, as he watched the number of heavily armed men waiting for night to fall, he realized that the game had become a great deal more dangerous.

That was why Matthew hadn't told Corbett what he was doing. Promising that he would explain once he returned to Los Angeles, he'd asked his agent to wire a thousand dollars to Jesus. He also requested that Corbett tell no one about his call. Since he was now an escaped felon, however innocent, he didn't want to involve Corbett in anything illegal. There was also the outside chance things might go wrong. If that happened, he didn't want to give Leigh any false hope.

The sun was slowly going down. The Baja air grew cooler. People began moving toward the doorways cut into the steel mesh.

"Soon," Jesus promised. "Soon, gringo, you will be home."

As a police car cruised by, Matthew suddenly felt as if he were back in the middle of a war zone. His stomach knotted and a heavy, sweet smell of death filled his nostrils, a leftover olfactory memory from Vietnam.

When the Mexican cops drove away, Matthew reminded himself that he'd always been a survivor.

Joshua watched Marissa soothe the damaged ego of a male computer student whose girlfriend had just dumped him for an illiterate, musclebound football player. The lighthearted sexual romp revolved around a young woman who'd been hired to be a house mother for a California fraternity. Although the premise was admittedly far-fetched, the vehicle was designed to display nearly every inch of Marissa's considerable attributes.

By the time the director yelled "Cut," Joshua would not have been surprised to discover that the young man's glasses were fogged.

Marissa had felt her father's presence the moment he'd arrived. Of course she'd been expecting him; the director had informed her that Joshua would be visiting the set. Fore-warned was forearmed, and after two little blue Valium and a belt of the Absolut vodka she kept stashed away in her dressing room, Marissa felt ready to face him. She had put everything she had into that scene. Now, as she walked toward Joshua, a confident smile pasted onto her face, she tried to read his expression.

"Well? What did you think?"

"Not bad."

Marissa beamed. It was the closest thing to a compliment she had ever received from her father. "You thought I was going to turn it into just another porno flick, didn't you?"

"It wouldn't have been your first one."

"That was just to get your attention."

"Well, it sure as hell did that."

"You're the one who's always saying to take risks."

He gave her a sharp look, surprised to hear his own words thrown back to him. "You rushed your lines toward the end. And you upstaged that poor kid every chance you got. But all in all, you pulled it off better than I would've expected."

"Corbett says I have a real future in romantic comedy."

"Corbett's your agent; he gets paid to say things like that."

"You said I was good."

"I said you weren't bad. There's a difference."

It was what he wasn't saying. Marissa had seen that grudging look of admiration in his eyes. The knowledge that he hadn't wanted to like her performance made his reluctant acceptance even more heartwarming.

"Mr. Baron?" The young grip looked extremely nervous about interrupting the conversation between studio head and star. "I'm sorry to bother you, sir, but there's a call from your daughter. You can take it on that phone over there."

Joshua's face lit up like the Las Vegas strip. Turning his back on his younger daughter as if he'd forgotten her exis-tence, he rushed off.

"Princess," he greeted Leigh expansively, "when the hell are you coming back home? Things aren't the same around here without you, sweetheart."

Damn, damn, damn! For the first time in as long as Marissa could remember, she'd had her father all to herself. And the miracle was, they had actually been getting along. Until that bitch Leigh had called and ruined everything.

She stood all alone in the shadows, watching Joshua laugh heartily at something Leigh said. Marissa nearly choked on the scalding bitter taste of envy that rose in her throat.

Abu Dhabi seemed to be a city built upon shifting sands. Dust was everywhere. Blowing down the narrow streets, making its way through back alleys, drifting over the meat and oranges in the marketplace. Even the buildings were the color of dust—brown, ecru, umber. There were times when Leigh found the unrelenting heat and dust debilitating. Now, even after a bath, she felt as if she had dust in her pores.

"This time next week, you will be lying on the California beach," Khalil said reassuringly.

They were sitting in the lobby of her hotel, drinking the ubiquitous overly sugared hot tea. The final scenes of *Arabian Nights* were scheduled to be shot in three days. And as much as Leigh was looking forward to leaving the oppressive heat of Abu Dhabi, she also knew that she was going to leave a little bit of herself here. It was frustrating, overcrowded, parts of it malodorous, even wretched. It was also one of the most fascinating cities she'd ever known.

"Do you know," she said with a slow smile, "there are times when I feel as if you can read my mind."

How many times over the past two months had she found herself wishing for something, only to have Khalil arrive with it in hand, as if by magic, moments later? He'd eased her work considerably, including keeping his pockets filled with piasters for the baksheesh, those tips and bribes that accompanied every transaction. Except for the usual cases of diarrhea that hit the American members of the crew, the filming had gone remarkably well. Even the scenes shot out in the desert had been achieved without incident, unless one counted spitting camels and dust storms.

Khalil smiled. "While I would like to claim that I possess an Eastern mysticism, the truth is that your lovely face is quite often an open book."

"How interesting that you should say that," she murmured. "People usually accuse me of being frustratingly enigmatic."

"They don't know you."

"And you do?"

"Yes." His dark eyes met hers. "I do."

How strange that he should remind her so of Matthew, Leigh thought, experiencing an involuntary sexual pull that was both painful and exciting. "Well, you certainly don't lack self-confidence," she said, pretending a sudden interest in the wizened old man wearing a red fez who was methodically sweeping away at the ancient Persian carpet with a palm frond.

Her hotel, located on the wide, newly constructed Corniche, retained a quiet gentility suggestive of the city's colonial period. Ceiling fans churned the air, leafy palm trees grew in bright brass containers and Bedouin baskets, the furniture was solid and overstuffed. In the adjoining café, a circle of men sat cross-legged on the floor, smoking hookahs and playing cards. As yet another example of the vast changes the oil reserves had wrought, next door to the hotel, beneath a red-and-white striped awning, a lifesize cutout of Colonel Sanders greeted diners eager to sample his finger-lickin' Kentucky Fried Chicken.

"I know that you are hurting," Khalil said. "More than you are willing to admit."

"No one gets through life without a few bruises." Leigh turned her gaze away. From her vantage point beside a high, latticed window (lattices, which Khalil had explained, were designed to protect women from view), she had a dazzling view of the harbor, where ships arrived daily from all corners of the world, their holds laden with apples from Washington State, Dutch canned milk, Chinese wheelbarrows, Korean tires. Wooden dhows bobbed beside the wharfs while workmen unloaded rainbows of silk, gleaming copper and gold, carpets and pearls.

"Spoken like a true American. I suspect next you'll be giving me that tired old bromide about rolling with the punches."

"You do know me, don't you?" she said with a slight smile.

"Not as much as I'd like." Before she could respond, Khalil changed the subject, leaving Leigh to wonder if she'd only imagined the sudden intimacy in his voice. "It went well today, I think."

They'd spent the day filming in several of the neighborhood marketplaces, where Leigh had almost succumbed to the lure of a lovely gold necklace. But when the old saleswoman, with a gold nose pendant and chin tattoo, had weighed the necklace on a pair of delicate scales, then pecked out the price per gram on a Japanese calculator, figuring in, she assured Leigh, a "most generous discount," the total cost came to more than fifteen hundred dollars. More than Leigh had been prepared to pay.

"Better than well. I can't thank you enough for talking that man into allowing us to film him." The moment she'd seen the bearded bargainer in the camel bazaar, Leigh had known that she had to capture him on film. Unfortunately, he had not been willing to cooperate. Until Khalil had stepped forward and murmured a few words. A coin changed hands. The deal was done.

"Many of the older people believe that photographs constitute a threat to God's creations."

"If he really believed that, I'm surprised you were able to bribe him."

"That was his bargaining excuse. Not his belief," Khalil corrected gently. "Contrary to popular opinion, Leigh, not everything or everyone in Abu Dhabi is for sale. We Arabs survived for thousands of years with nothing but our faith in Allah, our steadfast belief in his generosity, and the strength of our families and tribes. All this oil, while inexorably altering our landscape, has not changed who we are. What we are."

Leigh blushed and looked down at her hands. "I didn't mean to imply—"

"And I didn't mean to lecture." Khalil shook his head. "I'm sorry, but there are times when I get tired of being patronized by Westerners who didn't give a damn about this part of the world until they needed our oil reserves." He reached out, as if to take her hand, then, apparently thinking better of it, withdrew. "You, on the other hand, have been a model of diplomacy, Leigh Baron. In fact, if your State Department officials and oil company executives possessed even a fraction

of your discretion, the world would be a much better place."
His eyes, as they settled on her face, darkened with masculine
appreciation. "Not to mention a much lovelier place."

One again, Leigh felt herself blushing. But this time it was
not embarrassment that caused the soft color to drift into her
cheeks. "Thank you. That's a very nice thing to say."

"It's the truth. And now that today's work is completed, I
have a proposition for you."

"Oh?"

"How would you like to go horseback riding?

"Today?" Leigh glanced unenthusiastically out the window
where the brilliant yellow sun still rode high in the sky.

"Tonight. I raise Arabians at my house outside the city; I'd
enjoy showing them to you."

The chance to get out of the city sounded more than a little
appealing. "And I'd enjoy seeing them. Very much."

"Good." Rising from his overstuffed chair, he smiled down
at her. "I will pick you up at seven. It is only a short car ride
to my house."

"That sounds marvelous," Leigh said, standing as well.

Taking her hand, Khalil lifted it to his lips in an Old World
gesture that suited him perfectly. The light brush of his black
mustache against her skin was like a flare of sparklers, but
before she could pull away, he'd relinquished her hand and
was on his way out of the hotel, leaving Leigh to wonder what,
exactly, she'd just agreed to.

A large, unmarked delivery truck pulled up behind an abandoned mattress factory in L.A.'s warehouse district. The
driver, a heavyset, dark-complected man of indeterminate
age, lumbered to the back of the truck, unlocked it, then
disappeared around the corner. A moment later, fifty men
clutching hand-drawn maps from relatives living in the area,
dispersed in all directions. Matthew was the last man to leave.
He blinked, struggling to adapt his eyes to the bright California sun. He and the others had been in the truck for the last
eighteen hours.

His incarceration and near brush with death had given
him plenty of time to reevaluate his life. And although he
hadn't come up with any answers, he did know that he'd

spent a great deal of time thinking about Leigh. Wanting her. Missing her. Loving her. What they needed was time, he had considered. Time to get to know one another without outside influences like the studio, his goals, the vast differences in their upbringing.

The first thing he'd promised himself that he would do, if he survived this nightmarish ordeal, would be to take Leigh away to some distant tropical island, where they'd spend long, lazy days basking in the sun and feeding one another sweet, succulent fruit.

Passion fruit.

As he began walking toward Venice, Matthew smiled for the first time in months.

On a cool, clear night, a spirited gallop across the desert is an unforgettable experience. They could have been a million miles away from civilization; the shifting sands, dotted with oil wells painted to resemble bright birds, seemed to stretch out to infinity. A full moon hung in the wide sky overhead, lighting the world with an unearthly white glow. Spurring her sleek gray Arabian mount forward, Leigh experienced a surge of freedom like nothing she'd ever known. Beside her, dressed in fawn-colored jodhpurs, a loose white lawn shirt, and black boots, seated astride a magnificent black stallion, Khalil cut an undeniably striking figure.

"Where are we going?" she asked, after they'd been riding about thirty minutes.

"It's a special place I keep to maintain a bond with my past," he explained. "When I feel the need to escape the constant crush and clamor of the city, I come here. I think you'll like it."

Hard-pressed to think about anything she wouldn't like about this evening, Leigh returned his smile.

It was not long when she saw it. A large black-and-white tent, standing alone in what appeared to be miles of empty desert. "I'm amazed that you were able to find it."

"I may have adopted western clothes and western manners, but I still possess a few Bedouin instincts." He reined in his horse and dismounted.

"I'm glad," she said, handing him her reins. Although

Leigh was perfectly capable of dismounting by herself, she didn't argue when Khalil gripped her around her waist and lifted her down.

"Really?"

"Really. It adds a certain mystery."

He smiled at that. "Do you think so?"

"Definitely. The first time I saw you, I thought you had a hint of the mystic. These past two months have only intensified my feelings."

"I'm pleased to hear that." He pulled the flap of the tent open, gesturing her to go in. "Since my feelings about you have been building for fourteen years."

"Fourteen years?" Leigh stopped, gazing around the interior of the tent. Oriental rugs and tasseled cushions of gold- and silver-threaded Moroccan tapestry covered the floor. "But you've only known me two months."

"Ah, but I saw a picture of you when I was at Oxford. You were dressed in a long white dress with a pink satin sash. Your hair was tied back with a pink ribbon, revealing the pair of natural pearls that adorned your exquisite earlobes."

"It was the night of the Academy Awards," Leigh remembered, stunned by his total recall. Even she had forgotten the pearls—the first her father had ever given her. "I was thirteen, I think."

"You were twelve. And I believe that's when I fell in love with you."

His words hung between them, waiting for Leigh to pick up on them. She knew that he was leaving it up to her. She could turn away from what he was offering and, gentleman that she knew Khalil to be, he would never mention it again. Or she could give in to these sexual stirrings she'd been experiencing more and more frequently since arriving in Abu Dhabi.

For someone who had never thought a great deal about sex, Leigh was shocked to discover that she'd become a highly sensual person. It was as if Matthew had opened a secret door, exposing hidden desires, unknown needs.

"I can't believe you love me," she said.

The night was cool; Khalil knelt and lit a small brazier in the corner of the tent. "Why not?" he asked as he started some frankincense burning in a copper container. Leigh had learned that burning frankincense was a traditional method of entertaining guests. "You are beautiful, intelligent, sensual—"

"But you said you fell in love with me when I was a girl."

"I fell in love with the woman I saw in that little girl's eyes."

"There's something important I need to tell you."

He smiled up at her. "Do you think you could possibly impart this important information sitting down? Or do you plan to stand by the flap of the tent all night, looking as if you're prepared to bolt at the slightest touch."

Leigh entered the tent and sank into the silken comfort of the pillows. Khalil lay down beside her. In deference to the desert heat, she'd twisted her hair into a braid and tied it with a piece of white ribbon, leaving a fan of silky blond hair that Khalil brushed with a seductive touch over her cheek and down her throat. His gaze locked with Leigh's as he tugged lightly on the ribbon. A moment later it was lying on the blood red rug. Appearing fascinated with the intricate French braiding, he traced the weaving with his finger.

Leigh told herself that she should insist Khalil stop twining his fingers through the braid as he unwound it. But her words of protest remained locked in her throat.

"You have to understand," she said softly, "this isn't easy for me."

"I know." He freed her hair from the tight braid and lifted it over her shoulders.

"Until recently, I'd always kept my feelings hidden away. Where they'd be safe. Protected. But then I met"—she hesitated, unwilling or unable to say Matthew's name—"a man."

"The man who hurt you." His hands brushed against the soft slope of her breast as he arranged the silvery blond strands to his liking. If Khalil heard Leigh's soft intake of breath, he didn't comment on it. "The man you came to Abu Dhabi to forget."

"Yes."

"And now you are afraid to risk your heart yet again."

"Yes." Drawing her knees to her chest, she wrapped her arms tightly around them.

"I have never forced myself on a woman, Leigh. And I am certainly not going to begin with you." He bent his head and brushed his lips against hers. "But I am asking that you trust me. For this one night."

He pried her fingers loose, first one hand, then the other, murmuring soothing, seductive words that she recognized as Arabic. Then he lifted her right hand to his lips, slowly kissing each tingling finger, before pressing a provocative kiss against the tender skin of her palm.

Needs too long denied flared, months of pent-up yearning made her ultrasensitive flesh burn. Details blurred when Leigh slowly surrendered, luxuriating in the pure pleasure of silk being whisked over her warm skin. Through her swirling senses she could feel Khalil caressing her pliant body with wet, open-mouthed kisses. Heat from his mouth seeped into her bloodstream, causing searing flashes of pleasure.

His lips and hands were never still, moving over her flesh, leaving sparks in their wake. Wherever his lips touched, she burned—wherever his hands stroked, she flamed. Her body was molten, flowing wherever he sought to take her. The air surrounding them thickened with fire and smoke and blazing passions.

Khalil's mouth lingered at the inside of first one thigh, then the other, creating needs that grew increasingly unbearable. With fingers and teeth and tongue he drove her higher, relentlessly bringing her to crest after shuddering crest until her body hummed from a thousand erratic pulses and his lips were wet with her orgasms.

While Leigh was still gasping for breath, her love-slick body limp, Khalil thrust into her. He moved fast and hard, and she gave herself up to his driving rhythm. Falling back, he pulled her onto him, encouraging her to ride him wildly, his long, dark fingers grasping her hips, holding her firm. Although she would not have thought it possible, as Khalil rocked her back and forth, Leigh experienced yet another shattering climax.

When he felt her violent inner convulsions, Khalil came with an explosive shout that echoed across the vast, barren desert.

The feel of the sharp, hot needles of water pounded against his flesh. The first thing Matthew did when he arrived home was take a long, hot shower. The second thing he did was call Baron Studios.

"I'm sorry, Mr. St. James," an unfamiliar voice said, "but Ms. Baron is out of the country."

So what else was new? Although he would have preferred Leigh to have been desperately waiting by the telephone for his call, Matthew grudgingly admitted that she did have a studio to run. Perhaps she had discovered he was in Mexico and had gone searching for him. He decided he rather liked that idea.

"Where is she this time?"

He thought he detected a momentary hesitation. "Abu Dhabi."

What the hell was she doing in Abu Dhabi? He couldn't recall Leigh mentioning an upcoming trip to the Middle East. "Would you please give me her number?"

This time the silence was unmistakable. "I'm sorry, sir," the woman said after a lengthy, significant pause, "but Ms. Baron has instructed me not to give that number out."

"But—"

"I'm sorry."

"I'd like to speak with Mr. Baron."

"I'm sorry. Mr. Baron is out of town also."

"Is he in Abu Dhabi too?"

"No, Mr. St. James. Mr. Baron is in Las Vegas."

"I don't suppose you have a number for him there."

"No, sir," the secretary lied unconvincingly.

"Of course not." His mind spinning, he tried to think of a way to skirt this latest roadblock. "Okay, let's try Meredith."

"Meredith?"

"Meredith Ward. Ms. Baron's secretary."

"Ms. Ward is no longer with Baron Studios. I'm Ms. Baron's new secretary."

He'd come full circle. "And you have been instructed not to give me her number."

Again that uncomfortable little pause. "Yes, Mr. St. James. I am terribly sorry."

"You and me both, sweetheart."

Well, that was that. He knew things had been strained between them, that was why he'd wanted to go somewhere he could be alone with Leigh without the constant pressure of that goddamn studio.

Matthew could understand Leigh's drive to succeed. He could even respect it. But ambition was one thing, blind ambition yet another. As he sat in the dark and killed a bottle of bourbon, old emotions came bubbling to the surface. Feelings of resentment, mistrust, and a deep-seated insecurity he had never admitted, even to himself.

He felt betrayed that Leigh had abandoned him without so much as a backward glance. By the time the sun had risen over the nearby mountains, Matthew had vowed to never again let anything—or anyone—interfere with his plans.

Now that he had enough money to concentrate solely on his writing, he was going to become the best damn screenwriter in the business. And as far as he was concerned, Baron Studios, Joshua Baron, and particularly Leigh Baron could go straight to hell.

Because he damn well didn't need them.

Matthew St. James didn't need anyone.

He was, as the popular song lyric so succinctly put it, alone again. Naturally.

29

"Y̶ou're leaving."

Leigh reached out and took Khalil's hand across the breakfast table. "Location shooting for *Arabian Nights* finished three weeks ago," she reminded him. "I should have returned home then."

With his free hand he stroked her hair, enjoying the silken feel of it against his palm. "Ah, but think what you would have missed."

"Yes." Over these past months Khalil had become incredibly dear to her. She was going to miss him. Dreadfully. But she didn't love him, although there had been several times during these last pleasure-filled weeks that she had wished she could. "You've made me so very happy," she said quietly. More than happy. The nightmares had gone, vanquished to some dark, distant part of her mind.

His face was clouded with emotions too complex for her to easily read. "As you have made me." His palm moved to her cheek. "You would make me even happier if you would agree to stay."

"I'd truly love to, but I've played hooky long enough. I must get back to my work."

"Is it your work you're so eager to return to? Or Matthew St. James?" She'd told him all about Matthew the morning after they'd made love for the first time. Since then his name had not come up.

"My work, of course. What Matthew and I had—or what I thought we had—is over."

"Then your feelings for him should not prevent you from becoming my wife."

Stunned by his out-of-the-blue proposal, Leigh mistakenly took his words for more of the lighthearted teasing that had added spice to their relationship from the beginning. "Your first wife, you mean."

"The Koran only allows a man four wives so long as he can treat them all equally—which means not only giving them equal goods, but equal time as well." He smiled. "That being the case, monogamy tends to be the rule. Marry me, Leigh, and let me treat you the way that you deserve."

He really was serious, Leigh realized. "And how is that?"

"Like a princess. No," he corrected, "a queen. Equal to the king in every way."

Even if she believed such behavior possible from a man so steeped in Arab tradition, Leigh knew that she could never love Khalil in the way he appeared to love her. In the end she would end up hurting him the way she'd been hurt. And she did care for him too much to inflict such pain.

"I do love you, Khalil. But not in that way."

"Did I ever tell you that my parents had an arranged marriage?"

"No."

"They did. Which is, of course, traditional in our culture. My mother was twelve, my father twenty-three. They met for the first time on the day of their wedding thirty-eight years ago. Today you could not find a couple who loved one another more."

"Are you saying that I could learn to love you?"

"It's been known to happen. After all, at the risk of sounding vain, I am not a totally unlovable man."

"You're the nicest man I've ever met," she said honestly. "And one of the handsomest. And the smartest, and the wonderful way you make me feel when we make love is—"

"Wait," Khalil laughed, holding up his hand. "If I am, as you say in America, such a catch, why don't you grab me?"

"I don't know." She toyed with her necklace. The gold crescent was the one she'd priced three weeks ago in the marketplace, reluctantly deciding that it was too expensive. Khalil had surprised her with the necklace the morning after they'd made love in the desert.

Putting his fingers under her chin, Khalil lifted her downcast eyes to his. When she dared to meet his gaze, Leigh viewed tender affection, blended with undisguised sympathy in his ebony eyes. "I think," he said gently, "that you are still in love with this Matthew St. James fellow."

"That's ridiculous. Why, I—"

He pressed his finger against her lips, cutting off her words. "I also think you will always be in love with him."

No. His words tolled like a curse, reverberating alarmingly through her mind. He was wrong, Leigh assured herself.

She was over Matthew.

Completely.

Wasn't she?

April 1974

The California sun was setting in a glorious blaze of smog-enhanced pink and scarlet. Billboards soared above Sunset Boulevard in a promotional blitzkrieg, blatantly begging for Oscar votes. Fans lined the concrete canyon of downtown Los Angeles and crowded into bleachers, eager for a glimpse of their favorite stars; a fleet of helicopters hovered overhead, the cameramen and -women inside filming the scene. The gas crisis was forgotten as three hundred black limousines (booked up to a year in advance by the Motion Picture Academy for the royal procession to the theater) made their way up the hill to the glass-and-concrete palace of the Los Angeles Music Center for the annual Academy Award ceremonies.

The arrivals stepped out of their limos onto the red carpet leading inside. Reporters shouted, flashbulbs exploded, fans screamed. Across the street a small clutch of hecklers waved homemade placards quoting Scripture and accusing the stars of cutting deals with the devil. A long white limo pulled up to the curb and the liveried chauffeur, handsome enough to be a leading man at any major studio, leaped out and made a low, sweeping bow reminiscent of a royal footman as he opened the wide door. A perfectly proportioned leg, encased in glittering gold hose, slid out of the car. Moments passed before a flash of gorgeous thigh followed. Their attention successfully captured, the crowd waited with bated breath. When Marissa, voluptuously clad in a clinging, gold lamé dress dripping with black bugle beads, finally emerged from the luxurious backseat of the limousine into the glare of strobe lights, the fans in the bleachers roared their approval. Tossing her artfully tousled copper hair, Marissa smiled and waved. Her fans went wild.

In contrast to Marissa's golden heat, Leigh appeared regally cool. Eschewing the Hollywood tradition of a new, one-of-a-kind gown designed specifically to make a grand entrance, she'd chosen the same dress she'd bought for the premiere of *Scattershot*. She'd been wearing the silvery blue silk Valentino the first time Matthew kissed her and if the gown brought back painful memories, Leigh refused to dwell on them. Unlike that evening, when she'd worn her hair loose because Matthew asked her to, tonight she'd swept it back into a elaborate twist at the nape of her neck, revealing the matched pair of pale blue diamonds that glittered like chips of ice at her ears.

Seated five rows behind Leigh, Matthew realized that she reminded him of a character in *The Kalevala*, a Finnish national epic he'd recently read: Loviatar, Maiden of Pain, protector of the land of Pohjoloa. A beautiful, alluring, though ultimately deadly blonde, Loviatar's dagger of ice kept her immune from any magic spells a man might try to use against her. If anyone ever wanted to make *The Kalevala* into a movie, Matthew mused, Leigh would be a natural for the part.

Her cool composure had always fascinated and infuriated him. Matthew knew she had to be nervous—hell, even *he* had

unwillingly succumbed to a case of Oscar jitters—but outwardly she remained frustratingly calm. Watching Leigh politely accept accolades from stellar directors Mike Nichols and
Francis Ford Coppola, he had a sudden urge to climb over the
seats separating them and shake her. Or kiss her. The only
problem was, Matthew knew that if he gave into either impulse, he'd never be able to stop. The wound she'd inflicted
was still too raw.

Although officially billed as Hollywood's greatest show, the
Academy Awards could more accurately be described as a
four-hour series of prolonged after-dinner toasts, brightened
this year by the sudden appearance of a nude streaker who'd
sprinted across the stage. Still, the tedium of the evening did
nothing to detract from Leigh's satisfaction with the Academy's acceptance of her work. Since the kidnapping of Patricia Hearst two months earlier by the Symbionese
Liberation Army, *Dangerous*, which had already achieved both
critical and audience acclaim, had become the talk of the
town. Leigh watched with pride as her pet project garnered
Oscars in eight categories, including Best Picture, Best Director, and Best Actor. And although Marissa lost to Ellen Bur-
styn for Best Actress, everyone in attendance knew that the
younger Baron sister was the newest, brightest star in the
Hollywood firmament.

It had been fifteen months since Leigh had seen Matthew.
Although he had steadfastly refused (through Corbett) to do
any preballot hype for the picture, the members of the Academy had found his performance as riveting as Leigh herself
had, that long-ago day nearly two years ago when he'd first
read for the part.

Watching Matthew receive his Oscar from celebrity pre-
senters Shirley MacLaine and Warren Beatty, it would have
been impossible to miss the energy that surrounded him like
an aura. When he held the coveted gold statuette up for the
photographers, accepting the thundering applause of his
peers while at the same time seeming removed from it,
Leigh determined that he was still the consummate loner.
But instead of working against him in this establishment,
herd-mentality town, such an attitude only made him more
intriguing.

Matthew's gaze swept over the pavilion, unerringly settling on Leigh. For a heady second their eyes met and held and a flood of tumultuous, bittersweet memories flooded over her. It was then that Leigh realized she had unintentionally lied to Khalil. She had run from the truth long enough; it was now time to admit, at least to herself, that she'd never be entirely free of her feelings for Matthew.

He had inexorably changed her life. He had introduced her to a world of sensuality, awakened in her a hunger she'd never known existed and, when he'd cajoled, urged, and stoked it to a primitive, clamoring pitch, he'd shown her the mindless bliss of shared possession.

Matthew St. James had taken her to the very heights of ecstasy and then, in the end, he had taught her a basic lesson in human anatomy.

No woman had ever died of a broken heart.

BOOK TWO

1976

30

I t was a time of fireworks and John Philip Sousa bands. A time when America's Bicentennial celebrations served as a catharsis for events of the past years: Watergate, Capitol Hill sex scandals, Vietnam, presidential collapse, energy crisis, bankrupt cities, rebellion, riots, and recession.

It was also a heady time to be a woman. Independent spirits were breaking free of passive, home-clinging stereotypes in increasing numbers, achieving recognition in a society where values and standards had been long set by men. "Battling Bella" Abzug, known for her big hats and gruff voice, shattered the time-honored tradition that women—and freshman members of Congress—should be seen and not heard while a new kind of First Lady, Betty Ford, openly lobbied congressmen on behalf of the ERA. Sarah Caldwell, a former Arkansas iddler known as the Divine Sarah, became the first woman ever to conduct at the Met in New York and, in a move that made headlines all over the world, ABC spent an unprecedented five million dollars to lure former ornamental "Today" girl Barbara Walters away from rival television network NBC.

In Hollywood, during this second half of the tumultuous 1970s, owning your own production company was visible proof of power and prestige. It was viewed as the holy grail. After her dazzling success with *Dangerous*, Leigh declared her independence from her father by successfully lobbying for her own company within Baron Studios. Eighteen months later, it was obvious to everyone in town that Leigh thrived in the heady, autonomous atmosphere of her Sundown Production company. (Although there were numerous rumors floating about concerning Leigh's choice of a name, what only she knew was that one of the studio lawyers was calling every five minutes, insisting she name her company something, anything, so he could finish drawing up the papers. After racking her brain for an appropriate-sounding name, when Gordon Lightfoot's "Sundown" came over the radio, Leigh unrepentantly borrowed the title as her own.)

In a bravely independent move of his own, insisting that the only way to keep his ideas a secret was to never let them out of his head, Matthew had directed and produced a poignant story about an innocent Vietnamese laundry girl killed by U.S. artillery. The movie, *Friendly Fire*, went on to win an Oscar for Best Short Film.

"When are you going to use some of that money you've been making to buy yourself a decent house?" Corbett was sitting with Matthew on the front porch of the rented, gingerbread-encrusted bungalow in Venice.

"I like it here," Matthew said. "And you sure as hell can't beat the view," he tacked on when a willowy black woman, dressed in a fluorescent yellow bikini rolled by on a pair of skates.

"I suppose it's your business if you want to live like some throwback to the 1960s," Corbett conceded. "Actually, it suits that fuck-you reputation you're rapidly achieving. Speaking of which, you were missed last night."

"Not being one of the 'in' crowd, I doubt anyone noticed my absence."

"They sure as hell did when I showed up on stage to accept your Oscar."

Matthew heard the aggravation in Corbett's voice and, while he understood his agent's feelings, he could not change who he was. What he was. "Look, I took your advice and attended that three-ring circus two years ago. Once was enough."

"Well, however much you insist that you're not an insider, I believe this says differently," Corbett said, holding up the gold statuette. "Rona Barrett referred to you as Hollywood's newest wunderkind."

"She'll latch on to another one next year. Hollywood has never been short of boy wonders," Matthew said with a shrug. "Orson Welles was only twenty-five when he received four nominations. I'm thirty-two and this film is no *Citizen Kane*."

"Your next one could be."

For the first time since Corbett had arrived to deliver the award, Matthew looked interested. "You liked it."

"*Private Screenings* is the best thing I've ever read."

Matthew could hear the hesitation in his tone. "But?"

"But you're never going to be able to afford to produce it yourself."

"Well, I'm sure as hell not letting some damned commercial studio get their hands on it. I've seen what happens to writers in this town, Corbett. They slave over a story, honing it to the best it can be. Then they turn their work of love over to the philistines, who can't resist tinkering with it until it doesn't begin to resemble the original story.

"Finally, after all this fucking around, the movie comes out and the writer is forced to suffer the pain of his movie never getting made. Instead there's this other movie, which is, more often than not, a piece of shit." Matthew's jaw firmed. "I'd rather *Private Screenings* spend eternity in my desk drawer than have some schmuck executive with a pocket calculator for a brain screw it up."

"I don't want that to happen either," Corbett agreed. "But, like it or not, a crucial, if not the most crucial problem of making a film today, is what it's going to cost. And to do this baby right is going to take more money that you can swing by yourself, Matthew. So why don't you at least let me show it to a few people I trust?"

"Do you have anyone particular in mind?"

"Not yet. Let me give it some thought." It was the first time he'd ever lied to a client and Corbett hated having to do it. Worse yet, Matthew was more than a client, he was a friend.

As he drove back down Sunset Boulevard to his office, Corbett told himself that, in this case, the ends justified the means. But that didn't make him feel any better about his subterfuge.

Leigh was feeling on top of the world. It was the morning after the Academy Award ceremony and the Los Angeles sun had valiantly managed to slice its way through the smog, splintering the sky with shafts of brilliant gold. The clarity of the bright spring day intensified the lush landscaping outside her garden suite of offices, and although air conditioning precluded opening the French doors, Leigh imagined she could smell the piquant scent of the creeping rosemary that spilled from the Mexican clay planters.

Like too many of the city's residents, Leigh would have had to plead guilty to taking the weather for granted. It took days like this to make one stop and bask in the California sunshine and, although she had never considered herself superstitious, she couldn't help feeling that this glorious day was a portent of things to come.

Last night she'd read a screenplay, not that unusual an occurrence, certainly. But this was different; never had she stayed up all night, unable to put the screenplay down.

One of the principal reasons Leigh had formed Sundown Productions was so that she could make films that otherwise might not be made. Last year, five financially successful films—*The Godfather*, *The Exorcist*, *Earthquake*, *The Towering Inferno*, and *Jaws*—had changed the course of moviemaking. Impressed by box office receipts, all the major studios had jumped on the visceral shock bandwagon, producing a festival of blood and gore.

Private Screenings, the story of an unsinkable seven-year-old orphan determined to survive the abuse inflicted on him by overly strict nuns, uncaring bureaucracies, and neglectful, often cruel foster parents, definitely bucked what Leigh considered a distressing trend. The boy survived his unhappy existence by hiding in darkened theaters during Saturday afternoon matinees, taking refuge in a fantasy life where he imagined himself to be Mighty Man—righter of wrongs, conqueror of evil. By the time she finished reading, Leigh was in tears. She was also determined that Sundown Productions make the film.

She made the call herself, too impatient to play the power game of having her secretary call Corbett's secretary.

"Good morning, Corbett," she said warmly.

"Good morning, Leigh," the agent answered. "Don't you sound in a good mood. Hot date after the Awards party last night?" It had not escaped Corbett's notice that Leigh had left her father's Oscar party minutes after her arrival. Joshua, muttering something about desertion, had sulked all night.

"Don't I wish. No, I was working. As usual."

Corbett didn't warn Leigh about the need to maintain balance in her life; she hadn't listened innumerable times before and he doubted that she would today.

"Read any good screenplays lately?" he asked with feigned casualness.

"Could be," she responded, matching his easy tone. Then, unable to restrain her enthusiasm any longer, she said, "You knew that I wouldn't be able to resist *Private Screenings*."

"You liked it."

"I loved it. It's just what I've been looking for."

"It won't be the most commercial movie Baron Studios ever made," Corbett warned.

"No. But it will certainly be one of the best. How many studios are looking at it?"

"Only Baron. For now."

Leigh breathed a sigh of relief. As unenthusiastic as she was about becoming embroiled in a bidding war, she was more concerned about losing the script to a competitor. Something she could not allow to happen. "When can we get together?"

Corbett paused, seeming to ponder the matter. "How about lunch tomorrow?"

"How about dinner tonight?"

He laughed. "Are you sure you want to sound so eager?"

"I've never been one to play coy, Corbett, and I'm sure as hell not going to start now. This new writer you've found has a rare and special talent; I don't want to take a chance on him getting away."

"Tonight it is. Where?"

"Ma Maison? Eight o'clock?"

"Terrific." He paused, then added as an afterthought, "How would you feel about meeting the writer?"

"I'd love it." Leigh hung up the telephone, smiling. It was an absolutely glorious day.

Leigh's smile faded when she received a call from Ryan McIntyre, director of Marissa's new film. Although she had failed to win an Oscar for her performance in *Dangerous*, Marissa had forged a place for herself in romantic comedies and was in constant demand, despite a growing reputation for being difficult. Leigh spent a great deal of her time soothing irate directors.

"What is it now?" she asked.

"She's locked in her dressing room, claiming cramps."

"Perhaps she really doesn't feel well."

"Leigh, it's the third time in the last two weeks she's used the same excuse. How many fucking periods can one woman have in a single month?"

Leigh thought back to when Marissa was a freshman in high school and she'd been called to the school by the dean of girls to discuss her younger sister's repeated absence in PE, due, allegedly, to menstrual cramps. Then, as now, Marissa appeared to have accomplished the impossible biological feat of having three to five periods per month.

"How many, indeed?" she murmured.

"Well, you've got to do something. She's in there, blasting that damn disco music on her stereo and eating her weight in Mallomars—speaking of which, wardrobe had to let out her clothes again last week; if the kid doesn't stop shoving cookies into her mouth she's going to balloon up to the size of Shelley Winters and she can kiss her career as a sex goddess goodbye."

"Did you personally request her presence on the set?"

"Are you kidding? You know as well as I do that this is a question of protocol, Leigh. The director is supposed to be the unchallenged boss on the set. As director, that's where I belong. On the set. If I go and get the bitch, the balance of power will shift and then we'll all be in shit city . . . I sent the AD. Three times. She won't open the damn door. Anyway," he said, after taking a much needed breath, "everyone knows you're the only one who can talk her into working when she's like this."

"Give me twenty minutes to shuffle a few appointments and I'll be over." Leigh hung up the phone and sighed. Well, it had been a nice day, while it lasted. At least she had tonight's dinner with Corbett and his new discovery to look forward to.

Ma Maison had opened to a fanfare of publicity three years ago and had rapidly become a mecca for those Beverly Hills heavy hitters who wanted to indulge in a status meal without putting on a tie. It was five minutes to eight when Leigh walked into the restaurant, had her hand air-kissed by the ebullient manager, and immediately was whisked past the waiting celebrities to the table where Corbett had already been seated.

"You get more beautiful every day," the agent greeted her with a smile. "If you'd only chosen the other side of the camera, I could have represented you and we'd have made a fortune."

"I would think one Baron sister is all any man could handle," Leigh said dryly, sitting down. After giving her drink order to the waiter, she glanced at the silver bucket beside the table, where a bottle of Moët et Chandon was nestled in a bed of cracked ice. "It's not like you to count your chickens, Corbett."

"Ah, but I have good feelings about this deal," he said. "Something tells me that you and my client are going to hit it off right away."

She folded her hands on the table. "I love the screenplay, Corbett. And I want to make this picture. But I'm not willing to give away the store to do it, either."

"I'm sure we can come to terms, Leigh. Trust me."

She always had. But there was something about Corbett

tonight. Some devilish gleam in his eyes she couldn't remember ever seeing before. "Are you keeping something from me?"

"Who, me?" He flung his hand against his shirt. "Why, everyone in town knows that I'm an open book."

"Everyone also knows that you're not above a little manipulation when you're out to clinch a deal. So, what are you up to this time?"

Before he could answer, something over Leigh's shoulder caught his attention. "Ah, here he is now."

Leigh turned around, stunned to see Matthew walking across the room. When their eyes met with the power of a sledgehammer shattering crystal, dual emotions collided inside her—the raw pain of desertion and the unequaled joy at seeing him again. Fortunately, the waiter chose that moment to arrive with her drink. She took a fortifying sip of the vodka and tonic.

Matthew looked startled and extremely uncomfortable. "Hello, Leigh."

He hadn't changed, but Leigh wondered why she thought he'd might. Almost against her will, she'd found herself looking for him last night at the Awards ceremony. She hadn't really been surprised when he didn't attend; Matthew was gaining a measure of fame as Hollywood's most reclusive maverick.

"Hello, Matthew. This is quite a surprise."

Matthew shot Corbett a dark look. "Isn't it?"

"All right, I'll admit it," Corbett said. "I set this entire thing up. But I had a good reason."

"I'd like to hear it," Matthew said, pulling out a chair. Their knees brushed slightly, creating a small shock of unwilling desire for both of them.

"So would I," Leigh said.

Matthew looked at her. "You didn't know I'd be here tonight?"

"Of course not. I'm here because Corbett promised to introduce me to the man who wrote *Private Screenings*."

"*Private Screenings*? You read my screenplay?"

She bristled at the accusation in his tone. "I didn't know it was yours. The title page listed the author as William Seymour." She took another bracing sip of her drink. Dutch courage, her father called it. "May I ask why you used a pseudonym? Were you so afraid I'd turn the project down after what you did to me?"

"Hell, lady, I didn't even know Corbett was going to let you read the damn thing. I told him a long time ago that I didn't want anything to do with Baron Studios, especially your precious Sundown Productions . . . What I did to you?"

"Disappearing like that, driving me crazy, turning up with a wife you weren't even man enough to tell me about . . . Why didn't you want Baron Studios to produce your picture?"

"Wife? What the hell are you talking about?" Realizing that he'd just garnered the avid attention of the other diners, Matthew lowered his voice. "I don't have any wife."

"Then who was that woman I saw you with at the Academy Awards?"

"I didn't attend the damn awards."

"Not last night. Two years ago. When you won for *Dangerous*."

Matthew thought back. "That was Rosaria."

"And who, exactly, is Rosaria?"

"Not that it's any of your business, but she's a friend. She saved my life in Mexico, so when I got back to the States, I asked Corbett to help get her a job."

"That's right," Corbett confirmed. "She started out as a seamstress over at MGM, but she's worked her way up to assistant costume designer."

Leigh didn't give a damn about the absent Rosaria's couture skills. Something else had caught her attention. "She saved your life?"

"She broke me out of jail, then she took care of me when my bullet wound got infected."

Leigh felt as if she'd just fallen down the rabbit hole. "Your bullet wound? You were shot? And what were you doing in jail?"

"It's a long story."

"I wanted to tell you, Leigh, but Matthew swore me to secrecy," Corbett said. "To be perfectly honest, if you'd pressured me, I probably would have caved in and told you the truth, but when you came home from Abu Dhabi and refused to talk about Matthew, I figured whatever had happened between you two was your own business.

"But there's personal business and movie business," he continued. "And that's where I draw the line. I put the pseudonym on the pages I sent you, Leigh, because I knew Matthew's screenplay was something special and I wanted you to read it without prejudice. As for not being completely honest with you, Matthew, I was afraid that if you knew Leigh was considering the story, you'd refuse to sell it to her.

"I realize my behavior was unprofessional, but this movie deserves to be made by a major studio. Baron Studios is the largest, and currently the most profitable, due, in part, to Leigh's Sundown Productions company. Also, because I consider myself to be a friend to both of you, I think it's time you resolved your differences."

Speech made, he rose. "Enjoy the champagne. The check's all taken care of; I'll call you both in the morning." His knowing gaze went from Matthew to Leigh and back again. "Make that tomorrow afternoon."

They remained silent, watching him leave.

"Corbett's slipping," Leigh said finally. "He's always been a firm believer in the studio picking up the tab."

"Like he said, there's personal business and movie business. I have a feeling that this gesture was extremely personal."

"I think so too." She paused. "Congratulations on your Oscar."

Matthew shrugged. "All I wanted to do was to try and make a good film. To paraphrase Richard Burton, the Oscars are just a goddamned horse race. And to tell you the truth, it feels strange making a film about a war tragedy and ending up with a gold statue. Somehow, it just doesn't seem relevant."

Leigh was pleased that Matthew hadn't been blinded by Oscar's golden light, that success hadn't changed him. On second thought, she wondered why she thought it might have. He'd always had a firm vision of exactly where he was going.

"That reminds me of something I once read," she said. "They have an annual poetry contest in Barcelona. The third prize is a silver rose, the second prize is a gold, and the writer of the best poem gets a real rose."

"Sounds as if they've got the right idea."

"I thought so at the time . . . *Friendly Fire* was a marvelous film. Would you think me a hopeless case if I told you that I saw it three times, and cried each and every time?"

Matthew smiled. "That's worth more to me than any Oscar."

"It was really bad, wasn't it? Vietnam."

He was about to slough off her question, as he had so many times before. But something made Matthew tell the truth. "Yeah. It was rough. But I learned a long time ago that life doesn't come with a gold-plated guarantee."

"You really weren't married?"

"Never."

Leigh looked at him across a vast chasm of uncertainty. "But I went to your house. There was a woman there, a young Mexican woman who said she was your wife. She even showed me your wedding picture."

"You're joking."

"It's not exactly a joking matter, Matthew."

"Leigh, for the last time, I am not and have never been married."

She wanted to believe him. Dear God, how she wanted to believe that he had not just used her for his own ends, then thrown her away when he was finished. "But why would anyone lie about something like that?"

Matthew had had his own suspicions from the beginning, but no proof. "I've no idea. Perhaps it was one of Jeff's less than humorous practical jokes."

"Jeff? Not Jeff Martin?"

"You know him?"

"Of course. He and Marissa have been living together on and off since . . ." Her voice trailed off.

"Since that summer we met."

"Yes."

A comfortable silence settled over the table. Leigh was stunned at how right it felt to be with Matthew again. "I really did love *Private Screenings*. The story is compelling and it's written in a wonderfully terse, dramatic style that the director and actors are going to love."

They were talking about work, but their eyes were speaking

an intimate, remembered language all their own. "The same terse, dramatic style producers and executives can't understand," Matthew said with a slight smile.

"*Most* executives."

"That's right. You're one of the few studio people left in this town who loves movies."

She'd told him her feelings the night of the premiere they'd attended together almost four years ago. There were times that halcyon summer seemed a lifetime ago. Then there were those times that it seemed like yesterday.

"I'm surprised you remembered."

"Oh, I remember all right, Leigh. I remember everything."

They looked at one another and for a long, tantalizing moment the years slipped away and they were returned to that sun-kissed time when life was golden and their love shone brighter than the California sun.

"Where did you get your idea for *Private Screenings*?" she asked, seeking something, anything, to say.

"I think I could use a drink." Matthew lifted the bottle of champagne out of the ice and poured them both a glass. He downed his thirstily and poured another. "If I tell you, I wouldn't want Janet Bridges to make it part of the promotion. That is, if I decided to let Baron make the film."

"Agreed."

"Even Corbett doesn't know."

Leigh put her hand on his arm. "Matthew, I promise not to tell a soul."

He looked down at her hand, observing the way the pale shining ovals at her fingertips gleamed against his sleeve. When the vision brought back the memory of those slender hands on his body, creating havoc in every pore, he let out a long breath. "It's autobiographical."

Leigh tried to relate this remarkably successful, self-assured man with that lonely little boy. "I didn't know. You never talked much about your childhood."

"We didn't talk much about anything," Matthew reminded her. "Most of our time together we spent in bed."

"Perhaps that was part of our problem."

"Perhaps." Taking her hand in his, Matthew looked into her eyes in a way that made Leigh feel as if he could read her most innermost secrets. Remembered passion sparked, so electric it made her tremble. "How hungry are you?" he asked.

She thought about all the nights and weeks and years lost because once hurt, they'd both instinctively retreated behind the perceived safety of their emotional barricades. Even as Leigh warned herself that she could be hurt again, she found herself unable to resist. "For food?"

Matthew laughed. A deep, robust sound that Leigh had thought she would never hear again. "You're getting ahead of me."

Her heart was pounding so hard, she was amazed that the entire room hadn't heard it. "We have to talk."

"Absolutely." He touched her hair. "Your place or mine?"

"Where are you living these days?"

"I'm still renting my house in Venice."

"My place, then," Leigh decided. "It's closer."

31

The drive to Santa Monica seemed to take an eternity. Neither Leigh nor Matthew spoke. There was no need.

"Oh, shit," Matthew muttered as they walked up to the door.

Leigh looked up at him. "What's the matter?"

"When I went to the restaurant tonight I thought . . . It was supposed to be a business dinner . . . Hell, I don't exactly carry a rubber around in my wallet like some horny high school kid hoping to get lucky."

He'd always been so insistent about protecting her. That was only one of the reasons she had fallen in love with him. "Don't worry."

His jaw firmed. "I want you, Leigh. But—"

"I'm on the pill."

"Oh." Hating the idea of Leigh being with any other man, Matthew reminded himself that he certainly hadn't been celibate during their separation. But damn it, although he knew he'd be stoned by feminists the world over for harboring such a sexist thought, casual sex was different for women. Wasn't it? Okay, perhaps it wasn't. But that still didn't mean he had to like picturing Leigh in some other man's arms. Or worse yet, some other man's bed.

Sensing his discomfort, Leigh lifted her palm to his cheek. "My periods have always been erratic, remember? My doctor put me on the pill to keep me regular."

"Thank God for erratic periods. Because I'm not sure I could have walked away. Not after all this time." Bending his head, he kissed her with years of pent-up longing.

The minute they entered the house, they fell into one another's arms, kissing with a breathless lust that surprised them both. To reach the bedroom, they would have had to cross what seemed to be miles of glacial white tile. The journey was too far, their hunger too overpowering. They sank onto the soft white fur rug underfoot.

There were no words, no soft lovers' sighs. Only blurred movement, drugged sensations, blinding passion. Leigh heard the sound of silk ripping and welcomed it; unzipping Matthew's pants, she released his straining penis and ran her hot tongue along its length. A milky white droplet glistened on the dark, plum-hued tip. She licked it off, then took him deep in her mouth, sucking so hard Matthew thought he'd explode.

They made love without undressing, a fierce, feverish love tinged with animal lust. Parting her legs with his palms, he surged into her, his long strokes plunging deep and hard, crashing into the very heart of her. Her juices flowed in response to his thrusts and, when she came, it was with a series of violent shudders. When her body clutched at him, Matthew lost the last vestige of control. He poured himself into her, and said her name, softly, over and over, as if it were a prayer.

Marissa was in a rotten mood. She'd been up all night fighting with Jeff. During the marathon battle, he'd called her a selfish, ball-busting bitch; she'd shot back with the accusation that he was nothing but a spaced-out gigolo. It was then that he'd stormed out of the house, taking the Porsche, leaving her with the Mercedes convertible, which he knew she hated to drive because it had a stick shift. It wasn't until after he was gone that she discovered he'd taken their cache of drugs with him.

Not that she needed the stuff. She only popped a Dexedrine in the morning to get her started, a Valium or two when her bastard director acted like Adolf Hitler, some more little orange dexies before going out, then some 'ludes or a little grass before bed to come down. And once in a while a little coke, just to make the sex hotter. Everyone did it. It was the way of life in the pharmaceutical seventies.

Driving aimlessly, rage pounding inside her like the beat of ancient drums, she found herself at the waterfront with no memory of having driven there. A weathered tavern caught her eye; needing a drink, she pulled into the parking lot. Coming in from the bright sunshine, it took her eyes a moment to adjust to the darkness. Tanya Tucker was belting out an exuberant chorus of "Delta Dawn" on the jukebox.

When she could see, Marissa took a survey of the place. A layer of cigarette smoke hung over the room like a shroud. Against the far wall were two brightly painted pinball machines and a pay telephone. The center of the floor was taken up by green-felt pool tables, and an electro-dart game hung from the ceiling. Bottles were lined up behind the bar, beer signs glowed dimly in the smoky haze.

The Driftwood's clientele appeared to have come from the merchant ships docked outside the door. The unshaven men looked strong and tough. As her eyes swept over them, they looked back at her with a mixture of curiosity and lust.

One guy in particular caught her attention. Sitting alone at the end of the bar, he was definitely no leading man. His nose was flat, and leaned to the left, as if it had been broken more than once. He had a full black beard, long oily hair, and a ragged scar carved its way from the bridge of that battered nose to the corner of his eye. He was wearing a black T-shirt with the arms raggedly cut off, displaying a tattoo of a naked woman on one bulging biceps, a dragon surrounded by flames on the other. He also had, she noticed with a slight intake of breath, the most dangerous black eyes she'd ever seen. Perfect.

As she walked straight toward him, adrenaline pumping wildly through her veins, Marissa experienced the biggest rush she'd had in years. It was, she decided, even better than drugs.

It was not easy drawing Matthew out, but when he began to relate stories of his past, Leigh began to understand that his often brusque behavior was the result of his unsettled childhood. Matthew had never experienced the closeness of a family and became uncomfortable when people got too close. Learning about his past also helped her to understand why he found trust so difficult.

"So," she said as they lay in bed late one lazy Sunday morning two weeks after their reunion, "what do you feel like doing today?"

He reached out and trailed his finger down the slope of her breast, appearing fascinated by the way her nipple pebbled under his touch. "We could spend the day right here."

How was it that after all they'd shared, she could want him again so soon? "We could. Of course, there's also the chance we could starve doing that."

His lips followed the trail his fingertip had warmed. "We could send out for pizza. Much, much later."

"I've always liked pizza."

"Or we could go to Vegas."

"Las Vegas?" Neither she nor Matthew liked to gamble. There was more than enough risk in moviemaking. "What's in Las Vegas?"

"Sinatra." His tongue cut a wet swathe across her flesh.

"I think I'll pass."

"Wayne Newton."

"Ditto," she managed, just as he took her rosy nipple between his teeth and tugged.

"The Chapel of Lights."

"What's that? A new rock group?"

"It's a wedding chapel. Have I told you that I love the taste of your skin?"

"A wedding chapel. Like in marriage?"

"Yeah. Christ, you taste good. Like temptation. Warm, moist—"

"Matthew!" Grabbing hold of his hair, she yanked his head up. "Was that a proposal?"

"Actually, now that you mention it, I suppose it was. Should I have gotten down on my knees?"

"No. I mean yes."

"Yes, I should have proposed on bended knee? Or yes, you'll marry me?"

"Yes, I'll marry you." Leigh flung her arms around his neck. "Yes, yes, yes!"

Dressing quickly, they stopped only long enough to pick up Kim and a surprised but delighted Tina and Corbett on the way to the airport.

Nearly four years after they'd first looked into each other's eyes, Leigh and Matthew were married in the Chapel of Lights. Despite the haste, despite the fact that the music was canned and the minister yet another Elvis impersonator, the wedding was everything a wedding should be. The bride, clad in a Givenchy cream silk gown and carrying a bouquet of American Beauty roses, was beautiful and the groom was handsome. When they exchanged vows, the love they shared shone brightly in their eyes.

The call came the following morning. After hanging up, Joshua stared at the phone for a long, silent time. It couldn't be. She'd never desert him. Not his princess. Not Leigh.

But she had. She'd turned her back on everything they had built together, running off after that bastard writer like a bitch in heat. He pictured the two of them, coupled together like a pair of rutting dogs. Then, to block out the image, he went into the library and drank himself into oblivion.

Marissa had just returned home from an afternoon thrashing around in a sleeper cab with a trucker from Lodi. He'd been a big mean man, obviously used to knocking women around, but she'd managed him like a pro. For three glorious hours, she'd been in complete control.

Control. God, how she loved that word!

She was flying high until Leigh's phone call brought her crashing down to earth with a resounding bang. Her gut twisted with a spasm of raw jealousy, Marissa got back in her car. But instead of returning to the Driftwood, where she'd become a regular, she headed straight for the Beverly Hills Hotel. There, stretched out by the pool, clad in skimpy bikini trunks, were the money men, working on their coppery tans as they packaged million-dollar projects before lunch.

Her eyes scanned the current crop of moguls. She caught sight of a French film director with a known taste for buxom redheads and a penchant for leather. Licking her lips, Marissa grabbed a margarita off the tray of a passing waiter and walked toward his table.

Two days after reporting Leigh and Matthew's marriage, Rona Barrett took to the airwaves once again to break the unhappy news to men all over the world. Baron Studios' reigning sex symbol and the actress voted by *Playboy* readers as the Playmate they'd most like to be stranded on a desert island with was now Mrs. Philippe Corbière.

"What the hell got into you?"

Leigh looked up to see her father storming into her office. Although still technically on her honeymoon, she'd dropped in to the office to check her mail. "Good morning to you too."

"Don't good morning me, little girl. I want to know why you ran off with that bastard."

Leigh's gray eyes turned as cold as ice. "I am twenty-nine years old, which is a far cry from a little girl, and you will not refer to my husband in that manner again."

Husband. The word burned in his gut like acid. "Why not? Since that's what he is."

Angry color heightened her cheekbones. "That's unfair. Matthew can't be held responsible for his parents' behavior."

"How about his drug bust? Can he be held responsible for that? Or didn't he tell you about it?"

"He told me. He also gave me the report from the private detective Corbett hired to investigate the arrest."

"Corbett hired a detective?" That was news to him. Joshua wondered why his old friend hadn't mentioned a detective at the time.

"Yes, and it turns out that Matthew was booked into jail under a false name, which gives credence to his claim that he was framed."

Joshua felt icy sweat pouring from under his arms. "That may be what he's claiming, but does he have any proof?"

"He doesn't need proof. I believe him."

"If any of that drug business ever comes out, the guy is going to be a dead duck in this town, Leigh. I don't want anyone at the studio involved with him. Personally or professionally."

Leigh met his aggravated look with a calm, level one of her own. "I'm sorry you feel that way. Because not only do I love Matthew, I also plan to produce his new screenplay."

"I forbid it." The thunderous rage in Joshua's eyes would have cowed a lesser woman. "If he even tries to set foot on Baron Studios property, I'll have him arrested for trespassing."

Leigh had been prepared for an argument. Even so, the depth of her father's enmity surprised her. Not that she had any intention of backing down. She had spent her childhood playing poker with movie crews. Leigh could bluff with the best of them.

"Fine. If Matthew isn't welcome here, neither am I." She began emptying her desk. "Shall I call the publicity department with the news that I'm going into independent production with my husband, or will you handle the press release?"

Leigh had grown up at Baron Studios. Joshua knew she'd never carry out her threat to leave, but he didn't dare put her to the test. There was too much of Walter Baron's damnable stubborn pride in the girl and, personal feelings aside, she was too valuable to the studio to risk losing.

"All right," he said magnanimously. "St. James can stay. So long as he makes money."

The tension between them eased slightly. Leigh went around the desk and wrapped her arms around her father. "Don't worry, Dad," she assured him, tilting her head back to give him a dazzling smile, "Matthew is going to be the best thing to happen to Baron Studios since you took over after Grandfather's death."

At the mention of his father, Joshua recalled the Draconian power the former studio Titan had wielded during his lifetime. Walter Baron would have cheerfully crushed Matthew St. James underfoot without a backward glance. And although he would prefer to do exactly that, Joshua knew he couldn't, for fear of losing Leigh. Reluctantly, he decided to do nothing. For now.

Besides, he assured himself when he returned to his office and had poured himself a stiff drink, the marriage would undoubtedly end like the majority of others in Hollywood—in divorce.

And if it didn't? Joshua vowed to do whatever it took to reclaim his daughter and poured himself another single malt Scotch.

Leigh sank down onto her chair and buried her head in her hands. She had emerged from the argument victorious. Now she was shaken by how close she had come to having to chose between the two most important men in her life.

She left the office early and returned home to an empty house and a note from Matthew.

> *Sweetheart* [it read in his bold, black script], *Tina called. She closed the deal on that house in Topanga Canyon and, since Corbett's in New York, she wanted someone to celebrate with. We're having lunch at El Cholo; why don't you join us? Or better yet—start warming up the bed. I'll be home by three.*

As much as she adored Matthew, after six days of constant togetherness, Leigh was secretly pleased to have some time to herself. She spent the next hour walking on the beach, thinking back over the years.

She'd never had any friends her own age; she'd spent all her free hours after school at the studio, following her father from set to set, sitting in a corner, watching in awe the legions of world-famous stars who trekked in and out of his office. While the other girls were devouring Nancy Drew mysteries, she was reading *Variety* and the *Hollywood Reporter*.

When her schoolmates were glued to "American Bandstand," practicing the latest dance steps in front of the television, she was learning the proper tone to take in an audition meeting. And when those same giggling girls spent Saturdays at Neiman-Marcus, trying on dress after dress, looking for the perfect one to wear to that night's dance, she was standing outside a theater in Westwood, handing out response cards to audiences at sneak previews.

Her life, as far back as she could remember, had been entwined with the studio. And Joshua. Leigh thought of all the problems they'd overcome together, the triumphs they'd shared.

She loved her father. But she loved Matthew too.

Unfortunately, their antipathy for one another was only too obvious. Sinking down onto the warm sand, Leigh watched the sunshine reflect off the glistening water and wished that she didn't feel so torn.

32

Ninteen seventy-eight was a year of discontent. The women's movement had been the watchword of the 1970s, just as civil rights had defined the turbulent 1960s, but now, as the decade drew to a close, the nation seemed to be entering a time of retrenchment and appraisal. It was as if people wanted to stop and catch a breath, to try to access how far they'd come and where, exactly, they were going.

In Hollywood, money continued to prove a prime motivating factor as the power of the studios began to be eroded even further by a new breed of financiers, wildcat investors looking for a quick, one-shot deal. The vast amounts of dollars floating around town enabled a new batch of movie stars to demand—and get—contract amounts beyond the wildest dreams of a Tyrone Power or Norma Shearer.

Unsurprisingly, the ever rising crest of dollars extended beyond the walls of the movie studios. On Rodeo Drive, that world-famous altar of conspicuous consumption, prices rose into the stratosphere as the necessities of modern life were transformed into symbols of wealth by Beverly Hills matrons willing to shell out thousands of movie dollars for Egyptian cotton towels, silk sheets, chinchilla lap robes. Shopping became more than a pastime; it was an obsession, as New Money mavens outbid one another in an attempt to purchase Old Money class (or at least Hollywood's misguided idea of it).

Designer spectacles were currently in (fitted with clear glass for those with 20/20 vision and made of lightweight aluminum frames studded with diamonds and other precious jewels), as was anything from Gucci or Giorgio. The message silkscreened on a white, sixty-five-dollar cotton T-shirt displayed beneath the yellow-and-white awning in Giorgio's storefront window said it all: *He who dies with the most toys wins.*

Shopping wasn't the only indulgence: recreational drug use was common and sex was as popular as ever, providing constant grist for the rumor mills.

To Leigh's dismay, there had been more than one blind article in the gossip columns these past months, hinting at Marissa's reckless behavior.

> *What sizzling sexpot was seen riding off into the sunset on the back of a Harley last week? Word around the biker bars is that this twice-divorced star is no easy rider.*

On the May morning that particular column hit the streets, Leigh was forced to rush to the hospital, where Marissa had just been admitted.

"This has got to stop."

Leigh took hold of Marissa's hand, surreptitiously checking for needle marks on her arm, relieved when she didn't see any.

Angered by the concern she viewed in Leigh's eyes, Marissa turned her head toward the wall. "I don't know what you're talking about. I had a little accident, that's all."

"That's the official studio line. But we know the truth. Marissa, you were beat up. You could have been killed!"

"Don't be so melodramatic."

"I'm not being melodramatic. My God, honey, have you looked in a mirror?"

The emergency room doctor had warned her that her sister's injuries looked a great deal worse than they were. But Leigh had not been able to conceal her shock when she entered the hospital room and saw Marissa's battered face. Both her eyes were rimmed with mottled purple, one was swollen shut. Her cheeks and jaw were a canvas of black and blue, and an ugly row of neat black stitches cut across her top lip.

Marissa glared at Leigh out of her good eye. "You don't have to pretend to be so upset. We both know that you've always been jealous of my looks, of the way men ogle me. Now *you* can be the beautiful sister."

"I've never been jealous of you, Mar. Not ever. From that first day Mother and Daddy brought you home from the hospital, I loved you. I still do."

"You don't have the guts to love anyone. Not really. In fact, if you don't watch it, sister dear, you're going to lose that husband of yours. Matthew is not the kind of guy to sit around and play second fiddle to another man."

"There's no other man in my life."

"Isn't there?" Marissa's cracked lips curved into a lopsided, cruel smile. "What about our dear daddy?"

"Matthew understands that Dad and I work together; it doesn't bother him," Leigh said, not quite convincingly. "Why should it?"

"Why indeed," Marissa murmured. She reached out and turned on the transistor radio Leigh had brought to the hospital. As "Stayin' Alive" blasted over the airwaves, Leigh thought fleetingly about all the people in town, her father included, who'd thought the movie *Saturday Night Fever* to be merely a "nice little story." What she wouldn't give to have the box office receipts for that runaway hit!

"Speaking of Daddy," Marissa said, breaking into Leigh's thoughts, "I don't suppose I can expect a visit?"

It was the very question Leigh had been afraid Marissa was going to ask. "You know what a hectic day it is," she said, trying to hide the anger she felt toward Joshua for refusing to come to the hospital. "What with the Academy Awards tonight, and the party afterward . . ." Her voice trailed off. "Oh, hell, Mar, I'm so sorry."

Marissa shrugged, flinching as the movement caused a jolt of pain in her cracked ribs. "That's okay. It's no secret that he and I have never been close. Not like the two of you."

There was a strange edge to Marissa's tone. The familiar anger was there, but this time there was something else. A dark, ominous note Leigh was still trying to decipher as she drove back home to prepare for the evening's festivities.

"So how is she?"

Matthew leaned against the bathroom doorframe, enjoying the view as Leigh, wrapped in a fluffy peach towel, hurriedly applied her makeup. She'd gotten caught in a traffic jam on the Santa Monica Freeway and was running late.

"She has two black eyes, a split lip, and a pair of cracked ribs. But despite the fact that she resembles an extra from a low-budget horror movie, the doctor assured me that she can leave the hospital tomorrow and return to work in about ten days, after the swelling goes down."

"She was damn lucky."

"Wasn't she?" Leigh put down the gray eyeliner pencil with a soft sigh. "I am so worried about her, Matthew, I don't know what to do."

"Perhaps the first thing you should do is quit bailing her out of these messes."

"Are you saying I should just back away and let something terrible happen to my own sister?"

"No. I'm saying that if Marissa was ever forced to face the consequences of her own behavior, she might develop some responsibility."

"She's facing the consequences," Leigh snapped back. "You didn't see her face, Matthew. I did. Do you have any idea what this will do to her self-esteem? She's always gotten by on her looks; she thinks it's the only thing people value about her."

Personally, Matthew couldn't think of anything else to value about Leigh's younger sister but her looks. And even those were too blatantly obvious for his taste.

"You know, of course, that you have emotional astigmatism where your family is concerned."

"I do not!"

"Your sister's been married twice, she's screwed practically every guy in town, and she's got more drugs in her medicine chest than Walgreen's. But you're constantly viewing her as some innocent victim of circumstances. As for your father, you refuse to admit that he's always done everything he can to break us up."

"Because it isn't true." Turning back toward the mirror, she smudged the liner at the corner of her lids, giving her eyes a smoky appearance.

"Do you honestly believe that there was no one else at Baron Studios capable of handling that Irish problem last week?"

The assistant director had run his car into a farmer's hedge after imbibing too much Guinness at a local pub a few miles outside Cork. The farmer was seeking damages for not only the hedge, but emotional trauma suffered by his livestock: two sheep, an aged, swaybacked gray horse, and a dairy cow.

"We had to send someone with the authority to make a deal with the farmer on the spot."

"You've never heard of lawyers?"

Leigh frowned at him in the mirror. "All right, perhaps my presence wasn't needed, but—"

"How about last month? The trip to Guatemala."

A visa problem. Something that admittedly could have been handled over the phone.

"And let's not forget the little trek to India the month before that," he said before she could answer. "And the three weeks in Cairo last Christmas."

How could she? She'd been surprised to run into Khalil, looking as handsome and exotic as ever. When he'd congratulated her on her marriage, she'd read the questions in his smooth dark eyes and knew he had perceived that her life with Matthew was not the nirvana she'd professed it to be.

"I don't want to fight," she said, turning toward him. "Not tonight."

She'd been planning a special surprise for two weeks. First

they'd attend the Academy Awards ceremony, where Matthew, who was now being touted as Hollywood's new genius, was reported to be a shoe-in for two Oscars this time—for his original screenplay and directing of *Private Screenings*. Afterward, she was going to plead a headache, enabling her to skip her father's party and return home early, where a carefully prepared supper would be waiting. Along with a magnum of iced champagne and a tall stack of Billie Holiday and Smokey Robinson records. After drinking the champagne and dancing to the records, they'd make love. All night long.

She went up on her toes, brushing her lips against his. "I know how you hate these celebrity things. And I truly appreciate your agreeing to come with me."

"I don't like them, but I do understand why you have to attend. And that being the case, I'm not about to sit home and sulk while one of those studio hunks escorts you."

"Thank you, darling. I promise to make it up to you as soon as we get home." She wrapped her arms around his neck; the towel slipped to the white carpeting.

"I have an idea," he said, caressing her neck, her shoulders, her breasts. "Why don't you give me a little sneak preview of things to come?"

The sexual desire swirling in his dark eyes made her knees go weak. Leigh ran her hands over the tautness of his back, reveling in the feel of the rock-hard muscles beneath his white pleated shirt. "We'll be late."

His lips nuzzled her neck. "Our categories won't come up for hours."

"What excuse would we give?"

He cupped her breast, brushing his thumb over her nipple, pleased when it hardened in response to his touch. "The cleaners sent the wrong tux." His hand moved downward. "The dog jumped on your dress with muddy feet and you had to change."

His touch was like tongues of flame, whipping at her flesh. "We don't have a dog."

"You know that and I know that. But no one else does. I've got it." His hand slipped wickedly between her legs, making her gasp with arousal. "We'll say the car broke down on the way to the Music Center."

She'd been hovering on the brink of an orgasm, with the promise of more to come, when his words reminded her of something she'd forgotten. "Oh, no."

"What's the matter now?" A moment later, the buzzer at the security gate sounded. "Who the hell is that?"

"It's probably the chauffeur."

"Chauffeur?"

"Daddy insisted on picking us up in his limousine," she said flatly. "He wanted us to arrive in style."

The mention of Joshua Baron was all it took to curb Matthew's desire. He dropped his hands to his sides. "Then you'd better get dressed. We wouldn't want to keep Daddy waiting."

Scooping up his tuxedo jacket from the arm of the chair, he left the room without a backward glance.

Closing her eyes against an impending headache, Leigh considered that it could be a very long night.

Two days later, Leigh was sitting in a booth at the Polo Lounge, having dinner with Tina. Matthew hadn't complained when she'd informed him that she wouldn't be home for dinner, but Leigh had not taken that as a sign he was over his lingering irritation. He'd barely spoken two words to her since the night of the Awards ceremony.

"God," Tina groaned, "I think I'm going to die."

"You don't look it," Leigh said unsympathetically. "In fact, you look terrific. Exercise obviously agrees with you."

"Not me. If anyone's getting anything out of these torture sessions, it's the masochist I never realized was living inside this aching body." Tina took a drink of Perrier, then looked at the cut-crystal glass as if she wished it contained something stronger. "Who the hell ever invented aerobics, anyway?"

"John Travolta?"

"Uh-uh, although I do blame him for this disco fad; it had to have been the Marquis de Sade. I'm still trying to figure out why I let you talk me into taking that class with you. Sixty minutes of the Bee Gees is fifty-nine too many minutes for me. Whatever happened to Johnny Mathis, anyway?"

Tina reached into her bag before remembering she'd quit smoking six weeks ago. She'd give this damn health kick everyone was touting two more weeks. If she didn't feel like a new woman after that, she was returning to her unchic but highly satisfying bad habits. "By the way, what does Matthew think about eating dinner alone every Tuesday and Thursday while you're trying to reach your maximum heart rate?"

"I doubt if he'd notice."

"Corbett says he's been working awfully hard on his latest screenplay."

"Obsession is more the word," Leigh countered. "Did Corbett tell you that he's been working on this story off and on for nearly ten years, ever since he got back from Vietnam?"

"I knew that." Tina picked unenthusiastically at her dry romaine. Lord, what she'd give for a nice thick steak! "But, now that you mention it, I don't believe Corbett's told me what it's about."

"That's because he doesn't know. No one does."

Tina looked up from her search for nonexistent bay shrimp. "No one? Not even you?"

Leigh's lips firmed. "Not even me."

"How strange."

"He says it's because he doesn't want to risk the story getting out prematurely."

"Well, you can't deny he's got a point. You know as well as I do that this is the smallest back-fence town in America, Leigh. News spreads faster than a fire in the canyons during the Santa Anas."

"I know that," Leigh said softly. She traced small concentric circles on the pink tablecloth with her fingernail. "But wouldn't you think he'd trust his own wife?"

Not if he saw her as his enemy's pawn, Tina mused, thinking of how many times over the past two years Matthew had come over to their house, complaining bitterly about what he viewed as Leigh's unnatural attachment to her father. Despite everything she'd done to convince him that Leigh loved him desperately, Tina could tell that the wedge Joshua had instigated into their marriage was driving them farther and farther apart.

"Marriage isn't always easy, Leigh," she said now, covering the younger woman's hand with her own. "But you and Matthew love one another. And that makes it worth fighting for."

Her words blocked by the sudden lump in her throat, Leigh

nodded. But she couldn't help wondering if she'd already lost the battle.

Less than a week after her dinner with Tina, Leigh crept into the house at dawn, tiptoeing cautiously across the white ceramic floor. When she entered the kitchen, desperate for a cup of coffee, she found Matthew seated at the table.

"Matthew! You scared me!"

The icy look he flashed her was less than encouraging. "Then we're even. Because I was scared to death most of the night. In fact, I was going to give you ten more minutes before I called the police."

"I told you when I called to cancel our dinner plans that I had to run up to Santa Barbara."

"You also said that you'd be back by midnight."

"I know, but—"

"I kept thinking of what I was going to tell the police . . . You see, Officer, I know my wife's met with a terrible accident, because she promised that she wasn't going to let anything keep us from toasting our second anniversary. Especially since she was in Rio de Janeiro for our first—a little problem with filming permits at the Corcovado, and—"

This time it was she who cut him off. "Marissa took an overdose of Seconal. She was barely conscious when I got there. I had to rush her to the hospital."

"Interesting how you arrived just in the nick of time. Isn't that a two-hour drive?"

"A little more than that."

"Yet she managed to OD and remain conscious, waiting all that time for you to arrive. Fascinating."

"Are you accusing my sister of staging a suicide attempt?"

"Damnit, Leigh!" Matthew pushed away from the table, knocking the chair over as he stood up. "Are you that blind? Can't you see that Marissa just wanted to ruin our anniversary? She took those damn pills after she called you. That way she wouldn't risk anything but a sore throat from the stomach pump."

"You don't know that," Leigh countered. A lifetime habit of defending her sister kept her from admitting that the same thought had occurred to her while she'd been pacing back and forth in the corridor outside the emergency room, waiting for the secobarbital to be pumped out of Marissa's system.

"I know that she's a ruthless, self-serving woman who nourishes grudges like other women—healthy women—nourish children. And I know that both she and your father are determined to wreck any chance for happiness that you and I might ever have."

"That's not true."

"Isn't it? Why don't you make up your mind where your loyalties lie, Leigh? With your overly possessive father and that slut of a sister, or the man who loves you."

"I suppose you're referring to yourself?" He certainly hadn't displayed any great love lately. In fact, the last time he'd held her, or kissed her, had been while she'd been getting ready for the Academy Awards last week.

"Yeah. Remember me? The husband? The guy you promised to love, honor, and cherish. Until baby sister calls from an adult motel in some sick bid for attention. Or Daddy feels a need for his dutiful surrogate wife."

All the color drained from Leigh's face. "You can't mean that the way it sounds."

His hurtful words had come from the gut, not his head, but stubborn pride, and envy of the love she so willingly bestowed on two people who didn't begin to deserve it, kept Matthew from retracting his accusation.

"What's the matter? Did I hit a little too close to home with that one?" Pent-up grievances made him rash. "Tell me something . . . If Joshua had called from that motel, would you have rushed up to spend the night with him?"

Her hand shot out. A sound like a gunshot shattered the early-morning calm. Visibly shaken, Leigh stared at her palm, resting on Matthew's rigid cheek, as if wondering who it belonged to.

"Feel better?" His voice was low, deceptively calm, but Leigh could hear the intensity shrouded just below the surface. His dark eyes had hardened, the planes of his face turned to granite.

"No." She put her hands behind her back, twisting her fingers together. Her nervousness was pulsating in the hollow of her throat as she stared at the incriminating white mark left by her palm. She'd never hit anyone in her life. What was happening to her? To them? "Oh God, I hate this," she said, sinking down onto one of the kitchen chairs. "I hate fighting with you."

Matthew watched the unshed tears glisten in her wide gray eyes and fought the urge to go to her. To comfort her. He'd been going crazy all night long worrying that Marissa had gotten her involved in something dangerous this time. For the entire two years of their marriage, he'd lived with the constant fear that one of these days Leigh was going to arrive on her rescue mission and find herself facing one of Marissa's psychotic boyfriends.

He'd sat up, hour after lonely hour, drinking too many pots of strong coffee and waiting. Images flashed through his mind, Leigh bloodied and beaten on the floor of some motel room. Leigh raped. Killed.

This obsession she had with her father and sister, this need to please, her willingness to let the pair of them walk all over her—and her marriage—was tearing his heart out piece by piece. And the damnable thing was, he couldn't even hate her for it.

"I'm going for a walk," he said. He knew he had to get out of the house before he said or did something that would destroy the final fragile bonds between them.

Leigh watched her husband storm out of the kitchen, slamming the door behind him with enough force to make the copper pots hanging on the wall tilt.

And then, giving in to the tears she'd been too proud to shed in front of Matthew, she wept.

33

December 1978

"Did you see this?"

Leigh glanced down at the paper Joshua slammed onto her desk. She'd been forewarned about the story in today's *Variety*; the reporter had called Matthew last night to confirm it.

"I haven't seen it. But I knew it was coming."

"You knew? And you didn't tell me?"

"I only found out last night. What does it say?"

"That your husband has written a screenplay about an actor turned politician. A politician with organized crime ties."

"Is that all?" Leigh asked carefully. Matthew had finally let her read the script for *The Eye of the Tiger* last night and she'd realized immediately that it held bombshell potential.

"No. It also suggests that the primary character bears a striking resemblance to Brendan Farraday."

Whom everyone knew had political ambitions, Leigh tacked on silently. "There may be a few problems," she admitted.

"But the legal department can go over them with Matthew and hash them out."

"Impossible. I want the project dropped."

"Dropped?" Leigh stared up at her father in disbelief. "You haven't even read it."

"I don't care. Baron Studios is not going to make this film. And that's final."

"I'm afraid that's not entirely your decision," she said quietly. "You authorized my autonomy six years ago when you agreed that I could start Sundown Productions."

"Damnit, you can't make this movie!"

"Why? Do you really hate Matthew so much that you'd try to block a project he's been working on for years?"

"It's not a matter of how *I* feel about the screenplay. There are other players in the game, Leigh. Players who do not want this picture made."

"Who?"

"It's better you don't know. What you must realize is that it would be better—and safer—for all of us if this script was allowed to die a natural death."

"I understand your concern, but don't you see? If we give in to these people, these outsiders, we'll be compromising everything we've worked so hard to achieve. Everything Grandfather worked for." She took a deep breath before continuing. "Matthew has written a compelling screenplay and I'm going to turn it into the best movie of the decade. Perhaps the best movie Baron Studios has ever made."

Joshua knew that his own father would have admired Leigh's steely strength. But damnit, she could end up getting them all killed. "Isn't there anything I could say to change your mind?"

"Nothing."

Heaving a sigh, Joshua turned to leave the room. Halting in the doorway, he looked back over his shoulder at the daughter who'd never given him a moment's grief until that bastard St. James had entered her life. "I love you, Leigh. And I've always acknowledged your superb judgment."

She nodded. "Thank you."

"But this time, you're making a lethal mistake."

* * *

Her father's words of warning rang in her ears like a death knell, interrupting her work, disturbing her sleep. Only Matthew's unflagging enthusiasm for his project eased her unrelenting stress. For the first time in weeks—months—they were working together during the day and making love at night with an exuberant joy she'd worried they might never recover. And that, she decided as she dressed for her father's annual Christmas gala, was worth a few sleepless nights.

Joshua's elaborate holiday decorations could have put Fantasyland to shame. Every tree on the grounds had been strung with tiny white fairy lights, filling the night with bright, twinkling stars. A twenty-five-foot, white-flocked Douglas fir claimed center stage, dressed with antique gold ornaments, majestic in silver spotlights. Waiters, clad in gold, silver, and crimson metallic harlequin costumes, circulated with gleaming gold trays upon which rested slender silver goblets of Louis Roederer Cristal champagne. At the center of each silver lamé kilted table were graceful sprays of pungent pine and holly, adorned with shiny gold, silver, and scarlet balls. Continuing the theme, battery-operated lights added sparkle to the centerpieces.

"My God, Joshua's gone and re-created the courtyard of the Sun God," Tina said as she and Corbett arrived at the Baron estate. Dressed in a gold-shot Mary McFadden chiffon evening gown, her dark hair elaborately French-braided, she was Beverly Hills chic personified.

"Either that or King Midas's winter resort," Corbett murmured, eyeing a nearby fountain that for this one memorable night was frothily spouting champagne.

"Don't blame me," a feminine voice behind them offered. "Since I've been too busy with Matthew's new screenplay to arrange any parties, Daddy hired outside help."

Tina turned and hugged Leigh, exchanging cheek kisses. "Darling, I've missed you! That damn aerobics class just isn't the same without you to keep me in step." She backed up, giving the younger woman an appreciative glance. "You look positively delicious," she decided, eyeing the pencil-slim strapless white dress embroidered with silver flowers. Leigh's hair was a silver blond froth, left free and flowing at her husband's request.

"Like an angel," Matthew said, arriving in time to hear Tina's compliment. "My angel." He put his arm around her, drawing her close.

"Gracious." Leigh blushed as she looked up at her husband, resplendent in white tie. "You keep talking like that, Mr. St. James, and people will think we're newlyweds."

"That's the way I've been feeling lately, Mrs. St. James." It was wonderful to be able to enjoy Leigh out of bed as much as in! Over these past months Matthew had felt freer, happier, than he ever could have imagined, despite a faint, lingering fear that such unmitigated joy was tempting fate.

When Leigh and Matthew exchanged a long, intimate look, Corbett cleared his throat. "Well, it was great seeing both of you," he said expansively. "But from the way Tina's tugging on my arm, I think it's time to mingle."

Engrossed in one another, neither Leigh nor Matthew noticed their departure.

"Well, that's certainly a relief," Tina said, plucking a goblet from a passing tray. "I was afraid, for a while, that they weren't going to make it."

"You weren't the only one." Corbett reached out and touched her cheek. "Sometimes I think we're the only happily married couple in this town."

"I know." She covered his hand with hers. "But I do so want Matthew and Leigh to be as happy as we are."

His gaze held a warmth that belied twenty-one years of marriage. "Impossible."

Seeking a break from the barrage of questions about Matthew's screenplay, Leigh escaped to a far corner of the garden. Had the night ever smelled so fragrantly sweet? she wondered, breathing in the scent of the bright winter flowers. Somewhere out of sight a cricket clicked his lonely song. There was a ring around the white-misted moon and Leigh was looking up at it, marveling at how near it seemed, when Brendan Farraday's booming voice shattered her introspection.

"Leigh," he said, "you're looking absolutely gorgeous tonight."

"Why, thank you, Brendan. You're looking quite handsome yourself." It was true. Like so many of Tinseltown's aging

stars, Brendan actually seemed to grow more handsome—
more distinguished looking—with the years.

"Yessir," he said, nodding his head as his blue eyes moved
from the top of her head down to her toes, clad in silvery silk
high heels. "You're quite a vision." Farraday was famed for
his love of Western art and, at the moment, Leigh felt like a
piece of Remington bronze he was appraising for his collection. "Your husband's a very lucky man."

Leigh smiled. "I'll tell him you said so."

"I'll be the first to admit that Matthew and I didn't really
hit it off when we were working on *Dangerous,* but you know,
Leigh, I do admire that young man's talent. Yessir," he said
reflectively, "your husband has a rare and special gift. I'd hate
to see him ruin his career."

"That isn't going to happen."

"It sure as hell might if he ends up in court defending a libel
suit. Face it, Leigh, this is a company town; the powers that
be in Hollywood don't like controversy. If Baron Studios insists on making this movie, you may just find the ranks closing
against you."

His threat only strengthened her resolve. "Go ahead and
sue," she suggested, brushing past him on her way back to the
party. "It will only earn *The Eye of the Tiger* more publicity."

He grabbed hold of her arm, spinning her back toward him.
"Just a minute," he ground out. "I'm not finished talking to
you."

"Tough." She met his suddenly dangerous gaze unflinchingly. "Because I'm through listening."

"No you're not." As his fingers dug into the soft flesh of her
upper arm, Farraday demonstrated that he had not gotten
where he was by walking away from a fight. "You go ahead
and make your precious picture, baby. But you'll only have
yourself to blame if something happens to your husband
before you ever get it to the screen."

Leigh's blood chilled; his soft words seemed to come hurl-
ing directly at her, one at a time, shattering like glass at her
feet. "Are you threatening me?"

He shrugged. "Accidents happen." Point made, he released her and faded back into the shadows. A moment later,
she heard him loudly enjoying something one of the guests

had said, his robust laugh sounding as if nothing had happened.

Tina stood hidden in the shadows, listening to Farraday threaten Leigh. Some things—some people—never changed.

Thirty-seven years ago, she'd been a promising young actress at Baron Studios. She had appeared in three pictures when, cast in the role of a dancer who enrolls in college and falls in love with her staid mathematics professor, Tina brought three things to the screen that captured the audience's immediate attention: a pair of long, shapely legs that rivaled Betty Grable's, a cleavage that Jane Russell was rumored to have envied, and a sexy, comedic talent that Judy Holliday invented and Marilyn Monroe would later perfect.

In short, the former Teresa Salerno was a girl headed straight for the top, which was why Joshua Baron decided to cast the newcomer in Brendan Farraday's next picture. The only fly in the ointment was that Farraday had seigneurial rights, which meant, Tina's agent explained, that if Farraday didn't like her, she'd be off the picture. The agent snapped her manicured fingers. Like that.

The warning flew right over the top of Tina's head. Of course he'd like her; what was not to like? When the call came from his secretary, inviting her to a dinner party at his home, Tina vowed that by the time the evening was over, she'd have Brendan Farraday eating out of the palm of her hand. No one had ever accused Tina Salerno of not possessing self-confidence.

She arrived at Farraday's Laurel Canyon home clad in a velvet dinner dress worn by Joan Fontaine in her Oscar-winning performance in *Suspicion*. Her roommate, a costumer at RKO, had "borrowed" the dress for this important evening.

By morning, the dress was in tatters and Tina was back at her apartment, where Farraday's chauffeur had delivered her after a seemingly endless night of sexual abuse. Mottled purple and yellow bruises darkened her breasts, her legs, her buttocks. The smooth skin of her inner thighs was marred with teeth marks; blood and semen oozed out of her vagina and rectum.

"You have to call the cops," Tina's roommate insisted. "Star or not, you can't let the bastard get away with this."

"No," Tina managed through split and swollen lips. "No one would ever believe me."

"But I knew where you were going. I can testify for you."

"No!" Now that the shock was wearing off, Tina was on the verge of hysteria. Farraday's warning kept coming back to her. He had friends, important friends, who would not hesitate to kill her if she caused him any trouble. Something in his eyes had assured Tina that the movie star was telling the truth.

"At least I'm going to call a doctor."

Tina began to shake uncontrollably. "I can't risk it."

"Hey, don't worry. This guy is discreet. He does all the studio abortions."

"All right," Tina acquiesced. "But he has to swear never to tell anyone." As her roommate went out in the hall, where the building's single pay phone was located, Tina said on a ragged sob, "I got the part."

Leigh had almost managed to convince herself that Brendan Farraday's veiled threat was nothing more than the blustering of an angry man who'd drunk too much champagne, when Tina suddenly appeared from out of the shadows.

"Tina," she said with a start, "you frightened me."

"Not as much as Brendan Farraday already has, I imagine."

"You know Brendan when he's been drinking."

"Yes," Tina answered in a low, flat voice. "I know Brendan."

Leigh looked at the older woman more closely, alerted by her strangely trembling tone. Instead of the self-confidence Tina usually wore like a second skin, she looked nervous. But there was another expression on her face as well. Something that looked strangely like fear.

"Is anything wrong?"

"Yes. Something is terribly wrong." Taking a deep breath, Tina told her story falteringly, in vivid, unrelenting detail. "Of course I never went back to the studio," she said. "A few weeks later, after the bruises faded, I got a job answering the phone in a real-estate office around the corner from my apartment. After awhile, I got a license and began dabbling in sales, and one thing led to another and, well, here I am."

Leigh shook her head in shock and admiration. "This town is overrun with people who have reinvented themselves, but you've definitely outdone them all."

"I've done okay. Although I'll always regret that I couldn't have put that bastard Farraday in jail where he belongs."

"Now I understand why you've always hated him," Leigh said. "Does Corbett know?"

All the color drained from Tina's face. "Of course not. And you can't tell him."

"Why did you tell me?"

"I wanted you to understand that Brendan Farraday is a dangerous man. He's vicious, brutal, and he'd have someone killed without so much as a backwards glance." Looking nervously at the French doors, she said, "I've got to get back before Corbett starts looking for me." She placed her hand on Leigh's arm. "You have to do whatever it takes to stop this movie, Leigh. For Matthew's sake." And then she was gone.

Alone again, Leigh wrapped her arms around herself in an unconscious gesture of self-protection. She'd been so happy when she'd arrived at the party tonight. So hopeful. And then, in a few short moments, Brendan Farraday had managed to threaten everything that she held dear.

"There you are!" Matthew strode across the brick terrace toward Leigh. "I've been looking all over for you."

"I needed a breath of air."

"You're shivering." Taking off his coat, he slipped it over her bare shoulders. "Better?"

"I love you," she whispered softly, desperately. "Whatever happens, it's important that you know that."

"I do." He looked at her with a mixture of curiosity and concern. "Are you all right?"

"Of course." She took a deep breath that should have calmed her but didn't. "Can we go home now?"

Questions still lingering in his eyes, he lowered his lips to hers. "Sweetheart, I thought you'd never ask."

"I've got good news."

Leigh schooled her face to a calm, interested expression as

she faced William Zimmerman across her desk. The energetic, personable young attorney was one of Baron Studios'
latest acquisitions, hired after his graduation from Stanford
Law last June. In six short months he'd proven himself invaluable, and Leigh would not be at all surprised if he'd made it
to the top of the department before he turned thirty.

"I'm always in the mood for good news."

"*The Eye of the Tiger* isn't going to cause any major problems."

Her stomach dropped to the floor. It was not the news she'd
been hoping for. "Oh? Are you sure?"

"Well, there are a couple of scenes that could cause a problem, but nothing that can't easily be changed."

"Matthew is not willing to alter his script in order to avoid
a lawsuit."

"We're only talking about a few lines, Leigh. Nothing that
would diminish the integrity of the story." He looked at her
curiously. "You don't seem very happy about this. I figured
you'd be dancing on air."

Leigh forced a smile. "I appreciate all the work you've
done, William, but I'm afraid that after examining the matter
very carefully, I've come to the conclusion that making this
movie would put Baron Studios in jeopardy. Something I
cannot allow to happen."

"But, Leigh—"

"And that's why I'm going to ask that you render an opinion that Baron Studios should not finance this project."

He stared at her, thunderstruck. "But, Leigh, I've already
told you, there isn't any problem. I don't understand, it's a
terrific script, it's going to make a dynamite movie. My God,
it's your very own husband's project. How can you turn it
down?"

Leigh's gaze turned glacial, her words clipped. "I've explained my position. Now, will you write the opinion, or must
I ask another attorney in the department to handle it for me?"

Zimmerman's shoulders slumped visibly as he pushed himself out of the chair. "Of course I'll do it."

Leigh nodded, appearing coolly satisfied, even as her heart
was beating so hard and fast she wondered if she could be
having a heart attack. "Thank you. Oh, and William?"

He turned in the office doorway. "Yes?"

"I'd like to keep this meeting between us, if you don't mind."

His intelligent brown eyes searched her face. "Of course."

The moment she was alone, Leigh began to tremble violently. By behaving contrary to every rule of her life, she had saved Matthew's life. But at what cost?

34

Accustomed to overcoming obstacles, Matthew took Baron Studios' legal department report with a stoicism that was second nature. He was only sorry that the decision not to fund his film had caused a renewed rift with Leigh. For some reason he could not understand, when he announced his intention to seek independent financing, she had become almost hysterical.

It wasn't like Leigh to be so emotional, Matthew mused as he left the Polo Lounge. He'd just concluded an uneventful meeting with a potential backer—a Swiss banker from Zurich—when he ran into Jeff Martin.

"Hey, dude," Jeff said, swaying dangerously on his feet. "How're they hangin'?"

"Okay," Matthew said. "How are things with you?" Not that it wasn't obvious. Jeff's long, lank hair was unwashed, tied back with a leather thong, and his square jaw was covered with a three-day stubble of beard.

"Lookin' up, man. Looking better every day."

"I'm glad."

"In fact, I'm about to hit the big time."

How many times had he heard that? "Well, good luck."

"Yessir," Jeff mumbled, more to himself than to Matthew, "old Jeff's gonna be living on Easy Street pretty soon. Thanks to old man Baron."

He'd been on the way to his car, but at Jeff's words, Matthew abruptly turned around. "Joshua?"

"You know another Baron? Except the two chicks." Jeff giggled nervously. "Whoops, sorry, dude. I just remembered, one of those chicks is your old lady, huh?"

Matthew ignored the reference to Leigh. He worried that Jeff was involved in some new scheme with Marissa and, although he personally didn't give a damn about his sister-in-law, Leigh did. The one thing their already strained marriage didn't need right now was another crisis.

"What business do you have with Baron?"

"Old Josh is my ace in the hole." He grinned. "Which, I guess, makes you the king of the deck."

"Me?"

"Sure. The way I figure it, now that you're a big honcho, Baron should be willing to pay a bundle to keep anyone from finding out that he was the one who arranged your drug bust. Speaking of which," he said, "how the hell did you ever get out of that place? The old man just about had a stroke when he found out you'd escaped."

Matthew told himself that he should be feeling something—shock, anger, disbelief. But Jeff's words only confirmed a deep-seated suspicion he'd harbored for years. A suspicion he'd never shared with anyone. Who would have believed him?

"Sounds as if you've struck pay dirt," Matthew agreed easily. "Why don't we go get a beer and you can fill me in on the details."

"Great. It'll be just like old times. The two caballeros."

"Yeah," Matthew muttered. "Just like old times."

Two hours later, after Jeff had managed to recall specific details, Matthew confirmed that this was not some hallucination born in his old friend's sodden, burned-out brain. As he left the bar, Matthew decided that the time had come for Leigh to know the truth. About everything.

"I don't believe it!" Stricken, Leigh stared at Matthew. "You're only saying this because Baron Studios refused to finance *The Eye of the Tiger*."

Matthew understood that Leigh's first reaction would be denial. It was only natural, given her close ties to her father. He had laid it all out for her, including Jeff's participation in exchange for that small part in *Dangerous*.

"It's true, Leigh."

"No!" Hair pins scattered onto the tile floor as she shook her head. "Jeff's mistaken. Or he's lying." She grasped onto that idea like a drowning woman might cling to a life raft. "That's it," she said. "Don't you see? He and Marissa cooked this up. It's just another one of Marissa's schemes to get back at Father for treating her so abominably all these years."

"Leigh. Honey." He captured her wildly moving hands. "It has to be the truth. He knew too many details."

Pulling free of Matthew's light hold, she shrunk away from him. "It's a lie," she repeated. "A filthy, rotten, hurtful lie."

"Why don't you ask Joshua?"

"That's exactly what I intend to do."

As coldly furious as he was at Joshua, and as much as he wished Leigh had accepted his words at face value, Matthew understood her need to hear the truth directly from the source. "Let's go."

"No. I have to do this myself."

He grabbed her arm. "For God's sake, Leigh, you're in no condition to drive."

"Let go of me!" She shook him away. "Leave me alone!"

Matthew watched Leigh storm from the house. A moment later, he heard the roar of the Jaguar's engine and the squeal of tires as she tore away from the house.

Some days it just didn't pay to get out of bed.

Leigh broke every speeding statute on the books racing to Beverly Hills. A million thoughts tumbled around in her brain—spinning, swirling, colliding wildly. Questions without answers. Answers to questions she'd never dared ask.

She didn't want to believe her father capable of such treachery. But then she remembered that long-ago incident with Chance Murdock, when rumors had Joshua responsible for the teen idol's arrest, and wondered.

She found Joshua in the library.

"Darling," he said, greeting her with a broad smile, "what a nice surprise! Tell me that you're staying for dinner and I'll have Maria fix your favorite—veal piccata."

Leigh ignored both his welcome and his culinary bribe. "Did you have Matthew arrested in Mexico?"

He'd been waiting for this for years. Now that the moment of truth had finally arrived, Joshua found himself strangely calm. "Where did you get an idea like that?"

He looked like the MGM lion, confidently sprawled back in his leather-tooled chair. King of the jungle. Leigh had never realized, until now, exactly how brutal her father's jungle was.

"From Matthew."

"Honey, Matthew is angry about our refusing to finance his picture. Actually, I don't blame him; I'd be madder than hell myself, under the circumstances. He's just blowing off steam."

She had observed her father in enough meetings to know when he was bluffing. She watched him watching her and felt sick. "Matthew had lunch at the Polo Lounge today. He was meeting with a Swiss financier."

"I'd like to say I wish him luck. But we both know that would be a lie."

"And you never lie, do you, Daddy?"

There was something about Leigh's tone that made Joshua break out into a sudden sweat. "Never." He pushed himself out of the chair, experiencing an attack of vertigo when he stood up. "Since it's cocktail time, I believe I'll have a drink. Can I get you anything, princess?"

"No, thank you. Matthew ran into Jeff Martin. He was drunk."

"That's hardly surprising," Joshua remarked, pouring Scotch into a glass. "The man's no damn good; he and your sister are two of a kind."

"He may have a drinking problem," Leigh acknowledged. "But he seems to have a remarkable sense of recall. He re-

membered everything that happened when he and Matthew
went to Mexico.''

"Oh?'' The fingers of his right hand were numb, as if they'd
gone to sleep, and pressure was building behind his eye.

"He also had some interesting things to say about a deal
you supposedly made with him.''

Joshua tilted his head back and poured the Scotch down his
throat. The liquor coursed through him, warming his blood,
easing the painful tension that seemed to have his head in a
steel vise. "I knew it would have to come out one day.''

"Then you did conspire to have Matthew arrested? You
paid Jeff to plant those drugs on him?''

"Of course.'' Joshua refilled his glass. "I also arranged for
that Mexican extra to play the part of his wife.''

"The wedding picture was a composite.''

"An especially clever one, I thought. And if you're expecting me to apologize, you're going to be disappointed, Leigh.
In fact, not only am I not sorry, I'd do it all again, if it meant
keeping that bastard away from you.''

Leigh knew the pain and anger and recrimination would
come later, once the shock had worn off. Right now, she felt
numb. But she knew exactly what she had to do.

"I'm leaving Baron Studios.''

Joshua would have laughed at that, but his breath was coming in short puffs, and all he could manage was a ragged snort.
"You got away with that melodramatic ultimatum once,
sweetheart, but it isn't going to work this time. You'll never
leave Baron; the studio's in your blood. It's family. More than
that overrated bastard you're living with could ever be.''

Inside she was trembling like a leaf; outside Leigh appeared
calm. "Matthew's illegitimacy was none of his doing,'' she
responded icily. "Some other men are bastards by choice. My
resignation will be on your desk first thing tomorrow morning.'' On legs that felt like rubber, she turned to walk away.

"Grandstanding doesn't suit you, Leigh,'' Joshua called
after her. "Go ahead, leave if you want. After you discover
that there's not a studio in town who'll go against me and hire
you, you'll be back. On your knees.'' He shook his fist at her
rigid back. "On your knees, girl. Damnit, do you hear me?''

She turned, her eyes like cold gray stones. "I hear you. And not that my life is any of your concern, but I have no intention of seeking employment at any other studio. I'm going into independent production with my husband. Together we're going to make *The Eye of the Tiger*."

She was going to leave him. For that bastard. For Matthew St. James. He wouldn't allow that to happen. Joshua came after her, pushing Leigh against the carved mahogany door. His body pressed against hers; his large hands tangled cruelly in her hair and, before she could cry out, his mouth was eating into hers.

As his tongue thrust past the barrier of her teeth, a flood of memories came pouring forth from some dark, secret well inside Leigh. Memories she had blocked from her conscious mind years ago.

She had been a month shy of her sixth birthday when her father had come to tuck her in to bed.

"Whose little girl are you?" he asked the familiar bedtime question, his lips grazing her temple.

"Yours," she responded as she always did.

"Such a pretty girl," he murmured, his wide hand stroking her hair. "The prettiest girl in the world." He tugged at the pink ribbon at the ruffled neck of the white cotton nightgown.

"Prettier than Laura Lang?" she asked coyly, naming one of the studio's current child stars.

"Laura Lang looks like the Wicked Witch of the West compared to my princess," Joshua said, caressing the satiny skin revealed by the now open neckline. Something in his touch was strangely different tonight. Fear skimmed up Leigh's spine. Joshua felt her slight tremor.

"Shh. It's okay," he soothed. His hand trailed farther down her flat child's chest.

"Nanny says I shouldn't let people touch me," Leigh whispered as her father's treacherous hand crept lower, making slow, concentric circles against her stomach.

"Nanny means strangers. I'm your daddy. And I love you."

"I love you too, Daddy," she said, her voice muffled by the nightgown he was tugging over her head. "More than anything."

"I know." His hands trembled as they caressed her, stroking her body, playing with the soft pink folds no one ever touched. Even Nanny, after bathing Leigh, would invariably hand her the soft white towel, briskly instructing her to dry her "privates." Instinctively, Leigh pressed her legs together.

"Don't turn away from your daddy." His palms pressed lightly but firmly against her inner thighs. "I love you, princess. Let me show you how much."

He'd said the magic word. Leigh opened to him, allowing his long fingers to invade her most secret recesses. He was hurting her, but she didn't cry. Instead, she closed her eyes and reminded herself that her daddy loved her.

His fingers were deep inside her now, pressing, probing. Hurting. Daddy loves me.

His mouth covered hers, his tongue thrusting cruelly between her startled lips. Loves me.

He fumbled with his clothing, then grasped her hand and wrapped it around his penis. It was big and strong and pulsing. Leigh pulled away.

"No, damnit," he muttered harshly, curving her fingers back around his swollen penis, holding her hand in place with his own stronger one, moving their joined hands back and forth, faster and faster and faster until his body tensed and he pressed his mouth against hers again, expelling a tortured cry between her dry lips. Less than a heartbeat later, a hot, sticky substance shot out over her stomach and thighs. He loves me.

Her father lay atop her, heavy and inert, for what seemed an eternity. Finally he pushed himself up and, without a word, staggered unsteadily from the room.

Leigh lay alone on her rumpled, soiled sheets, tears streaming down her face. Pain radiated outward from her violated core like red-hot needles, and her heart was filled with fear. She began to shiver violently.

That was how Joshua found her when he returned with a warm washcloth and fresh sheets. Leigh concentrated on the now soothing touch of his hands—those same hands that had earlier caused such unexpected pain—as he bathed her in the scented water and changed her nightgown. Then he carried her over to the antique rocking chair in the corner, where she curled her legs under her and watched as he stripped the bed of the stained, flower-sprigged sheets and replaced them with crisp, ironed ones.

"Do you still love your daddy?" Joshua asked, tucking her back in the freshly made bed.

"Yes," she answered in a small voice that sounded as if it were coming from the bottom of the sea.

He ran the back of his hand down her cheek. "And I love you. More than your mother, or anyone. You're my own special princess."

She ignored a faint stab of guilt about enjoying her exalted position over her mother, choosing instead to bask in the warmth of her father's affection.

"But some people might not understand our special love." He frowned and brushed her silky hair away from her small, pale face. "Some people might want to hurt us."

"Hurt us?" Leigh asked uncomprehendingly. "Why?"

"Because they're jealous. They might even try to take you away from me."

Her child's heart froze; the shivering began anew. "No!"

Joshua took hold of her icy, trembling hands and lifted them to his lips. "I won't let them," he promised. "But you're going to have to help."

Her father was so strong. So brave. So important. How could a little girl like her help him with anything? "How?"

"We have to keep tonight a secret," he said, his eyes locking on to hers as if he could see all the way to the depths of her soul. "Our own special secret."

It would be years before Leigh fully understood the pact she had entered into that night.

"Our own secret," she repeated gravely.

"No!" Pushing against his shoulders, Leigh broke free of her father's smothering hold. "Let go of me!"

His face was the color of paste, his eyes glazed, beads of sweat glistening on his upper lip. "You've got the wrong idea," he stammered, reaching for her once again.

"Don't touch me," she shrieked, recoiling, slapping away at his outstretched hands. "Don't you understand? I remember. I remember everything."

Her words were an indistinct rumbling in his ears. A terrible pain stabbed into his temple like a sword of flame. "Princess—"

"Don't you ever call me that again, you selfish, unfeeling son of a bitch. Goddamnit, I remember!"

A veil was coming over his eyes. Fireworks were exploding in his brain. "You can't talk to me like that. I'm your father."

"You're a dirty, child-molesting pervert." Feelings of betrayal came boiling to the surface—furious, bitter feelings she had kept locked away for years.

He tried to explain, to tell her about Signe's infidelity, his own impotence, but the words were blocked by some towering, unseen barricade in his brain and wouldn't come.

Leigh's angry words were like bullets, coming fast and hard, striking him without pity. Joshua lurched, then crumpled to the floor.

35

The hours dragged by while Leigh waited for some word of her father's condition. She'd ridden with him in the ambulance to the hospital, racked with guilt as the paramedics struggled to keep him alive.

A pretty blond candy striper brought her a cup of coffee from the vending machine down the hall. It tasted like battery acid, but she drank it, in lieu of anything stronger. She listened to the anonymous, disembodied voices paging doctors, announcing indecipherable codes.

Shortly after arriving at the hospital, she telephoned Matthew, only to have their housekeeper tell her that he'd gone out. No, he hadn't said when he'd be back. Feeling as if her entire life was crumbling down around her, all Leigh could do was leave a message. And pray.

The shift changed. New nurses, their virginal white uniforms starched and clean, their manner brisk and efficient, came on duty. Leigh's vigil continued.

"Ms. Baron?" A solemn-faced doctor clad in rumpled white slacks, white shoes, and a long white lab jacket appeared in the doorway. He looked every bit as exhausted as Leigh felt.

"Yes?"

"I'm Dr. Britton. Since your father's doctor is attending a medical conference in New York, I've been assigned his case."

"I've been so worried. Is he—" She couldn't say the word.

"Your father has suffered a cerebral vascular accident. A stroke. But he's holding his own. For now. He's been moved to ICU."

"May I see him?"

He shook his head. "I'm afraid that wouldn't be advisable. He's still unconscious."

"But—"

"He wouldn't even know you were there." His intelligent blue eyes professionally examined her too pale face. "Go home, Ms. Baron," he suggested gently. "Get some rest."

"I can't leave without seeing my father. Please. Tell me. Is he going to live?"

"I can't promise anything at this point. The next few days will determine his prognosis for recovery."

Leigh wondered how she would ever be able to look at her father—think of him—without the treachery of his actions standing between them. She could not forgive Joshua, but neither could she ignore the gravity of his condition. Or the inescapable fact that she was responsible for his stroke. All her life she'd believed that if she could only avoid tension and controversy, everything would turn out all right. And what had she done? The first time she lost her temper and fought back, she'd nearly killed her father.

"If he dies, it'll be my fault. We had an argument." She drew in a long, shuddering breath. "I said some terrible things."

Putting aside professional distance, he took hold of her ice cold hand. "Every family argues."

"We never did. I always tried to live up to my father's expectations." Oh God, she thought, she was already talking about Joshua as if he were dead.

"Every family," the doctor repeated gently. "Even the famous ones." He squeezed her fingers. "Believe it or not, there are times my children dare argue with me. And in the event the worst-case scenario does occur, it's important for you to know that you didn't kill your father, Ms. Baron. His records indicate that he's had high blood pressure for several years. He could have had this stroke at any time—on the golf course, the tennis court, at work."

"But he didn't," Leigh said on something perilously close to a sob. "Don't you see, he had it with me. Because of me."

He eyed her more intently. "I don't normally believe in prescribing sedatives, but I think in your case—"

"No." Leigh drew in another deep breath. "I'll be fine. As soon as I see my father."

"You're a stubborn young woman, aren't you, Ms. Baron?"

"That's what I've been told."

The doctor rubbed his weary face with his hand, making Leigh suddenly feel sorry for him, surrounded by so much suffering and death. "You may see him for ten minutes," he decided.

"Every hour?"

"You're staying all night." It was not a question.

"I'm staying until my father regains consciousness."

"I'd hate to ever have to negotiate a contract with you," he relented on a sigh. "All right. Ten minutes every hour."

She had never expected any other outcome.

The ICU was blindingly lit. Nurses moved across the shiny tile floors on silent, rubber-soled shoes, their starched skirts making a soft, swishing sound as they went from patient to patient. The hushed room smelled like disinfectant and disease and death.

Joshua regained consciousness in the early hours of the morning. Leigh was standing beside his bed, watching the machines whisper and beep as they measured out his life. After a lifetime of thinking of her father as larger than life, she was stunned to see him looking so weak. So helpless. His skin was the flat color of putty, he was paralyzed, and he'd lost the power of speech. All he could do was stare impotently up at her, his pleading eyes moist with tears.

He was, Leigh reminded herself, guilty of the most pernicious behavior. She'd always thought of herself as a truthful person, yet in order to protect his own selfish interests, her father had encouraged her to spend years lying to herself. So many lies. So much deception.

Matthew found Leigh pacing the floor of the waiting room. She was wearing the same ivory suit she'd had on when she left the house late yesterday afternoon to go confront her father.

"I just heard."

His day-old growth of beard suggested that he'd spent the night away from home. With another woman? When that thought didn't wound her to the core, Leigh realized that even if her husband had been out committing adultery, at this moment, she was simply too emotionally drained to care.

"I left word with Ingrid."

"Have you been alone all this time?"

She looked around the deserted room as if surprised by his question. "Yes."

"Why didn't you call Tina and Corbett? Or Kim?"

She brushed at the wrinkles crisscrossing her silk skirt. "I didn't think of it."

"I'll call."

"No." Leigh lowered her eyes, terrified that he might view her secret shame. She felt as if a scarlet A had been emblazoned on her chest. "Really, Matthew, I just want to be alone right now."

He was going to lose her. Matthew could feel it coming and was damned if he knew how to stop it. "Alone with Joshua, you mean."

"They don't know if he's going to live or die. I'm all he has. If I desert him now, that might make a difference. And if he died because of me, I'd never forgive myself."

"You take too much responsibility onto yourself, Leigh. You always have. Your father, Marissa, the studio. You can't control the entire world."

They were standing at opposite ends of the small room, like combatants. "I don't want to control the entire world," she argued weakly. "Just my own little corner of it."

"Sometimes we can't even do that. No matter how hard we try."

"He needs me," she whispered.

If he dragged Leigh away now, with her father's life hanging in the balance, and the bastard died, Matthew knew it would haunt her—and their marriage—forever. "All right. I can understand the emotional strain you're under right now. So at least tell me that when I go to the studio to clear out my office, I can pack your things as well."

It was one thing to turn her back on the studio when her father was capable of running things. But now . . . oh, God, he'd been right about her all along, she realized unhappily. The studio was in her blood. It was the embodiment of the only family she'd ever known.

"Matthew, I can't. Not now." She dragged her trembling fingers through her hair. "Baron Studios has been in the family for more than half a century. It's my roots. I can't just turn my back on it and allow it to go under without a Baron at the helm. What about all the people who work there? I have to think of them."

He'd never known roots. There had been times, during his marriage to Leigh, that Matthew had actually believed that he might be developing some, putting them down in the sandy soil of Santa Monica, building a life not only for them, but for future generations. Obviously he'd been wrong.

It was bad enough that she was staying here at the hospital, with his enemy, but to choose Joshua Baron's empire over their marriage . . . Matthew could only view her behavior as betrayal.

"Is there any chance of changing your mind?" His voice was even. Calm. Only his rigid jaw and his white-knuckled clenched fists revealed his smoldering anger.

Leigh bit her lip. "No."

He exhaled a long, weary breath. "Then I'll be moving out of the house."

Why couldn't he understand? Her heart torn, Leigh could think of no words to stop him. It appeared that her choice was between the death of her marriage or the death of her father. Along with the business both her father and grandfather had struggled so hard to keep in the family. As much as she loved Matthew, as much as she wished she could bridge the distance that yawned between them, Leigh felt as if she had no choice.

"If that's really what you want to do."

"I'll be staying at the Wilshire."

"Fine." The problems between them could be ironed out, Leigh tried to tell herself. She loved Matthew. And he loved her. He'd be back.

"If you'd send my files and any mail I might get, I'd appreciate it."

"Of course."

They were hurting one another, but unable to stop, both had retreated behind their separate barricades of unbreachable pride. "Well, I guess I'd better be going."

Her throat burning, Leigh turned away, unwilling to watch Matthew walk away from everything they'd worked to build together.

Hours later Joshua's doctor put his foot down and threatened to withdraw her visiting privileges unless she got some rest. As she drove through the dark and deserted streets to Santa Monica, images and conversations whirled around in her mind. Her confrontation with her father, the horrible sight of him falling to the floor, the painful image of Matthew's rigid face as he forced her to choose between love and responsibility.

She entered her house, went into the bathroom, and stared at the wan, guilty face she saw in the mirror. "It was just a fluke," she whispered. "Just a one-time thing. He was drunk. I remember the smell of liquor on his breath." She dragged her hands through her hair. "It was just a fluke," she repeated. Then she dropped to her knees and was violently sick in the toilet bowl.

Much later, seeking something to do to take her mind off problems she was not yet prepared to confront, Leigh went into the kitchen and surveyed the contents of the refrigerator. Sitting down at the kitchen table, she made a list for the housekeeper, adding the beer Matthew preferred before she remembered she wouldn't need to buy it anymore.

Someday, she assured herself, all this would seem like a story. An old movie that Baron Studios had produced and then put away in the vault. A movie that was forgotten long before the delicate celluloid film turned to dust.

But as she stared unseeingly into the well of darkness out the window, Leigh knew that the scene she and Matthew had played out in the hospital waiting room was no movie. It was her marriage that had disintegrated to dust.

Unable to deal with such a devastating loss while her father's life hung in the balance, Leigh pushed it away, deep inside her brain, where she wouldn't have to look at it.

Only later, when her heart stopped pounding so painfully, perhaps she'd figure out how to go on living.

The princess was lying on a towering stack of fluffy goosedown mattresses. She was crying. Tears ran backward into her long blond hair. They turned to blood, staining her gossamer silk nightgown.

"I'm trying to get Donna Summer to record the title song for *After Dark*," Leigh said. She was feeding Joshua a spoonful of puréed lamb.

It had been four months since his stroke, a month since he'd been released from the hospital, and his recovery was progressing frustratingly but predictably slowly. His once hard body, unexercised for too long, had turned flaccid; his speech center had been damaged, causing him to become angry at his clumsy tongue. Since Leigh was the only person who could understand him, Joshua had grown more and more dependent on her.

In the beginning, she attempted to keep her visits to two a day—morning and evening—but Joshua's tantrums made her worry that he'd have another stroke. Rather than risk his life, she moved into one of the guest bedrooms of the palatial Beverly Hills mansion. Now that her memory of that infamous night had returned, Leigh's own room held too many painful memories. As it was, her feelings of love and hate and guilt were impossible to sort out, so she pushed them away into a distant corner of her mind and forced herself to concentrate on the present. And all the demands that had been placed upon her.

"Er," Joshua rolled his eyes. Lamb spattered onto the royal blue silk of his pajama top. She still hadn't forgiven him, but Leigh couldn't help pitying her father. All her life, she'd viewed him as strong, invincible. Now, his once vigorous body wasted, his razor-sharp mind dulled and increasingly forgetful, he was heartbreakingly pathetic.

"I know you wanted Cher." Leigh scooped the spilled food up and put it on the side of the plate. "But I got a call from Donna's agent last week and he told me that she's got a single on her new album that's really hot. In fact," she said, feeding him a bite of strained carrots, "it's titled 'Hot Stuff.' "

"Aater." Holding out a glass of water, she waited as he struggled to take a drink through the bent plastic straw. "I heard the song last night and it's going to be a big hit. If I'd only known about it a few months ago, we could have changed the name of the movie and used it for the title song. Also, Donna's first-lady-of-lust image certainly goes along with Marissa's role in the movie.

"So," Leigh said, patting his wet lips with a napkin, "I'm going to do my damndest to sign her." Ignoring Joshua's obvious irritation at the way she'd overrode his wishes, Leigh smiled encouragingly. "And now that we've dispensed with business, how about a little stroll around the room?"

She had hired round-the-clock nursing care and a therapist visited every day, putting Joshua through an intensive series of exercises to build strength back into his muscles. But he insisted that Leigh assist him in his effort to walk again.

Over these past months Leigh had begun to feel as if she was existing in two separate dimensions of time and space. During the day she divided her time between running Baron Studios and spending as much time as necessary with her father. But at night, after the large house grew quiet, she grieved for her fractured marriage. The nightmares, which she hadn't experienced for years, had returned with a vengeance, leaving her feeling exhausted, frightened, and ashamed.

Unsurprisingly, the columnists were having a field day with their separation. Rumors had Matthew sleeping with half the women in town, something that did not surprise Leigh. After all, she reasoned, he'd always been an intensely sexual man; she could not have expected him to remain celibate. Still, the rumors hurt. More than she ever would have thought possible.

Because the truth, as painful as it was to accept, was that she had not yet begun to get over Matthew. She wasn't certain she ever would.

36

July 1979

Matthew had not expected the divorce hearing to hurt so much. At least Leigh hadn't shown up; he wasn't sure he could have handled seeing her. He left the courthouse feeling a rare need for companionship. He drove to Tina and Corbett's house.

"How are you, dear?" Tina asked as she embraced him. Her sharp gaze took in the gaunt hollows under his cheeks, the bruised-looking patches under his eyes.

Matthew shrugged. "A little shell-shocked."

"Divorce is never easy," Corbett said knowingly. His first marriage had ended in a bitterly contested divorce. He'd met Tina while looking for some place to live after moving out of the Malibu Colony home he had shared with his wife of five years, a stunningly beautiful but manic-depressive actress. That painful experience had made him all the more determined to make this marriage work. "I know it's early, but you look like a man who could use a drink."

"I sure as hell wouldn't turn one down."

"So," Corbett said, handing him a glass of the bourbon he knew Matthew preferred on the rare occasions he drank hard liquor, "how's everything else going?"

"We begin shooting the outdoor scenes for *Unholy Matrimony* next week, if the weather holds in San Francisco."

Unholy Matrimony was a story about the disintegration of a marriage. Like all of Matthew's movies, the black comedy was intensely personal. Writing the screenplay had been cathartic; now he merely wanted to get it finished and in the can so he could get on with his life.

"You've been working awfully hard. Have you thought about taking a vacation after you wrap this one up?" Corbett asked.

"I don't need a vacation," Matthew said. "What I need is to go back to work and bring *The Eye of the Tiger* to the screen."

"That isn't going to be easy," Corbett pointed out. "In the first place, you're going to need Pentagon cooperation, and we both know they're not going to be enthusiastic about helping you make an antiwar movie."

"I can do it without the Pentagon," Matthew countered. "And it's not antiwar. It simply shows another side that the nightly news never revealed."

"Washington aside, there are a lot of people in the industry who don't want to see your movie made either."

"Since I've been having doors closed in my face all over town, that little fact sank in a long time ago."

"It's only 1979, Matthew. The war's only been over for four years; give people time to gain some perspective."

"I'll give them all the time they need. But once *Unholy Matrimony* wraps, I'm not going to let anything sidetrack me again. I've been working on this for more than a decade, Corbett. I refuse to give it up."

Corbett shrugged, knowing when he was licked. No wonder Matthew and Leigh's marriage had failed; he'd never met two more intransigent people.

"I certainly admire your fortitude, Matthew," Tina said with a smile. "Even if you are giving my husband ulcers."

The chiming of the doorbell forestalled Matthew's response. A moment later, the housekeeper appeared in the doorway with Leigh.

"Well, goodness." For a woman renowned for her ability to handle difficult situations, Tina was obviously flustered. "Leigh, darling. What a nice surprise!"

Leigh stood frozen to the spot, staring at Matthew, who looked unflinchingly back. "I had some papers for Corbett to sign. Allison Wainwright's contract." Was that soft, trembling voice really hers? Tearing her eyes from Matthew, she turned toward the agent. "I know how anxious Allison's been, so since your secretary said you were working at home this morning, I thought I'd drop them by."

Actually, Leigh had been depressed all morning by the thought of her marriage to Matthew being irrevocably severed. She'd come here seeking moral support, but Leigh was not prepared to reveal that little secret in front of the very man who'd deserted her. She watched Matthew turn his back on her and refill his glass. Bourbon? At eleven o'clock in the morning?

The atmosphere in the room turned as thick as winter fog. Corbett was the first to break the strained silence. "Thanks, Leigh. But you needn't have gone out of your way."

"I was in the neighborhood; it wasn't any trouble."

"Well, Allison will certainly appreciate your effort."

Another long, uncomfortable silence settled over them. "Gracious," Tina said suddenly, "I've forgotten my manners. Leigh, dear, have you had breakfast? Guadalupe made some marvelous blueberry muffins this morning, perhaps I could interest you in one. Or some coffee?"

"No, thank you, I've already eaten. Joshua refuses to do his exercises unless I have breakfast with him every morning before I leave for the studio." She'd been referring to her father by his given name ever since his stroke; although still irrevocably bound to him, she could no longer call him Daddy.

Hearing Joshua's name on Leigh's lips—lips he could still taste, after all this time—Matthew's eyes turned hard. "I've got to go. Thanks for the drink."

With that he was gone. Out of the house. Out of her life.

Back at her office, Leigh struggled to carry on while her soul was splintered. Determined never to be hurt by any man again, she vowed to direct her energies toward the single aspect of her life where she still maintained control—Baron Studios.

*   *   *

The walls were white and sterile. A white sink took up the corner of the room. The only furniture was a black swivel stool, an orange molded plastic chair, and a high, narrow hospital bed, covered with a clean sheet of white paper. Beside the bed was an aluminum tray upon which rested an assortment of stainless steel surgical instruments.

"Put this on," the nurse said, handing Marissa a muddy blue paper gown. The woman's expression was studiously remote, offering neither disapproval nor comfort. "The doctor will be with you as soon as he can, although I'm afraid he's running an hour or so behind schedule. It's been a hectic morning."

It wasn't exactly a banner day for her either, Marissa thought, undressing. Despite instructions to refrain from medication for twenty-four hours, she'd been popping Valium like Life Savers, but they could have been saccharine for all the good they were doing her.

It wasn't that she was all that upset about the abortion. Neither was she worried about the publicity; she'd used a false name and had arrived at the clinic wearing a long, straight brown wig, loose cotton top, and faded jeans that made her resemble all the other girls waiting nervously in the outer room. It was just that Marissa hated pain. Unless of course, that pain accompanied sex, which was precisely what had gotten her in this predicament in the first place.

Tossing her clothes onto the chair, she ran her hands over her still-flat stomach. Her breasts were unusually tender, but there were no visible signs of her pregnancy. Her eyes drifted to a calendar on the wall. July 25. The date rang a distant bell. Suddenly Marissa remembered that today was the day Leigh and Matthew's divorce was final.

An idea flashed through her mind. A thought so delicious that it caused goose bumps to rise on her bare flesh. There was so much to do. And so few hours in which to do it, Marissa considered, practically throwing on her faded top and jeans.

"I've changed my mind," she called out to the receptionist as she dashed out of the clinic. The woman, appearing accustomed to such behavior, merely shrugged and didn't bother to answer.

*   *   *

Matthew was alone in his penthouse suite at the Beverly Wilshire, methodically emptying a new bottle of Jack Daniel's and proceeding, for the first time in his life, to get roaring, disgustingly drunk. When he'd bought the bourbon that afternoon, the headline on the tabloid next to the cash register in the liquor store had screamed out at him: FAIRY-TALE MARRIAGE OF BEAUTIFUL BARON AND MAVERICK COMMONER REACHES FINAL FADE-OUT.

"Some fairy tale," he muttered, downing the liquor. The Eagles' "Heartache Tonight" prophetically came over the radio. Damn. The bottle was nearly empty. He'd have to call room service and have them send another one up. "A fractured fairy tale, maybe," he decided. "Written by the Brothers Grimm."

Perhaps he ought to have a woman sent up too, Matthew decided drunkenly. A tall blonde with big breasts and a willing eagerness to please. Despite the tabloid rumors to the contrary, he hadn't been with a woman since Leigh. Because the damnable truth of the matter was, as furious as he was with his ex-wife, he couldn't imagine making love to any other woman. He couldn't get Leigh out of his mind; it was as if her image had been imprinted on his lids, so that were he to close his eyes, he could still see her.

He was just about to dial the phone when there was a knock at the door. "That was fast." He opened the door to find Marissa clad in a filmy white dress that draped softly over her breasts. The dress was vaguely familiar; after a moment's consideration, Matthew remembered that he'd bought an identical one for Leigh for her last birthday. She was holding a bottle of vintage Krug.

"Hello, Matthew," she said, giving him a dazzling smile that showed all her straight white teeth. "I thought you could use some company."

"Even if I did, which I damn well don't, I sure as hell wouldn't send for you."

With a deftness that the most tenacious of vacuum salesmen would have envied, Marissa stuck her white high heel in the door, preventing him from closing her out. "Don't be so sure," she said silkily. "After all, brother-in-law, you and I have a great deal in common."

"That'll be the day. And as of this morning, I'm no longer

your brother-in-law. Good-bye, Marissa."

She glanced past him. "Do you have company?"

"Not yet."

"Good." Sidling past the half-closed door, she entered the darkened room. "Where are the glasses? I've never been good at this, but I think it's about . . . ah, here it goes." She nodded her approval when the cork popped with the retort of a rifle shot. Ignoring Matthew's blistering gaze, she poured the effervescent gold champagne into two stemmed glasses. "To freedom," she said, lifting one of the glasses in a toast.

Matthew shook his head wearily. "Marissa, I'm really not up to your antics tonight, I've had a long day and—"

"And you need a shoulder to cry on." She handed him a glass. She was standing very close to him, and Matthew could detect the painfully familiar scent of white roses that Leigh had always favored. "You're dead wrong about us not having anything in common, Matthew."

He took a long swallow of the icy champagne because the bourbon bottle was empty. "Name one thing."

"We've both been treated abominably by Leigh and Joshua. We both know the pain of betrayal."

"Leigh never betrayed me." He'd come to the reluctant conclusion that her own private sense of honor would not permit her to leave a helpless man, especially if that man was her father. The divorce was as much his fault as hers, he'd realized today while he sat in that courtroom, watching marriage after marriage disintegrate until it was his turn. He never should have issued such an impossible ultimatum.

"Don't tell me you didn't know?" she asked with feigned innocence.

"Know what?" Matthew refilled his glass, ignoring the froth of white foam that spilled over onto the carpeting.

"That Leigh blocked *The Eye of the Tiger*."

"That's not true." He was too startled to pretend not to be stricken by Marissa's information. He'd known that there was a conspiracy to keep his story from the screen, but never, in a million years, would he have ever suspected his own wife. Leigh had been completely supportive of the project. She'd told him so, hundreds of times. Thousands. "Leigh was behind me, all the way. It was the legal department's decision."

"At Leigh's instruction."

"I don't believe it."

"Perhaps this will clarify a few things." She reached into her white satin bag and took out a piece of paper. "It's a confidential memo William Zimmerman sent to Leigh, asking her to reconsider her decision to shelve *The Eye of the Tiger*."

The words blurred on the page as Matthew attempted to concentrate on their meaning. "Where the hell did you get this?"

She flashed him her deadly siren's smile. "I never reveal my sources. But it's not a forgery, if that's what you're thinking. In fact, you can ask Leigh yourself."

"I might just do that."

"Good. It really was to be expected, Matthew. Leigh would never go against Joshua. Not after all they've shared. Unfortunately for you—and your precious project—their relationship has always been a great deal more intimate than anyone would suspect."

"Now what the hell are you talking about?"

Her bright green eyes watched him with the clinical detachment of a physician about to pull the plug on a cancerous geriatric patient. "I'm talking about how many different ways there are for a father and daughter to love one another."

The all too obvious suggestion hung murderously in the air. Matthew reminded himself that Marissa had always been jealous of Leigh. For years she'd displayed an intense sibling rivalry that bordered on obsession. This was simply one more ugly example of Marissa's hatred for her sister.

"You're sick."

"Oh, one of the Baron sisters is sick, all right. But it isn't me." She dipped her finger into the champagne, then traced the outline of his rigidly set lips. "One night, when I was about nine, I heard my mother and father arguing. They were shouting, something that never happened in our proper, polite household. Being a naturally curious child, I sneaked downstairs. My father wanted a divorce to marry some slut of an actress he'd been screwing. It was then that Mother, understandably not eager to surrender her exalted position in Beverly Hills society as Mrs. Joshua Baron, threatened to reveal Daddy's little secret. The one about him fucking his own daughter." She gave him another sly, feline smile. "Believe me, Matthew, the daughter in question was not yours truly."

"Why should I believe anything you say? Besides, Leigh was a virgin."

Marissa laughed at that, a cold, cruel sound that ripped at his soul. "Goodness, you are naive, aren't you darling?" she purred, trailing her hand down his cheek. A muscle clenched under her fingertip. "Any girl can fake that; you've no idea how many times I've been a born-again virgin."

He wouldn't believe it. Despite his feelings about Leigh's defection, he had always considered her the single pure and beautiful thing in his life.

"Think about it," she suggested. "Think about all the times you've seen Joshua look at Leigh in a way that was anything but paternal. Remember how she ignored you every time Daddy crooked his little finger. And the way she stayed with him, even after she learned that he was the one who arranged for your arrest.

"Oh, yes," she said at his sharp glance, venom dripping from every word. "I know all about that too. I'm a clever girl, Matthew. I've had to be, you see, in order to survive. That's another thing we have in common." Her lips were but a whisper away from his; her breath fanned his face. The scent of white roses swirled in his head like an inhaled drug. "I make it a point to know everything about everyone, and I know that Leigh and her beloved daddy have been sleeping together for years."

Marissa taunted Matthew with intimate details of Joshua's sexual habits, Leigh's undaughterlike responses.

"What do you think they're doing now?" she asked. "locked away all alone together in that Beverly Hills mansion? What kind of physical therapy do you think your precious Leigh is giving Joshua, even as we speak?"

The devastating image of Leigh lying in her father's arms the very night their divorce became final was more than Matthew's alcohol-drugged mind could take. He struck out blindly, striking a woman for the first time in his life.

"Bitch!"

Marissa didn't hesitate to slap back. "Bastard!"

She began savagely attacking him, raking her fingernails

down his cheek, biting his hand when he tried to pull her away.

"Damn you," he growled, managing to jerk both her hands behind her back. Her champagne glass dropped to the carpet to lie unnoticed beside his. "Damn you to hell."

"You're just pissed because your precious wife liked fucking her own father better than you," Marissa shot back. Her shoulders ached, her ear was ringing from the force of his hand, and the murderous flame in his eyes was making her wet between the thighs. "What's the matter, Matthew, couldn't you make it in bed? Couldn't you get it up? Was that why Leigh ended up choosing Daddy?"

In response, he yanked her against him and Marissa experienced a surge of exhilaration like nothing she'd ever known She felt his tumescent penis against her belly. He'd freed her hands and she thrust her fingers into his hair, holding his head as she kissed him. A deep soul kiss that shattered the last of his self-control.

Her perfume confused him, even as his body, so long denied, reacted to her erotic, seductive movements. "Damn you," he said, dragging her roughly to the floor, "damn you for betraying me."

Marissa was like an animal in heat; moisture like warm honey flowed between her legs, every pore of her body painfully sensitized, like a thousand, a million, hungry little mouths. Yanking down the zipper of his pants, she clutched at him, pressing her palm against his groin.

Matthew shoved up her white chiffon skirt and pushed her legs apart. The lips of her vagina were darkly pink and glisteningly wet. He loved the taste of Leigh—a warm, seashell taste that had always reminded him of that first time they'd made love at the beach. He loved the softness of her public curls, like silver silk against his lips. But Joshua had been there before him. Touching. Taking.

"Goddamnit, I trusted you," he panted. "You're the only one." When he surged into her, Marissa cried out in victory and lifted her hips off the carpet to meet his angry thrusts. "The only one."

He pounded into her responsive body and, when he exploded in a violent and joyless climax, all Matthew could think about was punishing Leigh.

37

Joshua Baron was dead.

Newsweek called it "the passing of an era." *Time*'s cover story was "The king is dead." The *Hollywood Reporter*, proclaiming that "Baron Studios has lost its crown prince," ran a photograph of Marissa flinging herself atop the flower-draped coffin. The photo was picked up by the wire services and circulated around the world, which had been Marissa's intention when she'd thought up the dramatic stunt. Everyone who even aspired to be someone had shown up at the funeral, which was, *Variety* reported, "the media event of the year."

Father Timothy O'Bannion had to shout over the hovering helicopters. "Earth to earth, ashes to ashes, dust to dust; in sure and certain hope of the Resurrection unto eternal life."

He sprinkled holy water from a gold censor onto the gleaming ebony coffin. The sun glancing off the white marble angel standing eternal guard over Signe Baron momentarily blinded Leigh when she stepped forward to accept the handful of earth the priest extended her.

Keeping her eyes directed straight ahead, Leigh sprinkled the dirt into the grave. She flinched when she heard the small clods hitting her father's casket. The sweet scent of hothouse flowers nauseated her.

She'd been expecting this day for months, but Leigh was still benumbed with shock. During the mass for the Dead, the priest's words droned in her ear, as incomprehensible as the humming of a swarm of angry bees. A soft chorus of *Amens* signaled the conclusion of the graveside services. Leigh barely heard the condolences offered her.

"Leigh." Corbett touched her arm. "The limo's waiting."

She looked around, surprised to see that everyone but Tina, Corbett, and Kim had drifted away. Marissa was already in the limousine, reportedly attempting to compose herself. "I'd like a moment alone, if you don't mind."

"Of course," Tina said. "We'll wait for you in the car."

Leigh looked down at the coffin for a long, thoughtful time. "I want to forgive you," she whispered. "There have even been times when I think that I have." She drew in a long, shuddering breath. "The problem is, I'm not sure that I'll ever be able to forgive myself." Her head bowed by a combination of pain and guilt, Leigh turned away.

Matthew stood alone on a hillside, overlooking Joshua's Forest Lawn burial site. He could see the slender, grieving woman dressed in unrelieved black, and he felt as if there was a dark hole where his heart used to be.

Marissa was on her feet, her cheeks flushed. "What the fuck do you mean, I don't get any part of Baron Studios? Whether the prick bastard liked it or not, I was his daughter. I deserve half!"

Ira Friedman, Joshua's attorney, winced at Marissa's vocabulary. It was two days after the funeral and he'd been working overtime preparing for the reading of Joshua's will.

"Joshua left a letter explaining all that. A letter he asked that I read to everyone assembled here today."

"This had damn well better be good," Marissa said, flinging herself back down in the chair.

A stunned hush fell over the room after Friedman had read the brief letter in which Joshua revealed that he'd been in Greece when his wife had gotten pregnant with her second child. Signe had refused to reveal the name of Marissa's natural father. She had also admitted Joshua's lack of paternity from the beginning.

" 'And since I have generously given the girl known as Marissa Baron my name,' " Friedman concluded, " 'as well as providing her with a gracious upbringing and generous income, I feel I have dispatched any moral obligation I may have toward my wife's daughter. Therefore, in accordance with the agreement made with my wife, and witnessed by my attorney, Marissa Baron is not entitled to any further monies or property from my estate.' " He frowned as he folded the paper. "I'm sorry, Ms. Baron."

"Oh, you'll be sorry all right," Marissa exploded. "You'll all be sorry!"

Hating Joshua for striking back at her from beyond the grave, Marissa escaped the room, slamming the door behind her.

"I can't believe it." Leigh sat stunned, staring down at the papers Ira Friedman handed her. "Not only is Marissa not Joshua's daughter, now you're telling me that Brendan Farraday owns twenty-four percent of Baron Studios? But it's always been privately owned."

"It was owned by your father, who had authority to do anything he wanted with it. And apparently," Friedman said, "he gave twenty-four percent of it to Farraday as collateral."

All the little pieces of her father's strange behavior concerning Baron Studios' finances over the past years suddenly fell into place. There had been times when Leigh paced the floor for nights on end, worried that they'd be forced to declare bankruptcy. Each time, Joshua had shown up in the nick of time, just like the cavalry in those Westerns Baron Studios had made in the 1950s. Now that she knew where the money had come from, the image of Brendan Farraday wearing a white hat didn't fit.

"And how much did you say Kate Farrell owns?"

"Three percent."

"I hadn't realized she was still alive," Leigh murmured, trying to recall what she knew about the former actress.

Fifty years earlier, Kate Farrell had been a major star. Exuding sex from every pore, she had been able to suggest an amazing range of emotions with merely an arched eyebrow or pursed lips. Walter Baron had discovered her playing the piano in the sheet music department at Newberry's, recognized a gold mine when he saw one, and immediately signed her to a long-term contract with Baron Studios. Playing opposite such dissimilar talents as Valentino and Charlie Chaplin, her star took off like a blazing comet when the studio's publicity department blithely changed the birthplace on her biography from Maine to Georgia and began calling her the Vamp of Savannah.

By 1920 Baron Studios was paying her more than three thousand dollars per week, a mind-boggling salary for the time. That was one reason, many Hollywood wags suggested, that Walter proposed; always desperate for money to keep the studio afloat, by marrying his biggest star he kept her salary in the family.

Despite unequaled success in business, Kate and Walter found marriage a more difficult partnership. They divorced at the height of her success and, when the studio head could not afford the cash settlement her lawyers were demanding, a deal was cut for a percentage of the studio, where Kate continued to work to rave audience reviews.

Then, on October 6, 1927, Kate's star came crashing down to earth. In a Broadway theater, two thousand miles from where Kate was miming the part of Anna Karenina on a Baron Studios' sound stage, audiences were watching Al Jolson in *The Jazz Singer* and liking what they heard. The immediate success of that first talkie marked the end of an era. Kate's crisp New England accent was not only unsuited for a vamp from Savannah, Georgia, but her voice was too high to survive the temperamental performance of the early microphones. She retired, becoming more and more reclusive as she grew older.

"So," Leigh mused, "with Farraday owning twenty-four percent and Kate Farrell owning three, that leaves me with seventy-three percent."

"A majority," Friedman agreed.

Neither mentioned Marissa, despite the fact that her lingering fury settled over the room like a dark, wet blanket.

"God, Kate Farrell," Kim exclaimed. "I thought she was dead." It was a week after the lawyer's bombshell and, concerned about the weight Leigh had lost, Kim had invited her to dinner.

Leigh shrugged, pushing the untouched stir-fry around on her plate. "So did I. No one has seen her for years. I checked with accounting; they've been sending quarterly checks to her San Francisco attorneys."

"Then she must live in the Bay area. Unless she really is dead and her lawyers have been forging her name and cashing her checks. Hey," Kim insisted, as Leigh laughed, for the first time in months, "it's not that incredible. Why, just the other day, I was getting my hair done and heard the most amazing story about the lawyers who handled the Benny Todd estate . . . You know, that ninety-year-old character actor who married the sixteen-year-old daughter of his live-in nurse? Well, anyway . . ."

As Kim shared the outrageous, juicy piece of gossip, Leigh felt the chains that had been wrapped around her heart loosen ever so slightly. It was going to be all right. She was going to be all right.

Brendan Farraday sat by his pool, idly leafing through his mail. One letter in particular caught his attention. It was from Mark Longworth, the son of Reece Longworth, Signe Baron's attorney. The lawyer had died of a heart attack last month.

In the letter, the younger Longworth explained that while cleaning out his father's files, he had discovered a sealed envelope, along with a letter to Reece, instructing the attorney to forward the envelope to Brendan Farraday in the event of Signe Baron's death. Longworth had no idea why Signe's instructions had not been carried out and he felt obliged to deliver the letter to its rightful owner.

When he opened the enclosed envelope, a thousand memories flooded over Farraday. He'd met Signe at one of

Rocco Minetti's parties, and although he knew that the crime boss had slept with Joshua Baron's wife, he hadn't been able to understand the attraction. Until Signe practically attacked him on the floor of Rocco's sybaritic bathroom. Stunned to discover such unbridled passion lurking beneath that cool, elegant exterior, Brendan was hooked. Their affair had been one of reckless danger: they made love in her pink-and-gilt bathroom while one of Baron's famous parties was going on downstairs, in her Silver Cloud Rolls-Royce parked on Mulholland Drive, on the black leather couch in his dressing room at Baron Studios. It had been a period of insanity and, if he had been, as Signe had often claimed, like a drug flowing through her veins, he had been no less addicted. Time after time they'd break the affair off, only to come together again with a force more powerful than before.

Farraday's blood turned cold when he read the letter. He read it again. And again. But the faded lavender cursive handwriting never changed. Marissa was not Joshua Baron's daughter, but his. Farraday felt no stirrings of belated parental emotion, but he did realize that fate had just dealt him an extremely valuable card. Now all he had to do was figure out how—and when—to play it.

Who was he, the man who had fathered her, then abandoned her without so much as a backward glance? Was he someone in the industry? An actor, a director, perhaps even an agent? Did she know him? Did he know he had a daughter? Did he know that *she* was his daughter?

Part of Marissa was glad that she wasn't Joshua Baron's child. She'd hated the man all of her life, it should have come as a relief that she shared none of the bastard's blood. But then she thought of Leigh. And how, by an accident of birth, her sister had just been handed a multibillion-dollar business.

While she had received absolutely nothing. Nada. Zip.

Marissa stood in front of her dressing room mirror, glared into her own glitteringly furious eyes, and swore revenge.

38

"You have got to be crazy!"

Tina stared at Leigh as if she'd just grown a second head. It had only been three weeks since Joshua's death and, although Leigh seemed to be holding up well enough, this latest idea indicated that perhaps she was still in a state of shock.

"This is something I have to do," Leigh insisted.

They were in the foyer of the Beverly Hills estate, clipboards in hand as they took inventory of the furnishings. When she'd first decided to sell the home she'd grown up in, Leigh had expected to feel a pang of loss. Instead, whenever she looked at Tina's blue-and-gold sign on the rolling expanse of green lawn, she only felt relief.

Perhaps, by getting rid of the house that had harbored her secret sin for so many years, she could free herself from the demons torturing her mind on an almost nightly basis.

"You'll be making one of the biggest mistakes of your life

if you hand over that stock to Marissa," Tina warned.

"That's what Ira Friedman said." Leigh picked up a Sèvres vase. "What do you think? Storage? Or shall I throw it in with the stuff that stays?"

"Storage; it's too valuable to give away. And getting back to what we were discussing before you changed the subject, although I usually dislike lawyers on principle, Ira Friedman makes sense. Honey, I understand how you could feel some guilt about inheriting the studio, but it's not exactly as if Marissa were starving. She's making a fortune, as you well know, since she's making most of her pictures for Baron Studios."

"I know." Leigh sighed. "It's just that she missed so much. When she was a little girl, she would practically do cartwheels every time Joshua came home, trying unsuccessfully to get his attention. While I didn't have to do a thing."

"That's not exactly true," Tina felt obliged to point out. "You were a model daughter: bright, cheerful, hard-working, reliable . . ."

Sexually available, Leigh tacked on mentally, feeling the now familiar cloud of guilt settle back over her. What would Tina say if she knew the truth? "You're making me sound like a Girl Scout," she protested softly. "The point I'm trying to make is that Marissa has been looking for love her entire life and always ends up getting her teeth kicked in. I want to try and make it up to her. Besides, now that Joshua's no longer alive to come between us, there's an outside chance that Marissa and I might finally become friends."

"Well, I still think that you're making an enormous mistake," Tina said. "But it's your life. And your studio."

Leigh had spent a lifetime overlooking the obvious signs of her younger sister's malevolence and Tina knew that nothing she could say now would make one iota's difference. It was just too bad, the older woman considered. She resumed taking inventory, wishing that Signe had run off with Marissa's father, whoever he was, before the girl was born. That way everyone would have been spared a great deal of grief.

"Until death we do part." Matthew uttered his wedding vows with all the enthusiasm of a condemned man on the way to the gallows. Which was exactly how he viewed his situation.

He'd been stunned when Marissa had shown up at his suite at the Wilshire with the news that she was pregnant. The first time in his life he'd foregone protection and, here he was, months away from fatherhood.

He spent a long and sleepless night remembering his own tortured past, the childish taunts and jeers that had been the legacy of his illegitimacy. Unable to allow his child to grow up with such a stigma, Matthew had reluctantly agreed to marriage. It was, he told himself, his only choice.

Matthew lay on his back beside his new wife in their Reno hotel room, trying his damnedest to avoid touching her, and wished that it was Leigh who was having his baby.

Leigh couldn't have avoided the picture of Matthew and Marissa leaving the Reno chapel if she'd wanted to. Turning on the television midway through the evening newscast, expecting to view the reassuring presence of Walter Cronkite in his anchor seat, Leigh was stricken when instead, her sister and ex-husband's wedding picture flashed onto the screen. The scene caused a flashback in her mind. A flashback of another wedding photograph. That earlier picture had been a fake; this one, unfortunately, was all too real.

Why hadn't Marissa said anything? Leigh had called her two days ago with the news that she was giving her a significant block—twenty-five percent—of Baron Studios stock. At the time, Marissa had sounded ecstatic, reminding Leigh of the times she'd given in to Marissa's insatiable appetite for anything and everything belonging to her sister.

When Marissa was six, she'd stolen a stuffed tiger from atop Leigh's bed; at eleven, it had been a tube of lipstick and a crystal atomizer filled with Miss Dior. By her thirteenth birthday, she'd graduated to "borrowing" clothes; at fifteen with only her driver's permit, she'd taken some friends for a spin in Leigh's Jaguar. It had taken twenty-five hundred dollars and three weeks to put the car back in running condition after the accident.

Leigh had always overlooked Marissa's transgressions. But how could she overlook her own sister stealing the only man she'd ever loved?

*   *   *

Matthew stood in middle of the room, glaring down at
Marissa, who was sprawled on the bed. A half-empty bottle of
white rum sat on the bedside table beside a lipstick-stained
glass. She was dressed in the black satin nightgown she'd
been wearing when he left this morning for his meeting with
his banker. After the meeting, he'd had lunch with Tina and
Corbett, then attended a meeting of neighbors trying to protect the beach from encroaching development.

"What the hell do I have to do? Lock you up and post a
guard at the door?"

Marissa glared back. "If you were ever home, perhaps I
wouldn't have to drink. You've been ignoring me since the
day we got married."

"I haven't been ignoring you," Matthew insisted. "I've
been trying to get my movie produced."

"While I go crazy sitting around here with nothing to do all
day."

He'd tried to make the best of a bad situation. After returning from Reno, Matthew was determined that he would not
make the same mistakes with his child that Joshua had made
with Marissa. He would not be a father in name only. He
wanted the baby to feel from the very beginning that he had
been born into a real family. Something both he and Marissa
had missed.

With that in mind, Matthew had tried to treat Marissa with,
if not passion, at least respect. Unfortunately, his wife's un-
ceasing quest for attention reminded Matthew of trying to
capture the tiny beads of mercury that spilled out of a broken
thermometer. Just when you thought you had them, they
slipped out of reach. Little by little, he had begun to discover
that life with such an egocentric woman was a marriage made
in hell.

"The doctor told you that you're not supposed to drink."
He poured the rum down the drain in the adjoining bathroom.

"Hey, I just bought that bottle."

"It's not good for the baby."

"The baby, the baby," Marissa taunted. "Christ, that's all
I ever hear. Why don't you quit thinking about this damn kid

for a change and think about me?" She watched him take a clean shirt out of the dresser drawer. "Now what are you doing?"

"I've got to go out. I only came home to see how you were and to change clothes."

"Where are you going?"

"I have a meeting; I'll be at the Wilshire if you need me."

"You always say you're at a meeting. But you're really sleeping with Leigh again, aren't you?"

"Don't be ridiculous. I haven't seen your sister in months."

"Half-sister," she corrected bitterly. "And if you leave now, you won't hear my big surprise."

"What's that?" He glanced at his watch. If he didn't leave soon, he was going to be late.

"I've got a new role in a romantic suspense," Marissa said with a broad, excited smile. "It's called *Dangerous Passions* and I play a librarian who gets involved in a spy caper. I get beaten up and nearly raped by the villain, chased by the CIA, and ravished throughout the entire movie by the hero. Christopher Burke is directing."

"Well, that should certainly give you an incentive to get back on your feet after the baby's born." Matthew experienced a fleeting stab of pity for Marissa. How would he like it if he couldn't work for months? How would he feel if he was forced to sit around the house and watch soap operas and television game shows all day? He would, he answered himself with brutal honesty, go start raving mad.

"Not after," she corrected. "Before. We begin filming next week. It's going to be a real blast: Venice, Rome, Paris, Milan, Sri Lanka—"

"Wait a goddamn minute." He stopped in his selection of ties. "You can't make this movie. Not now."

"Why not?"

"Shit, Marissa, in case you've forgotten, you're pregnant. You can't be traipsing all over the world. Especially with Burke, who considers a movie some kind of damn Iron Man competition. If nothing else, how sexy do you think you'll look, running around Rome in a maternity dress?"

"Burke's already thought of that; the costume designer is working on a corset that'll hide everything."

"What about rest? Location shooting is rough enough, but

this one sounds like an absolute nightmare.''

"You're not going to stop me from making this movie, Matthew. Besides,'' she said dangerously, "think what fun you and my slut sister can have with me out of town.''

That did it. "I told you,'' he said as he took off his old shirt and put on the new, "I haven't seen Leigh in months. I haven't thought about her in months.''

"If I believed that,'' Marissa said, "you and I just might have something to discuss. But we both know that while I'm here alone tonight watching Barry James on television, you're going to be fucking Leigh's brains out.''

"Christ, you are really sick. Don't bother to wait up; I'll be late.''

"So what else is new?'' she screamed after him. She waited until she heard his car pull out of the driveway. Then she picked up the telephone. "He's gone,'' she purred into the mouthpiece. "Hurry over. Oh, and bring some rum. I seem to have run out.''

Matthew sat in the restaurant across from the man who held his future in his hands. "I'm sorry to be late,'' he apologized to his dinner companion. "A little family matter.'' He forced a grin he was a long way from feeling. "You know how pregnant women are.''

Khalil Al-Tajir studied this man who had, for so many years, held claim to Leigh's heart. "Never having been a father-to-be, I'm afraid that I wouldn't know firsthand, although I have heard tales of mood swings and strange cravings.''

"That's part of it.''

"Excuse my curiosity, but were you not once married to your wife's sister? The lovely Leigh Baron.''

Even her name could cause his heart to lurch. "Yes, Leigh and I were married.''

Khalil gave him a long, unfathomable look. "Some men are doubly blessed,'' he said finally. "Now, tell me about this screenplay of yours, *The Eye of the Tiger*. I hear it is quite controversial.''

"Oh, God, that was good.'' Marissa was panting and her skin glistened with a faint sheen of perspiration. The bedroom exuded a feral smell of wanton sex.

"You're not so bad, yourself. For an old pregnant lady," Jeff said, taking her hard brown nipple between his teeth. When he bit her, hard, Marissa yelped.

Jeff wondered how Matthew would react if he knew he was balling his wife. Since his acting career had stalled before it ever got off the ground, Jeff relished this personal triumph over his former buddy, who'd reached such an enviable pinnacle of success. Perhaps next time he ought to bring his Polaroid, he considered. Take a few candids for Matthew to put in the family album.

"New game," he decided, leaving the bed long enough to take four silk Hermès scarves from her drawer. In a flash, he'd tied her, spread-eagle, on her stomach. "You're a beautiful slave girl," he said, "captured in the Spice Islands." He retrieved his leather belt from a nearby chair and whipped her once across the buttocks.

"Ow!"

"Shut up, wench. I am the captain of this slave ship," he said, running his fingers over the red welt. "Every trip I select one woman to train into the proper ways of servitude." His hands, as they caressed her stinging flesh, were making her ache.

"I'll never submit," she said, getting into the spirit of this latest game. "I'd rather die."

"Now that would be a real waste of good pussy." He snapped the belt again, this time across the top of her thighs, and Marissa felt a delicious tingling between her legs. "No, I think we'll just break you in nice and slow."

As she wiggled beneath him, pretending to resist, Marissa hoped that her husband would stay gone for a very long time.

Sri Lanka was a world apart, a land of ancient mysteries. Ancient Arab mariners knew the teardrop island off the coast of India as Serendip, and an eighteenth-century British writer, describing it as a world of unexpected delights, coined the word "serendipity." To the Chinese, Sri Lanka was known as the Island of Gems, referring to its natural abundance of gemstones; rubies, cat's-eyes, sapphires the size of wrens' eggs. In Hindu epic, the name meant Resplendent Land.

A mystical island shrouded in blue-gray mist and antiquities, it was a place of scenic glories and ancient buried cities, home to beautiful, sari-draped women and saffron-robed monks. But to Marissa, the country formerly known as Ceylon was monsoons, a nearly impenetrable tangle of vines, sweltering shade, leeches, and the rank, unrelenting smell of decay as fallen limbs and dead trees rotted moistly underfoot.

She had been riding atop one of the country's ubiquitous elephants for hours, while Christopher Burke, demonstrating his typical perfectionism, struggled to capture the scene in all its glory before losing the day's light. Her dress, designed to conceal her pregnancy, had enough boning to qualify as heavy armor. She'd been suffering from cramps all morning and even the fresh coconut milk that their native guide had assured her would settle her distressed stomach had not helped.

It was late afternoon, and she'd been atop the beast for hours, when Marissa felt something warm and wet on the inside of her thigh. Lifting her skirt, she saw the dark red stain slowly oozing down her leg.

"Oh, my God," she cried out, her voice laced with panic. "I'm going to bleed to death in this fucking jungle!"

"I'm sorry." Matthew stood in the doorway, his expression as bleak as she'd ever seen it.

She'd been rushed by Land Rover to the capital city of Colombo, but Marissa could remember little of the trip. "You warned me the movie would be too much of a strain. So now you get to say I told you so. You should be feeling real smug."

Funny how the death of a child changed so many things. Matthew hadn't suddenly fallen in love with his wife when he'd heard about her miscarriage, yet he did regret the loss of a life they'd created together. And as furious as he was at Marissa for putting their unborn baby at risk, he also felt an unexpected surge of pity for what she'd been through.

He crossed the hospital room to stand beside the bed. Instincts older than time made him brush her damp hair from her forehead. "Smug is hardly the word," he said quietly. "How are you?"

"Sore as hell. When are they letting me out of this fucking place?"

"In a couple of days. You've experienced a lot of bleeding; the doctor wants to keep an eye on you."

Marissa cringed as she saw a gecko climbing the wall, searching out insects. "I hate it here. I want to go home. Now."

Her voice held an edge of hysteria. Matthew reminded himself that she'd been through a harrowing experience and deserved careful handling. "I can't see anything wrong with moving you to the hotel," he decided. "We can hire a nurse to stay with you until you're strong enough to travel."

"It sure as hell won't be soon enough."

"I spoke with Leigh as soon as I got Burke's call. She's chartering a plane to take you back to Los Angeles."

A familiar jealousy reared its ugly green head. "Interesting how Leigh was the first person you called."

Matthew recognized the tone immediately. It was the low, distant rumbling sound a volcano makes shortly before it erupts. "You're making this movie for Baron Studios; Leigh's head of the studio."

"How kind of you to remind me of that," Marissa snapped. "Let's also not forget how she wormed her way into those executive offices—by fucking her father."

Instead of feeling the shaft of pain her words had once caused, Matthew merely exhaled a weary sigh. This scene was so familiar he could act it out in his sleep. Marissa was on a tear and he decided that it definitely said something about her recuperative powers that she could suffer a dangerous miscarriage in the middle of a jungle and still muster up enough energy for a temper tantrum.

"Let's not get into that again," he suggested mildly. "You need your rest."

"What I need is to get even with that slut once and for all!" Marissa stormed, her beautiful face twisted with hatred. "I thought I'd done that when I took you away from her, but no, the minute I'm out of town, you two are back in bed together, laughing at me."

"That's ridiculous. In the first place, you didn't take anyone away from anybody. Leigh and I were divorced when you and I got married."

"But you loved her. Didn't you, Matthew? In spite of everything, in spite of her choosing to stay with your worst enemy, you couldn't get her out of your mind. Don't you think I knew that?" she snarled. "Why the hell do you think I bought a dress just like hers and wore her perfume the night your divorce was final? Because I knew that what you wanted most in the world was to fuck my sister. And what you wanted second most was to punish her for her dirty little secret. So I simply obliged you. On both counts."

He'd suspected as much for a long time, but his self-esteem hadn't wanted to admit that he could have been so easily manipulated. "I think it's time for me to go."

"Back to Leigh?"

"No. Back to my own life. Where I used to maintain some semblance of control."

He was walking away from her. Just like all the others. Just like her natural father, who hadn't even stuck around long enough for her to know his identity.

"Go ahead and leave," she shrieked after him. "But there's one more thing you need to know. That wasn't even your baby they tossed out in the trash this morning. It was Jeff Martin's. I was pregnant that night you raped me, Matthew. And I've been sleeping with Jeff every chance I could get since we got married. So what do you think of that?"

Matthew turned, his steady dark eyes those of a stranger. "I think," he said quietly, "that you and Martin are a match made in hell. And I'm sure you'll both make each other miserable, a state of mind which you, in particular, seem to enjoy. Good-bye, Marissa. It's been . . . interesting."

He walked out the door. When Marissa's water glass shattered against the doorframe, inches from his head, Matthew didn't bother to look back.

BOOK THREE

January 1981

39

Marissa read the listing of Academy Award nominations in the morning *Variety* and grew increasingly furious. As usual, Leigh and Matthew's names topped the list. It wasn't fair that their lives were going so well when hers was falling apart.

Marissa had carefully cultivated her resentment toward Leigh, feeding it regular doses of hatred and jealousy. She had thought that she'd ruin her sister's life by taking Matthew away from her, but Leigh seemed to thrive on running Baron Studios, which just went to show what a heartless bitch she really was. Only last week, she'd pulled Marissa off a movie, accusing her of being irresponsible and uncooperative. It wasn't enough that Leigh owned Baron Studios, she'd seen to it that her sister couldn't even work there.

And if that weren't enough, she'd actually had the nerve to suggest that Marissa enter a drug rehab program. Marissa hadn't been fooled by Leigh's phony concern; it was obvious that she just wanted to lock her away so that people would forget any other Baron sister had ever existed.

Marissa thought back to her sister's cool, collected attitude when she informed her that she was being replaced; anger curled through her like dark smoke.

"You made a big mistake, sister dear," she murmured, reaching for the pretty white stuff that always made her feel better. "One you're going to regret the rest of your life."

Leigh hadn't wanted to attend Christopher Burke's party to celebrate *Dangerous Passion*'s five Oscar nominations (Best Director, Best Cinematography, Best Original Screenplay, Best Actor, and Best Picture), but as head of Baron Studios, she knew she should at least put in an appearance.

Fortunately, Khalil telephoned with the happy news that he was planning to be in L.A. on business and would like to see her. When Leigh invited him to escort her to the party, Khalil had immediately accepted.

Burke's Malibu beach house overflowed with good cheer, fine wine, and congratulations. The guest list was strictly A, all the movers and shakers in the industry gathered to honor one of their own. By entertainment standards, Leigh supposed the party was a success—the rooms were too crowded to escape talking to everyone, the noise level too loud to hear what anyone was saying. When she couldn't listen to another word, when she'd had her fill of stuffed mushrooms, when the scent of cigarette smoke and perfume made her head ache, Leigh decided to go down to the beach for some fresh air.

"Can you believe all these people!" Jill Cocheran shouted over the din. The DJ hired for the evening had just put Eddie Rabbitt's "I Love a Rainy Night" on the turntable, while nearby a crowd gathered around the large-screen television to watch the arrival home of the American hostages after four hundred and forty-four days of captivity in Iran. "Ah feel like an itty-bitty sardine, stuffed into one of those funny flat cans. All we need is some oil to make things more interesting."

"Remind me to stop at a Ralph's on the way home," Matthew said. "We'll pick some up and make our own party."

"Matthew St. James!" She slapped his arm playfully. "Just when I begin to think you're the biggest stick-in-the-mud God ever put down on this green earth, you turn right around and surprise me." Jill smiled up at him. She was dressed like a lady pirate in a white satin blouse with billowy sleeves and black velvet knickers. A crimson sash was wrapped around her waist and enormous gold loops dangled from her earlobes. "Ah suppose that's why Ah allow you to drift in and out of my life, without ever stopping long enough to put down roots."

"I tried that once. It didn't work." He looked at her curiously. "Besides, since when did you want to settle down?"

"Ah don't, really. But Ah have to tell you, Matthew, if you ever got a hankering to get serious, Ah might just change my mind." When he looked concerned, she threw back her head and laughed. "Lordy, you shouldn't take a girl so literally. Go mingle, Matthew, before one of us says something we'll regret in the morning." Smiling at him, she melded into the crowd.

The glittery, gossipy gathering was the first time he'd been out on the town since his divorce from Marissa. Maybe Jill was right, maybe he was a stick-in-the-mud. Worse yet, perhaps he was getting old.

Now there was a depressing thought.

Ten minutes after his arrival, Matthew had already had enough. Since Jill seemed to be having the time of her life, boisterously lip-syncing "Nine to Five" to the delight of the guests gathered around her, he decided to take a solitary stroll on the beach.

Leigh saw him coming toward her. Telling herself that it was just a coincidence, that he hadn't followed her out to the beach, she leveled her eyes at Matthew and took a deep breath.

"Hello, Matthew."

"Leigh."

Standing beside the water, the moonlight tangled in her silvery hair, she was more beautiful than ever. But too thin, he thought, measuring her slender frame with a practiced eye. He'd explored every inch of her body, he knew it intimately. There were too many nights, even after all these years, that seductive visions of it infiltrated his sleep.

"I came out for a breath of fresh air," she said. "It was getting rather crowded."

"A typical Leigh Baron understatement." His tone softened his accusation.

The initial pain of seeing him passed. "I'm surprised to see you here, Matthew. This isn't exactly your type of party."

"I came with a friend. Jill Cocheran." Aching to touch her, he stuck his hands in his pockets and rocked back and forth on the balls of his feet.

"Ah." Leigh nodded. "The photographer who made your chest world famous."

A little pool of silence settled over them.

"Khalil says he's thinking of investing in *The Eye of the Tiger*," she said finally. She hadn't been surprised when Khalil had given up his cultural ministry position and established a syndicate to finance motion pictures. His interest in all aspects of the movie business had been more than obvious that long-ago summer he'd served as Abu Dhabi's liaison during the shooting of *Arabian Nights*.

William Zimmerman's memo to Leigh about rejecting his screenplay flashed through Matthew's mind. "That's right. It's taken a couple years of negotiations, but it looks as if we're finally on the verge of putting a package together. Now all we have to do is find a studio."

"I'm pleased things are working out for you."

"Are you?"

Leigh flinched at his cold tone as if he'd struck her. What did he know? "Of course."

He wanted to ask her why she'd blocked his project. Instead, he succumbed to temptation and reached out, brushing away the errant strands of hair the sea breeze had blown against her cheek.

"I've always liked your hair down."

Leigh swallowed. "I know."

"You were wearing it down that first night too." His hand moved down the side of her face.

"You've an excellent memory."

"You're a difficult woman to forget, Leigh. I know because I've tried."

"Matthew—"

"I remember thinking that you had the face of a Botticelli angel. I'd never seen a woman as beautiful—or as dangerous—as you."

"Dangerous?"

He wanted her so much at that moment that he experienced

a surge of anger at his lack of control. After all these years, after two painful separations, you'd think he would have learned his lesson where this woman was concerned. "Dangerous," he repeated. "Actually, a siren came to mind."

"Considering that sirens are infamous for luring men to their deaths, that's not a very complimentary description."

"Perhaps not." His gut twisted at the memory of her betrayal and he felt a dark sense of devastation that anyone so lovely could be so treacherous. Marissa's machinations, at least, had been blatantly obvious, so long as he'd remained sober enough to avoid her snares. Too many of Leigh's thoughts remained hidden. "But my feelings for you always seemed to prove fatal, in the end."

If he had struck her, it would have been less painful. Leigh let out a shuddering breath. She'd no idea he harbored such resentment. "I'm sorry you feel that way," she said, wrapping herself in her protective cloak of self-restraint. "Perhaps you should leave now, before you fall prey to my fatal attraction."

He could feel the steel curtain drop between them and Matthew realized he'd struck a nerve. When would they stop hurting each other? he wondered bleakly. When would they let go? "Oh, hell, I'm the one who's sorry. Come here." Putting his arm around her, Matthew drew her to him, feeling her familiar shape against his.

Leigh put her head on his shoulder and basked in the solid strength that had always been both comforting and exciting at the same time. "Why?"

Her mouth muffled against his jacket, he barely heard her. But he knew what she was thinking. Because the same painful thoughts were tumbling around in his own mind. He brushed her hair aside and pressed his lips against her fragrant neck. "Why couldn't we make it work?" he asked softly. "Or why can't we stay away from one another?"

She tilted her head back to look up at him. In the streaming silver moonlight, her lashes were tangled and wet. "Both."

A single tear glistened on her cheek like a diamond; he brushed it away. Matthew felt her heart thudding against his, felt her tremors, and he, a man who never gave in to impulse, lowered his mouth to hers.

Leigh moaned, feeling a shock like a seismic jolt shoot

through her. Wrapping her arms around his waist, she surrendered to the feel of his tongue sweeping her mouth.

"Christ, how I want you," he said, kissing her cheeks, her chin, her temple. Her face and lips tasted like tears. "I've wanted you from the first minute I saw you." His hands slipped beneath her royal blue velvet jacket, pushing aside the draped neckline of her dress to caress her breasts. Her engorged breasts filled his hands, his stroking fingers made her nipples tingle with anticipation. "Come home with me, Leigh. It used to make me crazy, thinking about the past, about you and Joshua, but being without you is worse." Matthew's words slashed through the passion clouding her mind.

"What are you talking about?"

"I know." Her warm flesh was like liquid satin, her scent alone was enough to make him hard, and the taste of her lips threatened to drive him over the edge. "About you and your father. But I can understand how it happened: in the beginning you were a child, he forced you. Later, you were afraid to reject him."

"You have it all wrong." Leigh backed away, nearly stumbling in the soft sand. "It wasn't like that . . . Oh, my God."

The shame of anyone—but especially this man whom she'd loved for so many years—knowing her sin was too much to bear. Emotions she'd kept safely locked away since that afternoon she'd remembered her father's betrayal came flooding back over her in waves. Sinking to her knees, she covered her mouth with her hands and began rocking back and forth. An eerie keening sound came from between her fingers.

"Shit, Leigh, I'm sorry." Squatting down beside her, Matthew tried to pry her fingers away, but his efforts only succeeded in intensifying her crying.

"Go away, Matthew. I don't ever want to see you again."

"That's going to be a little difficult. With both of us working in the same business. In the same town."

"Would you please just go?" Uncovering her face, she looked up at him. Her eyes had the fixed, glazed stare of combat veterans. An icy fear, like nothing he'd known since Vietnam, washed over him.

"I'll find Khalil."

"No!"

"Tina, then." When she didn't answer, Matthew took off

running across the beach toward the house.

He found Tina at the buffet table, and to Matthew's dismay, she was unmoved by his appeal.

"You and Leigh have been playing this same ridiculous game for nine years," she said, plucking a batter-fried hibiscus blossom stuffed with cheese from a nearby platter, "and I'm tired of watching foolish pride get between two people who obviously belong together. Might I suggest, Matthew," she said archly, "that if you really care about Leigh, you should be the one to take care of her."

"I tried, but she won't let me." His fingers closed around her arm. "Damnit, Tina, something's terribly wrong with her and you have to help. Before she does something that we'll all regret."

She looked up at him, surprised by his uncharacteristically emotional appeal. His dark eyes were filled with an unspeakable fear that touched a chord of apprehension deep inside her. "Where is she?"

Taking her arm, he guided her through the crush of people. Once outside, he pointed to where Leigh remained on the deserted beach, a small, isolated figure rocking silently back and forth.

"Damn you, Matthew St. James," Tina hissed, her own dark eyes shooting furious sparks. "What the hell have you done now?"

Not giving him a chance to answer, Tina took off her high heels and began running across the sand in her stocking feet.

Matthew stood on the balcony, watching and waiting. When he saw Leigh turn to Tina, and allow the older woman to take her into her arms, he felt a draining sense of relief.

"There you are!" Jill came out onto the terrace, a pair of stemmed glasses in her hands. "Ah brought you a drink."

Matthew cast one last glance toward the beach, where Leigh was rising unsteadily to her feet. "I think I'd rather go home."

Jill dumped the champagne into a nearby planter filled with ferns. "Lover, you must've been readin' mah mind."

"You have no idea how much I've missed being with you like this," Khalil murmured, taking Leigh in his arms. A change had come over her; a pall he was certain had something to do with Matthew's presence at the party. "How much

I've missed making love to you. I've never forgotten, you know."

"Neither have I." It was true. Her time with Khalil had been a magical, wonderful fantasy.

They were sitting in the moon-spangled darkness of her living room. Leigh had lit a trio of white beeswax candles immediately upon arriving home, and now, as he examined her face, illuminated by the flickering candlelight, Khalil considered that Leigh was a woman who would only grow more beautiful with the soft patina of years. He'd never seen her look so lovely. Or so sad.

"I had hoped that we might resume our relationship where it left off," he murmured, bending his head and giving her a slow, exploratory kiss.

So had she. Finally taking Kim's advice that she had mourned her dead marriage long enough, Leigh had had every intention of going to bed with Khalil tonight. But as his lips touched hers, it was Matthew's lips she was tasting, and when his hand slipped inside her dress to caress her breasts, it was Matthew's hand warming her naked skin.

"Oh, Khalil." She placed her palm on his dark cheek. "I know that I gave you that impression when you called, and again earlier this evening, but . . . oh, damn. I can't seem to do anything right anymore."

Turning his head, he pressed his lips against her fingertips. "You still love him."

"Yes."

"Then why do you not go to him?"

Such a simple question. Such complex answers. "It's difficult to explain," she insisted, rising from the couch. She began pacing the room.

"My grandmother used to cite an old Arab proverb," he said. "Perhaps you have heard it: Pride goeth before a fall."

She managed a weak smile. "That's an Arab proverb?"

"It could well be. After all, the West has borrowed many things from our culture. But whatever its origins, Leigh, it remains the truth."

"It's not anything as simple as pride. If that were the case, I'd go to Matthew on my knees and beg him to take me back."

It was Khalil's turn to smile. "Why do I have a difficult time picturing such a scenario?"

"All right, perhaps I wouldn't exactly beg. But it's a moot point."

Matthew knew. It did not matter how he knew—although she realized that once the shock had lessened, she would be frantic to know—but rather that he did.

"Whatever your problem, Leigh, you and Matthew are intelligent people. You can work it out, so long as you're both willing to take the risk."

He'd hit too close to the mark. "I know you mean well, Khalil, but I don't want to talk about this anymore." Leigh turned on a lamp, flooding the room with light. "Besides, there's something else you and I need to talk about."

"What's that?"

"*The Eye of the Tiger*. Matthew says you've got a package together. That you're looking for a studio."

Leaning back, he lit a slim dark cigarette and viewed her with interest. "Are you asking as a woman in love? Or as a studio executive who knows a good screenplay when she reads it?"

"You can't let him make that movie!"

There was an edge of uncharacteristic hysteria to her voice that had him instantly alert. "Why not? It's a compelling screenplay, as you no doubt know, since you were married to Matthew during the time he was writing it."

She sank back down beside him on the couch. "They'll kill him."

"Matthew thinks not."

She stared at him. "Matthew? He's been threatened too?"

Things clicked into place and Khalil finally understood the reason why Baron Studios had turned down Matthew's screenplay. "Darling Leigh," he clucked, "for a brilliant woman, you seem to wear blinders where Matthew St. James is concerned. Of course he's been threatened, you gorgeous, foolish woman. Did you think they'd stop with you? Knowing how obsessed the man is with getting this movie made? Matthew is not a man to run from a fight, Leigh. Surely that's one of the things that attracted you to him in the first place."

"He's too damn stubborn for his own good."

"This sounds to me like a case of the pot calling the kettle black."

When she shot him a sharp look, Khalil grinned. "Simply

another old Arab proverb." Standing, he took hold of her
hands and pulled her to her feet in front of him. "And now
that I have done my duty as an escort and bestowed my wealth
of knowledge concerning the war between the sexes, I think
it is time that I returned to my hotel. Unless you've changed
your mind about making love to me."

When he waggled his dark brows in a frankly lecherous
manner, Leigh laughed. "I really have missed you," she said
as she walked him to the door. "You always made me believe
that anything was possible."

He looked at her with astonishment. "But it is." Cupping
her chin with his fingers, he tilted her head back for a soft,
undemanding kiss. "He loves you, Leigh. And you love him.
That should be enough."

It should be, Leigh considered much later. But it wasn't.
When she lay alone in her empty bed, memories of Matthew—
the touch of his hands and lips—unleashed a flood of erotic
memories. Her body was seized with an expectancy bordering
on agony and, seeking relief, Leigh put her hand between her
legs, finding it to be, as always, a poor substitution for the real
thing.

They were lying in bed in Matthew's Malibu home. Not
eager to return to hotel life, he'd bought the house after his
divorce from Marissa had become final.

"It's okay, you know." Jill went up on one elbow and looked
down into Matthew's grimly set face. "It happens to lots of
men."

"Not me."

"Sugah, you are many wonderful things," Jill drawled, tracing his tense lips with a scarlet fingernail. "Smart, talented,
sexy as all get-out, but you are not Superman."

"So tell me something I don't know." Realizing how petulant he sounded, Matthew grimaced. "I'm sorry. I didn't mean
to be such rotten company."

"Don't apologize for being in love, Matthew." Leaving the
bed, she began to pick up her scattered clothing from the
floor. "Actually, Ah think it's kind of sweet," she said, step-
ping into a pair of red bikini underpants.

"What the hell are you talking about?"

"It's obvious what's wrong," she said, her voice muffled by

the billowy satin blouse she'd pulled over her head. "You are so in love with your first wife, making love to any other woman would be like committing adultery." She grinned at him, her blond head popping back into view. "Some girls might consider you old-fashioned, Matthew St. James. But Ah think you're the sweetest, most romantic man Ah've ever met." Bending down, she gave him a quick kiss. "Ah wonder if Leigh Baron realizes what a lucky woman she is."

"I rather doubt it."

"Well then, you're just going to have to see that she does. Aren't you? Don't get up," she said, pushing him back against the pillows. "Ah think Ah'm going to go back to the party. The night is still young and there was this cute little ole rock musician who looked as if he'd like a chance to ring mah chimes." Tugging on her impossibly high heels, she wagged her fingers at him and left.

Matthew laughed, thinking that Jill's carefree, no-strings-attached attitude reminded him a lot of Lana Parker. Or Lana as she'd been back when they were neighbors. The last he had heard from the attractive ex-hippie, she was married to a stockbroker from an establishment California family and had just given birth to a son, whom she'd named Jason Ashby Palmer Kirkland III. That, more than anything, had proven to Matthew that the flower generation had moved on to greener pastures.

So much had changed, he reflected. He'd come a helluva long way from that starving would-be writer with the hit-and-run sexual habits who seldom took the same woman to bed twice. He'd grown more successful than his wildest dreams, and he knew that there were any number of beautiful, sexy women who'd willingly tumble into bed with him at the crook of his little finger.

But he didn't want any of those women.

Damnit, he wanted Leigh. There. He'd finally put aside his wounded pride long enough to admit it. The next thing to do was to come up with some way to get her back.

In his bed. And in his life. Forever.

"I don't believe this!"

Marissa stared at the letter in her hand. The once ivory parchment stationery had yellowed and years had faded the lavender ink, but the handwriting was instantly recognizable.

"Since your mother would have no reason to lie about such a thing, I have to assume it's true," Brendan said, handing her the gin and tonic she'd asked for. "And the timing fits."

"You were having an affair with my mother? Right under Joshua's nose?"

"Yes."

"I love it," Marissa decided, leaning back in the chair and crossing her legs. "The old bastard was cuckolded by his biggest star. Delicious." She took a sip of her drink. "Did he know?"

"I didn't think so at the time. But of course I had no idea that he and Signe weren't sleeping together. When she got pregnant, she assured me it was Joshua's child."

Marissa glanced down at the letter again, then looked up at Brendan. "So, you're my father."

He nodded. "It appears I am."

"Well, imagine that."

She thought back to that time in Paris, during the filming of *Dangerous*. Furious at Matthew's continual rejections, she'd put on her most alluring nightgown and was headed down the hall to Farraday's room, where she knew, from the looks he'd been giving her all week, that she wouldn't be turned down. As fate would have it, that was the moment that Jeff had shown up with the news that he'd gotten a bit part in the movie. She laughed at how close she'd come to committing the same incestuous act that she'd held against Leigh all these years.

"I hadn't realized you'd find your paternity so amusing."

"Sorry. Private joke." She looked at him expectantly. "Well, Daddy dear, what do we do now?"

"Funny you should ask that question," Farraday said, opening a thick manila file. "I thought you and I might enter into a joint business venture. But since we're family, I'm going to be up front with you, Marissa, and tell you that it'll involve ruining your sister."

A burst of pure pleasure surged through her. Marissa licked her lips, leaned forward, and gave him her full attention.

"Where do I sign?"

40

"I can't believe you're doing this to me."

Leigh faced her sister across the room. Marissa was having a late breakfast in bed, clad in a white satin nightgown and matching bed jacket trimmed in ostrich feathers. The outfit could have easily belonged to Jean Harlow, but strangely enough, Leigh considered, it suited Marissa perfectly.

"For God's sake, Mar, we're sisters! Baron Studios has always been in our family. I never would have given you that stock if I'd known you'd go in with Farraday."

Marissa tossed her head. "To set the record straight, you're only my half-sister, remember? Actually, I'm relieved that Joshua wasn't my natural father. Considering his penchant for perversity."

Comprehension thundered down on Leigh, almost staggering in its enormity. "You knew," she said faintly. "All these years, you knew."

"Of course." The raw pain in Leigh's eyes thrilled Marissa and she was tempted to reveal her own father's identity. Then she remembered what Brendan had said about the damage such a revelation could do to his political career. Although Marissa was totally apolitical, the promises he'd made to her—money, power, half interest in one of the casinos planned for Palm Springs—kept her silent.

"You're the one who told Matthew," Leigh said, more to herself than her sister.

"Wow, when you start putting two and two together, you're a regular whiz kid." Marissa spread orange marmalade onto a toasted English muffin. "Are you sure you don't want breakfast?"

"I'm not hungry." Her stomach was gripped with escalating waves of nausea.

Marissa shrugged her satin-clad shoulders. "Suit yourself."

"Why?" Leigh whispered.

"Why?" Marissa eyed her over the rim of her coffee cup. "Why did I tell Matthew about you having sex with your daddy? Or why am I going to take your precious studio away from you?"

"Both, I guess."

"Christ, you are incredible!" Marissa slammed her cup down onto her saucer. Coffee splattered onto the peach satin comforter and went unnoticed. "I hate you. It's as simple as that. I've always hated you. For years I struggled in your shadow, waiting for a single word, a look from the man I thought to be my father. But all he ever wanted was you. It was always Leigh this, Leigh that."

She laughed, a dangerous, brittle sound that struck at the very core of Leigh's soul. "All those years," she said, her eyes glittering with absolute malice. "I knocked myself out to get the bastard's attention, when I could have simply spread my legs. Like his precious princess."

"You're disgusting."

"I've done a lot of things in my life. But at least I didn't get to the top by screwing my father," Marissa spat back.

Faced with her sister's naked jealousy, Leigh felt as if a blindfold had been taken from her eyes. She was finally forced to recognize a malevolence and ruthlessness she could only begin to understand.

"You and Farraday aren't going to succeed," she warned. "I've sacrificed too much for Baron Studios to simply roll over and let you two ruin it."

"Then I guess it's all-out war." Marissa lifted her fluted glass. The pale orange mimosa sparkled in the morning sunlight. "May the best woman win."

The sisters faced each other. Leigh's expression revealed cold, steely determination; Marissa's heated one was filled with provocative defiance. The rivalry between them was finally out in the open and Leigh realized that neither of them would emerge from the upcoming battle unscathed.

San Francisco was wrapped in its familiar blanket of fog. The American Airlines jet had been circling for what seemed like hours and, seated in first class, Leigh grew increasingly frustrated.

She'd come to the city to meet with Kate Farrell's attorneys. They had remained adamant on the telephone about maintaining the former actress's privacy, but she hoped that if she could only talk with them face to face, she could convince the lawyers to arrange a meeting with their client. Because if she couldn't talk Kate Farrell into voting with her, Baron Studios was going to end up owned by Rocco Minetti's development company and run by Marissa and Brendan Farraday.

Leigh glanced at her watch for the third time in five minutes, as if it might speed things up. It didn't.

Matthew sat out on his terrace, watching the waves wash against the shore. Something had been teasing his mind all morning. Something he'd read in this morning's *L.A. Times* article profiling gubernatorial candidates. Although the election was still months away, Brendan Farraday was considered an almost sure bet to win. Tax reform had cut deeply into revenues, which had caused a cutback in the services the taxpayers had come to take for granted. Apparently, increasing numbers of Californians viewed legalized gambling as the answer to all their fiscal woes.

He'd known Brendan Farraday had been a truckdriver

before becoming a star; the story had been the thing of leg-
ends, along with Lana Turner's famed soda counter stool at
Schwab's, and in a lesser way, his own discovery pouring
drinks at Joshua Baron's party. What he hadn't realized was
that Farraday was originally from Nevada, gambling capital of
America.

Interesting.

The last time he'd been in Las Vegas was when he and
Leigh had been married. Perhaps it was time he made another
trip.

"Are you saying that I enjoyed my incestuous relationship
with my father?"

Harriet Singer, a motherly-looking psychologist in her fifties, leaned back in her chair and observed Leigh over linked
fingers. "I was merely suggesting that when a relationship
which begins in innocence and trust takes on undercurrents
of secrecy and danger, that danger can become enticing," she
said calmly. "Fear, mixed with pleasure, can be like playing
with fire."

Leigh had spent three hours a week for the past two months
with Dr. Singer, trying to untangle the Freudian knot that was
her relationship with her father, and not one minute of those
hours had been the least bit easy. "But I didn't remember
anything for so many years. And even then I didn't begin to
remember all the other times." There'd been too many to
count, she'd discovered under hypnosis. Beginning when she
was five, ending when her period had begun at thirteen.
"How could I have blocked something like that out?"

"It wasn't that difficult. You simply created another self, a
little girl with memories and experiences separate from your
own. Whenever your father approached you, you turned into
that other little girl."

"She sent messages to me. Through my dreams."

"Yes."

Leigh dragged her hands over her face. "The monster
wasn't just my father, was it? It was also my other self. My
mother's jealous rival. That precocious little girl who liked
having her daddy all to herself." Leigh exhaled a long, rippling sign. "No wonder my mother never displayed any

warmth or love. She must have hated me."

"You can't take the blame for whatever problems your parents had with their marriage," Harriet advised sternly. "Whatever pact they made, they were adults. While you were merely a child. A child who survived by forgetting."

Not entirely. The shadows had always been there, disappearing before she could make out their shapes.

For eight weeks, Leigh had done all the talking. Now, for the first time, Harriet seemed inclined to offer the reassurance Leigh needed. "You have to understand that while you went to school, or work," the psychologist continued, "made friends and gained experiences, your other self remained a child, unable to deal with complex emotions, difficult moral decisions."

"Is she the reason I've always been afraid to love?"

"Perhaps. Love is never easy. Even for a rational adult." She smiled. "Do you know, every once in a while, I look across the breakfast table at my husband—who I've loved for nearly thirty years—and ask myself, who is this man? And what the hell is he doing here in my kitchen?" When Leigh smiled, as she was supposed to, Harriet Singer nodded, satisfied. "There's something else you need to consider."

"I'm not certain I can take much more," Leigh said.

"You're a tough lady, Leigh Baron. What you've achieved proves that. Which brings us to my next point: growing up in a dysfunctional family, you viewed home as a dangerous, treacherous place, while the outside world—the public arena that frightens most children—was an unknown place, therefore a place of hope."

"Are you saying that part of my success comes from the fact that my father molested me?"

"That's a bit simplistic, but yes, it's possible that besides causing you a great deal of pain and mental anguish, his behavior also contributed to your willingness to take risks."

Leigh thought about that for a long moment. "I still can't understand what made him do it," she said quietly.

"You'll probably never be able to understand," Harriet advised. "But what you must do, Leigh, is to forgive. You must forgive your father, so you can forgive yourself."

* * *

Something was in the air. The sun was low, though it wouldn't set for another hour. The cool wind whipping off the ocean carried the pungent scent of salt and a Pacific storm that had been threatening all day. The sea swirled angrily, the white spray rising high and wide; dark clouds raced by overhead.

The turbulent weather fit Leigh's mood perfectly. Needing to be alone, she walked along the hard-packed sand at the water's edge. Her mind was in turmoil: thoughts spun wildly, memories colliding into shattered dreams, reckless hopes overrun by fears.

She'd always thought of herself as a survivor. If anyone had ever asked, she would have said her best attributes were her resiliency and her persistence in the face of seemingly overwhelming odds. Her determination to save Baron Studios, at whatever the cost, was a prime example of her perseverance. Unfortunately, her marriage had been a different story.

When it came to Matthew, she'd been a coward from the first. She'd run away from her feelings for him, and even after making love, she remained afraid to open herself up to all the relationship could offer. Instead of tracking him down and confronting him about his alleged marriage, she'd gone running off to Abu Dhabi like some flighty heroine out of a nineteenth-century novel. Even after that misunderstanding had finally been smoothed over enough to allow them to marry, she continued to hold something back.

Matthew had been right all those times he accused her of running all over the globe on errands any mid-level employee could have performed. The cold, unattractive truth was that she'd welcomed those trips because they kept her marriage—and Matthew—from becoming the single most important thing in her life. She had stood impotently by while he walked out of the hospital the day after her father's stroke; she had remained silent when he subsequently filed for divorce. She hadn't even raised a hand to stop him from marrying Marissa, even though the thought of him making love to her sister was almost more than she could bear.

During the sessions with Harriet Singer, she had come to understand that her almost obsessive perfectionism stemmed from a child's mistaken belief that she should have been able to control something that was beyond her control. She also was finally able to believe that she was the victim. She had nothing to feel guilty about.

And perhaps most important, she realized that she had become a prisoner of her own defenses; her shell, which had always protected her from being hurt, now seemed like a cage.

A cage she desperately wanted to escape.

The man lay in the shadows, watching. Waiting. He was clad in a hooded black wet suit and his face was darkened, as if for jungle combat. The waterproof bag he carried with him contained coils of double wire, four small round blasting caps, a radio receiver, and enough C-4 plastic explosive to powder the Coliseum. The fog had rolled in, wrapping the house in a thick gray blanket, obscuring the thin sickle of moon, muffling the night sounds. Crickets chirped; nearby a dog barked. As the hours passed, the fog became thicker and the night grew silent. And still the man waited.

Master Sergeant John Hill had been a member of Delta Force, an elite team that originated in the jungles of Vietnam. While stationed in Nha Trang, he'd seen a recruitment flyer stating that the Army was looking for a few good infantrymen, men guaranteed a medal, a body bag, or both. They should be loners, able to work independently, and possess a streak of paranoia.

Although Hill qualified in all three categories, so did a lot of other in-country soldiers. What earned him a coveted place on Delta Force was a passion for demolition and a love of loud noises.

Earlier, the lone commando had disabled the complex alarm system with a skill that suggested such sabotage was all in a night's work, and now, as he made his way toward the house, blending quickness with a pantherlike agility, Sergeant John Hill was smiling. It was good to be working again.

41

The shrill ringing of the phone jerked Matthew from a deep, dreamless sleep. Groping for the receiver, he muttered, "Yeah?"

There was only silence on the other end of the line.

"Hello?" he said with obvious irritation. "Who's there?"

Another pause. Then finally, "Hello, Matthew? It's Leigh."

She need not have given her name. Did she think he could ever forget her soft, musical voice? He turned on the bedside lamp as he sat up. "Leigh? Are you all right? Is something wrong?"

No, I'm not all right and everything is wrong. "I need to talk with you," she said instead. "Could I come over?"

"Leigh, it's"—he glanced at the clock radio—"almost two o'clock in the morning and there's a bitch of a fog out there. You know how dangerous this road can be." She sure as hell should, Matthew considered, since her mother had died on it. "Tell you what, why don't I come to you?"

"I couldn't ask you to do that. I'm sorry, Matthew, I didn't realize how late it was."

"But if it's important—"

"It's nothing that can't wait until a more reasonable hour. Are you free for breakfast later this morning?"

"Sure."

"Fine. Why don't you come by around eight and I'll make a Mexican omelet."

"Sounds great," he agreed instantly. "Leigh?"

"Yes?"

"Are you sure you're all right?"

"Positive. My only problem is that I have difficulty reading a clock properly. Good night, Matthew, I'm really sorry to have bothered you."

"No bother," he said to the dial tone. She'd already hung up.

"What the hell was that all about?" he wondered out loud. He turned off the lamp and prepared to go back to sleep.

The explosion lit up the sky, shaking the earth with such force that neighbors, jerked from sleep, could only surmise that Southern California had just been hit with a major earthquake. The Big One. Windows shattered, the shrill shriek of burglar alarms rent the night air, followed by the wail of sirens as fire trucks and police cars rushed to the site.

Where the house had once stood, a pile of rubble was engulfed in flames. A crater large enough to house the Goodyear blimp had swallowed two bedrooms and the den.

"Wow," one rookie cop breathed in awe as he stared at what had only minutes before been a prime piece of California real estate. "Whose place was it?"

"Belonged to that movie guy," his partner said, watching the sparks shoot into the sky. "St. James. Matthew St. James."

While the firefighters waged a futile battle, far out on the darkened water, beyond the breakers, Master Sergeant John Hill looked on with a rush of physical satisfaction that was almost sexual. His assignment completed, he started the engine and piloted the Zodiac down the coast, toward Mexico.

* * *

"You really needn't have come," Leigh said. She put a pot of water on for tea. "I would have never forgiven myself if something had happened to you on that road."

"You sounded upset," Matthew said simply. "And I couldn't get back to sleep, knowing that something was bothering you bad enough to have you pacing the floor at two in the morning."

"Oh, Matthew." Leigh sank down onto a rattan barstool at the counter. "I really don't know where to start."

"How about at the beginning?"

She dragged her hands through her hair. "There's something I have to say first."

She looked so distressed, so uncharacteristically unnerved, that it was all Matthew could do not to take her in his arms. "What's that?"

"I love you. I always have."

"I know."

"What?"

"There was a time when I was so angry at you that I didn't believe you knew the meaning of the word. Perhaps I'm finally growing up, because lately I've decided that perhaps it was the very fact that you loved me which made you so unreachable."

How could he know something that had taken her so long to understand? The sudden whistle of the teakettle shattered the moment into a thousand crystalline pieces. "The water's ready." She crossed the room, taking the steaming copper kettle from the burner. "How do you know me so well?" she murmured, as she poured the water over the tea bag.

"I've been thinking about us, Leigh. A helluva lot, actually, if you want to know the truth."

"Really?" She carried the tea to the table, the sudden rattling of the china cups against their saucers sounding unnaturally loud in the nighttime stillness of the house. Leigh was appalled to discover that her hands were shaking.

"Really. And I've come to the conclusion that part of the problem was that we were too much alike."

"We were both afraid to open up."

"I'm not one of those people who think our entire futures are determined by when our mothers stopped breast feeding.

But it doesn't take a Ph.D. in psychology to realize that our pasts do play an important part in our futures. I think our major problem was that you were always afraid of losing my love, while I expected to lose yours."

"Which made us overly defensive."

"That thought has crossed my mind."

Leigh took a deep breath, garnering the strength to continue. "Marissa didn't exactly lie."

"About you scuttling *The Eye of the Tiger*, or . . ." A muscle twitched along Matthew's jaw, but his voice remained calm. "The other."

He couldn't even say it out loud. This wasn't going to be at all easy, Leigh thought. "I think I'd like a drink." She reached up in the cupboard and took down the bottle of Courvoisier Napoleon. "Would you like a glass?"

"Am I going to need one?"

She met his steady gaze without flinching. "You just might."

Matthew reminded himself that he loved Leigh enough to forgive her anything. "Perhaps I will have a drink," he decided.

Leigh poured the cognac into a pair of glasses. She handed one to Matthew, then took a sip of her own. The alcohol warmed her, but it didn't make what she had to say any easier.

"I did ask William Zimmerman to block your project," she admitted. "But I was trying to save your life."

She told him about Brendan Farraday's threat and the reason she'd taken it seriously, leaving out Tina's revelation, which was, Leigh had determined, no one's business.

"So, as much as I hated doing it, I honestly didn't feel I had a choice."

"You could have come to me."

"And you would have refused to drop the project."

"Of course. But at least we could have worked together to get Farraday out of the picture. And if we had taken care of the guy back then," he pointed out succinctly, "he wouldn't be trying to take Baron Studios away from you today."

"You know about that?"

"Leigh," Matthew said patiently, "you're the one who taught me what a small town this is, remember?"

"Are you saying that everyone knows about Farraday and Marissa trying to take over the studio?"

"I'm afraid so."

"How does the grapevine view my chances?"

"Do you want the honest answer?"

"Yes."

"Slim to none."

She tilted her jaw in that way he remembered with a mixture of fondness and frustration. "I'm going to stop them, Matthew. I don't know how, but I will."

He lifted his glass. "I have no doubt you will, sweetheart. Besides, I'm working on something myself; we just might manage to kill two birds with one stone."

"What does that mean?"

He shrugged. "I'll tell you later, if my hunch pans out. So, now I finally understand about *The Eye of the Tiger*."

"And?"

"And although I wish you'd told me, I appreciate your doing your wifely best to save your husband's life."

A pregnant silence settled over them. "Now comes the hard part," Leigh said softly.

Her hands were trembling as she refilled her glass. Matthew put his hand over the top of his, declining her offer. Whatever she had to say about her relationship with her late father, he knew that if he didn't stay sober, he'd only end up making a bad situation even worse.

They were facing one another, barstools swiveled together, knees touching. "Let's continue this conversation somewhere else," he suggested, taking her hand. "Somewhere a little more conducive to intimacy."

He led her down the hall, into the sitting area of their former bedroom. The cozy niche had always been a refuge from the turmoil of their lives, a place where they could shut out the rest of the world.

"All right," he said, putting his arm around her and drawing her close, "I'm ready." And he was, he realized, feeling the familiar warmth of her body against his. There was nothing she could tell him that would make a difference.

Basking in his solid, reassuring strength, Leigh put her head on his shoulder and closed her eyes. "It happened a long time ago," she managed in a voice that was little more than a whisper. "For years, my mind blocked it out."

Matthew felt a flood of relief. If she'd been routinely sleeping with Joshua, like Marissa had alleged, how could she have blocked out such behavior? "He raped you?"

"No. Well, not exactly. Oh God, it's so complicated."

In a faltering voice, she told him everything—about Joshua's betrayal, about her repression that never allowed her to understand or admit, the power her father had wielded over her. She told him about her shock when the truth had come hurtling back, fear that she had caused Joshua's stroke, and the lingering sense of guilt that by setting herself above her mother and sister, by being Joshua's "princess," she had willingly contributed to her own molestation.

When she finally finished, the sky was tinged with a soft pink tint. Leigh felt drained.

"Christ, we really do belong together," he said.

Leigh looked up at him. "You don't sound very happy about that," she ventured.

"It's not that. I was just thinking that for two supposedly intelligent people, we've been a real pair of jackasses." He bent his head and brushed her trembling lips with his. "I never, ever, loved Marissa. I only married her because I didn't want my child to grow up a bastard."

She remembered what he'd told her of his own childhood. "I'd hoped at the time that might be the case." She pressed her hand against his cheek. "I'm sorry you lost the baby, Matthew," she said compassionately.

He laughed at that, but the sound held no humor. "It turned out that it wasn't mine after all."

"I suppose I should be surprised, but I'm not."

There was one thing more, one thing he needed to tell her. "The reason I thought it might be was because I did have sex with her the night our divorce was final," he admitted.

"You don't need to tell me—"

"Yes," he cut her off. "I do. Because I don't want any more secrets between us, Leigh. Never again."

She nodded, her heart in her eyes as she looked up at him.

"After seeing you that morning at Corbett and Tina's, looking so beautiful and unattainable, I went back to the hotel and indulged in a bout of self-pitying, solitary drinking. Not that it's any excuse, but I was pretty drunk when Marissa showed up, goading me about your blocking my project. I thought I could handle that, but when she told me about you and Joshua . . ." He paused. "Well, I don't want to go into details, but her accusations hit pretty hard."

"I've got a good idea of what they were," Leigh murmured.

He ran his hand down her hair. "Even then," he said, "in my mind, it was you, Leigh. I wanted to punish you, to hurt you like you'd hurt me, but all I succeeded in doing was punishing us both even more."

"Oh, Matthew." Tears streamed silently down her cheeks. Leigh dashed them away with the back of her hand. "What a mess we've made of things."

"Shh." The years of separation fell away as he nuzzled her neck and throat with his lips. "That's all in the past." Unfastening the ribbon tie at her waist, he slipped her ivory satin robe off her shoulders. She was wearing a sea green satin chemise, the lace bodice so sheer it could have been spun from spiderwebs.

Leigh's hands delved under Matthew's black fisherman's sweater to stray over his chest. Her fingers wove their way through the forest of dark curls as her lips sought his.

They kissed a long, luxurious time; then they stood and held each other, swaying together in the misty pearl light of dawn, as if dancing to music only they could hear.

They walked hand in hand the few feet to the bed. They undressed each other, slowly, reverently. Then they were lying naked on the crisp Porthault sheets, Matthew kissing her sensitive breasts as he caressed her from her shoulders to her thighs. His hands tempted, his mouth seduced. His tongue, as it slipped between her parted lips, promised.

In turn, Leigh made love to him, her lips and hands moving over him in blissful familiarity, like a love song whose music stays forever in your mind. Wherever his fingers lingered, she flamed; wherever her hands played, he burned.

Their lovemaking was so intolerably beautiful, so exquisitely sensual, that Leigh could only close her eyes and ride the spiraling passion that carried her higher and higher. Outside, the sun rose over the horizon, drowning them in a shower of golden warmth. The pace quickened; hands that were once content to loiter now moved more urgently. Soft sighs became throaty moans. Tender kisses grew eager, hungry.

When he did not thrust into her as she expected, but instead penetrated her with tantalizing slowness, her hot wetness surged forward to welcome him. She was already on the brink and he'd no sooner begun to move inside her when the first pulsating wave crashed over her, followed by another, then another. Feeling her contractions along the length of his penis excited Matthew to new heights of passion, and he plunged into her with a deep, rhythmic stroke. The sound of the surf roared in his ears as Matthew was overcome by an incomparable pleasure that went on, and on, and on. A blood red haze appeared before his eyes. Then everything went dark and hc collapsed on Leigh's pliant flesh, his body spent.

Their lovemaking had been both redemption and pledge and, when she lay quietly in his arms, Leigh wept again. This time, however, her tears were born not of sorrow, or regret, but love.

42

For some reason she knew had everything to do with Matthew, Leigh felt uncharacteristically domestic. She was briskly whipping eggs in a blue Pyrex bowl for that omelet she'd promised while he showered, when the phone rang.

"Hello?"

"Leigh, it's Tina."

"Good morning, Tina. Isn't it an absolutely beautiful day?"

"Actually, dear, it's begun to rain."

"Really?" Leigh glanced out the window. "Goodness, I could have sworn the sun was shining." She laughed.

"I'm afraid I didn't call to give you a weather report."

Belatedly noticing the strain in Tina's voice, Leigh put the bowl down on the counter. "Something's wrong. It's not Corbett?"

"No, he's fine. Well, not fine, but considering . . . Leigh, dear, I think I'd better come over."

Dread was a cold, wet thing, covering her like a shroud. "Just tell me. Is it Marissa?"

"No." Tina's ragged intake of breath came over the wire. "Honey, it's Matthew."

"Matthew?" Involuntarily, Leigh glanced in the direction of the bedroom with its adjoining bath. "What about Matthew?"

"There's no easy way to say this. He's dead."

"Dead?" For one horrible second, the words struck at the very core of her heart. But relief quickly swept over her when the man in question entered the kitchen, clad in a pair of low-slung jeans, water sparkling like diamonds in his black chest hair. "Tina, wherever did you get an idea like that?"

"His home was blown up last night, honey. The arson squad is going through the rubble, but the police say they don't expect to find any suvivors."

White spots swam on a sea of black velvet behind her eyes. Leigh slumped down onto the barstool, dropping the receiver.

Alarmed, Matthew put his arm around her while scooping up the phone with his free hand. "Who the hell is this?"

There was a startled gasp on the other end of the line. "Matthew?"

"Tina?"

"Oh, thank God, you're safe."

She sounded every bit as bad as Leigh looked. "Of course I'm safe. Why wouldn't I be?" Listening to Tina's explanation, Matthew's frown deepened. "Thanks for calling," he said. "If you don't mind, I think I'd better take care of Leigh. Sure. We'll come by right after I talk to the police." He replaced the receiver in the wall cradle. "Tina says the news is reporting that the explosion occurred at two-thirty."

"Oh, my God." Fate was such a delicate, unpredictable thing. If she hadn't called him, if he hadn't decided not to wait until morning . . .

"Looks as if this time you really did save my life," he said, wrapping her in his arms and pressing his lips against her brow.

Leigh slumped against his reassuring strength. "What do we do now?"

Putting his fingers under her chin, he tilted her head back and kissed her. "First we have breakfast. Next I suppose we ought to call the police. Then I promised that we'd drop by to prove to Tina and Corbett that you didn't just finish making mad, passionate love to a ghost. And after we take care of all those mundane social duties, we come back here and see how many ways we can think up to drive one another crazy."

As he unfastened the sash to her short robe, Leigh could think of innumerable ways without even trying. "There's one thing we have to do before that."

"What's that?" He lowered his lips to her breast, his tongue flicking enticingly at her nipple.

"We have to stop by the studio."

"Take the day off."

"But there's a contract I want to draw up."

He lifted his head, instantly alert. "What contract is that?"

"You are going to let Baron Studios make *The Eye of the Tiger*, aren't you?"

A few hours ago, nothing could have pleased him more. But that was before Farraday's hired killer had blown his house to kingdom come.

"I don't want to do anything that might put you at risk, Leigh."

"For just one fleeting moment, when Tina told me that you were dead, I felt as if I'd died." She pressed her hand against his cheek. "We're in this together, Matthew," she insisted. "This time we're going to be partners. In everything."

Matthew thanked whatever gods or fates had seen fit to give him yet another chance with this woman. "If you really want to make this movie, there's something you should know. Something you never asked."

"Whether the story really is true."

"Yeah. Remember Farraday's entertainment tours?"

"Of course. They practically made him a hero. With the government facing more and more protesters, they appreciated having a famous name like Brendan Farraday support their undeclared little war. And even those of us who didn't approve of the war gave Brendan credit for trying to make life a little better for the soldiers who were risking their lives over there."

"Yeah, the guy was a real Boy Scout," Matthew muttered. "The real reason Farraday made all those trips to Vietnam was to keep a tight control on the drug cartel he'd built."

"How can you know such a thing?"

"One of the guys in my unit was working for Farraday. Trouble was, after about three months he got a little greedy and began doing some dealing on the side. Shortly after that, Farraday came into camp with a bunch of pretty blond USO girls. When he left the guy was dead. Shot right through the right eye on his way to the latrine. The official report was death by a VC sniper. But there were a lot of us who knew Farraday had ordered the hit."

"Other people knew about this?"

"There's no point in killing someone unless you let other people realize that it could also happen to them. I think Murphy was killed more as an example than for revenge."

"Why didn't you tell anyone?"

"Are you kidding? Who'd believe the word of a bastard grunt like me against a man like Brendan Farraday? You said it yourself, sweetheart, the man was a hero."

"So why are you opening things up again?"

"In the first place, I'm only admitting to you that this story is factual. And in the second place, I'm more of a match for Farraday now." He gave her a long, probing look. "And now that you know the truth, if you don't want to get involved in making this movie, I'll understand."

Leigh told herself that after Tina's horrendous story about Farraday brutally raping her, she shouldn't be surprised to discover that the actor had been leading a double life. But she was. "I meant what I said, Matthew. We're partners, all the way."

He'd never loved her more than he did at this moment. "Well then, partner," he drawled, punctuating his words with kisses, "how about going back to bed and consummating the deal?"

"But I was going to make you breakfast."

"Leigh, darling . . . man does not live by omelets alone."

He lifted her into his arms and headed decisively for the bedroom. Leigh could not think of a single objection.

It wasn't easy being a woman in these new, undefined 1980s. Betty Friedan, who'd once jokingly referred to herself as "the Pope of women," the very same woman who'd written the feminist bible, *The Feminine Mystique*, founded the National Organization of Women, and led the nationwide Women's Strike for Equality (the largest demonstration of its kind since the days of the suffragists), had published another book proclaiming that a new set of constraints was forcing women to deny themselves the pleasures of home and families.

On the other hand, *The Cinderella Complex* claimed that personal psychological dependency was the chief force holding women down.

She was certain that she'd never suffered from the Cinderella Complex, but Leigh had to admit that perhaps Friedan's new Second Stage idea had merit. Because the more time she spent with Matthew, the more she found herself fantasizing about a real home. With children.

There were no witnesses to the violent demolition of Matthew's house. After rumors of mob threats against him were uncovered by a reporter at WBC, Matthew's script became front-page news and the pressure from the press built with each passing day. Along with the media attention, the armed guards stationed at Leigh's house and the studio only added to the unrelenting stress.

"I only have two days until that damn stockholder's meeting Marissa and Farraday called," Leigh complained when she returned to Matthew's office at the studio after a meeting with her attorneys. "What am I going to do?"

Matthew glanced up from the stack of computer sheets he'd been studying. The cost estimates were substantial; fortunately Khalil had offered unlimited resources. "I'd suggest that you talk Kate Farrell into voting with you, instead of those two rattlesnakes."

"How can I do that, when I don't even know where the woman is?"

Matthew handed her an envelope.

"What is this? A plane ticket? To Klamath Falls, Oregon?"

"Kate Farrell has a ranch there," he said mildly. "She's expecting us for lunch tomorrow."

"What?"

"Her lawyers called while you were out."

"There are two tickets here . . . Us?" She stared at him as his words sank in. "You're coming with me?" In the past, aside from his own films, he'd never displayed a modicum of interest in Baron Studios.

"Hey, we're a team, remember? Partners."

"But I thought you resented my feelings about Baron Studios."

"It was your father's interference I resented," Matthew corrected quietly. "There were admittedly times I thought you were overly obsessive about the studio, but I didn't really want to change you, Leigh. I merely wanted you to expand your horizons, to realize that there was a lot more to life than work."

Like love. And commitment. She perched on the edge of his desk. Her emotions, no longer guarded, were in her eyes, on her smiling lips, in the trembling of her hands as she framed his face between her palms. "I love you, Matthew St. James. And as soon as we get home, I'm going to spend the rest of the night showing you exactly how much."

Matthew closed the cover on the cost sheets. "Sweetheart, that's the best offer I've had all day."

Their lips were inches apart when the intercom buzzed. "I could learn to hate that thing," Matthew muttered. He pressed the button. "Yes, Marge?"

"I'm sorry to bother you and Ms. Baron," the secretary said, "but there's someone waiting in the lobby I think you'll want to see."

"Not another reporter?"

"No, sir. It's Miss Farrell."

Matthew and Leigh exchanged a look. "Kate Farrell?" Leigh asked.

"That's the name she gave to the guard," the secretary confirmed.

"Please," Leigh said, "have the guard send her up. On

second thought," she decided, "we'll go meet her."

"Yes, Ms. Baron."

"I wonder what made her come here?" Leigh said as she and Matthew left the office.

"Your guess is as good as mine. It's too bad, though."

"What's too bad?"

"That she decided to come here. Personally, I liked the idea of visiting her ranch."

"Really?" She glanced up at him. "I wouldn't have thought rural life to be your cup of tea."

"True enough," he agreed easily. "But the idea of tumbling you in a hayloft was extremely attractive."

"You're incorrigible," she said with a smile.

"I know; actually, I've always considered it one of my more endearing traits. . . . My God, look at that," he said as they approached the lobby. "It really is her."

The small, reed-thin woman was obviously in her late seventies or early eighties, and the unmistakable aroma of horses and hay clung to clothing more suitable to a ranch hand than a former movie queen—jeans, a red-and-black checked shirt, and cowboy boots. Still, the resemblance to the earlier silent movie sex symbol was unmistakable. Her warm brown eyes still slanted catlike at the corners, her heart-shaped face possessed those same amazing cheekbones, and in a burst of old Hollywood glamour, her once sparkling auburn hair had been dyed a vivid orange.

"Miss Farrell," Leigh greeted her warmly, taking both the woman's hands in her own, "how nice to finally meet you."

"I'll bet you thought I'd died years ago," Kate said with a forthrightness usually attributed to the very young or the very elderly.

"Not at all," Leigh responded, not quite truthfully. Only a few months ago, had anyone asked, she would have guessed that the former actress was no longer living.

Kate gave Leigh a long, measuring look. "You've got your grandfather's chin," she determined. "Are you as stubborn as Walter, as well?"

"I've been accused of being tenacious."

The old woman nodded. "Good. Women have to be tough if they're going to succeed in this business. I'm still furious at

Lillian Gish for saying that directing was no job for a lady. That was, of course, after she'd tried directing that silent movie in New York. Hell, just because she couldn't cut it on the business end of a camera was no reason to help the men keep the doors closed against the rest of us." ·

"But you did direct a flapper flim for Paramount," Matthew recalled.

Kate's dark eyes lit up. "I've heard you were an intelligent man, Matthew St. James. But I hadn't known that you were a collector of ancient movie trivia. There are very few people who know about that film." She sighed. "You know, I rather liked telling people what to do. I think I would have made a successful director, but Walter had other ideas about the direction my career should take, and once Walter Baron made his mind up about something, it was no longer up for debate." She gave them both an appraising look. "But of course you two young people have already discovered the perils of mixing moviemaking and marriage."

Matthew put his arm around Leigh's waist. "We're working on it."

Kate nodded, apparently satisfied. "Good. I've followed both your careers with interest and, although each of you is quite successful on your own, together I believe you can build an even greater dynasty than Walter—or Joshua—ever dreamed of."

"Thank you for the vote of confidence," Leigh said. "Does that mean I have your support at the stockholders' meeting?"

"My dear, you had my vote even before those thugs showed up at my ranch last night."

"Thugs?" Matthew asked, instantly alert.

Kate glanced around the room, as if seeking out spies. "Why don't we go for a drive along the beach," she suggested.

They drove up the Coast Highway, with Kate explaining about the pair of men who'd shown up unannounced and uninvited at her Oregon ranch, suggesting that Brendan Farraday would appreciate her vote.

"Of course I feigned ignorance in the entire battle," she said with a self-satisfied grin. "Then, when they pulled out the proxy for me to sign, I simply fainted. Oh, not really, dear," she said at Leigh's concerned look. "I was merely acting. I still can, you know," she said to Matthew.

He smiled. "I've no doubt of that. Talent like yours doesn't disappear, it merely ages, like fine wine."

"Oh, I do like this man," Kate said to Leigh. "You mustn't let him get away this time."

"I've no intention of it," Leigh answered, exchanging a quick, fond glance with Matthew.

"Good. Now where was I? Oh yes. Anyway, my housekeeper, who isn't such a bad actress herself, assured the men that I often have such spells and that I'd be fully recovered by morning. Or at least well enough to sign their papers."

"And that satisfied them?" Matthew asked, his doubt obvious.

"They didn't have any choice but to agree. I was, after all, unconscious. They left, promising to return first thing in the morning. Of course the moment they left the house, I called the airline and booked a seat on the first flight out of Klamath Falls. Then, afraid they might be watching the house, I put on the clothes I wear to muck out the stalls, figuring that if they did see me leave, they'd think I was one of the hands.

"That's why I'm dressed this way," she explained. "Usually I'm much better turned out for traveling. Anyway, I went out to the barn, took the old pickup we use for hauling hay, and hightailed it to the airport." She cackled delightedly. "I figure that, by now, Farraday should be chewing their behinds off for letting a senile old woman get the best of them."

"I am glad you've come," Leigh said, "but you must understand, Miss Farrell, these are very dangerous men."

"You must call me Kate, dear," she said, patting Leigh's hand with her beringed one. Blue veins crisscrossed the back of Kate Farrell's hand, but her soft skin was the color of gardenias, free of the age spots suffered by so many of her contemporaries. "And of course I know that those men were dangerous. I may be old, but I'm not stupid. If their suits hadn't tipped me off first thing—they looked like extras from an Edward G. Robinson movie—the guns they were wearing under their jackets would have probably given me a clue." She peered at them with bright brown eyes that reminded Leigh of a curious bird. "Now that I've managed to escape their trap, what do we do next?"

"The first thing we need to do is find you someplace to stay where we can keep you under wraps for the next two days," Matthew mused. "Unfortunately, while they may look like something from an old gangster movie, the bullets these guys use are all too real."

"I heard about your house," Kate said matter-of-factly. "Lucky you weren't in it; they'd still be picking up pieces of you off the Catalina coast."

When Matthew chuckled appreciatively at Kate's forthright speech, Leigh repressed a shiver. She'd tried to put it behind her, but she couldn't forget how close she'd come to losing Matthew forever.

"How about Corbett and Tina's house?" Leigh suggested. "I don't think Farraday would ever think to look there."

Matthew nodded. "Good idea."

"I'd like that," Kate decided. "Corbett Marshall's grandfather, George, was my banker, you know. Back when I was still working at the Famous Players Lasky Studio on Long Island. He even proposed to me. Three times. I turned him down each and every time."

Her eyes turned thoughtful. "I'd already decided that if he asked once more, I'd accept. But he didn't, and I ended up marrying Walter Baron instead, which didn't last the year. Walter was a hard man. I've heard his son was nearly as ruthless." She looked at Leigh expectantly, as if expecting Joshua's daughter to confirm her statement.

"Joshua Baron was an extremely complex man," Matthew said quietly, coming to Leigh's rescue. He squeezed Leigh's hand, assuring her that he'd managed to put the past—and Joshua's treachery—behind them.

"That's probably what they said about Genghis Khan," Kate offered on a cackle. "The way I've heard it, other movie moguls may kill to eat, but Joshua Baron killed for fun."

Neither Matthew nor Leigh answered. Unfortunately, it was all too true.

"I have a gift for you. Something you might just find exciting," Matthew said later that evening. They were sitting out on the bedroom balcony, watching the sun sink into the ocean.

Leigh smiled up at him. Soft pleasure lingered in her eyes. "Something else?" They'd made love earlier, and for some reason she was not about to analyze, each time she and Matthew made love, it was as if it were the first time. "I'm not sure how much excitement I can take for one day."

He went back into the house. Moments later he returned with a manila envelope. "I thought you might like to take this to your meeting."

Leigh pulled out the sheaf of papers. She began to read, her curiosity replaced by incredulity. "Farraday used to transport contraband for Rocco Minetti?" she asked unbelievingly. "How did you find that out?"

"I've had a detective digging into the guy's background for a few months. They did a pretty good job of covering up, but these prove that Brendan Farraday—the former Arnie Stoller—is not the Boy Scout he's perceived to be."

"If this ever got out, his campaign would be finished," she murmured.

"Deader than a doornail," he agreed cheerfully, leaning back in his chair and stretching his long legs out in front of him. "The way I figure it, Farraday will gladly sign over his twenty-four percent in the studio in exchange for this little blast from his past. As big a fish as Baron Studios is, it's still small potatoes compared to the power he'd gain if he was elected governor."

The idea was so tempting. Even though now, thanks to Kate Farrell, she would be able to fend off Farraday and Marissa's takeover attempt, so long as he possessed his stock, Farraday would still have a vote on the board of Baron Studios, something that was anathema to Leigh.

"If I make that deal with Farraday," she said slowly, "I'll practically be putting him and his mobster cronies in the governor's mansion." She shook her head, giving the papers one last wistful glance before sliding them back into the envelope. "I have to turn these over to the attorney general."

"My darling Leigh," Matthew said on a slow sigh, "sometimes, for an intelligent woman, you demonstrate a remarkable lack of street smarts. Didn't your father teach you that when you're negotiating, you should always hold one vital piece of information back?"

"Yes, but—"

"Was it Hedda Hopper or Louella Parsons who said that the deeper you dig, the dirtier it gets?" Matthew asked. "Anyway, here's the smoking gun that's going to get Farraday out of our hair for good," he said, handing her one more piece of paper.

Leigh's eyes widened as she read the information on the page. "I don't believe it! Brendan Farraday killed his father?"

"Actually, Arnie Stoller is the one who blew his old man away," Matthew said. "But since they're one and the same, I believe that the Nevada police will be quite pleased to be able to close their files." He grinned. "I would have notified them earlier, but I wanted to give you an opportunity to buy back Farraday's shares before he's arrested. There's no point in tying up so much of the studio's stock in a civil lawsuit for the next twenty years."

"I hesitate to say this, because it's going to sound like dialogue from an old silent movie, but you really have saved the studio." There was a tremor in her voice. She stood up and looked down at him with uncensored admiration and love. "How can I ever repay you?"

"Don't worry," Matthew said cheerfully. He pulled her down onto his lap. "We're both intelligent people. If we put our heads together, I'm sure we'll think of something."

43

To Leigh's vast relief, the stockholders' meeting held no surprises. Farraday's eyes had narrowed dangerously when she'd entered the room with Kate Farrell, but the voting was cut and dry and over in minutes. Relieved to have won, Leigh experienced a stab of regret for lost opportunities when Marrisa stormed out of the conference room, swearing to make Leigh pay once and for all. She'd heard those words too many times to count. Still, Leigh couldn't help wishing that there had been some way to reach her sister. Unfortunately, the seeds of jealousy planted by Joshua so long ago had borne a bitter fruit.

"Oh, Brendan," Leigh said casually as the actor turned politician left the room, "there's just one more little thing."

He turned in the doorway and glared back at her. "What?"

"I'd like to purchase your shares."

Had it not been for the reassuring presence of Matthew, waiting just outside the door, Leigh would have been frightened by the rage in his stormy blue eyes. "It'll be a cold day in hell before I sell those shares to you."

"Better bundle up, Brendan," Leigh countered. "Because there's a blizzard on the way. You see, I have big plans for Baron Studios. Plans which do not involve crooks." She held out the detective's report, holding back the same pages Matthew had initially kept from her. "I don't believe the voters would be so eager to elect a man with crime ties."

"What the fuck are you talking about?" he growled, snapping the pages from her hand. He perused them quickly, his complexion turning grayer with each line.

"I'll pay exactly what my father owed you," she said, taking out her checkbook. "Not one penny more."

He snapped the check from her outstretched hand. "Your sister's right. You are a cunt."

Her cool expression didn't waver. "Please close the door on your way out, Brendan."

A moment later he was gone, leaving Leigh bathed in a cooling flood of relief.

"Hey, bartender." Marissa waved her empty glass. "Why don't you hustle that good-looking ass? A girl could die of thirst in this joint before she got a refill!" She had been drinking steadily for four hours, but unfortunately she still wasn't drunk enough to forget the way Leigh had treated her. Fucking bitch. Where was it written that she always won?

The shift had changed and the evening bartender, a good-looking Muscle Beach Adonis, and new to the Driftwood, gave Marissa a long, surprised look. "Hey, you're Marissa Baron."

"Bull's-eye. Give the hunk a Kewpie doll." She leaned her elbows on the bar and licked her lips lasciviously. "Unless there's something else you'd rather have, Mr. Tall, Dark, and Hung."

Taking away her empty glass, he replaced it with another. "Sorry," he said easily. "But I'm afraid you'd be wasting your time."

"Shit. I should've guessed from the tight pants. Only queers advertise that openly."

Instead of appearing offended by her attitude, he grinned. "My daddy always said that if you don't have any meat to sell,

take the sign out of the window. On the other hand, sometimes it pays to keep the sign up."

"Well, from what I can see, you'll never be accused of false
advertising," Marissa said, her gaze dropping pointedly to his
groin. "But that still doesn't solve my problem of what I'm
going to do tonight."

"Perhaps the gentleman at the end of the bar might have
some ideas," the bartender suggested. "He offered to buy
your drink."

Marissa turned. When she viewed the familiar face, her lips
curved into a slow, sensual smile. "Jeffy. It's been a long
time."

Jeff Martin slid off the stool and came to stand beside her.
"Too fucking long, if you ask me. I've missed you, babe."

He didn't look anything like the drop-dead handsome
gigolo she'd met nine years earlier. His complexion was sallow; his once sun-gilded hair hung lank; there was a faraway,
remote look in his eyes; and, as he wiped his nose with the
back of his hand, she noticed a distinct tremor.

But what the hell, Marissa decided, so long as the guy could
still fuck like Superman, what did she care what he looked
like?

"You got any stuff?"

He grinned, reminding her of the devil-may-care Jeff of old.
"Funny you should bring that up. I just scored some ace coke
that should make a dynamite speedball. If you've got the guts
to try it."

She tossed back the rest of the rum. "Sweetie, you are
playing my song."

After Leigh's treachery, she needed something special to
lift her spirits, Marissa told herself as she left the Driftwood
with Jeff. Tomorrow she'd figure out a way to get even.

"You are an extremely accomplished actress, my dear,"
Kate said. Leigh and Matthew had taken her to dinner to
celebrate their victory. "That was quite the scene you pulled
off this afternoon."

"Are you sure Farraday couldn't see my knees shaking?"

"She looked as cool as a cucumber," Kate told Matthew.
"You would have been proud."

"I always am."

"Are you certain that you can't stay a few days longer?" Leigh asked.

"More than sure," Kate said emphatically. "I've enjoyed my visit, but I've got a mare set to foal and a garden to plant. Besides," she said with a wink, "I need to leave before those pesky reporters discover that I'm in town and plaster my picture all over the front pages of those horrible supermarket tabloids. I've always felt it's better for fans to remember me the way I was—a vamp—instead of a shriveled up old woman."

"You're not that at all," Leigh protested. "In fact, you look lovely." Kat had discarded her disguise. She was wearing a vintage forest green Mainbocher suit that carried a faint, underlying scent of mothballs and a matching green hat with a perky yellow-and-black feather. An exquisitely matched pair of Canary diamonds set in antique gold twinkled at her ears. "I don't know how to thank you," Leigh said.

"Simple. As as stockholder in this studio, I want to see some profits. And although I realize that three percent doesn't give me a very large voice in the day-to-day operations, if you ask me, you ought to get this fellow back on the payroll." The feather bobbed when she tilted her head toward Matthew.

Leigh's eyes met Matthew's. "That's precisely what I intend to do."

The police were waiting for them when they arrived home. "What in the world?" Leigh murmured when she saw the marked cars parked in her driveway. "Did you turn Farraday in so soon?"

"No. I wanted to give you time to file the papers."

"Then if it isn't about Farraday . . ." Ice skimmed up her spine. "Oh, my God. Marissa," she whispered, clinging to his arm.

"You don't know that for certain." But Matthew had seen the way Marissa had stormed out of the office. He had lived with her for those few hellish weeks. He knew exactly how self-destructive Leigh's sister could be. And that was before she'd slipped so deeply into her Götterdämmerung of drugs and alcohol.

"Ms. Baron?" The officer's face was solemn, his blue eyes offering sympathy.

"Yes, I'm Leigh Baron." Her fingers closed more tightly on Matthew's arm as her premonition increased. "Is something wrong, Officer?"

He took his cap off. "I'm sorry, Ms. Baron. But it's your sister."

Leigh had been expecting this for years. But that didn't stop her knees from almost buckling. "Is she—"

"I'm sorry, ma'am. But she's dead." He looked nervous, as if expecting her to fall apart, to get hysterical, or start scream-ing or something, Leigh thought. "We can't be certain until the autopsy, but from the drug paraphernalia scattered around the bedroom and the needle marks on her arm, the suspected cause of death is an overdose."

An image of Marissa, lying dead on her peach satin bed, her arms riddled with needle marks, made Leigh's heart clench. She closed her eyes, hoping that when she opened them the patrolman would be gone, that this would turn out to be a horrible nightmare. She opened them again. No such luck. Unfortunately, it was all too real.

"Uh, if you don't mind, Ms. Baron," the young patrolman said hesitantly, "we need someone to come to the morgue and identify the body."

Body. She'd never noticed what a final ring that word had to it. Feeling strangely faint, she leaned against the reassuring pressure of Matthew's arm around her waist. "Of course," she murmured. Her words were a distant hum in her ear, like the sound of the sea that supposedly lingered in a conch shell.

Leigh was grateful for Matthew's lack of conversation when they returned from the Los Angeles County morgue later that night. Her brain felt strangely numb and her stomach felt as if it were riding a rollercoaster. She couldn't get the sight of Marissa sliding back into that horrible drawer, as if she were being hidden away in some oversize safe deposit box, out of her mind.

Even her father's death had not left Leigh feeling so bereft; after the horror of his initial stroke, Joshua's death had been expected; the second stroke, which had taken his life during his sleep, had seemed peaceful by comparison. But Marissa had died violently. The bruises on her face and body and the needle marks in her arm had attested to that.

The unwelcome vision lingered before her eyes. Leigh moaned softly and pressed her fingertips against her closed lids. Without taking his attention from his driving, Matthew took her hand in his.

It had definitely been a day of contrasts. When she continued to see Marissa's atypically calm but waxen features, Leigh tried to remember that a few short hours earlier, she'd been floating on air.

If Joshua's funeral had resembled that of a head of state or Far Eastern potentate, Marissa's was a media circus, the likes of which Tinseltown hadn't witnessed since the death of Valentino. Guards had to be posted at the funeral home to keep the hordes of fans from storming the doors in order to catch a glimpse of Marissa's body. Cars were backed up for miles on both the Golden State and Ventura Freeways and, on the surface streets surrounding Forest Lawn, traffic had ground to a standstill. Crowds of fans covered the lush, rolling green hills.

"My God, it looks like a Rose Bowl float," Tina said to her husband, when they saw the flower-draped white coffin. "I doubt that there's a flower left growing anywhere in the Western world."

"You know what they say," Corbett answered quietly. "Give the folks a good show, and they'll all come. And Marissa, for better or worse, gave the people one helluva show."

"Amen to that," Tina murmured.

The helicopters were back, circling the burial site, their rotors blowing delicate petals from the acres of hothouse flowers. Leigh ignored them. She'd said her final good-byes to her sister at two o'clock this morning, in the privacy of the mortuary's silent chapel. She found this elaborate ceremony something painful to endure, but she knew it was what Marissa would have wanted.

"Marissa would be pleased by the turnout," Leigh said.

Matthew decided not to state his opinion that Marissa had lost her ability to be pleased by anything years ago. "Ironic, isn't it?"

She looked up at him. "What?"

"The goddess of love, eventually dying from a lack of love."

His words, Leigh considered, were unhappily all too true.

They were leaving the funeral, Khalil on one side of Leigh, Matthew on the other, when one reporter burst from behind the police barricade. "Ms. Baron, Mr. St. James," Peter Bradshaw of WBC shouted. He ran across the lawn, his jean-clad cameraman, attached by an electronic umbilical cord, following on his heels. "If I could just have a minute."

Matthew's arm curved possessively around Leigh's shoulder. Khalil hovered protectively beside her. "Can't you see Ms. Baron is in mourning?" Matthew growled. "What is it with you guys, anyway?"

The TV reporter appeared uncowed by Matthew's blistering glare. "I'm just doing my job, Mr. St. James. There's a rumor going around that Marissa Baron's death was a mob hit. Those same rumors say that Baron Studios is going to cave in to mob threats against your life and shelve *The Eye of the Tiger*. Would either of you like to comment?" He thrust a microphone in front of them.

"Damnit," Matthew complained, "don't you have any respect for the dead? Why don't you let it go?"

"I'm sorry, Mr. St. James," Bradshaw persisted unrepentantly, "but this is a big story; it isn't going to go away just because you don't want to talk about it."

"Look." Matthew brushed the microphone away as if it were a pesky fly. "I'm giving you ten seconds to get out of here; then you'll be arrested for trespassing."

Determined not to allow the reporter from the upstart television network an exclusive, the other reporters descended on the threesome as they walked toward the waiting limousine. Flashbulbs exploded, blinding Leigh; microphones were shoved into her face; the unintelligible shouted questions were a cacophony of raised voices.

Realizing the futility of answering their questions here, Leigh stopped long enough to issue a brief statement. It took an effort, but she remained calm, drawing herself up to her full height. "Mr. St. James and I will be holding a press conference tomorrow morning at ten o'clock in the press room at Baron Studios. We'll both make a brief statement and then we'll answer any questions you wish to ask." She took off her sunglasses, her soft gray eyes looking directly into Bradshaw's. "Now, if you don't mind, I would like to mourn my sister in peace."

Peter Bradshaw hadn't gotten what he wanted—an exclusive—but at least he'd gotten the ball rolling. Beside, he decided as he looked up into Matthew St. James's glowering face, it would definitely be pushing his luck to stay around here any longer.

"Ten o'clock," he said, backing away as he saw the policemen headed his way. "I'll be looking forward to it."

"Are you sure you want to do this?" Matthew asked concernedly as they entered the back seat of the limousine.

"We can't keep dodging the issue, Matthew," she said wearily. "It's time to face it head-on."

Khalil, seated across from the couple, looked at Leigh, his concern evident in his solemn dark eyes. "Are you certain you're up to the rigor of a new conference? It has been an exhausting three days, made worse by your insistence to plan every detail of your sister's funeral yourself. Why don't you simply issue a statement through your attorney?"

"Khalil's right," Matthew said. "A statement should keep the vultures at bay for a while. Besides," he pointed out, "once the police arrest Farraday, Minetti won't have a candidate to run, so the mob will back off."

"Until the next time," Leigh tilted her chin. "I'm not going to allow myself to be bullied by anyone, Matthew."

Khalil and Matthew exchanged a look. They both knew Leigh well enough to realize that attempting to change her mind would be a waste of time. And they both loved her enough to worry that, by standing up to Minetti publicly, she could be risking her life.

44

Jeff Martin was desperate.

His hands, seldom steady these days, shook like a leaf in a hurricane as he clung to the telephone receiver. "Hey, Mr. Minetti," he whined, "you got the wrong guy."

"No. I don't. You see, Martin, Marissa Baron called Brendan Farraday the night of her death. She said she had left the Driftwood with you."

"Hey, the chick didn't make any calls!"

There was a momentary silence on the other end of the phone. "Now that you've admitted you were with her, after all, let me tell you she told Farraday you were in the john."

"Okay, so I was with her. So what?"

"I have to assume the man who was with her that night is also the man who injected her with the cocaine and heroin that killed her."

Sweat poured down Jeff's face, from under his arms, his

crotch. "Hey, Mr. Minetti, it was an accident, okay? I didn't mean to kill the chick. Hell, I liked her. Besides, she had this habit of picking up guys, strangers, you know. It could've been anyone."

"But it wasn't anyone, Martin. It was you."

Jeff dragged his hands through his lank dishwater blond hair. "I told you, it was a fucking accident!"

"And the bruises?"

"What can I say? The chick liked it rough, and I didn't mind obliging her. Is there a law against a little S & M between friends?"

"You're not getting my point, Martin," Rocco Minetti said with a cold, deadly calm. "If it hadn't been for those fresh bruises, the police undoubtedly would have written the Baron woman's death off as accidental. Now they've called homicide in, which is more attention than we'd like with Brendan's upcoming campaign on the line."

"I'll tell you what, just extend me a little bread and I'll blow town," Jeff said. "I'll go to Mexico. Colombia. Brazil. Somewhere the cops'll never find me."

"I'm sorry, Martin," Minetti said, "but you've become a dangerous liability. There's nothing I can do to help you." He hung up.

His final words rang in Jeff's ears like a death knell. "Shit!" The shout echoed off the bare walls of the apartment. Minetti was going to have him killed. And there was nothing he could do about it. Not a fucking thing. Except run like hell.

Throwing his few possessions into a duffel bag, Jeff ran from the apartment, no destination in mind. He only knew that he had to get the hell out of here before Minetti's hit men arrived.

His head was pounding and a needlike pain was radiating under his skin. When he realized Marissa was dead, he'd taken off, leaving all his stash behind. He'd been three days with nothing but some grass and a few 'ludes and he was about to go out of his fucking mind.

Desperate for relief, he went into a liquor store and bought a pint of whiskey. As he counted the rumpled bills out onto the counter, he noticed the L.A. *Times* headline: STUDIO TO BREAK SILENCE ON ST. JAMES'S SCREENPLAY. Rubbing his watery eyes with his fingers, he tried to focus on the swimming black print, his alcohol-sodden brain remembering something about Minetti wanting to keep Matthew's script from the screen.

That was it!

The way to get back into Rocco Minetti's good graces.

He'd blow Matthew away.

"Damnit, Leigh," Matthew said the next morning, "you don't have to do this." He looked like a man who wanted to lay down the law, if he could only figure out how to make it stick. "The police should have Farraday in custody before the news crews ever get their cameras set up. It'll be over."

"With men like Minetti, it's never over." Leigh pushed herself up from the table. "Unless people stand up and refuse to be intimidated." She pressed her hand against her stomach, where giant condors were flapping their wings. "Are you ready to go?"

"In a minute." He drew her into his arms and kissed her long and hard. "Now, I'm ready," he said, when they came up for air.

Flashbulbs popped like gunfire the moment they entered the room. Along with all three major television networks, WBC had sent a camera crew, which certainly wasn't surprising, since Peter Bradshaw had broken the story, setting off the chain reaction that had brought them all here today.

Jockeying for position with the network crews were jean-clad, T-shirted cameramen and -women from local television stations. Beside them stood the field reporters—the men bronze, blond, and handsome; the women tawny, blond, and beautiful, proving that the California girl popularized by all those Beach Boys songs was alive and well and living in Holly-wood. Behind these uniformly attractive golden individuals, notebooks in hand, were the print journalists, delegated, as always, to the back of the room.

Posted on either side of the doorway were two Brinks guards, their eyes alert as their gazes continually swept the crowded room. Only moments earlier the uniformed men had delivered a million dollars in newly minted thousand-dollar bills to Leigh Baron. They had remained to ensure that none of those crisp green portraits of Grover Cleveland fell into the wrong hands.

Leigh was not surprised by the turnout. Viewed by many to be Hollywood's reigning royalty, she and Matthew had lived in glass houses for years.

As they'd decided, Leigh spoke first. "Ladies and gentlemen, I have a few things to say before turning the microphone over to Mr. St. James. The first is of a personal nature. As you all know, I had the unhappy task of burying my sister yesterday. During the past four days, I have been informed of stories suggesting that her death was a homicide. There have even been rumors that she died of a mob hit. Those stories are blantantly false.

"The sad fact is that my sister was a very troubled woman. She had become addicted to drugs and alcohol, and although her friends and family did everything in our power to help her, unfortunately, in the end, it wasn't enough. And while I will always regret not being able to save her from the destructive powers of her addictions, I hope that her death will serve as a warning to those in our community who consider recreational drugs to be both safe and fashionable.

"I also want to say that Marissa's addiction did not take away from her tremendous talent, nor did it diminish the pleasure she gave so many moviegoers during her too short career. And although we had our differences, both personal and professional, there was never a time when I stopped loving my sister. And I can only hope that she has found the peace which eluded her for so much of her life."

The room was as still as a tomb. Leigh took a deep breath, glancing down at Matthew for moral support before continuing.

"Now, for the persistent rumors that Baron Studios intends to shelve *The Eye of the Tiger* because of certain unsavory elements in our community, I will admit that both Mr. St. James and I have received numerous threats."

A low murmur of interest rippled through the assembled group of reporters.

"Most of those threats were anonymous, which only proves the cowardice of the people we are dealing with. Others were

more forthright, Brendan Farraday being one of the individuals who felt obliged to warn me against making Mr. St. James's
movie."

The murmurs turned into a noisy buzz of excitement.

"But Baron Studios will not bow to pressures from people
like this," she insisted, her voice growing stronger with each
word. "We will bring *The Eye of the Tiger* to the screen. Baron
Studios believes that the period of national denial concerning
the Vietnam war has gone on too long. It's time people had
an opportunity to view a slice of life from this era, written by
a man who was there.

"And we are so certain that there is a demand for this film
that we are pledging a one-million-dollar advertising budget." Reaching into the attaché case, she pulled out the neatly
stacked bills and held them up for everyone to see.

Flashbulbs exploded. Portable videocams hummed. Excitement rippled through the crowd like a shot of adrenaline; it
was obvious that the reporters were dying to dash out of the
room and file the story of the year. But they wouldn't. Not
until they'd heard from the man standing next to her.

"And now I'd like to introduce the writer of *The Eye of the
Tiger*, a man whose credentials speak for themselves, Matthew
St. James."

Introductions were unnecessary, Leigh knew as she sat back
down. They all knew him. For much of the last decade the
name had appeared, larger than life, on movie screens in
darkened theaters all over the world. SCREENPLAY BY MAT-
THEW ST. JAMES. DIRECTED BY MATTHEW ST. JAMES. A MAT-
THEW ST. JAMES PRODUCTION. Once he had been the bane of
Joshua Baron's existence. Today Matthew St. James was the
ace up the sleeve of Baron Studios. In Hollywood vernacular,
he had the world by the balls.

Leigh watched Matthew weave his seductive spell over his
audience. Then her gaze drifted slowly over the rapt crowd,
returning momentarily to a man standing at the front of the
room, his eyes unblinkingly riveted on Matthew. The lack of
a camera revealed that he wasn't a photographer. And he
wasn't carrying one of those long slender notebooks favored
by reporters the world over. Nor did he have a portable recorder in the hand that was visible. His other hand, she noted

with slow-building apprehension, was tucked away in the pocket of his faded denim jacket.

Too late, she recognized him. Jeff Martin. Before she could determine what he was doing here, staring through watery blue eyes at Matthew with such concentration, she saw it. The gun. Pointedly directly at Matthew.

No! Events seemed to slow to the agonizing pace of ten frames per minute. She grabbed the bronze bust of her father, Joshua Baron, from its marble pedestal beside her, and hurled it at the gunman. Then she screamed.

The sudden sound of the shot ricocheted around the room like the snap of a firecracker. The riveting explosion was instantly followed by another. Then a third.

After what seemed an eternity, the reporters began to react, shouting and shoving violently, trying to force their way to the front of the room. A blood red haze covered Leigh's eyes; someone a long distance away was calling for an ambulance. Instinctively she reached out for Matthew.

"Matthew?" she asked in a voice that was little more than a whisper.

Matthew was on his knees beside her, brushing the strands of blood-splattered hair from her forehead. "I'm here, Leigh. Don't worry, darling. Everything's going to be all right."

She was going to die. Just when things were finally beginning to work out for them. "I love you." Her lips moved, but no sound escaped.

Just as their fingers touched, Leigh surrendered to the darkness.

45

I t was bedlam.

At the same time Leigh was being rushed into the hospital emergency room, a parking garage under construction next door to the hospital had collapsed, burying three construction workers and injuring scores more. Within minutes, the emergency room was overflowing with patients, doctors, nurses, and paramedics.

Matthew could understand that he was in the way, hovering beside the gurney, but he didn't want to leave Leigh's side. Finally, a harried young resident, clad in unconventional wrinkled chinos, a Grateful Dead T-shirt, a pair of high-top basketball shoes, and a blue L.A. Angels baseball cap managed to convince him that he'd be helping Leigh more by allowing the doctors to get on with their work.

"What the hell is taking them so long?" Matthew ground out. He paced the floor of the private waiting room the hospital administrator had commandeered for him, away from the prying eyes of reporters. The rigid lines bracketing his mouth were deeper and harsher than usual.

"Matthew, you saw the chaos in that emergency room," Khalil said. "The fact that Leigh is not their first priority can only mean that she's not as badly injured as the others." His voice was calm, but the ashtray beside him, filling up with cigarette butts, told its own story.

Triage. Matthew remembered lying on the ground, watching the nurse at the evacuation unit in Vietnam separate the incoming wounded by the gravity of their wounds. "If anything happens to her . . ." His voice drifted off, his words choked by the gigantic lump in his throat.

"I know." Khalil ground out his cigarette and immediately lit another. "I suppose it is no secret that I love her."

"No."

Khalil eyed Matthew through a haze of blue smoke. "Will that present a problem?"

Matthew stopped pacing long enough to consider Khalil's question. "There was a time when I found trust an impossible thing," he said finally. "In those days I would have seen you as a threat."

"And now?"

"And now I consider you my friend. As well as Leigh's."

Khalil nodded, satisfied. He hadn't wanted to give up his ties, however innocent, to Leigh, but at the same time, he didn't want to be responsible for keeping Matthew and her apart. "I tried to make a place in her heart," he said. "But you were always there. You are, my friend, a very fortunate man."

"I know." He resumed pacing the floor. Matthew hoped that his luck held up.

Leigh opened her eyes, disoriented by her strange surroundings. She blinked in an attempt to clear her mind.

"Thank God, you're awake."

At the wonderfully familiar voice, Leigh concentrated on focusing on the man seated beside the bed. "Matthew?"

"Right here, sweetheart." He stood up, coming to stand over her. "How are you feeling?"

"Thirsty," she decided. "My mouth feels all fuzzy."

"That's from the shot they gave you before they stitched you up."

"And I feel like I'm riding a merry-go-round. A flying one."

He brushed her blood-matted hair back from her forehead. "Think of it as a cheap drunk."

She half smiled. "But I never get drunk." She pressed her fingertips against her temple, where a row of dark black stitches cut a path through her hair. "I'm so dizzy."

He bent down and brushed a kiss against her dry lips. "Why don't you get some sleep," he suggested.

Exhausted from trying to keep her eyes open, she allowed her lids to drift down. "You'll stay?"

"Forever," he said.

It was early evening when she woke again.

"How are you feeling?" Matthew asked.

"I'm fine," she assured him.

"Are you sure?"

She nodded, wishing she hadn't done so when boulders tumbled around in her head. "Did you say something about stitches the last time you were in here?"

"Don't worry, the scar will never show under your hair."

"I wasn't worried about that. I was trying to remember what happened."

"Jeff tried to shoot me, but that bronze bust of Joshua you threw at him made his shot go astray and it grazed your scalp." He frowned. "You had no damn business risking your life like that. If anything had happened to you . . ."

Leigh could remember the panic she'd felt when she saw the gun aimed at Matthew. "I couldn't let you be killed. What happened to Jeff?"

"The guards shot him. He's dead." It took every ounce of Matthew's self-control not to shout at her for putting herself in danger. Realizing that she'd already been through enough, he took her hand and lifted it to his lips. "That's twice you've saved my life. I'll have to think of some way to repay you."

"Jewelry is always nice," Leigh mused. "I've always been a sucker for sapphires. And emeralds aren't too bad either. But do you know what I'd really like?"

"Name it and it's yours."

"A plain gold band," Leigh suggested softly.

"Funny you should mention that." Matthew reached into his pocket and pulled out a box. Leigh's heart was pounding a million miles a minute. She lifted the lid.

"Oh, Matthew." Tears sprang to her eyes when she viewed the ring resting on its bed of royal blue velvet. Three brilliantly cut diamonds glittered on a wide platinum band. "It's absolutely exquisite."

"Three stones," he said, taking her hand and slipping it on her finger. "One for each of the times we've been together, but don't get any ideas about going for a quartet, lady, because this time is going to last forever."

"Forever," she agreed, holding her hand up. The diamonds caught light, breaking it into tiny white hot flames.

He bent his head, intent on kissing her, when there was a knock on the hospital room door. "Mr. St. James?" The floor nurse popped her head into the room. "I hate to interrupt, but you asked me to tell you when the news came on."

Matthew smiled. "Thank you, Mrs. Wilkinson." He picked up the remote control beside Leigh's bed and aimed it at the television hung on the wall.

"I'm not certain I'm ready to see myself being shot, Matthew," Leigh said hesitantly.

"Sorry to disappoint you, sweetheart, but you are old news."

"Then what . . . ? Oh, it's Brendan."

"Uh-uh. Arnie Stoller." They both watched the actor being taken from the backseat of the patrol car, his wrists bound by a pair of stainless steel handcuffs.

"Well, that's that," Matthew said, turning the screen black again. "Farraday's out of the picture and, thanks to you standing up to him publicly the way you did, Minetti won't dare do anything to disrupt *The Eye of the Tiger*. So, as soon as we spring you from this joint, we can start celebrating our upcoming nuptials in style."

"In bed, you mean," Leigh said with a saucy grin.

"Hey, don't blame me if that's my favorite style." When he bent his head and kissed her lingeringly, Leigh forgot all about her headache. "I have another proposition for you," he said.

"What's that?"

"We've been doing so well working together on *The Eye of the Tiger*, what would you say to collaborating on another Baron Studios production?"

"Any time," she answered without hesitation. "Do you have something in mind?" She hadn't known he'd been working on another screenplay.

Matthew sat down on the edge of the bed, took her hand in his, and laced their fingers together. "All my life, I avoided becoming involved with anyone," he said. "And then I fell in love with you and discovered that I wanted commitments. Strings. A long, luxurious lifetime of strings."

"I want that too," she said softly.

"I know. And as happy as that makes me, I've recently discovered that I'm a selfish man. I want it all, Leigh." He took a deep breath. "I want to have a child with you."

"Only one?"

"That depends on you. Although I'm certainly open for negotiation on the number and gender."

She looked up into the dark eyes that were filled with promises. "There's nothing I'd love more than to have babies with you," she answered truthfully. "And now that you bring it up, two would be nice, three even better . . . But, there's just one thing."

His heart clenched. "What's that?"

"Well, I *am* thirty-four years old, Matthew. Do you think that's too old to begin a family?"

Matthew had never loved Leigh more than he did at that moment. He drew her into his arms, unable to remember when he'd ever felt so happy. "Positively ancient," he said. "All the more reason to get started as soon as possible."

OPEN WIDE – IT WON'T HURT

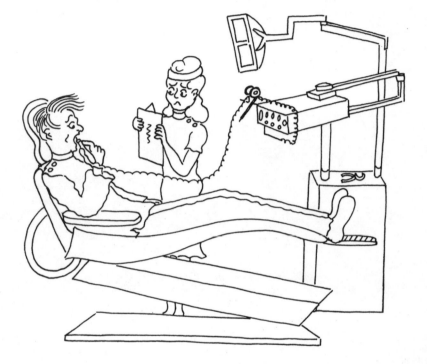

Open Wide –
It Won't Hurt

by

LEONARD WILDER

Illustrated by
Joan Wilder

ST. MARTIN'S PRESS
New York

ROBERT HALE LIMITED
London

© Leonard Wilder, 1978

First published in Great Britain, 1978

ISBN 0 7091 7087 4

Robert Hale Limited
Clerkenwell House,
Clerkenwell Green,
London, EC1

St. Martin's Press Inc., 175 Fifth Avenue,
New York, N.Y. 10010

Library of Congress Catalog Card Number 78-19659

First published in the United States of America 1979

ISBN 0-312-58677-9

Printed in Great Britain by
Lowe & Brydone Ltd., Thetford, Norfolk
Photoset and bound by Weatherby Woolnough.

CONTENTS

This book is dedicated to our children, Andrea and Lucien, whose patience with us during its preparation has been exemplary

1

Embryo Student

"Excuse me a moment, can I have a word with you?"

Out of the dark shadows of a building loomed a large, scruffy man. He was wearing a dirty fawn raincoat and he had a black patch over his left eye. He was unshaven and on his head was a dark brown cap, shiny with grease. This was a tough part of London and I had heard of people being attacked and knifed in broad daylight. The man's hand darted into his pocket and almost as quickly he withdrew it. Instinctively, I ducked to avoid the blade which I was sure would strike me. The hand stopped short and the man smiled.

"Sorry if I startled you," he said in a quiet cultured voice.

"Military Intelligence," he went on.

7

"Military Intelligence?" I echoed.

"Military Intelligence," he repeated. "We're checking up on possible army deserters and you look as though you might be the right age to be involved."

I looked down at his hand. It held an official, well worn document of identity and a photograph of himself, correct to the black eye patch, which, to my surprise, was covering his other eye. Although the war in Europe had been over some weeks, the armies of occupation were still having a busy time. Desertion was still a reality.

"Can you produce your identity card, please?"

He was most respectful although his manner carried an air of authority. I showed him my blue identity card.

"I see you come from North Wales," he observed. "What are you doing in London?"

I explained that I was up for the day for an interview at the Dental Hospital. I showed him the letter I had from the Dental Dean.

"Oh, you're a student." His manner softened.

"I hope to become one," I said.

He fumbled in the other pocket of his raincoat and produced a pair of spectacles. Then removing his black eye patch he put on the spectacles and shielding his eyes with a hand from the glare of the sun he inspected my documents. His left eye appeared as sighted as his right.

"That's just part of the disguise," he explained. It also explained the eye patch over his other eye in the photograph. I wondered if he wore it over a different eye on alternate days.

"That seems to be in order," he said. "Good luck with the interview," and he withdrew into the shadows with the same suddenness as he had appeared.

My day had started very early on the north-west coast of Wales. I had been evacuated there with my family since the outbreak of World War Two had disrupted our home in London together with so many thousands of others. In the beautiful setting of hills, dales and long sandy beaches I had completed my general education. The time had come to think of the future.

Choosing a career when one is still quite young and inexperienced of life is a difficult task. It is a choice that so many have to make when, perhaps, they are the least equipped so to do. I had always been attracted to 'something medical' and as I enjoyed doing things with my hands, especially small and precise things, dentistry seemed to be the right choice for me. The family doctor and dentist in Wales had both qualified from the same hospital in London. After I had had discussions with them they had offered to give me letters of introduction when I decided to become a dental student. I wrote away for an interview. My scholastic attainments having been satisfactory I was soon granted one. So, on a warm, sunny morning in July I boarded a train at the local station and was soon travelling south towards the Capital. I had put on my best Welsh tweed suit and matching cloth cap. Everyone wore a cap in our part of Wales. By early afternoon the train was grinding to a halt at Euston Station. Suddenly, I was in London. Suddenly, I was overwhelmed by an awareness of its size. Suddenly, I was coughing from the acrid smoke that stung my eyes and burnt my throat as it belched from the engines. I had almost forgotten what London was like, having known no town larger than twelve thousand people since I had come away to Wales. As I made my way by bus along the streets, the war-torn ruins of a once proud city made a deep impression on me.

The sun was high and the day was getting warmer. Inside my thick tweed suit I was perspiring freely, partly because of the hot day and partly because of the growing feeling of apprehension toward my forthcoming interview. I prayed that all would go well. In moments of fantasy I had seen myself one day as an established dental surgeon, wearing a long, starched, white coat, engaged in intricate fillings or the skilful removal of a wisdom tooth. I was somewhat lost in this reverie as I alighted from the bus and started to walk the short distance to the underground station from where I would take a train to the Dental Hospital. So it was with something of a shock that I had been shaken from my day-dreaming by the sudden appearance of the large man with the black eye patch. I quickly recovered from this incident and had a hasty glance at my watch. It showed me that I had better hurry were I not to be late for the interview. I descended into the welcome coolness of the underground station. My cool reprieve was, however, short-lived. For when the train arrived it was crowded, hot and stuffy. Within moments the perspiration was flowing freely again from every pore of my skin. I was forced to stand and joined several other passengers who were hanging on the nearby straps. Fortunately, I had but three stations to go. I would just make it without having to hurry. The train slowed as it pulled into my station and then came to a halt. I waited for the doors to open. I waited and nothing happened. A gentle lurch and the train started up again along the platform, quickly gathering speed. Now I would be late. Above my head was a red lever. "£5 Fine for Improper Use" it warned. In a flash of panic I found myself pulling hard on it! It was as though the train had hit a brick wall. It stopped quite dead and I was almost thrown over. Hats, handbags and briefcases came showering on the floor as pandemonium broke out.

"Silly idiot," a woman cried.

"Damn fool," shouted a man to me as he extricated himself from a lady's lap on to which he had fallen. My carriage being the last one it was still alongside the platform, the front part of the train having already entered the tunnel. Suddenly a loud bell started to ring. I waited for the doors to open but they did not. Instead, an official appeared through the door leading from the adjoining carriage. He took some persuading that my action was an attempt to prevent myself from missing a vital interview. He carefully wrote my name and address into a little red note book, warning me that I would shortly hear from the London Passenger Transport Board. In fact I never did. He did, however, open the doors of my carriage and I escaped like a frightened rabbit from the irate passengers.

Time was preciously short and I ran all the way to the hospital. Fortunately, the directions I had received through the post were very accurate and I covered the quarter of a mile in record time. With minutes to spare I arrived, sweating profusely at the front gate of the hospital. I darted through the entrance. Seemingly from nowhere a blue-jacketed arm swung down in front of me. I collided with it and grabbed it to prevent myself from falling over. The arm remained rigid.

"In a hurry, mate?" came a rich cockney voice.

The sudden impact left me more breathless than I had been as a result of my dash from the station. My gaze travelled along the arm and I found myself looking into two pale blue eyes set deeply in a round, ruddy face topped by a crew-cut hair style. I learned later that this gate keeper was affectionately known as 'Blue Eyes'.

"Yes, I am in a hurry," I panted.

"Then hurry along round to the side entrance," came the crisp reply. The arm maintained its rigidity.

"Side entrance?" I repeated his words.

"Yes, mate, side entrance." He paused briefly and added with deliberation, "tradesmen's entrance."

"Tradesmen's entrance?"

"Yes, this front gate is for the hexclusive use of staff and students. So off you go, mate," and he pointed to the side of the building.

"B-but, I've come here for an interview and I'm almost late," I added pleadingly.

He hesitated and his arm disclosed that it had a functional elbow joint as he slowly removed it. He inspected me à trifle suspiciously.

"Gotcher papers?"

And so for the second time that day I handed over my letter from the Dean. He read it slowly and then checked my name with a list he had concealed under a newspaper on his desk. The change in his manner was reminiscent of a comic opera. He sprang to attention as his ruddy complexion turned crimson.

"Beg your pardon sir, sir." He offered the second "sir", no doubt as a peace offering. "You see, sir, I thought you was one of the tradesmen, what wiv your cloth cap on. I've not never seen a student wiv a cloth cap on before." He then added hurriedly, "Not meaning no offence, like." He inspected his list again. "I see you've come down from Wales," he observed.

"That's right. I have."

"Well, sir, if you don't know it, students don't never wear caps. Don't be offended but I suggest you leave it here and pick it up on the way out. If you hurry, you'll just be in time. It's at the end of this corridor, third door on the right. Good luck," he called as I hurried away. That was the third good-luck wish I had received that day. The first having come from my family early that morning.

Down the long corridor I went. One, two, three and I stopped at a plain oak door with a notice pinned to it. It gave

a list of names and confirmed that my interview was due at
3.30 p.m. The time was exactly 3.30 p.m. I had barely time to
straighten my tie and mop my dripping brow when the door
opened and a voice from within the room called me by name.
My racing pulse increased by several beats a minute. After
the hectic experiences of getting from Euston Station to the
hospital, the interview was quite a pleasant experience. Professor Walters, the Dean, immediately put me at my ease. He
had just one other companion with him. I never discovered
his name and, in fact, I never ever saw him again. But he, too,
was most courteous to me. The twenty-minute conversation I
had with them was of a very general nature and I sensed that,
much to my surprise, I seemed to be pleasing them. This was
confirmed, a little more than four months later, when I
received information that a place had been reserved for me as
a first-year student to start 1st October of the following year.
This, in fact, would be the commencement of the next
academic year.

Some two months before I was due to become a dental
student and after an exile of six years, the family and I returned to the London area. We settled in north-west Middle-
sex, just on the London perimeter. Soon it was 1st October. I
still re-live that day in all of its vivid reality. The morning
broke bright and sunny with the merest suggestion of
autumnal crispness in the air. As I had my breakfast I
switched on the radio and listened to Eric Coates's "Knightsbridge March" on the Home Service which has since become
Radio 4. The music had a sedative effect on me, relaxing the
feeling of excitement I felt in anticipation of my first day as a
student. The half-hour journey on the underground seemed
endless to me. I remember having to shut my eyes for a
moment in the blinding glare of the morning sun as I
emerged from the station near the hospital. Just four
minutes later at nearly 9 a.m. I was approaching its front
gate. The strains of the "Knightsbridge March" seemed to
fill my ears again. For me, like so many young men that
morning, a new life was about to start. Eric Coates's music
was like the overture to a new opera. As the rousing,
heraldic chords echoed in my head, I strolled nonchalantly
and capless through the front gate, nodding casually to the

man on duty. It was Blue Eyes himself.

"Good morning, Mr Wilder," he smiled.

He had actually remembered my name after over a year. This did my little ego a power of good. I smiled back as the final notes of the March sounded inside my head.

Forty-two new students had assembled in the Biology Department. Forty-two strangers, who were shortly to form friendships and associations according to their individual temperaments. We were a motley crowd. The war with Japan was now over and thousands of young men were being demobbed to start life again as civilians. So, in addition to the more customary young students who had come from school about half our numbers were men who had fought in the War. These found the adjustment to the discipline of student-ship quite a challenge after the rigours of service life. There was the ironic coincidence of an army major sharing the same dogfish dissection in biology with his former corporal batman. Fate takes many strange routes in life. At the end of that first academic year, having survived the War, the major fell at his first M.B. examination and failed. He decided to discontinue his studies. In due course the corporal went on to become a consultant at one of our foremost hospitals.

Looking back, I suppose my first year as a student was the most uneventful. It took some time to settle down to the exacting routine of study and more study. It took time to get to know my fellow students. It took time to readjust to the big city after the vast freedom of the sea and country which I missed so much. Competition was very keen. We knew that there would be many others anxious to fill our ranks were we to do badly in the first M.B. examination at the end of the academic year. That first professional examination did take its toll and somewhat depleted in numbers, we re-formed our ranks, turned our backs on biology, physics and chemistry and prepared, after the summer vacation, to do battle with the unexplored terrain of human anatomy and the mysteries of physiology. The mixture of 'boys and men' had been an interesting success. The maturity brought in by the somewhat older and more worldly ex-service men had enabled those fresh from school to grow up a little more readily, to their advantage. The lance-corporals, majors, sub-lieutenants and squadron leaders had quickly learned to shrug off their wartime images and adapt to just being students. Although, for just a few this re-adaptation took a little longer. I remember having a rough time one morning dissecting a rabbit in zoology. Peter Dawes, who had been a lieutenant on submarines and who still sported a magnificent beard, eyed the dissection almost woefully. "It's not looking too ship-shape on the starboard side," he observed.

"That rabbit's had a bit of a prang, I'd say," came the comment from John Warren, a former flying officer. By the end of that first year, the army, navy and airforce jargon had almost been replaced by the language of dental and medical students. We had become integrated.

Before going away on my summer holidays I decided to purchase a human skeleton and skull in readiness for the start of the forthcoming course on anatomy and physiology. Such a purchase was quite a good investment for at the end of our studies and the use of the 'bones', it was customary to re-sell them to another second-year student and so one could always be sure of getting one's money back. I had little difficulty in acquiring such an outfit from a senior student for the sum of just ten pounds. The bones came neatly stowed away in a very old and battered leather attaché case. I decided to keep them safely at my home during the long summer break. On my way home with them from the hospital I called in at my barber's. I set the attaché case with its contents on to an empty chair while I had my hair cut. Some fifteen minutes later and immaculately shorn I picked up the case to leave the shop. As I did so, there was a slight click and the old and rusty lock chose to fail at that moment. Before I could do anything the lid burst open and the skull and bones cascaded across the barber's shop, the skull coming to rest at the feet of the next customer who was about to occupy my vacated chair. He froze, gave me a long stare as though I were either Burke or Hare, took a backward step, turned on his heels and stalked out of the shop. Mumbling apologies, I scampered about the place, diving under chairs and between people's legs in a frantic bid to retrieve the scattered bones of my skeleton.

"If this is your idea of a funny joke," shouted the owner of the establishment, "then I suggest you take your business elsewhere. You've just lost me a customer!"

"I'm very sorry," I stumbled, "but it was an accident. Really it was."

"A likely story," he said and he turned to one of his assistants. "These students are all the same. Don't know where to stop." He turned to me. "Now get that sickening head and bits of bones out of here!" and he advanced towards me. Realizing that he was in no mood to be appeased, I escaped from the shop, feeling very cross with the attaché case. I decided to change to another barber after that. The next morning I transferred the skull and bones to another, more reliable container. By the afternoon I was sitting on a train, heading north-west to Wales on the start of a well-deserved holiday.

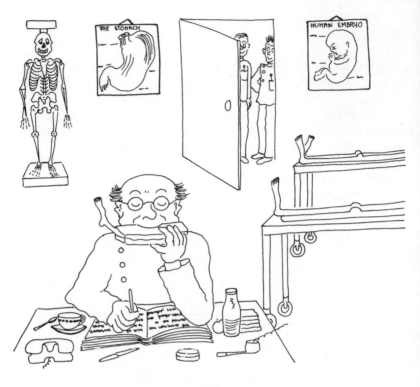

2

One Man's Meat

October came round all too quickly and with it the start of
the second year. Back once more at the hospital, I made my
way to the top floor of the Anatomy Department and to the
dissecting room, where I was to be presented with the preserved cadaver of a human being. The dissecting room had
during our first year been a mysterious strongroom on the
third floor where, from time to time, sweet, sickly, pungent
odours would percolate down the stairs to the lower floors; the
unmistakable smell of preserved 'specimens'.

I had spent the summer vacation swimming, lazing and
tanning on the golden sands of the North Wales coast where,
as the guest of old friends, I had escaped again to the wide

16

open spaces. I had returned to London the evening before and the sudden anticlimax of finding myself confined in a white-tiled room with a bare stone floor and almost featureless but for a row of marble-topped tables, was almost unbearable. The Professor of Anatomy sorted us out into groups of four. Peter Dawes, John Warren, Charles Martin and I were set at table E. Four students at each of seven tables. Twenty-eight out of the original forty-two were embarking on a year's exploration into the construction and workings of the human body. My three colleagues had each purchased a brand new book on anatomy, the famous *Gray's Anatomy* and a companion book, a step-by-step guide to dissection. I had managed to get my books second-hand but in good condition from a local bookseller. The money I had saved had gone toward the train fare for my holiday. Peter, John, Charles and I waited around the clean, washed dissecting table E. The other six groups were doing likewise at their tables. The low murmur of our voices echoed and re-echoed from the bleak walls of the room as we waited in nervous anticipation to be given our cadavers for dissection. The faint smell of formalin made me feel sick. Away and outside down the corridor some footsteps sounded and gradually came nearer to the room. The noisy clatter of wheels accompanied them, the wheels of a trolley. Suddenly, the door burst open and for the first time my eyes set gaze on Street, the dissecting room attendant. He wore a stained white coat. He was about five foot three inches in height, almost as wide and was completely bald. His moon-like face and head shone with a pale yellowish luminosity. John Warren coughed nervously. "Fancy anyone actually wanting to do this for a living," he said.

"I bet he's sold his body to the hospital already and spent the money," added Charles Martin. Street trundled the trolley up to table A. On it was the corpse of a woman. Her body had a slight greyish tinge as a result of the preservatives used. It was difficult to assess her age. It might have been seventy. I had never seen a corpse before. I had hardly slept the previous night in anticipation of this morning. But it hit me worse than I expected. I suddenly felt physically ill.

"I can't possibly go through with all this," I thought. "A whole year spent slowly taking one of these to pieces . . . a whole year!" I shuddered inwardly.

"I really don't think I can take this," John Warren voiced my thoughts.

"It's one thing shooting at some stranger in an enemy plane, but this, ugh!"

By the time we had composed ourselves and realized that no doubt all our fellow students felt the same, Street was trundling our specimen over to table E. On it was the cadaver of a man, well over seventy and of medium stature. Street and his assistant lifted it on to the marble dissecting table. I had not expected the body to be quite so stiff as it was. I had overlooked the fact that it might have been in the preservation tank for some considerable time. The rest of the morning was spent meeting the anatomy demonstrators, who would guide us through our dissections and test us at regular periods on what we had learnt. The required standard was high.

In addition to our anatomy text books, we each had a set of dissecting instruments, consisting of a pair of tweezers, three or four different sized scalpels and a couple of instruments for probing called 'seekers'. We would be spending the first term studying the chest.

"Good morning, gentlemen, have you decided who is going to make the first incision?" Dr Davies, one of the anatomy demonstrators was addressing our group but had his eyes fixed on me. He had a high-pitched boyish voice.

"F-first incision?" I repeated.

"Yes, got to make a start sooner or later." He rubbed his hands together, took his pipe out of his mouth and holding bowl in his hand pointed along an imaginary line on the cadaver's chest. The mouthpiece was so close to the body that at one point it actually touched it. "You'll need a large-bladed scalpel for this," he said and put the pipe back into his mouth without even wiping it. I shot a quick glance at John who raised an eyebrow.

"Ah, now this will do the job," and Dr Davies handed me my largest scalpel.

"Is this yours?" he asked.

"Yes, it's mine." I answered. I was caught.

"Right now, Mr . . .?"

"Wilder," I informed him.

"Right now, Mr Wilder," and he said my name slowly and

deliberately as if trying to remember it in addition to all the other new ones that morning, "show us how to do it."

"I've never done it before," I heard myself say, having lost all shreds of a sense of humour.

"Of course you haven't," he responded ironically. "That is why you are here." He removed his pipe again and this time he actually drew a line on the chest with the mouthpiece about eight inches in length. The merest of perfunctory wipes on his white, starched coat and it was back in his mouth. "Come along now," and impatience entered his voice. Trying to conceal the tremor of my hand I placed the scalpel onto the cadaver's chest and ran it along the line Dr Davies had indicated. I had expected the blade to sink into it like a sharp carving knive into the Sunday roast. But nothing happened.

"Now use a little pressure, Mr Wilder."

"I thought I was," I said.

"Obviously not enough," he responded. "Let's do it together."

His large hand enveloped mine and he directed it to the cadaver again. I felt it being forced down, some resistance as the blade met the preserved skin and then a downward plunge as it cut through the body. A moment later I felt further resistance as it met the underlying bone. I broke out into a cold sweat and the room seemed to swim. From afar I could hear Dr Davies's voice.

"Steady, old chap, don't pass out now that you've started."

I struggled within me and came slowly back. The collar of my shirt was drenched with perspiration.

"Are you all right?" he asked dispassionately.

"Fine thanks," I lied.

"Then let's carry on," and he guided my hand and scalpel along the line of the incision and then removed his hand. I sank slowly down on to the stool we each had. The cadaver lay still, silent, motionless, unperturbed and indifferent. There was no flow of blood from the eight-inch incision. It all seemed remote and impersonal. I had started! I had already crossed the first barrier. I handed my scalpel to John Warren who was seated on my side of the cadaver.

"It's a nice strong scalpel," I teased. "Would you care to make the next incision, Doctor?" In a few minutes time John, Peter and Charles would be initiated as well. For a few brief moments I intended to enjoy the distinction of being first.

Needless to say I had no lunch that day. The sight of the roast beef served up to me in the hospital restaurant brought me out in another cold sweat. In fact, I turned almost complete vegetarian for several weeks. But as the days lengthened into weeks and the weeks into months, I found to my relief that my initial repugnance for practical anatomy was waning. The daily practice of dissection was becoming routine. I hardly noticed the now familiar smells of the dissecting room.

Slowly our cadaver was taken carefully to pieces. 'Arthur', as we had affectionately come to call him had become a friend. We, of course, knew nothing about him, his whereabouts or his life, but in death he was serving well the cause of medicine. Without Arthur, the four of us would never become dental surgeons. At the end of each week, the various 'pieces' were removed by Street and his assistant. As Arthur became less and less, so our knowledge of anatomy became more and more and our note books grew into several volumes as we carefully recorded every organ, nerve, muscle and blood vessel, and their positions and relationship to each other. Working closely as I was with three other colleagues, we soon became good friends and we found that the four of us were remarkably compatible. I was always under the impression that the other three were brighter than myself. I, consequently, worked and studied hard to keep up with them. Charles Martin had a delightful sense of humour and the fine ability of keeping us going at the end of a particularly difficult dissecting session. On one occasion I had been reading a couple of paragraphs in the dissection manual. When I returned my attention to Arthur I was surprised to see a cigarette smouldering in his mouth. This inoffensive joke had also been noticed by Dr Davies from the other side of the dissecting room. He bore down on Charles Martin.

"Mr Martin, if you wish to continue here as a student you'll kindly refrain from these childish practical jokes!"

After that poor Charles could do nothing right although he was easily the cleverest of our group. Our year in the anatomy department would have been a happy time to think back about were it not for Dr Davies. He was the only thorn in our side. His early hint of facetiousness grew and grew. He would delight in catching Charles Martin out on some remote point during our fortnightly oral examinations. We discovered that he had been having some matrimonial trouble and although we felt some sympathy for this we did resent the venting of his emotions on us and especially on Charles. Charles had come to the hospital straight from school. He obviously had a successful career ahead of him. I admired his tenacity in side-stepping the frequent caustic remarks that Dr Davies would direct at him.

"I don't know how you tolerate him," I said to Charles one day after he had suffered from a particularly vicious on-slaught over a trivial error. "If I were you, I'd have socked him."

"I'm biding my time," replied Charles.

A few days later, a somewhat distraught Dr Davies approached me. "My wife hasn't been able to prepare my lunch box today and I'm not in the mood to go down to the restaurant. Would you mind getting me some sandwiches, Wilder. Anything will do. I don't want much. Just leave them on my desk."

Dr Davies's room was a little glass partitioned area in the dissection room. It had no door but did, at least, offer him a little privacy. In it were a simple wooden desk and a chair. As I had intended having a sandwich lunch in the library that day over some books, I had brought with me a packet of cheese sandwiches. I had overlooked the fact that it was Peter Dawes's birthday and he had invited our group of four to the restaurant for lunch. When at lunch time he had reminded me of this I decided to leave my cheese sandwiches on Dr Davies's desk. "Why waste them," I thought. John, Peter, Charles and I set off for the restaurant In the doorway of the dissecting room Charles Martin hesitated. "I just want to finish writing up some notes before I forget them," he said pensively. "It won't take more than a few minutes. You three go on and order my lunch for me. See you soon," and he darted back through the door. Lunch was a long, pleasant affair and over an hour later the four of us wandered back to the dissecting room feeling more like an afternoon's nap than a dissecting session. However, we settled down to work on Arthur. It might have been fifteen minutes later when Dr Davies appeared at our table. He was in an unusually affable mood.

"Thank you, Mr Wilder, for those delicious cold meat and cheese sandwiches you got me for my lunch. How much do I owe you?" Cold meat and cheese!? I had left him only cheese sandwiches. Then a ghastly thought struck me as I noticed that there seemed to be fewer 'pieces' lying around on the dissecting table than before lunch. I looked up and caught Charles Martin's innocent expression. He gave me a slow, knowing wink. Suppressing any outward sign of emotion I turned my head to the dissection. To this day I am sure I detected the very faintest of smiles on Arthur's face!

By the time there was literally nothing left of Arthur the year of anatomy was over. By good fortune all four of us passed our second year's examinations. Of the other twenty-four in that year, sixteen of them passed, two were referred to take the examinations again a year later and six decided to relinquish their studentships. From the original forty-two there were twenty of us who had survived the first two gruelling years. Now there were six weeks of summer vacation to enjoy and after that the pleasant prospects of entering the Prosthetics Department as third-year students.

3

Fools Rush In

I was nearly half way through my third year at the dental school, the year spent studying the gentle art of denture prosthetics. The snow that had fallen the previous week had miraculously disappeared in the night. The wind had changed direction and had backed from north-east to the warmer prevailing west. Suddenly, the long winter seemed to be cracking and here, at last, was the early promise of spring. The crocuses that had stoically thrust their way through the soil and into the blanket of snow were now adding a splash of colour to the dark background of the earth. Winter's long wait was over. Nature was progressing to its next stage. After this long winter, studying how to construct dentures in the laboratory, today was to mark the start of the next stage in my dental training. Today, I was for the very first time going to attend to my very first patient.

The prosthetics room was situated on the first floor of the dental school. It was separated from the technicians' laboratory by a short, featureless corridor. An incessant clatter of leather soles on the stone floor of the corridor was a constant reminder of the busy traffic of students between the prosthetics room and the laboratory. Students were hurrying to keep their appointments with their patients while others were returning to the laboratory with impressions, plaster models and partly constructed dentures. During those first few months I had spent in the laboratory, the prosthetics room had become the promised land and with one's eventual entry there had come the attainment of that much coveted title of 'pre-clinical student'. Today, I and a few of my colleagues, who by some interesting coincidence were all attired in their best suits, had become, or perhaps to be more correct, were just about to become 'pre-clinical students'.

"Hello, Wilder. Feeling nervous?" Mark Travers caught up with me as I passed through the heavy green doors of the dental school.

"Very," I said. "Are you?" I asked hopefully anticipating some comfort in sharing his apprehension.

"Not really," he replied confidently.

I was at an immediate disadvantage. But then I should have expected this. Travers was the grand master of gamesmanship. He was also very bright and obviously had a brilliant career ahead of him. At that very moment I hated him! Outside the prosthetics room we joined the short queue of students who were waiting to go in. Travers and I must have been the last to arrive for as we did so the door opened and Professor Glenn smilingly welcomed us. This was it. I hurried in through the door. I was a pre-clinical student. I was in the promised land; keen, young, inexperienced. Fools rush in where wise men fear to tread!

"Mr Travers, will you go to chair number four," requested the Professor. "You, Mr Wilder, to chair number five and you Mr . . ." The student who should have attended chair number six had not yet arrived and so I found myself virtually alone with Travers in our part of the room. Seated in the chair was a genial gentleman of about seventy. He was dressed in a well worn grey suit and he wore a pair of old and very polished brown shoes. I found myself seeing a similarity in the wrinkles in the leather of his shoes to the wrinkles in his weather-tanned face. He looked like a retired market porter. His hands were enormous and they were screwing up his cloth cap as I offered him a "Good morning".

"Good morning, Doctor," came the throaty reply in undisguised cockney. I warmed to him and found some secret comfort from my nervousness in his brown, trusting eyes. No doubt, to so many who had lived and worked their lives in the shadow of the hospital, the 'doctor' was part of an infallible institution. This morning I had just been recognized as belonging to that institution. This morning I was the 'doctor'. This morning I was infallible. Little did he know!

My patient, Archibald Curran, was a well preserved seventy-six. He had, indeed, been a market porter and over the years had from time to time left small pieces of his anatomy behind him in various operating theatres of the hospital, not the least being his entire set of upper and lower teeth.

"They done it, Guv, wiv a dose of the larfing gas. But I didn't see nuffink to larf abart when I gits 'ome and sees me old mug in the mirrer! So 'ere I am and you can make me all young and 'andsome again wiv a nice set of nashers." He laughed long, heartily and chestily. So much so, that it produced a slight broncho-spasm and I had to suppress his splutters by giving him a drink of water.

Archibald Curran had lost his few remaining teeth six months previously. His gums, having now healed, were ready for a full set of upper and lower dentures. This visit was to be a matter of first impressions. Having made upper and lower plaster models from the impressions, time could then be spent in the laboratory setting the teeth up on a wax base ready for the fitting or try-in. I had many times watched Professor Glenn demonstrating the taking of impressions and I had admired the dexterity with which he manipulated the dental plaster, spatulating carefully measured amounts of plaster and water in a plastic bowl until, when it was the consistency of thin, smooth cream, he had poured it into an impression tray and then skilfully inserted the whole thing into the patient's mouth. Two minutes later, when the impression had set, he had removed a perfect negative replica of the edentulous jaw with a soft cry of "There!" I was reminded of Little Jack Horner!

Now it was my turn. I was relieved that my first dealings with a patient would be the simple taking of an impression. As I mixed the plaster and water, out of the corner of my eye I noticed that Travers had already inserted his impression tray on to his patient's upper jaw and was timing the setting period. Holding the handle of the tray gently with a hand, he stood there, implacable and confident. I spent rather longer mixing the plaster than the stipulated time, as I found difficulty in smoothing out several large lumps of dry plaster that somehow refused to mix with the water. By the time I had filled the impression tray I was aware that the mixture was rapidly losing its fluidity. With a hurried "Open wide", I frantically shoved the tray and its contents into Mr Curran's mouth only to find to my horror that the tray was upside down and that the plaster that should have been taking an upper jaw impression was facing his bare lower dental arch. I just stopped myself from pressing the white mass onto his tongue and coughing nervously I removed the tray from his mouth. By which time the plaster had set!

"I'll just re-take that," I mumbled, casting a hasty glance first at Mr Curran and then at Travers. My patient was quite oblivious as to what had happened and was sitting there with his mouth open and his eyes closed. Travers's beady eyes, however, had observed the whole episode.

"Try getting the tray the right way up next time!" His remark hurts me to this day. I turned my back on him and carefully proceeded to mix a fresh plaster and water impression. This time the lumps were more controllable and although I again took a little more time getting a smooth mixture than I should, I quickly inserted the tray the right way up into my patient's mouth, pressed it firmly on to the roof of his mouth and upper gums and stood slightly back to admire the scene. It was then that I noticed a bulk of plaster oozing down from the back of the tray and slowly approaching his open throat. He was breathing through his mouth and in a flash I had a vision of the plaster breaking away, falling into his windpipe and blue-faced, choking patient struggling in his death throes on the floor of the prosthetics room. As I stood, frozen to the spot, the plaster rapidly grew harder and it set, leaving a gap of barely half an inch between the back of his throat and the edge of the plaster. Mr Curran sat there relaxed, breathing gently. A familiar cough behind me made me turn my head. Travers was pointing to the corner of his mouth and shaking his head wisely. I had no idea what he meant. He then pointed to my patient and at once I realized the significance of his behaviour. The handle of the impression tray was protruding not from the centre of his lips but right out of the corner of his mouth. In my concern to get the impression in at all, this time I had overlooked the angle of insertion. I carefully removed the tray. The impression was, of course, quite useless. Being rotated in the tray, it had missed vital areas of the mouth. I laboriously removed the impression and set about preparing yet another mix of plaster. Travers had by now completed the taking of both upper and lower impressions and was tidying up his instruments.

"O.K. Guv?" Archie Curran smiled at me enquiringly.

"Fine thanks," I murmured, feeling hot under the collar.

"Making good progress," I added unconvincingly.

This time I added a drop or two more of water to the plaster than before so that I should have a little more time to get the tray into the right position. I loaded the mixture into the tray. It was quite smooth and devoid of lumps, albeit just a trifle on the thin side. With a muffled sigh of "Here we go," I placed the tray and its contents into the correct position. This time there was no excess coming from the back of the tray and the handle was correctly protruding right from the centre of his mouth. A gentle calm came over me.

"I'll just wait a couple of minutes for that to set, Mr Curran," I said reassuringly. My patient grunted his assent, opened his eyes and winked one of them at me.

"It's a bit thin, isn't it?" Travers's voice.

"It's what?" I asked.

"That plaster looks a bit thin," observed Travers. He was inspecting the plaster left in the mixing bowl.

"Do you really think so?" I asked nonchalantly, casting a proud look at the impression tray which was seated so correctly in my patient's mouth.

"I doubt whether it will ever set," said Travers and he added, "How long has it been in?"

"Nearly three minutes," I said.

"Then it should have set by now."

"I'm sure it has," but my newly acquired confidence was deserting me. I pulled gently down on the tray handle. There should have been considerable resistance due to the suction between the set plaster and the gums. But the tray fell easily away and to my disgust on inspection I found a thin watery powder residing as a shapeless mass in the tray.

"Can I help you?" he offered in a loud superior voice.

I pushed him away from the dental chair. "Don't make me out to be such an incompetent idiot in front of my patient," I said angrily. "I don't want him to know that he's my first patient."

"I was only trying to be helpful," Travers said. "The way you're going, you'll be here all day!" he added.

"That's my worry," I snapped.

Travers shrugged his shoulders, picked up his perfect upper and lower impressions and slowly walked out of the prosthetics room.

I returned to Archie Curran. "Last impression coming up," I said as I inwardly prayed. This time everything went according to the text book. The mixture was just right, the angle of insertion was correct and the final impression that came out after just two minutes was a treat to see. Curran and I were the only two occupants of the prosthetics room by now. There was no-one to proudly show my hard-won results. By now it was lunch time.

"Can you come back tomorrow for the lower impressions?" I asked.

"I fought you only 'ad to take two?" he said.

"That depends on the shape of the mouth," I lied. "In difficult cases we have to take each jaw in four segments!"

"I see, Guv." He appeared to understand. Which was more than I did as my remark was meaningless. It did, however, win for me the opportunity of taking four impressions for the lower jaw, should it be necessary, on the following day. I

picked up my solitary impression and escaped into the sanctuary of the laboratory.

Four weeks and two impressions later, for I had, indeed,
obtained an excellent lower impression at only the second
attempt – I was learning, which was the very reason for being
a student – I found myself greeting Mr Curran again in the
prosthetics room. I had spent many hours under the guidance
of a skilled dental technician setting up the teeth on a pink
wax base. At this stage the dentures look quite completed and
ready to wear. The teeth are the ones carefully chosen to suit
the patient's mouth for function, colour, shape and general
appearance. They are set up in wax so that should an alter-
ation be necessary at the try-in stage it is relatively easy to
move the teeth in the wax in order to achieve this. When the
dentures are eventually considered correct the wax is replaced
by hard, pink acrylic in the laboratory and the dentures given
to the patient in the finished state. Mr Curran had then come
for his try-in. It was a creative moment and I can well
remember my sense of anticipation as I slipped the wax
dentures into his mouth. "Do be very careful with them," I
cautioned. "They are only made out of wax and I don't want
them damaged."

I stood back to admire the quite remarkable improvement
that they made to his appearance.

"My word, you really do look great," I observed.

I handed him a mirror. He inspected himself carefully for
some time and then fighting back tears he grabbed my arm.

"Blimey, you're a ruddy hartist," he exclaimed. "Cor," and
he chuckled, "just wait till the missus sees me."

"That's just what she'll have to do, Mr Curran," I said.
"She'll have to wait until they're completed. I'll have them
finished in the real plastic for you for next week. Just wait a
moment while I get Professor Glenn to inspect them at this
stage."

Professor Glenn was pleased with my first attempt at
denture construction. He suggested one or two minor altera-
tions which when I had carried them out certainly made
Archie Curran look a good fifteen years younger. I was
beginning to forget the trauma of the impression sessions.
Needless to say, Travers's wax try-in was excellent. His
patient, a charming little lady of about sixty-five, was having

quite a busy time at the hospital. In addition to her dentures she was currently being fitted with a hearing-aid and attending the clinic for arthritis. She had lost her teeth nine months previously and was impatient to face the world looking normal again.

"What do you think of that?" Travers invited me to inspect his work.

"I see you've managed to catch up somehow," he added. Without waiting for my comments he went on, "I'll just get the Professor to approve the try-in," and he brushed past me in search of Professor Glenn.

I carefully removed the dentures from Archie Curran's mouth and placed them in a bowl of chilled water to prevent the wax which had become warmed in his mouth from distorting.

"Would you please make an appointment to see me at the same time next week," I requested.

I was now really enjoying these early days of being a pre-clinical prosthetics student. The personal contact with patients was a fascinating challenge, even if one had to learn the hard way. It was lunch time. I had used up so much nervous energy attending to my patient that my appetite by now was nothing short of being ravenous. I decided to postpone tidying up my instruments from the prosthetics room until I had eaten my lunch in the students' canteen and restored my blood sugar level to its physiological normal. The standard of lunch that day was well above the usual beige taste of the canteen, a welcome reward for my endeavours. Engrossed as I was in my thoughts about Archie Curran's dentures, I hardly noticed Travers's absence from his usual place about three tables away from mine.

On my return after lunch to the prosthetics room, I was met by a white-faced, agitated Travers.

"Have you seen my patient?" he barked at me as I entered the room.

"Your patient?" I echoed. A quick glance at chair number four confirmed her absence.

"The bloody woman's disappeared," he raved, "and she's still wearing the wax try-in dentures!"

I had never in two and a half years ever seen him distressed or agitated. He was now almost hysterical.

"I went to get the Professor over an hour ago," he explained. "By the time I found him and got back to the chair – I suppose it was a good ten minutes – the idiot woman had gone!" He slumped down into the dental chair. "If she ruins that set-up," and he hesitated while he contemplated the situation, "I'll just about murder her!" he spat out.

"She's hard of hearing, isn't she?" I asked.

"Yes, she is," confirmed Travers.

"Perhaps she didn't hear you say it was only a try-in," I suggested.

"Perhaps she thought the dentures were finished and went home. Travers, you did tell her it was only a try-in, didn't you?"

His face turned several shades whiter. "I think I did," he said hesitatingly. "Yes, I'm almost sure I did," he added uncertainly. "Well, er, well, I might just have forgotten."

I felt sorry for him. It looked as though the great Travers had fallen at the last hurdle. At that moment, the receptionist made her way along the row of dental chairs towards us.

"Mr Travers, there's a Mrs Brown on the telephone for you. She sounds rather distressed." Throwing me a frantic stare, he ran to the reception desk. Two minutes later he returned.

"She did think that the dentures were finished and ready for wearing," he said. "When I went to get the Professor she assumed it was all right to go home. Being deaf, we hadn't been able to communicate much at any time. Well, she went home and had a piping hot cup of tea. What that hot tea did to her wax dentures I leave to your imagination." He sank down into the chair again. "Oh hell," he moaned. "Bloody hell!"

One week later I fitted a delighted Archie Curran with his dentures. I had become attached to my creation over the weeks and it was with somewhat of a wrench that I parted with them. However, my next patient was waiting for me. I went to the waiting room. "Mr Atkins for Mr Wilder, please. Would you kindly come this way." I led the way to the prosthetics room and over to chair number five. As I carefully measured the dental plaster and water into the plastic mixing bowl and set to work on the impressions for my second set of full upper and lower dentures, a loud voice came to me from the direction of chair number four.

"Now, Mrs Brown, if you would kindly sit quite still, I'll start once again to take the impressions for your dentures."

"There's really no need for you to shout like that, Mr Travers," came the response. "I'm not deaf, you know!"

4

The Truth That Leaked Out

"Bang goes my summer holiday," I cursed. "After the price of that little lot, I shall be stony broke for the rest of the year." That 'little lot' was, in fact, a complete set of dental instruments for my use as a fourth-year clinical student. It contained a full range of everything that would now see me through my final two years of study. I had ordered them from the dental supply company as soon as I had heard that I had successfully passed my prosthetics examination. Now, at the start of the fourth academic year, they were ready for me to collect from the showrooms near the hospital. The instruments were beautifully arranged in the drawers of a shiny new mahogany cabinet. It was about eighteen inches high and had an equally shiny chromium carrying handle. In accordance with the custom, I had had a small chromium plate engraved with my name on it. This was securely screwed on to the top of the cabinet, proudly proclaiming my hard-won status of 'clinical student'. The price had been suggested in a pamphlet on equipment sent out by the Dean. However, under considerable pressure from the dental company's salesman, I had purchased a great number of supplementary instruments which, he assured me, "were absolutely necessary. That list from the dental school is always inadequate. You don't want to be caught out short when you start the new year".

In the feeling of euphoria of just having passed the pros-thetics examination, I was influenced enough to take his advice. Now, several weeks later and in the cold grey of a January morning, I was beginning to think that I had been caught out short in rather a different way. "You'll need all the gear when you have qualified," came the attempt at reassurance from the salesman.

"If I ever do," I replied sourly as I struggled with the weighty cabinet out of the showroom doors.

The cabinet seemed to get heavier as I made the two hundred yards to the hospital and then up two flights of stairs to the Conservation Room. By the time I had set it down on a stand beside one of the dental chairs my arms were aching. However, my concern at the cost and the discomfort of getting the cabinet to the hospital were quickly dissipated by the feeling of achievement of at last being let loose on patients – not merely the taking of impressions – but actually giving injections, and filling and extracting teeth.

I had for three long years watched with secret envy the senior medical students as they wandered about the hospital with their stethoscopes peeping nonchalantly from their pockets, and their dental counterparts who always seemed to have a mouth mirror nestling conveniently at hand in the top left pocket of their jackets. Somehow or other one of these mirrors found a similar repose in a similar pocket of my jacket during the short journey between the dental company's show-room and the hospital. With the sudden acquisition of this badge of seniority I became lost in a reverie as the 'dental surgeon' found himself struggling into a freshly starched, white clinical jacket in the company of some sixteen other new clinical students.

"Well, Leonard, this is it." Charles Martin placed his dental cabinet on the stand by the next chair to mine. "Mind if I work next to you? I might learn a thing or two."

"Not from me, you won't," I replied. "But stay right there, I'd be glad to have you as a neighbour."

Charles and I had become good friends over the years. We had spent many hours together over the telephone at weekends, sorting out some problem or other with our studies.

The Dental Conservation Room was a large, rectangular room, built around a square glass-windowed well, which went down to the ground floor. Two rows of chairs ran along each of the four sides of the room and faced inwards towards the well. The chair I had chosen was in the outer row and at the end of it. This had one great advantage. It was the nearest chair to the hand basins. In this position I had only to take about two or three paces to wash my hands and so spare myself the inconvenience of having to walk several yards each time from a chair further along the row. Although, by present standards the dental units and chairs could be considered somewhat out of date, at the time they were the very latest in equipment. They had, in fact, only been installed brand new the previous year and looked very smart in shiny mid green.

A whole year had passed since my first traumatic attempts to take impressions for dentures. I had learnt a lot in that time, a lot about dentures and a lot about dealing with patients. It was this latter aspect which I found fascinating. People varied so very much but tended to have one thing in common. That was a reluctance and frequently a dislike and even horror of going to the dentist. I felt that the dentist could do so much to put his patients at ease.

I remembered my trepidation when I had attended Archie Curran, my very first patient, in the prosthetics department, and my hope that he would not know this fact. These sentiments now came back to me even more strongly. I had spent the three previous months to this in the 'Phantom Head' room, learning to inject and drill and fill and clean and extract on model teeth in model jaws in a model head. But this was for real. There was no leeway for error! At 9.30 a.m. I and Charles Martin went to the waiting room which was

annexed to the Conservation Room. I had during the past few
months grown a moustache. I hoped that this would add a
look of increased maturity about me and might even lend an
air of professional authority. One feels so very vulnerable at
this stage of one's training.

My first patient, Mr James Anson, was a small, thin man of
thirty-eight. He had a slight limp of his left leg, the result of
having had poliomyelitis as a child. He eyed me pensively as I
called his name and introduced myself. Did he know that I
was a first-timer, I wondered? I brushed my moustache with a
finger in an attempt to attract his attention to it. By the time
I had led the way through the Conservation Room to my
chair I was feeling more and more like Sheridan's character
Bob Acres in his play, *The Rivals*. Like him, I could feel "the
valour oozing out through the palms of my hands"! He sat in
the chair and as I bent over him to inspect his teeth I prayed
inwardly that I would find nothing wrong. Courage had
deserted me and I wanted so much to win some time and
have a quick desperate look at my notes again. But luck, too,
was against me. Arrayed along his jaws were teeth in various
stages of decay. Large holes and even larger ones. How I
hoped to find just one little cavity on which to make a start.
My sweating fingers gripped the dental probe as I system-
atically inspected each tooth. In the Phantom Head room the
synthetic teeth were all clean and polished. James Anson's
were black with tobacco tar and the odour that came from
them had a bitter, sour aroma that hung in my nose. Then,
quite suddenly, the fine point of the probe located itself in a
tiny cavity on the side of his first left upper premolar tooth. I
suppose it was about the size of a pin head. This would make
a good, safe, start. There was another attraction to this tooth.
Being near the front of his mouth I could drill it without the
hazards of working upside down and back to front on the
reflected image in the mouth mirror. There was also no tooth
either side of it, which made access that much easier.

"I'll make a start on this one," I said, nonchalantly tapping
the tooth with the probe. The patient shut his mouth with a
snap and turned his head to one side.

"Didn't think there was anything wrong with that one," he
challenged.

"There's a hole in it," I responded.

He gave me a long, cold stare. "That's funny. The other dentist didn't say so."

Other dentist! What other dentist?

"You've been to another dentist, have you?" I asked.

"Yes, my regular one," he replied.

With his teeth in their advanced state of neglect, I wondered how regular that meant.

"I had a check-up a couple of months ago and he said, (stressing the "he") that I had seven large holes to be filled, four nerves to be took out, five teeth to be pulled, and part top and bottom false teeth to go in." He leaned back in the chair, turned his head away, a thin smile creasing his face.

"He said what?" I asked.

"Seven very large holes, four nerves, five out, falsies in!" He repeated his inventory in a high sing-song voice.

"No mention of the small one in the top left tooth?" I almost pleaded.

"No mention at all," he said challengingly. "Just seven large holes, four nerves, five out, and new falsies in."

He had certainly learnt his lines.

"Then why didn't you go back to him for the treatment?" Hope was faintly stirring within me.

" 'Cos they took him away." He was enjoying every minute of this exchange.

"Took him away?" I asked with surprise at his remark.

"S'right. He went bonkers."

"He went bonkers?" I repeated slowly.

"Yer. Most of them do after a bit, don't they? It's all that strain, looking in that tichy mirror, ain't it?" He threw me another of his long, cold stares. "Just you wait and see. Just you wait and see!"

I had obviously chosen the wrong profession, but I was committed. In my fourth year it was too late to change. How I loathed this wretched man with his soothsaying.

"Well, Mr Anson, you are now in my care and I have decided to make a start on the small cavity on your upper left tooth." I said the words without a trace of confidence in my voice.

"It don't need doing!" he snapped. "Just seven large holes, four nerves, five out, and two falsies." I heard myself repeating the jingle in my mind along with him. He leaned forward in the chair and staring at me unblinkingly asked, "How long have you bin at this game?" I felt homicidal.

"Er, long enough," I replied non-committally.

"Huh!" he snorted. "I was just wondering, that's all."

Then suddenly, inspiration hit me and I saw a legitimate way of ridding myself of this pest.

"Very well then, Mr Anson, we shall be pleased to carry out your treatment." By using the word 'we' rather than 'I', I hoped to speak with the authority of the 'Institution'. "But as you appear to require several extractions, we shall arrange for these to be carried out first so that your gums can start to heal as soon as possible in preparation for your dental prostheses."

"Me dental what?" For the first time he appeared a little unsure.

"Dental prostheses," I reiterated slowly, realizing that he did not know the word. I was starting to learn the early rudiments of gamesmanship.

"I dunno that. All I want is some falsies when me teeth come out."

"My dear chap," I said somewhat patronizingly, "they are one and the same thing."

"Oh, is they?"

The tide was beginning to turn.

"If you would care to go along to the Reception Desk and make an appointment to be seen in the Extraction Department, your fillings, large and small, can be attended to afterwards. Would you like to have them out under gas?"

"Gas?" He appeared startled at this suggestion.

"Yes, gas," I stressed slowly.

"I'm not having no gas, thanks very much."

"Why not? Just a quick whiff and it's all over."

"I'm not having no gas," he insisted, gripping the arms of the dental chair. "I knew a bloke what kicked it under gas. Just a quick whiff and it was all over for him. You can do mine with the needle."

He hesitated and added, "Please, sir."

I had won. It would have been unkind to pursue the battle any further. Mr James Anson hobbled out of the conservation room door and closed it behind him. I never saw him again. My annoyance dissipated, I felt rather sorry for him and I hoped his treatment would go well. I also realized the strength of the 'Institution'. It was the ultimate weapon, the atom bomb which I decided rarely ever to use except as a last desperate resort.

The time was nearly 10.30 a.m. and I realized that I was starving. It had been the same during the first few weeks in the Denture Room. My expenditure of nervous energy had been most extravagant. I had burnt up my blood sugar to an uncomfortable low. Replenishment was urgent. At this early hour I was ready for lunch. I made my way to the canteen where, to the astonishment of the catering staff, I consumed a hearty three-course meal.

It was 11.30 a.m. Half way through the morning and I felt I had done a hard day's work. Yet the new clinical student had still to perform his first filling. My next patient had been waiting for me since 10.30 a.m. I hurried to the waiting room and escorted Sidney Lake to the chair. Mumbling something about "Sorry to have kept you waiting but that last patient was a difficult case" (which was not altogether untruthful), I made him comfortable in the chair. Sidney Lake was a pale-faced young man of eighteen and patently terrified of dentists. He needed two medium-sized fillings in adjacent teeth. His mouth was well cared for and I felt that I could cope with the work with some degree of confidence. I also wanted to help this nervous young man. I saw myself twenty-five years into the future, surrounded by appreciative patients who had once suffered the same nervous anguish as Sidney Lake and had, as the result of my reassuring manner, lost all vestiges of fear.

"Would you like to have an injection?" I politely asked him. His eyes grew wide and he sat in the chair quite motionless. I laid a hand gently on his shoulder.

"Would you like to have an injection?" I cooed quietly. He drew himself away from me and I could see the perspiration forming in small shiny beads on his forehead and face. He turned a shade paler. I watched, fascinated, as the beads grew larger, joined together and then ran down his face in glistening tracks to be absorbed by the collar of his shirt.

"If you have an injection," I explained, "then you won't feel the drill." At the mention of the word "drill" he shuddered and turned his head towards the spittoon. I waited for him to be sick but after a moment or two he recovered and I was spared that inconvenience. After several minutes of careful coaxing, he finally agreed to have an injection and so with rapidly increasing heart rate I went to find a house surgeon to supervise the giving of my first injection.

Tony Ainsworth had been qualified nearly two years and was one of the senior house surgeons. He had the reputation of being a patient instructor and I immediately warmed to his easy, unassuming, yet quietly confident manner.

"Just give the local analgesic slowly," he advised, "and don't forget to warm the solution first," he went on.

"Why warm it?" I asked.

"Would you like cold liquid squirted into your gums, especially if you were terrified?" he asked. "If you inject gently with a warm solution then you reduce shock to the patient."

It was all so obvious when one came to think of it. I was learning.

"Open wide, please, Mr Lake," I requested. "It won't hurt." I stood there for a moment with the needle of the syringe poised like a snake ready to strike. My heart was pounding in my chest. I glanced briefly at Tony Ainsworth who nodded his head.

"Okay," he said gently.

At last the moment had come. In a few moments I would have crossed the threshold that can be crossed but once in a career. For with the giving of that injection I would become a member of an exclusive club. I was on the way to becoming a dental surgeon. The door was opening and I was about to enter.

"Hold it, Wilder!" A curt command rang out.

Tony Ainsworth grasped my arm with a hand. I froze and felt like a boxer who, being obviously well ahead on points, had unexpectedly run into a barrage of blows. With his other hand he pointed to the floor around the dental unit. A shallow pool of water extended from it to the hand basins near by.

"I think there's a fault in the unit," he said. "We had better get it checked before you use it, so don't give that local yet. If the water spray fails in the middle of a filling, you'll overheat the tooth."

He turned to the patient, motionless in the chair with his mouth open. "Sorry to delay matters now that you've got yourself all worked up," and he hurried away to find the dental engineer. I was just as worked up as the patient. No-one had said sorry to me! It was nearly midday and my total achievement so far had been nil. The golden gate was still shut tight.

The engineer was a man who had never heard the word 'hurry'. He was also very thorough. Which meant that the simple changing of a tap washer could easily take him half an hour. He arrived with Tony Ainsworth some fifteen minutes after the leak had been noticed, chewing on an unlit cigarette end and beaming benevolently at the world in general. He slowly inspected the damp patch on the floor.

"Well, it might be coming from the unit. On the other hand it might be coming from the hand basins. There's no doubt about it, it's either one or the other," he murmured pensively, sounding as though he were tackling one of the world's greatest problems. As he spoke the cigarette end moved up and down on his lower lip as if it were firmly stuck to it. I waited to see if it would fall off but it never did. I learned at a later date that he was nick-named 'Fag End' by students and staff alike.

"Let's take a look at the sinks first," he suggested. Half an hour later and after much banging and tightening of nuts and washers, he slowly scratched his head. "Definitely not the hand basins," he proclaimed wisely. "So it must be the unit."

By one o'clock precisely Fag End had packed the last spanner into his tool box. He stood up and mopped his brow. "Well, I've tightened everything I could. You'll have no more trouble with that. See ya," and he ambled away with his distinctive unhurried gait. Of course, it was too late to do anything at all for Sidney Lake and, in any case, I was ravenous again and ready for my second lunch. I made another appointment for him to see me at the same time the following week.

Tony and I had our lunch together. By the time I had got through my second helping of apple crumble I was feeling replenished enough to face the world again. Came two o'clock and I was escorting Mrs Jean Mellish to the dental chair in the Conservation Room. Under Tony Ainsworth's careful surveillance, I prepared to give her an injection for a small filling in her right upper second premolar tooth. Mrs Mellish was an attractive, petite lady of thirty-five, with golden hair cut short. She was so relaxed that some of her mood transmitted itself to me. Tony stayed quietly in the background as I held her upper lip to one side and pressed the sharp end of the syringe needle against the mucosa above the tooth. Despite my apparent outward calm, I was trembling inside. The slightest of forward pressures and I watched as the needle entered her mouth. I threw her a hasty glance. She was sitting there quite unperturbed. I received a short nod from Tony and I started to inject very slowly. After several seconds I withdrew the empty syringe. I had done it! After the morning's delays and frustrations I had actually given my first injection. It was a big step forward. Mrs Mellish smiled. "What a gentle touch you have," she said." "I can see you've had a lot of experience." The words were a magical tonic to my ears. I looked at Tony, hoping for further approval and was rewarded by his nod of commendation. The preparation of the tooth presented me with no problem and by 2.45 p.m. a grateful patient was thanking me for my "excellent attention". I walked with her to the door in the hope that she might throw me a few more compliments before she took her leave. At the door she stopped.

"Who was that other young man watching you?" she asked. "Was he a junior student learning how to do it all?"

"There is always something to learn," I replied cagily.

I had a lecture to attend at 3 p.m. and with a profound feeling of achievement I packed my new, shiny instruments away in my dental cabinet. But I was impatient for the next day to come. The drama of being the 'dental surgeon' had fired my imagination. The future was full of smiling and appreciative Jean Mellishes.

The rest of the week passed uneventfully. With Tony Ainsworth's ever-vigilant eye always on me I performed a number of injections and carried out several successful fillings. By the end of the week the feeling of newness had slightly worn off. I was beginning to get the feel of it all. So when the second week started and I went to collect Sidney Lake from the waiting room it was with a sense of growing confidence. Which was just as well for the week's wait had added considerably to his anguish and I found him at least as nervous as the time before. For his sake I decided not to waste time and as soon as I had him settled in the chair I hurried away to find Tony Ainsworth. But he was busy with another patient and I had to wait nearly ten minutes for him to come and supervise my giving of the injection. Once again, I prepared a warm solution for this purpose. Turning to my patient, "Open wide, please," I requested, "It won't hurt." I have often read about the experience of *déja vu*, the sort of feeling that 'it has all happened before'. *Déja vu* or not, my hand was poised just as the week before, and then, "Hold it, Wilder!" and I heard a mocking echo from the past. A ghostly hand seemed to grab me by the wrist and with a sinking feeling I heard, "I think there's another leak in the unit." I turned my eyes from Sidney Lake's open mouth to the floor and I saw what, by now, I expected to see, a thin pool of water extending from the unit to the hand basins. We then proceeded to go through a replica of the pantomime that was performed just seven days before: the checking of the hand basins and taps, followed by the laborious dismantling of the dental unit and the consequent tightening up of everything. Once again Fag End was slow, laborious and thorough. Once again, at the end of it all, Sidney Lake had no treatment carried out and was given yet another appointment for yet another week. Once again, during the rest of the week, the dental unit and the water taps to the hand basins behaved themselves and gave not one moment of trouble. Once again, the week passed and yet once again, I led Sidney Lake from the waiting room to the dental chair in the Conservation Room. This time Tony Ainsworth had been prudent enough to get Fag End to check the equipment on the morning of Sidney Lake's appointment.

We were beginning to think that there was some kind of a jinx on this patient's treatment. We were even considering the possibility of using another unit this time. But as Tony said, "Let's give it another try. Third time lucky." The equipment all checked out in good working order. By the time I had the patient settled in the chair, Tony had the injection all pre-pared for me to administer. We wasted not a moment, not one unnecessary second for the capricious unit in which to start its neurotic behaviour. Sidney Lake was in a high state of nerves. He looked like a man facing a firing squad for the third time having experienced two previous reprieves just as the rifles were being levelled at him. He was trembling visibly as I advanced with the syringe poised. I briefly laid my other hand reassuringly on his shoulder but in his tenseness I doubt if he noticed it. For a fleeting moment I hesitated and then repeated my party piece, "Open wide – it won't hurt." My hand with the syringe moved forward. Now.

"Hold it, Wilder!!" My racing heart missed a beat and then went pounding on. There, sure enough with obsessional reliability I felt a hand grasp my wrist. The room seemed to spin, recede and come back with a shock.

Tony Ainsworth's voice sounded softly in my ear. "Look at that," he whispered.

I followed his gaze and saw to my surprise a thin, steady trickle of liquid flowing gently from the patient's right trouser leg on to the floor and form into a pool between the dental unit and the hand basins. Tony's face broke into a wide smile as he tried to suppress his mirth. "He's pissing himself with fear," he chuckled, "and that's what it's all been about. Now we know the truth about the leaks! He must have been too embarrassed to admit it. Now, just press on or we'll never get his treatment started. Let's have a nice, gentle and professional technique."

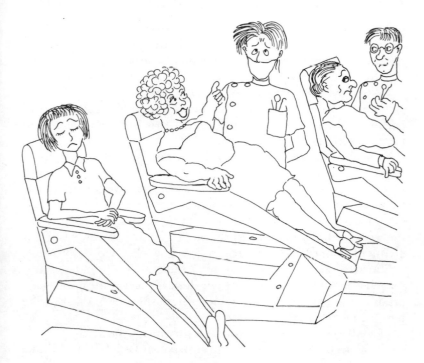

5

Nothing to Hide

I tapped respectfully on the door of the dental sister's office.

"Come in," called her voice from within the room.

Sister Meadows was ageless. She was small, round, grey-haired and always bustling. She had been sister to the dental hospital longer than anyone could remember and looked as though she were good for another hundred years or so. I liked her a lot. She had frequently invited me in for a morning coffee with her, no doubt as an inducement for me to relate one of my humorous experiences with patients. Although barely six months had passed since I had become a clinical student, even at that early time in my career, I could always see the lighter side of events. Life is so full of responsibilities and disappointments that I was determined to enjoy its sunnier aspects while I could. I believe that this philosophy has served me in good stead ever since.

"Do you have a face mask I could wear?" I asked her.

"Why, has your patient got bad breath?"

"No, it's not her breath. That I can live with. It's her cheap perfume. She reeks of the stuff and in this hot summer I'm in for an overpowering afternoon."

By way of a response Sister Meadows stared at me for a moment and then briefly changing the subject, "I thought you looked different today," she said, scrutinizing my face. "You've shaved off your moustache."

"I got fed up with it," was my reply. "So I shaved it off at the week-end. If you don't approve, it's all the more reason for giving me a mask to hide behind."

She treated me to one of her delectable chuckles, rummaged about in the drawer of her desk for a few moments and produced a new packet of white linen surgeon's masks. She handed me one.

"I shall expect a laugh from you for that," she said.

"That seems a fair price," I promised and I left her to make my way to the waiting room.

Spreading herself over the largest chair was Mrs Agnes Jarrow. She was by far the biggest woman I had ever seen. Although she was sixty-five, I believe she had never learnt to count beyond eighteen. Consequently, she thought, spoke and acted this very age. She always wore red and carried a matching handbag. She would poise herself precariously on a pair of very high-heeled stiletto shoes. With her size and weight it was, indeed, quite a remarkable balancing feat. Her hair was dyed a yellow blonde and had so much lacquer on it that it appeared to consist of a mass of tightly coiled springs. All this was grossly aggravated by the stench of the cheap perfume. No doubt, she had anointed her large frame with copious amounts of the stuff before attending for her dental appointment that day. The few other patients who were in the waiting room were all bunched together in the other chairs on the furthest side of the room to Agnes Jarrow. I can remember the look of relief on the face of the waiting room secretary as I led the way through the door and into the Conservation Room. I had prudently removed one of the arm-rests from the chair before going to call for her, otherwise it would have been quite impossible for her to have got into it.

"How are you today?" I dutifully enquired.

"All the better for seeing you, Mr Wilder." She spoke in a small squeaky voice with assumed cultured tones. It was very like a pantomime caricature. The first time I had heard this small, affected voice issuing from so large a lady, I had to turn away to avoid her seeing me smile. As usual she fluttered her heavily made-up eyes at me and small flakes of black mascara showered down on to her cheeks. In the heat of the day these quickly became absorbed into the damp perspiration on her face so that as the session proceeded she adopted an ashen hue. As she settled into the chair, I adjusted my face mask.

"Have you got a summer cold, Mr Wilder?" she asked.

"Yes, that's right," I lied.

"You poor boy. You need someone kind to look after you," and she gave me a long knowing look. I decided to busy myself choosing an instrument. This was her sixth visit to me, by which time she had had eight teeth filled and I was now ready to polish her fillings and start to scale her teeth.

"I'll get them all cleaned up today," I said, "and then you won't have to come back again, Mrs Jarrow."

She looked disappointed. "I shall miss my little sessions with you, Mr Wilder," she replied sadly. "I suppose you know that I have become rather fond of you over the weeks," and she gave me a fat smile. In the heat of the summer's day, I broke out into a cold sweat while the mask clung to my nose and face.

"It's always good to establish a rapport between patient and practitioner," I said, avoiding reference to myself as 'student'. As her mouth was now open again, she gave a half grunt and to avoid further conversation along these lines I inserted the saliva ejector. After several minutes of careful polishing I had her new fillings sparkling bright and as I moved away to admire my work I became aware of the heavy perfume engulfing me in its aroma. The mask was quite useless. I tore the thing from my face.

"That's better," she beamed. "Now I can see you, Handsome."

I glanced hurriedly around the room lest any of my colleagues had overheard her remarks. But the nearest ones to me were too engrossed in their own problems to notice mine and those who were some distance along the row of chairs would never have heard her anyway. All I could think of saying was, "Rinse out, please." She sucked in half a glass full of pale pink mouthwash and taking careful aim directed it from a distance of nearly two feet in a powerful jet towards the centre of the spittoon. The arm-rest I had removed was the one on the left of the chair, that is the one nearest the spittoon. As she leaned towards the bowl to ensure the safe delivery of the last drop, she slipped slightly and fell against the polished stainless steel basin. She reflexly put out her hand to steady herself and in so doing knocked the half full tumbler on to herself. With a squeal of "Ooh!" she leapt out of the chair with amazing agility while I hurried forward to mop her down with a towel.

"Don't worry, Mrs Jarrow," I said. "It's only water and will soon dry off in this hot weather."

"Even so, I shall have to rush home and put on some-thing dry. I shall have to come back again for the scale and polish," and she smirked with a look of triumph in her eyes. I cursed the chair, cursed the spittoon and cursed the mouthwash. Fate had played a cruel trick on me. Now I would have to endure her adolescent suggestions and the sickly perfume yet again. I could not decide which of the two was the worse. To my relief, no-one had even noticed the little episode. It had all happened so quickly. In my usual manner I escorted her to the door of the Conservation Room.

"Just one more visit, Mrs Jarrow," I said. "You need only make one more appointment."

Her response was to ask me a question. "Tell me, Mr Wilder, are you married?"

I took a backward step. "Am I married?"

"Are you married?"

"Married, no, I'm not married."

An undisguised look of relief crossed her eyes.

"Why do you ask?" I enquired.

"Ah!" she mysteriously went, wagging a chubby finger under my nose. "See you next week."

I stood there puzzled by her remark as she waddled towards the appointments desk. That was the last straw! I was hot. I was tired. I was ruffled. I'd had enough! London was sweltering with temperatures well into the eighties. I decided that a long week-end away from the hospital would do me good. It was Wednesday afternoon. Fortunately, I had no lectures to attend on either the Friday or the following Monday. So I rearranged my patient's appointments and on the Thursday night I caught a train to the cool open spaces of North Wales. All I wanted to do was to lie in the sun on the sandy beach and cool off from time to time in the sea. A quick phone call to my old friends there assured me that I would be welcomed with their usual hospitality.

By the time I had returned to the hospital on the following Tuesday I was ready to face the pressures of student life again. I had even almost forgotten Agnes Jarrow. However, 2 p.m. on the Wednesday came around with its inevitable precision. I went to collect her from the waiting room. It was then that I received the shock of my life for in the space of just one week it seemed that she had lost at least three stones in weight. Although still far from being slim, the improvement was quite breathtaking. She was seated in a chair beneath a window on the far side of the waiting room facing the door.

"Mrs Jarrow," I gulped, looking towards her and trying to conceal my surprise. She stood up and came towards me. She was dressed in a tight, short, navy skirt and a white blouse buttoned to the neck. These were obviously brand new as none of her previous clothes could now have fitted so well.

"Mr Wilder?" There was a trace of uncertainty in her voice.

"Yes," I replied.

"It is Mr Wilder?" she enquired.

"Yes," I confirmed with surprise, and as I had another hard look at her I received yet another one. It wasn't Agnes Jarrow at all but a slimmer, younger version!

"I'm Miss Jarrow, Dolores Jarrow," came the explanation. "Mother caught a chill here last week and so she sent me to keep her appointment instead. I hope it's all right? I do need a check-up."

It was all beginning to add up. I felt myself being carefully snared. I decided to play it with professional courtesy.

"I'm sorry to hear about your mother, Miss Jarrow. She accidentally spilled a glass of water over herself. I'm surprised she caught a chill in this hot weather, though."

But she wasn't listening to me. As I spoke, she was looking me over with an undisguised analytical eye. I wondered if I matched up favourably to the description she had, no doubt, been given. From her expression, I feared this to be very much the case. The resemblance to her mother was quite staggering; the same height, similar voice, even the blonde spring-like hair and the stiletto-heeled shoes, and even the same sickly perfume. The only distinguishing difference was her weight and age. I guessed this latter to be around forty. I directed her to my chair in the Conservation Room and invited her into it.

"I shall have to take a few routine particulars about you, Miss Jarrow," I said. "I presume your address is the same as your mother's?"

"That's right," she replied. "We share a nice cosy flat. It's just right for the two of us although we do get lonely at times." She fluttered her eyes in the unmistakable Jarrow manner. "My parents split up about twenty years ago and so I just stayed on at home."

"What is the year of your birth, please?"

She thought before replying. "Is that really recessary?" she asked warily.

"Just for the records."

"Well, I'm – er – I'm twenty-nine, so you can work it out."

I worked it out by deducting forty years from the current year and accordingly recorded this on to her record card.

"I presume this is just a routine examination and that you are not having any trouble with your teeth," I said.

She did not seem to have heard the question but just sat there staring right at me with the same unself-conscious look that a child has when it is completely engrossed in some activity. I repeated the question a little more loudly. This appeared to shake her from her thoughts. "Mmmm?" she asked dreamily. I repeated the question for yet the third time.

"Trouble with my teeth? Oh no, no trouble," then hastily

corrected herself. "Oh yes, I have a lot of trouble with my teeth, a lot of trouble."

"What trouble are you having?"

She looked a little surprised. "Why – er – toothache of course. What did you expect?"

I could hardly admit that I had hoped for nothing at all. My one thought was to terminate the visit as soon as possible. I was quite inexperienced at dealing with a situation such as this and I knew that the longer it went on the more difficult would be my attempts to extricate myself.

"Where is the toothache, Miss Jarrow?" I enquired.

"All over," she assured me. "All over," and she nodded her head to emphasize her statement.

"Well, I'll just take a quick look," I said airily.

As I moved towards the chair her perfume wafted towards me in relentless concentration. I took a deep breath and dived into the cloud. "Open wide, please," I requested. The quickest of glances showed me that hers was one of those mouths which enjoyed a natural immunity from any form of dental disorder. In a society where sugar is consumed in enormous amounts such a situation is uncommon. In my short experience it was by far the healthiest mouth I had seen. She had all sixteen teeth in each jaw regularly placed in uncrowded dental arches and her gums were pale pink and healthy. Despite the sickly perfume, I heaved a sigh of relief. I could now quickly dispense with her. I spent a couple of minutes going through the pretence of examining each tooth.

"You have a very healthy mouth, Miss Jarrow," I smiled. "Congratulations, you require absolutely no treatment at all."

Her face dropped with disappointment and so I added as a form of consolation, "Come along for another check-up in about six months time." I started to untie the tapes of the protective plastic napkin I had placed around her neck. With a quick, sharp gesture she hit my hands aside.

"No you don't!" Her manner changed quite dramatically and I saw her as a bird pecking at its companion who had tried to eat the last crumb of bread on a lawn.

"I want a proper examination," she demanded. "I want a proper examination," she reiterated, "not just a quick flick with your prong!"

"You have had a proper examination, as you call it, Miss Jarrow," I said. "There is so obviously nothing wrong with your mouth that all I required was a few minutes." I tried to appear experienced and confident.

"Few minutes?" she shot at me. "More like a couple of bloody seconds!" Her thin veneer of culture was wearing even thinner.

"I do assure you, Miss Jarrow, that there really is nothing wrong whatsoever with your teeth," I insisted.

"How do you know?" she snorted. "You're only a student!"

I was instantaneously deflated. It was her trump card in gamesmanship. The few words were fired at me with the accuracy of the skilled marksman and they had found their target. I was hurt. I was no longer the experienced dental surgeon in full control of the situation. I had by that short remark been reduced to an incompetent schoolboy. The heat of the day grew hotter as I boiled within.

"If you have so little confidence in my professional ability, Miss Jarrow, perhaps you would prefer to be transferred to someone else who would, no doubt, tell you just the same as I," I said trying to maintain my composure.

"No, no, no, don't take it that way. Don't take any notice of me. It's the hot weather. It makes me nervy."

"Nervy,'" I thought. "Down right aggressive" would have been more appropriate and I looked for the bruises on my arms where she had just thumped me aside.

"If it will please you, I'll have another look."

This time I spent considerable time inspecting each of her teeth. It only confirmed my previous observations. "Your teeth are quite, quite perfect," I said. "There really is nothing to do. There is no point in discussing it further."

"Then I don't have to come back?"

"Not for six months. Not until your next check-up."

"Then what about the toothache?"

I returned her gaze unflinchingly. "What toothache, Miss Jarrow?"

I have since learnt not to contest such a situation with a direct reprise. Realizing that she was being put at a disadvantage her feminine guile was brought to the fore again.

She put her hand to her throat, closed her eyes and sank her head back on to the head rest of the chair.

"I don't think you like me," she said weakly. I was at a loss for a reply. "All this aggravation with you has given me a turn. I think I'm going to faint!"

It was difficult to tell if she had turned pale in view of the abundance of make-up she was wearing. I had to play it safe. "I'll just remove the waterproof," I said as I swiftly untied the tapes. "That will get some air to you."

She lay quietly in the chair as I did this. "That's a little better," she whispered softly. "Could you undo the buttons of my blouse?" I hesitated and cast a furtive look around the Conservation Room. In the sweltering heat I doubted if my fellow students had even noticed my presence that day. She moaned very gently as if to add a little weight to her request. Trying to look as if I were inspecting the water flush in the spittoon for some obscure reason, I bent forward and undid the two top buttons of her blouse. She moaned gently again. The wretched woman was getting ahead on points! I could feel the perspiration running down my back as I undid yet another button.

"How do you feel now?" I asked guardedly.

"Better," she said. "Getting better but I shall have to come back next week for the scrape."

"What scrape?"

"I always have them scraped and polished even when there are no fillings to do. But I'm too upset to have this today, so I shall have to come back." I had to admire her persistence. However, by now my back was well and truly up and I intended to get her out there and then.

"Miss Jarrow, I'm not prepared to carry out treatment that you don't require. As you now seem to have recovered I won't detain you any longer. I'm expecting my next patient any time now."

At my remark, she slumped right back in the chair with her head lolling awkwardly downward. She may or may not have fainted. I decided to take no chances. There was only one thing for me to do. I quickly operated the foot pump, raising the chair up a couple of feet. I then lifted the foot-rest as high as I could and lowered the back of the chair right down so that her feet were higher than her head. This should short cut any faint by increasing the flow of blood to her head. She opened her eyes, looked around her and realizing the position into which I had put her, threw me a withering look, leapt off the chair and stalked towards the door with loud shrieks of "Disgusting, disgusting!"

I sank on to the dental chair and had a long, cool drink of water. When I felt a little more composed, I suppose it must have been four or five minutes later, I made my way to the Reception Desk outside the Conservation Room. To my relief, Dolores Jarrow was nowhere to be seen. The Appointments Secretary was looking my way, her face wreathed in smiles.

"What's so funny?" I asked her.

"You," she answered without offering further comment.

"Why me?"

"The things you students get up to," and she laughed into her hand. I was in no mood for any mysteries by this time.

"Explain," I simply requested.

"That last patient of yours, Miss Jarrow," she laughed. "Do you know what she told me?"

"Well, what?" I was prepared for anything now.

"She said," and she gave quite a creditable impersonation of Dolores Jarrow, " 'I think I'll report that Mr Wilder to the Superintendent. You see, I never wear knickers in this hot weather and he pumped the dental chair all the way up to the ceiling and tilted it right back for all and sundry to have a good look. Disgusting he is, right disgusting!' "

Neither Agnes nor Dolores Jarrow showed their faces, teeth or otherwise at the hospital again. On reflection and in retrospect I felt very sorry about the incident. I had learnt no dentistry from them as patients or prospective patients. I had, however, had a painful lesson in human relationship and I suppose that was just as valuable as any clinical experience I may have acquired. I have often wondered how Dolores Jarrow eventually fared in her quest for a 'medical' husband, whether he be tall, short, fat, thin, young or old.

As the years passed and one or more of my colleagues would find himself a wife and get married, I would from time to time be invited to a wedding. It is always good to know that one is remembered by old friends at such a time of celebration.

I must admit to a feeling of relief when having opened each invitation to the ceremony I have found the bride's name has never been Dolores Jarrow.

6

Soda Water

I crammed forward with twenty or so other students to read the typewritten sheet recently pinned on the notice board of the dental hospital. Looking down the column of alphabetically listed names, I found my own at the lower end under the Ws. Alongside it was typed, "Professor Francis". That was good. My final appointment which would end the last few weeks for me as a fourth-year student was about to start and this would be with the Professor himself, Head of the Conservation Department. I read further along the line and my heart sank just a little when I discovered that I would have to be working with the Professor's recently appointed house surgeon, Victor Rockman. Although I hardly knew him, he had the reputation for being a difficult man and a stickler for perfection. He was one of those rare people who had come from a family which boasted to have a long list of brilliant and successful members of the medical profession. Rockman's father was a neurologist. He had an uncle who was an ophthalmic surgeon and there was another uncle in America who was a leading psychiatrist there. He, himself, was good at almost every sporting activity, especially tennis. All this was in addition to a highly successful academic career, so far his having won two scholarships since starting at the hospital as a student. It was difficult for anyone not to know all these facts as he wasted no time at disseminating all the information at a first meeting. One could hardly say he was popular or even liked but rather that the hospital, and that is students and staff, had healthy respect for his achievements and ability. It would be interesting to see Victor Rockman in close professional association with Professor Francis who, in contrast, was the most unassuming of men and a fine dental surgeon and teacher as well.

"I see you're stuck with cocky Rocky," observed Peter Dawes with whom I had shared my days in the Anatomy Department.

"I've also got the Prof. thrown in for good measure," I said.

"That's some consolation," came the reply. "You know where his room is, don't you?"

"Yes," I said, "first on the left, down the corridor."

"That was his old room," observed Peter. "He moved only last week to that old clinical demonstration room round the other side of the Conservation Room. You should see it now, beautifully decorated and with a brand new chair and unit. I envy you in there."

"Where are you?" I asked, looking for his name down the list.

"I'm in 'Kids,'" he said a little deflated. "Six weeks of hard labour and not so much as a 'thank you' at the end of it. You know what it's like in there; screaming children and organized chaos. Wish me luck," and he wandered off in the direction of the Children's Department.

I found that the old Clinical Demonstration room had been completely transformed. It was, as Peter Dawes had said, beautifully redecorated in an egg-shell-finish pale blue. The unit and chair were brand new but unlike the standard mid green of the equipment in the students' main Conservation Room this was in a shade of delicate silver grey. I suspected a woman's touch in the choice of the colours and wondered what part Sister Meadows had played in this. The room was empty when I got there and so I spent some time inspecting my new surroundings and admiring the whole set-up. In front of the dental chair was a curved three-tier wooden stand with metal rails in front of each tier so that up to thirty students and other visitors could observe any demonstration on a patient in the chair. How wonderful, I thought, it would be, being the Head of the Department and to be able to display one's clinical skills to students and post-graduate visitors. I became engrossed in these thoughts and was soon lost in the kind of reverie to which I was prone. In my mind I saw myself demonstrating to a group of internationally famous dental surgeons. I was half-way through the removal of an imaginary impacted wisdom tooth when a sudden sound awakened me from my day-dream with a jolt.

"Who are you?" a superior voice was coming from a sallow-faced young man. He wore a pair of heavy horn-rimmed spectacles which were perched on the end of his nose and he was observing me over the top of them. His dark hair was neatly trimmed and he looked older than the age he would have been as a House Surgeon. He wore grey flannel trousers and highly polished black shoes. To complete this picture, his white clinical coat was so clean and starched so hard that I am sure it would have stood up on the floor by itself. It was, of course, Victor Rockman. Rumour had it that his wardrobe consisted exclusively of grey flannel trousers, seven pairs to be precise, and five hospital blazers, each one emblazoned with the appropriate stars around the hospital crest depicting his various sporting successes.

"I'm Wilder," I said. Then realizing that I would be working closely with him during the next few weeks, I added cordially, "Leonard Wilder. I'm the new dresser to Professor Francis."

"Good morning, Mr Wilder," he said, brusquely ignoring

my more personal approach. "I'm Mr Rockman," and he accentuated the "Mr".

"How do you do," I said and I proffered my hand. He inspected my limb through his spectacles for several seconds and then responded by crushing it in the vice-like grip of his own hand. I regretted making the gesture. He seemed surprised at my friendly approach. I sensed that he felt safer behind a more professional exterior.

"You can start by getting the instruments ready for the first case this morning," he said. "It's the preparation of two upper central incisors for porcelain jacket crowns. The patient, aged eighteen, fell over at school when she was twelve and fractured off the incisal edges. Now that the pulps have become smaller she is old enough for crowns." He appeared to have forgotten that he was talking to me and was apparently enjoying every moment of listening to his own voice.

"When does the Prof. get here?" I asked.

"Oh, don't worry about Professor Francis," he said superciliously, "I shall be doing most of the demonstrating here. Now you can bring the students in who should be waiting outside the room."

As I opened the door to invite the sixteen students in for the demonstration, I was beginning to think that perhaps, after all, it was Peter Dawes in the children's department who was going to be the lucky one, even with all its constant pandemonium in there. I shepherded the students into the room. They were all immediate colleagues of mine, having come from the various other departments to which they were attached, for the morning's clinical demonstrations in my new department.

"Mr Wilder, go and get the patient," ordered Victor Rockman. "Her name is Adrienne Shaw."

There were five people in the waiting room: a mother with two children, an elderly lady and a rather nervous looking young man. As none of these appeared to answer to the description of an eighteen-year-old Miss Adrienne Shaw, I returned to the Clinical Room.

"She's not there," I informed him.

"What do you mean, she's not there?" he snapped. "She was due five minutes ago, so she must be there. She's five minutes late!"

He had obviously not learnt something that I already accepted as part and parcel of patients' appointments. That is, that they are often late, and often very late. Only the month before, one of my patients turned up three days late for an appointment! Broken appointments were far from uncommon too.

"Go back to the waiting room and bring her along," he said testily. Back at the waiting room, I noticed that the group of five had been added to by a middle-aged gentleman with a military air about him.

"Miss Adrienne Shaw?" I said in a whisper, looking vacantly at a wall. The patients all inspected each other critically to see if anyone would respond and then settled down again to reading their out-of-date magazines.

"Miss Adrienne Shaw for Professor Francis," I said again, appealing to another wall. I dreaded an empty-handed return to Rocky in the Clinical Room. There was, of course, no response. As I turned to go out of the room, the young man stood up. "Excuse me, sir," he said.

"Yes?" I asked.

"Did you say Miss Shaw or Mr Shaw?"

"I said, Miss Adrienne Shaw. Why, do you know her?"

He coughed uneasily. "Well, sir, I have an appointment to see Professor Francis to have my front teeth crowned."

"What is your name?" I asked.

"It's – er – it's Adrian Shaw," he said. "Mr Adrian Shaw."

I stifled a laugh. Fancy Rocky making a mistake! "Then you'd better come with me," I said. 'Sorry if we got your sex wrong."

"It frequently happens," he sighed.

As I ushered Adrian Shaw into the Clinical Room, we were met by a "Who's this?" shot at me by Victor Rockman.

"This," I said very slowly, trying to keep a straight face, "is your patient for crowns, Mr Adrian Shaw!"

The room burst into a roar of laughter. I waited for Rocky to talk himself out of the situation, but to my surprise his reply came as, "That stupid secretary is dimmer than I thought. How can she expect anyone to read her atrocious handwriting. She's put me ten minutes late already!" He addressed the patient. "Sit down," he barked, pointing to the chair.

Adrian Shaw drew himself nervously into the chair. Rocky placed himself behind the chair with the mouth mirror in his left hand and a dental probe in his right. He looked like an orchestral conductor about to conduct an opera.

"I will commence by infiltrating 2.2 millilitres of lignocaine hydrochloride into the mucosa of the buccal sulcus superior to each of the maxillary central incisors. This will inhibit the afferent nerve impulses, thereby producing regional analgesia. Otherwise he will find the procedure to be very painful." He looked up at the students perched on the observation stand in front of the chair and patient. Satisfying himself that they appeared to be suitably impressed with the start to the overture he turned to me. "Give me the syringe," he ordered. I filled a tumbler with some warm water and placed a cartridge containing the injection into it.

"What on earth are you doing?" he asked in amazement.

"Warming the solution," I said and then I added, "Tony Ainsworth always does it this way."

"Does he, indeed," came the acid reply. "Mr Ainsworth is at liberty to conduct himself as he chooses. This is my clinic, so hand me the injection."

I inserted the cartridge into the barrel of the syringe and handed it to him.

"Open your mouth, patient," he commanded. Adrian Shaw gave me a nervous glance. I winked back at him in an attempt at reassurance. Rocky then performed one of the quickest injections I have ever seen. Quite contrary to the book, it was all over in a flash.

"Did that hurt?" he asked.

"No, Professor, it didn't," came the reply.

Rocky gave a smug smile, not bothering to correct the error in identity. "Huh," he snorted, "Of course it didn't, not if it's performed correctly."

There then followed such a fascinating example of jacket crown preparation that I soon realized why this egocentric man had won almost every scholarship and honour that had come his way. As he was completing the fitting of temporary crowns on to the prepared teeth of Adrian Shaw, the door opened and in came Professor Francis. He had a full head of silvery grey hair, was of medium stature and spoke in a quiet unassuming voice. He also spoke in somewhat of a monotone with little variation in his inflections. He had, consequently, earned for himself the reputation of being able to send an audience to sleep quicker than any other member of the teaching staff.

"Good day, gentlemen," he courteously addressed the assembly. "Have you made a good start, Rockman?" he asked.

"I have just finished," came the confident reply. With a flourish Victor Rockman laid the instruments he was holding down on to the bracket table. The performance was over.

"Finished?" Professor Francis sounded surprised. "I was under the impression that there were two teeth for crowning. Was it just one, then?"

"There were two teeth and I have prepared them both."

"That was quick." The Professor stared unbelievingly in the direction of the patient's mouth.

"They were very easy," claimed Rocky.

"No crown preparation is very easy," commented Francis.

Victor Rockman did not reply but instead addressed the patient.

"I'll see you again next week for the fitting of the permanent crowns." He turned to the hand basin and started to wash his hands.

"As I appear to be superfluous here," said the Professor, "I think I'll go and have a coffee," and with a wry smile on his face he slipped out of the door. Needless to say, when the crowns were fitted a week later they were a delight to see. The fit was perfect, the colour matching to the natural teeth was perfect, and the shape was perfect. Then, of course, everything that Victor Rockman did was perfect!

As the fourth year drew to its close so did also my appointment to Professor Francis. I saw little of him during this time. He must have realized that despite Rocky's irritating conceit, the man was both a brilliant operator and teacher. To avoid unnecessary friction Professor Francis allowed him to conduct most of the clinical demonstrations. It also gave the Professor the extra time he required to complete a text book he was writing on crown and bridge procedures. I soon learned to live with Rocky's personality. I believe I was one of the few who ever did. It was well worth it, as I acquired so much useful knowledge from him in those few weeks that it has been quite invaluable to me ever since.

On the very last day of each academic year it was the custom for the various dental departments to hold a series of clinical demonstrations. This was always successfully organized and enabled students to visit the departments and watch various demonstrations again before moving on to the fifth and final year. In our clinical room we had planned demonstrations on crown procedures to be held during both the morning and afternoon sessions. These were to be taken by the Professor and Rocky respectively and assisted by myself. I had, therefore, a busy day ahead of me but one that I welcomed as I would go out of the department, as it were, in a blaze of glory. On the day set aside for the meeting I arrived at the hospital half an hour earlier than usual in order to prepare the Clinical Room and check over the equipment. When I came to light the gas burner attached to the unit I found to my dismay that no gas was coming out of it when I turned on the tap. With a sense of growing urgency I rushed off to look for Fag End, only to find him upside down in a hole in the ground trying to repair a water leak in the basement of the building.

"I'll be along as soon as I can," came his muffled voice from way down inside the hole.

"But it's urgent," I appealed to him. "We need gas for the clinical meeting to warm the compound for taking crown impressions."

"I can't be in two places at the same time," came the languid reply in his typical slow manner. "According to Matron, this 'ere 'ole is urgent."

"What's going on?" Victor Rockman's voice at my elbow made me turn my head. "Someone said they saw you go down here, Mr Wilder. What's the matter?"

"There's something wrong with the gas," I explained. "There's nothing coming out of the burner on our unit."

Rocky bellowed to Fag End down the hole. "Come out at once and attend to my unit. It's urgent."

"So's this leak," came the muffled reply.

"You won't get any change out of him," I said to Rocky.

"Curse the stupid man," he cried angrily. "It's time they

pensioned him off. Come on upstairs and I'll fix the thing myself."

With the precious minutes to the start of the demonstration ticking away we hurried back to the Clinical Room and Rocky in a frenzied hurry started to dismantle the access plate at the back of the dental unit.

"If you can't get it repaired in time, we can always postpone the start of the session for a few minutes," I said. "Everyone will understand. Mechanical breakdowns do happen, you know."

"Never!" He snorted defiantly. "I'll get it fixed and we will start on time. My units never go wrong."

Sure enough, with about two minutes to spare, he tightened the last screw on the access plate of the unit. He inspected his watch.

"There you are," he claimed proudly. "I bet no-one could have done it in such a short time."

"Do you think we had better test it?" I asked.

"Of course it's all right," he cried. "Anyway, there's no time now. Let them in."

I flung open the door of the Clinical Room as in poured a crowd of students and a few members of the staff followed by Professor Francis. It was a customary gesture of courtesy for members of the staff not demonstrating at the meeting to visit other departments. I was pleased to see that the Dean and Professor Glenn had chosen to grace us with their presence for the morning's session. The group arranged itself on the viewing tiers which had just sufficient capacity to accommodate them all. The Dean and Professor Glenn were accorded the best viewing places in the middle of the front row. The first case was our old friend Adrian Shaw for whom two more crowns had been recommended by Rocky for the teeth adjacent to the ones already crowned. Adrian threw me a look of relief as I settled him in the dental chair. "I'm glad you're here," he whispered in confidence, "this crowd is a bit off-putting."

"Don't worry," I said. "The Prof's attending to you himself today. He's very nice."

A hush fell on the group as Professor Francis started the session. "This case is the routine preparation of two lateral upper incisors for jacket crowning. The central incisors were crowned by Mr Rockman about six weeks ago and as you can see he has done a fine job on them." Direct and to the point, Professor Francis was a most unpretentious man. He turned to me.

"Would you please light the gas, Mr Wilder." I struck a match, turned on the tap of the gas burner and a gentle hissing confirmed the presence of gas issuing from the pipe. I lit it.

Rocky, who was standing next to me whispered, "I told you I'd do it." At that moment three loud clicks came from somewhere inside the dental unit, followed by a couple of clunks and then a gurgling sound. Rocky moved towards the unit. "That's all right, Professor," he said with an air of authority, "I'll adjust the jet on the burner."

As he grasped the flame adjustment ring on the burner the flame went out. With a puzzled expression on his face he bent over the burner to inspect it. It was then that several things all happened in very rapid succession. It started with a whooshing sound, followed immediately by a solid column of water which shot with great pressure out of the gas burner. The water hit Rocky full in the face and as he staggered away the water went on up and hit the light which was angled carefully over the dental chair. With a vigorous ricochet it plunged down at an angle on to Adrian Shaw, bouncing off him all over Professor Francis. The Professor shot out a hand to move the gas burner away which was now spurting water like a fountain. In so doing he swivelled it around and the column of water struck the ceiling, rebounded and finally cascaded in a torrential shower over the Dean, Professor Glenn and most of the students on the viewing tier. As I was standing on the other side of the chair to Professor Francis and Rocky, by some remarkable stroke of good fortune very little of the cloud-burst rained down in my direction and so I escaped with the merest sprinkling of light drizzle. Drenched as he was, Rocky managed to turn off the tap of the gas burner and within seconds of the incident starting, it was all over. At that moment Fag End's head appeared round the door.

"Do you still want me to repair that gas tap, Mr Rock-man, or did you manage to do it okay by yourself?" he asked. Then in his own slow manner he noticed the sad, drenched group inside the room. His eyes widened as he stood there in the doorway.

"Oh," he said mournfully as he took in the scene. "Oh hell! oh blinking, bloody hell!"

PLEASE
REMOVE
SPECTACLES
AND
DENTURES
BEFORE
EXTRACTIONS

7

Sleeping Sickness

Roll out the barrel,
We'll have a barrel of fun;
Roll out the barrel,
We'll have the blues on the run;
Zing, boom, tarrarrel,
Ring out a song of good cheer;
Now's the time to roll the barrel,
For the gang's all here

The strains of this war-time song floated down the road as I made my way over the slippery cobbles. It was cold, it was raining, it was grey, it was miserable. It was also Saturday morning in late February. In the four and a half years since I had become a student I had always enjoyed the delight of having a 'lie-in' on a Saturday morning. After a gruelling five days at the hospital when each evening would end for me over my books into the early hours of the following morning, I felt entitled to this one small luxury; a long, lazy reward. Thinking back, I am sure that the promise of my weekly 'sabbatical' was the spur that kept me going during the week. Now that gift had been taken from me and at 8.10 a.m. I found myself walking between two, tall grey stone buildings towards the Surgical Out-Patients Department. Not ever having seen the hospital on a Saturday before, I was amazed at the transformation. Gone were the groups of pre-clinical students flirting with the nurses even in the rain. The hustle and bustle of late-comers dashing to a lecture or a white-coated professor hurrying to the same appointment, all this was gone too. There was a quiet air of organized urgency about the place as the senior clinical students went about their business. Four years or so of experience were adding to their maturity. Soon they would be qualified and accepting vital responsibilities for themselves.

As a final-year senior dental student, my responsibility that morning lay in the general anaesthetics department. I was on my way to receive the first of many instructions in the administration of 'gas' for dental extractions. The idea of putting someone to sleep on this bleak morning filled me with a yearning for my warm, comfortable bed sixteen miles away and I longed to escape into the cosy oblivion of my own sleep. As I neared the wide, green doors that led into Surgical Out-Patients, the song was now well into its second chorus. There seemed to be a good twenty or thirty voices which were giving a fair rendering of it. To my surprise the sounds were issuing from a half-open window on the second floor of the building. Mystified, I hurried through the doors. I had never been inside this place before. The bare, brick walls, painted brown on their lower halves and cream on the upper parts gave it all an institutionalized atmosphere. The echoing of footsteps in the uncarpeted corridors and the faint smell of antiseptic took me back to the age of four when I had my tonsils and adenoids removed at the Great Ormond Street Hospital for Children. I followed the arrowed instructions painted black on the cream part of a wall. "Dental Extractions – 2nd Floor", it unsympathetically indicated. I felt sorry for the patients even before I had met them. Up the well worn stone stairs I went as the familiar strains of the song echoed in my ears. On the second floor I stopped outside a door from where the singing had now reached its maximum volume. A large notice on the door reiterated, "Dental Gas Extractions". Beneath this was another sign which said, "Waiting Room". I tentatively turned the old brass knob and opened the door.

The sight that met my eyes is something that has etched a vivid and permanently indelible picture on my memory. In a bleak, almost featureless room were three rows of long wooden benches. These were crowded by a varied assortment of people whose ages seemed to range from about sixteen years to sixty. Facing this group and standing up was a small, wiry man of around thirty-five. He had dark, sleek hair cut extremely short. He was conducting the 'choir' with an air of hysterical enthusiasm. Along the wall and facing the 'choir' were several plain wooden chairs and on one of these sat a white-faced young woman holding a handkerchief up to her mouth. As I took in the scene a door to the left of me marked "Surgery" opened and a middle-aged man wandered into the room and sat down on one of the chairs. He, too, was holding a handkerchief to his face and I could see that it was slightly blood-stained. In response to this man's entry, the 'choir-master' held up a hand and the singing abruptly stopped. He followed this by a quick gesture with his other hand a loud cheer rang out followed by "He's a jolly good fellow, for he's a jolly good fellow . . .". This was then skilfully led back into "Roll Out the Barrel" again. No-one appeared to have noticed my presence as I stood there enthralled by the scene. It was, indeed, a novel way of keeping up their spirits while waiting for their extractions under general anaesthesia. The door to the left opened again and a pretty hospital staff nurse came through and went up to the 'choirmaster'. She shouted in his ear above the singing. Another sharp signal from him and the voices quietened again. "'Enery Bates for the slaugh'er," he half ordered. A young man of about twenty stood up on the edge of the second row. "Wish me luck, Alf," he almost pleaded as he followed the nurse through the door into the surgery. I decided to tag on behind him, closing the door behind me as the singing resumed with renewed vigour.

"Mr Wilder?" the question came from a tall, slim man, aged about forty. He was balding quite considerably and had a large, beaky nose on which were perched an incredibly small pair of pince-nez spectacles. He was wearing a green gown and I assumed him to be Dr Harrison, the anaesthetist in charge of the session.

"Yes, sir," I nodded.

"You're late," came the brief observation.

I inspected my watch. It was sixteen minutes past eight. Before I could offer an excuse about the poor train service on a Saturday morning, he went on, "We start precisely at eight o'clock and you should be ready by then. Remember, the patients have been fasting all night! Hurry along and put on a gown."

Someone handed me a green anaesthetist's gown and I struggled into it. It was much too long and several sizes too big. I was forced to hitch it up at the waist with a length of white bandage that I found in a dish. It made me look slightly pregnant. There was a suppressed air of urgency about the place. In addition to Dr Harrison and myself there was the nurse I had seen, the Department Sister, resplendent in dark blue, and three other students, John Warren who was on gas instruction with me, Dick Sefton and Mike Bean who were performing the extractions. They were being supervised by Tony Ainsworth who had recently been appointed Junior Registrar. Four students, one dental surgeon, one anaesthetist and two nurses. I could well imagine the terrifying scene these eight presented to a nervous patient. All this on an empty stomach too!

"Mr Wilder, take off your shoes," came Dr Harrison's strange request.

Noticing the look of surprise on my face Tony whispered in my ear. "Take off your shoes and put on a pair of rubber boots," and he indicated a row of these arranged on the floor along a wall. "That's to insulate you against static electricity," he explained, "and so prevent a spark from possibly igniting the oxygen."

I hurried into a pair of short Wellington boots. During the several Saturday mornings that I spent in Surgical Out Patients I never found a pair to fit my size-eight feet. I'm convinced that they were all size twelve. The only way to keep them on was to walk with a long, slow, gliding motion. They all did it. I learned the art quickly and found myself performing 'the glide' with remarkable success. The room contained one rather old-fashioned dental chair which stood right in the middle of it. There was no dental unit and no spittoon. On a glass trolley to one side was a comprehensive array of forceps, elevators, bone chisels, mouth props and throat packs. Behind the chair was the gas machine containing cylinders of oxygen and nitrous oxide, the anaesthetic. Tony Ainsworth, in his reassuring manner, settled Henry Bates into the chair. The Sister produced a large, brown, rubber apron which she tied carefully around him.

"Which teeth?" asked Dr Harrison.

Tony inspected the patient's record chart. "Upper left first molar and upper right first molar," he said.

"Right," came the reply from Dr Harrison. He turned to the patient.

"What time did you last eat?" he asked.

"Seven o'clock," came the nervous reply. Harrison looked up at the surgery clock on the wall.

"That's only about one and a quarter hours ago," he snapped. "You were instructed to be fasting for at least four hours before you came here. You could be sick under the anaesthetic. You'll have to come back next session. And don't waste our precious time again." Henry Bates squirmed uncomfortably in the chair. "It is more than four hours, sir," he stuttered. "I meant seven o'clock last night when I had my tea."

Harrison turned crimson. "Why didn't you say it was last night," he growled.

"I'm sorry, sir, but you just asked what time."

Dr Harrison controlled his anger and asked instead. "Have you been to the toilet?"

"Yes, sir."

"When?"

"About five minutes before I came in here," and he glanced nervously around the room. The strains of "She'll Be Coming Round the Mountain" broke through the heavy door that led into the waiting room.

"Then we're actually ready," came the caustic remark. He turned to me.

"As Mr Warren has already attended to two patients this morning, I think you had better take over this one. My pulse rate immediately increased. To my surprise, his manner dramatically changed and he suddenly became the skilled and patient teacher. I saw the analogy to the actor standing nervously in the wings waiting to go on stage and then utilizing all his pent-up energy in his subsequent rendering. He inserted a rubber prop between Bates' upper and lower teeth on the right side of his mouth.

"I want you to breathe gently through your nose," he quietly instructed the patient. "Just close your eyes and let yourself drift off to sleep. I shall be looking after you very carefully."

He adjusted a dial and with a gentle hiss the mixture of gas and oxygen wafted down the rubber tube from the machine and out of the nose piece which he placed over Henry Bates' nose. Without saying a word, he took my hand and placed it on to the nose piece. He then removed his hand leaving me in apparent control.

"Increase the oxygen by five per cent," he instructed me. I increased the oxygen by five per cent. Several moments passed in complete silence. I was interested to see that Henry Bates had opened his eyes and had them fixed intently on me. Perhaps he found it reassuring to do so. I wish I could have shared his confidence. No doubt he would shut them again at any moment as he went under. But they remained unblinking and gazing directly at me. Just as I was expecting Harrison to increase the percentage of nitrous oxide he said, "He's ready."

"But sir," I whispered, "he's not under. His eyes are still open."

"He's under all right," came the reply. "They frequently have their eyes open. Carry on," and he nodded to Tony Ainsworth. Dick Sefton, Mike Bean, the nurse, the Sister and Tony who had been standing there motionless as statues suddenly burst into life. In a flurry of movement someone shone a bright light at the patient. Standing behind him and slightly to his left I also received the full glare of its 150-watt brilliance. I was completely blinded for several seconds. Someone else held a chipped white enamel dish under his chin. Out of thin air a large gauze throat-pack made its way into his mouth while a pair of forceps gripped his upper left first molar tooth. I felt his head rock from side to side and then with a cry of "That's the first one out," the whole performance was repeated with his other tooth. It was all over in just four minutes. All this time Henry Bates' eyes were rooted steadily on me. Although he was fast asleep, it gave me an uncanny feeling. I felt as though I were being scrutinized in case I should commit an error. It even gave me a feeling of guilt. Twelve minutes after entering the surgery Henry Bates was awake again, back in the waiting room, seated on a wooden chair with a handkerchief to his mouth, and learning that it was "A Long Way to Tipperary"!

The rest of the session proceeded in a similar manner. John Warren and I would assist Dr Harrison on alternate patients while upper teeth, lower teeth, front teeth and back teeth in various stages of decay flowed in an endless stream into a variety of chipped, white, enamel dishes. The chorus in the adjoining room grew thinner until a quartet trimmed down to a trio, to a duet, to a soloist, and then eventually silence. Alf had waited patiently through to the end, giving encouragement with his sharp cockney humour. As I waited for him to be brought in, I wondered how his own courage would stand up to the ordeal and how many ivory castles he was going to lose that day.

"Well, that's it for this morning," said Dr Harrison. "Same time next week and please be on time." He turned away to wash his hands.

"How about that fellow called Alf?" I asked Tony Ainsworth. "Haven't we got him to do?"

"Oh, he's not a patient," came the unexpected reply. "He's one of the hospital porters. He comes in on his day off, whenever he can, to help cheer up the scared and needy."

I went into the waiting room but Alf had already left. Having made his valuable contribution that morning he had no need for thanks. His reward had been in the satisfaction of helping thirty or so people over their hurdles. In the ensuing three months Alf gave us his unpaid administrations another seven times. I missed him whenever he was not there. My first session as a student anaesthetist had been an exacting one. The morning had seemed endless to me. The surgery clock now pointed to just past twelve noon. I was exhausted. I had a quick lunch in the students' canteen and promptly fell asleep on the underground train on my way home. By 1.45 p.m. I was tucked up snugly in my own bed again. I was warm and cosy; the morning's gas session gradually receded from my mind: soon I was fast asleep.

With each succeeding Saturday, I found my energy expenditure decreased. So that by the time I entered Surgical Out-Patients for my last session not only had I learnt a great deal about general dental anaesthetics but I found that a gruelling four-hour session would leave me quite unaffected. I had hoped that Alf would be conducting his choir on this my final gas session but he was away on a spring holiday and so we were left to manage the patients ourselves. I was not unduly concerned about this as, over the weeks, my confidence had grown under the expert tuition I had received. This session proceeded in the usual manner. There were rather fewer patients than on an average Saturday morning, only eighteen to be precise. So taking our time leisurely over each case we had them all completed by 11 a.m.

"Mr Wilder, would you please ring downstairs to Reception and see if there are any late-comers," requested Dr Harrison. I did so on the surgery telephone and heard that a lady was already on her way upstairs with her young daughter. Two minutes later, Mrs Kent was being ushered into the surgery with her daughter, Mary, aged seven. The little girl had long golden hair and delightful blue eyes. To complete the picture an abundance of freckles covered her face and nose. She was remarkably composed and quite unafraid. Her mother, in contrast, was in a high state of agitation. Mrs Kent had obviously dressed herself up for the occasion and was wearing a well cut fawn two-piece suit in gaberdene. Mary had an abscess on her lower right deciduous first molar tooth. At the age of seven this should be quite a quick and easy extraction.

"If you would care to wait in the other room," said Dr Harrison to Mrs Kent, "it won't take long."

"I would prefer to be present when my daughter goes under," came the reply. Dr Harrison hesitated. "It's very unusual," he said.

"Please, Doctor, I insist."

"Very well," he sighed. "Just sit down on one of those chairs by the door then." He indicated a couple of chairs on the far side of the room.

"Oh no," and Mrs Kent held firmly on to her daughter's hand. "I want her done sitting on my lap."

"That's out of the question," responded Dr Harrison.

But the mother clutched even more firmly on to the little girl.

"She's terrified and won't leave me out of her sight. I must insist, as her mother, that she sits on my lap. I'm the only one who can control her when she's so nervous."

Being the last day of this course of instruction and this being the last patient, I sensed that Harrison did not want to end it with a tussle. "Very well," he sighed again. "Very well, just climb up on the dental chair and put Mary on your lap."

"As it's a young child, sir," I said, "will we be using the Vinesthene instead of the nitrous oxide?"

"Yes, of course," came the reply.

"What gas are you going to give her?" asked the mother suspiciously. "She's very sensitive, I'll have you know, just like me. I've always been sick under gas even when I'm fasting. It's that feeling of suffocation when the bag goes over your head."

Dr Harrison looked peeved as he said, "May I respectfully point out, Mrs Kent, that it is Mary who is receiving the anaesthetic and not you. Furthermore, we don't put a bag over the head, and if the anaesthetic is administered correctly there is never a sense of suffocation."

"Can't you do it with some sort of spray," asked the mother. "I read about it in a medical book. It's call Ethel something or other and you spray it on a bit of gauze and give it to the patient to sniff. It said that this sends them to sleep and then you can pull out the tooth. I don't know if you've heard about it, have you? The book said it's done without gas that way."

"Thank you for the advice," came the icy reply from Dr Harrison. "The 'spray' as you call it is ethyl chloride and it is a highly volatile liquid whose vapours do have an anaesthetic effect. However, as it is difficult to control we hardly use it. I would recommend Vinesthene in Mary's case."

"But you do have some, do you?"

"Yes, of course we do. We have a full range of anaes-thetics."

"Then I want it on Mary. The book said it was very good."

Dr Harrison considered his answer and I saw a gleam come into his eyes. "Then 'the Book' should know," and he sighed yet again. "As this is the last patient of the course," he said to me, "I think I'll do this one myself." He lowered his voice. "I'll show you and Mr Warren how to really give an ethyl chloride general anaesthetic." He produced a round metal frame which had a diameter of about four inches. Over this was stretched a piece of fine gauze. He held this in front of Mary's face. "Just close your eyes, Mary, and breathe in and out quite normally. It's all very pleasant, dear." Standing in front of the chair, he directed a fine jet of the ethyl chloride from a glass container on to the gauze, spraying it to and fro over the surface. After less than a minute he called, "She's ready," and within moments Mike Bean had removed the abscessed tooth. I looked at Mrs Kent. Her eyes were closed and her head was lolling to one side. She was breathing rhythmically and snoring gently as she did so.

"Her mother's gone under as well, sir," I called.

"Really?" came the reply full of mock surprise.

At that moment Mrs Kent opened her eyes, blinked, looked around the room, heaved once or twice and was violently sick. As the Sister and the nurse rushed forward to help Mrs Kent to come round and to tidy her up, Dr Harrison turned to his students and said, "As you can see, gentlemen, learning the gentle art of general anaesthesia is not always such a pleasant affair. Now, if you will all excuse me, I've just remembered that I promised my wife I'd be home early for lunch today. I hope you have found the course valuable."

He removed his gown, washed his hands and within seconds was out of the door.

8

Honours Among Thieves

With the sound of "Good Luck", ringing in my ears, I closed
the front door of my house and started off on the ten-minute
walk to the local underground station. It had been raining
steadily for three days and, being mid-June, the humidity was
uncomfortably sticky. I was nearing the latter part of my
qualifying final examinations and this Friday morning was to
be a three-hour test in practical conservative dentistry. To
this day I am sure I have the number '142' indelibly engraved
on my memory. That is the number that had been designated
to me as an examinee for the duration of the examination.
At odd moments I had worked out all sorts of permutations
with the digits 1, 4 and 2, and finally decided that their sum

total of 7 might be a good omen, as this was generally regarded by the superstitious as being a lucky number. But on this warm, rainy day, I was feeling anything but lucky. In fact, I felt that Lady Luck had deserted me. I did not consider that I had performed particularly well in the examination so far. I could not put my finger on any one disastrous event but it was just that I had an uneasy feeling about it all.

Considering myself somewhat of a stoic, I had for years spurned the use of an overcoat in the coldest of winters, always finding the warmth I needed from a thick polo-necked sweater under my jacket and a warm pair of gloves. By the same token I also did not possess a raincoat. However, this morning, my father had insisted that I borrow the old fawn one to which he had become sentimentally attached and which I remember him wearing since my early childhood. "If you get drenched through in this rain it will spoil your concentration in the examination," he had warned me.

Somewhat reluctantly, I had attired myself in this paternal heirloom. My father was considerably broader than I, a fact that had pleased him as it always deterred me from borrowing one of his best suits for the occasional social engagement. The raincoat hung about me like a loose bell-tent in a gale and to restrain it from flapping too much I tightened the belt as far as I could. A light wind was blowing and my umbrella was quite inadequate at keeping the rain off the lower part of me. Consequently, by the time I had reached the station my trousers were wet through from the knees down and they clung to my legs like a cold second skin. As the train made its way from station to station, I suppose I must have half dozed off. Not that I was in the habit of sleeping on the train but this, I am sure, was a subconscious attempt to escape the overwhelming feeling of tension building up inside me in anticipation of the examination.

It's interesting how accurate one's sense of time can be when in a familiar situation. Without looking at my watch or even the names of the stations, I could invariably know, after five years of making the same journey, when the train had arrived at my destination. It was as though some inner mental clock had given me the time. As the train stopped that morning at each station, in my half-waking half-sleeping state, I mentally ticked off the names of the stations. I had already passed several of the eighteen stations when the train came to a halt much too soon for the next one. I heard the doors start to open and then almost immediately shut again. I opened my eyes. The train had stopped in the tunnel between stations. The doors opened about three inches and then closed again. This was repeated a number of times. Then it seemed as if all the power had been cut off and a heavy silence fell upon the train and its commuters. I inspected my watch. I had forty minutes before the start of the examination. The journey in the train would normally take another twenty minutes and then I needed another fifteen minutes to get to the hospital, change into my white coat and get to the Conservation Room where the examination was being held. Provided we got going again pretty soon I still had time – just. And then the lights went out! The British are a remarkable people. No-one stirred, no-one said a word, no-one seemed to be breathing. It was as though I were all alone in an inky void. I had no idea that silence could be so powerful. It completely engulfed me. Down the carriage a tiny light went on as someone shone a small pocket torch on to the financial page of the morning's *Times*. I suppose three minutes must have passed when the door between the carriages opened and in the light of a hand lantern I could see the figure of the guard.

"Power failure," he said briefly. "We'll get it fixed." As he passed down the carriage, I leaned forward in my seat.

"How long will it take?" I asked urgently.

"Not long, Guv," he replied without stopping.

I wondered just how long "not long" was going to be. I remembered my experience with the communication cord on the day of my interview some years before. I promised myself that if ever I qualified I would buy a car as soon as I could and rarely travel underground again. In the solid darkness I peered at the luminous dial of my wrist-watch. Five minutes had passed. The train and its load of passengers was still motionless. And then there was a faint distant whirring noise which grew nearer and louder as the train started to throb gently again with all the familiar underground-train sounds. The lights went on with such startling suddenness that the brightness hurt my eyes. The doors went through their opening and closing routine again several times, there was a slight lurch, a stop, another lurch, another stop accompanied by loud popping sounds coming from the direction of the driver's cabin and then the train started up and continued towards the next station. The man reading *The Times* put his torch into his jacket pocket without at any time looking up from the paper. I had lost eight minutes. If nothing went wrong now and if I hurried at the other end I would still not be late. Nothing else did go wrong. I did hurry and at 9 a.m. precisely I was filing with the other candidates into the Conservation Room.

We are all creatures of habit and having become conditioned to the routine of my own dental chair and its position in the Conservation Room I found it rather disturbing to find 'No. 142' hanging from the back of a chair in a different part of the Department. The chair was, in fact, right in the middle of a row several yards from my old familiar place. I found that I was positioned between the two Donovan brothers, Jason and Howard. They were identical twins, so identical that I had never really been able to find one small unique distinguishing feature. The only thing I had ever noticed when they were together was that Jason appeared to have slightly larger features than his brother, Howard. I am sure that this was not really so and that any measurements would have verified it but I clung to this conception and it frequently spared me the embarrassment of getting their names wrong. No doubt, they were accustomed to constantly rectifying mistaken identities. They were striking in appearance, over six feet tall, thin in build with carroty red hair and a pale complexion under a profusion of freckles. All this was set against a pair of grey-blue eyes. They tended to be rather quiet and had not particularly shone academically but were considered to be good 'steadies'. Their progress and marks in the various tests over the years had been remarkably and consistently close together. They came from County Galway in Eire and they spoke with an attractive Irish brogue. Their uncle, who practised as a dentist in South London was waiting for them to qualify so that he could hand over his practice to them jointly and then retire. Qualification for them was, therefore, something rather urgent. I was almost certain that I had Jason on my left that morning with Howard on the other side. A quick look at their numbers soon confirmed this. One of the examiners had been imported from one of the other dental hospitals, a Professor Butler. I noticed him leaning against a wall surveying the Donovans intently. He then carefully noted their numbers and checked this against his list. As well as the responsibilities of an examiner, he had the additional responsibility of not confusing their results. I exchanged a brief "Good morning" with each one of them, their reciprocations coming in their characteristic Irish brogue.

My patient was a Mrs Elton who was already seated and waiting for me. By an interesting coincidence the Donovans had a husband and wife as patients, Mr Edwards in Jason's chair and Mrs Edwards in Howard's chair. The first part of the test was to be the preparation of a tooth for a gold inlay. The standard required was high. There was no leeway for mistakes. I gave Mrs Elton an injection and was soon absorbed with my work on her second right upper premolar tooth. As I completed each stage, I had this inspected by Professor Butler so that I could proceed with the next. To my delight, after the disturbing journey and wet start, it turned out to be one of those mornings where everything seemed to be going just right for me. The patient was completely relaxed and I was making good time. Even my trousers had dried off by now. Not so, apparently for Howard Donovan. It was more than obvious that he was having a difficult time. Mrs Edwards was very restless and kept moving about in the chair. His pale complexion had turned several shades paler and I noticed that he had stopped working and was inspecting the lady's tooth with a worried look on his face. He wandered over to Jason's chair and engaged him in conversation.

"Candidate 143," Professor Butler bore down on Howard. "Discussion with other candidates is not permitted during examination. Kindly return to your patient."

Howard returned to chair No. 143. Professor Butler went with him. "Is anything wrong?" he enquired.

"Nothing at all, sir," he shot out nervously and immediately busied himself on the patient with a weak attempt at nonchalance. Butler stood by him for several moments and then said as he walked away, "Let me know when you are ready for me to inspect the preparation."

"Yes, of course, sir," came the reply.

Having satisfied himself that all was apparently well in our part of the room, the Professor strolled to the other end of the row from where he could still keep us under his surveillance. Howard moved as near to my chair as he could without attracting attention. I sensed that he wanted to talk to me and so I positioned myself nearer to him as well.

"Wilder, I'm in serous trouble," he whispered.

"What's wrong?" I asked, keeping a careful eye on Butler.

"I've gone and exposed the nerve!" admitted Howard, giving me a look of despair.

"Hell! that's serious," I said.

"When Professor Butler sees it, I've as good as failed," he almost whimpered. To expose the nerve of a tooth, was, indeed, an unforgivable sin and failure of the examinee was almost assured.

"Wilder," he called in a whisper again.

"Yes,"

"I've thought of what to do."

"What's that?"

"Can I steal a spot of your dentine?"

"Some of my dentine?"

"Yes, can you drill a spot more dentine out of your patient's tooth and give it to me. If I place it over the nerve I've exposed and pack it in tight the professor may just miss it when he looks at the preparation."

What an ingenious if completely dishonest idea! It meant I would be aiding and abetting him. I thought of Jason possibly passing and poor, unfortunate, Howard having to wait another six months to take finals again. I thought of his indignity at having to face his brother every morning at breakfast with Jason in practice and himself only a mere student. I thought of his aged uncle still having to slog away at dentistry and having to wait while his second nephew joined the practice. Jason would not be sufficiently experienced to manage a practice alone yet. So I thought that the only decent thing for me to do was to supply him with the dentine that might well be the elixir of life for him. I sidled back to Mrs Elton. "Just a few moments more," I said, "and I'll have completed my work on your tooth." Drilling carefully and as far from the nerve as I could, I removed a small speck of dentine. I retrieved this as a powder and carefully depositing it on a glass slab placed it on Howard's instrument table which was only a couple of feet from where I was. I threw a hasty glance down the row of chairs in the direction of Professor Butler. He was busy checking another candidate's preparation. Furtively and frantically Howard Donovan collected the precious morsel and quickly introducing it into the unsuspecting Mrs Edwards' tooth, he quickly packed it on to the exposed nerve.

"How are you getting on?" Professor Butler was approaching our group of chairs again.

"I'm just ready, sir," I said.

He carefully checked my preparation and muttering, "No undercuts there. That's good. Carry on," he moved towards Howard.

"I'm ready, sir," said Howard turning crimson. At that moment a short queue, consisting of Jason and two other students formed for Butler and realizing he was under pressure, he gave Mrs Edwards' tooth a somewhat cursory inspection.

"That's all right," he said and moved away to Jason. I thought Howard was going to faint.

"Have a cold drink," I whispered to him. Howard's face gradually returned to its usual pallid shade and the examination proceeded untrammelled again. One hour after this incident, I had taken a wax pattern of the preparation, cast it in gold and had cemented it into Mrs Elton's tooth. Professor Butler was obviously satisfied with my efforts. Without too much display of emotion he said, "I believe this lady requires a filling in her upper left central incisor. Would you please do this and fill it with silicate. Make sure you get a good colour match."

Mrs Elton was a model patient and within minutes of administering an injection for her second tooth I was busy preparing this for a 'white filling', as so many patients call it. All was going well for me and I had to suppress a feeling of growing confidence for it is in this state of mind that things can go wrong. Having survived the ordeal of the nerve exposure, Howard had fitted a gold inlay over it and was now engaged on filling a second tooth. Mrs Edwards had left and another patient had taken her place for this, a middle-aged gentleman. Out of the corner of my eye I could see that Jason was also working on his second tooth. Like myself, he still had the original patient in the chair, Mr Edwards.

"P-sst, Wilder!" an urgent whisper from Jason Donovan.

I turned my head in his direction. He was staring towards me with a maniacal expression on his face.

"What's wrong?" I whispered.

"I've just gone and exposed the nerve!" he exclaimed in an Irish brogue which was more marked than I had ever known him speak with. Here was a situation with which I was becoming increasingly more familiar! In a nightmarish dream-like state I carefully removed some more dentine from dear Mrs Elton's second tooth and once again I placed it on to a glass slab. I looked round to make sure that Professor Butler was not too near and to my concern saw him wandering amiably in our direction. I hurriedly covered the tiny heap of dentine with a clean piece of gauze.

"You should be nearly ready to fill the tooth now, gentlemen," he beamed. "I am sure you are all looking forward to a hard earned lunch." He looked at the clock on the wall. "You have exactly twenty more minutes."

He positioned himself between Jason and me, watching me working with a bland smile on his face. Suddenly I noticed him looking intently at my instrument table. Cold fingers ran down my spine. "Just interested to see what instruments you are using," he said, completely ignoring the dentine concealed under the gauze. He picked up my mouth mirror from the table and had a look at Mrs Elton's upper left central incisor.

"This is ready for filling," he observed.

"Yes, sir," I agreed.

"Then why didn't you invite me to inspect it?" he asked.

"I was just going to," I said.

"Carry on then," he continued and settling himself once more between Jason and me, he continued to watch me working with a vacant expression in his eyes. Over Butler's shoulder I could see the anguished look on Jason's face. He dare not, with the Professor almost touching him, 'pinch some dentine' from the candidate at chair No. 140. I was his only hope, and the one thing that might bring him salvation was right under the very nose of Professor Butler. I looked at the clock. It was fifteen minutes to noon. It looked as though Jason was not going to share in his brother's escape.

At that moment Peter Dawes appeared between the rows of chairs. "Can you check my cavity preparation, please?" he asked the Professor.

"Certainly, where are you working?"

"It's the other side of the Conservation Room," said Peter and he and the Professor disappeared down the room. With a trembling hand Jason Donovan inserted the precious powder into Mr Edward's tooth and within seconds the red spot indicating the exposure had been carefully concealed. At eleven minutes to noon Professor Butler passed his preparation of the tooth and in the dying seconds of the examination Jason just managed to complete the filling.

Weeks later, the brothers confessed to me that they had prepared Mr and Mrs Edwards for the event of there being "a reaction from the treatment". The Edwards had been told that in such an event the Donovans' uncle would be prepared to see them at any time. I understand that at 8 a.m. on the Saturday morning the couple had presented themselves at the front door of his surgery, both suffering from considerable toothache. I further understand that he had dealt appropriately with the Edwards as he did most certainly also with his two young nephews.

The examinations drew to a close two weeks later. Weary from the strain, I escaped to my favourite haunts in North Wales where, for one whole month, I renewed my friendship with the mountains of Snowdonia, the craggy passes, the lush valleys, the golden sands and the cool sea. Refreshed and invigorated I returned home again. The results of the Final Examination were due by the first post on 1st August. That day arrived and with racing heart I watched from my bedroom window as the postman made his way towards my house. He delivered several letters to the house next door and then without so much as a glance in my direction passed my gate and continued on down the road. I felt my heart miss several beats and I sank down heavily on to the end of the bed. Had I really failed after all that endeavour? To have come this far, having passed every examination to date, I had been most fortunate. I had also worked very hard for my successes. The anticipation of qualification and the promise of at long last venturing out into the world as an assistant dental surgeon in an established practice had been an exciting goal for which to aim. Was this to be denied me for at least another six months when I would have to sit the examination again? The thought of this ordeal threw me into a state of deep depression. I composed myself and waited for the second postal delivery that day. It was the longest morning of my life. But inevitably, midday arrived and with it the familiar figure of the postman pushing his bicycle with one hand and holding a bundle of letters in the other. I died a thousand deaths as he approached our house and then, as before that day, he passed us by. No letters! No notification that I had passed my Finals. I was still just an ordinary student. Most of my colleagues would by now be celebrating their results. There would be wild hectic parties. I had been looking forward to all that. The telephone bell rang. I answered it. The excited voice of Charles Martin informed me that he had received his results and, as I had expected, he had passed. He had just heard from John Warren and Peter Dawes. They, too, had passed. I offered him my congratulations, trying to conceal my own bitter disappointment. He took some convincing that I had apparently fallen at the last fence. It eased the pain to know that my friend had so much faith in me. I made some excuse and discontinued the conversation. As I put down the telephone, I heard the front door chimes sounding. At the door was the daily domestic who helped out next door.

"Hello, Mr Wilder," she smiled. "This letter was delivered this morning to next door by mistake. I see it's addressed to you. I hope it's not important." Important?! The long, buff coloured envelope bore the crest of the hospital and had printed on the top left-hand corner, "Personal". I thanked her and made my way into the kitchen. With a cold, clammy hand I tore open the envelope and carefully withdrew the typed letter from within. I tried to read it but my eyes failed to focus. With a determined effort I was, at last, able to discern the print. It spelled out the magical message for which I had toiled so hard for so many years. I had, indeed, passed the entire set of final examinations. I read, re-read and re-read yet again the wonderful news until I was quite certain that I had made no error. I cannot remember how many telephone calls I made that day. I am sure the Post Office did rather well out of them. It took me several days to accept the fact that my student days were over. But having looked forward to this for so long I now felt a wave of nostalgia towards the hospital that I would be leaving and increasing trepidation towards the wide open world that I would now have to face. The time had come for me to look for an appointment as an assistant in a practice, for me to accept my own professional responsibilities and to start to make my own decisions without supervision. The time had come for the fledgling to leave its nest and make its first uncertain flight. Three days later I went to see the Appointments Officer at the hospital and from him I received a list of 'assistants required' in and around the London area. The time had also come for me to buy the motor car I had promised myself, and so to the 'assistants required' list I added another one of 'good quality used cars'. The days immediately ahead were going to be very full and busy ones. I hoped they would be successfully productive.

But what of Jason and Howard Donovan? Several weeks after qualifying, I met them at a re-union dinner. They had both passed the final examinations. With honours!

9

Seven Down, One to Go

"Assistant Dental Surgeon required for busy, well established practice in good residential area of Welwyn Garden City. Experience preferable but not essential. Apply, Cartwright, Bowden & Peacock." There were just eight practices advertising for assistants which were situated within reasonable driving distance of my home. I decided to try these in the order in which they were printed on the list. This was as good a reason as any other. The name heading the list was a practice in Finchley, London. A telephone call there had informed me that the position had already been filled. The Welwyn Garden City practice was second on the list. Although in Hertfordshire it was on my side of London and easily accessible along the A1 road. I telephoned and was given an appointment to come and meet Mr John Cartwright the following day at 1 p.m. "He won't be able to give you long," came the efficient and rather aseptic female voice over the phone, "as it's during his lunch break." The next day I set out well in advance for my very first interview. As the little black Ford nosed its way away from London and along the dry road, hot in the summer sun, I was overcome by an increasing sense of insecurity. The success of my final examinations had, during the previous month, given me a wonderful feeling of confidence. Letters had arrived with my new degree blazing like a beacon after my name. Friends and neighbours had stopped me in the street to offer their congratulations and like a newly discovered film star I had revelled in the glory of success. Suddenly, this had dissipated. Messrs Cartwright, Bowden & Peacock had never heard of me. I was, no doubt, just another face for them to peer at and decide whether they liked it or not. I was, in a sense, back at the beginning, starting all over again with an interview. I wondered whether it would occur to them that I should like them or their aseptic, indifferent receptionist. I suddenly felt angry and resentful and then reproached myself almost at once. I had transferred my sentiments of nervousness and apprehension to one of aggression. This was wrong.

Some twenty minutes later I pulled up on the edge of the town. Built to be a model town, its spaciousness and sense of symmetry had always fascinated me on the few occasions I had been there. The practice was at 15 Dale Farm Road. I called from the car to a solitary person walking along the tree-lined road. The man had a ruddy complexion and wore a tweed pork-pie hat. He was carrying a pair of well-worn and well-oiled garden shears.

"Can you tell me where Dale Farm Road is?" I asked.

His face clouded as he thought for a moment and then from the frown melted and was replaced by a large, friendly grin. "Oh aye," he answered in a gravel voice. "Dale Farm. It's right on down this road beyond those dark trees. Then it's either third or fourth left down Welwyn Way, straight on over the bridge and then either second or third right down Farm Road. About a mile, no more. There," he concluded making a gesture with the garden shears, "it's as simple as that."

Either third or fourth left and then either second or third right, I reflected on the uncertainty. As there was no-one else in sight to either confirm or refute these directions, I thanked him and drove off down the road towards the dark trees. It was a good fifteen minutes to 1 p.m. and so I reckoned I would get there well in time for my appointment at 1 p.m. Welwyn Way was, in fact, the third on the left. This took me over a little hump-backed bridge which crossed a large, still pond. I noticed that there were a few white swans, some mallard and a water hen or two on it. It was quite pretty and I resisted the temptation of stopping the car to enjoy the scene. Third on the right indicated Farm Road. After about another half mile the road petered out into a stony track much too narrow for a car to negotiate. A wooden sign pointed to Dale Farm. I put on the hand brake and hurried on foot along the track. Dale Farm, yes, but as yet no indication of Dale Farm Road. About a hundred yards along the track I went and then it turned abruptly right to reveal a delightful old farmhouse with a cosy, thatched roof. "Afternoon Teas", stated a weather-worn sign. The time was nine minutes to 1 p.m. A blind horse could have sensed that this was not Cartwright, Bowden & Peacock, Dental Surgeons of 15 Dale Farm Road. In the early stages of panic I rang at the bell and waited while from somewhere deep inside the house twin bells, slightly out of harmony, burst into life and almost as suddenly, faded. A young girl, dressed in a black dress and wearing a neat white apron came to the door.

"I'm looking for Dale Farm Road," I said, hopefully praying that the farm would magically be transformed into No. 15. I would even, with the minutes ticking by, have exchanged her warm, friendly smile for the aseptic dental receptionist.

"I'm afraid you've come the wrong way," she said. "It's the other side of the farm. When the new road was built it cut us off from Dale Farm Road and it gets a lot of people confused. Did you come over the bridge by the pond?"

"Yes, I did," I said, glancing hastily at my watch.

"Then it's first left over the bridge, then first left again and then almost immediately first left again. You can't go wrong." Couldn't I, I wondered as I thanked her and sprinted the hundred yards to the car? Her directions were impeccable and at one minute to 1 p.m. the car was parked outside No. 15 and with a shaking hand I was pressing the front door bell. The house was a large, red brick pseudo-Georgian building and in keeping with the general atmosphere, quite symmetrical. There were two upstairs front rooms and two on the ground floor, the front door being situated between these. There were three brass plates fixed to this door. The one which bore the name of Mr Cartwright had been so much polished over the years that his name had been almost obliterated, whereas, Messrs Bowden & Peacock's plates, although no doubt also having been treated to the same polishing enthusiasm, were still quite new and hardly worn. There was a space from where a fourth plate had obviously recently been removed. The door was opened by an imperious looking lady in her early fifties, dressed in dark grey two-piece suit.

"Mr Wilder." I recognized the aseptic voice and wasn't sure whether this was meant to be an observation or a question. Before I could answer, she went on, "Come this way, please," in a voice devoid of any emotion. I followed her across a bare, dark hall and through a door marked, "Waiting Room". The inside was white; white walls and ceiling, window frames white, white spartan furniture and a white shade over the solitary hanging light bulb in the centre of the ceiling. The floor was covered in a light grey, marble effect linoleum. The rest of the room was featureless and like my companion devoid of emotion. Despite the warm afternoon I felt quite cold.

"My husband will be with you almost immediately." So the aseptic voice belonged to Mrs Cartwright! She left me alone. "Almost immediately" was so correct for within seconds of her departure the door opened to admit a tall, thin man in his late fifties. His receding hair was a light gingery colour. He wore a short white jacket, immaculately starched. I sensed an air of extreme impatience about him. I also noticed that his tie was that of a hospital other than mine, a hospital with whom we had frequently clashed on the sports field. I felt sorry I had put on my own hospital tie that morning with such pride.

"Mr Wilder?" He offered me his hand. Without sitting down himself or inviting me to do so he plunged straight into the interview standing up, while I shuffled uneasily from one foot to the other.

"How long have you been qualified?" he asked.

"Recently."

"Yes, yes," he said impatiently. "How recent?"

"I left teaching hospital last month."

"I see, then you have no experience?"

I felt deflated. "Well, as a clinical student," I offered weakly. It was then that his eyes noticed my tie and I sensed him recoil for a moment. It was as though a curtain had been dropped between us.

"That doesn't count!" he said tartly. "I really wanted someone as an assistant who had had at least some little experience in practice. I haven't the time to supervise an inexperienced, newly qualified man. Thank you for coming to see me."

Within moments, I found myself driving slowly away from the bleak, Georgian house with its bleak waiting room and even bleaker occupants. Back home, I crossed the names of Cartwright, Bowden and Peacock from my list. I re-read the words "Experience preferable but not essential". Cartwright obviously had a deep prejudice against my hospital. I tried to reassure myself that it was nothing personal about me. It was, however, an unhappy start and enough to give anyone a profound sense of insecurity.

I had a late lunch with my parents who were most sympathetic and a glass or two of my father's favourite red wine soon had me buoyed up again. I telephoned the next two names on the list only to be told that these vacancies had already been filled. I thought of Charles Martin, Peter Dawes, John Warren and my other former colleagues. Had they found themselves suitable assistantships yet? I remembered that Charles had wanted to stay on at the hospital as a junior member of the staff and eventually make a career for himself as a researcher and teacher. That thought had crossed my own mind once or twice, only for me to dismiss it. The conception of ultimately having my own practice and running it in my own individual way had grown steadily with me over my years as a student. It was still my firm ambition But I had to launch out first as an assistant in a practice where I could be happy and then I could give of my best.

The fifth name on the list was a Mr Roy Birch, in Hackney, London. In the event of my going there, this would mean a drive each day into London and in heavy traffic. The idea did not really appeal to me but with the list now shortening, I telephoned Mr Birch. I was flattered that he actually left a patient in the chair to come to the telephone to speak to me himself. I found myself talking to what sounded like a pleasant and patient gentleman. He offered to interview me at his surgery at 5.30 p.m. at the end of his day's work. This gave me sufficient time to tidy up and compose myself and then head the car in the opposite direction to Welwyn Garden City. Before leaving home I took the precaution of changing my tie for one with a nondescript pattern on it. The practice was situated on a main bus-route. I had no difficulty in locating it and finding a parking place just a few streets away. The surgery was on the first floor of a long parade of shops. Beneath it was a bank and the entrance to the practice was through a door to one side of the bank and up a steep flight of stairs. Roy Birch answered the door himself. He was a man of good stature and well preserved for what I thought to be in his early sixties. He had, as yet, not one grey hair in his head.

"My nurse has had to go off a little early today," he explained as he led me inside. "But I'm very resourceful and often work alone." I followed him into the waiting room which was furnished in a conventional manner. It had, however, a certain warmth and colour so painfully absent from the one I had experienced that morning. He seemed unconcerned to hear that I had qualified just recently and had no experience in general practice.

"That's all right, my boy," he assured me. "I don't mind teaching you the tricks of the trade. When can you start?"

At that moment his door bell rang and he excused himself to answer it. I heard voices in the hall for a few moments and then he appeared at the door of the room. "Mrs Blatching has just turned up with a bad toothache," he said. "If you don't mind waiting five minutes I'll just whip it out for her and then we'll arrange for you to start soon if you like." I waited for about six or seven minutes while he attended to his patient. He was soon back again. "Doesn't take long when you know how, does it," he smiled, proudly.

"I'm impressed with the speed your injection works, Mr

Birch," I commented, making polite conversation. "I have to wait at least ten minutes before extracting."

"Injection? I gave her gas."

"Then you have a colleague here?"

"Of course not, I gave it myself."

Acting as both anaesthetist and surgeon was something I had never considered. It struck me as being a very risky procedure. I started to have an uneasy feeling about his readiness to engage an inexperienced assistant with virtually no interview. The startling contrast to the morning's experience was so great that I was unprepared for his easy-going attitude, but I sensed a slight unprofessionalism which put me on my guard.

"Do you have a mechanic on the premises?" I asked him.

"No, I don't. As you know, most dentists send their denture work to an outside laboratory these days. It keeps the overheads down."

"What about crowns and bridges?" I added.

"Crowns and bridges? Bless my soul, we don't do that sort of stuff here. That's for the clever boys. You'll have plenty of time for all that in years to come, if you want to. My advice to you, young man, is to get all the practice you can with the bread and butter stuff, fillings, extractions and dentures. Don't worry son," and he gave me a wink, "I'll soon sort you out."

Here was a honest to goodness, forthright man, a plain, hard-working, old-fashioned dentist. He obviously took great pride in his practice and was, no doubt, well loved by his patients. But it was patently clear that the scope of his work was very limited. I had one more try. "Do you do any endodontics, Mr Birch?" I enquired.

He looked at me for a moment and a suggestion of disappointment entered his eyes. "You mean root canal treatment, do you?"

"Yes, that's right."

"No son, I don't. If a tooth is all that gone I put a pair of forceps to it and extract." He became a little pensive. "Where did you qualify from?" I told him. "Then I suppose this place can't offer you the type of work you want." He sighed. "That's been my problem lately. All the nice fellows, like yourself, don't want a good old-fashoined practice like this. Dentistry has changed so much in the forty years since I started. The trouble is that I haven't changed with it. I really would love to have you here. You see, I have no son of my own to take over when I quit one day. I was hoping to get some nice chap all set up so that he would step into my shoes when the time comes. I don't think I can ever see that happening now. I suppose that's the price for progress."

I was at a complete loss for words. The contrast between Cartwright and Birch was like comparing black to white. I had, of course, to decline accepting the assistantship and I left Roy Birch with a deep feeling of regret. I had learned a lot during my first day out in the big world. I had started with a feeling of rejection and ended it feeling almost apologetic for my training.

The following morning I telephoned the sixth name on the list only to learn that the assistant there had changed his mind about leaving and had decided to stay on. There were now only two practices left to contact. I hoped one of these would be suitable as the next list would not be out for another month. I telephoned Mr Hans Trimmelwasser, who practised in Cricklewood. Over the telephone he told me that he was looking for an assistant to stay for at least two to three years. He performed a full range of dentistry with particular interest in crown and bridge work. There would also be scope for me to develop any speciality I wanted. He would be pleased to meet me at 4 p.m. His house and practice were situated at the junction of two roads in a residential part of Cricklewood. It was also within just a few minutes walk of the nearest underground station and several bus routes. I realized the importance of this for patients. As the front garden had been concreted over I had no problem in parking the car. The door was opened by a middle-aged lady who spoke in a marked continental accent.

"Dr Trimmelwasser vill see you soon," she said, showing me into a small room that was obviously the private sitting room. I noticed her reference to him as "Doctor" and I remembered that this courtesy title came from the continent. "I didn't sink you vould like to sit in ze vaiting room viz ze patients. Vould you like a cup of tea?"

I readily accepted this gesture and she left me alone. A few minutes passed and then she returned without the tea. "Ze

Doctor said perhaps you vill join him for tea in ze surgery."

I followed her out of the room and into a surgery brilliantly illuminated with a multitude of fluorescent tubes which ranged all over the ceiling. My immediate impression was of a busy, well equipped, if untidy practice. It had a comfortable atmosphere about it. Mr Trimmelwasser was a large man and completely bald apart from a grey fringe that ran from one temple around the back of his head to the other side. He was wearing a very long white coat which had only one button on it, the top one, and this was fastened. He had on a pair of small rimless spectacles through which he inspected me rather short-sightedly.

"Ah Dr Vilder," he boomed in an equally continental accent. "You're just in time for tea." To my surprise, there was a patient in the chair, a girl of about eighteen, and on the bracket table alongside the instruments was a steaming cup of tea, presumably for her. Mr Trimmelwasser was leaning against the dental cabinet holding a cup and saucer. The receptionist who wore a black skirt and floral blouse but no white coat handed me my tea. She then poured one for herself from a teapot standing on the cabinet.

"Vould you care for a biscuit?" he invited, indicating the plate of assorted biscuits on the instrument table. I dutifully took one. He followed suit, choosing a large wheatmeal biscuit which he then thoughtfully dunked into his tea, watched it solemnly as the tea soaked in and then inserted the entire thing into his mouth. There was silence for a few moments. The patient treated herself to a biscuit and we all munched and sipped at our mid-afternoon break. If only I had a camera to capture the scene, I thought, and I had to stifle a laugh.

"Ve alvays have tea at four o'clock," he observed as though the future success of his practice depended on this ritual, "and ze lucky patient in ze chair is our guest. By ze vay, zis is Dr Vilder, a dentist and zis is Hildegard, mine receptionist and nurse. She is ze boss here. She," and he stressed the "she" each time, "tells me vot to do and I do it. But you see, zere is a politic here," and he chuckled deep down in his throat. "If somesing goes wrong, zen it is her fault," and as he chuckled, he turned up his nose in her direction and the chuckle grew into a hearty laugh. He put a hand on his patient's shoulder.

"Zis is Miss Susan Godfrey who has come in today to have a new crown fitted. She broke a front toos ven she vas younger. Now zat ze pulp and root canal have grown smaller, I have made for her a beautiful jacket crown in vacuum-fired porcelain. Fortunately, ze toos remained vital, ozervise I vould have carried out root treatment. Now, as soon as Susan has finished her tea, I vill carry on ze good vork."

He handed me a plaster model of the patient's mouth and I inspected the artificial crown that had been constructed for her upper right front tooth. "Vot do you sink of zis?" he asked proudly. The workmanship was superb and at least as good as anything I had ever seen at the hospital.

"I'm most impressed," I said.

"I'm glad you like it. And now if Hildegard vould kindly remove ze tea sings, I vill cement zis crown and zen Susan can go and decide vich boy friend to go to ze pictures viz tonight."

The next ten minutes passed as he cemented the crown in place, waited for the cement to set and then carefully removed the excess. The colour match was perfect. The patient thanked him and left the surgery. I waited for the interview to start.

"And now Dr Vilder on mine next patient I shall be removing stitches I put in one veek ago after I removed a mesio-angular impacted visdom toos. Have you taken out many visdom tees?" I admitted to only having observed two such operations. "Nevermind, zis vould not be expected from you yet." I felt relieved, and as Hildegard ushered the next patient into the surgery, I started to wonder when, if ever, I was going to be able to discuss an assistantship with him. The patient, a young man of about twenty-two, had had his lower left wisdom tooth surgically removed seven days previously and I was impressed to see no sign of swelling and that he was quite able to fully open his mouth. Spasm of the muscles of the jaw can persist for quite some time after such an event. Trimmelwasser deftly removed the stitches and another patient happily departed. "After ze next patient, ve vill talk," he assured me, just as I was despairing of this happening. Mrs Beloff was next brought in. She had a large, painful ulcer about half an inch long inside her lower lip. "Tell me, Doctor, vot is ze diagnosis?" He invited me to inspect her mouth and at once I recognized the lesion to be an aphthous ulcer.

"It looks like recurrent oral aphthae to me," I said.

"Vot can you do for her?"

"I would prescribe the local use of hydrocortisone sodium succinate in the form of Corlan pellets," I replied.

"Excellent, mine dear Vatson!" he exclaimed. "You see, Hannah," he said addressing Mrs Beloff, "I have a clever doctor here zis afternoon. Now, I vill give you tventy little tablets and you should put one near ze ulcer and make it last as long as you can. You must not use more zan four a day."

"Why is that?" asked the patient.

"Vhy is zat?" he repeated her words. "It is vhy because I say so. Zat is, vhy is zat," and he wrote out a prescription, handed it to her and sent her on her way. He turned to me. "Now, Dr Vilder, ve talk." He placed the chair from his desk next to the dental chair, indicated that I sit on it and eased himself into the dental chair. "You have now had a chance to see me, to see Hildegard and to meet some of mine patients and find out a little how I conduct mine practice. Tell me, doctor, are you interested?"

"Yes, I'm very interested," I replied truthfully. This was a practice where I knew the standard of dentistry was good and the range of work varied. It was what I was looking for. It was also colourful and human. I liked his informal, first-names-only approach with his patients. He was right to have given me the chance to see how he worked.

"How long have you been qualified?" he enquired.

"I'm afraid to say I've only been on the Dentists' Register one month."

"Don't be afraid to say it," he said reassuringly. "Ve all have to start once. If you are keen and villing and have a good sympasetic approach, zen zere might be a place for you as an assistant here. I'll tell you mine position. I have promised to see anozer three more applicants. Like you, I don't know zem from Adam. But betveen now and two days time I vill meet zem and zen I vill make some sort of a decision. I suppose you have also ozer interviews to keep?"

"A few," I replied non-committally.

"Can you telephone me in two days time and zen ve vill talk again?"

I agreed to do this and took my leave of him with mixed

feelings. Had he offered me the appointment there and then, I would have accepted it. Did he like me? Did he not like me? Did he prefer someone with a little experience? If so, how did anyone ever start in a good practice or was one forced to gain initial experience at a Roy Birch's? I was having to wait two days to find out and so I crossed the seventh name from the list of 'assistants required'. There was just one to go. In the event of Mr Trimmelwasser not offering me the assistantship, I made a telephone call and arranged to be interviewed by Mr Hector Leafe at his practice in West Ealing, the following day.

10

Don't Kiss Me, Kate

"Leonard . . . Leonard . . . wake up . . . wake up!" My mother's voice. I stifled a yawn and tried to pretend that I had not heard her. I felt a hand on my shoulder shaking me gently. "You'll be late for your appointment. Wake up," she persisted. Her voice was coming from the left of my bed and her hand was on my left shoulder. Now this was strange because the left side of my bed is against the wall and anyone coming in to my bedroom could only ever be on the right of the bed. "Come on, dear, now wake up!" What was she doing on the left of my bed? That was impossible! I should have opened my eyes but this would have broken the cosy sensation of sleep. Then I noticed that the sound of the

100

birds that would normally be coming to me from the garden
outside was much louder than usual, in fact much nearer. I
forced my eyes open with a jerk. As they tried to focus on
the white, pebble dash pattern of the ceiling, I noticed with
surprise that I was not gazing up at the ceiling as I had
expected but at a blue sky, broken by small, fluffy cumulus
clouds which were drifting on the breeze. Then as full
consciousness filled by mind, I realized that I was not in bed
at all, that I had not overslept for breakfast, but that I had
dozed off in a deckchair in the garden, that the time was
4.30 p.m. and that I had an appointment to be interviewed
by Mr Hector Leafe in Ealing at 5.30 p.m. In a frenzied
hurry, I tidied myself, swallowed a cup of tea that my
mother insisted I have and within ten minutes I was driving
furiously in the direction of Hector Leafe's. Looking back
over the years most of my interviews seemed to have got off
to a traumatic start. Was this to be a life-long pattern, I
wondered? Then Fate took a kind turn for on that warm
and sunny August afternoon most of the usual busy traffic
must have decided to go by another route. The road opened
up to me like the Red Sea to Moses and even the traffic
signals were all green for a change. I found myself pulling
up at my destination at exactly 5.20 p.m. I became calm
and composed.

The house was situated on a main road but had a large,
wide, tarmacked drive which swept round in an arch, giving
access on the left side with an exit on the right. The house
was of a broad, double-fronted design, most probably built
in the mid 1930s. It had large, bay windows with diamond
shaped leaded glass. Smoothing my hair and straightening
my tie, I wandered slowly up to the front door. A shiny brass
plate stated, "Hector W. Leafe, L.D.S., R.C.S. Eng., Dental
Surgeon". Below this was another, newer plate in brown
plastic with white painted letters which said, "Edward
Richards, B.D.S., U.Lond., Dental Surgeon". A gentle
"meeow" made me look down to find quite the largest cat I
had ever seen. It had the appearance of a doctored tom. He
really was enormous; a piebald mosaic of black and white
with just the merest suggestion of tortoiseshell on his chest.
He came right up to me and proceeded to rub his back
against my legs, accompanying this sign of affection with a

deep, rattling purr. He was so strong that I had to brace myself against him. "I wonder if you belong here?" I thought. Then I noticed that he had a metal chain around his neck which carried a small inscribed plate. I bent down and read, "Henry VIII, Leafe, Ealing".

"Good afternoon, your Majesty," I heard myself say. "Would you please stop banging against me and let one of your humble subjects pass."

I shall never know whether he really did understand me but he stopped short, looked up at me with his grey-green eyes and majestically stalked off around the house, still purring with sheer contentment. I inspected my watch – 5.24 p.m. Just right for my appointment; not too early and certainly not too late. A movement from within the bay window to the left of the front door made me look in that direction. I observed that it was a pleasantly furnished and equipped dental surgery. The dental unit and chair were in a conventional ivory-tan colour and the rest of the room in matching cream. The afternoon sun was shining from behind me and streaming into the room so that I doubt if anyone in there would readily have seen me at the front door. A man, wearing a high-necked white dental coat was standing in the room with his back to the window. He was quite short and well built. The sun was picking out a balding patch on the crown of his head. With his back to me, it was difficult to tell his age. A door opened into the room and in came a young lady in her mid twenties. She had dark blonde hair, worn shoulder length and she was wearing a green print dress. I assumed her to be a patient. She cast a hurried look around the room and seeing that he was the only occupant rushed over to him, threw her arms around his neck and kissed him quite passionately on the lips. His reciprocation was to clasp her in a bear hug and return her kisses with several of his. I watched, enthralled, as he showered her with a multitude of little kisses, working his way from her mouth down and around her chin and finally in a flurry of passion to every part of her neck. I could hear her giggles through the closed window, punctuated with little sobs of "Oh darling, oh darling!" The door leading into the room suddenly opened.

Fortunately, for the dentist and his patient in there, the

door opened towards them, which gave them just a second
to disengage themselves from each other's arms before the
entrant appeared from around the door. This, I saw to be a
dental nurse, dressed in a white coat, neatly kept in place by
a blue shiny belt. She was quite an attractive brunette with
a fresh complexion. The patient, turning slightly pink, sat
herself into the dental chair and the dentist started to wash
his hands in the hand basin on the far side of the room. If
this was a possible employer of mine, then what sort of a
practice was this? I had been brought up in a most ethical
and professional background! However, the time was nearing 5.30 p.m. and so I pressed the doorbell. Immediately,
from within the house, came the loud barking of a dog and
it sounded as though the bark belonged to a particularly
large dog. Within seconds the door was opened by the
dental nurse I had seen through the window.

"Mr Wilder for Mr Leafe at 5.30 p.m." I said. "I have an
appointment for an interview."

"Yes, of course," came the reply as she opened the door
wide for me to enter. She led the way straight across an
oval-shaped hall to the waiting room. Right in the centre of
the hall was a wooden desk with two telephones and appointment books on it, and there was a leather padded chair
behind it. The waiting room was cosily furnished and carpeted. On the walls were several paintings and engravings of
World War I aeroplanes, most of them being Sopwith
Camels.

"Mr Leafe will see you as soon as he can," said the nurse.
"He is busy with a patient at the moment." I had no doubts
about that!

The barking of the dog that had accompanied me into the
waiting room abated and the only sound then came from
the loud and regular ticking of a tall, mahogany grandfather
clock that stood in a corner of the room. I settled myself into
a comfortable chair and studied the house prices in Surrey
from a copy of *Town & Country* magazine. Some fifteen
minutes must have passed and I was deciding on whether to
buy a seven-bedroomed mansion, one and a half miles from
Esher with well stocked gardens and riding stables, or go on
a world cruise in a luxury liner, when the waiting room door
opened and a gentleman in his mid-sixties came in. He was

tall and angular, his head of silvery hair giving him a rather
distinguished appearance. He was wearing a black jacket
and black striped trousers and a gold chain ran from one
pocket of his black waistcoat across to another pocket. It
reminded me of my father's 'special' suit that he wore only
for very important occasions. I had tried it on once and
quickly decided that it was not my style at all.

"Mr Wilder? I'm Hector Leafe. How do you do?" His
voice was soft and unhurried and I recognized a northern
accent that had apparently not been lost during his sojourn
in southern England. He held out his hand and as I shook it
he said, "Nice of you to come and see me."

This was most certainly not the dentist I had seen express
himself so amorously with his patient about twenty minutes
previously. Perhaps that was his outgoing assistant. Within
minutes of meeting Hector Leafe it was more than obvious
to me that I was dealing with a most ethical, honest,
forthright and reliable man. From a brief clinical discussion
with him I knew that here was a well balanced practice
where I could consolidate my undergraduate studies. He had
a patient and sympathetic manner and readily understood
the early problems that a newly qualified dental surgeon
would inevitably have to encounter. I would have been
pleased to place my own dental care in his hands. In the
space of barely twenty-four hours I had come from the
painful experience of almost instantaneous rejection from
Messrs Cartwright, Bowden & Peacock, through the antithesis of Roy Birch to the present situation of possibly being
offered two assistantships at the same time, Hans Trimmelwasser in Cricklewood and Hector Leafe in Ealing. Two
practices, poles apart, but both run by highly competent
and experienced dental practitioners.

"I would be pleased to have you as an assistant," came the
invitation. The confidence I had lost in Welwyn Garden City
was rapidly returning to me. "But before you accept or
decline Mr Wilder, perhaps you would like to view the
surgeries and meet the staff?"

We made our way across the highly polished parquet
flooring of the hall to the surgery on which I had so inadvertently been a 'peeping Tom'. We stopped outside the
door. "This is my present assistant's room, Ted Richards,"

he explained. So that's who the amorous gentleman was. He tapped respectfully on the door. "I don't like to disturb him if he is engaged on something important with a patient," he said. In view of recent events I appreciated, probably more than he did, the possible relevance of his remark! The door was opened by whom I recognized to be the dentist I had seen. Ted Richards was considerably younger than he had appeared to be through the window and with his balding head towards me. I assessed his age to be in his late twenties.

"Am I disturbing you, Ted?" enquired Hector Leafe.

"Not at all, Hector, come right on in," came the reply in a rich West Country burr. "I've just finished for the day."

As we entered the surgery, I noticed that the young lady in the green print dress was just getting out of the dental chair. The nurse was busying herself tidying the instruments from the bracket table.

"May I introduce Mr Leonard Wilder who may be taking over from you, Ted." Ted Richards looked keenly at me, decided at once that he liked me, and smiled warmly at me.

"Been qualified long?" he asked.

"Only just," I replied.

"Then you can't do better than start off here with Hector. He's taught me all I know. I'd still be staying on if I weren't getting married in ten days time. My future father-in-law is a dentist in Yeovil and insists that I join him there in readiness for his retirement. By the way," and he nodded in the direction of the nurse, "that's Christine. She's a brick and a delight to work with." He then turned to the patient. "Now come and meet my fiancée, Catherine. She's just come in for a scale and polish to get the old nashers all sparkling for the wedding."

My heart rose. Suddenly everything was explained. Suddenly I liked the set-up at Hector Leafe's very much. There appeared to be no snags. I also liked the set-up at Trimmelwasser's. The situation put me in a dilemma. Ted Richards' fiancée was a charming young lady. Coming from the West Country, she, too, spoke with a warm burr in her voice. From what I had seen, I had no doubts that they would make a very happy couple.

Hector Leafe was very thorough. He not only let me inspect all the equipment and instruments in the assistant's surgery but also led me into his which was diagonally across the entrance hall, occupying the lower front room with the large bay window on the other side of the house. His surgery was almost identical to the other one except that the equipment was a little older in appearance and certainly looked more worn. "My wife and I live in the upper part of the house," he explained. "In this way there is no intrusion between the domestic and professional quarters." He went to the foot of the stairs. "Helen!" he called up the stairs. "Helen! come and meet Leonard Wilder."

The now silent dog broke into a series of loud, throaty barks from somewhere on the first floor of the building. These were accompanied by a lady's voice calling, "Charming, Charming, steady now boy." The barks and the voice grew louder as, at one and the same time, a large white and black-spotted Dalmatian appeared at the top of the stairs as did a grey-haired, compact lady in her early sixties. Although rather slight in build, she had a somewhat athletic manner about her. The family obviously had an attraction for oversize animals as, with the cat, this dog was the largest Dalmatian I had ever set my eyes on. For a few moments he stood there quite still, like a statue, scenting the air with his nose. Then having decided that like the rest of the household he approved of me, he gave one high-pitched yap and came bounding down the stairs straight at me. Before I had time to think he leapt on to his hind legs and with his front paws on my chest started to affectionately lick my face amid a staccato of more excited yaps. If Henry VIII had been strong then Charming was indeed a Hercules, and it was with great effort that I prevented myself from being knocked to the floor. "Down Charming, down boy!" ordered Mrs Leafe as she followed him down the stairs. A certain amount of physical restraint was necessary from her before he was persuaded to relinquish his attachment to his new-found friend. However, after a little tussle, he stood by her side panting while she clung with determination to his collar. I produced my hwndkerchief and quietly dried my face from his expression of welcome. "I think he rather likes you," observed Mrs Leafe. If this were 'liking' someone then I shuddered to think how he might express 'intense love'. During this brief encounter, Hector Leafe had stood there quietly with a pained expression on his face, waiting for his wife to control the animal. He, himself, had made no move.

"Helen, let me introduce Leonard Wilder."

"Are you coming here?" she asked with interest. I wondered how much her own sentiments had been influenced by her dog's obvious approval of me.

"I'd like to very much," I replied truthfully but noncommittally.

"By the way," she said tugging hard at the dog's collar, "this is Prince Charming. We call him Charming for short. We're very fond of animals here. We normally keep a budgie in the waiting room but he's upstairs having a few days holiday."

I could not determine just how serious that remark was meant to be. Not being familiar with the recreational inclinations of budgerigars I could only assume that for them a change of environment was, indeed, a holiday. Then why not? I was inwardly amused at the regal names given to the cat and the dog and speculated on the exotic name the bird might have to endure. I had not long to wait. In a matter of moments, Helen Leafe had disappeared up the stairs still holding on to Prince Charming's collar. She reappeared seconds later struggling with the dog in one hand and a large bird cage in the other. As she descended the stairs to the hall, the cage swung quite wildly in her hand but its occupant seemed unperturbed by this movement. It just sat there on its perch as though it were stuffed. Having reached me she proudly held the cage under my nose for me to inspect.

"Come on Colonel, say 'hello' to Mr Wilder." Colonel sat on his perch, motionless and voiceless. She shook the cage rather violently.

"Now Colonel, do your act and say 'hello' to Mr Wilder." To prove he wasn't stuffed, Colonel stretched a wing and then opened his beak twice in rapid succession but no sound issued from it. I wondered if all the vigorous movement to which he had been subjected had made him motion sick. But my question remained unanswered as I had no idea how to assess when a budgerigar was suffering from motion sickness. Then it occurred to me that very likely birds never did.

"He's a little shy today, is our Colonel Bogey." I should have guessed that 'Colonel' by itself was insufficient for so distinguished a bird! Then I noticed that he, too, was considerably larger than most average budgies. It was either that the Leafes specialized in large members of every species or that with all the love, affection and no doubt, food bestowed on their pets, these had grown to such outsize proportions. Then just as I was beginning to think that Colonel Bogey was the exception and that he, alone, did not approve of me, he performed a series of neat side steps on his perch which brought him up against that part of the cage which was nearest to me. "Hello fella, hello fella!" I'm sure he said. This was followed by a delightful short song of melodious chirps, whistles and flutes. "He likes you. He likes you," exclaimed Helen Leafe with unconcealed delight. My paranoia promptly vanished.

"I am sure that Mr Wilder has seen quite enough of the Leafe ensemble this afternoon," interrupted Hector Leafe glaring at his wife. "Have we put you off completely or would you like to consider the assistantship?" he asked me with forthright frankness.

I admitted my interest. How could one otherwise with such a delightful set-up. But I went on to explain that I had already tentatively accepted an offer from Hans Trimmelwasser in Cricklewood. As I had only about a one in four chance of being engaged by that gentleman I had, consequently, come along that afternoon for the interview. "If you could let me know your intentions within a day or two," he said, "then I will make appropriate arrangements. As Ted is leaving at the end of next week you could start the following Monday." This I promised to do and took my leave of the Leafe family.

I had thought that interviews would be a straightforward, almost impersonal affair, based mainly on academic ability. Although I had always appreciated the importance of a patient/dentist relationship, somehow any such sentiment between an assistant and the principal of a practice, let alone his family and pets, had never ever occurred to me. But I liked what I had quickly learned during the past few days. I decided to let Fate play its own hand and decide for me which practice I would launch out in as a fresh dental graduate. As I parked the car in the driveway leading to our garage, my father opened the front door. "Mr Trimmelwasser telephoned while you were in Ealing," he called. "He is offering you the job but says there is a slight snag to sort out. He left his telephone number for you to call back."

Curious, I dialled the number in Cricklewood. The telephone rang for some considerable time and I was just about to replace my instrument on the assumption that the house was empty when the ringing tone stopped and the guttural tones of Hans Trimmelwasser broke through the ear piece. "Ulloo."

"Dr Trimmelwasser?"

"Speaking."

"Leonard Wilder here. I believe you telephoned me. I hope I'm not disturbing you?"

"No, no," came his reassurance. "I'm just about to start mine supper. But it's okay. Just a moment." I heard him calling to someone in the house. "Rosa! Rosa! Put mine supper back in ze oven. I'm on ze phone. I von't be long." His voice returned to the telephone. "Dr Vilder, I vill come straight to ze point – no side turnings. I vould like to offer you ze assistantship. Zere, I've said it. But zere is quite a but. You see, mine present assistant, who is Australian, is going back to Australia. He had planned to do zis in three veeks time. Now he vants to stay on until ze end of September. Vould you be prepared to vait nearly two months? I can't kick him out just because he is changing his mind. He is a good boy and has been vis me over three years. So zat is mine position. Now you tell me vot you sink."

The idea of waiting two months in idle leisure was not exactly appealing to me. I was eager to exercise my newly authorized skill as soon as possible. The assistantship at Ealing could start in just over a week's time. Fate had, indeed, made the decision for me. I explained all this to Hans Trimmelwasser. Although he had anticipated my reply, I noticed a marked note of regret in his voice as he put down his telephone. I did, however, promise to keep in touch if "sings don' quite vork out ze vay you vant", as he put it. What an encouraging day it had been. I had almost forgotten by then my experience at Welwyn Garden City. To complete the day I telephoned Hector Leafe and arranged to start at his practice on the following Monday week. The next week passed very quickly. I invested the time by purchasing some new, white dental coats, revising one or two books that I considered might be of value and catching up with social visits to some of my relatives whom I felt I had neglected during my final year as a student. They were all pleased to hear of my forthcoming assistantship and one or two even promised to become patients of mine at Ealing.

On the following Monday week and with mixed feelings of anticipation and apprehension I arrived at Hector Leafe's for my first professional day as a dental surgeon. The sun was shining as it did on the day of my interview with him. Even Henry VIII was there to greet me on the doorstep. He went through his previous purring and leg-rubbing ritual with the same vigour. I noticed that Ted Richards's professional plate was now absent from the front door and that it had been replaced by a similar one which bore my name and qualifications. I stood back and admired it proudly for several minutes. It was beautifully new and shiny. Almost too new and shiny. The nameplate of a newly qualified dentist, an inescapable beacon to tell all who see it that "This man is inexperienced". I hoped that time would mellow the plate and also the person whose name it bore.

The door was opened by Christine, the dental nurse, whom I had briefly met ten days before. She gave me a cordial welcome and then went on, "Mr Leafe forgot to tell you that he holds a dental clinic on Monday and Friday mornings at the local hospital," she said. "So you will be here alone this morning."

"Alone?" I repeated as the full impact of my responsibilities hit me. As a clinical student there had always been a house surgeon or a registrar within easy call to help me or extricate me from any problems. I had unconsciously put Hector Leafe into this category, someone on whom to lean during my early days of initiation. Quite unexpectedly, I was alone. The thought frightened me. Christine sensed my thoughts.

"Don't worry, Mr Wilder. We have given you a very easy

start to your first day," she said reassuringly. "In fact most of this morning's patients will be only routine examinations and perhaps an X-ray also." I felt a little more at ease. "Your first patient is new to the practice, a Mrs K. Morris. She's already in the waiting room, but don't rush as it's only ten to nine."

By 9 a.m. I had briefly refamiliarized myself with the surgery lay-out and done up the last button on my new white dental jacket. The basic instruments were neatly laid out on the instrument table and a glass of pink mouthwash had been carefully set out. I was ready for my debut. The front door bell rang and Christine peeped through the window.

"That's a patient to make an appointment," she observed. She inspected the patient a little more carefully. "Oh dear," she sighed. "It's Mrs Peters. She's the practice gossip. She can talk the hind-leg off a donkey. It takes about fifteen minutes to make her an appointment."

"Would you like me to bring in Mrs Morris?" I asked her. "After all, as a student I always collected patients myself."

"Thanks," she replied. "I'll be as quick as I can. Good luck with your first one," she called over her shoulder as she made her way to the front door. By the time I had combed my hair and polished my shoes with a dental tissue the hands of the surgery clock were pointing precisely to 9 a.m. I walked across the hall. Mrs Peters was already engaging Christine in lengthy conversation at the desk. Christine was smiling benevolently but I doubt if she were really listening. I opened the waiting room door and stood there in the doorway.

"Mrs Morris for Mr Wilder please," I called. The last words had hardly left my mouth when, in a flurry of movement, the patient leapt out of her chair, charged right at me, flung her arms around my neck and kissed me violently on the lips. For a moment I was rendered immobile with sudden astonishment. "Congratulations, dear Leonard," I heard coming from the mop of dark hair into which my face was buried. With great effort I disentangled myself from the lady's embrace. "Kate!" I exclaimed. "What are you doing here?"

"You told us last week that you were starting today so I thought I'd be your very first patient. I telephoned for an appointment and the nurse was able to give me a cancellation." The patient was one of my favourite cousins, Kathryn. She had married quite recently and so I was, as yet, not accustomed to thinking of her by her new name of Mrs Morris. Through habit, I still thought of her as Miss Kate Leigh.

A snort from behind me reminded me that my cousin and I were not the only occupants of the hall. Mrs Peters had turned crimson and glaring first at Kathryn and then at me, declared to Christine, "What flagrant immoral behaviour. Kissing a patient!" She almost spat the words out. "Huh, if this is the new assistant, I wouldn't be surprised if he were struck off the Register pretty soon. I've a good mind to report him myself. You can cancel that appointment with him for a start. I'm not having him touch me!"

"But Mrs Peters," pleaded Christine, "didn't you hear? This lady is Mr Wilder's cousin. She was only congratulating him on his new assistantship."

"Don't expect me to swallow that yarn," came the disbelieving cry. I prayed for the ground to open and for it to swallow me up. It refused to comply with my request. What a way to start off! I looked at Kathryn appealingly.

"I *am* his cousin," she said to the indignant Mrs Peters. "There was nothing unprofessional about his behaviour. I am allowed to kiss a first cousin, aren't I?"

I retreated to the surgery and left Christine and my cousin to placate Mrs Peters. The last thing I wanted was for her to file a complaint to Hector Leafe about his new assistant, unjustified as it might have been. The voices in the hall gradually became subdued and I heard the front door open and close. Through the leaded glass window I watched Mrs Peters stalk down the drive and go off down the road.

"She won't breathe a word to Mr Leafe," said Christine entering the room with Kathryn.

"She won't?" I asked incredulously.

"She's moving to Brighton in two weeks' time and only wanted a check-up and a scale and polish before she goes. I persuaded her to wait until her move and then find herself a dentist down there."

"She didn't need much persuading, either," added Kathryn.

As my blood pressure returned to normal and the tightness of my collar slackened from around my neck, I settled Mrs Kathryn Morris in the chair and started to examine my first professional patient.

"Open wide, please," I requested, "and whatever you do, don't kiss me, Kate!"

11

In at the Deep End

"What are you doing about lunch, Mr Wilder?" Helen Leafe's head appeared around the surgery door. Kathryn Morris had just left, after only requiring a scale and polish, and I was preparing to see my 9.30 a.m. patient who, as yet, had not yet arrived.

"Lunch?" In the excitement of starting on my first day with Hector Leafe, I had completely overlooked bodily refreshments. "I suppose there must be a café somewhere not far," I speculated. "Can you recommend one?"

"I was hoping you'd do the same as Mr Richards," she said. "He always joined us for lunch upstairs. Didn't Mr Leafe mention this to you?"

"No, he didn't."

"Trust a man to overlook a thing like that. I make lunch just after one o'clock each day and you'd be very welcome to join us."

"You can't possibly entertain me like that every day, Mrs Leafe." Although her invitation was very welcome, I felt that I had to make a gesture of declining.

"Well, I shall expect some reciprocation from you," she said mysteriously.

"Mr Richards would offer to take Prince Charming out for a walk now and then after lunch. Do you think that's a fair offer?"

"I think it's an unfair offer," I smiled. "I think it goes very unfairly in my favour but I'll readily accept it. Thank you."

"Then I'll see you at one o'clock," and she disappeared into the hall.

"What do you do for lunch?" I asked Christine.

"I go home," she replied. "My flat is only a quarter of a mile away. I can get there in five minutes."

The door opened and the head of Mrs Leafe appeared again. "Have you any dietary dislikes?" she asked.

"None at all," I assured her.

"Then as it's your first day, I'll make something special. Hector and Freda will be back by about 1 p.m., that is if they are not kept late at the clinic," and the head was gone.

"Who's Freda?" I asked Christine.

"Of course, you haven't met Freda yet, have you? She's Mr Leafe's personal dental nurse. She's been with him nearly forty years," and she sighed. "I believe she's had a thing about him for all that time but I doubt if he has ever suspected it." She looked wistful. "Love at arm's length," she added.

"How about Mrs Leafe? Does she realize how Freda feels about her husband?"

"I don't know?" she reflected pensively. "In the four years that I've been here, I've not really been able to make Mrs Leafe out. Most of her life seems to rotate around the pets. It's just as well for you that you hit it off with Charming. That was your test as far as she's concerned."

The doorbell rang.

"That will be Mrs Sandra Powell. Shall I bring her

straight in?" The surgery clock indicated 9.35 a.m.

"Please do," I requested.

A quick inspection of the patient's record card showed me that she had already been given two fillings during her current course of treatment and that all that was required was a small silver amalgam restoration in her upper first, left premolar tooth. What a strange coincidence. For I remembered that it was at such a location that I started on my very first patient as a student some years before. How things had changed for me in that time. The raw undergraduate was now a dental surgeon, qualified and on the Register. I had learned a great deal about dentistry. There was now the period of consolidation before me and above all the challenge of coping with a variety of patients and becoming integrated into the dental world of Hector Leafe.

Into the room, preceded by Christine, came an attractive woman in her mid thirties. Her raven hair was cut quite short in a tulip style and she wore a simple summer dress of light beige which had a tie-up belt in matching material. A single string of white synthetic pearls adorned her neck. She stopped short in the doorway.

"You've changed, you're different!" she exclaimed. I was unprepared for this welcome. She turned to Christine. "This isn't Mr Richards. I was expecting Mr Richards. I'm Mr Richards's patient!" And then to me, "You're not Mr Richards," almost accusingly. A feeling of guilt swept over me as I threw a hasty glance at the mirror on the wall which confirmed without a shadow of doubt that I most certainly was not Ted Richards.

"I'm terribly sorry," I offered her in weak defence. "You see, he's got married."

"Oh!" She half sobbed, half shrieked. "Got married? Got married! He can't possibly have done that!"

"Why ever not?" I asked with genuine surprise.

"Because he never said anything to me."

"Should he have done?" I wondered what sort of obligation he was under to Sandra Powell.

"Well, I have been coming to see him for three years," she said. "Regularly every six months, too," she added. "You do get to know your dentist quite well in that time. I somehow always thought of him as a confirmed bachelor. Married? Is

he really married? I was only in here two weeks ago and he
didn't say a word."

"I can't help what he did or did not tell you, Mrs Powell," I
said. "All I know is that he has left to live in Somerset with his
wife. I have taken over from him now." And then I added as a
gesture of reassurance, "I shall try to be as kind and as gentle
as he was." I assumed that Ted Richards had been kind and
gentle.

"He was a marvellous dentist," she reflected. "Somerset did
you say? What part?"

"Yeovil."

She thought for a moment and then becoming more
composed said, "Ah well, that's much too far away." She
inspected me carefully for several seconds. Then her manner
dramatically changed. "And what is your name?" she asked.

"Mr Wilder," I told her.

"Mr Wilder . . . Mr Wilder. . . . Very well, Mr Wilder, I
will let you attend to my teeth," she condescended. "Now,
you do promise not to hurt me?"

"Yes, of course," I said.

She moved slowly into the surgery and up to the dental
chair.

"He's very young," she remarked to Christine.

The memory of my early days in the Conservation Room at
the hospital flooded back to me. For a moment I regretted
having shaved my moustache. Christine, who was arranging
the instruments, returned the comment with a sickly smile
and played safe by not saying anything. I was at a loss to
compete with this gamesmanship. "I suppose you've only just
qualified, have you?" It was more of a challenge than a
question.

"Er yes . . . I suppose I have." I was completely exposed
and vulnerable.

"Ah, well," she sighed as she seated herself in the chair,
"there's only one small filling to do. I don't suppose you can
do much wrong with that." Whereupon her head sank back
into the head rest and she closed her eyes. I felt she had turned
the external world off including me, and had retreated inwardly for safety. I moistened a pledget of cotton wool with a
drop of surface anaesthetic and then carefully retracting her
upper lip on the left side I gently applied it to her gum over

the tooth to be filled. She sat motionless, breathing deeply and rhythmically. I waited a full minute for it to take effect and then very carefully I pressed the sharp end of the hypodermic needle against the mucosa of her gum. The slightest resistance and the point slowly entered up to a depth of a few millimetres. I looked up at Sandra Powell's face. Her eyes were still shut tight; she was still out of contact with the outside world. I then administered one of the gentlest injections I had ever given and carefully withdrew the syringe. Christine's open hand appeared under mine and I gratefully placed the syringe into it. Still no change in Sandra Powell. I selected a bur from the dental cabinet and inserted it into the handpiece of the drill.

"It's going numb?!" Sandra Powell suddenly exclaimed, opening her eyes wide with amazement.

"Of course it's going numb," I said.

"But you haven't given me an injection yet."

"I have given you an injection."

"But you couldn't have done," she insisted. "I didn't feel anything."

"You're not supposed to feel anything," I said as my confidence came surging back.

"He didn't really give me an injection, did he?" she asked Christine.

"Yes, Mrs Powell. Mr Wilder gave you an injection all right."

A beige-covered arm swept up from the patient in the chair and her hand grasped mine. "Thank you, thank you very much," she said with a catch in her voice. "I've always been terrified of injections. I just couldn't see how a newly qualified dentist could avoid hurting me. That's why I was so facetious with you. I was trying to cover up my stupid fear. You see, I had so much faith in Mr Richards that I couldn't imagine his successor being as gentle." She relinquished her grasp of my hand and closed her eyes again. "You can do what you like now," she said. She was as good as her word. By fifteen minutes past ten, I had completed her filling and she left thanking me profusely, "for being just like Mr Richards".

I had only seen two patients and already I was running fifteen minutes late. Hurriedly washing my hands, I asked Christine to show in my ten o'clock patient. Mrs Thorn was about fifty, well spread and none too tidy in appearance. She gave the impression of having just left off washing the kitchen floor to rush round to the dentist. She shuffled over to the chair without even noticing me, slumped into it and then looked up. The words "Good morn . . . ," tailed off as her eyes took me in. "Oh," she said, "I've not seen you before. You're different!" I was prepared for it this time. I took a deep breath. "Mr Richards has left to get married and has gone to live in Yeovil in Somerset with his wife," I said mechanically. "My name is Mr Wilder. I have just qualified but I am as gentle as Mr Richards and I promise not to hurt you." I stood back and watched to see the reassuring effect it would have on Mrs Thorn.

"Mr Richards? Who is Mr Richards?" came the totally unexpected reply.

"The dentist who was here before me." I explained. "The dentist who attended to you last time," I added.

"That was no Mr Richards," she responded. "That was a lady dentist, Miss Gardener."

From the other side of the surgery Christine's voice floated over to me. "That's quite right, Mrs Thorn. According to your record card you were last here six years ago when Miss Gardener made your dentures for you. When she left, Mr Richards took over and now that he's gone we have Mr Wilder."

"Oh, I see. Well, if you are good enough for Mr Leafe then you are good enough for me," she said, readily accepting me as a satisfactory replacement. Even with Hector Leafe away at the clinic it was some reassurance to have his moral support behind me. "Will you make me a new set of teeth?" she enquired. "My jaws have sunk in since I had these and Mr Thorn says they make me look older than what I should."

It required only a short examination to confirm that there had been considerable resorption of the bone of her dental arches and that her "jaws had sunk in". I agreed to construct new dentures for her and offered to take the first impressions right away. By 10.40 a.m. Mrs Thorn had left and I had somehow survived my first three patients.

"It's not always like this," laughed Christine as I treated myself to a long, cold drink of water. "It's bound to be trying for the first few weeks until you settle in and the patients get to know you."

"I should live that long," I said as I downed another glass of water. There was a determined rap on the surgery door. Christine started to open it. It was barely a few inches open when a husky voice barked at her from the other side. "Will he be long?" it asked impatiently. "I have a train to catch."

"He's ready now," said Christine, fully opening the door. "Please come in Mr Hooper." The thick-set figure of a man in his late fifties marched across the floor and leapt into the chair. He nodded at me.

"Morning, Mr . . .?"

"Wilder," I added and waited for his response.

"Morning, Mr Wilder," he repeated. "Sorry to be in a rush but I have a train to catch to Scotland." He spoke in short sharp phrases. "I only want a quick ease to my lower denture. It's the same spot the chappie before you had some trouble with. Giving me sheer hell it is. Can't eat and I like my food," and he slapped his abdomen three times. He reminded me of the ringmaster at a circus I loved to go to each Christmas when I was a child. I could just imagine him cracking his whip into the sawdust. Mr Hooper did, indeed, have quite a large ulcer caused by his lower denture. I admired his ability to suffer what must surely have been considerable discomfort. Within ten minutes I had removed just sufficient from the fitting surface of the denture to afford him considerable relief. "It should feel even more comfortable in a couple of days when the ulcer has healed," I told him as he thanked me and rushed off to catch his train.

"Would you like a cup of coffee? It's nearly eleven o'clock,' asked Christine. Coffee? I suddenly realized that I was starving. I could have eaten my lunch even at that hour. It was the old story all over again. The nervous strain of a new situation and I was burning up energy at a great rate. Christine disappeared into a small room which led off the entrance hall of the house. This room had, I later learned, started its life as a cloakroom-cum-storeroom, but at a later date the storeroom part had been converted to offer limited facilities for brewing tea or coffee. Just after eleven o'clock and somewhat refreshed, I prepared to do battle with the rest of the morning's patients. By 11.25 a.m. when my 11 a.m. patient had not yet arrived, Christine wrote 'Appointment Failed' against the name of Simon Fisher. "He's sitting for his eleven plus in two weeks' time and has most probably forgotten his appointment here," she suggested. "It's a good excuse for not coming," she added.

At precisely 11.30 a.m. Mr Stan Hawkes parked his battered green van in the driveway and was ringing the door bell. He came darting into the room. He was short, with sleek dark hair and had a long, thin nose. His shiny blue suit reflected the almost midday sun which was streaming in through the window. Without looking at his chart, I put him at about forty. He seemed to land in the dental chair from about half way to the door. He shut his eyes as if in pain.

"It's no bloody good, I've been up all night wiv it!" he complained in a strong London accent.

"What's the trouble?" I politely asked.

"You know. That ruddy toof what you done!" I was taken aback.

"I beg your pardon?" was all that I could say. He opened his mouth and jabbed a grimy finger at a tooth. He raised his voice aggressively.

"That toof what you done abart ten days ago. Well, it's been giving me fair ole murder it 'as. I've been down South on a job and I couldn't get to you. And as I hate all ruddy dentists, I didn't fancy going to some strange bloke. Cor!" and he held a hand against his cheek in self-pity. "Whip it out, mate. Do me a favour."

I hastily inspected his record card. From it I saw that ten days previously Ted Richards had treated a lower right molar for a suspected exposed nerve.

"I'm sorry to hear of your pain, Mr Hawkes, but it wasn't I who attended you last time."

He slowly opened his eyes, stared at me, fumbled in a pocket of his crumpled jacket, produced a pair of steel-rimmed spectacles, placed them on his nose and inspected me more carefully. "Well, stone the crows!" he exclaimed. "So it ain't. Where's the other bloke?"

"Mr Richards has left and I have taken over from him." I hoped that this brief explanation was all that would be required. I was right.

"I see," he said slowly, suddenly subdued. "Will you take it out for me? I've had fair ole hell wiv it, I 'ave."

An inspection of his tooth showed me that most of it had decayed away and that Ted had placed into the cavity an enormous temporary filling. By twelve noon, Stan Hawkes, minus the offending molar, was starting up the engine of his green van. He pulled out of the drive and turned in the direction of Birmingham on his way to 'another job'.

"What does he do for a living?" I asked Christine.

"I've never found out," she said. "He's always going off somewhere on a job. Actually, he only ever comes in when he has toothache. We've never been able to impress on him the importance of regular treatment."

The doorbell sounded by the next patient. "That will be Miss Chidworth. She's a remarkable lady of nearly eighty. You're fitting a new lower denture for her this morning. Mr Richards carried out all the other stages but didn't have time to complete it before he left. She's a dear but rather slow."

Agatha Chidworth certainly was slow. Although physically sound for her age, she obviously had spent the latter part of her life quite uninfluenced by the hustle and strain of the twentieth century. It took her several minutes to remove her light coat, then her hat, then her kid gloves, place her umbrella, despite the cloudless day, in a corner of the surgery, make her way to the dental chair and settle herself into it. She smiled at me endearingly. "Good morning, Mr Wilder," she said. "I'm very pleased to meet you."

This cordial reception and knowledge of my name was quite unexpected. I had been preparing myself for a "Where's Mr Richards?" approach. For the first time that day I felt myself relax. "Good morning," I responded. "May I ask how you know my name?"

"That's very easy," she replied. "When I heard from Mrs Leafe that Mr Richards was leaving, I asked the name of the new gentleman and I was told that it was going to be a Mr Wilder and that you would be fitting my new denture for me."

"That's quite right," I said as I inspected the denture that Christine had placed on the bracket table. There was little for me to do other than ask her to remove her old lower denture and insert the new one into her mouth. A few adjustments here and there and it was ready for her to wear. "There you are, Miss Chidworth," I said. "Do let me know if you experience any discomfort and I shall be pleased to make any necessary adjustments for you."

"I'm sure that won't happen," she said. "They feel comfortable already." She studied my face and continued. "I do believe you are a very clever dentist. Fancy knowing what size to make it without even seeing me first."

"That's no problem," I hurried to explain. "You see, it was Mr Richards and the dental technician who did all the work. All I have done is to give them to you. It's been no more difficult than the milk roundsman delivering the milk."

But she shook her head wisely. "I can see that you are modest as well as clever," she smiled. "Fancy getting it right without knowing the size of my mouth."

"But Miss Chidworth, you mustn't give me the credit that belongs to Mr Richards. It was he, who made the denture for you, not I."

"Yes, yes, I know he took the impressions. I've had all that before but this is the finished denture. I think you are very clever and I shall tell Mr Leafe how lucky he is in having you here." She had shut her mind to any other explanation and so I realized that the matter would have to rest there. I hoped that Ted Richards would have understood my getting the credit for all his good work. If she were slow in coming into the room then she was even more painfully slow in leaving. By the time she had put on her coat and adjusted her hat and then had several long looks into the surgery mirror at her new teeth, my 12.30 p.m. patient had been waiting over ten minutes. With my first luncheon date with the Leafes barely twenty minutes away, I tried not to appear impatient as I helped her out of the room.

"What am I doing for the next patient?" I asked Christine as I inspected the last name on the morning's list of patients. "Miss Fournier," I read. "Sounds French."

"She is French," Christine explained. "Annette Fournier is a French *au pair* girl. Although she's been here nearly two years, her English is only fair. She spends most of her time with other French *au pair* girls. And as the English family with whom she is staying speak French, she hasn't really had much of a chance to learn English. I'll bring her in. She's here for a routine examination."

In the few moments that Christine was gone I tried to recall what little French I had learnt at school and had since forgotten. Languages had never been my strong point. Annette Fournier was a pretty girl of twenty. Traditionally French in appearance, she was a petite brunette with dark piercing eyes. She wore a navy suit with a white polo-necked jumper.

"Bonjour, Mademoiselle," I greeted her somewhat self-consciously, hoping that my attempt at detente would offset the French equivalent of "Where is Monsieur Richards?"

"Bonjour, Monsieur," came the warm reply. "Vous parlez français?"

"Très peu," I replied. "Very très peu."

Christine hid a smile behind her hand. "What's your French like?" I asked her. "Non-existent," came the immediate response. "But don't worry. She does speak some English."

I addressed the patient. "Do you speak English?" I found myself talking deliberately in monosyllables.

"A leetle," came the shy response.

"I believe I have to examine your teeth this morning," I continued slowly."

"Examen, oui, of course, yes," and she sat in the chair, leaned her head on to the head rest and opened her mouth.

She had a very high standard of dental health. I did, however, find the beginnings of a small cavity in an upper molar tooth.

"You have a small cavity in this tooth," I said tapping the tooth in question. "It will need a filling."

Christine leaned across the patient. "I doubt if she will understand the word 'cavity'," she said. I cleared my throat and rephrased it.

"You have a hole in this tooth," I tried to explain. I looked at Annette's face to see if she had understood me.

"'Ole, what ees 'ole?"

I searched for a synonym for 'hole' and 'cavity' that would be suitable in this situation. Not being able to think of one, I tried, "This tooth is very slightly bad," but felt that this was a poor description of a minute speck of early caries.

"Bad, bad?" she reflected. "It ees bad! On doit enlever?" and she turned pale.

"Oh no!" I said, placing a hand reassuringly on her shoulder. "Not extracted. Non, non, not enlever! Fill, filling, amalgam." And then from somewhere in my memory something stirred as I remembered the words that had eluded me. "Trou!" I exclaimed. "A hole. Il y a un trou dans ce dent. I will make a filling, plombage," and I looked at Christine triumphantly.

"Ah, oui!" Annette exclaimed with relief, "Okay, plombage, feelleeng, okay, d'accord."

With the surgery clock at nine minutes to one I realized that with my present limited experience I could never have carried out a filling, even small, in less than nine minutes and arrive for lunch in a state of composure. Somehow I managed to get it over to her that I would like her to return again the following week. She readily agreed and as she departed, she treated me to a delightful smile.

"You speak good French," she slowly said!

Ten minutes later, having survived my first morning as a dental surgeon, I climbed the stairs to the Leafes' residential part of the house and was welcomed by Prince Charming who treated me to another burst of friendly face-licking.

"Would you care for a drink before lunch, Mr Wilder?" offered Helen Leafe. "Perhaps a glass of sherry?" She watched me thoughtfully as the golden liquid sent a mellow flush through me, restoring my tried nerves to a feeling of well being. "I suppose Mr Leafe will be here at any minute," I said, trying to make polite conversation.

She coughed a little uneasily and replied, "My husband telephoned from the clinic just a few minutes ago. He is having to extract two impacted wisdom teeth as an emergency at 2.30 this afternoon and so he and Freda won't be home for lunch today."

"Impacted wisdom teeth?" I said thoughtfully. "That could take a long time."

"It could," she agreed. "So he has asked me to cancel his afternoon's patients for him. If I can't contact all of them, he would be most grateful if you would fit those into your afternoon's surgery list." She stared at me hopefully. I already had seven patients for the afternoon, more than I would ever have seen as a student during an entire day's work. After my morning's initiation, the idea of having to fit goodness knows how many more in was a terrifying thought to a new graduate.

"I'm sorry to throw you in at the deep end like this," she said refilling my sherry glass.

"It's one way of learning quickly," I reflected, trying to appear unmoved. "It's sink or swim, I suppose."

"I had better start the telephone calls," she said. "So do you mind if I serve your lunch for you now? Please don't wait for me."

She had obviously gone to some effort with the lunch. The silent solitude in which I tried to consume the fried liver and onions, sauté potatoes and green peas, albeit a little over-cooked, was something I shall always remember. The antici-pation of another new batch of patients was enough of a challenge by itself, but the thought of Hector Leafe's own personal devotees was sufficient to make me nearly choke on the rice pudding. I hoped he would consider a third glass of sherry fair compensation for what I might have to face up to that afternoon as I poured myself another glass. By 2 p.m. I knew the worst. Helen Leafe had managed to postpone only three of her husband's seven patients. "We dare not send the other four away when they arrive," she said. "It goes against Mr Leafe's principles. It looks as though you'll have a busy first afternoon." I thanked her for the meal, assuring her that it had fortified me for what lay ahead, but I doubt if my words carried any conviction in them.

The afternoon passed in a kaleidoscope of new faces, forests of teeth, men, women, boys, girls, all shapes and all sizes. Christine was superb but I felt that my greatest hurdle was the time factor. Hector Leafe's patients were accustomed to a gentle, efficient and quick operator and expected the same from me. Gentle, I tried to be; efficient, yes, if I took my time and consequently the word 'quick' had to be replaced by 'slow'. It became the nightmare dream of running to escape from danger when, somehow, one feels that one is running in treacle and is unable to go fast enough. I cannot remember individual names or what I did for whom. But I stayed the course and collapsed into the dental chair at 6.30 p.m.

Christine made me a welcome cup of tea. "After a day such as this I think you'd better have an early night," she said. "But you coped very well," she added encouragingly.

It certainly had been a hard start. It was over and with a feeling of achievement I closed the front door and on my first day as a dentist. My employer and his nurse had not yet returned. I wondered which of us had experienced the tougher day. As I drove towards my home, the evening sun was beginning to dip low over the houses in the western sky. I was tired, tired and yet completely fulfilled. This is what I had wanted – to be a dentist – and now I had my first day as such behind me. It was something that could never be taken away from me. Irrespective of what professional problems I might encounter in the future, I had survived the first plunge in at the deep end and I had swum to safety.

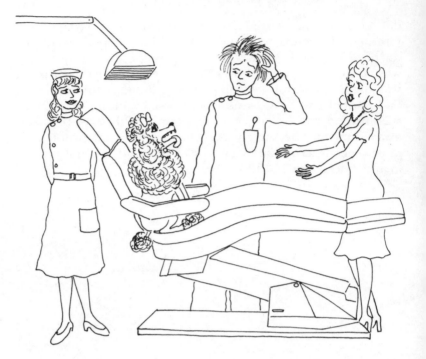

12

Thereby Hangs a Tail

"Br -r-i-n-g, Br -r-i-n-g, Br -r-i-n-g." I lazily stretched out an
arm, switched off my alarm clock and buried my head under
the bedclothes. Five seconds later I sat up with a start. The
night had flown and in the bright dawn of a summer's
morning I realized that my second day as an assistant with
Hector Leafe was about to start. I leapt out of bed. Three-
quarters of an hour later, I was fighting my way through
mounting traffic in the direction of Ealing. As I parked the
car at the side of the drive, I noticed a grey-haired, chubby
little lady making her way to the front door. As she did so,
Prince Charming appeared through the open door and went
bounding up to her, wagging his tail. She stopped and patted

his head saying, "There's a good boy, Charming. Come to
say 'Good morning' to Freda, have you?" I had by then
caught up with her, whereupon the dog transferred his
attentions to me and treated me to yet another of his
affectionate welcomes. "You must be Leonard Wilder," she
said.

"Yes, I'm the new assistant. Good morning," I replied,
fending off another barrage of canine exuberance.

"I'm Freda Picton," she said. "Mr Leafe's personal dental
nurse." She stressed the word 'personal' and I sensed a slight
air of possessiveness. She spoke with a soft, rather cultured
voice. There was just the slightest suggestion of a Scottish
accent, possibly Edinburgh, but it was only just discernible. I
assessed her age to be in her early sixties. I stood aside to let
her through the front door. "I hear you had a hectic first
day," she said as she turned towards her surgery.

"It certainly was a testing start," I replied. "But as you can
see, I have survived."

"You did more than survive." Hector Leafe's voice came
from the stairs that he was descending. "I understand from
Helen and Christine that you managed most admirably.
Incidentally, little Miss Chidworth thinks you're very clever.
She telephoned last night to tell me how lucky I am to have
you on the staff. Well, I wish you good luck on your second
day. If you have any problems just come and tell me. I'm only
across the hall," and he and Freda went into their surgery for
their morning's session.

Unlike the previous day, that day passed quite easily.
Perhaps I was prepared for the unexpected and the "Where's
Mr Richards?" approach, but I finished the day on time and
returned home almost impatient at having to wait for the
next day's surgery to start. As the days lengthened into
weeks, I gradually settled down at the Leafes and realized
that I had made the correct choice in my first professional
step. Christine was a constant source of encouragement. She
had been engaged to a student teacher for the past year,
Michael Digby. Having recently qualified, he was teaching
English at a school in Harrow and they were both saving
hard in order to get married. During my third week, he
became a patient of mine. As I felt that this was a result of
her recommendation, it was a great boost to my confidence, a

most important consideration during my early days.

After Helen Leafe's initial burst of enthusiasm, her cuisine gradually declined in standard if not in quantity. Her early attempts at exotic preparations gave place to a singular lack of culinary imagination. I noticed that her husband would discreetly consume the occasional antacid tablet from time to time. Having committed myself to being a permanent lunch guest, I accepted the daily rounds of fried cod, fried corned beef or cold meat, all served with none-too-crisp chips and the inevitable tinned green peas. As the helpings were more than I could cope with or even fancy, Prince Charming's frequent presence under the table presented me with a courteous way out. In a short time I developed considerable skill at feeding two mouths from the same plate without being noticed. In retrospect, I must confess to a twinge of guilt at my lack of appreciation of my hostess. For though deficient in imagination, the food was certainly not of poor quality. The experience did bond a deep and lasting friendship between myself and Prince Charming whose obvious affection for me was something that Helen Leafe was not slow to observe.

"I do like a man who gets on well with animals," she said one day over the bread pudding and custard. "My one regret is that my husband has so little time for our pets," and she threw him a bitter glance. I believe he might have made a suitable comment but had chosen just the moment before to insert a couple of antacid tablets into his mouth.

Freda Picton, despite her easy outward manner, was rather difficult to get to know. In those early days it seemed to me that she lived in a kind of fantasy world in which she was married to her employer and that the real part of her life existed between them confined within the four walls of their surgery. Once inside each morning, she rarely ventured out except for her brief visits to the waiting room to collect his patients. She did not dine with the family but chose to eat a packed lunch "quietly in the surgery". Whether she did so to avoid Helen Leafe's cooking or to avoid Helen Leafe herself or a combination of both these factors is something I still speculate about. But she rarely ever mentioned Helen Leafe's name. It was as though she negated the lady's very existence. Somehow, this set-up worked very well, the effect being to have produced a most efficient and devoted employee.

After several weeks of fine, warm, sunny weather, the British Summer true to its unpredictable nature, deteriorated dramatically one night and I was greeted the following morning by a leaden sky and the mournful weeping of the heavens. Because of the sudden change in driving conditions, traffic was much slower that day and so for the first time since I had started I arrived several minutes late for my first patient. I was met in the hall by Christine. "To save you time, I put your first patient in the chair as soon as I saw you turn into the drive," she said. "Here, I'll help you into your white coat," she added, flourishing a well-laundered dental jacket.

"Who is it?" I enquired.

"It's Mrs Purlin," she answered and then hesitated as she continued, "Er, actually, it's her little girl first, before you see her," and she turned her head as she stifled a laugh.

"What's so funny?" I asked, casting a glance at the long mirror on the wall of the hall in case my hair was ruffled or I had a smut on my face. I was relieved to see that I presented a conventional professional appearance. "Well, what's so funny?" I repeated.

"Nothing, really," and no longer able to contain her mirth she let out a girlish burst of laughter. I gave myself another hasty inspection in the mirror on the wall.

"I can't see anything to laugh about," I said, completely mystified. Suppressing another outburst of mirth, Christine put her hand on the knob of the surgery door.

"How old is the patient?" I asked, trying to ignore her inexplicable behaviour.

"Three," she chuckled as she stood aside for me to enter the room. As the door opened from behind the dental chair, I was unable to see Mrs Purlin's little girl who was hidden by its tall back. Mrs Purlin, herself, was standing next to the chair. She was quite a striking lady in her late thirties. She was dressed simply in a plain but expensive-looking black dress which I noticed was particularly well fitting and tended to accentuate her shapely figure. It came down to just above her knees. Around her neck was a diamond choker, matching a similar one on her right wrist, while on her left hand she wore a diamond-studded wedding ring. Her hair fell about her shoulders in long golden tresses and had plainly received much careful attention. With warm, dark eyes, she was by no means unattractive. It was obvious that she knew this and was accustomed to using it to good purpose.

"Mrs Purlin?" I smiled. "Sorry to have kept you waiting but I ran into unusually heavy traffic. It's all this rain, I suppose." I made my way to the chair to greet my little patient of three. I know that Mrs Purlin said something to me but her words failed to make any intelligent impression on my cerebral cortex. For to my surprise, amazement and astonishment, there seated in the dental chair was not a little Miss Purlin as I had expected but a whiter than white immaculately trimmed poodle! The shock to me of seeing this dog actually in the chair was so sudden that for a moment I became completely disorientated. It was so utterly unexpected that I almost lost sense of my own identity. I looked hard at Mrs Purlin who smiled sweetly at me.

"Is this the patient?" was all I could say.

"That's right, Sonia. This is Sonia, my little girl," she said in a soft cultured voice. My faculties came rushing back to me.

"You can't possibly be serious, Mrs Purlin," I gasped.

Her big brown eyes opened wide. "Why ever not?" she asked.

"Because this is a dog and I'm not a vet!"

I tried to contain my emotions. She looked hurt. "Mr Richards always gave her an inspection before seeing to my teeth," she said with obvious honesty. I transferred my gaze from her to Christine who was discreetly hiding her amusement behind the dental unit. She quickly confirmed this comment by a vigorous nodding of her head.

"Mr Richards actually attended to this dog?" I asked incredulously.

"Bitch," corrected Mrs Purlin. "Sonia is a bitch," looking even more hurt.

"Very well, bitch then," I conceded.

"Don't worry," she said. "There is nothing ever to do for her. Her teeth are in perfect condition."

I was just about to ask her why it was necessary to carry out an inspection when the teeth were perfect when she added, "It's just that I like to be reassured. I know that Sonia would appreciate it, too. Wouldn't you, darling?" she concluded by asking the occupant of the chair.

Sonia sat there indifferently staring through the window at something in the far distance. Her long, pink tongue was lolling, moist and shiny from the left corner of her doggy mouth and her front legs were trembling slightly with a rapid rhythm. "Mr Richards was always such a sweetie about it," cooed Mrs Purlin. "I'm expecting the same from you." What was I to do, or not do?

My indecisiveness was answered by Christine handing me a mouth mirror. "Mr Richards just had a quick look," she urged. "It only took him a moment."

By way of further inducement, Mrs Purlin grasped Sonia's jaws in her hands and firmly but gently opened her mouth for me. In somewhat of a daze I tried to remember the comparative animal dental anatomy I had studied as a second-year student. I recalled the dentition of a camel, a snake, and even a shark's continuous dentition, as it is called, but at that crucial moment the teeth of the canine species were replaced by a void in my memory. However, that knowledge was really hardly necessary for as I peered into the long open jaws of Mrs Purlin's "darling Sonia" and felt her hot breath waft over my face in short, sharp, pants, it was immediately obvious that her teeth were in excellent condition. It certainly did not require the knowledge of a vet or even a dentist to make that assessment.

"A perfect set of teeth in a healthy mouth," I declared with relief as I handed the unused mouth mirror to Christine.

"Thank you," smiled Mrs Purlin as she picked Sonia from off the chair and set her down in a corner of the room. "You are a darling." She moved towards me and for a moment I half expected her to kiss me but she hesitated, looked me up and down approvingly and climbed into the now vacant chair. "You are a pet," she smiled as if to confirm her approval of me.

I doubt if she had meant that last remark as a pun. I refrained from replying and picked up another mouth mirror from the instrument bracket table. Ten minutes later I had confirmed that Mrs Purlin's teeth were also not in need of any attention. "You just require a scale and polish," I said. "I'll do it for you now," and without waiting for any response from her I started to remove the tartar from her teeth. Although the time was by now already 9.30 a.m. I decided to run in to my next appointment and to complete her treatment there and then. The contemplation of having to postpone her scaling to a subsequent visit and to face another possible confrontation with Sonia was more than I could bear. Within a few minutes I had completed this short treatment. "There you are, Mrs Purlin," I said, "both you and Sonia can be pleased to know that your mouths are in perfect condition. I'll see you for a routine check-up in six months time."

"Both of us, of course."

"Er . . . both of you?"

"Yes, of course, both of us."

I looked appealingly at Christine who quickly avoided my gaze. With no-one to support me, I conceded defeat. "Very well, both of you."

"But not six months time," she objected. "We usually come in every four months. Don't we, darling?" she called to Sonia.

Taking this as some sort of cue that the time had come to leave, the poodle sprang to the surgery door and pushing against it with her front paws, started to bark excitedly. From somewhere upstairs came a deep-throated response from Prince Charming. Amid this canine duet, Mr Purlin picked up her pet and holding her firmly, departed the surgery. "See you again soon," she smiled, throwing another approving look at me.

I waited until she had left the room and then I turned to Christine. "If I knew you better, I'd have throttled you for not warning me about Mrs Purlin's little girl," I said as I advanced on her with my hands outstretched.

"If you do that," she laughed as she ducked away from me, "you'll be even later for your next patient. I'm sorry but I honestly forgot that she usually brings her poodle, not that she comes in all that frequently."

"But she suggested every four months," I reminded her. Christine inspected Mrs Purlin's record card.

"It's just over a year since she was last in," she observed, checking the dates on the card. "The time before that was eighteen months previously, so that's two visits in two and a half years." She gave another girlish chuckle. "I think she's got a thing about you," she teased.

I mopped the perspiration from my forehead. "Bring in the next patient, please," I asked her.

"I'm glad you got on so well with Sonia Purlin," Helen Leafe said as she served me with a copious helping of veal and ham pie, potato croquettes and green peas. It was a welcome change to sample the new-style potatoes after the daily routine of chips. Perhaps my successful encounter with Sonia Purlin had stimulated this fellow dog lover into another attempt at imaginative cooking. "She's a prize-winning poodle," she added proudly as though the Purlins's association with the Leafes gave her some share in that success.

"She certainly is a beautiful specimen," I had to agree. If only I could have regarded her a little more dispassionately.

"She and Charming are such good friends." She looked at her husband for his approval but he just ignored her remarks, grunting quietly as he attacked the veal and ham pie. During the following two weeks I noticed through the surgery window that Mrs Purlin came to the house on no fewer than four occasions. Each time she was dressed in something quite different, quite exclusive, quite expensive. Each time she brought Sonia with her and each time she would look in the direction of my surgery window as she went past.

"Sonia has been to visit Charming again," declared Helen Leafe at lunch on the third occasion. "She's such a darling. I'm sure she knows that she is welcome to come here as often as she likes. I believe that Mrs Purlin thinks very highly of you as a dentist, Mr Wilder. She always asks how you are. I thought you would like to know that." I took a large mouthful of sago and mumbled incoherently.

It was just three weeks after my first encounter with the lady and her poodle. I had started to attend the practice on alternate Saturday mornings. This was at Hector Leafe's request to cater for those patients who found it inconvenient to come during the week. But he was very fair and he and Freda would be in their own surgery on the alternate Saturdays to mine. On the particular Saturday in question, I had just completed the last patient and was bidding Christine goodbye for the week-end when the telephone rang. Christine answered it.

"It's a personal call for you," she said, handing me the instrument. "I'm dashing off now," she whispered as I took it from her. "I'm meeting Michael for lunch and I'm late," and with that she was gone.

"Hello, Mr Wilder speaking," I called into the mouth-piece.

"It's Cynthia Purlin here," came the voice from the other end.

"What can I do for you, Mrs Purlin?" I asked in a controlled professional manner.

"I've got terrible trouble with my wisdom tooth," she said. "Could you come round and examine it, please?"

"It would be better if you were to come here," I answered. "After all, I have my equipment here. I was just about to leave but I'll wait for you if you could come straight away."

"I couldn't possibly come to you, Mr Wilder. I'm much too ill." In my limited experience I had never seen a wisdom tooth that had suddenly become so troublesome that it had prevented its owner from attending for an inspection. I had examined her but three weeks previously when her mouth had been in excellent condition. Only a few days before she had been round for tea with Helen Leafe in apparent good dental health. Could it be that bad? I was on my guard.

"It really would be more convenient if you could come here, Mrs Purlin," I urged.

"No, Mr Wilder, I can't come to you," she insisted. "You are my dentist and I'm calling on you in an emergency. I expect you to honour your obligations and make a domi-ciliary visit to my home."

"Very well then," I sighed. "What is your address?"

She gave it to me, a block of flats about one and a half miles from the practice. I promised to be there in ten minutes. Gathering a few simple instruments I hurried off in my car. The flats were an imposing building standing in colourfully laid-out gardens, set well back from the road. Hers was the penthouse at the top of the eighth floor. I imagined that the view from there would be quite impres-sive.

The large, glass entrance doors automatically slid open as I stepped on to the rubber mat outside. A grey-uniformed commissionaire was on duty in the entrance hall. He was a fine, handsome man, weather-tanned from his semi-outdoor duties. He directed me to the lift which speedily ascended to the penthouse. As I stepped out of the lift and on to the landing, I noticed that there was only one door in sight and on this was a simple brass plate which bore the single word "PURLIN". I pressed the bell button and waited as the faint tones of the chimes sounded from the other side of the door. From a metal grille above the button a voice issued.

"Mr Wilder?" I recognized my patient's voice.

"Yes," I replied, "Mr Wilder here." At that I heard a click and the door opened about half an inch as though controlled by a remote internal opening signal.

"Do come in, please," she invited. I did as requested and found myself sinking into the deepest pile carpet I had ever seen. It was in chocolate brown and ran from wall to wall along a long corridor at the end of which was a partly open door. The walls were lined with teak wood panelling, broken here and there with some small, original oil paintings, predominantly of nude women. As there was no-one to greet me, I walked to the door and through it into a spacious open-plan lounge-dining room. The flat had been tastefully furnished in a contemporary style. Much attention had been given to little details and particularly to the pleasant blending of soft furnishings and colours which created a pleasing symphony of beiges, tans and warm browns. A faint but distinctive scent of expensive perfume hung gently on the air. Despite my apprehension of finding myself in Mrs Purlin's home, the atmosphere had a calming and relaxing effect on me. From a door on the other side of the room her voice called.

"In here Mr Wilder, please." I made my way across the thick carpet and entered through the door. In a large double bed in the middle of the facing wall lay Mrs Purlin. She was wearing a pale lime-green négligé in a flimsy material and a matching frilly bed-jacket. She was looking remarkably fit and healthy. Suspecting that I had been tricked, I felt my anger rising. Suppressing this I said, "I came as quickly as I could, Mrs Purlin."

A growl made me turn my head to see Sonia standing in the doorway baring her teeth at me. "No, Sonia. It's Mr Wilder, the dentist," she called to the dog. This only pro-

duced another growl from her pet who advanced towards me
a few paces. The gentle, cuddly animal I had met at the
surgery some weeks before had been transformed into a
fierce, threatening, guard dog. I moved away from her.

"No, Sonia," Mrs Purlin repeated. "Friend, friend, nice
friend. Nice Mr Wilder," and she leaned across the bed and
taking my hand proceeded to stroke it. "There, Sonia, see,
Mr Wilder is a friend, there," and she repeated the stroking
several times as the gesture eventually convinced the dog
that I was the person she had met before. The growling
stopped and was gradually replaced by much tail wagging as
she sniffed at me. Within moments, Sonia had completely
accepted me. She lay down on the carpet by the door and
lost all interest in me. Mrs Purlin relinquished her hold on
my hand.

"With my husband away so much, Sonia is the only
companion I have. But as much as I love her, it is a bore
being left alone. Now, come and sit down." I looked around
the bedroom. The only place to sit was on the dressing-table
stool which was pushed hard up under that piece of furniture. I moved across the room to get to the stool.

"No, not there silly, sit here," and she patted the side of
the bed on which she lay. I hesitated and coughed nervously.
If I didn't escape at that very moment, I knew that the
wretched woman was about to draw the net even more
tightly around me. Why had I not insisted on her coming to
the surgery?

"You're not afraid of me, are you?" she challenged.

Lost for an answer, I ignored the remark and said, "I've
come here to examine your wisdom tooth, Mrs Purlin. So can
I do that and go as I have to be home for lunch?"

"Lunch? Now you don't think I'd ask you here and not
offer to entertain you, do you? I've already arranged lunch,"
and she pointed to a low coffee table standing by the wall on
the far side of the room where I had failed to see it. On it was
laid out lunch for two; fresh salmon mayonnaise with mixed
vegetables, fruit salad and cream, and coffee, all on a most
expensive-looking set of delicate china. She had contrived her
trap well and with experience. The dentist-patient relationship had become reversed. I was no longer the professional
man, the supreme king in his clinical domain. In the space of

a few minutes, I had been reduced to a blushing schoolboy with thumping heart, sweating hands, awkward and inexperienced.

Unable to think of a suitable reply, I just said, "Which side of your mouth is the tooth, Mrs Purlin?" At that she lay back on the bed and laughed loud and long. So much so, that it brought tears to her eyes.

"Which tooth, er – Doctor?" she teased.

"Your wisdom tooth, Mrs Purlin," I snapped turning hot.

"Tooth? er – tooth?" she mocked as though it were the first time the question of a wisdom tooth had ever entered her mind. "Oh, yes, of course, wisdom tooth. That's right. You've come specially to look at my wisdom tooth. Now let me think. Which side was it that gave me all that trouble? I do believe it was on the right side. You see, as you came in, it became much better. But come and have a look just to make sure."

She opened her mouth, placed her hands behind her head and stared at me with an exaggerated expression of girlish innocence. I knew by then that I would find nothing wrong but I moved to the bed to inspect the back of her mouth. The bed was a large double one and as she was lying right in the middle of it I was quite unable from a standing position to see anything at all. Consequently, I was forced to sit on the side of the bed beside her and lean over her to make my examination. A fleeting look of triumph flashed across her eyes. I completed the examination in a matter of seconds.

Jumping up I said, "Your mouth is as healthy as it was the day I saw you two or three weeks ago. I doubt if you've had any trouble with it at all."

Her eyes opened wide with assumed amazement. "You don't believe me," she exclaimed. "Are you suggesting that I've made the whole thing up just to get you into my bedroom?"

She sat up and drew the bed-jacket around her in a dramatized gesture to conceal herself from me.

Somehow, I found just the words I needed at that moment. "Mrs Purlin," I said. "Shall we stop playing games? Just let me take my leave and I suggest we both forget this ridiculous situation."

That was the worst thing I could have said. For in response, she burst into a flood of tears which put me at a total disadvantage. "You horrible, hurtful man," she sobbed. She rolled over on the bed and buried her head in the pillow.

"There, there," was all I could say ineffectually. "Please stop crying. It really isn't necessary."

She looked up at me through red eyes. I produced a large clean handkerchief from my pocket and handed it to her. As I did so I prayed to be able to extricate myself from the situation without loss of face or any further emotional complications. Fate has a strange and unpredictable way of behaving, for it was as though my prayers were answered. Like a boxer who is suffering a barrage of blows from his opponent and who is saved by the bell, I heard the door chimes sounding from the lounge. "There's someone at the front door," I exclaimed as I leapt over Sonia on the floor and dashed towards the bedroom door. "Just a moment," she called from the bed. Opening a drawer in the bedside table, Mrs Purlin produced a pair of dark sun glasses and placed them on her nose. "I don't want anyone to see me like this." She then pressed the button on the base of a microphone set into a small stand on the table.

"Who's there?" she called.

"It's William, madam." The voice I recognized as belonging to the commissionaire of the flats issued from the speaker in the stand. "Just to remind you, madam, that it's two o'clock. Will you require me for the usual?"

My imagination ran riot as I edged away from the nymphomaniac on the bed. One man was obviously not enough for her that day. She even had a standing arrangement with the hall porter!

"That's right, William," she called into the speaker as she pressed the door release button. "Come straight in. I'm in the bedroom." I felt a sickening, sinking feeling in the pit of my stomach. The brazen hussy was so lacking in a sense of shame and morality that, thwarted in her attempts to seduce me, she was openly flaunting her lover – goodness knows how many she had – right before me. I became paralysed with shock and found myself rooted to the spot. William, the porter, came into the bedroom. He removed his peak cap.

"Will the usual half an hour be long enough today, Mrs Purlin?"

"Yes, thank you, William," she replied. "As it's a warm day you can go at a nice steady pace. You'll find your money in an envelope on the dressing-table."

I felt my heart racing very fast. William collected his money – tainted money! – from where she had indicated and went over to the bed. At this point I nearly fainted!

"Thank you, madam," he said. "Will that be all?"

"Yes, thank you, William," she replied. "By the way, this is Dr Wilder, who is attending me this afternoon."

I gave him a weak, sickly smile. I attempted to run from the room but my legs refused to function. I remained glued to the floor. Then to my surprise, he turned on his heels, picked Sonia up from off the carpet, tucked her under an arm and moved off into the lounge, saying to her as he went, "A nice half hour's walk in the gardens will do you a power of good, my girl. And no running away from Uncle William today, eh?"

With a surge, the power returned to my legs. "Wait for me William," I shouted into the lounge. "I'll come down with you in the lift. I was just about to leave." With a call of, "You'll be all right now, Mrs Purlin," I hurried after him into the lounge and then out of the flat into the safety of the lift.

I ran the short distance through the grounds to my car. Once inside, I locked the doors and sat there breathing heavily. I felt an utter idiot. I should have coped with the situation much better than I had. Here was a comparatively young woman, who being neglected by her husband, was almost desperate for some male company. On reflection, I realized that she had made no real improper suggestions to me, but even so, as a young man it was a situation still new to me. I had never anticipated anything like this. I had always seen myself as the image of the 'professional' man with a growing retinue of patients who would always honour and respect the patient-dentist relationship. I had discovered a lot about dentistry. There was more, so very much more for me to discover about the people whose teeth I attended. From the car I looked up at the penthouse, perched on the top of the building. The figure of a woman, wearing a flimsy lime-green négligé was at the window, looking up and down the road. I let in the clutch and sped homeward.

When I arrived at the Leafes the following Monday morn-

ing, I was met in the hall by Christine. "Mrs Purlin telephoned a few minutes ago," she said. "She would like you to
call her back. She says it's urgent. Something about a
wisdom tooth." I chose a moment when the telephone and
reception desk in the hall were unattended and with a
shaking hand I dialled the number. Within seconds the now
familiar voice of Mrs Purlin came to me.

"Cynthia Purlin," she announced.

"Mr Wilder here. You telephoned?"

"Oh hello, Leonard," she said in soft feminine tones. I was
on my guard. "I think I owe you an apology. Could you call
in for a few minutes on your way home this evening and I
will explain everything." I was just about to phrase an excuse
for not complying with her request when Hector Leafe
descended the stairs on the way to his surgery. He stopped
right by my side to inspect his appointment book. Somehow,
I could not face telling him about my incident with her.

"How is your wisdom tooth this morning?" was all I could
think of saying.

"Are you trying to be sarcastic?" came the reply from the
telephone.

"I'm sorry to hear it's still troubling you a little," I was
forced to say. "Just continue with the mouthwash for a few
days more. That should soothe the gum for you. Good
morning." I replaced the instrument on to its stand. "Peri-
coronitis around a wisdom tooth," I explained half to the
reflection of myself in the mirror and half to Hector Leafe.
"I'm treating it with a zinc sulphate mouthwash. If that
doesn't settle it, I'll perform an operculectomy."

"I'm sure you know what you are doing," he replied
approvingly. "By the way, I would like you to take my place
at a medico-dental symposium at the Royal Society of
Medicine next week. I sent for a ticket for myself months ago
but now Helen insists that I accompany her to the Annual
Richmond Dog Show. She's one of the judges and expects
me to watch her perform. Blasted animals! For the sake of
peace and quiet I've agreed to go with her. Can I give you
my ticket? It's for Friday week. You should enjoy it if you've
not been before. It gives one a chance to meet up with
medical colleagues for an evening."

I accepted his offer and he retreated into his surgery

muttering something about "damn dogs", and "I was looking forward to that meeting", under his breath. During the following ten days, Cynthia Purlin made no fewer than three attempts to entice me to her home. But by the use of increasing tact, I managed to avoid a personal confrontation. I was relieved that she had not pursued her advances to the surgery itself. I wondered how long that stronghold would remain free from assault.

It was my first visit to the Royal Society of Medicine. As I entered through the imposing doors, I was enchanted by the aura of medical knowledge that seemed to pervade the entire building. Generations of doctors, dentists and surgeons had met within its walls to discuss, debate, teach and learn. So it was with a sense of professional pride that I took my place in one of the lecture theatres in the company of men, mostly much older than myself. The room was almost completely filled but I was fortunate to find a vacant seat at the end of a row. Seated next to me was a well-dressed gentleman whom I assessed to be in his late forties. He wore an immaculate blue suit with a faint chalk stripe. The end of a white silk handkerchief protruded discreetly from his top jacket pocket, while a white rose adorned the lapel. I detected the aroma of a particularly expensive after-shave lotion. As the meeting had a few minutes before the start of the first speaker, he and I indulged in casual conversation. He was a psychiatrist, practising in central London, within walking distance of the Royal Society of Medicine. He told me that he specialized in matrimonial problems which were "very much on the increase these days", he said. At that, our conversation had to end as the first lecturer was preparing to start his contribution to the symposium. But during the interval, the psychiatrist and I resumed our conversation. "May I treat you to a coffee?" he offered. I was impressed by his self-assurance and abundance of confidence, and I hoped that after twenty years or more in practice I would mature into the successful professional man such as he. He was interested by my accounts of my early days as a dentist and particularly by my, as yet, comparative inexperience in coping with the older, sophisticated patients. One thing led to another and I found myself telling him about my recent involvements with Cynthia Purlin. He listened intently. When I mentioned her name, he appeared to be startled.

"I'm sorry if I should not have disclosed her name," I hastened to say. "Was it unprofessional of me?"

"Not at all," he quickly answered. "That's all right."

Then I realized that she could have been a patient of his. What side of her character had I presented that, perhaps, even he did not know about? But he recovered his composure and silently listened to my words without comment as I concluded the tale.

"So you see I have a problem," I said. "I just don't know how to discourage the lady's advances. If I knew her husband would be understanding, I would risk going to see him and telling him about her."

A strained, glassy look entered his eyes and he laid an unsteady hand on my shoulder. "There's no need for you to look any further, young man," he said in a trembling voice. "You just have. You just have!"

13

The Tooth that Turned Up

"How would you like to do a locum?" My last patient for the
day had just departed and I was preparing to go home when
Hector Leafe appeared in the doorway of my surgery.

"A locum?" I asked. "What locum and why?"

"Emrys Jones, who was at dental school with me telephoned just now. He slipped over in the snow this morning
and has sprained his wrist. His doctor has immobilized it for
him and so he will be out of action for a while. As he is a
one-man practice, he hoped I might lend you to him until his
wrist gets better."

"Where's his practice?" I asked.

"It's in Acton," explained Hector. "Less than two miles from here. I shouldn't think it will be for more than a week or two at the most."

He looked at me hopefully.

"When would he want me to start?" I asked.

"It's Friday today," observed Hector. "It would be nice if you could go there on Monday."

"But what about my patients? I'm almost fully booked for the next two weeks."

"I'll ask Christine to rearrange them for you. Things haven't gone too easily for Emrys. He's never really made a success of practice. I'd like to help him if I can."

I considered the matter. It might be interesting to have experience in another practice for a short time. I had been with Hector Leafe about six months and was just beginning to feel a sense of consolidation about my dentistry. Hector had seen to it that I had reaped the benefit from as wide a range of dentistry as I could. I was grateful to him for this. So why not? It might be fun trying to cope in a different environment, if only for a week or so. Here was an unexpected challenge. I decided to meet it.

"Very well," I agreed. "I'd be pleased to help him out."

"That's champion! Then I'll telephone him to say you'll be there on Monday," said Hector. I followed him to the telephone in the hall where he dialled his friend's number. "Hello, Emrys. Hector speaking. I've had a word with Leonard Wilder and he'll be delighted to start on Monday morning. How's that for service?"

The speaker on the other end of the line said something and Hector responded with, "It's a pleasure. Old friendship dies hard . . . yes, of course. Here he is." He handed me the telephone. "He wants a word with you."

"Hello Mr Jones," I called into the instrument. "Leonard Wilder here."

"Hello there. It's nice of you to offer to help me out after my stupid accident." His sing-song Welsh tones produced a sudden wave of nostalgia in me for the Wales I had loved so much as a boy and in my teens and had seen less and less of during the past few years. It would be great to reminisce with him about Snowdonia and the valleys, that is if he came from that part of the country.

"What time do you want me to be there on my first day?"
I enquired.

"We start promptly at 8 a.m." came his reply. "So can you
get here by 7.30 just to give you time to look around first
like?"

"Did you say 7.30 a.m.?!" I was not the best of risers,
particularly on a cold February morning in mid-winter. At
the Leafes, I had by now got it down to a fine art. If I rose at
7.45 a.m. and left my house at 8.30 a.m. I would normally
arrive at the practice by five minutes to nine and be ready
for my 9 a.m. patient with seconds to spare. I did a quick
calculation. It meant getting up at 6.15 a.m. – in the middle
of the night! I knew that to thousands of people 6.15 a.m.
was by no means early but I had never got up at that
unearthly hour.

"Yes, 7.30 a.m. why, is that too early for you, boy?" came
his question. I swallowed hard. "No. Not at all, Mr Jones. I
just wanted to confirm the time, that's all." We exchanged a
few more words and as I replaced the instrument on to its
stand I consoled myself by remembering that I could have a
long lie in until 6.45 a.m. on the days subsequent to my first!

I was so concerned not to oversleep or not hear my alarm
clock on the Monday morning that I hardly slept at all and
kept waking at frequent intervals during the Sunday night.
So when the alarm did sound at 6.15 a.m. I awoke feeling
tired and heavy-eyed. As I lay there in my bed staring
vacantly upwards and letting consciousness slowly dawn, I
became aware that the ceiling of my bedroom was particularly brighter than usual and I realized that new snow must
have fallen during the night and was being reflected by the
street lighting upwards and on to the ceiling. Snow! I threw
off the bedclothes and went to the window. A soft blanket of
white covered Mother Earth as far as the eye could see. It was
thick and beautiful. Everything had lost its sharpness. There
were no harsh points or angles to be seen anywhere. The
roofs, houses, pavements and roads all merged gently into
each other. The snow as unbroken and virgin, for in our
suburban back road no foot-print or car tyre had yet disturbed the blanket of white down. I looked at our long
driveway leading from the garage to the road. It was impossible to see where it started or ended. I decided to clear a

path for the car to get out through were I to hold surgery at Acton that day. I slipped into my clothes and armed with a spade and broom proceeded to dig and sweep until I could at last see the concrete of the driveway. By the time I had finished, I had worked up a ravenous appetite for breakfast. But discretion made me decide to bring the car out on to the road first. I got into the driving seat and with frozen fingers turned the ignition key. The engine turned over a few times but the plugs did not fire. Like myself, the car was not the best of morning starters. I tried a full range of various positions for the choke and then after an age, when it seemed that the battery was fading fast, the engine trickled into life and by my careful manipulation of the choke it eventually developed a fine and healthy running. I inspected my watch. 7 a.m. precisely. No time for breakfast now! Starving as I was, I let in the clutch and pulled carefully off into the road. Due to the snow, going was very slow but the traffic was also comparatively light. The two factors compensated for each other so that I arrived in Acton by 7.25 a.m.

Hector Leafe had told me that Emrys Jones' surgery was in the main shopping centre. I had no difficulty in locating it and I was amused to find it situated over 'Fred's Fried Fish'. Parking the car, I discovered a narrow entrance alongside the fish shop which bore a list of names of the occupants of the various offices in the building which ran to three storeys: a solicitor, an accountant, Emrys Jones, a firm of insurance brokers and an organization calling itself 'Sales Products'. This latter name intrigued me, as it had no real meaning. At 7.30 a.m. I was ringing the bell on the faded green door leading to 'Emrys Jones – Dentist' that led off the cold stone corridor on the first floor over the shops. The door was opened by a short, ruddy-faced man of about Hector Leafe's age. He was quite stout for his height. His full head of grey hair was curly and crinkly, and cut very short around the neck and temples, so that he appeared to be wearing a fur hat. As his right arm was heavily bandaged, I assumed at once that he was Emrys Jones. He was attired in a well-worn heavy tweed suit which had a faint check pattern against a lovat green background. He really looked more like a Welsh farmer than a dentist. I could imagine him controlling the black and white collie sheep dogs in the heart of the mountains.

"Mr Wilder," he said rather than asked.

"Good morning, Mr Jones," I answered and then added by way of a friendly gesture, "Bore da".

"Bore da y chi," he responded. "Good morning. Do you speak Welsh?" and he stepped aside to let me enter his premises.

"A little," I said. "I spent six years there during the war before I became a dental student."

"Then you are indeed welcome here. Croeso!" he smiled as he slapped me on the back with his good hand.

The surgery and contents looked as though they had come straight out of a museum. My heart sank, for there in the centre of a small dark room and facing the window stood an old black dental unit and an uncomfortable-looking dental chair in matching black. Although clean, neither of these items looked as though they had seen any polish for years. Right next to these was a large gas and oxygen machine that gave the appearance of being strategically close at hand for constant use. At Ealing we firmly believed in the conservation of teeth and Hector prided himself on his infrequent recourse to extractions or general anaesthesia. As I stood there I became aware that the faint smell of antiseptic and clove oil which is so characteristic of a dental surgery and to which I had become so accustomed that it no longer registered at a conscious level on my mind was strongly suppressed by a powerful aroma of fried fish and chips which, no doubt, over the years had permeated up from the shop below until it saturated every molecule of the surgery. I had decided to come here for new experiences. That was certainly what I was about to get. But what kind? To my surprise I could not see a hand basin or any water supply in the surgery. Then through a door which opened on to a tiny office I noticed a small sink on the wall. Did this mean that each time I wanted to wash my hands, which would be very frequent, I had to go into the office? Apparently it did! Emrys Jones may have sensed my thoughts as I looked around because laying his hand on my arm he said, "I'm sure this is not quite what you have been used to at Hector's but I'd be grateful for your help until this heals," and he indicated his right arm.

What could one say in response to this? "Please don't worry, Mr Jones," I said. "I'm here and I'll stay as long as it is necessary."

"Thank you, my boy. Then come and meet Iris." He led the way into the minute office and introduced me to his one and only employee. Iris must have been at least seventy years old. She was slightly built and rather taller than he. Her white hair was gathered tightly back across her head and tied at the back in an old-fashioned bun. The whole setting could have come out of a Dickens novel.

"This is Mr Wilder whom I told you all about, Iris."

"How do you do, Mr Wilder," and she offered me a frail hand to shake. I greeted her appropriately and then spent a little time familiarizing myself with the surgery lay-out, such as it was. An inspection of the appointment book was quite a revelation. For unlike the half hour appointments to which I was accustomed, this practice was seeing patients at fifteen-minute intervals. I noticed that against each patient's name was written either a 'D', an 'S' or an 'F'.

"What is the significance of these letters?" I asked Iris.

"Well, the 'F' stands for a filling, the 'D' is for dentures, and the 'S' is for scaling."

"How about crowns or bridges?" I asked, half anticipating the answer.

"We never see those here," she said, as if they were as rare as ice crystals on a sunny beach.

Noticing that no appointments had been made for that afternoon, I enquired why.

"This afternoon is a gas session," she explained. "Dr Matthews will be here at one o'clock for that, directly after lunch."

"But how do you know who is coming?" I asked.

"Because they've all been given appointments," she said. I decided to leave it at that.

A buzzer sounded over the door between the surgery and the office. "That will be the first patient, Mrs Cordell, for a scaling," she said, peering through rimless spectacles at the appointment book.

She shuffled over to the surgery door and opened it to admit a lady in an advanced state of pregnancy. She wore an almost threadbare red coat, unbuttoned and revealing a tired-looking floral dress underneath. Accompanying her was a small child of about two whom I took to be a little girl and an older one, also a girl, of about four. They were dressed quite inadequately for the cold weather. Had it been at the Leafes I would have asked Christine to brew a hot drink.

"Sit on that and don't move," ordered Mrs Cordell in a strong London accent, indicating the one and only wooden chair in the room. The two children clambered on to the chair and kneeling on the seat with their arms around each other entertained themselves by watching the growing traffic in the snow laden streets outside.

"I've hurt my hand, Mrs Cordell," explained Emrys Jones, "and Mr Wilder here, will be seeing you for me today."

"Okay," came the patient's reply without any sign of concern or even interest for her dentist's incapacitation.

"She's having trouble with her gums and they just won't clear up," said Emrys Jones. "They keep bleeding a lot. So I have advised her to have frequent scaling. I did them for her two weeks ago."

I invited her into the dental chair and inspected her gums. "She's got pregnancy gingivitis," I observed and then I added courteously, "Don't you agree, Mr Jones?" He looked into her open mouth.

"Is that what it is?"

"I would say so," I confirmed. "How long have you been pregnant, Mrs Cordell?" I asked her.

"Over eight months."

"And how long have your gums been bleeding?"

"They started a few months ago." She ended each answer with a loud sniff.

I refrained from suggesting that she might blow her nose.

"Since you became pregnant?"

"Oh yes."

"Did you have this trouble during your other two pregnancies?"

"Four pregnancies," she corrected.

"Four pregnancies?"

"I've got a boy of nearly seven and another girl of nine. They go to school."

"Well, did you have this trouble before?"

"Oh yes, they always bleed."

"Have you told Mr Jones this?"

"No."

"Why not?"

"He never asked me."

"Well, Mrs Cordell, there's nothing wrong with your gums. You have what is called pregnancy gingivitis, and it will clear up as soon as you have your baby as, no doubt, it did on the previous occasions."

"That's right."

"You can go now," I said as she made no move to leave the chair.

At my request she levered herself out of it and bawling, "Come on you," to her children, opened the door for them and following them out into the corridor called, "Ta," to me over her shoulder.

My next three patients did not keep their appointments. Broken appointments at the Leafes did occur but were infrequent. In my half year there I had come to recognize the loyalty exhibited by most of the patients to the practice; a loyalty built on trust and appreciation. But Emrys Jones's practice was so very strikingly different that it presented an almost complete antithesis. So much so, that neither he nor his faithful Iris seemed unduly concerned by the omission of the patients to honour their appointments. I spent the half hour familiarizing myself with the instruments in greater detail and trying not to notice the ever-growing hunger pangs that I felt. I wondered what time there would be a mid-morning coffee or tea break, if at all. My 9 a.m. patient arrived on time and then came an unbroken run of appointments, twelve in all, so that by 12.15 p.m. I had completed countless fillings, several 'scrapings', as most of the patients would refer to a scale and polish, and fitted two sets of dentures. I was also exhausted and in an advanced state of starvation. I made what seemed to me to be my one hundredth trip into the office to wash my hands, hoping as I did so that I might survive the afternoon's gas session. I thought back to my training in this at the hospital and the hectic conditions under which I had frequently to operate there and felt grateful for so valuable a background.

"If you're ready for lunch, boy, then we'll all go down now." Emrys Jones's very mention of the word 'lunch' triggered off a copious salivary response in my mouth, accompanied by a muffled rumbling sound from my abdomen.

"Go down, did you say, Mr Jones?"

"That's right. We always go downstairs to Fred's for lunch. It's quick and not expensive. You will join us?"

In my condition the short trip to 'Fred's Fried Fish' was about as far as I wanted to go for lunch that day. I followed him and Iris down the stairs, up which I had climbed barely five hours previously but which, by now, felt more like five days ago. At the foot of the stairs, instead of going out into the street as I had expected and then in through Fred's entrance they turned back along the corridor for a few yards and then went through a door on which were painted the words 'Fred's'. I found myself at the back of the 'Fried Fish Shop' looking forward towards the front of the premises and the street outside. It was quite narrow, more so than I had expected. Along the entire right side ran the counter and the range from which a grey, blue pall of oil fumes rose slowly, then to be sucked into an air filter which formed a long canopy along the length of that wall. I doubt whether the filters had ever been changed as an equal amount of fumes appeared to issue from the upper side of the extractor and then to be spewed upwards by the fans towards the ceiling. This certainly accounted for the smell in the surgery directly above. It was, however, pleasantly warm inside the shop despite the bitter wintry cold and snow in the street. I wondered to what unbearable heat the temperature would rise to on a warm summer's day and I hoped that Emrys Jones would restrict any future mishaps to the winter months. Five square tables were arranged along the wall on the left. These, presumably through lack of space, had been set right up against the wall so that only three chairs could be placed at each table, giving accommodation to fifteen people in all. Four of these tables were by now fully occupied by a motley assortment of people. The table nearest the rear of the shop carried a 'Reserved' sign and it was at this one that Emrys Jones and Iris seated themselves, indicating to me that I should occupy the third and vacant chair.

"Fish and chips?" he asked me.

A quick inspection of the menu chalked up on a black slate on the wall told me that it was either haddock and chips or cod and chips or plaice and chips or hake and chips, all served with peas. From the almost obliterated chalk I guessed that the menu had more than likely been the same for some considerable time.

"Fish and chips?" he repeated.

As there seemed to be no other choice, and so wondering whether the alternative to fish and chips would be no lunch at all, I quickly accepted the same diet to which I had been conditioned with monotonous regularity by Helen Leafe every Tuesday lunch time. But there the similarity ended. The piece of haddock with which I was served tasted as though it had come from the sea that very day. It had been fried to a delicate golden brown and was tender and succulent. The chips were dry and crisp, and the peas had a fresh-from-the-garden taste about them. If for no other reason, my locum at Emrys Jones's would be well worth the 'fish, chips and peas' each day. I was almost glad for the hunger I had suffered. As I sat there tucking into a second helping of haddock, I speculated whether karmic judgement had so rewarded me for my altruistic act of helping out an incapacitated colleague. The anticipation of my ultimate return to Helen Leafe's cuisine, or lack thereof, was a sentiment I tried to ignore. Full of sea-food, no longer hungry and slightly sleepy, I returned at one o'clock with Emrys and Iris to the surgery on the floor above.

Within moments of our return six patients had presented themselves for the afternoon's gas session. It was then that I discovered that they had all been given appointments for one o'clock. By 1.15 p.m. when no Dr Matthews had yet arrived, Iris telephoned his home to learn from his wife that he was "out somewhere on his rounds. But don't worry, he would never forget his Monday afternoon at the dental surgery". As she completed the telephone call, the door burst open and into the room came a man who bore a remarkable resemblance to Emrys Jones, only that he was a bigger person, quite large in fact and had a ruddier complexion. He was even wearing a heavy tweed suit. Despite the lower than freezing weather he had no overcoat, this being replaced by a voluminous long red scarf which had a home knitted appearance and which he had wound around his neck several times. As he removed this and brushed a thin layer of snow from his greying hair, I detected quite a high percentage of alcohol in his breath.

"Sorry I'm late, Emrys," he breathed in a gruff voice, "but I just stopped off for a quick warmer at the local on the way. This bloody cold weather has produced another 'flu' wave and I'm working my guts out at the moment. So I've got to keep my spirits up somehow," and he gave a deep and insensitive guffaw.

"How's the arm?" he went on.

"If I don't try to use it, Doc, then it doesn't hurt me," said Emrys Jones.

"Then don't try to use it. It'll mend. Be patient." As he moved to the gas machine, he said to me, "Hullo to you. You're the assistant, are you?"

"How do you do, Dr Matthews," I replied. "I suppose I'm more of a locum than an assistant."

"Uha," came his indifferent response and then he asked me, "Can you extract?"

"Of course," I replied, surprised at his question.

"What I don't mean is 'Can you take out teeth?' Any damn fool can do that. I'm used to dentists who do a complete clearance of uppers and lowers in six or seven minutes without breaking a root." He looked at me challengingly and I moved aside to avoid his alcohol-laden breath that wafted my way.

"As a student I used to perform full clearances but in my present practice there isn't such a necessity for the removal of teeth."

"Where's that?"

"In Ealing," I told him.

"Then what's so bloody special about Ealing?" he demanded.

"It's quite a different practice from this, Doc," explained Emrys Jones for me. I was grateful for his intervention as I found my early contact with Dr Matthews devoid of any sort of rapport. "I'm sure he is as good at extracting as I am. He wouldn't be Hector Leafe's assistant were he not."

"We'll soon find out," Dr Matthews growled. "Who's first?"

"Mrs Sparrow, Doctor," said Iris.

"What, Mrs Sparrow with the twins?" he asked.

"That's right, Doctor," she said.

"Bring her in," he ordered.

According to her record card, Mary Sparrow was due to have an abscessed upper left first molar extracted. "Hullo Mary," the doctor welcomed the patient. "Sit in the chair, open your mouth and just breathe through your nose." Mrs Sparrow followed his instructions and he placed the nose piece of the gas machine over her nose as he switched on the mixture of nitrous oxide and oxygen. I was concerned to see from the dials on the machine that he was using a rather lower percentage of oxygen than was considered to be the minimum safety level as recommended by the hospital. However, he was the anaesthetist, sober or not. But I still had my niggling doubts. Within moments, Mary Sparrow was sufficiently under for me to start the extraction. He nodded his head for me to begin. I depressed her tongue and placed a gauze swab on to the back of it.

"You don't need that!" he snorted.

"It's an absolute precaution I've always been taught to take to prevent anything going down into the trachea," I said in defence of my action.

"If you know what you're doing then nothing will go down the wind pipe," he almost spat out. I had never had a rub with any professional person. Now, for the first time, I felt my anger rising inside me but exerting self-control I avoided a reply. Instead, I picked up the forceps and applied them to the tooth.

"Now make a good job of it, if you can!" came his snide remark.

The gauntlet was down! "I'll show him," I thought, as I promised myself a quick and perfect removal of the tooth. But then I had not reckoned with Mary Sparrow's upper left first molar. I exerted a degree of sideways pressure. As there was no response, I increased the pressure. There was still no response. I leaned heavily on the forceps, first one way and then the other. All that happened was that the patient's head moved from side to side as a result of my exertions. First molar teeth are notoriously difficult to remove, especially if the bone supporting them is dense and strong as in a young person, and Mary Sparrow was twenty-four. I gripped the forceps with renewed vigour and almost pulled the patient's head off. The tooth's reluctance to be parted from her mouth was a challenge to my determination to remove it. After several minutes of doing battle it rested unscathed and rock like in her jaw. For a moment I took my eyes from her teeth and had a look at her face. She was beginning to turn an unhealthy shade of blue.

"Oxygen!" I called to the anaesthetist. "She's going cyanosed! Her face is blue! She needs more oxygen!"

He glared at me through bleary eyes and cursing under his breath he retorted, "Don't tell me how to do my job, you bloody amateur!" and for a moment I thought he was going to strike me. My temper snapped and with my new-found energy I submitted the tooth to an herculean pressure. This was too much for even Mary Sparrow's tooth. There was a "bang" from her mouth. I fell heavily against her as the bone yielded and with a wave of triumph I held up the forceps with my extracted prize completely intact with all three roots!

The next two patients were children who had each come in for the removal of some badly decayed baby teeth. I had not seen such a degree of deterioration in any of Hector's young patients and wondered at what early age their inevitable set of false teeth would be supplied. These extractions proceeded uneventfully. I worked at great speed as I was determined that Matthews would not subject these youngsters to the deprivation of oxygen which appeared to be a hazard with his administrations. Patient number four was an Irish labourer, named James O'Rourke. He was aged thirty-eight but looked at least ten years older. He had been suffering from toothache in a lower molar tooth and had been given an appointment that day for its removal.

"When did you last eat?" I made the usual enquiry.

"At breakfast, dis marnin'," he said in a brogue so thick that it could have been cut with a knife. "The lady said for me not to eat after."

"Nothing since then?"

"Not a t'hing."

As I approached him in the chair I was caught by an unexpected gust of beery breath so violent, that in comparison the whisky-laden atmosphere around Matthews was like a refreshing breeze on a spring day.

"Anything to drink?" I asked, looking him straight in the

eye. He avoided my gaze by looking down at his black unpolished boots and said,

"Not a drop. Oi'd swear it on the Boible!"

"Are you quite sure?" I challenged.

At this, Dr Matthews interrupted. "Why don't you stop asking damn fool questions. Just let me give him the gas and then you can whip out his tooth. I've got my rounds to get on with!"

At the sound of the word 'gas', James O'Rourke stiffened in the chair.

"Gas!" he half shouted. "Oi'm not havin' no gas!"

"But that's what you've come for, Mr O'Rourke, an anaesthetic for your extraction," I said.

"Oi'm not havin' no gas!" he reiterated vehemently. "Folks die under gas and oi'm no good to me if oi'm dead, to be sure. You can take it out wit de needle. No-one said anyting about gas to me. Just come in for the tooth pullin'."

This was not the first patient I had met with such a repugnance for gas. I looked hopefully at Emrys Jones. "I suppose I could give him an injection if that's what he prefers."

"This is a gas session," snorted Matthews. "I'm not wasting my bloody time hanging around while your injection either works or does not." He addressed the patient. "Now look here, you. I've come specially here to give you a general anaesthetic, so stop wasting my time and let's get on with it."

With an incredible turn of speed, O'Rourke shot out of the chair pushing the doctor against the gas machine as he did so. He rushed to the door shouting, "Oi'm not havin' no gas! Anyway, it's stopped hurtin' so oi'll keep the tooth," and with a trembling hand he opened the door and disappeared down the corridor.

The last patient but one was an elderly lady who had three very loose lower teeth. While she was seating herself in the chair, I noticed Dr Matthews eyeing her very thoughtfully. Then to my relief he turned the percentage of oxygen up several marks on the gauge of the gas machine. Despite his outward brusqueness, I noticed a certain professionalism creeping into his manner. Whether this was in response to my earlier observations on Mary Sparrow or that he had sobered up a little I do not know. He then proceeded to administer a creditable general anaesthetic and within moments I had removed her three loose teeth. I suppose I would have welcomed a small comment of commendation for so quick a technique but instead he grunted quietly to himself as Iris led the patient from the surgery. He delved into a pocket of his tweed jacket and producing a flat third-size bottle of whisky said to me, "I don't suppose you drink when you're seeing patients, do you?"

"Not when I'm working, Doctor. I like to keep a clear head," and than realizing the implications of my remark, I felt myself turning red.

Fortunately, he seemed to miss this and said, "Then if you don't mind I'll just have a little warmer. I need a constant nip to keep me going through the day. How about you, Emrys?"

Emrys Jones held up his bandaged hand. "Indeed no, Doc. Not for me, thanks."

By way of response Matthews removed the cap from the bottle and giving a powerful suck at the open end almost drained it down to the last drop. "Ah, that's better!" he exclaimed as he returned the bottle to his pocket. "Now I can face the world again. Come on, let's do the next one."

The next patient for gas was a Mr Patel, an Indian gentleman who, according to his record card, had been a patient at the practice for over five years. I learned later that he was the manager of a shoe shop in the main street, some few hundred yards from the surgery. He came in wearing a long grey linen shop coat and looking very cold. He spoke in a very soft voice and with only a suggestion of an Asiatic accent. "Good morning, Dr Jones," he addressed my temporary employer. Then nodding respectfully to Matthews and me welcomed us in a similar manner. He was a slight man of forty-three, not very tall, with smooth dark hair and piercing brown eyes. Reading his notes I saw that he was due to have his six upper front teeth removed. As the result of chronic gum disorder over some years they had become loose. A partial upper denture had been made for him to have fitted straight away. An inspection of the denture, which Iris brought in from the office, showed me that it had been robustly constructed by whichever dental laboratory Emrys

Jones employed. There had been, however, a singular lack of attention to the importance of appearance and in consequence the six teeth on the plate had an unnatural and monotonous regularity about them, something I had always in my short experience sought to avoid. But in comparison to the gross ungainly angles which his own front teeth had presumably assumed over the past few years, there would, no doubt, be some improvement, albeit unimaginative. He confirmed that he had taken no food or drink since his breakfast at 8 a.m. and sat quietly and composed in the chair.

Dr Matthews reduced the oxygen percentage on the gas machine to its earlier low and, giving me a defiant look, applied the nose piece to the patient as he switched it on. No doubt the alcohol in his blood had again risen to the required level to revert him back from the brief glimpse I had had of 'Dr Jekyll' to the formidable personality of 'Mr Hyde'! Fortunately, the teeth were quite loose and within a few moments I was applying the forceps to the sixth and final tooth. As I subjected it to a careful rotation and eased it gently from the socket, the patient moved his head unexpectedly to one side, perhaps as a response to early oxygen deprivation. Matthews, despite his blood alcohol, demonstrated a reasonably quick reflex and attempted to restrict the movement with his large hands. But the sudden jerk had been sufficient for the forceps to be jolted sharply in my hand with the result that in the space of a few seconds the tooth that was held firmly in the beaks of the instrument was nowhere to be seen. I looked in Mr Patel's mouth and at the back of his throat. I inspected his clothing and the floor. I even examined the pockets of his grey shop coat. The tooth had vanished! I had completed the extractions but now, instead of six teeth, which should be lying on the white vitreous instrument bracket table, there were but five!

"You've dropped it down the back of his ruddy throat," accused Dr Matthews.

"I don't think so," I responded.

"You must have done," he snorted. "If you can't find it around here then it's gone down his throat. I said you were a bloody amateur!"

I'd just about had enough of his arrogance. Something snapped inside me. "If you hadn't deprived him of oxygen and started him off in anoxic convulsions then he would not have jerked his head. And what is more," I added before he had time to answer, "if you had permitted me to use a throat pack in the first place and not violated a cardinal anaesthetic principle, the chance of such an occurrence would have been nil. You haven't been giving these patients anaesthesia. You have been rendering them unconscious by suffocating them!" I was furious. It was quite unlike me to behave in such a manner but under his constant provocation the volcano had erupted.

"You impudent young pup!" he shouted, turning crimson, and leaving the patient who was by now showing signs of recovering from the gas, he lurched towards me. At that Emrys Jones sprang in front of him and pushing against him with his good hand exclaimed, "Please calm yourself, Doc. You've had a little too much to drink. Remember that time at the Rotary lunch. So just calm yourself, man." Matthews halted in his tracks and briefly considered "that time at the Rotary lunch". Whatever had, indeed, happened on that occasion, its contemplation had a magical effect on him. For he breathed heavily for a few seconds and then without saying a word he returned to Mr Patel in the chair. He also seemed to undergo, to some extent, a dramatic sobering up again. For several moments he stood quite still staring at me and I could almost hear him thinking aloud as he tried to understand this "impudent young pup". He calmed himself and for the time being an uneasy truce existed between us. As soon as the man in the chair had regained his faculties, Matthews said, "We have not been able to locate one of your teeth. Just in case it's gone down your throat you will have to go to the local hospital for an X-ray."

Mr Patel looked frightened. "Is that serious, Doctor?" he asked.

"I'll answer that question when I've had the radiologist's report," replied Matthews. "But first the dentist will fit your denture."

Despite its unflattering appearance, the denture fitted well and by the time the gas had completely worn off Mr Patel was able to leave with an intact dental arch again. But before he did so, Matthews had telephoned the hospital and arranged for an immediate X-ray. Mr Patel left a worried man. As soon as the door closed behind him, Matthews turned to me and Emrys Jones.

"He's gone and swallowed that tooth all right. Just you wait and see. The X-ray will show it in his stomach. That's when the fun and games will start!"

"Not wishing to be disrespectful, Dr Matthews," I said, trying to re-establish communication between us with a courteous, if uncomfortable, approach, "I doubt if it would be in his stomach. Surely, with his airway open, any tooth would fall down his trachea and into his right bronchus. In which case the X-ray would show it in his lungs. But I am certain that hasn't happened, otherwise he would complain of pain and be experiencing a paroxysm of coughing, which he is not. No, I'm quite sure that even without a throat pack it has not gone down anywhere."

"Then where the bloody hell is it?" shouted Matthews. The trumpets of war were beginning to sound again! Matthews, Emrys Jones, Iris and I conducted a search of the entire practice. For thoroughness, we even turned the little office inside out and went as far as looking in the corridor outside. But the five extracted teeth rested on the instrument table incomplete without their sixth member and the mystery of the missing tooth remained unsolved.

The time was by now 3 p.m. and I was more than feeling the strain of the day's work. But the day was far from over yet for me. The next batch of patients for 'gas' was arriving; another eight in fact. After the incident of Mr Patel's missing tooth, Dr Matthews became almost silent, almost morose, and the session proceeded without a hitch. He still persisted with his low oxygen content anaesthetics and so I extracted at breakneck speed to avoid unnecessary distress to the patients. By 5.15 p.m. and with another twenty teeth more behind me, I finally escorted the last patient to the door and made my ultimate visit to the office to wash my hands. "Tea is ready," called Iris as she served four piping hot cups of tea around the desk in her tiny room. From an old tin box, so worn that most of the red paint on it had been rubbed off, she produced a packet of ginger snaps and offered them round. I remembered the 'Mad Hatter's Tea Party' at Hans Trimmelwasser's practice the previous year. Dr Matthews completely ignored me as he broke a biscuit in two, placed each half in turn in his mouth and then washed it down with a loud slurping noise. He became quite talkative again with Emrys Jones, punctuating his conversation here and there with caustic remarks about "blundering amateurs", and "it's experience that matters, not learning!" By now I was composed and determined to retain my dignity, and so I quietly sipped my tea and munched my ginger snaps.

It must have been about 5.20 p.m. when the telephone rang. Iris answered it and then handing it to Matthews said, "It's the hospital for you, Dr Matthews. It's the radiologist." Taking it from her he barked into the instrument.

"Hullo, Dr Matthews here. Yes . . . yes. . . . Oh, really?" and he gave me a sheepish look. "Nothing at all? Are you sure? It's quite clear?" He sounded almost disappointed. "I see. Thank you, Doctor." He slowly replaced the telephone. "Mr Patel's X-ray is clear," he admitted to Emrys Jones, half turning his back to me. "There's no sign of the tooth anywhere on him."

I experienced a feeling of elation as I heard the news. Here was partial triumph over my adversary. I could now afford to be polite. The tide was beginning to turn.

"Then shall we search the surgery once more?" I suggested.

"You won't find it there," growled Matthews with persistent pig-headedness, "We know it's not here, so why bother?"

I looked him straight in the eye and asked, "Then where do you suggest it is, Dr Matthews? If it's not here and it's not on the patient, as we've searched him, and it's not in his chest, where do you suggest it might be?"

He gulped a couple of times and then opened his mouth to reply. But I shall never know what he was going to say for at that moment I dropped the ginger snap I was holding in my hand and bent down to retrieve it from the floor. And then I saw it! Nestling in the turn-up of Matthews's right trouser leg was Mr Patel's upper left lateral incisor tooth! Emrys Jones must have noticed it at the same moment as I did as his eyes followed the biscuit to the floor.

"The tooth has turned up, Doc!" he proclaimed. "It's in your trouser turn-up!"

Dr Matthews closed his mouth and let his gaze fall in the

direction of his feet. He slowly bent down and removed the tooth from his turn-up, placed it in an ash tray on the desk, removed the almost empty whisky flask from his pocket and drained the last few precious drops. He walked out of the office into the surgery and then, picking up his scarf, he went into the corridor outside. Without a word he closed the door behind him.

Emrys Jones's wrist conveniently healed by the end of the week, sufficient for him to be able to resume work himself on the Monday. I was relieved not to be confronted by Dr Matthews at another 'suffocation' session on the Monday afternoon. With a little regret I had my final haddock, chips and peas at 'Fred's Fried Fish' on the Friday. By 5.30 p.m. I was driving through the now slushy snow towards my home. I had done my duty to another colleague. It had been a long arduous week. The week-end's break ahead would be a welcome reward.

14

Open Wide

"He's found Methuselah!" These strange words greeted me
as I put on the hand-brake and stepped out of my car in the
drive of Hector Leafe's home in Ealing. Helen Leafe came
rushing excitedly towards me. "Prince Charming has found
Methuselah," she cried pointing in the direction of the privet
bushes which separated the front garden from the main road.
Yapping almost in a frenzy was her canine pet, his attention
focused on some object just under the bushes. Taking me by
the arm she propelled me towards the scene of the activity.
Made curious by her biblical reference, I allowed myself to
be led. There, almost hidden by the shrubs, was by far the
largest tortoise I had ever seen. I know little or nothing about

165

these reptiles but it was easy to assess that this one was of considerable age.

"He's found Methuselah!" she exclaimed for the third time. "I thought we had lost him last year but this clever boy has found him for us," and she bent down and embraced her large Dalmatian with maternal affection. "You clever, clever boy," she whispered in his ear. But he shook himself free from her grasp to continue his prancing around the tortoise.

"What's all the noise about, Helen?" Hector Leafe stood framed in the doorway of the house.

"Prince Charming has found Methuselah," called his wife with renewed delight. My employer gave the dog and tortoise a bored look and turning on his heels disappeared into the house.

"It's almost nine o'clock," I observed to his wife. "I'd better get ready for my first patient."

By now, Prince Charming had stopped his noise and was standing in front of the tortoise wagging his tail furiously and glancing first from it on the ground and then up to his mistress as though to say, "Yes, I am a clever dog." Sensing that she had almost forgotten my presence, I followed on Hector's steps into the building.

It was late May and about nine months had passed since I first set foot in these premises as Hector Leafe's assistant. I was nine months older and considerably wiser. I had consolidated a lot of what I had learned about dentistry. But I had, by comparison, learned more about people and human nature. The one week I had spent during the winter's snow at Emrys Jones's practice in Acton had been the salt and pepper with the meal. I had, by now, got to know many of the patients who attended regularly for their six-monthly dental inspections. It was nice to meet people again whom I had met before and spend a few minutes of each visit just engaged in light conversation. It was some time since I had been subjected to the "Where's Mr Richards?" syndrome. I was now being accepted in my own right. My confidence was growing and with it, I hoped also, a steady improvement in my work. I glanced down the list of patients for the day.

"Mrs Penny at 12 p.m." I read out to Christine. "I see she's been given an hour. Have I seen her before? I don't remember her name."

"No, you haven't," said Christine, inspecting the patient's record card. "She only comes in when she has a problem."

"Then I'll have to lecture her on the advantages of regular attention," I said.

"I doubt if she'll respond to that."

"Why has she been given a double appointment?" I asked. Christine smiled and replied mysteriously, "You'll find out when you meet her." Realizing that she was not willing to expand on this, I suppressed my curiosity and prepared to start the morning's work. It was one of those mornings where I really needed about thirty-five minutes for each appointment as against the thirty minutes I normally allocated. Everything took just that little longer. Either the fillings I did were very large or there was a particularly heavy deposit of tartar to remove from the teeth or a new denture required longer to fit than I would have anticipated. The result was that I gradually slipped more and more behind with my timetable and it was not until 12.25 p.m. that Christine went to the waiting room to collect Mrs Penny. During the few moments she was out of the surgery I briefly read the patient's record card. Mrs Ursula Penny was aged just fifty and lived in Chiswick. She had last been in for treatment a little over one year previously when she had received two small fillings and had her teeth scaled and polished. For some reason, as yet unknown to me, Ted Richards had concluded the treatment notes on her with an exclamation mark! I heard voices approaching and the surgery door was opened by Christine to admit a pleasant-looking lady. She was somewhat on the stout size yet moved daintily despite this. She was also not very tall. She was dressed in a simple paisley patterned dress of non-specific colour. She wore no make-up and her greying dark hair was trimmed rather short. As her dress was cut well away from her neck it gave the impression that she had a particularly large and long neck. I introduced myself and invited her to sit in the dental chair. Why the double appointment, I still wondered? Perhaps Christine had anticipated that she might require considerable treatment. From her card I saw that this was not the pattern of her previous visits. And why Ted Richards's exclamation mark? She hesitated before getting into the chair.

"You've got the back of the chair inclined rather steeply," she commented, looking critically at the chair.

"Do you think so?" I said. "It's only in the position I usually have it." I inspected the chair. It was inclined at a gentle angle. No-one had ever made that observation before.

"I can only sit in a chair with a perfectly straight back," she said. "If I lie down I get a choking feeling in my throat."

I contemplated whether she slept standing up or sitting bolt upright in bed, but said, "If it pleases you, Mrs Penny, I'll straighten the chair back."

I made a few quick adjustments, setting the back of the chair at precise right angles to the seat. This is a particularly awkward angle for a dentist to work in as one is forced into taking up a position requiring considerable gymnastic skill in order to obtain any suitable access to the patient's mouth. I was beginning to understand the significance of the exclamation mark. Thanking me for "being so understanding", she climbed into the chair and then promptly slid several inches down it so that her chin was almost touching her chest.

"Mrs Penny, could you possibly come a little bit higher up the chair as I cannot get to your mouth while you are in that position," I requested.

She looked at me with big round eyes and I watched as they slowly filled with tears. She uttered not a word.

"All right then, all right," I urgently said, patting her on the shoulder reassuringly in an attempt to stem the impending flood. "You can stay as you are. I'll do my best."

In response to this, her salty pools retreated and I went on, "Just open wide please and I'll give you a check-up." It was at this point that I discovered that the lady's idea of "open wide" and my interpretation of the words were at considerable variance. Now I'm not unreasonable and when I say "Open wide", I'll settle for a comfortable one inch to one and a half inches from the middle of the top lip to the middle of the lower lip. But what on earth can anyone do with a gap of half an inch? It is physically impossible to get a mouth mirror into a mouth and see into it as well under such conditions.

"Mrs Penny, could you please open just a little bit more?"

I entreated. With what seemed to be a great effort she forced her mouth open to the minimum one inch. Standing on one leg and bent over like a question mark, I started to perform as good an examination as I could in the prevailing situation. I suppose not more than a minute had passed when quite suddenly her hand grasped mine, forcing the probe I was using for the inspection away from her.

"I wasn't hurting you, was I?" I asked.

"Oh, not at all. You're ever so gentle. But my jaws are aching and I'd like to rest them for a while."

Aching after only one minute? What would I do if she needed treatment that required several minutes work? So far I had found nothing wrong and I prayed that the inspection would find her dentally fit. As if in answer to my thoughts she looked up at me and said.

"I've come because I've lost a filling in this tooth," and she indicated a premolar in her right upper jaw. With a sense of threatening disaster, I persuaded her to open her mouth again. Fortunately, the deficiency in the tooth was not large and I assessed that about six or seven minutes work would be sufficient to refill it. The rest of the mouth was in good condition. I confirmed that this was the only tooth that needed treatment and in a moment of rashness I offered to do it there and then. It was customary at this stage for Christine to tie the waterproof bib around the patient's neck in preparation for the treatment. However, on this occasion she found reason to be engaged on some other duty on the far side of the surgery. To save time I advanced on the patient with the bib myself.

"You're not going to put that on me, are you?" came the nervous question.

"Yes. It's to protect your clothing."

"I can't have anything round my neck," she exclaimed, holding one hand to her throat, "it makes me want to choke. That's why I wore this old dress. I don't mind if you mess it up." And then she added slowly, "Please." I decided there and then that if I ever managed to perform the filling on her tooth I would promote her to two exclamation marks on the field of battle!!

"Would you care for an injection?" I offered.

"I never have injections," came the reply. "They make me

want to choke! I'm sure you'll be gentle, Mr Wilder."

"I promise to do my best, Mrs Penny."

So exercising considerable agility and working at lightning speed I completed the preparation of the cavity in the tooth in one and a half minutes. Fortunately, being only a lost filling there was not a great deal to do. As I finished, her hand was beginning to creep upwards to grasp mine again. But I beat her to it this time and moved away from the chair with a flourish.

"There, I've finished," I proudly claimed.

"It didn't hurt one bit," she told me.

With a justified sense of achievement I requested her to "Rinse out, please." To my astonishment, instead of picking up the tumbler containing the mouthwash and complying with my request, she swung herself out of the chair, stood up, walked around me and the unit to the other side of the chair and then picked up the tumbler and rinsed out into the spittoon standing up. I glanced across at Christine. She put her head on one side and gave me a butter-wouldn't-melt-in-my-mouth smile. Oh yes, it all made sense to me now! Nothing less than a double appointment would be sufficient to get anything done to this patient. It was already five minutes to one o'clock and I could smell faint wafts of Helen Leafe's cottage pie seeping in from under the surgery door. I wondered if I would finish Mrs Penny in time for lunch that day. Not that the cuisine would be anything to make a mouth water but, at least, it was good food of a kind. Eventually, Mrs Penny returned to the chair. The actual filling of the tooth was a nightmare of coaxing her to open her mouth "just a little bit more please, Mrs Penny", frequent stops to prevent her from choking, several short perambulations by her around the surgery, "just to get my breath back", and a number of ritualized circuits from the chair to the spittoon in order to rinse out. By 1.30 p.m. I had completed the filling and developed a stiff neck as a token. Her one saving grace was her appreciation of my patience with her.

"You've been very kind and very painless. I'm sorry if I'm difficult but I just can't open my mouth wide and then only for a minute or so at a time."

Her comment was by now quite unnecessary. I saw her to

the front door and dashed upstairs full of apologies for being late for lunch. As I waded through a particularly tasteless cottage pie, which by now was little more than tepid, I consoled myself that it would not be earlier than the November before Mrs Penny would be due for her next six-monthly check-up. But then I had overlooked the capricious whims of Fate. It was precisely one month to that very day and I was making my customary morning inspection of the appointment book. To my dismay, there, written clearly in Christine's distinctive handwriting was the name "Mrs U. Penny" for 12 p.m. and a double appointment had been reserved for her too.

"What's Mrs Penny coming in for?" I demanded of Christine. "She's not due for a check-up for months yet."

"I'm afraid that filling you did for her has fallen out. She's coming in to have it re-done," came the reply in a voice full of mock sweetness. I am sure that my standard of work from that moment until twelve noon fell well below the level I normally set myself but the anticipation of another 'Penny performance' had devastated my concentration. When she arrived, she was most apologetic for "having brought out the filling you did, Mr Wilder, on a sticky toffee". I set to work to repair her tooth once more. By 1 p.m. I had almost suffered a slipped disc, my left knee was aching from being bent against the joint, I had a painful ache in my neck again and I'm sure I had developed a permanent squint. For her part in the act, Mrs Penny had made her usual insistence that she sit bolt upright. She also seemed to sink even further down the chair than on the previous occasion so that access to her mouth was nigh impossible. I had to stop thirteen times for her 'breather' and to "rest my jaws as I can't keep my mouth open for more than a minute at a time". She also made six excursions from the chair around the room to the spittoon in order to rinse out. As she left the premises, I prayed that Providence would keep her away until her next six-monthly check-up.

The days passed and lengthened into weeks and in time the weeks added up to yet another month. I set the appointments with Ursula Penny to the back of my mind. There would now be at least another four months until her routine check-up and possibly next time all that might be required would be just a simple scaling and polishing of her teeth. Being now the end of July, the children had all started their summer vacations. Consequently, there had been a sudden influx of boys and girls of all ages whose parents wanted to ensure their offspring had sound healthy teeth for the holidays. In the space of a few days the practice had been transformed virtually into a children's clinic. Hector Leafe's surgery had undergone a similar change. Christine and Freda in their wisdom had taken good care to leave sufficient spaces in the appointment books to accommodate the flood of requests for the children to be seen. Christine, as always imaginative, had even scattered a few toys around the surgery. It was a pleasant surprise one morning to find the bowl of blue African violets missing from the window ledge and to have it replaced by a giant furry teddy bear. This outsize cuddly toy was obviously of vintage age as, in places, the fur fabric had been so worn that only the base material was showing. "He belonged to my mother," explained Christine with nostalgic affection, "and she gave it to me. I always bring him here for his summer holidays."

It was the end of the first week of the 'children's clinic'. Christine had already left to keep a date with her fiancé, Michael Digby. I was just finishing writing up my clinical notes and checking a few X-rays when the telephone rang in the hall. I waited for Freda to answer it. When this did not happen after some seconds had passed, I assumed that she, too, had gone home and so I went to the desk outside the surgery and picked up the telephone.

"Can I speak to Mr Wilder, please?" It was a lady's voice and one that had a familiar ring but, as yet, one whose identity I could not place.

"Mr Wilder speaking."

"Oh, I'm glad I caught you before you left. This is Mrs Penny." It was Friday evening and with both dental nurses gone, I nearly dropped the telephone! In a fleeting second I saw a brief picture in my mind of a nightmare session with her lasting well into the week-end while I wrestled with her in an attempt to replace all the fillings she had "brought out on a sticky toffee". I mopped the perspiration from my forehead with the back of my hand.

"Good evening, Mrs Penny. What can I do for you?" I said, endeavouring to conceal the sudden tremble in my voice.

"Do you like music, Mr Wilder?" came the unexpected question.

"Music?" I asked, trying to switch off the dental tussle before my eyes.

"Yes, Mr Wilder. My husband and I are giving a musical evening tomorrow at our house and we wondered if you would care to come along. We have a lot of musical friends and we often go round to each other's homes for an evening of music." In nearly one year of practice, this was the first time that a patient had ever suggested a social contact with me. I preferred not to consider the episode with Cynthia Purlin as a 'social contact'. It would be interesting to meet patients in a different environment from the dentist-patient relationship of the surgery and have them regard me as just Leonard Wilder, rather than Mr Wilder, the dental surgeon. I found myself accepting the invitation to be at the Pennys' residence in Chiswick at 7.30 p.m. the following evening. "Come nice and hungry," she had prepared me, "as there will be plenty to eat."

The Saturday evening was warm and sultry with an overcast sky and not a breath of wind. In the seclusion of my bedroom I tried on my father's grey, lightweight suit, only to find, as I had expected, that it was too big for me. Consequently, I decided to wear a pair of grey trousers and a blazer which would suggest an air of professionalism and yet still be informal. The Pennys' house in Chiswick was remarkably like the Leafes' in Ealing. It had probably been built around the same time and by the same property developers. Mrs Penny welcomed me, dressed in a long black dress and looking considerably younger than when she had attended the surgery. I was not quite sure whether to dispense with the professional formality of surnames and to replace this with the less starchy use of first names. This was solved for me by my hostess. "This is Mr Wilder, my dentist," she said, introducing me to her husband. Once a dentist, always a dentist I would be, even at a musical evening on a Saturday night! In retrospect, perhaps it was better that way.

By 8 p.m. a total of some twenty guests had arrived and by 8.30 p.m. I had consumed more than my fair share of smoked salmon, cold meats, a great variety of salads and mounds of black bread, all topped up with delicious strawberry gâteau and washed down with chilled Bordeaux wine. At 8.40 p.m. I settled into a comfortable chair to be entertained by a string quartet drawn from the guests. As a non-musician, but one who appreciates music, I was impressed by the fine standard of playing by these amateur musicians. The time passed quickly and by 10 p.m. the quartet had been followed by a recital of Chopin Etudes, played creditably by a local solicitor and then, in complete contrast, a selection of popular old songs from World War I, sung by a lusty gentleman of about seventy who completed his presentation by wearing white flannel trousers and a striped blazer. As the applause for him died away, Mr Penny who had been acting as Master of Ceremonies stood up. He introduced the last performer for the evening, his wife, who was going to sing some German Lieder.

As well as being an excellent hostess, Ursula Penny was also a fine mezzo-soprano. From her rendering, which was ably accompanied by her husband at the piano, it was apparent that she had received professional instruction at some time. What a welcome contrast she now was to the impossible dental patient I had known her to be in my surgery. I realized that as patients might sometimes find difficulty in forgetting that their professional attendants were normal human beings outside their working hours so, too, was it easy for a dentist to assess his patients solely from their behaviour in the unnatural environment of sitting in a dental chair with their mouths open wide or otherwise. Ursula Penny's reception at the end of her last song was a fitting climax to an enjoyable evening. So much so, that she required little persuasion to sing yet another song as an encore. She had, obviously prepared herself for this as her husband already had the music at hand on the music stand of his piano. I settled down to listen to a few more minutes of her singing. As her song entered the final bars, she reached for a particularly high note and I was marvelling at the surprising stretch of her mouth when she put a hand to her face, staggered slightly and turned to her husband as the note died away in her throat. A stream of unintelligible sounds issued from her as she held both hands to her head, her mouth still kept awkwardly open. I made a lightning diagnosis. Mrs Penny had suffered a 'spontaneous dislocation of her jaws due to an over-excursion of the condyloid process of the ascending ramus of the mandible in the articular fossa of the temporal bone'! I could still see in my mind's eye the words printed plainly on page 108 of my text book of dental pathology under a photograph of a lady whose mouth had undergone a similar contortion to Ursula Penny's.

"I-- -islocated -y -aw!" came from her overstretched mouth. Mr Penny peered down her throat and then at her, by now, white face. The impact of what had happened had not yet struck him. "What's wrong, dear?" he simply asked.

"I-- -islocated -y -aw!" she frantically shrieked at him. He looked back at her with an expression of bewilderment in his eyes.

"I can't close -y -outh," she wailed, her distress made worse by her sudden inability to communicate with her husband.

"Oh! Oh dear!" he gasped as the situation eventually dawned on him. Turning to me, he asked, "Mr Wilder, you're a dentist. Can you help her?"

"Yes, I can reduce the dislocation for her," I said making my way to the piano. I had seen such a demonstration at the hospital by one of the teaching staff when I was a student and although not having been put to the test before myself, I knew just what to do. "It won't take a moment," I added confidently.

The technique was just a matter of grasping the lower jaw with the thumbs held over the back teeth. Then by exerting a firm downward pressure followed by a backward move-ment and then as the chin is swung upwards the dislocation is immediately reduced. I seated Mrs Penny on the piano stool and standing astride her, I grasped her lower jaw in my hands.

"It may feel a little unpleasant, Mrs Penny," I said, "but not too bad."

The scene had suddenly changed. The Pennys' lounge-cum-concert-hall had been transformed into an operating theatre. I now saw the guests at the concert as international dental surgeons eager to see me perform a new revelation in surgical technique. Mrs Penny was once more the patient. For a brief moment I held the glory of the stage.

"Ready?" I asked her. She nodded her head. I pressed down with my thumbs on to her lower back molars. I then pressed a little harder and then even harder still. At this, both her hands shot up and gripping my arms restrained me from further endeavours.

"It's -ain-ul!" she cried resentfully. I stopped all movement and looked her in the eyes. "You're hurting -e!" she shouted.

This triggered off the complete picture of the demonstration I had seen at the hospital and it was then that I realized that the reduction of the dislocation had taken place under a general anaesthetic. I relinquished my grasp on her jaws as though I were holding a hot brick. Trying not to lose face I said, "I'm afraid it's rather worse than I had anticipated. I shall have to do this under a general anaesthetic. We shall have to take her to the surgery right away."

And then I remembered. It was past 10 p.m. on a Saturday night. The Leafes had gone away for the week-end to Sussex, with the cat, dog and bird hustled off to Freda Picton for the night. With no Hector to administer an anaesthetic where could I locate an anaesthetist at this inconvenient hour? I was her dental surgeon and the responsibility for her well-being lay with me. I decided to telephone Dr Westbury, Consultant Anaesthetist at a London hospital and the practice anaesthetist on the occasions when either Hector was at his clinic or I might be away. But there was no reply from Dr Westbury's number when I telephoned there. Who else did I know who might help out? With reluctance I remembered Dr Matthews from my bitter clash with him at Emrys Jones' practice in Acton. With mixed feelings I telephoned his house only to learn that "the Doctor is away for a few weeks at a Health Clinic". I interpreted this as meaning that he was away drying out from excessive alcoholism. As I put down the telephone a quick inspection of my wrist watch showed me that Ursula Penny had by then kept her mouth open for over ten minutes. This was already ten times longer than at any time before.

It is at moments like this that one's subconscious mind

frequently supplies the answer to a problem. From the hidden depths of that part of my brain welled up a name, Charles Martin. Charles, from my former student days and who was now established as a house surgeon at the hospital, lived at Streatham. Here was a hopeful chance for my patient and myself. In my diary I found his telephone number. The time was 10.15 p.m. Would he be in or away for the week-end I wondered as I listened to the regular ringing of the bell? After what seemed an age, the ringing stopped and I recognized Charles's voice. I explained the situation and implored him to help out in the role of anaesthetist. To my relief he offered to drive over and meet us at the surgery in Ealing. "When did she last eat?" came his cautious request. The buffet had finished at 8.30 p.m. It was now one and three quarter hours later. "She should be safe enough for a nitrous oxide gas by midnight," he said. "I'll be over by 11.45 p.m."

So Ursula Penny was forced to wait with her mouth wide open for another one and three-quarter hours.

As the first minutes of the Sunday morning gently nudged aside the end of the Saturday night, Ursula Penny sank into a pleasant controlled sleep under the expert control of my old friend of student days. Charles Martin, with his usual perfection, administered a model anaesthetic. Encouraged by this excellence of technique I found just the right pressure and just the right direction to enable me to reduce her dislocation in a matter of moments. This renewed team-work of ours was a pleasant ending to an unpleasant situation. Mrs Ursula Penny spent the next two days resting quietly at home and telephoned me on the Tuesday to say she was none the worse for her experience.

Just before Christmas she attended for her routine half-yearly dental examination. She came smiling into the surgery and without waiting for me to adjust the chair she seated herself in it, in the usual inclined position to which it was normally set. Sitting well up in the chair she opened her mouth wide, but not too wide, just in case! She required one small filling and a scale and polish. Allowing me uninterrupted access to her mouth I was able to complete the treatment within the half hour, during which she undertook her periodical mouth rinsing from the chair in the normal manner. Somehow, we both avoided any reference to the incident of four mouths previously. Somehow, she had lost all her former eccentricities in the dental surgery. Somehow, she had become a model patient!

15

When The Cat's Away

Mr Alexander Katz was completely square. He could hardly
have been more than five feet four inches in height and gave
the impression of being almost as wide. He was in his mid
fifties and apparently of mid-European origin as he still
retained a trace of an accent which was interestingly mixed
up with a South African one. I discovered that he had been
in business for several years in Cape Town. He had a glorious
head of sandy hair, a feature to which he must have devoted
some considerable attention as it was always neatly trimmed
and groomed. "You've been highly recommended to me,
Doctor," he announced at his first visit to the surgery, still
retaining the use of the European courtesy title of 'Doctor'

179

when addressing me. It was good to know that I had made sufficient a favourable impression on the patients I had inherited at Hector Leafe's that they had considered me worthwhile a recommendation. I had been Hector's assistant now for two years and during that time had come to consider myself very much a part of that establishment. Yet despite the passage of those two years, my employer's wife still referred to me as "Mr Wilder". To Hector, I had been "Leonard" from the onset, yet he had never bothered to suggest to his wife that she might be less formal with me. I doubt if he had even noticed it. It was late August and, as yet, I had not been able to get away for a holiday that summer. Hector had developed some arthritis in his hands and he had been advised to rest them for a month. This had thrown considerable additional strain on me as the only working dentist at a busy practice. I longed for a break. Despite his inability to work, Hector was in 'attendance' most days and would wander about the surgeries wearing a crisp, white coat. In defiance of medical advice, he still attended his clinic at the hospital on Monday and Friday mornings, though I am sure this did not do his hands any good. "I am pleased to see so many patients sending you their friends," said Hector encouragingly to me as he inspected my appointment book and saw that Mr Katz had come to me that way. Such a comment from Hector was indeed something as, on the whole, he was a man of few words and not over generous with his compliments.

"I want four new jacket crowns on my upper front teeth," requested Mr Katz, struggling to squeeze himself into the dental chair. He was wearing a fawn, lightweight suit of expensive cut and a pale blue silk tie over a white shirt. There was an immediate air of success about him. I examined his upper front teeth and found that he already had them crowned. As these crowns appeared to be several years old, his gums had receded from the edges of them and in addition they had also become worn and stained. Here, certainly, was justification for replacing them. I agreed to construct the crowns for him. A complete examination of his mouth displayed the presence of extensive but excellent replacement of some missing teeth by fixed bridgework. "Done by the best man in Cape Town," he lost no time in telling me. I subjected his teeth to a thorough cleaning and polishing, took X-rays of them and asked Christine to arrange for his crown appointments to start the following week. He thanked me and followed Christine into the hall to make his appointments. Several minutes later, through the surgery window, I saw Alexander Katz get into his shiny grey Bentley and drive off.

"What a strange man," said Christine on her return to the surgery. "He's very inquisitive."

"Why do you say that?" I asked.

"He started by asking me my name, then how long I had been here and then if I was happy in my work. He even had the audacity to ask me how much I was getting paid," she said angrily.

"He was just making friendly conversation," I said, trying to placate her.

"Then I'd thank him to take this kind of friendly conversation elsewhere," she replied. "By the way, he's made an appointment for his wife as well next time he comes," she informed me as she left the room to go for the next patient.

Mr Katz's appointment had been made for 3 p.m. on the following Tuesday. At about ten minutes to this time I noticed his Bentley pull up in the driveway and I watched him get out. He was accompanied by a lady whom I assumed to be his wife. Through the window I could see that she was a good twenty years younger than he, which would put her in her mid thirties. She was of average height and had a shapely figure. She was dressed in a white suit with accessories in pale green. Whatever the original colour of her hair, it was now a honey blonde and had that just-come-from-the-hairdresser look about it. It was lacquered in a piled high set, having the effect of making her considerably taller than her husband. When they got out of their Bentley, instead of coming up to the front door, they proceeded to wander about the drive subjecting the exterior of the building to some intensive scrutiny. This continued for several minutes until, eventually, Mr Katz rang the doorbell. By 3 p.m. he was easing himself into the dental chair. It is always a relief to undertake any extensive dentistry on a docile patient. Mr Katz proved to be just this. He sat in the chair motionless while I carried out the work necessary for his

crowns and then provided him with four temporary ones
until the fitting of the permanent crowns at his subsequent
visit. Throughout the preparation of his teeth I felt he had
been deep in thought all the time. I thanked him for being a
co-operative patient as I helped him from the chair. His wife
was due next for a check-up.

"Busy?" he suddenly asked.

"Yes, very, Mr Katz," I replied. "You see, Mr Leafe isn't
working for a few weeks as he has arthritis and so I have had
to bear the full weight of the practice. I expect him back,
though, shortly."

"I think you got a good business here," he said looking
round the surgery. I had never encountered such an observation from a patient.

"I've always considered dental surgery as a profession, Mr
Katz. I'd hardly call it a business."

"Call it what you like. If it makes money then it's a
business and I think this place could make good money if it
was run well. But first of all it needs proper organizing."

I was so taken aback by these comments that I found
myself short of a reply. This gave him a chance to continue.
"First of all, if you were to ask for my advice, I'd put a
dentist in to work while your Mr Leafe is not able to work
himself. Fancy letting good machinery and tools stand idle
when they could be earning money. That's what I call bad
business. Is Mr Leafe here?"

I looked enquiringly at Christine. "I believe he is dictating
letters to Freda," she said.

"I'd like to speak to him," requested Mr Katz.

"Mr Leafe is busy at the moment," I said as a little alarm
bell sounded in my brain. "Can I help you at all?"

"Yes, you can," came the quick reply, "by taking me to see
him. Busy or not, when he hears what I have to say he won't
even think about being busy."

In somewhat of a daze after his criticisms of the organization of the practice I led the way to Hector's surgery. I
tapped on the door and opened it when he called "Come in."

"May I introduce my patient, Mr Katz," I said, ushering
him into the room. "I hope we're not disturbing you but he
has asked to have a word with you." Sensing that some
indelicate comment was about to be forthcoming, I was

frustrated by my inability to prepare Hector for this.

"I understand you are supposed to be busy, Mr Leafe," said my patient, subjecting Hector's room to a quick but searching survey as he spoke, "so I won't waste any time. I believe you may have to give up your business because of ill health. So before the practice starts to drop off I'm prepared to make you an offer for it."

Hector opened and closed his mouth several times like an expiring fish but no sound came from it. He stared hard at Mr Katz as though he were a being from another planet. With an effort he found some words.

"What did you say?" he slowly asked.

"I said if you're thinking of getting out because of your health then I'm prepared to make you a good offer for the whole place, lock, stock and barrel," and he smiled as if pleased with his final turn of phrase.

Now, Hector being the most civilized of men, I had never seen him show any outward sign of aggression. Despite his wife's considerable attention to her 'menagerie', as he referred to the animals, and which he found a constant irritation, he had always observed great tolerance towards her and her pets. I had never seen him irate with Freda or Christine or display any irritation towards a difficult patient. But Mr Katz's remarks must have sparked off some deep latent emotions within him that, I believe, even he did not know existed. As all the colour drained from his face and I sensed the adrenalin pounding through his veins, he gripped the top of his chair behind which he was standing so tightly that his knuckles turned white.

"Are you suggesting that I sell you my practice?" he asked in a voice charged with emotion.

"Yes, I am," replied Mr Katz. "I'm prepared to make you a good offer for your business as a going concern. Look at it my way. I can see that you will have to give up soon. If your hands are giving out then how can you expect to work? It stands to reason. If I buy you out now then you can retire to a small place in the country, invest the proceeds in gilt edge and live a quiet secure life of leisure. Now it makes sense, don't it? But don't rush at an answer. Think about it."

Despite his inner turmoil, curiosity won the better of Hector. "And what would you propose doing with my practice?" he asked acidly. "After all, you're not a dental surgeon." His northern accent became more marked as his anger rose.

"If we do a deal then it's my business what I'd do," came the sharp reply, "but all right, since you're a gentleman, I'll tell you. If there's enough work here for another surgery, I'd bring in two more assistants. I'd put Mr Wilder in charge as I think he's all right and I'd run it as a going concern. That's what I'd do."

Hector looked first at me then at Freda, sitting amazed at her desk. Then back at me and finally at Alexander Katz. Yes, the man was still there, still so very real in his immaculate lightweight suit and sleeked down hair. Hector had been hurt, very hurt. I don't think the question of retirement had ever occurred to him. I am sure that in his own mind he could see himself carrying on indefinitely. The practice and his patients were his life. The idea of a happy retirement in closer contact with Helen and the animals was something he had, no doubt, banished to the deepest depths of his mind. Now that Mr Katz had blatantly brought out this possibility, Hector had been visibly shaken.

"Mr Katz," he said in a voice that trembled, "I am in perfect health as you can see. I have no intention of retiring or disposing of my home or my practice. The temporary set back," and he stressed the word 'temporary', "with my hands was quite minor and I am at this very moment arranging to start my work again quite shortly." He stared hard at my patient, who displayed no outward emotion at all in response to Hector's reply.

"Are you quite sure you wouldn't like to consider it?" came Mr Katz's insensitive insistence. Hector's white face turned bright red in the space of a second.

"There is nothing to consider," he said emphatically. "The practice is not for sale. Good afternoon, Mr Katz!" then at a loss for further means of communication, he seated himself at his desk and promptly ignored his intruder.

Without batting an eyelid, Mr Katz led the way out of the surgery and into the hall. With a shrug of his shoulders he declared, "Nothing ventured, nothing gained," dismissing the whole incident as would an habitual gambler who had lost a small chip at the roulette wheel. Opening the door to the waiting room he called to his wife. "Betty, you're next."

She replaced the magazine she had been reading on to the table that stood by the wall and looked up at him expectantly. "Well?" she asked. "Did you have any luck? Did you see him?" she spoke with a strong London accent and I detected a trace of resentment in her voice.

He grimaced at her and turned his head to one side. "He's no businessman, is that Mr Leafe. He wouldn't even let me make him an offer. All right then, if that's how he wants it, I'll take my business elsewhere. I reckon that once a dentist's hands start to give out then he'd better think of packing up. You'll see, he'll regret turning me down." As he spoke he stressed his point by making a series of forward jabs in the air with the index finger of his right hand.

"I told you not to start business with your own dentist," she reproached him. "The trouble with you is you don't know where to stop. He's your dentist, isn't he? Then let him be your dentist. Don't mix him up with business," and she turned the palms of her hands upwards as if appealing to his stubborn reason.

"Now look here, Betty, don't you start telling me what to do or what not to do," and his manner became aggressive as he now directed his finger jabs in her direction. "I did very well in business before I even married you and I don't want no advice from you now!"

This heated exchange between Alexander Katz and his wife, Betty, was taking place completely oblivious to my presence. I found myself looking first at him and then her as the words were bandied from one to the other like a ball over a tennis net during a hard game. He abruptly terminated the banter by saying, "Come on or you'll be late for your appointment," and just as abruptly his manner softened as he became aware again of my presence. "By the way, this is Mr Wilder, Mr Leafe's assistant. He's making my crowns for me. He's good, very good," he smiled sweetly as he reached up and patted me on the back. He sank into an arm-chair and picking up the fashion magazine his wife had been reading, he stared at it vacantly as he produced a cigar from a gold case.

"This way please, Mrs Katz," I said and I led the way across the hall to my surgery.

"You mustn't take any notice of Alex," she said with some

concern as she seated herself in the dental chair. "I hope he didn't upset you all."

"I think his suggestions were rather disturbing to Mr Leafe," I said, trying not to get personally involved with the recent occurrence.

"You see, business is his life," she said pensively, "that's the only thing that really matters to him." A far away look entered her eyes and she sighed. I decided to steer the conversation away from her husband and to get on with her examination. Her teeth had obviously been subjected to a good standard of care in recent years. All that she required were two small fillings and a scale and polish. She asked me to do the scaling first. "I'd like them all clean and shiny for a social function tomorrow night. I'll come back for the fillings when Alex comes for his crowns."

I complied with her request and then appointments were duly made for Mr and Mrs Katz to return the following week for their respective treatments, and they then drove off in their Bentley. Hector made no further reference to Alexander Katz or to the offer 'to buy him out', but I knew that he had been rattled by it. He became obsessed with his hands and I would see him inspecting them from time to time and examining his finger joints. Whether or not he was feeling any better he, nevertheless, went ahead with his arrangements to start again in his surgery about a week later.

In due course, Mr Katz and his wife arrived for their appointments. As before, he came into the surgery before her, and as I had anticipated, he seemed to have forgotten the incident of the previous week and was now completely absorbed with his new crowns. I was pleased to find that they were a perfect fit, a perfect shape and a perfect colour match. The dental laboratory that constructed our crowns and bridges for us was always to be relied on to produce excellent work. I was particularly pleased about this in the case of Mr Katz as I shuddered to think of his reactions had they not satisfied him. He was delighted with them.

"You've done a good job," he exclaimed as he admired himself in the hand mirror. "Now I can smile at the girls again," he said beaming at Christine who avoided his glance and busied herself at the hand basin. "I'm going to South Africa soon on a business trip and this will give me confidence."

I didn't think he needed any more than the abundance of it he already displayed! "How much do I owe you?" he asked me and then went on, "Now be a good boy and keep the price down, after all I did bring you my wife as a customer."

I refrained from correcting his use of the word 'customer' to 'patient' and said instead, "I don't normally conduct the financial side of the practice myself. If you would care to go to the desk with the nurse, she will give you an account."

"I'd be delighted to go with her to the desk," he said rubbing his hands together. "In fact, I'd be delighted to go anywhere with her," and he gave me a broad wink behind Christine's back. As he left the room I prayed that his business trip to South Africa would keep him there for a long time.

His wife's two fillings were no problem. She declined my offer of a local analgesic, saying, "I don't like injections. I don't want a frozen face for the rest of the day. Don't worry, I'll be a good girl and sit still. If you hurt me, I'll just scream." True to her word she was 'a good girl' and sat quite still until I had put the finishing touches to the last filling.

"I understand you are going to South Africa soon," I said, making polite conversation as she prepared to leave. "Oh no, I'm not going," came the reply. "Alex always goes alone. What interest is it to me to meet a crowd of boring businessmen? He might enjoy it but it's not for me. I'm taking myself off to a Health Clinic in the country instead. I usually do when he goes away."

"I believe they are quite popular these days," I said, as I opened the surgery door for her. "Is it far from London?"

She hesitated before replying. "Not too far," came the slow answer. "Now let me see, which one am I going to this time? Oh yes, it will most probably be the one in Bedfordshire. That's right."

Just one hour after their arrival, Betty and Alexander Katz had driven away from the practice.

The car I had run for two years and which had been far from new when I had bought it was now exhibiting the signs and symptoms of rapid decline. I was constantly having to have something replaced or repaired. I realized that the time had come for its permanent total replacement. Deciding on its successor presented no problem as within a few days of making my decision I had seen just the car I wanted and at the right price. It was one size larger than the one I had been using and a good three years less in age. But I had no idea how attached one could become to something which, after all, is just a machime. In two years my old car had become personified, a friend whose every whim and ailment was personally known to me. So it was with something of a wrench that I said goodbye to my old friend and drove away from the car showroom with my next one, a highly polished and shiny fern green model. I now had a new toy and I could hardly wait for the warm summer evenings during which to tinker with it and adjust it in order to get just that extra mile or so out of each gallon of petrol.

"Aren't you going to have a break this summer?" asked Hector over lunch one day. He had been back at his surgery for just one week and gave the outward appearance of being able to cope again.

"I had been postponing it until I felt happy about leaving you all alone," I said.

"I'm perfectly fit," he assured me. "So don't worry about me. If you don't get away soon, the summer will be over. Why don't you go down to Brighton at the end of next week. The Dental Conference will be on and so that might be worth attending." It was an excellent idea. Two of my former colleagues from student days were assistants in the Brighton area. It would be nice to meet up with them again after two years. But getting hotel accommodation in Brighton in September was no easy matter. Being a popular south-coast resort, most of the hotels gave me the same reply to my enquiries; "Fully booked up for several weeks." I suppose I must have made a dozen or more phone calls and was working my way up through the price range when I was fortunate in being offered a cancellation at one of the better hotels on the sea front between the two piers. "We can only let you have the room for one week," came the hotel receptionist's voice over the telephone. I readily accepted this. So with my luggage stowed in the boot of the car and final rub of polish on the metal work, I was all set for my late summer's break. I had arranged to attend the Saturday morning at the surgery and to drive down to Brighton from Ealing immediately after lunch. This was very convenient as

Ealing was on the direct route from my home to Brighton. In my usual manner I inspected the appointment book on my arrival at the surgery.

"Mr Katz at 12.30 p.m.!" I exclaimed as I looked down the list of names. "What's he coming in for?"

"I believe he wants an adjustment to one of his crowns," explained Christine.

Punctually at 12.30 p.m. Mr Katz arrived and Christine brought him into the surgery. Any fears I might have entertained about his new crowns were unjustified. All that was required was a small easing at the back of one of them where it was pressing on his lower opposing tooth. The whole procedure took no more than ten minutes.

"Well, I'm off to Cape Town in a week's time," he said as he left the surgery. "First thing next Saturday morning I'll be on my way. So I'll settle my account with the girl now," and he made his way to Christine who was at the desk in the hall. As I removed my white coat and washed my hands, I soon lost myself in thought as I planned the route I should take to Brighton in order to avoid, if possible, the Saturday traffic. I was disturbed from these thoughts by Christine who came bursting into the surgery.

"What a nerve he's got!" she exclaimed.

"What's up?" I asked her.

"He's just invited me to go to South Africa with him. He said it would be a pleasure to share a room with someone who could appreciate the good things in life!"

"What did you say to that?" I asked.

"I told him in no uncertain terms that I was engaged to get married and that I would be spending the week that you are off with my fiancé's family in Luton."

"What did he answer to that?"

"He just shrugged his shoulders and said that he hoped my fiancé appreciated a girl like me. Gosh, he really is brazen."

The hotel in Brighton was excellent and the week passed all too quickly. The Dental Conference, held at the famous Dome, was well organized but the weather was too hot for me to be able to concentrate on the latest dental equipment and techniques. I paid two brief visits and then succumbed to the greater temptation of sun, sea and fresh air. I did, however, locate my two former colleagues and passed a couple of pleasant evenings with them. I discovered that they, too, like myself, had been unprepared for the cold plunge into the river of life. Like myself, after two years, they were beginning to come to terms with the fact that dentistry was more than just the treatment of teeth. Like myself, they had found that the world outside the safe monastic confines of a teaching hospital could be tough going and that one was forced to mature rapidly, if sometimes painfully, in order to survive.

With its inevitable certainty the final day of my holiday arrived and with the feeling of reluctance that most holiday makers experience when packing their luggage, I fastened the catch on my suitcase and made my way to the hotel foyer to settle my account at the reception desk. The week's vacation had done the trick. My town pallor had been replaced by a healthy tan. My nerves had regained their calmness again after the stresses of professional life. I felt well and rested. It was midday and, as is usual on a Saturday, there was a fair exchange of guests taking place. Some arriving and others, like myself, leaving. I waited behind a gentleman who was already speaking to the receptionist on duty.

"I have a reservation," he said to the girl. I smiled inwardly as I looked at him. He reminded me somewhat of Mr Alexander Katz whose very existence I had almost forgotten about since coming away to Brighton. It did, however, please me to remember that he would, by now, be on his way to Cape Town.

"Did you make the reservation in writing?" she asked the man as she opened the hotel reservation book.

"No, I telephoned some time ago," he answered. "We have stayed here before." He certainly did remind me of Alex Katz, except that he was much younger, about forty perhaps. But his height and stature were fascinatingly similar. His diction, though, was very English and in this quite unlike my patient.

"What is the name, sir?" asked the receptionist.

"Mr and Mrs John Smith," came his reply. She inspected the book and then crossed the names off as she confirmed the reservation.

"Would you and your wife please sign the hotel register," she requested, placing it before him. Taking a pen from his jacket pocket he signed the book. Then turning to some seats arranged in the centre of the foyer he called. "Darling, would you come and sign the register."

A lady who had been seated stood up and slowly walked towards the reception desk. She was aged about thirty-five, had a good shapely figure and honey blonde hair, lacquered in a piled high style. She was wearing a well tailored white suit with pale green accessories. As she advanced, my heart missed a beat as I recognized her to be none other than Betty Katz herself! At the moment of my recognition her eyes met mine and bore into them unflinchingly. Then without any hesitation she turned away and picking up the pen wrote, "Mrs Mary Smith – Bedford".

16

Bursting to Go

"Weddings always make me cry." Helen Leafe wiped a tear from each eye and returned her white lace handkerchief to her handbag. Christine and Michael Digby were a striking couple at their marriage ceremony. They had chosen a quaint little church for it about three miles from Luton. With the spring daffodils in full bloom and on a pleasant sunny day it was a delightful setting for the girl who had been my dental nurse for over two and a half years. After a protracted engagement the day had at long last been fixed. Christine made a beautiful bride in a long white wedding dress and Michael looked amusingly uncomfortable in his slightly over-size grey tails, hired for the occasion from a well-known London dresswear shop. The wedding had been the main topic of interest at the Leafes for several weeks, reaching a degree of high intensity as the day approached. But here it was, and now Christine was Mrs Michael Digby. I clicked enthusiastically at my camera shutter as they emerged from the shadows of the church and stood in the bright afternoon sunshine of this fresh April afternoon. The reception was held at an hotel about five minutes drive from the church and I estimated that about seventy guests were present.

Fond as I am of champagne, there is something about my metabolism that induces in me a state of drunkenness were I ever to drink more than one glass. Now, it's very difficult to assess one's consumption of champagne when there is always some helpful person at hand only too eager to top up one's glass when it is barely half empty. Consequently, as the afternoon wore on and as I sampled this and that and washed it down with a drink from a glass that persisted in staying full the events and speeches and congratulations seemed to recede further and further from the conscious level of my mind. I do, however, remember one incident that stood out above most of the rest. I had become aware that a rather small elderly gentleman with a completely bald head had been eyeing me thoughtfully for some time. Eventually, as I was tucking into a savoury cheese bridge roll, he approached me. "Mr Wilder?" he asked a little hesitatingly.

"U-hum," I agreed through a mouthful of food.

"You're Mr Leafe's assistant, aren't you?"

"U-hum," I replied, swallowing the last piece of savoury cheese.

"Do you mind if I talk dental shop with you for just a minute or two?"

With the blood level of champagne rising pleasantly in my veins, it was something of a shock to be brought out of my euphoria and to be reminded that I was a dental surgeon, especially at a wedding. I made some non-committal gurgling sound as I downed another drink of champagne. Presumably, he interpreted this to be my assent for at that he drew very close to me and lowering his voice said, "How do you know if your dentist has made you a good set of false teeth?"

I tried to bring him into focus as he and the room swayed

gently before my eyes and I grasped the side of the buffet table to steady myself. "I beg your pardon?" I asked. "I didn't quite hear you with all this noise going on."

He then repeated his question lowering his voice even more. "How do you know if your dentist had made you a good set of false teeth?"

As the champagne was now flowing freely within me his remark just did not register. "But I don't wear false teeth," I vaguely remember myself deny.

I don't know whether he heard my reply but at that he took me by the arm and propelled me out of the hotel lounge and into a comparatively secluded corner of the corridor outside. "I had a full set made about a month ago by a man in Harley Street and I have a feeling they are not the best quality," said my enforced acquaintance. With that he deftly removed his upper and lower dentures and waving them before me asked, "What do you think, Mr Wilder?"

In two and a half years of general practice I had seen dozens and dozens of people with their dentures out. In the professional atmosphere of a dental surgery this is quite normal. But to be presented with a set of false teeth in cold blood in the corridor of a hotel somewhere in the country and at a wedding reception was more than I could stomach. The tidal wave of champagne within me gave a surge. The dentures in his hand suddenly multiplied into four sets, then eight sets, then sixteen . . . then he, the corridor, the hotel and the world spun into a mosaic of meaningless shapes and colours as reality and consciousness slipped away from me.

"Feeling better, Leonard?" My mother was standing over me with a steaming cup of tea in one hand and a bottle of aspirins in the other. I took in my surroundings. I was in my bed in my home! I started to move and as I did so it was as though some giant had struck me on the head with a mallet.

"What happened?" I groaned, putting a hand to my head.

"Mr Leafe brought you home in his car after the wedding yesterday," she smiled. "It looks as though you had a good time."

"Yesterday?!" I tried to sit up in bed, only to be reminded that the giant was still there with his mallet. "Then this is Sunday?"

"You've slept right round the clock," she said, getting me to sip some of the tea. I stayed where I was until late afternoon of that day and when I eventually escaped from the giant on guard it was 6 p.m. Whatever happened to the gentleman with the dentures I shall never know as I never saw or heard from him again. I have often wondered if he existed.

Christine and Michael had gone on a two weeks' tour of Scotland for their honeymoon and Hector had decided to take advantage of this by going to a Health Hydro for treatment of his arthritis. Despite his former aspirations that the trouble with his hands was "only a temporary set-back", his diminishing ability to work was beginning to give him some concern. Helen Leafe went with him. Being a health enthusiast, she could not resist "spending two weeks in good healthy surroundings", she had declared. The various pets were farmed off to accommodating friends and so Freda, I, and Methuselah the tortoise, were left to hold the fort alone for two whole weeks. With Helen Leafe's absence from the house, Freda Picton took over with vigorous possessiveness. On the Monday after the Sunday after the Saturday of the wedding, at my usual starting time of 9 a.m. I was back, completely sober again in my surgery. The premises had an unnatural ring of emptiness about them. Freda came bustling into the room. She pottered around with the instruments for a few moments. Then turning to me she asked slightly uncomfortably, "Would it upset you to work in Mr Leafe's surgery? After all these years I can't get the feel of this room."

When a lady makes such a request how could I refuse. So within minutes I had transferred to the surgery on the other side of the hallway and taken up residence in what was to be my surgery for two weeks. Now the interesting thing is that the two surgeries were almost identical in lay-out so that despite Freda's plea that she could not get the feel of my room, by the time I had completed my morning's list of patients I felt I had always worked in there.

It was then that I made a pleasant discovery. Freda Picton was a fantastic cook! Given freedom to reign supreme in Helen Leafe's domain, she excelled herself. No doubt with a strong sense of competition she produced for me a mouth-watering lunch. Considering that she had assisted me most ably and attended to all the telephone enquiries herself, I really do not know how she had managed to cook a more than welcome dish of traditional roast beef, Yorkshire pudding and two veg. The apple pie that followed was absolutely delicious. I felt sorry that this able lady had never married and given some lucky man the benefit of her excellence. Then I sadly remembered Christine's words when I joined the practice. "She's been in love with him for nearly forty years." How true it was. Poor little Freda. This was as near as she could ever get to being the 'mistress' of Hector Leafe's household. By the time the two weeks were over Freda seemed to have become rejuvenated. I found her a pleasant, good-humoured and most efficient companion. Soon, however, the practice had returned to its former atmosphere. Hector was back with Freda in his surgery. Christine, in her new status of 'Mrs' was with me in my room and Helen Leafe, once more in command of the upstairs domestic quarters, had returned to the preparation of her overcooked meals.

Hector avoided any comment about the value of his stay at the Health Hydro. I had my doubts and decided not to broach the subject.

"Leonard, I've decided to retire!" Hector Leafe had been pensive and silent during lunch. Helen, too, had served us without hardly a word of conversation. Even Prince Charming, in his usual position under the table, had been unusually inactive for so playful a dog. I had hardly set eyes on Henry VIII for several days and Colonel Bogey had been remarkably untalkative recently. It was as though the Leafe family, sensing the impending bombshell, had prepared itself for the inevitable.

"Retire?" I echoed his word.

"Yes, Leonard, retire," he said with the voice of someone who knows he is playing a losing game. He looked wistfully at his hands. "After forty-five years, I suppose it's time I laid down the instruments for the last time," and he sighed.

I felt a sudden lump in my throat. "Well, I'm sure you've earned yourself a good long retirement," I said and felt immediately the total inadequacy of my attempt at consoling his distress.

"I never wanted to retire," he said resentfully. "But these," and he held up his arthritic hands, "these have decided otherwise. It's no use fooling myself. I've got to give up and give up soon."

"How soon?" I asked, my mouth going dry. He stared at the table for a moment and then looked straight at me.

"Christmas, Leonard, this Christmas," and he hurriedly turned his head away. It was September. I had been with him for three years and was now one of the family. In my heart I had known that he could not continue working for much longer but since Christine's wedding I had negated such thoughts in my mind. It was time, too, for me to stop fooling myself and to realize that the sand in Hector Leafe's professional hour-glass had almost run out.

"How about the practice? What will happen to the practice?" and I remembered the offer that wretched man had suggested to Hector the year before.

"Helen and I are hoping to buy a chalet bungalow in Surrey. It will give her more elbow room for the menagerie and keep them out of my hair," and he forced a smile. "I'll find plenty to do there for myself."

"We've just seen the place we want and made an offer for it," said Helen Leafe with considerable enthusiasm. "It will have a spare room for guests so we shall expect you down frequently."

"And it's much nearer to London than your favourite spot in Wales," added Hector.

"But what about this place?" I asked, steering him back to my earlier question. "I've given that a lot of thought, Leonard, a lot of thought. I just couldn't face selling it as a going concern. After all these years I'm damned if I could see someone else running my practice in their way. No, it might sound a bit stupid but I'm just letting the place go. The estate agent has introduced me to someone who would like to convert it into a small nursing home and the financial side is very attractive. A complete change like that would not upset me. It would make a nice nursing home." He paused for a moment. "So I'm telling you our plans now to give you three months to sort yourself out and move on into fresh pastures where you know you'll be happy. I've just heard that Christine is having a baby early next year, so I won't have to worry about her. As for Freda," and sadness entered his eyes, "she wants to go and live with her sister in Dorset. I shall miss Freda. It's been a long time now." The lump in my throat returned.

After that day, Hector Leafe's practice could never be the same for me. Things had changed permanently with the knowledge of Hector's decision. I had three months to find myself another appointment. In a way it was almost too long for it gave me time to think and contemplate. Where could I ever be as happy again in another practice? The question of starting my own practice did not even arise yet. It was too soon for me to accept total responsibility for such an undertaking and, of course, the financial commitments were still beyond my means. The ideal situation would be to find a position which could offer me some increase in responsibility and yet shield me from the ultimate decisions. At one stage I even considered taking a short service commission in the army. The Royal Army Dental Corps offered to start me as a Captain with promise of early promotion to the rank of Major. I resisted the temptation and doubtful delights of seeing myself in uniform with three pips up and decided instead to try the Appointments Registrar at my former hospital. But in late September most of the new graduates had been snapped up as assistants. "We'll put you on our list," promised the Registrar, "and keep you posted should anything suitable turn up." During the following two months I went to see about four or five practices in and around the London area, but none of them came anywhere near the happy atmosphere I had known for the past three years at Hector Leafe's.

I was beginning to despair at ever finding myself a really suitable assistantship when during the first week of December I received a telephone call from the Registrar. "Mr Wilder," came the voice on the other end of the line, "I believe I have the very practice for which you are looking. A Mr Arnold Tomlinson is looking for two assistants for his practice in South Kensington. He is a former graduate of the hospital and would welcome someone like yourself as possibly the senior man. I suggest you go and see him." Hector was closing down and moving out in two weeks and time for me was short. This might be the very straw for me at which to clutch. Through the Registrar I arranged to meet Mr Tomlinson at 6 p.m. that evening. Making sure that I had finished

my last patient at Hector's by 5.30 p.m. I hurried to my car
and drove off in the direction of South Kensington. The
traffic was kind and with no hold-ups I arrived at my
destination well in advance of my appointment. The weather
was remarkably mild for early December. It had almost a
spring-like air about it. I somehow felt it was the right day to
be interviewed as a prospective assistant. I had been told that
the practice was in a main road over a chemist shop and that
access to the surgeries was through the shop itself. An unusual arrangement, I thought. By five minutes to 6 p.m. I
was standing outside a rather quaint and rather old fashioned shop which bore a sign declaring, "Pharmacy – Duncan
Holmes & Son". In the window were three giant swan-
necked bottles containing fluids coloured red, amber and
green respectively. The interior of the pharmacy was designed and set out in a similar idiom. There was a faint
medical smell about the place and it had a pleasant atmosphere of cosiness about it. The counter ran along the entire
length of the wall on the left, its position reminding me a
little of the fish and chip range at 'Fred's Fried Fish' in
Acton. At the far end of the shop was an illuminated sign
bearing the word 'Dispensary'.

A staircase started about half way down the shop on the
right and a brass plate at the foot of the stairs had an arrow
on it pointing up the stairs and the words 'Arnold Tomlinson, L.D.S., R.C.S., Eng. Dental Surgeon'. I made my way
up the stairs and found myself in a small square vestibule
confronted by a large brass doorbell button. I pressed this
and waited. Within a few moments the door was opened by a
lady wearing a starched dark green drill coat. She looked
somewhere in her early forties and was of medium height
and stature. Her greying hair was swept back across her head
and tied at the back, leaving it rather long around her neck.
"Good evening," she said. "Mr . . . ?" "Wilder," I completed.
"Mr Wilder for Mr Tomlinson. I have an appointment at 6
p.m." and I inspected my watch to confirm that I was still on
the right side of the hour. "Will you come this way please,
Mr Wilder?" and she led the way through the door, across a
carpeted hall and through another door marked "Waiting
Room," in black letters on a white background. "Mr Tomlinson is running late this evening," she said. "He will see you

as soon as he can." Then she added, "Would you care for a cup of coffee?"

"Please don't go to any trouble," I said.

"No trouble at all," and she left me in the room. She spoke with a quiet cultured voice and I sensed an air of great efficiency about her although, as yet, I did not know who she was. As I waited, I reflected as to whether this new and unfamiliar place to me was to be my new home. It had a more Spartan atmosphere than the Leafes'. The waiting room contained a simple table, set in the middle of the room and a dozen or so plain wooden chairs ranged around the walls. In addition, there were two large, very square arm-chairs either side of the window which overlooked the main road. These chairs must have been of some age as they were covered with linen loose-covers which had a faded floral pattern. The only other piece of furniture was an old oak bookcase completely devoid of any books. No more than three or four minutes had passed when I heard the doorbell ring, a pause, and then two voices nearing the waiting room. The door opened and the lady in the green overall ushered a pale-faced young man into the room. He looked to be in his early twenties. He was quite tall, thin and with dark hair trimmed rather short. He wore a clerical grey suit, white shirt and a tie which I recognized as being from my old hospital. His face looked rather familiar to me. Having been told that Arnold Tomlinson was also a former student of the hospital I had prudently worn my tie as well that day. The young man noticed it right away. He looked at me for a moment and then as some colour entered his cheeks he exclaimed, "Leonard Wilder, isn't it?"

"Yes, that's right," I affirmed, flattered by his recognition of me.

"You were in your final year when I was in the Anat. and Phys. department," he said. "I remember you well." As he said this the door opened again and a girl of about twenty-two, wearing a white surgery coat entered carrying two cups of coffee. She was rather petite with short dark hair and a fresh complexion.

"Mrs Hitchin, the secretary, asked me to bring these in for you." She set them down on the table. "Sorry to keep you waiting," she said, "but we're rather behind this evening."

She smiled and left the room.

"I'm Keith Barlow," said my companion and offered me a cold moist hand to shake. He was in a marked state of agitation and beads of perspiration stood out on his forehead. "Have you come for the job as well?" he asked me. "If you have, then I won't get it. You must be very experienced by now."

"Well, I wouldn't say very experienced," I said, stressing 'very', "but after three years I suppose I have learnt a thing or two." I could afford to be generous with my modesty. "But didn't the Registrar tell you that there are two appointments vacant here?"

"Are there?" he breathed as a little more colour entered his cheeks. "It would be great being here with you in my first job. But I heard you were in practice in Ealing."

"Did you?" I said, surprised that my whereabouts were known to him. "Well, the Principal there is retiring and the practice is closing down, so like you I'm job hunting."

"You've nothing to worry about," he said. "Anyone would be pleased to have you."

"Good of you to say so," I replied, my ego nicely inflated. He fidgeted nervously on his chair, stood up, stared through the window, ran his fingers through his hair and paced the room uneasily. "It's quite an ordeal waiting to be interviewed," he exclaimed. "Worse than taking Finals!"

"When did you qualify?" I asked him.

"I got the results two days ago and I haven't got used to the idea yet."

"You will in time," I said trying not to appear too superior. The door opened and Mrs Hitchin beckoned to me. "Mr Tomlinson would be pleased to see you now, Mr Wilder." I took my departure of Keith Barlow, leaving him my untouched cup of coffee. Straight across the hall we entered a white painted door. Sitting on the end of an old oak desk was a large man in his mid fifties, wearing a very long white coat. What he had of his hair, for he was considerably thin on top, was dark and sleeked down. He was powerfully built and had an athletic appearance about him. Like myself, he was wearing the hospital tie, albeit old and well worn.

"Ah, Wilder," he welcomed me in a deep booming voice,

rubbing his chest with two large hands. "Sorry to keep you waiting but that last extraction was a bit of a B." He spoke with a slight London accent and his manner was friendly and down to earth. "I've heard a lot of good things about you. You're with old Leafe, aren't you?" I was put at my ease by his comments and surprised that he should know about Hector. "Don't worry, I've not had any spies on you. It was the Registrar at the hospital who told me all that. Damn shame about old Leafe having to retire. His loss may well be my gain. I've had a couple of Australian assistants who are going back home just after Christmas and so I'm looking for replacements. With your background I could offer you the post of Senior Assistant."

It was as simple as that! No discussion or even mention of dentistry or technique. My three years at Ealing had been an invaluable foundation for me. Perhaps the 'old school tie' had done the rest. In a way I suppose I was pleased to find a practice where the principal was so completely different to Hector Leafe. In this way I could make no comparisons and still retain a happy memory of my time with him. I also knew at once that Arnold Tomlinson and I could work well together, a relationship that was so essential. He showed me round the practice. His surgery and waiting room were on the first floor. In addition to this there was a smaller room that may once have been a kitchen but which was now a staff room and had limited cooking facilities. With a staff of seven; three dentists, three nurses and a secretary, this was a welcome amenity. On the floor above there were the assistants' surgeries, well equipped, if lacking in colour, and also a toilet-bathroom. It looked as if a four-roomed maisonette with kitchen and bathroom had long since successfully been converted into this dental practice over Duncan Holmes & Son.

"If you are interested, I could start you at the beginning of January," he offered.

That would be in four weeks' time. Nothing could have been more convenient. I had two more weeks to go at Hector's and then Freda and I had promised to help the Leafes pack up their complicated household ready for their final exodus. Helen had refused Christine's offer of similar assistance as by her rapidly increasing size it looked as though she might be carrying twins. At almost the last hour Arnold Tomlinson's offer had been Hobson's choice but one that required no further consideration. Fate had dictated that I and the Leafes part professional company. Here were the fresh pastures to which Hector had referred. Under the circumstances I welcomed the new challenge. I also could not deny the pleasure I derived from the anticipation of becoming the senior assistant.

By the time I had taken my leave of my forthcoming employer the time was 7 p.m. and my interview with him had lasted over fifty minutes. I wondered how Keith Barlow had survived the long tantalizing wait for his interview. I went into the waiting room to collect the coat I had brought with me as Mrs Hitchin invited him in to see Arnold Tomlinson. "Good luck," I whispered to him as he followed her out of the room but he made no sign of even noticing my presence. His face was ashen again and glistening with perspiration and as he stumbled after her his eyes had a glassy expression in them. For my own sake I was glad my interview was over. As I closed the practice door behind me at the top of the stairs leading down into the chemist shop, I could hear Arnold Tomlinson's booming voice. "Ah, Barlow. Sorry to have kept you waiting. Now, you've just qualified, haven't you?" I went off in my car.

Those last two weeks with Hector Leafe were a slow agony for all of us. We all carried on with our duties as if no change were ever likely to take place. But it was like a condemned man counting the hours to his execution. With due concern for everyone, Hector had circularized all his patients suggesting alternative dental practices for them to attend in the area. A number of my own stalwarts had even promised to follow me to South Kensington. As a final gesture at the end of the last professional day, Hector invited Christine, Freda and myself upstairs for a glass of sherry with himself and Helen, and he then said a few words of appreciation to us. The most bitter blow of all was to Freda Picton. She tried hard to hold back the tears but her emotions won in the end and they burst out in a torrent.

The following four days were hard physical work; packing this, wrapping that, searching for something else, looking for string and labels and more and more brown paper. It threw

the Leafes, Freda and I together in a temporary new relationship and somehow dispersed the sadness of the previous
weeks. Christine insisted on being with us, "if only to lend
moral support and make the tea," she had said. But I
suspected it was a weak attempt to delay the final farewell.
When it did come, on the Christmas Eve, somehow it was
not as bad as I had anticipated. We had all found something
important to do, no doubt to help us over that last goodbye.
Freda was catching a train to Dorset, the Leafes were following the furniture van down to their bungalow, Christine and
her husband were leaving to spend Christmas in Luton with
his family and I had decided to service my car, a thing I
rarely did myself. Suddenly, it was all over and I was the last
one of 'the family' left standing in the drive of the house in
Ealing, a house now empty save for the happy memories of
nearly three and a half years for me and forty years for the
Leafes. As I climbed into my car a representative from the
local estate agent was nailing a 'Sold' sign over the board
which had been erected near the bushes.

The new year started and with it the start for me of a new
life in dental practice in South Kensington. It was also the
first start in general practice for Keith Barlow for despite his
concern and anxiety he, too, had been engaged as an assistant. Unlike Hector who infrequently came into my surgery,
Arnold Tomlinson give the impression of being in all three
surgeries at the same time. He would also make short visits to
my room to chat up the patients and have a quick look at
their record charts. He was a man of great vitality and
considerable stamina and during my first week with him he
worked right through the day on two occasions without even
a break for lunch. In retrospect, I missed the unimaginative
cooking of Helen Leafe and Prince Charming's persistent
presence under the table. There was, however, an excellent
Greek restaurant less than fifty yards away, owned by a
permanently smiling gentleman whom I got to know as
'George'. When he had learnt that I was the new assistant,
and I somehow managed to slip in the title of 'Senior
Assistant', at Arnold Tomlinson's, he welcomed me most
cordially. "If you are with Tom," he beamed, "then I'll give
you special service. Come into the kitchen any time you like
and you can choose for yourself the best and at no extra cost."

Keith Barlow discovered that trying to get through a day's work nearly killed him. I was reminded of my own early struggles. Consequently, he decided to bring sandwiches for his lunch and gulped them down with a cup of tea in the space of barely ten minutes. I doubt if it did his digestion any good but it did help him to compete more hopefully with his timetable. My dental nurse, Janet, was an angular girl in her mid twenties. She had long fair hair which would often fall about her face. She had been in the profession since she was eighteen and certainly knew all there was to know about the running of a surgery. Like Christine at Hector Leafe's, she had the wonderful ability of complete anticipation and within two days was able to hand me the very instrument I required without my even asking for it. I quickly discovered that she had a delightful sense of humour, a characteristic so desirable in a large, busy practice. In this respect, I saw the similarity to Christine as well. By the end of my first week I realized that I was settling in rather better and quicker than I had hoped I would in so short a time.

Arnold Tomlinson rented a fully equipped surgery in Harley Street which he attended for one day a week and so on Friday when he was away I had the total responsibility of the practice. I must confess to the delight I had when on my first Friday there Keith Barlow came nervously to my room to say, "Could you help me with the extraction of my patient's lower left second molar. I just can't get it out. He's an old patient of the practice and I feel so embarrassed."

Feeling very much the Consultant, I led the way back to his surgery which was adjacent to mine. In the chair was a burly man in his forties. Keith bit his top lip and handed me the forceps.

"I understand you have a difficult tooth to extract," I remarked casually, trying not to make it appear that it was Keith's lack of experience that might be the important factor in his inability to remove it.

"My teeth are always rock solid," the patient agreed. "The last dentist here had a fight to get a double tooth out for me about two years ago."

"Well, let me just have a look at it, shall I," I suggested breezily.

After three and a half years and the experience of a great

many extractions, a quick examination disclosed to me that Keith had already considerably broken down the socket in which the tooth was held and although still apparently firm it would require very little additional effort to remove it. Keith had not realized this. I placed the forceps on the tooth and five seconds and a couple of deft twists later I was placing it on the bracket table for all to admire. The look of respect that the patient shot at me lifted me right up for the rest of the day. I was beginning to look forward to Fridays.

It was during my second week at the practice that Janet said to me one day, "Have you noticed that unpleasant smell in the waiting room?"

"What smell?" I asked.

"It's a sort of chemical smell. Come and have a sniff."

We went down to the waiting room. There was no doubt about it, there was a noticeably pungent odour in the room. It was quite unpleasant.

"Perhaps someone has spilt something on one of the arm-chairs," I suggested.

However, an inspection of these revealed no contamination there. We conducted a quick search of the waiting room and examined the carpet but drew a blank. I returned to my surgery and forgot the matter. But the following day Janet brought the subject up again as we completed the last patient.

"That horrible smell in the waiting room is getting stronger," she declared as I was preparing to go home.

I dutifully went and sampled the atmosphere in the waiting room again. The bad odour most certainly was more noticeable than the day before. "Do you think it might be coming up from the chemist below?" I suggested.

"I doubt it very much," she replied, "these buildings are too solid for that. It has never occurred in the three years I have been here. I'll turn the room out tomorrow when Mr Tomlinson is in his Harley Street practice."

That Friday was a particularly busy day for me. Two of Arnold Tomlinson's patients required emergency treatment and in his absence their care naturally became my responsibility. Keith Barlow had made several requests for my assistance and by 6 p.m. I was grateful the week was over, grateful yet gratified with my ability to have held the fort. I wandered into Keith's surgery to bid him a good week-end. I had barely been in there a minute when the door was flung open and in stalked Janet holding a large ornamental flower vase at arm's length and at the same time pinching her nose between the forefinger and thumb of the other hand. She released the grip on her nose.

"This is the cause of the stink in the waiting room," she exclaimed.

"This," I recognized as the flower vase that stood on top of the bookcase in the waiting room. She held the vase out for me to inspect.

"Some dirty bugger has gone and peed into it!" and she placed the vase on to the desk by the wall and collapsed in uncontrollable laughter. I peered into the vase. It was three quarters filled with a cloudy, yellowish liquid which glinted in the reflected light from the surgery ceiling. A pungent smell of ammonia caught at my throat and I drew my head away as I started to cough.

"By the look and smell of it, it's been there for weeks!" she laughed. "What filthy person would want to do that? Fancy peeing into the flower vase!" and gurgling to herself she removed the object, saying as she left the surgery, "I'll throw it down the loo and leave the vase soaking in antiseptic over the week-end."

I turned to Keith whose face had become crimson, presumably embarrassed by the whole situation.

"Don't let it worry you," I said to him. "The world is full of strange people with strange habits. It's a pity that we shall never find out who did it."

He did not appear to have heard my words but just stood staring vacantly ahead of him, moaning softly to himself. "Oh dear, oh dear!"

"Keith, are you all right?" I asked, taking him by the arm. But he shook me off and turned away. Then in a flash the whole thing became crystal clear to me. "Keith!" I exclaimed. "The day of the interviews, six weeks ago! Keith, I'll never tell a soul but please satisfy my curiosity."

He turned slowly towards me and looked at me like a small boy who had just spilled the milk over the best carpet. "I didn't expect to get the job and forgot all about it until now," he simpered half to himself. Then with some effort he said to me, "You were so long with Mr Tomlinson that evening that to pass the time I drank the coffee you left and mine. Then after a bit I found I was dying for a leak and I couldn't find the lavatory. There was no-one around to ask and the vase was so convenient. I'm thoroughly ashamed of myself but I was simply bursting to go!"

Christmas 1997

Dear Mom—

I doubt this book will have any direct tie-ins to your research, but I thought you might find it interesting just the same to explore connections between two states our family has lived in.

Love,

Volunteer Forty-Niners

Volunteer Forty-Niners

TENNESSEANS AND THE CALIFORNIA GOLD RUSH

Walter T. Durham

Vanderbilt University Press
Nashville and London

This publication is made from recycled paper and meets the minimum
requirements of American National Standard for Information Sciences—
Permanence of Paper for Printed Library Materials. ∞

Photo credits: 1: Museum of New Mexico, Santa Fe; 2, 3, 29, 30: *Harper's New Monthly Magazine* 20 (April 1860); 4: Arizona Historical Society, Tucson; 5: Wells Fargo Bank, History Room, San Francisco; 6, 7, 31: Calaveras County Historical Society, San Andreas; 8, 13, 14, 15, 17, 18, 23, 25, 26: Tennessee State Library and Archives, Nashville; 9: Jourdan George Myers, Deer Creek, Calif.; 10: Negative #CN021773, Oregon Historical Society, Portland; 11: Frank H. McClung Museum, W. Miles Wright, Photographer, Univ. of Tennessee; 12: Kenneth Thomson, Gallatin, Tenn.; 16: United Methodist Publishing House Library, Nashville; 19: Tennessee Historical Society, Nashville; 20: Jean Marschall Hibbett, Gallatin, Tenn.; 21: James Totten, Hendersonville, Tenn.; 22, 28: The Huntington Library, San Marino, Calif.; 24: Sumner County Archives, Gallatin, Tenn.; 27: Ann Harris Anderson, Gallatin, Tenn.; 32: Dr. James W. Thomas, Gallatin, Tenn.

Library of Congress Cataloging-in-Publication Data
Durham, Walter T., 1924-
  Volunteer Forty-niners : Tennesseans and the California gold rush
  / Walter T. Durham. -- 1st ed.
    p. cm.
  Includes bibliographical references and index.
  ISBN 0-8265-1298-4 (alk. paper)
    1. California--Gold discoveries. 2. California-
  -History--1846-1850. 3. Tennessee--Population--History--19th
  century. 4. Migration, Internal--United States--History--19th
  century. I. Title.
            F865.D94 1996
    979.4'05--dc21   97-21090
                                                   CIP

to those who could see beyond the gold

Contents

Illustrations

(Sketch maps by Robert C. Durham)

Preface

Volunteer Forty-Niners: Tennesseans and the California Gold Rush fills the author's self-imposed requirement that a study of this length should be made in an area that for the most part has escaped serious scrutiny. Although students of the California gold rush have produced thousands of books and articles, they have paid little attention to the gold seekers who came from the southern states. That scant attention has left significant original materials to be examined and shared with readers even at this relatively late date.

Reports of the gold rush that were overdrawn, exciting, romantic, and at times boring have appeared in newspapers, magazines, journals, and books published since the mid-1800s. Fortunately there are also many evenhanded portrayals of the period based on thoughtful letters, well-kept diaries, and other dependable records. But exciting or dull, accurate or self-serving, most of the firsthand accounts in print have come from the pens of men or women whose personal origins were in the northern, eastern, and midwestern states.

This book attempts to adjust the imbalance. It focuses on the experiences of Tennesseans. But those men and the few women who emigrated were also Southerners, and although they were strongly oriented to westward expansion, they were products of a regional culture significantly different from cultures in other sections of the country. The author has chosen Tennessee as a case study because the ready response of its gold seekers in 1849 was representative of what might be expected of emigrants from other states of the South and because Tennesseans simultaneously provided vital leadership at the very highest levels in organizing the government of the state of California.

Who were the Tennesseans? The term is used here not only for the native born but also for those who had spent at least a few years of their lives as residents of the state. Thus many "Tennesseans" actually set out for California from more recent residences in Louisiana, Texas, Missouri, Arkansas, and Illinois. Yet they were of the same cut as people who left from homes in Tennessee. A moving frontier was in their blood, and this move, westward to the Pacific, was the most expansive of them all. Notwithstanding their Southernness, most Tennesseans would experience the gold rush in ways similar to those of most Ohioans or New Yorkers.

This book makes no attempt to identify or count all of the many men and women who left Tennessee for California between 1849 and 1856. It does seek to identify and relate the experiences of representative forty-niners from all over the Volunteer State and from as many different cultural backgrounds as possible. The text and appendix include the names of a multitude of them both to show their participation in the exodus and to tease researchers into exploring further the experiences of individual miners. The most difficult identification task was to learn the names of persons from the ranks of slave blacks, Native Americans, and women in general.

This story of the gold rush is possible because Tennesseans wrote about their daily life and adventures while en route to the West, while in the gold country, and while on their ways home. It has been distilled from those letters and from diaries, public records, newspaper reports, reminiscences, and other accounts written by them. It is the story of emigrants attracted by gold and by the enchanting promise of the California country.

While researching and writing this book, I received help from so many that the limits of space preclude identifying all of them by name. County historians shared freely. Many Tennessee newspapers printed my letters seeking gold rush information and often their readers responded. Librarians and archivists were unfailingly helpful whenever I invaded their premises in person, by mail, or by telephone.

I found important caches of materials and the ready assistance to examine them at the Tennessee State Library and Archives, the Nashville Room of the Public Library of Nashville and Davidson County, the Jean and Alexander Heard Library of Vanderbilt University, the United Methodist Publishing House Library, and the Southern Baptist Convention Library and Archives, Nashville; the Sumner County Archives, Gallatin; the Hoskins Library Special Collections, University of Tennessee, and the McClung Historical Collection, Knox County Public Library System, Knoxville; the Archives of Appalachia, East Tennessee State University, Johnson City; the Huntington Library, San Marino, California; the California State Library, Sacramento; the History Department, Wells Fargo Bank, San Francisco; the New York City Public Library; Rutgers University Libraries, New Brunswick, New

Jersey; the Virginia Historical Society, Richmond; the Southern Historical Collection, University of North Carolina, Chapel Hill; the William R. Perkins Library, Duke University, Durham; and the Library of Congress, Washington, D.C.

No one was more helpful than the distinguished scholar J. S. Holliday, Carmel, California, who generously shared his experiences as a longtime student of the gold rush. The counsel of Professor Don Doyle of Vanderbilt University was vital. I am grateful for suggestions offered by Professor Emeritus Robert Corlew of Middle Tennessee State University.

Help came from many other friends, but especially useful contributions came from Jourdan George Myers, Deer Creek, and Peter J. Blodgett, San Marino, California; Edward M. Steel, Jr., Morgantown, West Virginia; and Tennesseans Neal O'Steen, William B. Eigelsbach, and Steve Cotham of Knoxville, Shirley Wilson, Hendersonville, Jean Marschall Hibbett and Albert A. Bennett, Gallatin, and Mary Glenn Hearne and Fran Schell, Nashville.

I recognize again the patient, excellent work of my secretary and research assistant Glenda Brown Milliken. I am indebted to Dimples Kellogg for her usual clean and forthright copyediting. It has been a pleasure to work with Charles Backus, director of the Vanderbilt University Press, and with editor Bard Young and their entire staff. Once again, the time for the undertaking was made possible by the gracious understanding of my wife, Anna Coile Durham, and my business partner, John R. Phillips, Sr.

The book is much the better because of all who assisted, but the author accepts the final responsibility.

Walter T. Durham
Gallatin, Tennessee

Introduction

Since its earliest settlement, Tennessee had been a principal staging area for the American westward movement. By the 1840s, many of the state's residents were members of second or third generations of the early settlers who had established European culture west of the Appalachians. Most of the rest were immigrants who had opted to make the mountain crossing into what had been known for the past half century as the Old Southwest. With the exception of blacks,[1] most of whom were then in slavery, nearly all people in the state owed their presence to their own or their family's conscious decision to migrate westward.

Largely because of its geographical location, Tennessee had received much of America's first westward migration and, after the Louisiana Purchase, had funneled immigrants west of the Mississippi River into territories that became the states of Louisiana, Arkansas, Missouri, and Iowa. Smaller numbers passed into Kentucky, Illinois, Indiana, Alabama, Mississippi, and the upper Northwest. From wherever they next stopped, many of them ultimately drifted toward destinations farther west.

Beginning in the early 1830s, Tennesseans had been active participants in the settlement and development of Texas. They had been prominent in the councils of those who declared and fought for its independence from Mexico, who established it as a republic, and who ultimately brought it into the United States of America. A former governor of Tennessee, Sam Houston, became the president of the republic and the first governor of the state of Texas.

The presidential terms of Tennesseans Andrew Jackson (1829–37) and James K. Polk (1845–49) not only broke the monopoly on the presidency held by the eastern seaboard states, but also proclaimed the rising political power of the expanding West. Jackson reinforced and reinvigorated the concept of a union of states and confirmed the course of American empire westward. Polk followed by annexing Texas and acquiring Oregon and the Mexican cession lands. Before he left office, the United States stretched from the Atlantic to the Pacific Ocean, and Manifest Destiny had become much more than a slogan.[2]

For the two decades prior to 1849, Tennessee held political power that was disproportionately large for the size of its population. Jackson, Polk, and several highly influential senators and congressmen had shifted national attention from Virginia to Tennessee as a training ground for presidents. Earlier, Polk had been Speaker of the House of Representatives, and Senator John Bell, who sought the presidency as nominee of the Constitutional Union party in 1860, first served in the House. The dynamic Felix Grundy was a congressman and later a senator and attorney general of the United States. Senator Hugh Lawson White was the Whig nominee to be Jackson's successor as president, but he lost the canvass. Balie Peyton was elected to the House and won national attention for his oratory and his decision to switch from the Democratic party to the Whig party. Andrew Johnson was a member of the House before moving successively to the Senate, the vice presidency, and the presidency.

At the state level, Democrats and Whigs shared political control of the governor's office throughout the 1840s. Each party won three of the six gubernatorial elections between 1839 and 1849. Even Polk's election to the presidency in 1844 did not disturb the balance of power in Tennessee politics. In fact, he failed to carry his own state, falling short by 113 votes.

National issues were reflected in the posture of both state political parties. Democrats and Whigs alike were committed to the Union, but challenges to the practice of slavery that emanated from the East and North increasingly concerned Tennesseans, although the majority of whites were not slave owners. Surely many slaves within the state welcomed the talk of freedom, but just as surely most slave owners were opposed or wanted to expand slavery into the West and throughout the country. Most local members of both parties opposed the Wilmot Proviso of 1846 that would have excluded slavery from all territory acquired from Mexico. They agreed with President Polk that such a requirement would be "mischievous and foolish."[3]

The first time that Tennesseans were greatly stirred during the 1840s was the outbreak of the war with Mexico. When President Polk asked the governor of Tennessee for 2,800 volunteer soldiers, more than ten times that number came forward. The response caused Tennessee to become known as "the Volunteer State," a tribute since perpetuated in the state's proud tradition of loyalty and readiness.[4]

By the end of 1848, the union of thirty states represented a nation growing at a fast rate. The area of the country had more than tripled in size since 1790. The population in 1850 was nearly six times that of 1790. The spirit of nationalism was exuberant, but nowhere more so than in the South where Jackson and Polk had nurtured it. Like their neighbors in the region, Tennesseans were excited.[5]

At midcentury, Volunteer forty-niners were leaving behind a state with a population of 1,002,717. Small towns had arisen in great number, but Nashville, the capital with a total population of only 10,165, was the largest city in the state.[6]

1850

see also
on p.245

Reflecting the preponderant agricultural economy, most of the white population were farmers. Iron forges and furnaces and mills to saw lumber and process grains furnished most industrial employment. The first cotton factories had just appeared. The impending spread of a network of railroads, some of which were then under construction, had created new interest in establishing industrial plants, but the development of the rail systems was the largest and fastest growing industry in prospect.[7] All in all, the industrial economy of Tennessee was not strong enough to attract much attention outside the boundaries of the state or to create much opportunity within them.

Most of the slave population, 239,459 in 1850, worked in agriculture in West and Middle Tennessee where cotton, corn, and tobacco were the principal cash crops. In locales throughout the state were 6,422 "free colored." From 1819 to 1824, emancipation had been advocated by the *Manumission Intelligencer* and the *Emancipator* at Jonesborough and by the *Genius of Universal Emancipation* at Greeneville. Yet in 1849, Tennessee was a slave state, and no significant public opposition to slavery existed among the all-white male electorate.[8]

By the midsummer of 1848, reports of the discovery of gold in California were trickling back to the states. In fact, a local rush to the area of the discovery soon developed at San Francisco where sailors abandoned their ships in the harbor and merchants closed up shop and all hurried to the gold field.[9]

Responding in 1849 with the same enthusiasm shown by the Mexican War volunteers, Tennessee gold seekers rushed to be among the first from outside the region to reach the mines.[10] They faced momentous questions: How and with whom would they make the crossing? How would they fare in the mines? What would they contribute to the development of govern-

ment and commerce in California? Who among them would become leaders in public life? What kind of enterprises would attract them? How
would the mining experience affect those who returned to Tennessee?

Preoccupied by the riches they anticipated, few gave serious thought
to the national implications of what they were doing. Like other
Southerners, Tennesseans left home even as the Mexican cession had agitated anew the slave-free issue and threatened the existing balance of an
equal number of slave and free states. Volunteer forty-niners were only
vaguely aware that their arrival in California would raise vexing national
questions. Had they and other Southerners come to extend the South and
the practice of slavery to the West Coast? Would their presence intensify
the sectional tug-of-war between North and South? Or was it possible
that regional economics and a national negrophobia[11] would combine to
prohibit slavery and severely limit the migration of black Americans, free
or slave, to the new Canaan? Would the rush to California require unlikely congressional compromise to save the Union for another decade and
enable California to achieve statehood?[12]

The answers to all of these questions would come soon, but some
would be only temporary and none without pain.

Volunteer Forty-Niners

CHAPTER I

California Gold!

W HILE a restless nation awaited authentic information about the reported discovery of gold in California, President James K. Polk prepared the farewell speech of his presidency. Honoring his pledge to serve only one term if elected, he was ready to give a final accounting.[1] Although few cared to review Polk's remarkable accomplishments in office, all would listen attentively when he spoke of California. They wondered whether the discovery by James Marshall[2] at Sutter's Mill was a fluke or a valid indication of what the future held for those who would go for the gold.

In the speech delivered December 5, 1848, Polk launched the gold rush of 1849 by calmly explaining the situation in the region. When California was acquired by treaty with Mexico earlier in the year, he said, it was known that "mines of the precious metals existed [there] to a considerable extent," but the value and magnitude of the deposits were not then known. From reliable evidence and the most recent field reports, the president concluded that the region held gold in large amounts:

> The accounts of the abundance of gold in that territory are of such an extraordinary character as would scarcely command belief were they not corroborated by the authentic reports of officers in the public service who have visited the mineral district and derived the facts which they detail from personal observation. . . . The explorations already made warrant the belief that the supply is very large and that gold is found at various places in an extensive district of country.[3]

To document his provocative claims, President Polk submitted to Congress copies of Col. Richard B. Mason's reports to the War Department made after a visit to the "mineral districts" during the preceding July. Mason found nearly the whole male population of the region, some four thousand men, in the gold fields.[4]

Recognizing that government had a role to play in the discovery drama, the president recommended that Congress authorize establishment of a branch of the United States mint in California to "more speedily and fully avail ourselves of the undeveloped wealth" of the mines. The proposed mint would raise "gold to its par value" in California and would also provide for the ready processing of gold bullion and specie imported from the west coasts of Central and South America, he said.[5] Samples of gold were at that very moment in the hands of assayers at the Philadelphia mint. And within a week, they found it met their highest standards: it was "genuine" gold.[6]

When news of the president's speech reached Jonesborough, Tennessee, the local newspaper editor could not believe Polk had discussed the gold mines in such a matter-of-fact way. Instead, he needled the president for the serious mien of his presentation. He wished that Polk had spoken "with an enthusiasm that ought to characterize the delivery of a sermon, calling sinners to repentance." But the contents of the message created public excitement that obscured the allegedly unenthusiastic style of its delivery.[7]

Polk's fellow Democrats in Tennessee gave him credit for adding California gold to the national inventory of natural resources. At the same time, they took the Whigs to task for their presidential campaign contention that the value of the entire territory gained from Mexico "was not worth a dollar."[8]

The politics of California gold notwithstanding, Tennesseans and Americans throughout the land faced the prospect of having gold if not for the asking, then certainly for the taking.[9] Repeated reports that deposits were extensive and the mineral easy to harvest caused public expectations to soar. The only recognized hardships that lay in the way were in the crossing to California.

Gold fever swept Tennessee.[10] Newspapers fed the frenzy, and even editors who pointed out the considerable pitfalls of rushing to the West had to admit that the rewards might be astonishing. The fever did not abate quickly and in 1850 was still in a contagious stage. Letters to Montgomery

County families brought by traders returning from California during the latter part of March "put the people into a ferment of excitement." A Clarksville editor acknowledged that "half of the men we meet, and even some of the girls, are talking and thinking about nothing but fortunes to be made in that blessed country."[11]

From points as distant as Boston, Massachusetts, and Springfield, Missouri, a young Tennessee collegian and a former resident of the state could not ignore the rising passion for California gold in their areas. Nashvillian Randal W. McGavock, then in school at Harvard College, noted in his journal on December 20, 1848, that "the President's message has caused the people to run mad almost about this gold region."[12] A former Greene Countian in Springfield, Missouri, wrote to Jacob Lintz of Greeneville: "The 'gold fever' is now raging here to a great extent, and will probably carry off a great many of our citizens."[13]

Even before the Philadelphia mint made its validating report of the purity of California gold samples, Americans throughout the land had begun to plan to go to the gold fields. Tennesseans were among the first. On December 16, John H. Quisenberry of Memphis advertised his intent to recruit a company of fifty to leave March 25, 1849, for Fort Smith, Arkansas, there to "fall in with the Fort Smith Company, on the 1st of April following." Anyone could reserve a place with Quisenberry by making an advance deposit of $20.[14]

At the far eastern end of the state, a group of men at Jonesborough announced the organization of the California Mining, Laboring, and Trading Company. They invited applicants to join by making an investment of $300 in the firm and providing "satisfactory recommendations" as to health and morality. The organizers, who had adopted "stringent laws against gaming and intemperance," warned that violators would forfeit their investment and suffer dismissal from the company.[15]

Few communities, if any, in the state escaped the gold fever. As at Memphis and Jonesborough, local prospectors usually banded together, and often the press noted their enthusiastic departures for the West. In East Tennessee a group was readying itself to leave Athens while at Knoxville former United States Senator Alexander Outlaw Anderson[16] began recruiting what would be one of the largest Tennessee companies to undertake an overland crossing. At Memphis, out-of-state groups mixed with large numbers of Shelby County men, almost all destined to make the first leg of the journey by river to one of the outfitting towns of

New Orleans, Fort Smith, Independence, or St. Joseph. Others departed for the West from Madison, Carroll, and Henry Counties. In Middle Tennessee several groups set out with men drawn principally from Davidson, Sumner, and Lincoln Counties, but including several representatives from Cannon and probably every other county in the region.[17]

Some saw the west-bound men as representing much more than a lust for riches. One observer ascribed high purposes to them:

> They go as agents of social comfort, moral progress, expanding civilization and diffused thought, and (noblest of achievements) run high up into the heavens of strange lands, the cross-crowned spire, symbol of a true faith and prophecy of a sure eternity. Those who go to California may not know it—but they are society's, or rather God's, agents to these wonderful ends.[18]

Although "God's agents" may have feasted on spiritual food, they had also an appetite for the kind of California boosterism that emanated from the Far West. Reassurances from the region boosted their faith in the presence of gold, if not in the omnipresence of God. The Memphis *Daily Eagle* quoted excerpts from a private letter written February 2, 1849, by former Tennessean Peter Hardeman Burnett who had just arrived in California from Oregon:

> I am here at this point, having been attracted hither by the unlimited gold region of California. . . . Men are here nearly crazy with the riches forced suddenly into their pockets. . . . The accounts you have seen of the gold region are *not overcolored*. . . . *The gold is positively inexhaustible*.[19]

Such enthusiasm was a virtual invitation to charlatans to become involved in the gold rush. Advertisements proclaiming the virtues of Signor Jo. E. De Alvear's Goldometer and *Gold Seeker's Guide* appeared in many Tennessee newspapers. Customers ordered the "instrument" and booklet by mail from an address in New York City by sending $3, but they soon discovered that the offer was a fraud. There was no such person as De Alvear.[20]

"California Gold Grease" was an obvious humbug. Newspaper accounts noted: "A Yankee down east has invented this specific for the use of the gold-hunter. The operator is to grease himself well, lay down on the top of a hill, and then roll to the bottom. The gold and nothing else will stick to him."[21]

A Knoxville shoemaker, B. H. Reed, of previously impeccable character absconded with $9,000 in cash entrusted to him at Nashville for delivery to a Knoxville bank. He successfully reached the port at Charleston, South Carolina, loaded up with supplies, and about February 10, 1849, boarded the ship *Othello* for the first segment of his bank-rolled crossing to El Dorado.[22]

Many prospective travelers to California sought help from Memphis and Nashville book dealers who sold "travel notes," including routes to the gold fields. They advertised books with maps of the region: *The Gold Mines of California* by G. G. Foster, *California and its Gold Regions* by Fayette Robinson, *What I Saw in California* by Edwin Bryant, *A Tour of Duty in California* by J. W. Revere, and *The California Guidebook* by John C. Fremont. For inspection at its office, a Nashville newspaper offered a map of the route to California from Corpus Christi, Texas, to San Diego through El Paso del Norte.[23]

Nearly all the books described the land between St. Louis and the West Coast in glowing terms, yet a Clarksville man who crossed to Oregon in 1849 vowed the country was quite different. The representations in Fremont's book were almost wholly incorrect, he said, "and as to his pictures of 'beautiful valleys' of [the] Bear and other rivers, he has certainly drawn extensively on his too fertile imagination." Calling Fremont "*the* humbug of the 19th century," the Montgomery Countian said the general glossed over the realities and waxed unjustifiably poetic:

> Those beautiful plains are nothing more or less than vast sandy deserts covered partly with wild sage, with here and there a green spot of grass, affording tolerable pasturage for our animals. Those mountains, whose picturesque scenery has been heralded to the world, are immense heaps of bleak, barren rocks, from whose gray tops, or deep chasms, I was unable to trace out anything beautiful, grand or sublime.[24]

Other books were more helpful, however. Edwin Bryant's *What I Saw in California* contained practical information for cross-country travelers and served as a guide to the kinds of data and experiences to include when writing their letters or making entries in their diaries.

Forty-niners could find suggested lists of equipment for both the crossing and the mines at the local hardware store. Memphians, for example, would have no trouble purchasing all of their hardware supplies at the store of J. M. McCombs, according to his advertisement:

FOR CALIFORNIA

Persons going to California would do well to call and examine our stock of the following articles, which we have rec'd direct from England and the manufactories in the East, viz:

Stub Twist and Damascus double and single bbl. shot guns; Stub Twist Rifles and Shot Guns, combined; American Rifles, assorted sizes; Powder and Pistol Flasks and Shot Pouches; Every article of gun-trimmings; Shot and Lead; Long and short handled Fry Pans; Pick Axes, hand and chopping Axes and Hatchets; Curry Combs, Drawing Knives; Trace Chains and Hames; Stretcher, Stay, Tongue, and Fifth Chains; Shovels, Spades and Hoes; Pocket Knives, every variety.[25]

Not all advertising was as directly focused. Hoping to exploit the gold fever, a Pulaski merchant headlined his newspaper notice "California Gold Wanted." Readers found that his purpose was to sell his merchandise at a "very short profit"—and for any kind of money. Although he indeed "wanted" California gold, he must first sell his stock of goods to provide funds for traveling to the mines.[26]

A Nashville publisher was more direct in his approach to disengaging from business and migrating to the gold fields. William M. Hutton, co-publisher of the Nashville *Daily American*, was eager to go. He advertised:

A valuable investment can be had in the *American* office, in the way of a lease, for three years, all of my interest in the establishment, consisting of one-half. It will be a good investment for anyone who has not got the "California fever" so bad as I have. The *American* is firmly established and in a prosperous condition.[27]

Some advice to would-be Californians dealt with what they should do before their departure. A Memphis wag targeted debtors who might be fleeing their Tennessee creditors by suggesting "it would be well for some of those who talk of making settlements in California to make a settlement at home before they go."[28] Some made a clean getaway, however. In 1849,

James R. Fitts of East Tennessee avoided answering a bill of complaint filed against him in the chancery court at Rogersville when he "removed himself to the country of California." There he was beyond the reach of a Tennessee court.[29]

With tongue in cheek, a Memphis jeweler advertised that a locomotive of superior power would soon leave his place to pull a train through to California in three days. Headed "Ho! For California!" the claim was all farce, but it called public attention to the jeweler and his store.[30]

Serious men made serious proposals about employing railroads to reach the gold fields. On January 8, 1849, a native Tennessean, Senator Sam Houston of Texas, introduced resolutions in the United States Senate for the appointment of a committee "to inquire into and report upon the expediency of the government establishing a railroad from some point on the Mississippi to San Francisco, across the country—the first proceeds of the California gold mines dug at the rate of an assessment of eight percent rent, to be applied to its construction."[31]

It was easy for Tennesseans to believe that Memphis could be the eastern terminus of such a transcontinental road. Even the distinguished naval scientist Matthew Fontaine Maury had anticipated the construction of rail lines from California to the Mississippi River, and he wrote extensively about the advantages of having the eastern end of the road anchored at Memphis.[32]

Tennessee wanted the railroad. Rallying February 22 at the Commercial Hotel to advance the cause, Memphians cheered former Governor James C. Jones as he reeled off a list of blessings that the western road would bring to the state. Before adjourning, the assembled citizens endorsed an earlier Arkansas call for a convention to be held July 4 at Memphis to harness the energy of both states "to procure construction of a National Railroad from the Mississippi River to the Pacific Ocean."[33]

Business leaders throughout the state hastened to support a transcontinental railroad. The East Tennessee rail promoter J. G. M. Ramsey chaired a public meeting at Knoxville that elected delegates to the Memphis convention, later postponed until October 16 because of the presence of cholera[34] in the Mississippi valley. Public meetings in the other major cities and towns elected delegates to the railroad meeting.[35] The Memphis committee on arrangements begged for widespread representation at the convention to set a course that would "lead to the completion of the most magnificent work which has been attempted in the tide of time."[36]

[handwritten margin note: 1829 - logical time for Preston + others to have gone to TN]

Public preoccupation with western gold quickened local sensitivities to the possible presence of gold and/or other undiscovered mineral deposits in Tennessee. Some remembered that gold had been "mined" in Tennessee as early as 1829, principally from gravel beds in the mountain streams of the Coker Creek District of Monroe County. The recoveries were not sufficiently large to warrant continuing commercial interest, however.[37]

Newspapers in February printed the unauthenticated report that "silver and gold mines" had been discovered in Benton County, Tennessee, near Wyatt's Mill. The mines purportedly held large amounts of silver and gold ore of unusually rich yield. Excitement in the area was at such a pitch that the owner of the land had it guarded day and night.[38]

There were reports that a copper mine and "several lead mines" had been discovered in northeastern Sumner County. The mineral deposits were located not far from a valuable sandstone deposit near Hartsville. The Gallatin *Tenth Legion* promised that the mines would soon be worked.[39]

Subsequent discoveries of copper, zinc, lead, marble, and gypsum in East Tennessee rendered that section "a more desirable country in which to make a fortune than California," one booster asserted. Land values increased dramatically; unidentified buyers purchased three-quarters of a section of land in the copper region for "a million and a quarter dollars."[40] For the next century, copper was the mineral most profitably mined in Tennessee. Polk County was the site of most of the first mining activity with twelve mines in production by 1854.[41]

Notices of mineral "discoveries" always made good reading. On July 22, 1853, the Athens *Post* reported a display of specimens of gold brought into its office from discoveries in "an adjoining county." Reports from East Tennessee of the 1854 discovery of lead ore within two miles of Rogersville and silver ore near Taylorsville appeared in the crowded columns of the state press.[42] Some readers raised an eyebrow and others guffawed when a Nashville journal reported that someone had discovered gold on the public square of Bolivar, Tennessee.[43]

Tennesseans would have preferred to mine gold at home, especially when they contemplated the rigors of journeying to the West Coast. The overland crossing could be devastating to one's physical well-being, Williamson Countians learned from a firsthand account written by a New York soldier and printed in their local newspaper.

I have seen those who started from the borders of Missouri hale and stalwart men, hobble down into the plains of California crippled for life. I have seen brothers, who in the madness of hunger, have fought for the last bit of their father's dead body. . . . Maidens who left their homes . . . [for] this far-off land . . . despoiled of their loveliness and bloom, withered into mature old age.[44]

Editorials counseled caution to anyone who would race to the West. An East Tennessee newspaper editor, who elected to remain at home, warned that Europeans who had sought gold in Mexico and South America had been reduced in the process to "rags, starvation and beggary." He recalled, "Spain . . . was reduced to poverty by the neglect of her commerce and manufacturing in order to dig for gold." Pointing out that California was federal territory, he doubted that the United States government would permit anyone, citizen or foreigner, to pocket "the public treasure with perfect impunity." The government would most certainly put a stop to "this system of promiscuous piratical plunder," William G. Brownlow wrote in his Jonesborough *Whig and Independent Journal*, January 17, 1849.[45]

The editor's observations suggested the question: Why did not Spain or Mexico, both known for skill in locating and mining precious metals, discover California gold? Its presence was no less obvious than deposits they had discovered in other Mexican provinces or in South America. Apparently, Spain and, later, Mexico failed because they settled only a few coastal areas in California and their people seldom ventured into the central river valleys and the lower western Sierra Nevada, the site of an extensive gold region. A part of the answer may be that the situation of California at the extreme northwestern reach of Mexico resulted in its receiving little attention from the central government. It was simply too expensive to settle and supply the region on more than the very modest basis they had employed.

That explanation was not convincing to those who thought Providence had played the key role in the American discovery. Among those anxious to give credit where it was due was a Tennessee newspaper published at Lebanon for the Cumberland Presbyterian Church. Both the gold and the silver of that region "belong to the Lord" who had concealed it from the savages and Catholic Spaniards only to reveal it to Anglo-Saxon Protestant Christians, the editor explained. As with every blessing there was an obligation, in this case to "preach the word and bring the church to California," he concluded.[46]

The gold discovery sent some Christians scurrying for their Bibles. Could this be the biblical land of Ophir that furnished from afar the gold for King Solomon's temple as discussed in 1 Kings 10:11? The *Presbyterian*

Record, published weekly by the West Tennessee Synod at Nashville, raised the question in its issue of March 3, 1849, and a year later answered it in the affirmative.[47] But, citing Proverbs 3:14, the Presbyterian *Christian Observer* reminded that there was "Something Better Than Gold," and most other religious publications readily agreed.[48]

There seemed no way to quell the excitement, even though discouraging advice abounded. The counsel "stay at home" frequently headed the suggestion lists for those "feverish to go to California."[49] Nerve-racking reports of lawlessness and violence, including riots and numerous incidents of bloodshed, did not stay the forty-niners. A Memphis correspondent boasted that "men of character" were among the first emigrants of 1849, but few, if any, expected the situation in El Dorado to change overnight.[50]

Some deliberately circulated discouraging reports, hoping to coax others to stay away from the gold fields. The *Presbyterian Record* reprinted one such article from the Liverpool [England] *Albion*, which, if true, would have ended all gold hunting and left California "desolate." The *Albion* reported that a citizen of Liverpool claimed to have discovered a process by which he could "convert iron to gold and produce the material in tons." If the English newspaper intended for the purported claim to dampen the enthusiasm of American gold seekers until their British cousins could arrive and join the hunt, it failed totally.[51]

The passion for gold was often a subject for editorial ridicule. "The cholera and the gold mines of California are all the rage now. . . . To tell the truth, we don't know which to regard the greatest evil," observed the editor of the Maury *Intelligencer*, December 21, 1848. Noting the exasperation of the citizens of Mexico at their government's having given up a province so rich in gold, another commentator remarked that California gold was like all other gold: "The root of all evil."[52]

Certain skeptics employed verse in their dire warnings. The Pulaski *Western Star* compiled "A Patriotic Song for California" in four-line verse, borrowing from comments in other journals. The last stanza came from the Franklin *Review* and spoke knowingly to the miners:

> Yes, wise men will make your graves —
> And all your gold fall heir to,
> And say — "poor fools, they're broke and gone
> We know not — care not — where to."[53]

CHAPTER II

By Land and Sea in '49

NOTWITHSTANDING belittling criticism by cynics and warnings of real dangers by thoughtful observers, many Tennesseans chose to join the rush for gold. Coming from all sections of the state and from virtually every county, the forty-niners were principally young white males. Underlying the response was widespread poverty, much of which was concentrated in families living on farmlands worn out by overcultivation. When compared to that of other states, personal income in 1849 was extremely low. In earlier times poverty level personal incomes had pushed young men out of the state to seek their fortunes, but the pull of gold combined with the push of poverty at home was powerful indeed.

 *already! by 1849*

Many who had gone to Mexico during the war with that country saw the gold rush as an extension of their prior adventure. Probably an even larger number of Mexican War volunteers who had been turned down because of the vast oversubscription in Tennessee viewed the risky rush to California as compensation for the opportunities denied them in the recent war.

For young men with families and burdensome debt, the gold mines offered an irresistible opportunity. For adventurers, what greater challenge and reward than crossing the continent and reaping untold riches? Peer pressure sent many hurrying to the mines. Others chose deliberately, thinking the prospects too promising to ignore. Among them were young lawyers, doctors, dentists, and other professionals who seemed more interested in going than their counterparts in agriculture and business, yet there were some from every imaginable category. At first only a few women responded, and most went with their families. Many of them entertained doubts about the adventure, but just as many looked forward to a new life in a land flowing with milk, honey, and gold. The few black men and women, nearly all of whom went as slaves, had little or no choice in the matter.

Because the costs of going to California were higher than most could muster, people who made the earliest decisions to go were often of financial means or were of sufficient standing in their communities to merit the financial support of others. "The emigrants I have met . . . are a loss to the districts from which they came," one enthusiastic correspondent wrote from Little Rock where he had met large numbers of the California-bound, most from Tennessee and other Southern states. "They are . . . attorneys, physicians, theologians, mechanics, and the hard-fisted yeoman."[1]

It was not in the interest of all to embark on the gold adventure. Obviously those of advanced age or in less than robust health should have no place in the rigorous outing. Those whose careers were well established as farmers, professionals, and businessmen had more reason to remain at home than to venture away. Others remained behind because of personal responsibilities at or near home. And numerous persons, for various reasons, simply did not care to undertake the risky enterprise.

As the gold rushers began preparations for the crossing, their first concern was selecting an appropriate route to California. Consulting books and newspapers that provided a variety of choices, they excitedly weighed the advantages of each. Many made their selection after discussions with others who became fellow travelers.

Because West Tennessee had direct access to the Mississippi River and the rest of the state had indirect access by way of either the Tennessee or the Cumberland River, emigrants looked to New Orleans as a point of departure. Regular steamboat service provided a generally risk-free trip of five to six days from Memphis and nine to twelve from Nashville.

In 1849, New Orleans offered two principal choices for the California-bound. The first was the all-sea, all-weather route that required sailing vessels or steamships. It led travelers across the Gulf, down the long east coast of South America, and westward around Cape Horn at the southern extremity of the continent. Once in the waters of the Pacific, it continued in a northwesterly direction along the west coasts of South and Central America and Mexico to San Francisco. The advantages of this passage were considerable. It required no overland travel, no change of carrier, and

MAP 1. Sea Routes to California, 1849

no participation by the passengers in camp duties such as standing guard, repairing equipment, and attending to dray animals and cattle. Travelers would encounter no hostile Indians. They could go at any time of the year, and they had no demands on their time or health except those occasioned by seasickness.

On the other hand, the disadvantages spoke persuasively to inlanders. The journey of nearly 15,000 miles from either New York or New Orleans was long and slow with few port calls and many uninterrupted weeks at sea. Even landlubbers knew that navigation around Cape Horn was hazardous. But the main objection was the time required, usually five to six months or more.[2] The rushers of '49 believed that the first arrivals in the gold fields would have substantial advantages over those who followed. Tennessee forty-niners looked for a faster crossing.

The second and most popular option at New Orleans could provide a relatively quick passage by employing a combination of sea and land travel. By that method, a gold rusher could reach San Francisco in less than one-half the time and distance by Cape Horn.[3] The crossing began when ships under steam or sail delivered passengers and freight across the Gulf of Mexico 1,400 miles to the tiny port of Chagres[4] on the Atlantic side of the Isthmus of Panama. Travelers did not linger at Chagres. They rushed on not only because of their mission, but because during the rainy season, the town was a breeding ground for tropical diseases, and even in dry times, accommodations were meager.[5]

To cross the Isthmus to the Pacific Ocean, travelers had to take small riverboats or dugout canoes up the Chagres River about 60 miles to Gorgona or about 67 miles to Cruces. The remainder of the trip from either point was overland for 20 or 25 miles to the Pacific port of Panama City. The road from Gorgona to the coast was low and muddy and essentially impassable during the wet season; from Cruces the road was "high, rocky and rough." They were approximately the same length, and both required the use of pack mules, which were readily available for hire. The last segment from Panama City to San Francisco was 3,000 miles by sea.[6] Depending on the time lost while waiting at Panama City and the choice of sail or steam, passage from New Orleans to San Francisco required sixty to one hundred days.[7]

Cornelius Vanderbilt, a New York financier, whose philanthropy later made possible the establishment of Vanderbilt University at Nashville, opened an ocean-to-ocean route across Nicaragua in 1851. It employed small steamboats to navigate the wildly meandering 120 miles of the San Juan River to Lake Nicaragua, then larger steamers for the next 75 miles across the lake, and mules for the remaining 12 miles overland to the Pacific Coast. Frequent portages on the river prevented the somewhat shorter route from making serious inroads on the Chagres-Panama crossing, and a revolution in Nicaragua closed the connection in 1857.[8]

Other less popular crossings began at New Orleans. One that attracted only a few Tennesseans began with a voyage to Veracruz, Mexico, from which point a stage line delivered passengers westward about 800 miles through Jalapa and Mexico City to Guadalajara. There travelers purchased horses and mules for the rest of the journey either to San Blas, a Pacific port distant 200 miles, or to Mazatlán, a port city 350 miles farther north. Promoters claimed that the trip from Veracruz to San Blas could be made in sixteen or seventeen days. At either Pacific port, passengers usually experienced long waits for ships to California.[9]

Tennessee newspapers reported another trans-Mexico possibility for those setting out from New Orleans. Suggested by a company of Louisiana gold seekers who planned to follow it, the crossing involved traveling by ship to Matamoros, Mexico, thence overland about 700 miles through Monterrey, Saltillo, Parras, Durango, and across the mountains to Mazatlán. About 1,500 miles of sea travel would complete the journey to San Francisco. The Louisianians touted it as the cheapest way to reach the gold fields.[10]

Another route from New Orleans led by sea to a choice of either of the Gulf ports of Brownsville, Matamoros, or Port Lavaca and from thence overland to San Antonio and El Paso, Texas. There the course veered southward by way of Chihuahua to Mazatlán. The rest of the journey was by ship to San Francisco.[11] A variation of this route, beginning at El Paso, followed the valley of the Gila River to the crossing of the Colorado River and into California at Fort Yuma. It then crossed the state westward to San Diego where gold rushers could go north to San Francisco by sea.[12]

Although many Tennesseans opted to go by a route with one or more sea segments, most at first chose to make the crossing by land. They preferred land routes probably because few of them had experienced sea travel, but almost all could ride horses and most men could drive teams of mules or oxen.

Newspapers from Jonesborough to Memphis printed descriptions of the land routes to California, each heavily promoted by the city at its eastern terminus.[13] Merchants of the three gateway cities of Fort Smith, Independence, and St. Joseph were well prepared with supplies, essential and nonessential. And each city was easily accessible from Tennessee by riverboat.

The southern route to California began at Fort Smith, and the press throughout Tennessee publicized its advantages.[14] This route had minor variations, especially in the Oklahoma country. The version first traveled led from Fort Smith across the prairies by tracing the valley of the south fork of the Canadian River to a point near its source, and from there into Santa Fe. The trail turned southward along the Rio Grande to Doña Ana and then westward along Cooke's Wagon Road[15] into southern California.[16]

Advocates of the southern route hailed its accessibility to the "eastern and middle states" where combinations of railroad and riverboat travel could bring the gold rusher to Fort Smith "within *three weeks at farthest*." By continuing without delay, one could expect to be in San Francisco 120 days from the time he left home, it was claimed, "and that too over a route which, for safety, certainty and freedom from disease has no rival."[17] Also, the southern route was shorter than the 2,000-mile crossings from Missouri by approximately 300 miles, its proponents maintained.[18]

About 300 miles north of Fort Smith, both Independence and St. Joseph offered travelers access to the celebrated Santa Fe Trail through the later states of Kansas, Colorado, and New Mexico. At Santa Fe were three options for completing the crossing to Los Angeles: the Old Spanish Trail, Cooke's Wagon Road, or Gen. Stephen Watts Kearney's trail across the later state of Arizona along the Gila River.[19]

Furthermore, Independence and St. Joseph were gateway cities to the Oregon Trail, which attracted the preponderance of land travelers from Tennessee and elsewhere. After passing the Rocky Mountains but before reaching Oregon, it provided several opportunities for travelers to turn onto overland passages to Sacramento, California. The Oregon Trail became so popular with gold seekers from all points that it was soon known as the California-Oregon Trail or simply the California Trail.

Connecting trails from the Missouri cities merged near Silver Springs about 150 miles northwest of Independence to form a single route leading to Fort Kearney. Following the Platte River until its junction with the Sweetwater River, the California Trail passed Fort Laramie, and it crossed the Continental Divide over South Pass. It continued past Pacific Springs, turned onto Sublette's Cutoff, and later took Hudspeth's Cutoff through

Soda Springs. At the nearest point, the route circled about 85 miles north of the Great Salt Lake en route to the headwaters of the Humboldt River, which it followed until the stream disappeared underground about 250 miles northeast of Sacramento.

The final, and often most torturous, obstacles to reaching the gold fields were 40 miles of desert and the towering Sierra Nevada. The desert crossing offered no choices, but there were two principal trails across the mountains. One of them traced the Truckee River to its source in the lake of the same name, and from near there moved down the Yuba to the Feather and Sacramento Rivers.[20] The other, known as the Carson Trail, was south of the Truckee and followed the valley of the Carson River into its higher elevations. Once the trail passed the summit, it continued along the headwaters of the American River down to its main stream and finally to the Sacramento River.

As the forty-niners contemplated the various overland routes, they were reassured by news that the army was taking extra mules and horses westward to provide assistance to emigrants in distress along the trails. Small detachments would set up emergency supply posts and send wagons of corn and other provisions to patrol. The aid was planned so "that our people will not perish without help and die for want of food," a Tennessee newspaper reported.[21]

A railroad from Memphis to San Francisco existed only in the dreams of its advocates in 1849. Without it, the gold seekers faced a long and tedious journey that included elements of the unknown. What about storms at sea or times of calm when a sailing vessel made no progress whatsoever? What about illnesses of all types, especially cholera and tropical fevers? Would overland travelers be prepared for attacks by hostile Indians?[22] Or how could they avoid snows in the mountains and find water and grass enough to cross deserts? These obstacles and many others threatened their safe passage.

Most planning to go would have been surprised to know that other Tennesseans were already on the scene. Several had crossed to California during the two decades prior to the discovery of gold in 1848 and remained to participate in the developing life of the new state. They had come in the various roles of explorer, hunter, trapper, trader, businessman, soldier, and family settler.[23]

Notable among them for the parts they would play in the New West were the American consul at Mazatlán, a Mexican War veteran, a trapper-trader, an attorney who had westered to Oregon, and a postal agent who was ordered to the territory in the latter part of 1848. Although all were native Tennesseans, not one of them had a prior acquaintance with another. Their common interest was California and the future it offered.

Few Tennesseans, indeed few Americans, knew as much about California before the gold rush as John Parrott, United States consul at Mazatlán, Mexico, 1837–46 and 1848–50. In 1845, he purchased a one-twenty-fourth interest in the New Almaden quicksilver mine in Santa Clara County and made what was probably his first visit to California.[24] Born in 1811 in Jackson County, Tennessee, he had lived much of his life in Mexico after following his older brother, William S. Parrott, to Mexico City in 1829. Forced from his consulate in 1846 by the Mexican War, John lived in Havana, Cuba, until returning to Veracruz, Mexico, on April 14, 1847. In 1848, he traveled to Washington, D.C., to seek and receive "reappointment as consul of the United States at Mazatlán."[25]

Before becoming consul, John Parrott had lived in Mazatlán working as a clerk for Parrott, Talbot and Company, a mercantile firm jointly owned by his brother William and United States Consul Samuel Talbot. When Talbot resigned from his governmental post, John Parrott was appointed in his place December 30, 1837.[26]

With the appointment as consul, Parrott positioned himself for mercantile trade along Mexico's northern Pacific Coast by establishing Parrott and Company, the successor firm to Parrott, Talbot and Company, in Mazatlán. For the next nine years he performed banking and business services through his new company. From these practices and his visits to California in 1845 and again in early 1849, he became well acquainted with the gold country. The best information about the size and composition of the California population available to the United States secretary of state as late as 1848 was Parrott's estimates based on inquiries made during his visit in 1845.[27] He also had the best estimate of the quality of California gold when on October 6, 1848, he responded to suggestions that it was bogus by asserting it was "17 or 18 carats fine."[28]

Parrott made his 1849 journey to California to deliver in person certain urgent dispatches from the Navy Department to Commodore Thomas Ap Catesby Jones, the Pacific fleet commander, but the consul had the gold rush very much on his mind. After looking over "the gold region in California" and assessing prospects for the area during January and February 1849, Parrott became even more enthusiastic. "[It] is much more than it has been represented to be," he wrote. His only fears were that the value of gold could "suffer from the abundance of the yield" and the safety of the country could be endangered by the growing emigration from South America and other quarters.[29]

Believing that he had gathered information relative to California that would be of "more importance to the Government" than his remaining at his consulate, Parrott made his way from Mazatlán to the nation's capital. He brought a quantity of gold dust valued at $80,000 and "for the use of the United States government . . . the most complete map of the gold region which has as yet been made." On arriving he expressed "an entire confidence in the vast extent" of California's mineral wealth and estimated the amount of gold "which will be obtained the present year at thirty millions of dollars."[30]

When Parrott reached Washington, he was incensed to learn that a Mexican government official had intercepted and seized a requisition of 469 mules that he had filled and dispatched to the United States Army quartermaster at San Francisco. He valued the animals at about $250 each. The seizure resulted in Parrott's losing the whole shipment. "For the sole purpose of personal aggrandizement and private gain," the official had invoked a law that did not exist, Parrott charged. He petitioned Secretary of State John M. Clayton to demand reparations from the government of Mexico in the amount of the lost sale, approximately $120,750. After the United States assumed American citizens' claims against the Mexican government under the terms of the Treaty of Guadalupe Hidalgo, July 4, 1848, Parrott was forced to negotiate with the United States and ultimately to settle for significantly less than his claim.[31]

Enjoying the public attention that he received in the East, Parrott nonetheless left Washington on October 18 to return to Mazatlán. He wintered there before he resigned as consul on April 9, 1850. Within a week he departed by steamship for California.[32]

David F. Douglass of Sumner County traveled from Mexico to California in 1848 as a wagoner with Maj. Lawrence P. Graham's First Dragoons. Two years prior in Texas, he had enlisted in Jack Hays's Mexican War regiment and had served with distinction until the end of hostilities. Douglass had moved to Arkansas in 1836 where in 1839 he killed Dr. William Howell in a duel. Imprisoned because of his actions for about a year, he returned to Tennessee when released. Relocating to Mississippi, he engaged in the "Choctaw speculation" and later moved with the Indians as their commissary. He lost money in that venture and left them to go to New Orleans and, in the winter of 1845–46, went to Texas. Later in California, he became a noted Whig political leader.[33]

A native of Nashville, Benjamin Davis Wilson came overland in 1841 with the Workman-Rowland wagon train from New Mexico where he had spent eight years as a trapper and trader. At first planning to book passage from the West Coast to China where he wanted to seek his fortune, Wilson was unable to make that arrangement and decided to settle in California. In 1843, he purchased the Jurupa Rancho, a frontier station of three thousand acres. He increased his landholdings by purchase and, in 1844, by marriage to Ramona Yorba, a daughter of Don Bernardo Yorba, a wealthy Mexican landowner.[34]

Orphaned at the age of eight, Wilson became a mountain man who was fearless almost to the point of foolhardiness. Barely escaping death in encounters with hostile Indians, he came even nearer losing his life when mauled by a grizzly bear that had slain one of his cows. Undaunted by that experience, he later led an expedition into the San Bernardino Mountains where the hunters located a large colony of grizzlies. He and his comrades killed twenty-two bears at a place they named Big Bear.[35]

Active in defending settlers' rights against discrimination by the Mexican government, he was a leader in their successful effort to expel the abusive garrison troops of Gen. Manuel Micheltorena from Los Angeles in 1845. Soon after the war with Mexico began, Wilson accepted a temporary commission as captain in the United States Army, raised a volunteer force of twenty-two Americans and undertook scouting duties in his district under orders from Commodore Robert F. Stockton. Later he and his men barely escaped a firing squad when they were captured by the Mexican army and held in military prison for about three months. Afterward, he returned to his ranch and, thereafter known fondly as Don Benito, maintained an influential interest in the changing scene in California. Wilson's beloved Ramona died in 1849, and four years later he was married to Margaret Short Hereford who bore him two daughters, Ruth and Annie. Ruth Hereford Wilson later became the wife of George S. Patton and mother of Gen. George S. Patton, Jr., of World War II fame.[36]

Just north of California another Tennessean was close enough to the gold fields to beat the rush from the East. Peter Hardeman Burnett, born in Nashville in 1807, was living in Oregon when the discovery news reached that country in 1848. As a youth, Burnett had followed his family to Missouri, but returned to Tennessee in 1826 to read law and work in and, for a short time, own a general store in Hardeman County, near Bolivar. While in West Tennessee, Burnett was married to Harriet Rogers, formerly of Wilson County, and in 1832, he, his wife, and their young child moved to be with others of his family in Missouri.[37]

Burnett spent his Missouri years first as the unsuccessful operator of a mercantile business, next as a practicing attorney, and finally in 1842, as an organizer of a large wagon train to take settlers to Oregon. When the wagons rolled out in the spring of 1843, Burnett was captain of the train, and his wife and child were among the approximately one thousand persons in the entourage. The crossing from Missouri was made in "the first and perhaps the largest single immigrant wagon train ever to cross the North American continent all the way to the Pacific settlements."[38]

After a successful crossing to Fort Vancouver, Burnett promoted the settlement of Oregon by sending his accounts of the journey to eastern newspapers. Arguing that it was a much more desirable place to settle than California, he demonstrated his conviction by laying out a town, but the venture was a failure. Public service soon claimed him; the legislature of the provisional government elected Burnett a justice of its high court in August 1845. Old debts plagued him, however, and on January 1, 1847, he resigned from the bench to go into private practice, which he hoped would be more lucrative.[39] When Congress created the territory of Oregon in 1848, President Polk appointed him associate justice of the United States Supreme Court for the territory.[40]

Burnett's preference for Oregon over California was quickly dispelled by the discovery of gold in the latter state. Putting aside his latest judicial robe, he again became a wagon train captain. On October 29, he and many of his Oregon neighbors, including his nephew Horace Burnett, arrived near Sutter's Fort in the Sacramento Valley. His wife and other family joined him the following spring at San Jose.[41]

Burnett began mining at Long's Bar on the Feather River, but on December 19, he forsook the mines and soon afterward opened a law office in Sacramento. He made the change in order to accept appointment as agent for John A. Sutter whose opportunities and problems associated with his gold-rich landholdings apparently had become overwhelming.[42] Brought into the public domain once again by his law practice, Burnett actively participated in the movement to achieve statehood for California.[43]

A few weeks after President Polk's address of December 5, 1848, attorney William Van Voorhies of Maury County was at sea aboard the steamship *Falcon* out of New York bound for Chagres on the first leg of a journey to San Francisco. A Democrat and neighbor who had "taken the stump" for Polk during the election campaign of 1844, Voorhies had recently accepted appointment by the president as special agent of the Post Office Department in California.[44]

After crossing the Isthmus to Panama City, Voorhies took passage on the new Pacific mail steamship *California*, which was on its maiden voyage from New York City to San Francisco. He reached his destination February 28, 1849.[45] His arrival was one of the first by anyone who had left the United States after the president's gold speech.

Voorhies carried with him instructions from President Polk drawn by Secretary of State James Buchanan "to make known . . . to the citizens inhabiting that territory his views respecting their present condition and future prospects." The president wanted them to know that the California country was then and since May 30, 1848,[46] had been a part of the territory of the United States.[47] He ordered Voorhies to welcome all in the region, including former Mexicans, to the privileges and protection of the United States Constitution and to assure them that their new government was vitally interested in them and the future of the territory. "In the not too distant future," Polk predicted, one or more "glorious states" would spring into existence in California. He promised military protection against any "civilized or savage foe." Expressing regret that Congress had failed to establish a territorial government for California in 1848, he predicted favorable congressional action early in the next session. In the meantime, he said that the region would operate under the de facto government that was in existence at the end of the war with Mexico. It was the only practical alternative to anarchy.[48]

Just how Voorhies delivered the message of reassurance is not known, but he was chosen for the assignment, Buchanan said, because he was charged with opening postal routes and post offices in the region to facilitate communications up and down the West Coast and with the eastern states as well. Thus he would have many opportunities to communicate with local leaders because the nature of his work required him to visit throughout the region. The purpose of the message was clearer, however. The president wanted the citizens of the newly-acquired territory to be patient, and he wanted to discourage the development of any kind of independence or separatist movement among them.[49]

Coincident with the accession of Whig President Zachary Taylor of Mexican War fame, Voorhies resigned his federal appointment on March 30,

1849, surely before he had completed the delivery of President Polk's message. He went directly to the gold fields, but after a single month gave up mining and established himself with the former postmaster and future alcalde of San Francisco, John W. Geary, in the firm Geary, Voorhies and Company, General Auction and Commission Merchants, Montgomery Street, San Francisco.[50]

Tennesseans already in California were far ahead of the eastern gold rushers who, in addition to selecting a plan of travel, had other decisions to make. How would each forty-niner pay his expenses for the crossing? What kind of equipment, supplies, and provisions would he need? Would he go alone or with a partner or partners? When would he go?

CHAPTER III

Going for the Gold

THE FIRST three months of 1849 were frantic times for people bound for the gold fields. With a built-in anticipation of high yields and quick riches, gold mania made sane planning for the adventure difficult. Yet there were sobering requirements to be faced, not the least of which was money enough for the undertaking.

How much money would be necessary for equipment, supplies, provisions, and transportation? There were so many variables and unknowns that no two answers would be the same. An approximate budget for a prospective miner, whether going alone or with others, was in the range of $500 to $700, no small sum in 1849.[1]

For those traveling altogether or largely by water, most of the expense was in the purchase of tickets. Their first outlay was for river or rail travel to an ocean port city where they could buy tickets to California. Those who chose the Isthmus route had to pay for the land crossing on the spot. Upon reaching Panama City, they frequently experienced long delays because there was not enough shipping along the eastern Pacific Coast to accommodate them. As a result, they often had to pay an additional premium to be permitted to board a ship for which they had been holding a ticket from two to eight weeks. Such unplanned delays caused unexpected outlays for food and lodging.[2]

Those who made the land crossing incurred comparable expenses. They invested first in horses, mules, and/or oxen and next in wagons and harness. Also, they purchased foodstuffs, arms, camp supplies, and repair parts for the harness and wagons and anything else repairable. The crossing provisions for one man could amount to 150 pounds of flour, 150 pounds of bacon, 25 pounds of coffee, 30 pounds of sugar, a small quantity of rice, 50 or 75 pounds of crackers, dried peaches, salt and pepper, and a keg of lard.[3]

Each forty-niner required certain minimum mining equipment. A typical list might include clothing, boots, a tent, cooking pans, mining tools, a rifle, a pair of pistols, 5 pounds of powder and 10 of lead, a Bowie knife, and a hatchet.[4]

There was speculation that emigrants going most or all of the way by sea could make handsome profits by taking goods to sell in California. The practice would surely increase their requirements for capital, but not so surely yield profits at the end of their journey, a newspaper editor counseled.

> Most of the emigrants from Tennessee . . . take the overland route, and consequently will not be tempted to take out any kind of goods on speculation. This is the best course. The emigrant should take his fortune . . . and when there, purchase what he may want. . . . But take no "ventures," for you will have to wear out and use yourself every thing you take.[5]

With expenses high and little chance of offsetting them by selling goods on arrival, how could young men afford the trip? Probably most of them borrowed money from family and friends to bridge the gap between what they could raise from their own resources and what the trip expenses were projected to be. Some, of course, had the necessary funds and invested them without hesitation.

A few forty-niners found financial backing from silent partners or sponsors at home who advanced expense money in exchange for a share of their earnings in the mine fields. G. C. Crenshaw of Hartsville assumed the role of sponsor when he sent a company of nine men and two wagons across to California in 1849. Agreeing to pay their travel expenses both going out and coming back, Crenshaw remained at home but sent his son James along as manager of the party. The miners agreed that they would split their earnings over and above the cost of living while in the mining country on a fifty-fifty basis with their sponsor.[6]

Some signed on with an outbound company of miners, agreeing to split their earnings in the mines during a specific period of time in exchange for having their travel expenses paid for them. Sumner Countian James C.

Shackleford contracted with a local company to pay one-half of "the neat proceeds of his labor" for two years in exchange for the firm's furnishing him "the necessary equippage and funds to defray all . . . expenses . . . to California."[7]

Many miners organized stock companies. Although each company had its own distinguishing characteristics, two approaches were commonly used. One established stock ownership for all who participated in the crossing and mining; the other provided stock ownership for both stay-at-home investors and those who went to the mines. In both instances the sale of stock was to raise enough money to send the working members to California and provide their living expenses until their work became profitable. Then all would share in the profits.

Infrequently mining companies included blacks—either slave or free—even though slavery was prohibited in California by the old Mexican law and, in 1850, by the California state constitution. That there was little or no enforcement of those prohibitions may have been due to representations made by slave owners, their slaves, and free blacks, all of whom at first seemed to consider their presence to be temporary with a return to Tennessee very much in their plans.

One of the first stock companies organized in the state was the East Tennessee Gold Mining Company with forty-seven working shareholders and a number of stay-at-home investors. Established at Knoxville early in 1849 and led by Gen. Alexander Outlaw Anderson[8], the company accepted cash or subscriptions in kind such as "horses, provisions, and other articles" from its members for stock. A surviving manuscript stock certificate issued to N. S. Crozier of Knox County on May 1, 1849, sets forth the arrangement made with stockholders who subscribed cash for their shares.

EAST TENNESSEE GOLD
MINING COMPANY

This Certificate is issued to Mr. N. S. Crozier of Knox County Tennessee for the sum of Six hundred dollars by him paid to me for stock in the aforesaid company and which will entitle him to receive thereon the full proportion of the net proceeds of said capital, counting seven hundred dollars to be equal to a miners share, and which is the same pro rata with investments made by all others. The said proceeds he will be entitled to receive at the dividend of the gold obtained by the said company in California, and which will be made there in the presence of the said company, in twelve months after the commencement of the mining operations of the said company.

This Certificate will, in addition thereto, entitle him to receive at the dividend made in California, the amount of the capital stock for which it is issued, out of the first proceeds of the gold obtained by the mining operations of said company.

In testimony whereof, I have hereunto set my hand and official signature this 1st day of May A.D. 1849—having signed Duplicates hereof.

> A. Anderson
> Conductor of the East Tennessee
> Gold Mining Company[9]

Although Anderson had reported before they left that the company's financial condition was satisfactory and sound,[10] David Anderson Deaderick, his cousin, brother-in-law, and company treasurer, later said that the company's position would have been much stronger had they sold all the stock for cash. The general, his son James M., and Deaderick had been very deliberate in planning the expedition, but in-kind subscriptions so overloaded the wagons that their early progress was materially delayed.[11]

The governance of the East Tennessee Gold Mining Company embodied elements of both military and corporate organization. Although he signed stock certificates as "conductor" of the company, General Anderson was clearly in command of his traveling stockholders to the point of dividing their number into three "squads." He assigned "teamsters" to each squad, designated a driver for the forge and another for the ambulance, and appointed his son James and David Deaderick to be his "staff."[12]

Later, just before setting out across the prairie, the company accepted five new shareholders. None was from Tennessee, but each bought in with cash that reinforced the treasury. The new members were able, also, to make professional contributions to the crossing. One was an experienced traveler among the Plains Indians, another was a pharmacist, and the remaining three were physicians.[13]

During January and February 1849, Mexican War veteran and peacetime attorney Maj. Robert Farquharson[14] organized a company at Fayetteville in which the thirty-four traveling members owned all of the stock. Operating under a constitution and bylaws that governed their activities, the men elected Farquharson to be their captain or chief officer. Each paid $250 into the company treasury in cash or supplied wagons, mules, harness, or other equipment of comparable value. When ready to depart, the organization had six wagons, one "strong carriage," forty mules, six tents, and various provisions including two thousand pounds of bacon contributed by the citizens of Fayetteville.[15]

Staff officers for the company included R. E. Gilliland, a law student who apparently functioned as the captain's deputy. R. McKinney, druggist, was first lieutenant; S. Edmondson was second lieutenant; W. A. Russell, physician, was the surgeon; and James Russell, merchant, was treasurer. The commissary was J. A. Zively whose skills were listed as "cabinet maker, painter, daguerrean and chemist"; A. M. Beattie was wagonmaster.[16]

When the emigrants were ready to set out for California, the *Lincoln Journal* noted that their departure would have no small impact on Fayetteville. "The company is composed principally of young men who have been raised in town or resided there for a long time," the editor wrote, "and their absence will make a vacuum in society that will require time to fill."[17] Farquharson's quick success in organizing local forty-niners inspired imitation, and before he could get his men out of the state, Captain G. V. Hebb, a fellow Mexican War volunteer, was signing up members for another company in Lincoln County.[18]

Responding to President Polk's announcement of gold in California, eight men from his home county of Maury banded together in February 1849 to go to the mines. They organized neither partnership nor stock company, but agreed informally to share travel expenses. In a memoir written many years later, one of the group, James C. Cooper of Mt. Pleasant, explained their arrangements:

> Each member was required before starting on this trip to own a saddle horse and to deposit into the expense fund one hundred dollars to pay for cooking utensils and equippage. Thomas Ridley, who drove a four-horse team belonging to the company, was allowed fifty dollars for his services. Some of the party were fortunate in having their outfits presented to them by philanthropic friends and were all in due time well equipped and ready to begin our long journey.[19]

In addition to Ridley and Cooper, the Maury team included Thomas Dunham, William Lawhorn, James Starkey, Thomas McMillan, Joseph

Cooper, and "Parson" William G. Canders. With a wagon carrying supplies and equipment, the men departed from Mt. Pleasant on horseback to go to Fort Smith by way of Memphis.[20]

A West Tennessee-North Mississippi contingent for the gold fields materialized at Memphis in 1849 in the gathering of fourteen Tennesseans and eleven Mississippians, all prepared to leave about March 15 for Fort Smith. Inasmuch as La Grange, Tennessee, was the home of nine of the men, probably the core of the company was organized there with invitations to others to join forces. Certainly the number of La Grange forty-niners gave them a formidable voice in all matters affecting the venture.[21]

There was no simpler way to organize a company than that employed in March, 1849, by five Carter County gold rushers. Styling themselves the Tennessee Company, the Carter Countians invested equal funds and agreed to an equal split of the profits to be made twelve months after their arrival at the mines. They planned an overland crossing after final outfitting at Independence. Samuel Murray Stover kept a diary of their travels, and the other four men were William C. Taylor, John E. Brown, Charles Mason, and J. E. T. Harris.[22]

The California-bound in Trenton, Gibson County, could join a small company there by contributing $250 in cash and supplying a good mule valued at about $80. When seven men had paid their cash to Dr. Lewis Levy, treasurer, the company welcomed a party of five that had formed for the same purpose at nearby Yorkville. The twelve left Trenton for St. Louis on April 18, 1849, their sixteen mules pulling four covered wagons loaded with clothing and camp equipment.[23] Anderson Davis, "the patriarch of the expedition" and veteran of camp life in the Florida Seminole wars, led the joint company. At St. Louis, the Gibson Countians enrolled five additional members increasing their strength to seventeen. They set out for California via St. Joseph.[24]

Maj. George H. Wyatt of Memphis rallied a company of thirteen to leave for the gold fields in August 1849. Few details of that organization have survived, but it is known that its members crossed by way of the Isthmus. Those who made the journey were Maj. Wyatt, his son, Dr. J. N. Bybee, William C. McLemore, D. H. Keeling, Fred P. Goll, a certain Dr. Shelton, a man named Reid, three whose names are unknown, and two unidentified slave blacks.[25]

Not all crossing parties were organized or even assembled prior to departure for California. Some seem to have developed almost by happenstance as gold rushers joined forces two or three at a time. These ad hoc parties had informal agreements about sharing the labor and expense of crossing to the gold fields, but rarely anything about sharing profits from mining.

Consider the experiences of Rebecca Foster Reeve and her brothers Clayton and Robert Reeve of Pactolus, Tennessee. Planning to go by water to Independence, the three Reeves acquired a flatboat, which on March 12, 1849, Robert and Rebecca put into the Tennessee River just above Knoxville. Clayton was to finish liquidating his iron operations and join brother and sister below Knoxville within a week or ten days.[26]

After his last frantic days at the rolling mill and cupola, Clayton and Henry Bridleman of Sullivan County set out in a horse-drawn wagon to overtake the flatboat. Upon reaching Knoxville where Robert and Rebecca were waiting, they met three young men from Greene County, also California-bound. When Clayton invited them to buy a flatboat, put their horses and wagon aboard, and "lash their boat to ours and go in company," they accepted. Another Sullivan Countian P. White signed on at the same time, and an unidentified Presbyterian minister, his wife, and family came aboard, also.

The only known agreements governing the party on the two lashed-together flatboats were oral and impromptu, having to do with duty assignments for the working crew of eight men. "We now divide our time four serving from sun rise to sun rise, that is twenty-four hours duty. When [there are] no winde or shoals [we] have but little to do, but at other times, have to work verry harde to keep the boats from striking the banks; nearly all covered with large leaning trees," Clayton Reeve wrote.[27]

The Reeve entourage was one of the first Tennessee gold-seeking parties to include women. Their presence meant that they and their families planned to settle in California whereas members of the many all-male mining companies usually expected to return home within a year or two.

An effort at Nashville to gather a company of family immigrants to California in the spring of 1849 apparently failed, probably because the promoter John L. Brown based his appeal only on land speculation. Seeking to enroll the A. R. Wynne family of Castalian Springs in the venture, Brown professed March 7 to be "succeeding finely with the project for the emigration of fifty or more families to California." He assured Wynne that "a number of first-rate families will go from Nashville" and entreated him to recruit families of his neighbors for the settlement party.

Focusing on the prospects of skyrocketing land values, Brown urged Wynne to sell out his Tennessee holdings, principally land, and to relocate and reinvest in California. Time was of the essence because Brown believed it imperative to arrive in California during 1849 and establish a settlement before the area should be engulfed by people with like intent. He explained:

> By going now we can select the best portion of the country. . . .
> Our land will enhance immensely in value. Even if we have to
> make sacrifices in disposing of property here, we will much more
> than make it up in three months after our arrival in that country.[28]

The Wynne family did not join the projected settlement nor, apparently, did others in sufficient number to make the emigration possible. The prospect of land ownership in California in 1849 did not attract as powerfully as the lure of gold.[29]

Investors organized the Nashville and California Mining Company, Dr. I. H. Harris, superintendent, during January and February 1850. Featuring substantial ownership by Nashville stay-at-home shareholders, the company elected its officers from their number. N. Hobson was president; W. F. Bang, vice president; George W. Morton, secretary; and Robert Lusk, treasurer. In the traveling company, in addition to Superintendent Harris, were A. A. Adams, engineer; Randall M. Ewing and Benjamin B. and Hardy Brett of Wilson County; and seven slave blacks: Ned, Thornton, Solomon, Moses, Henry, Elias, and Hector.[30] No records of the actual stock subscription or the total capitalization have been discovered.

During the early months of 1850, some Sumner County men organized a stock company at Gallatin under the name of "Wilson, Love and Co. for the purpose of mining in California and in such other pursuits" as its field managers Frank B. Wilson and George Love "shall agree upon." Shares of stock were priced at $500 each with a total cash capitalization of $9,000 authorized and paid in by twelve subscribers, nine of whom were stay-at-home investors. Although records identify only one officer, the secretary-treasurer William M. Blackmore, it is reasonable to judge that the president of the company was the prominent midstate attorney Josephus Conn Guild. He was its largest shareholder, and at that time his presence in any organization usually assured him of a leadership position. The cash subscribers were Guild, four shares, $2,000; J. A. Blackmore,

William M. Blackmore, and Joseph M. Robb, each investing $1,000 for two shares; James Alexander, R. D. King, John W. Moss, William Moore, B. M. Jenkins, Simon Elliott, William Tyree, and the partnership of C. H. Wallace and William Moore each holding one share of $500. Only three of the cash investors, Elliott, Tyree, and Wallace went to the gold mines, and each of them received an additional share valued at $500 for being members of the working party. As "head and managers" of the miners, Wilson and Love each received two shares of stock. Neither made a cash subscription. Others who owned single work shares were Jacob A. Tyree, William Patterson, William Wright, James D. Cartwright, William Love, Richard Charlton, G. D. Blackmore, James S. Allen, and Lycurgus Charlton.[31]

The stay-at-home shareholders agreed to make available to Wilson and Love the entire cash capital of $9,000 upon their departure for California. The money was to be used first to pay travel expenses. Should any surplus remain, Wilson and Love were authorized to use it for the purchase of provisions, tools, or other supplies needed by the firm "and in case of sickness the party afflicted shall be sustained and supported in like manner."[32]

Confident and enthusiastic about their prospects, all members of the mining party, including Wilson and Love, agreed to work in California for the firm until November 1, 1852. Each accepted a contract provision that he would forfeit all interest in the company and "pay by way of agreed damages one thousand dollars" into the company treasury should he fail to work in good faith or should he "abandon or quit the firm and cease to labor for it."[33]

When the Wilson, Love and Company miners passed through Nashville on their way to New Orleans and an Isthmus crossing, four other Sumner men were traveling with them. Though not original members of the company, they had probably linked up for their own and the company's added safety.[34]

In 1850, forty-two men from Clarksville and Nashville formed the Nashville and Clarksville Havilah Mining and Trading Company.[35] Twenty-three of the company were "Home Officers and Stockholders," and nineteen were the "Officers and Operatives," active members of the expedition. The entire group subscribed seventy shares of stock valued at $500 each for a total capital of $35,000. Available records do not separate cash from in-kind subscriptions, but it is known that two "Operatives" put in "Negro fellows as cash stock." J. M. McClelland subscribed the services of the "Negro man John," and Dr. E. M. Patterson the services of the "Negro man Walker."[36]

However the stock was paid in, forty-five shares were owned by the men going to California and twenty-five by the stay-at-home investors. A constitution bound the company members to remain together for eighteen months or, failing to do so, forfeit their respective interests.[37]

The "Home Officers" were Dyer Pearl, president; G. H. Warfield representing G. H. Warfield & Co., vice president; William James, treasurer; and John Ramage, secretary. Each owned a single share. "Home Stockholders" of two shares each were E. P. McGinty and E. R. W. Thomas & Brother. Each of the remaining home investors owned a single share.[38]

Committed to an overland crossing, the Havilah "Operatives" were headed by a corps of officer-shareholders. T. A. Thomas was general superintendent and owned two shares; William M. Mathews, first assistant, four shares; M. B. Moorman, second assistant, three shares; Samuel M. Kingston, expedition treasurer, four shares; Oliver Hart, engineer, two shares; and Dr. P. H. Thurston, "physician to the mines," three shares.[39]

Planning to extract gold from quartz, the Havilah Company invested in a steam engine to furnish power for a stamping mill to crush the ore and in other equipment heavier than that usually improvised for washing gold particles from soil or gravel deposits. Before leaving for the West, Havilah also acquired "a select assortment of drugs" and sent it and the heavy equipment by sea accompanied by a supercargo.[40]

On April 20 as the company approached a state of readiness for its departure from Nashville, First Assistant Superintendent Mathews went ahead to St. Louis to make advance arrangements for its arrival. Five days later Havilah announced that its gold seekers would set out from Nashville on April 27 on the steamboat *Sligo No. 2*.[41]

Smaller companies sprang up across the state, but records of their organization are scarce to nonexistent. Editorially skeptical about the gold discovery for the first fifteen months after its validation, Nashville newspaper editor A. M. Rosborough organized the Tennessee Mining Company during January and February of 1850 and became its superintendent. When introduced to the prospect of quartz mining in which machinery pulverized the ore to break out the gold, Rosborough changed from doubter to promoter.

The former editor had five associates in the mining company: J. Litton Bostick, treasurer; Dr. W. H. Farmer; James Bostick; E. Taylor; and E. W. Taylor. "A Negro boy," probably E. W.'s slave, would accompany them.[42]

The six shareholders were obligated to work as "a joint stock company, eighteen months from the time of their departure."[43]

During March, 1850, two Sumner County men organized a joint stock company for "acquiring gold or money for the term of two years in California." The brief agreement between Jesse D. Bond and John J. Hibbett, the only shareholders, specified that each would hire three "hands" to work in the gold fields and that their "forces" would be united. Bond agreed to hire himself, his son Thomas Bond, and J. L. McGowen. Remaining at home, John J. Hibbett agreed to furnish his three "hands" in the persons of his son James L. Hibbett, John W. Gilmore, and a slave black known as King.

Naming Jesse D. Bond "foreman or manager of the company," the agreement called for the management of the affairs of the company to pass into the hands of James L. Hibbett in the event of the death or disability of the foreman. It was the agreed duty of the foreman "to use his greatest industry and endeavors to accomplish the object" of the association.

There was no reference to a cash investment by either principal nor was there any mention of a common expense fund. It was agreed, nonetheless, that after two years "shall have expired and after having deducted all expenses of the enterprise," the resultant proceeds of the expedition would be divided equally between the two organizers.[44]

On the date of the Bond and Hibbett agreement, Jesse D. Bond, Thomas Bond, and James L. Hibbett left Nashville in John B. Moore's company, recruited principally in the Hartsville area. Twenty-two other men were in the group listed by the Nashville *Daily American* on April 20, 1850. It is presumed that McGowen, Gilmore, and King were with the party, but their names were not included in the published list.[45]

Early in 1850, John T. O'Brien, captain of a company of Tennessee volunteers in the Mexican War, organized a group of six at Knoxville. O'Brien, his brother James, Jesse S. Wall, David Ross, James Henry, and Dr. William Hunt were dedicated to retrieving gold from "quartz rocks." They planned to work the rock with mortars and pestles and a "machine" not further described. James Henry did not go with the others to California and was probably interested only as an investor.[46]

Although articles of agreement were signed by all parties and left in the care of publisher William Gannaway Brownlow, the document itself has not survived.[47] Brownlow's interest was limited to the family dimensions of the company; the O'Briens were his wife's brothers, and Dr. Hunt was married to Mrs. Brownlow's sister. Somewhat tempted to join the growing East Tennessee emigration, the acid-tongued editor decided to remain behind to keep the *Whig* alive and to deny his enemies the pleasure of his absence. Hunt went ahead, and the other four miners soon set out for California by way of Charleston, South Carolina, and the Isthmus crossing. They purchased mortars in Charleston and seemed to have had all equipment ready for departure for Chagres on April 29, 1850.[48]

The firm of Harris, Ellis, Day, and Holloway was the core of a company of seventeen Sumner Countians who made the overland crossing from Independence in 1850. James O. Harris, Tyree Harris, William Ellis, Henry B. Day, and James Holloway were the members of the firm and organizers of the expedition.[49]

Led by Col. David Cook, investors and miners raised $12,000 for a stock company at Lebanon in the spring of 1850. Shares were sold for $500 each. Planning to recover gold by the quartz mining process, the company sent Colonel Cook to Cincinnati to purchase the "machinery necessary to carry on the business." The only two shareholders mentioned in the newspaper account of the venture were Colonel Cook and Col. William B. Stokes.[50]

Among the many for whom California was an elusive dream because of the cost of crossing was a former circuit court clerk of Sumner County, George F. Crocket. After leaving public office in 1848, Crocket moved to Memphis where he said he soon lost everything he had. Going to California seemed to be the best prospect open to him as he explained in this request for assistance to William Bowen Campbell:

> I have been and am still trying to raise the means to take me to California, that land of promise, but am afraid I will not succeed. My only hope is to get some appointment near this El Dorado. Now do you think, Colonel, you could procure me through the government an appointment to California no matter what? I will do anything, *I can*.[51]

Crocket was only one of many who dreamed the golden dream yet remained at home. J. B. R. Lyon, editor, manager, and part owner of the Greeneville *Spy*, expressed a desire to sell his interest in the newspaper so that he could go for the gold. A fellow Greenevillian George W. Foute, a physician who was holding the office of Greene County court clerk, was

reported to be "determined to go to the golden region." Congressman Andrew Johnson was skeptical about the westering intentions of his Greene
County neighbors. He expressed the opinion that, should they go, Foute
would be making "a bad move," and Lyon could be one of those who "will
take off more than they bring back."[52]

Joining a company, large or small, seemed to be the best way for Tennesseans to approach the mines, and thousands followed that course. Organizing the companies was comparatively easy and was usually done at
home with people who knew each other. Legal consultation was available
and laws were followed. Friends were at hand, free advice flowed like wine
at a wedding feast, and little or no physical exertion was required.

Crossing to California was entirely different. The gold seekers were no
longer at home, and they knew only the members of their own company in
an environment where often there was no code of law. Travel was debilitating, whether for the relatively passive passenger on a ship or for the extremely active overlander. Often they had to resolve questions of command
that might involve a slow-moving train on the prairie or a becalmed sailing
ship on the seas. And there were the everlasting questions of personal relations, from civil arguments to brawling fights that more than once ended
in death.

Although few who chose to go could envision the experiences they
would have along the way, it was time to move out. And that is precisely
what they did.

CHAPTER IV

Trailing Southern Routes

A S THE first Volunteer State forty-niners began their long journeys to the gold fields in the spring of 1849, many chose the southern routes that permitted passage at any time of the year. A Memphis company of five men led by F. Pinckard was one of the few that took the Isthmus route in 1849, leaving New Orleans April 27, reaching Chagres May 27, Cruces June 4, and Panama City June 8. In a letter written home from the latter port, Pinckard extolled the virtues of his passage. He even enjoyed a slow crossing by sail to Chagres and found the east coast port much more agreeable than he had anticipated. He reported little sickness there at the moment, and although it was the rainy season, the streets were free of mud. His was very different from most reports that typically described it as "the abode of pestilence and fevers, surrounded by a swamp, and overhung by a miasmatic cloud of noxious vapors."[1]

Hobbled by "a considerable quantity of freight," Pinckard and his four associates required five canoes to transport them up the river to Cruces. While waiting there for enough saddle mules to return from the west coast to take them to Panama City, they arranged to have their freight sent ahead to the port. Although others had not found it so pleasant, Pinckard said he had "rarely enjoyed a trip more than that from Chagres to Cruces."[2]

The trek over the mountains to Panama City was not so enjoyable. Riding a mule over a mountainous trail that was "rocky beyond any possible conception of rocky roads" was a challenge to the uninitiated. "It is a villainous road," he wrote, and for the first three or four miles the novice is in constant dread of broken bones, but if he will ride with a loose rein, ready to check in case of a stumble—which rarely occurs—and suffer his beast to choose his own steps, unhurried and ungoverned, he will soon gain confidence, and look around and above instead of before and beneath him.[3]

While waiting for a ship to San Francisco, they had time to examine the old Spanish-built Panama City. It was different from most cities in the United States, and he described it:

This wall which surrounds the city proper is about one mile in circumference; the houses compactly built, frequently a whole square united by a single outer wall, but divided by interior divisions into 40 or 50 dwellings. The streets are narrow, but remarkable well paved in every quarter, are concave, and well drained and cleanly. About half the houses are three stories high, and nearly all of the balance two stories. There is great similarity in the appearance and quality of the houses—no splendid dwellings and no miserable hovels, and this may be remarked of the inhabitants, also, there appears to be no extremes in grades, and, altogether, a republican, comfortable sort of people.[4]

Further information about Pinckard and his unnamed companions is lacking. It is presumed that they reached San Francisco and proceeded to the mine fields.

Pinckard's party seemed to escape disease in the tropics, but not all were so fortunate. A young Nashvillian, Charles W. Hart, died in Panama City on June 16, 1849, of cholera contracted while crossing the Isthmus.[5]

Maj. George H. Wyatt chose the same route for his Memphis company of thirteen. Eleven left from Memphis for New Orleans by riverboat on August 19, and the other two joined the party there. Characterized by the Memphis *Daily Eagle* as "active, intelligent and enterprising," the men departed across the Gulf for Chagres on August 26. After taking the steamship *Oregon* from Panama City to San Francisco, Wyatt reported from California on November 1, 1849, that he, his son, and two black slaves were at work in the mines.[6]

Former Tennessee Congressman Isaac Thomas, born in Sevierville in 1784, journeyed to California in 1849 from his adopted state of Louisiana where he had become wealthy from ventures in sugarcane, sawmills, and steamboats. It is thought that he followed the Isthmus route. He returned to his fields of sugarcane sometime before his death there in 1859.[7]

Colonel of the Third Tennessee Regiment during the Mexican War, Benjamin F. Cheatham was superintendent of a company of fourteen from Nashville who chose the Isthmus route in mid-1849. Cheatham and six of the group left Nashville for Memphis by riverboat on August 21, 1849. Three others left by stage the next day to join them at Memphis from whence the party, then ten in number, steamed down to New Orleans to embark for Chagres. Four of their fellow travelers had left two or three weeks earlier to make arrangements at Panama City to expedite the group's Pacific passage to San Francisco.[8]

Cheatham's party arrived in California in the late autumn of 1849, although details of the crossing are lacking. Subsequent letters he wrote from the gold country do not mention their journey, but focus on the prospects for gold and other gainful opportunities.[9]

Maj. Ben McCulloch, a native Rutherford Countian who had left Tennessee to become a Texas Ranger, set out from Memphis for California in the early part of August 1849. Traveling to the gold fields with him were D. C. Gowan, A. F. Martin, and W. W. Hanks.[10] Because of the late summer departure, the party probably followed the Isthmus route, although details are unavailable.

Dr. John Jefferson Franklin of Sumner County must have gone to California—and returned—via the Isthmus because he had visited the gold fields and was again in Nashville by October 1, 1849. He was so enthusiastic about opportunities in the mines that he lost no time in preparing his family and slaves to go back with him. The precise size of his party is not known, but his commitment to the West was total. When he reached California the second time, he remained there until his death in 1875 at Sonora.[11]

The all-sea trip from New Orleans or New York to California by way of Cape Horn attracted few Tennesseans in 1849. One exception was Charles H. Randall, a native of Rhode Island who had moved to Tennessee in 1846. He completed the crossing by September 9, 1849. No other details of his travels have been discovered.[12] Another was George W. Seay of the Havilah Mining Company. He traveled that route in 1850 with equipment and supplies shipped by his company.[13]

Nashvillian Thomas B. Eastland chose the Port Lavaca-Mazatlán route for himself, his son Joseph G. Eastland, his slave Dow, and a hired driver John Morehead, and on April 21, they set out from his home city by riverboat. Eight days later they arrived at New Orleans, and after a two-week delay they departed by steamboat on May 11 for Port Lavaca, Texas, where they planned to "fit out" for the long journey. At New Orleans the "useful and obliging" George Douglass of Gallatin, a former navy mid-shipman joined them.[14]

Seeking to purchase mules at Lavaca, but finding none for sale, East-land's party bought horses to take them over the 160 miles to San Antonio. Seventeen miles short of the city, they purchased six mules but found it necessary to stop for nine days to break them "for the saddle and harness." On May 31, they pitched camp just outside San Antonio.[15]

Before leaving Nashville, Eastland had made plans for his small cadre to join a party of emigrants leaving San Antonio[16] about June 1 under the leadership of Col. John Coffee "Jack" Hays, a Texas Ranger of note and a former Tennessean.[17] He found that Hays, who recently had been appointed Indian subagent to the Gila tribes, and the emigrants were following a detachment of army troops commanded by Maj. Jefferson Van Horn. Although the "upper" or northern route via Fredericksburg had been recommended by Hays who was familiar with it, Van Horn received orders at the last minute to evaluate the southern route by following it to El Paso. By June 10, Hays's contingent, including several families and the East-lands, was following about one mile behind the troops.[18] When they were camped in closer proximity, the emigrants were "treated with the music of the army's fine band every evening."[19]

Exploring the route ahead, making changes in course to avoid natural hazards, and working at times on the road to make it passable for the wag-ons slowed the progress of the troops and the emigrant train. Eastland spoke for many of the forty-niners when he wrote on June 17:

> I trust we shall have no more stopping, thus far we have made but little headway, and lost a great deal of time. California is yet afar off and many a weary, long day will pass ere we reach it, but the word is *Onward*, and our band is composed of men who will not turn their backs.[20]

Encamped on the banks of Devils River June 28 to July 1, the forty-niners hunted, fished, and harvested a few wild grapes to supplement their provisions. The natural beauty of the area inspired Eastland.

The scenery at this point is beautiful, immense cliffs of rock on all sides, seeming as if they had been rent asunder by some great convulsion, leaving between, small valleys overhung by immense precipices, some of which look like invulnerable fortresses, others, like regular walls built by the hands of men.[21]

The entire train stopped at Cherry Springs on July 4 to celebrate the anniversary of American independence. Beginning with a salute of guns fired at sunrise, the celebration continued throughout the day with much eating and the drinking of many toasts. The liquor "was potent enough to produce all sorts of toasts and songs, a fight or two between some outsiders, and the stealing of a horse at night." There were few other troublesome incidents, and "the day passed off pleasantly."[22]

Traveling slowly westward, the army-led train crossed the Pecos River on August 7. When he noted the crossing in his male-oriented journal, Eastland corrected an oversight:

I forgot to mention in the proper place that a woman of our party, gave birth to a fine boy on the 5th at our camp on Live Oak Creek. I suggest Hard Times as a good name for the little stranger. Both are doing well.[23]

The route at times defied the engineers' ingenuity and frequently was so difficult of passage that the train was delayed for several days. Such unplanned stops confirmed Eastland's evaluation of the way chosen as "a *failure*." He regarded the engineers as inept and saw their ineptitude as "certain evidence that *gross ignorance*, or *willful design* has governed those who induced the Government to make a road [of] this route."[24]

The engineers were continually on the lookout for grass and fresh water, but seemed to find them where they were least expected and to find nothing where they expected either or both. But they frequently found rattlesnakes, and Eastland periodically noted that he had killed an especially large one.[25] The recurring presence of reptiles along the trail reminded him of the naturalist Gerard Troost, a professor at the University of Nashville. He observed, "If Dr. Troost had given me an order for specimens of rattlesnakes, tarantulas, centipedes, scorpions, and '*sich like varments*, I could have filled it *completely* — we sometimes had them for bedfellows."[26]

As they approached El Paso, they met Mexican peddlers with carts loaded with "grapes, peaches, apples, onions, etc.," their first opportunity in three months for all to eat fresh fruits and vegetables. Typical of the experience of overland travelers, they had been "living on meats altogether."[27]

The emigrants reached El Paso on September 10, 1849, after "ninety-seven days of irksome delays and travel since leaving San Antonio." Eastland abandoned his plan of continuing with the train via the Gila River and San Diego because he was not interested in *another experimental* journey." Instead he chose to go into Mexico and proceed by way of Chihuahua and Durango to the port of Mazatlán. It was a case of the "farthest way round is the nearest way through," and he believed it would save both time and

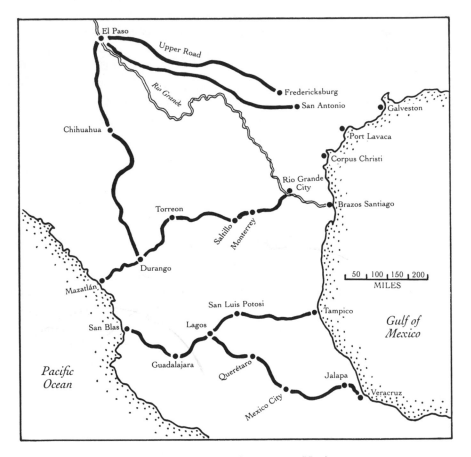

MAP 2. Forty-Niners across Mexico

money. His choice would also avoid possible confrontations with warriors of the Apache nation, then in arms against Americans, and would follow a proven road all the way.[28]

Eastland prepared quickly for the journey to Mazatlán. He sold his wagon and dray animals at El Paso, reserving only enough for his party of four to ride, and arranged for their baggage to be sent ahead by a "large train of merchant wagons." Eastland was delighted to be depending on his own judgment, "being determined not to be a *follower* any longer."[29]

On September 12, the Eastland four left Colonel Hays after promising to meet him in San Francisco and took the Chihuahua Road and soon fell in with the wagon train that bore their baggage. After a relatively quick and easy passage of 237 miles, they reached Chihuahua on September 23, but a "violent attack of the fever" confined Eastland to his room for several days.[30]

After he recovered, Eastland arranged for his small party to travel with a wagon train leaving for Durango on October 7. Although on one occasion thieves stole a few head of cattle from the train and on another made an unsuccessful attempt, the journey was otherwise uneventful. They arrived at Durango on November 2.[31] The city of approximately twenty-five thousand was the largest they had seen since leaving New Orleans.

Eager to move on, the forty-niners set out for Mazatlán on November 6. Their route led across the Sierra Madre and the Sierra de Costa, the most difficult passage that they had experienced. In places the road was too narrow "to admit of two animals passing," and it often followed along the bottom of deep channels worn by traffic and erosion. At times it crossed steep ridges and deep canyons. "Sometimes the ascent is nearly perpendicular for many hundred feet, so is the descent, and over huge piles of rocks seemingly impassable. Immense gulfs frequently bound the passway, and certain death would be the fate of the traveler if his animal should make a misstep," he noted.[32]

They arrived at Mazatlán on November 15 and immediately bought steamship tickets to San Francisco. Eight days later they boarded the already crowded steamer *Oregon*, and on December 1, they docked at San Francisco. The "long and fatiguing journey" was over; it had required 225 days from Nashville.[33]

While Eastland was on the way to Mazatlán, Jack Hays took a more direct, if slower, course to California. Determined first to treat with the Gila in his capacity of United States Indian subagent to them, he announced that he would lead the train over a new route through Apache country. He expected to talk with representatives of at least one of the several Apache tribes in a meeting clandestinely arranged by himself and John Gordon, a young white man adopted by the Indians who had become "their principal war leader."[34]

On the morning of September 24, Hays rode out of camp at the head of a caravan of about 150 emigrants and turned up the Rio Grande, leaving their military escort behind. Stopping briefly at Doña Ana, they went farther up the river, forded it at a crossing called San Diego, and turned west toward the Pichacho de los Mimbres.[35]

Visited by John Gordon of the Apache, Hays agreed to a meeting with representatives of the tribe at the base of Ben Moore's Peak. But he was not destined to treat with them. On the designated day as Hays and his caravan drew near the mountain, they heard repeated gunfire a short distance away. By chance a detachment of Mexican cavalry had intercepted the Apache party coming to meet with him and had killed nine of them. The Indians perceived the meeting and the ambush as part and parcel of a scheme to annihilate them, and Hays had to abandon his plan for negotiations.[36]

From camp at Ojo de la Vaca, Hays set a course due west through the Chiricahua Mountains, a stronghold of another tribe of the Apache. The course was a new one; Cooke and others had avoided it because they believed it had no water. Fortunately for members of this train, they found enough grass and plenty of water high in the snow-capped mountains.[37]

After a tortuous descent, the emigrants left the Chiricahuas behind, crossed a wide plain to the San Pedro River, and three days later reached Tucson. Planning to try again to meet Apache representatives, Hays suggested the emigrants could proceed at their own pace along Cooke's Wagon Road to the Colorado. Eight of the group and two white servants remained with Hays, and the others went ahead.[38]

While waiting six weeks in Tucson for the recovery of an ill member of his party, Hays had plenty of time to evaluate prospects for treaty making with the Indians. Taking into consideration the end of the Mexican War, the continuing Mexican practice of bounty payments to those who brought in Indian scalps, the lack of a federal policy for dealing with the western Indians, the absence of United States troops in the area, and the gold rush migration to California, he decided that prospects for timely success in dealing with the various tribes were poor indeed. When he considered additionally that there was no "head chief" of the Apache nation and that periodic indiscriminate killing of their people by whites assured their ongoing hostility, Hays declared his assignment impossible. He drafted a letter of resignation to mail as soon as he reached San Diego.[39]

The former Tennessean and his small company made their way from Tucson to the villages of the Maricopa and Pima and turned down the Gila River 180 miles to its junction with the Colorado. Hays moved his company at the brisk rate of about thirty miles each day. Aided by Yuma who were selling dried pumpkins and beans at the mouth of the Gila, the company crossed the Colorado on December 5, 1849.[40]

Hays led his people down the Colorado for about twelve miles and then turned due west onto a desert plain, eighty miles wide. Fifty miles into the desert they replenished provisions at Camp Salvation, maintained by a government commissary to assist emigrants. It was then ninety-six grueling miles to Warner's Ranch,[41] but they reached that haven for travelers on December 23. After a brief pause, they pushed on to San Diego, arriving just before the end of the year. There on January 3, 1850, Hays posted his letter of resignation as Indian subagent on the Gila to Secretary of the Interior Thomas Ewing.[42]

Impatient to continue to San Francisco, Hays and his party took passage from San Diego on the *Colonel Fremont*, a small brig that accommodated about fifty passengers. Not long after they had put out to sea, a violent storm that lasted four days blew the brig off course, and waves fifty feet high almost swamped it. Nevertheless, on January 25, 1850, Jack Hays stood on deck to watch the small vessel pass through the Golden Gate into San Francisco Bay.[43] His crossing from San Antonio, calculated from the day he left until the day he arrived at San Francisco, spanned 229 days.

During the first part of September 1849, as Hays and Eastland neared the end of their travels together, they had met John Heckendorn and some of the twelve members of his Clarksville Mining Company near El Paso. The Clarksville company, which had left Montgomery County sometime in April, went by river to New Orleans, crossed the Gulf to Texas, and set out for El Paso by the route that took them through San Antonio and Fredericksburg. The principal correspondents and leaders of the company were John Heckendorn and F. A. Piercy.[44]

Moving in a sixty-two-man train that included other separate companies of six and eight men from Tennessee but not further identified, and thirty-six men from New York, the Clarksville Mining Company passed through Fredericksburg on May 21. The landscape offered little but arid mountains and desert wastes.[45]

Death claimed two brothers of the party before the train reached El Paso. Elbridge Bradshaw drowned in the Rio Pecos while bathing, and Joshua Bradshaw died while recuperating from a serious illness at Socorro in the care of "an American family."[46]

Near Pecos Pass, Thurston, Ferguson, and Newton of the Clarksville company and five men from New York became lost while searching for water. They were able to survive only after a timely rescue by a volunteer search party from the train. Heckendorn wrote of their desperate condition: "Having thrown away their arms and ammunition and set their horses free, [they] with their tongues swollen, and perfectly blind, had laid down on the ground to die."[47]

"Much fatigued and worn down by the long marches, hot sun, large plains, and scarcity of water," the Clarksville company reached a village fifteen miles below El Paso on July 16, 1849. The train rested there for several days during which time Heckendorn, Piercy, Glenn, and Hereford decided to postpone the remainder of their trip to California until spring. They sold their interest in the company's mules and equipment to six of their fellow travelers and rented a house in El Paso for the winter.[48]

The rest of the Clarksville Mining Company set out for San Diego by way of Corralitos on July 26. They were to pick up Cooke's Wagon Road from the lower Gila River. One of their number, Sidney Herring, died of congestive fever when they were about fifty miles south of El Paso.[49]

During the fall and winter months, Heckendorn and his associates worked to replenish their exhausted funds. With Hereford in charge, they put up a blacksmith shop at El Paso where they also repaired watches and guns. Dick Glenn branched out to cutting and sawing timber on Organ Mountain about sixty miles from the shop. Piercy handled the cooking duties for the four and oversaw the operation of their large still, boiler, and fixtures for making brandy from local grapes.[50]

Although untrained in medicine, Heckendorn brazenly represented himself as a physician. He soon enjoyed a larger practice than the town's "one regular bred" doctor. Bragging that death had not claimed a single patient of his, he admitted it was a "great wonder, for I have dosed some of those greasers awfully." When Heckendorn ministered to a young man thought to be dying of cholera morbus, the patient recovered quickly, and the "doctor" suddenly had a reputation that attracted a lucrative practice.[51]

After wintering in and near El Paso, Heckendorn, Piercy, Glenn, and Hereford made their way across northern Mexico to Mazatlán and from there arrived at San Diego on May 15. Within forty-eight hours they were aboard a steamship bound for San Francisco. From a chance meeting with Dr. Harris of Nashville, they learned that it was reported in Clarksville that Indians had killed the entire company. The truth was that they had experienced no casualties inflicted by Indians. Of three deaths suffered, two had been from natural causes and one by accident.[52]

The four Clarksville Mining Company men reached San Francisco on May 20. Heckendorn observed, "I am in luck, and if I do not get some of the lumps [of gold] it will not be from want to exertion in getting to the mines."[53]

The six Clarksville men who had continued on their journey when Heckendorn and his colleagues stopped for the winter called a halt at Corralitos and went to work in silver and copper mines. It is believed that they arrived in California in the spring, but details of their further travels are missing.[54]

A woman born in Lawrence County, Tennessee, traveled overland with her husband and two young children from Lamar County, Texas, directly to California in 1849. About ten years before, Louisiana Erwin had come to Texas from Tennessee with her parents, the Sam Erwins of Lawrence County. In 1843, she had become the bride of John Theophil Strentzel, a young expatriate medical doctor from Poland. Six years later, on March 22, 1849, the family set out in a train of wagons for the gold fields.[55]

The Strentzels faced the customary challenges of trail life. They encountered the same natural obstacles that others faced: mountains, deserts, and the lack of water for people and animals. The strain on the latter was especially severe. "A great many animals died and a great many so broke down that they were fit for nothing anymore," Louisiana wrote.[56] When they reached El Paso, the train dispersed. After resting twelve days, the Strentzels left with another company and traveled up the Rio Grande about eighty miles to connect with Cooke's "large, plain wagon road." They found good water and grass in adequate supply for the next 220 miles.[57]

Navigating a sixteen-mile-long mountain pass over roads that challenged the drivers' skill and patience was a different story. On one six-mile stretch, "we had to back our wagons seventy times," Louisiana recorded, but they came through without breaking wheels or axles. One hundred miles west of the pass they were able to cross "a very bad mountain" only by doubling their teams. On the west side of the mountain at the isolated village of Santa Cruz, they purchased fruits, green corn, onions, and flour.

They pushed ahead 108 miles to Tucson and another 75 miles to the Pima Villages. Louisiana recognized that they were about to cross a desert that would challenge the company to its utmost.[58]

Sixty-five miles beyond the villages, the Strentzels and company began to plan their travel around the survival of the dray animals. They lightened their wagons by discarding all heavy articles they "could possibly dispense with." They rested the animals at every opportunity and traveled in "the cool of the day" at a slow pace.[59]

For nearly all of the remaining 130 miles to the crossing of the Colorado, they saw dust and sand and very little grass. "The dust was almost insufferable; it was generally from six to twelve inches deep," Louisiana wrote. "It was almost impossible for our wagons to travel nearer than fifty yards to another." Their way was further impeded by their predecessors' discarded equipment and provisions, wagons, boxes, and trunks.[60]

The Strentzels reached the crossing of the Colorado on October 15 and came onto California soil four days afterward. Following the Colorado downstream fifteen miles, they turned away from it for another fifteen to "the emigrant wells" where there were good water and mesquite beans or "breadfruit." After three days of rest, they filled their vessels with water and, late in the afternoon, "started across the main desert." For the first thirty-seven miles, they were without water or grass. By traveling as much as possible at night and by resting the animals at every opportunity, they reached Camp Salvation on the Poca River where they rested several days before resuming travel. They reached Warner's Ranch on November 9 and arrived at San Diego on November 29.[61]

Another Tennessean, who, like the Strentzels, had westered to Texas, chose an overland route to Sonora, California, from El Paso that included significant mileage in Mexico. Benjamin Butler Harris was born in Virginia but came to Tennessee at an early age, was educated at the University of Nashville and, after graduation in 1845, taught school for two years at the Springfield Academy in Springfield, Tennessee. While there he read law and was admitted to the Tennessee bar.

In 1848, Harris relocated to eastern Texas to practice law, first to Harrison County, and soon after to Panola County. A debilitating siege of malaria encouraged him to look farther west for his future, and after the discovery of gold in California, he left Panola County for the mines on March 25, 1849.[62]

At Johnson's Station, an army cavalry post twenty miles west of Dallas, Harris cast his lot with a company of fifty-two men led by Isaac H.

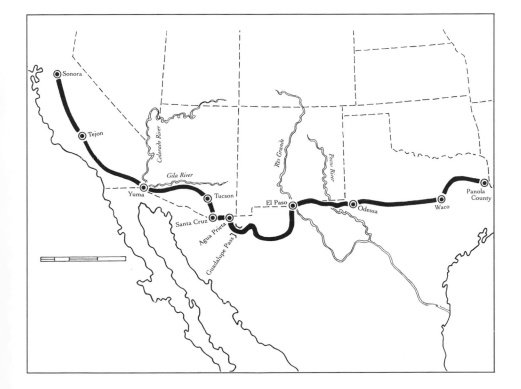

MAP 3. Trans-Texas Route to California

Duval, an experienced Texas Indian agent. By making the crossing by saddle horse and pack mule, they expected to be one of the first Texas groups at the gold fields. The experience did not prove an easy one, however.[63]

To reach El Paso, the Texas company took a new route across the dry Staked Plain and the Sand Hills to the Pecos River. Before they reached the river, the men nearly revolted against Duval because they had found no water along the untried route. They spoke openly of killing him, but finding cool water calmed their outrage.[64]

After ascending the Pecos River about ten miles, they turned westward in the direction of the pine-covered Guadalupe Mountains. Crossing over the Guadalupe Pass, they rested in camp at Cerro Alto Lake and then moved toward another mountain range. The pass was narrow, but it led them onto a plain called Hueco Tanks,[65] which held the only reliable source of water between the Pecos and El Paso.[66]

"Massed boulders" between the Tanks and the village of Ysleta, twelve miles below El Paso, slowed their progress considerably. During that stretch they were encouraged when they found notes posted by members of a second party that had left Johnson's Station about the time that the Duvals set out. That group of about fifty men had split into small squads in an effort better to deal with the chronic lack of water. Some squads were only one or two days ahead of Duval's company.[67]

When Harris and his cohorts reached Ysleta, they found it an oasis in every sense of the word. The few hundreds who lived in the oldest permanent settlement in Texas offered food, drink, and dancing, and the forty-niners enthusiastically accepted their hospitality. Before—or after—they wore out their welcome, the gold seekers moved to Socorro, a larger town about three miles down the valley. Then they crossed into Mexico, taking the shortest route to El Paso, which they reached on June 6.[68]

During that period Harris noted that the farther they traveled from home, the more the "piety" of his group waned. By the time they reached the Rio Grande, all signs of personal restraint had vanished. "A Negro [man] was the only one whose piety did not wane and who got his religion safely into California, delivered C.O.D.," he observed.[69]

From El Paso, Harris turned again into Mexico. By July 3, they were at Santa Cruz. Although chosen by his fellow travelers to deliver the company's Fourth of July address, Harris declined and focused his thoughts on reaching San Diego. He was not so focused that he failed to remark see-

ing the giant saguaro cactus for the first time as they approached a campsite at San Xavier. The next day they rode into Tucson, the last Mexican
town they would visit before reentering the United States.[70]

The route from Tucson to the Gila River was across a desert plain, but
the men were spared crippling hunger and thirst by Pima Indians who met
them with food and water about a day's travel from the Pima Villages.
Next, they went to the Maricopa Village and then followed the Gila River
to its junction with the Colorado. They crossed the Colorado into California at Yuma.[71]

After reaching the California bank of the river, Harris and his fellows
watched some Yuma Indians skillfully drown a fat mule that belonged to a
Tennessee party they were helping across the Colorado. When the large
animal was brought to shore, the Yuma swarmed around it, cut it up, and
divided it within a few minutes. It was a trick that they were reputed to
employ whenever they could seize the opportunity.[72]

Changing original travel plans that would have taken them to the port
at San Diego for a sea connection to San Francisco, Harris and his colleagues chose to proceed overland to the gold fields at Sonora. They
reached Vallecito on August 18, San Felipe on August 19, and Warner's
Ranch soon afterward. Onward they rode to Lake Elsinore, William
Workman's ranch and, finally, Los Angeles, which Harris thought contained "two or three thousand people," but only "three or four Americans."
One of them was "Don Benito," Benjamin Davis Wilson, a Tennessean
who had become a leading figure in the political and economic life of Los
Angeles County. The forty-niners replenished their supplies for the trip to
the mines at his store.[73]

Wilson gave them directions to Sonora, and on September 1 the gold
rushers moved out on the last stretch of their crossing. On September 29,
1849, they dismounted at Sonora. For Harris the long "pilgrimage" to the
gold fields was at an end, six months and four days after he departed from
Panola County, Texas. He would not return to Tennessee until the end of
the Civil War.[74]

One of the first Tennesseans to migrate to California by way of Mexico
City and Mazatlán was Dr. H. Fischel, a Nashville dentist. Apparently traveling alone, Fischel crossed the Gulf of Mexico to Veracruz and made his
way to Mexico City during the early days of March 1849. For the remainder of his journey across Mexico, he rode horseback with a party of Americans for mutual protection against robbers and thieves. They proceeded by

way of Guanajuato and Guadalajara to Mazatlán, boarded a steamship there, and arrived in California sometime in May.[75]

Former Nashville physician Dr. O. M. Wozencraft made his way from New Orleans in 1849 with a party of seventeen. They went by ship to Matamoros and from thence overland to Monclova, Chihuahua, and the Gila River. The rest of their route is not known, but they reached San Francisco before the end of the year. In 1850, Wozencraft returned to New Orleans and took his wife and daughter to California by the Isthmus route.[76]

Although the all-seasons passages offered miners the convenience of departing anytime they chose, many of them elected to travel overland from a gateway city situated farther north. The location of Fort Smith, accessible from the Mississippi by riverboat via the Arkansas and White Rivers, promised that forty-niners from the Upper South would soon throng its streets and patronize its outfitting stores.

CHAPTER V

Via Fort Smith and Sante Fe

CROSSING to California was a reminder to many Tennesseans that they or family members of prior generations had crossed overland from the seaboard colonies to the Tennessee country. When the state was organized in 1796, it was the second west of the Appalachians and the second to be created as an expression of the westward movement. Before they came and after they arrived, the pioneers had dreamed of pushing the frontier toward the setting sun.

Prior to 1849, Tennesseans of all generations, including those who settled the area before statehood, had played important parts in the westward movement. Not only had they explored, surveyed, and settled the land, but they had organized government in all its branches, had built schools and churches, had initiated agriculture, trade, and commerce, and had done all of that with an expectant eye on the ever-beckoning West.

To choose a crossing by land in 1849 was thus a natural extension of successful practices of the past, although the vast expanse of plain, desert, and mountain offered challenges on a scale few could reasonably anticipate. Early season departures enticed Tennesseans to Fort Smith and were possible because the southern spring supported the growth of grass for livestock long before there was similar forage along the northern routes. The promise that the first groups to leave Fort Smith in April would be escorted by army troops made the course even more attractive.[1]

In the spring of 1849, many from Mississippi joined Tennessee gold rushers to take riverboats to Fort Smith. On March 15, 175 such emigrants at Memphis sought steamboat tickets. Loaded heavily, the *Pontiac*, the *J. L. Webb*, and the *Kate Kirkwood* provided passage for them and many more

within the next few days. Soon afterward four other river steamers transported an additional 350 California-bound men, nearly all from Tennessee
and Mississippi, to Fort Smith. An Arkansas newspaper reported April 6
that 400 emigrants had passed through Little Rock by land or river during
the previous week.[2]

Advance agents for the Washington company of about one hundred
from Memphis, E. Houston and E. H. Williams, arrived at Fort Smith on
March 15 to purchase oxen, mules, horses, and supplies. Identification of
members of the company, organized at Camp Disappointment near Memphis with Morgan Cook of Nashville as captain, is limited to the "Memphis
mess" of thirteen and an "Independent mess" of four, all of whom left Memphis by riverboat on March 21 and reached Fort Smith ten days later.[3]
They expected to be joined within two to three weeks by Mississippi companies of sixty and thirty from Holly Springs and Pontotoc, respectively.[4]

Traveling from Fort Smith with the troop escort as far as Santa Fe,
the Memphis forty-niners encountered no resistance from any of the
Indians whose territory they crossed.[5] When they resumed their journey
westward, however, mountains and deserts posed serious obstacles to
their progress. At the Pima Villages, Dr. Lucious Lucullus Battle and two
companions disposed of all their equipment and gear except what each

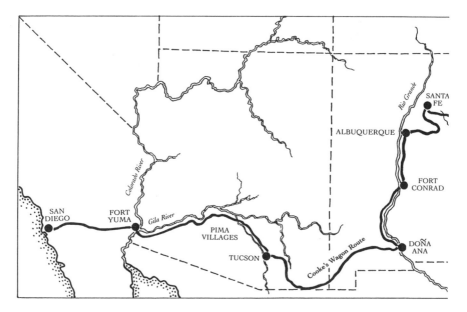

MAP 4. Southern Route from Fort Smith via Santa Fe to San Diego,
Adapted with permission from William E. Hill, *Reading, Writing and Riding along the*

could load on a single mule. Battle left behind his pocket watch, medical books, and medicines. Although they soon abandoned their guns because they were too weak to carry them, they completed the crossing to San Diego. Physically devastated and their funds exhausted, they booked passage to San Francisco on the steamer *Oregon* with the financial assistance of Maj. George H. Wyatt, Dr. J. N. Bybee, Roscoe Field, and other Memphians already on the ship.[6]

Captain R. S. Miller's company from Carroll County was another that set out from Memphis for Fort Smith during the month of March.[7] John H. Boardman's Memphis party of eight members left their hometown on March 17, 1849, in time to make the April deadline for Fort Smith.[8] Waiting there when they arrived was William K. Newman, another Tennessean, who had been elected third lieutenant in an Ohio company, the Western Rovers.[9]

Other Tennessee parties were bound for Fort Smith. Prominent among them were Maj. Robert Farquharson and the Lincoln County company and James Carlisle Cooper and his company of eight from Mt. Pleasant.[10] All seem to have made their crossing to Santa Fe as part of the train escorted by Captain R. B. Marcy's detachment of soldiers or in separate units traveling just ahead or close behind it.

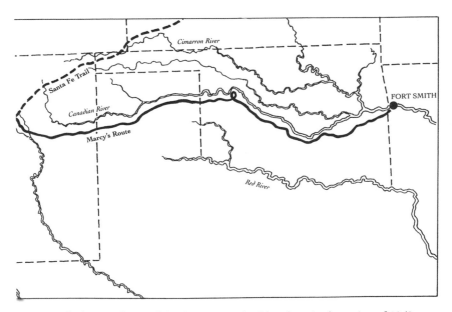

over which passed one of the first trains of gold seekers in the spring of 1849. *Oregon-California Trails*, Oregon-California Trails Assoc., Independence, Mo., 1993.

Robert Farquharson and his well-organized Lincoln County company of thirty-seven men had set out from Fayetteville on March 3 for Memphis, where they planned to load onto steamboats for the trip to Fort Smith. Traveling in a train of mule-drawn wagons, they crossed the Tennessee River at Savannah on March 9 and arrived at Memphis on March 14. Unable to send the entire company on a single steamboat, Farquharson sent some on the *Pontiac* and the remainder on the *J. L. Webb*. They were reunited April 5 at their destination. One of the company, T. Ewen Clark, was stricken with cholera en route and died soon after reaching the fort.[11] P. A. Taylor, an unattached Tennessee forty-niner from the town of Denmark, was a passenger on the *Kate Kirkwood* ascending the Arkansas in late March when he fell overboard and was drowned. Ironically, he was virtually assured a watery death by the weight of his money belt that contained $500 in gold and silver.[12]

The several Tennessee parties found themselves among a large number of emigrant companies that had assembled in response to the Fort Smith promoters and were ready to cross the plains. The others had come from Missouri, New York, Ohio, Kentucky, Louisiana, Mississippi, and "almost every state in the Union."[13] On April 10, two thousand emigrants camped in and around Fort Smith, with more arriving each day. By month's end they and later arrivals had approximately nine hundred wagons strung out across the prairie in what must have seemed to be an endless train.[14]

Heavy rains at Fort Smith made preparations for departure slow and tedious. Mules strayed, surface water flooded tents, and any attempt to move a wagon usually resulted in its wheels miring down in the mud.[15] The two Lincoln County preachers, Marshall and Small, held nightly prayer meetings, but not all of their Lincoln County associates attended. One who absented himself wrote that he had "never fancied either one of the men enough for that." He believed they were "two of the laziest men in camp."[16]

The Lincoln County company moved out of Fort Smith on April 14. During the first day's travel their wagons mired down four times while going ten miles "through a barren country filled with bogs and swamps." When an axle broke, "all hands had to stand in the mud ankle deep, raise up the bed and put in another." The first occasion to cheer was when they crossed the state line into the uncharted West, and a few of the men "who had got some liquor" straddled the line and drank to their days ahead.[17]

Plagued by breakdowns, the wagon train pushed slowly ahead. The Lincoln Countians often took two or three days of each week to repair damaged doubletrees, axles, and wagon tongues. Muddy bogs, sand hills, stream fords, and steep descending grades seemed to guarantee problems.[18]

Although preoccupied with equipment failure, the Lincoln men were alert to the threat of Indians, some of whom were accomplished thieves of horses and mules. On May 13, Farquharson agreed for his men to camp together with certain Little Rock companies for mutual protection for the remainder of their trip through Indian country.[19]

Along the Canadian River, the Tennesseans for the first time saw large herds of deer and antelope. On May 23, they enjoyed their first buffalo meat. And when they saw an immense cloud of dust raised by a herd of wild horses, they thought at first they were about to be attacked by Comanche![20]

On June 11, the first intracompany animosity surfaced when two of the men fought until one received a pistol shot wound that resulted in his death a few hours later. Cornelius Slater, harness maker, died when, according to one account, his own gun discharged accidentally as he struggled with John P. Homan. Soon after Slater was buried, a company committee investigated the shooting and reported to the entire membership. After hearing the evidence, the members of the company ruled that Homan had "committed murder on the person of Cornelius Slater" and in so doing "committed an offense against the company." They expelled him by a vote of "24 to a scattering." Forced out, he took up with another group in the train.[21]

After the shooting but before the investigating committee was appointed, Farquharson sensed displeasure with his leadership and offered his resignation. The company refused to accept it, however, and he continued in his role as captain, though stricken ill the same day.[22]

Farquharson and his men reached Santa Fe on June 18 and, after consulting local guides, decided to take the southern route from there to California. It was reputed to be a relatively safe passage, a consideration of no small importance since Captain Marcy's soldiers were remaining at Santa Fe.

The Lincoln Countians moved out on June 22 to Galisteo where they rested their mules, overhauled wagons, and inventoried supplies and equipment. The company received wagon master A. M. Beatie's petition for permission to withdraw from membership in it, and after debating the matter, the members voted to grant his request. They also permitted another member, Jesse S. Franklin, to withdraw.[23]

J. A. Zively, who had remained in Santa Fe to make and sell daguerreotypes, rejoined his companions at Galisteo in time to leave with them on July 3. When they quickly reached the Rio Grande, C. A. Mc-Daniel noted on July 6 that nearly two and one-half years had passed since he first saw the river during his Mexican War experiences along its lower reaches.[24]

Once across the Rio Grande, the Lincoln forty-niners moved out again over a rough, arid terrain that led them to the edge of the Guadalupe Desert on August 2.[25] An unexpected discovery of some good water coupled with a few days of rest strengthened their exhausted mules enough to be put in harness again. The company moved slowly across to Tucson where men and mules again recruited,[26] and on August 22, they resumed their journey. Passing the Pima Villages in three days, they reached the Gila River four days later. There the only plant growth that could be used for feed was mesquite beans, and the mules devoured them. Ahead in the train, oxen dropped out daily.

After ten days in the sand hills along the Gila, the plodding company came upon an area covered with grass enough to restore its famished mules. While the animals were regaining their strength, the men prepared to cross the Colorado River near the mouth of the Gila, not far from their camp. On September 19, the day after their last mule was safely across, John N. Horton died. He had been "sick for some time with fever" and was the third member of the Lincoln company to die since leaving Fayetteville.[27]

October brought the Lincoln men into an area of mountains and valleys where they saw western ranches for the first time. Although the mountain roads connecting them were far from easy to travel, the ranches usually had water and grass and occasionally orchard fruit. Most were attended by their Mexican owners, but some had been deserted when the Mexican War began. The forty-niners were astounded when they came upon a ranch whose owner had four thousand horses and twenty-seven thousand head of beef cattle grazing on thousands of acres of wild clover and other grasses.[28] The great deserts were behind them. Southern California lay at their feet.

Farquharson and his loyal company arrived at Los Angeles on October 14. While they rested there for five days, nine of the men decided to approach the mines by taking a steamship to San Francisco, and the others chose to continue by land to Hangtown, later to be known as Placerville. The nine, Dr. W. A. Russell, James Russell, D. W. Russell, John C. Russell and his son, J. A. Zively, H. K. Street, W. W. James, and E. B. Reinhart, proceeded by riverboat from San Francisco to Sacramento, and then overland to the mines. The larger party traveled overland to Buena-ventura, followed the coast northward to Santa Barbara,[29] and then crossed the San Joaquin River to reach Hangtown about December 1, 1849. The Lincoln company had been en route from Fayetteville to the mines for nine months.[30]

James Carlisle Cooper's Maury County company of eight young men rushed to the early spring rendezvous at Fort Smith. With eight saddle horses and a team of four more pulling the company wagon, they set out from Mt. Pleasant sometime in February and reached Memphis in ten days. The extensive bottomlands of Arkansas were so flooded that the men were compelled to go by riverboat to their destination.[31]

Arriving at Fort Smith in March before grass was far enough ad-vanced for grazing, the Maury Countians waited about three weeks and then left with the army-escorted wagon train for Santa Fe about the mid-dle of April. The small company made cause with twenty-seven other men to create a traveling party of thirty-five. They were in the same train that included the Lincoln County company and other Tennessee companies and individuals.[32]

On one occasion the thirty-five were isolated from their fellow travel-ers by a large party of Comanche who met and surrounded them on the trail and traveled with them for most of a day. All were greatly relieved when the Indians left them and they could reestablish contact with the train.[33]

Upon reaching Santa Fe, the Cooper company met a neighbor from Mt. Pleasant, identified only as "Puryear." He had been with a party of Missourians, but was financially destitute. For "old acquaintance sake," the company accepted him as a member and "paid his way." Fourteen oth-ers joined the traveling group, raising its number to fifty.[34]

Following approximately the same route taken by Farquharson's Lin-coln company from Santa Fe, the Maury Countians arrived near Los An-geles during the latter part of October. They were at work in the mines around Mariposa at their journey's end December 1, 1849. One of them, William Lawhorn, died a few days after they reached the mines. The other seven had arrived in good health, though nearly exhausted.[35]

Details are lacking, but two other groups of Tennesseans were parts of the large wagon train that left Fort Smith in mid-April 1849. They were the Memphis Exploring and Mining Company and one of the several companies from different parts of the state that styled themselves the Tennessee Company.[36] At least two Wilson Countians were in the train.

Paulding Anderson and Joseph Sumner had left home about the first of March to be among those departing from Arkansas in April.[37]

Individual gold hunters, traveling on their own, gravitated early to Fort Smith. John Barton of Campbell County was one of them. Leaving two days behind the Lincoln County company, he followed in their wake to Santa Fe and continued with them until they reached the confluence of the Gila and the Colorado.[38]

Barton found the extent of the desert areas depressing:

All the road upon the Gila, 200 miles, was a desert—little or no grass. Then from the Colorado to Warner's was a desert, 120 miles, but about fifty miles from the Colorado a new river broke out last summer, making an abundance of grass at that point—but for this, all the animals must have died.[39]

In retrospect he would not recommend the Gila Road, but suggested instead a new route discovered by J. M. Washington, governor of the territory of New Mexico, lying between the Gila and the Old Spanish Trail. Based on the train's experience with thieves, he advised those who followed to protect their animals at night not by confining them but suffering them to graze "with a guard around *them*, instead of a guard around the encampment."[40] On December 21, Barton terminated his crossing at Monterey, short of the mines. He had been en route eight months from Fort Smith.[41]

Among those of the early spring train was Memphian J. B. Mallory. Characterizing his journey to Santa Fe as "quite a pleasant tour across the Comanche plains," he continued westward along the Old Spanish Trail but soon veered away from it to reach Salt Lake City several days later.[42]

The Mormon settlement was an impressive sight. "They live in a delightful valley—I saw fine buckwheat, corn, melons, and vegetables . . . growing luxuriantly," he noted, adding that while there he had heard "a Mormon sermon, which was truly rich, rare, and peculiar."[43]

Turning westward from Salt Lake City, Mallory followed Hastings Cutoff as he passed the southern end of the Great Salt Lake and crossed the great salt desert, "ninety miles wide, without a drop of water." He and others had chosen the cutoff to save time and miles. It did neither. "This was a route we should have avoided," he said,[44]

Following the California Trail along the Humboldt River for what seemed to be a great distance, Mallory took a wrong turn, and pushing resolutely ahead, he later found himself in Oregon, three hundred miles out of his way. Nevertheless, he trudged on to California, arriving in Sacramento about November 1, 1849.[45]

Another Tennessean in the Marcy train was H. Haralson, a drifter who had accompanied Sam Houston from Nashville west to the Cherokee country in 1829. Haralson was far along on his journey when, on September 25, he met Lieutenant Cave Johnson Couts, a fellow Tennessean, near Carrizo Creek. Couts was leading an army detachment from San Diego mission to the mouth of the Gila.[46]

Not all who chose Arkansas as a gateway to the gold country persevered to complete their journeys. In 1849, Joe Pearson of Bedford County depopulated the community of Flat Creek by leading a company comprised of members of its Reece, Brown, Watson, and Womack families across the Mississippi. Only Pearson went as far as Oregon. Others stopped to settle in Nashville, Arkansas, and a few went on to Beaumont, Texas.[47]

Although most who traveled the Fort Smith route in 1849 reached California safely, they did not recommend it to others. If, as had been claimed, it was appreciably shorter than the California Trail, it could not be proved by those who tried it, many of whom were eight or nine months en route. They were further disillusioned when they discovered that among the first to arrive at the mines were other Southerners who had come by way of the Isthmus of Panama. Their communicated dissatisfaction quickly had the effect of sending later Tennessee gold seekers principally to the Isthmus route or to the California Trail via Independence or St. Joseph.

CHAPTER VI

The California Trail in '49

A FTER the wagon trains from Fort Smith were already under way, hundreds of other Tennessee forty-niners poured into Missouri to undertake the crossing from Independence or St. Joseph. Arriving in numerous companies, they checked their equipment, laid in supplies, rested their animals, and then shoved off across the prairie over the California Trail.

Most came in time to start out as soon as there was grass enough along the route for forage. They knew from the tragic experience of the Donner party during the winter of 1846–47 that crossing the Sierra Nevada before the early snows set in was a matter of life or death. About one-half of that party of eighty-five had died from cold and starvation while snowbound in the Sierra. Some of the last to be rescued had survived by eating the flesh of dead fellow travelers. Sixteen of the Donner party were Tennesseans, thirteen from a single Weakley County family. Five of them and an infant from Montgomery County died in the snow. Another of the Weakley Countians had died from an accidentally self-inflicted pistol shot earlier on the trail.[1]

Three of the many companies[2] that stopped at Independence before setting out for the gold region in 1849 were the Tennessee Company of Carter County, the Reeve party of Sullivan County, and Maj. Richard B. Alexander's Sumner County company. Like most of the others who chose the California Trail, they must have been attracted in part by Forts Kearney, Laramie, and Hall, which though located far apart along the route, provided way stations and islands of security for weary travelers.

Leaving in one of the season's earliest trains, the Tennessee Company of Carter County "started for the plains" from Independence on May 2.

The company diarist Samuel Murray Stover, a twenty-five-year-old medical doctor, left the first night's camp to visit a cousin, Elizabeth Bowers and her husband, Jonathan, who had migrated westward a few years before and were then living near Independence. Stover felt like he was in "old Carter" again when he discovered that his company camp was on the prairie farm of a Mr. Rice, a cousin of Abraham Nave, "an old associate" of his in East Tennessee.[3]

Delayed at Rice's for a week by rain, the train resumed its journey on May 8 by which time Stover had made arrangements for his company to travel with Gen. John Wilson, a native Tennessean who had migrated to Missouri where he had become an attorney, newspaper editor, and Whig party activist. He was on the way west with his wife, two daughters, and three sons to undertake the duties of United States Indian agent at the Salt Lake. A military detachment commanded by Captain R. H. Morris escorted Wilson's company. While waiting for the general to break camp, Stover visited more former Tennessee kin, including "Aunt Deborah Stover" whom he had not seen for twenty years.[4]

The Tennessee Company and General Wilson's entourage shared the experiences of many other companies. They found places in long, loose trains, traveled when they could, and stopped when necessary. As a result the relative positions of companies in the lineups were almost constantly changing. For example, Stover's party overtook the "Pioneer train"[5] on May 15, and six days later the Pioneers passed them. By May 28, they were ahead of the Pioneers, but when they pitched camp that night, the Pioneers rode past them again. While the Tennessee Company rested June 1 and 2, the Reeves passed them, but they in turn overtook the Reeves on June 4 in time for Stover to take "supper and breakfast with them." They traveled apart for several days, but later would visit together at Fort Laramie.[6]

By the time the train reached Fort Kearney, several members had become dissatisfied with their slow progress and attributed it to having too many commanders. Although grumbling and complaining were fairly common among crossing parties, the complaints were so serious that the companies agreed to put the train under a single commander, Gen. John Wilson. Nevertheless, "the slowness and manner of travel" continued to be a disappointment to many.[7]

Occasionally tensions between travelers became so taut that when they snapped, violence resulted. In a small party of Kentuckians that seems to have attached itself tightly to the Carter Countians, one of the forty-niners shot another of the group. Called to the scene, Dr. Stover found the victim only superficially wounded. His fellow travelers voted to expel the assailant, and he left the same day.[8]

After a two-day stop at Fort Laramie, the Tennessee Company moved on through the Black Hills, and continuing the gradual ten-mile ascent to the South Pass, they crossed the Sweetwater River where snowdrifts along its banks suggested they had reached higher altitudes. But the actual South Pass crossing of the Rocky Mountains was not as exciting as Stover had expected. Expressing the sentiment that would be echoed by thousands who followed, he wrote, "There is no appearance of a mountain there and no one would ever suppose they were on the top of the Rocky Mountains unless they had been told so."[9]

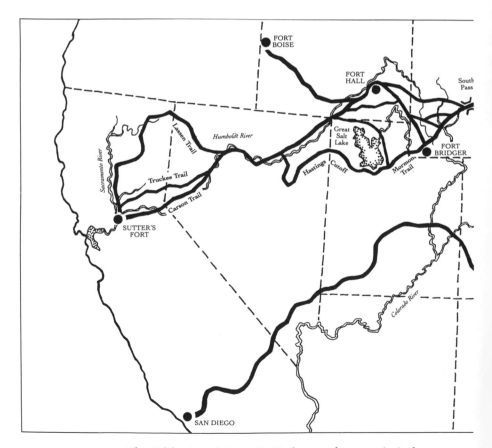

MAP 5. The California and Santa Fe Trails were the two principal routes
Adapted with permission from William E. Hill, *Reading, Writing and Riding along the*

As they traveled in the vicinity of the Continental Divide, marked by the crests of the Rockies, the Carter Countians periodically encountered persons from Tennessee. On July 9, Stover was asked to treat a sick man in a nearby train, a certain Vestil, traveling with his wife, formerly a Miss Mann of Tennessee. The next day they met Henry Bridleman who had left the Reeve company and was traveling with eight Virginians. On July 16, Stover was "greatly surprised to meet a young lady" of his acquaintance, Elizabeth White of Sullivan, and her parents who were relocating to California. The Whites were in the Pleasant Hill Company, but for a few days traveled with or near the Carter Countians who were cheered by Elizabeth's riding horseback with them. Later members of the Tennessee Company met J. L. Carter, a former Johnson Countian who had lived in Arkansas prior to joining the gold rush. His brother John Carter and

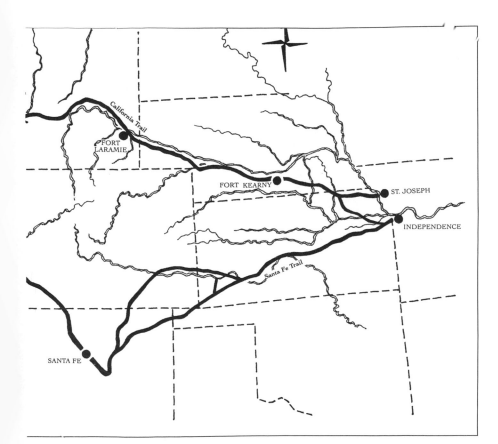

for overland crossings from the Mississippi Valley.
Oregon-California Trails, Oregon-California Trails Assoc., Independence, Mo., 1993.

Robert Williams, also former Tennesseans, were "on ahead" in the train.[10]

At the South Pass, General Wilson gave up command of the train and took leave of his military escort. He planned to stop for a few days at Salt Lake City on government business before continuing on the route that followed Lassen's Cutoff into the Sacramento Valley. He, his family, and unidentified fellow travelers arrived at San Francisco on December 8, 1849. A relief team sent out from Sacramento materially assisted them in their mountain crossing.[11]

Hoping to save as much as eighty miles or more, the remaining train, including Dr. Stover's company, took Hudspeth's Cutoff south of Fort Hall, followed Raft River to the headwaters of the Humboldt, and traveled down it to Lassen's Meadows. There on August 21, the train leaders chose Lassen's Cutoff, believing that its prospect of water at "twelve, sixteen, and twenty miles and grass at sixty" was better than the Humboldt route on which there was no water for sixty miles and no grass for one hundred. For the Carter Countians the decision was made easier by the disappointing conditions along the upper Humboldt: poor water and "indifferent" grazing with no oats or clover as expected. Stover noted that he "had never been so grossly deceived in anything as I was in this river."[12] Other diarists referred to the Humboldt as the "Humbug River" because its muddy waters were "seasoned with alkali and salt."[13]

Lassen's Cutoff severely tested the Carter Countians' stamina. Planning to travel after dark to avoid the devastating heat of the day, the train was forced to stop in the middle of the second night because they could not negotiate their way through "the dead and tired oxen that had fallen in the road." Suffering from a lack of feed, their horses awakened them at daylight by gnawing on "the wagon . . . their blankets and bridle rein." Moving out, the train picked its way deliberately, sending scouts ahead to search for water and grass. What did they find? Other trains and companies. After a few days the number of persons and dray animals along the immediate route was so large that there was competition for access to any water and grass.[14]

The Carter Countians reached "good grass" on August 24 and found themselves in the company of "several hundred wagons." Many belonged to the large trains commanded by Benoni Hudspeth and John J. Myers, professional captains of emigrant trains. Several were in a train from Oregon City with supplies for the troops at Fort Hall and for others making the crossing. After taking two days of rest, Stover and his associates joined a company from Dayton, Ohio, for the remaining journey to the mines.[15]

On August 28, the Tennessee Company traveled through twenty-six miles of canyon before halting for the night. Two days later the company reached "the base of the Sierras," where the weather was warm, although the mountain peaks were "tipped with snow." On the following day Stover logged triumphantly, "Today we crossed the Sierra Nevadas." His wagon had needed to "double team" only about a half mile in the process.[16]

Although the Carter Countians thought they had crossed the Sierra Nevada on August 31, they had crossed instead the Warner Range, just north of the northern extremity of the Sierra Nevada. They were not yet in the valley of California, and they faced the extremely rough canyon and steep hills of the Pit River. Carefully executing the many crossings necessary to follow the Pit, the forty-niners next forded a branch of Feather River and followed Deer Creek until, on September 15, they arrived at the Peter J. Davis ranch.[17] Stover concluded his journal with their arrival at Davis's, and in the absence of other records, the further experiences of the Tennessee Company are not known. Their crossing from Independence required four months and fifteen days.

Brothers and sister Clayton, Robert, and Rebecca Foster Reeve of the village of Pactolus were the nucleus of a party of eight men, two women, and an unrecorded number of children that left Knoxville March 26, 1849, on two flatboats lashed together. After negotiating the full 652-mile length of the Tennessee River, they reached Paducah, Kentucky, on April 13, disposed of their flatboats, and took the steamboat *Washington* to St. Louis. Steaming up the Missouri River on the *Alexander Hamilton*, they reached Independence on April 22.[18]

Following a few weeks behind the Tennessee Company, the Reeves experienced no serious problems as their train[19] rolled slowly across the plains, over the South Pass, through Soda Springs, and finally to Fort Hall. After resting a few days, they turned southwest to the Humboldt River and followed it to Lassen's Meadows. Although the entire train had planned to go the traditional route to the Humboldt Sink, the leaders changed their minds when confronted at the Meadows by signs urging the advantages of Lassen's Cutoff. The claims were especially persuasive as the Reeves read them against a background of alarming reports about the dangers recently encountered by other travelers along the lower Humboldt.[20] Trailing twenty-four hours behind the Wolverine Rangers, the train turned onto

Lassen's Cutoff on September 22, about a month behind the Tennessee Company, and into the most difficult part of the journey.

The resulting passage was over the most forbidding country. Sand, rock, and hardened lava dominated the landscape; steep grades and narrow canyons challenged wagoners. Little water and even less grass were available. Only the strongest dray animals survived it.[21]

Passing through the Antelope Hills, Lassen's Cutoff led to Rabbit Hole Wells and across Black Rock Desert to Black Rock Springs. An extended mountain pass opened the way next to High Rock Canyon, across another desert, and to the base of a wall of formidable mountains that appeared to be their last barrier before reaching the gold fields.[22]

After rest and preparation for the climb, the Reeves broke camp and began a strenuous day. At times having to attach nine yoke of oxen to a single wagon to complete the steep ascent, the forty-niners successfully crossed over the summit of the Warner Range. Enraptured by their breathtaking view of what she mistakenly thought was the valley of California, Rebecca Reeve thought they were near the end of their crossing.[23]

The journey was far from over, as all discovered the next day when they met a government relief train. Lassen's Cutoff added 350 miles to their route instead of reducing it. The relief party sternly reminded them that they "must by all means keep in large companies, as the Indians were troublesome and dangerous."[24]

The train followed the cutoff to the south end of Goose Lake and then wound southward along a sixty-mile stretch of the upper reaches of the boulder-strewn Pit River. One morning, the Reeve brothers discovered that a wagon wheel needed repairing, and they and Rebecca remained behind for that purpose. When they completed the repairs, they harnessed their team and set out to overtake the train then about five miles ahead of them. After they had traveled about one thousand yards, Clayton suddenly remembered that he had left his fishing rod on the riverbank where they had camped. He returned on foot to get it, but a party of Modoc[25] lying in wait, shot a volley of arrows at him. The eighteen that penetrated his body brought a loud, stunned outcry and then death.

Hearing the cry, Robert raced toward his brother, but seeing that he was dead and spying a Modoc in ambush, he turned back to protect Rebecca. Abandoning their wagon, Robert and she rushed away from the river into "the rocks" on the slopes above. Rebecca refused to hide while her brother went for help, but ran with him for about a mile until they saw one of their train on the bank below with his gun in search of game. Robert left Rebecca with the hunter while he ran after the others.[26]

When Robert overtook the train, a large contingent of men responded and rode back to escort Rebecca to safety. Before camping for the night, the train commander sent a detail of several men to recover Clayton's body. The next day fellow forty-niners placed Clayton Reeve's remains in a grave, marked it with his name, and posted a placard warning other emigrants coming behind them.[27]

Grief stricken, Rebecca found her strength restored by the thoughtful care of her many traveling companions. The death of Clayton was made no easier for his sister to bear by a group of mounted Modoc who shadowed the wagon train for more than a week after his burial. Well-armed guards kept them at a safe distance, however.[28]

An early snowfall caught the train as it reached a branch of Feather River near the desert. There the companies had intended to cut hay to provide for their teams as they crossed the vast wasteland ahead, but the snow was deep enough to prevent hay making. Eager to move beyond the snow-covered area around them, the companies pushed their starving, nearly exhausted animals ahead for another forty-eight hours and camped near a branch of Deer Creek. It was too much for many of the oxen; they could go no farther. The train members decided to abandon everything they could not pack on the backs of the remaining animals.[29]

The Reeve company was no exception. Rebecca recalled later:

> We left our tent filled with valuable clothing and treasures I grieved to part with. We could not take them, our animals would give out . . . beautiful dresses, bonnets, my treasured books, table linen and valuables of all kinds.[30]

Proceeding in snow two and a half feet deep, the train formed a long line. At the head of the Reeve company were their five packed animals followed by the members of the company on foot, except Rebecca who rode on a "good firm mule" that had been given to her by the captain of the relief train. On the first day, two of their animals collapsed in their traces. Rain and snow fell on the company for the next twelve days and nights before it reached the Peter J. Davis ranch.[31]

Scores of emigrants who had arrived before the Reeves and whose progress had been impeded by widespread flooding in the vicinity crowded

Davis's ranch. After waiting two weeks for the flood waters to recede, Robert Reeve convinced Rebecca that she should remain at the ranch and journey to Sacramento later with others of their train. He navigated down the Sacramento River in a small boat that he fashioned and reached Sacramento in mid-November.[32]

Later, Rebecca had an uneasy adventure on a newly constructed riverboat as she and the other twenty-one passengers made their way down the flooded river. "Head winds tossed us about for near two weeks, the river rose very high with the rains, almost the whole country was inundated," Rebecca recalled. "We could scarce find ground sufficiently high to encamp upon at night." She arrived at Sacramento City in the latter part of December 1849, "nine months and one week" after leaving Pactolus, Tennessee. When they left Independence, the Reeves had expected to be in the Sacramento Valley by the latter part of August or a month after at the latest.[33]

Maj. Richard B. Alexander's company of twenty-eight Sumner Countians, most of whom were from Hartsville[34] and vicinity, left Gallatin en route to Independence via Hopkinsville, Kentucky, on or about March 27, 1849. Although accounts of the early part of their journey are lacking, Alexander's company was 120 miles past Independence at the upper crossing of the Kansas River on June 1, hoping that they were beyond the range of cholera, the malady still prevalent in cities behind them.[35]

Hartsvillian Thomas P. Duffy was enchanted by the rolling prairie, even though those who had passed before them had "used up the grass and dry wood convenient to water." Duffy said that while traveling over the prairie with no defining features on the horizon, they were "as the boys expressed it . . . very frequently out of sight of land." During the first 120 miles, Duffy and his associates worked six mules to each wagon and the men walked, and they expected to continue in that manner for the next 200 miles unless the roads improved.[36]

From time to time the Sumner company met small groups of emigrants who had turned back. They justified their course by telling "terrible tales" of the likelihood of travelers facing starvation or having their throats cut by Indians. Observing that they had "taken fright and are making back for 'home sweet home,'" Duffy was not surprised. "We had expected to meet such chicken-hearted fellows before we started from Independence," he said, "and we expect to meet plenty more of the same sort."[37]

The company followed the California Trail through the South Pass and along the Mormon Trail to "the Mormon city of the Great Salt Lake."

Picking up the headwaters of the Humboldt, they followed the river down-stream to Lassen's Meadows, and like the Carter Countians and the Reeves before them, they left the river there and proceeded by way of Lassen's Cutoff. Surviving the desert, they crossed the main ridge of the Warner Range on September 26. The men pushed ahead for three weeks and reached Lassen's ranch, the easternmost settlement in the Sacramento Valley, on October 19, 1849, 206 days after leaving Gallatin.[38]

The company lost a member who had joined it en route. Michael Duffy died October 28, 1849, about sixty miles from Sacramento. Apparently he was not related to the family of fellow gold seekers Francis M. and Thomas P. Duffy, the former of whom reported that Michael "was buried by the light of the moon, by the way side, under a willow bush, *far, far* from home and friends, except seven persons then present."[39]

Among those seeking early departure from Independence was an eager company of Middle Tennesseans consisting of James Quinton, William Beaty, Thomas J. Stump and his two sons John T. and Thomas J. Stump, Jr., of Nashville, and M. Smith, W. M. Clark, and John Harris of Rutherford County. With oxen, a wagon, a tent, and suitable equipment, the party crossed to the mine fields by the California Trail. While Quinton and his associates waited, another party from the Nashville area was on its way to Independence on board the riverboat *Susquehanna*. It included an unnamed "gentleman and his family and C. Daniels, H. Billiod, Rufus Smith, and [a man named] Leslie."[40]

Small parties of Volunteer forty-niners continued to gather throughout the spring at Independence. During the first week in March, "several small parties of four and eight each" were preparing to leave Nashville for the Missouri town. F. M. Weams of Franklin joined a waiting Kentucky train there led by Captain Edwin Bryant who had written instructively of his previous visit to the West. Another Tennessean, C. D. Atkins, was camped nearby with the Louisville Kentucky Emigrating Company.[41]

A company of six men from Knox County was at Independence on April 9, 1849, preparing to attach a single oxen-pulled wagon to a train about to leave for the gold fields. The men were John L. Osborne, A. P. Osborne, C. Harvey, D. F. Wood, Samuel Hunter, and A. W. Rogers. A few days later a company of four and another of five reached Independence from Tennessee. H. H. Means, Alfred Means, and "two servants" had come from Shelby County; David Roger, James Davis, R. Dellmarch, James Walker, and Thomas Elrod were from DeKalb County.[42]

Emigrating was a family matter for Jackson Countians Joshua Draper, his wife, Christina Lyles Draper, and the four youngest children of their nine. The parents and Sarah, Leonidas Hogg, Nancy Malvina, and Susan Sweezy Draper are known to have journeyed by wagon across the plains to California. They settled at Sutter's Mill in the Sacramento Valley in the autumn of 1849.[43]

Warren County raised a company that followed the California Trail. A letter written from the mines by B. M. Morton of Tarlton suggests their journey was far from easy.[44] Ill by the time they began the crossing, Morton "had to be hauled" from Fort Laramie to the gold fields. At some point along the trail, ten men left the company.[45] The remaining members, more numerous than those who broke away, included a few women. Morton's letter mentioned five deaths including one woman, Ann McFatridge, "Dr. Perkins [and] Edwards from Greenfield," all of whom died in California; William Tatem who died "on the plains"; and Merideth Hailey who died at Chagres on the way home.[46]

One of the first Tennesseans to set out for the gold country in 1849 died somewhere in Missouri in April of that year. A brief entry in the minute book of his Sumner County church records it: "April, 1849. James Hall Martin departed this life in Missouri, being there on his way to California."[47]

Choosing St. Joseph as a gateway to the plains, a Monroe County company of nine men left Knoxville April 16, 1849, by riverboat. Col. James W. Bicknell, a former postmaster at Madisonville, was leader of the party whose other members were the cousins Hugh Brown Heiskell and Tyler Davis Heiskell, the brothers Richard L. White and Dr. Oliver P. White, Cornelius Howard, Nelson Cannon, John Brown, and Andrew A. Humphreys.[48] They arrived at St. Joseph on May 9 in plenty of time to begin their crossing to California on May 23. Several other Volunteer forty-niners had been in camp there on April 14, 1849, and probably had moved out by the time the Monroe company arrived.[49]

Traveling with forty-one other argonauts, including J. W. Campbell of Knoxville and J. C. McIntosh of Memphis who had reached St. Joseph with them,[50] the Monroe men[51] and their oxen-drawn wagons followed the California Trail at the rate of about sixteen miles per day. Soon after crossing South Pass, they took Sublette's Cutoff, passed north of the Great Salt Lake, and then turned southward to the headwaters of the Humboldt.

The Monroe company shared the travails of others who passed that way but, like them, had special trials of their own. Blinding clouds of fine dust rose from the trail at the slightest disturbance. On September 8, Hugh Heiskell noted, "The train started at half past eight . . . traveling eight miles down the valley, parched and dry, the dust rising in clouds as the train moved on and for miles down the road as far as eye could reach we could see clouds enveloping the cavalry which were on ahead." Along the lower reaches of the river, the water was so alkaline that neither human nor animal could safely drink it.[52]

The Monroe Countians found a card on September 11 at a campsite with the names of a party of East Tennesseans scrawled on it: H. Hood, A. Hood, A. Hardin, J. C. Hardin, and B. F. McCarty. Although that group had left Knox County "several weeks" before Bicknell's men, they had left the card only the day before. The Monroe men never overtook them, however.[53]

Another reminder of home came when the gold rushers learned of the presence on the West Coast of two men formerly well known in East Tennessee, Stephen L. and Joseph Meek. Recently Stephen had joined the rush to California from Oregon where they first had settled, but Joseph remained behind. Earlier he had somewhat complicated his life by taking an Indian wife. Hugh Brown Heiskell noted that Joseph was "trying to get clear of [her] as the country was settling with whites, but she clings to him."[54] Joseph had become marshal of the Oregon Territory five days after it was created on August 13, 1848.[55]

Although they would reach California before death claimed any of their members, the Monroe men stopped on the way to assist in the burial of a fellow traveler. "We spent the morning digging the grave for Mr. Crocker," Hugh Brown Heiskell wrote. "Having seen divers bodies exhumed by the wolves, we dug it deep. . . . The place selected . . . is a pretty spot with a fine bush of the hawthorne species shading his head. . . as the sun turned itself behind the mountains, we buried him, whose sun has set forever on earth."[56]

The beginning of a harsh desert crossing was signaled when the coalition of travelers with ten wagons and teams reached the Humboldt Sink. After the river disappeared underground, there was virtually no water left at the surface for the next forty miles. There were a few saltwater wells dug by others who had passed that way, but the water was not fit to drink.[57]

Only five of the wagons survived the devastating passage. The "Monroe boys" brought both of their vehicles through successfully. When one of their wagons mired in deep sand, they doubled their teams and pulled it ahead several hundred yards until they reached solid ground. After a day of rest they returned and similarly retrieved the wagon left behind.[58]

The other six messes of the traveling company were less fortunate. Tyler Heiskell told of their experiences:

> Mr. [Donald] Campbell's[59] mess lost five oxen, their wagon, their clothing and provisions, but what they could pack on their backs and one steer. A second mess well provided with everything, and a doctor with a fine stock of medicines, lost five head of cattle, their wagon, much fine and laborers' clothing, got through with an ox and cow packed and what they had on their backs.

He continued:

> A third mess lost four oxen out of eight, a wagon and first-rate outfit, getting what they could pack on four broken down oxen. A fourth mess lost three oxen out of six, and abandoned their outfit. A fifth abandoned all but what they could pull in a cart with two poor steers. The sixth mess got a cart through, abandoning half their outfit.[60]

The last twenty-eight miles of desert trail were "one continued scene of destruction of property, horses, mules, oxen, wagons, provisions of all kinds." For the last fifteen miles, there was on average one abandoned wagon every two hundred yards. The stench of dead animals was unrelenting, and the trail was piled high with "thousands of pounds" of bacon, flour, and other foodstuffs left behind.[61]

Once across the desert, the emigrants selected the Carson Trail to Sacramento and soon after met "government relief parties, with mules, oxen, and provisions." For many of them it was "just in time." Having fared better than most of their fellow travelers, the Monroe men directed the relief to families not far behind them who were in dire need of assistance.[62]

Warned by the relief parties to push ahead before autumn snows blocked their mountain crossing, the Monroe Countians rested their animals for a day and set out on October 15. They followed a plain stretching about twenty-five miles to the southwest, and before night they could see the Sierra Nevada behind the hills that walled their valley. On the next day the granite hills closed in, forcing the river into a canyon strewn with large boulders. The travelers did not stop "as there was no possible retreat."[63]

Fearfully aware of the Donner party's experience three years earlier, the Monroe men began their ascent of the Sierra Nevada on October 18. They reached the summit of the first of the two main ridges and descended to a valley from which they would attack the higher pass the next day. Just before reaching the valley, they met another relief party that brought "six yoke of cattle" to assist them. Hugh Heiskell minimized the value of the cattle when he noted, "We could have [made it] without danger, but we will not insult Uncle Sam by refusing his aid."[64]

On October 19, the Monroe company scaled the "last and highest ridge of the Sierra Nevada," a "toilsome ascent" of five miles. The men had arrived dangerously late in the season for the mountain crossing, but good luck attended them. Just a few days before they reached the highest elevations of the Sierra, a snowstorm dropped three feet of snow and closed the pass for two or three days. Fortunately a quick thaw permitted them to cross over before a massive snowfall closed the pass on October 30 for the season.[65] They had survived a flirtation with disaster.

Descending the western slopes of the Sierra Nevada, the company came upon John Campbell "lying by the side of the road his horse dead by him." Campbell, "so affected in his legs that he cannot walk," had been left by a nearly exhausted partner "to the mercy of the Indians and Sierra Nevada or the doubtful tender mercies of the emigrants behind." Men of the company placed him in a wagon and resumed the pace.[66]

The Tennesseans were awakened during the night of October 19 when two arrows flew at close range. The first intended for the guard Cornelius Howard missed, but the second aimed at Jack Johnson penetrated six plies of blankets, three shirts, his "webbing belt," and his left side, "stopping against the lower rib." He recovered from the wound, however.[67]

Though an isolated instance, the Indian incident caused the gold seekers to hurry on to Weaverville, about sixty miles east of Sacramento, where they arrived October 24. There on Weaver Creek they decided to spend the winter and start digging for gold in the spring. They had been on the way six months and eight days from Knoxville, five months and one day from St. Joseph.[68]

The Gibson County company of twelve from Trenton and Yorkville embarked on its western adventure from St. Joseph. The men had left

Trenton on April 18, 1849, with "four covered wagons drawn by sixteen mules, loaded with clothing, camp equipage, etc." They went by land and "consumed several days to reach Hickman, Kentucky," from which place they took passage on a riverboat to St. Louis.[69]

There the twelve banded with five other gold seekers from Williamson County led by Dr. R. M. Freeman[70] in a traveling arrangement for mutual protection. Before taking the steamboat *Alton* to St. Joseph, the enlarged party purchased clothing and "some mining machinery and implements." After seven days aboard the *Alton*, they reached St. Joseph, camped a few days on the banks of the Missouri River, and then crossed it and began the long haul westward.[71]

Near the South Platte River, the combined company met numerous small parties of Indians, principally Pawnee fleeing from the Sioux, but encountered no hostility from them. After fording the Platte, they came upon thousands of buffalo making the plain "black . . . for miles and miles." The forty-niners killed four for meat the same day.[72]

Crossing the larger streams was always difficult, at times an ordeal. At the North Platte River, "a deep bold stream, some three hundred yards wide," the Gibsonians had an opportunity to test their ingenuity. They removed the undercarriage from one of their wagon beds that was designed in the shape of a boat and made ready to use it as a ferry. To guide it across the river, they connected it to a cable that had been stretched from bank to bank and made fast at both ends. Six large connecting rings and hooks permitted the wagon-boat to slide along the cable but held it against the strong current. It made repeated trips, and by the end of the day all of their freight was safely across. They maneuvered the other wagons over the river by using the cable, and the mules swam the stream, all except one that was drowned in the attempt. Soon afterward, the wagon-boat was employed successfully to move their supplies across the Green River, but the absence of a cable such as they had used on the North Platte made the process slow and more arduous.[73]

The trail was busily traveled, and after Fort Laramie the vistas changed constantly. The only thing that remained the same was the number of dead animals—cattle, horses, mules, and oxen. Dr. Freeman often counted "as high as 100 a day."[74] Undeterred, they pushed ahead and several weeks later reached Fort Hall in Oregon.

A lingering English army company was in charge of the fort and had it garrisoned by Snake Indians. The emigrants hardly noticed their unlikely combination of hosts. They were elated to have the chance to buy fresh milk and butter supplied by a large dairy herd. It was one of the reasons they remained there for two weeks, then "started on a long hike to the Sierra."[75]

By following the Humboldt River, they reached the "hot springs" with their mules almost "worn out."[76] Recognizing that the teams could not possibly pull their wagons over the intervening desert and the Sierra Nevada, the men packed the mules and abandoned their wagons. For reasons not explained, Dr. Freeman left the company and went with another, trading the wagon discarded by his company for the transportation of his baggage the rest of the way. In a forced march beginning at dark, the remaining combined company crossed to the Truckee River and camped on its banks for three days. Then, refreshed, they began the ascent of the Sierra Nevada.[77] When they finally reached the summit and passed over to the Pacific slope, they found an empty cabin in which, three years prior, several members of the Donner party had perished.[78]

The long crossing ended for the Trenton men in the mines, about one hundred miles north of Sacramento. There they began mining at a place about two miles from the American River that later grew into the city of Auburn. The Yorkville forty-niners chose to enter the mine fields at a site about fifty miles east of Auburn.[79]

Dr. Freeman and his newly chosen colleagues negotiated the first crossing of the Truckee River September 17 on their way by wagon to the summit nine winding miles away. He recalled, "We crossed the river thirty times, and most of the crossings were almost impassable, the river being hemmed in by high mountains, the water running at a most rapid rate, and the bed of the river being full of cobble stone." They reached the top on September 27, but they had frequently doubled their teams to do it and even more often had stopped to rest them.[80]

Having to bring wagons down the mountainside compounded the usual difficulties of descent. Although they at times locked the wheels, in almost every case they dragged a "large tree top foremost" to retard the vehicles' inclination to run away or just tumble down the slopes. Nearly exhausted, they came into Bear River Valley on September 29, rested two days, and then followed the river down to Stupe Hollow, where, on October 6, they began washing gold *for the first time.*"[81] Dr. Freeman had been en route from Williamson County for six months.

A Tennessee company of seventy is known through the presence of Col. Joseph S. Watkins, for fourteen terms a member of the House of Representatives of the Virginia General Assembly and subsequently a citizen of Memphis.[82] Departing from St. Joseph in the latter part of April 1849, the company was known to have "a republican and military form of government, a constitution and bylaws, a president and vice-president, a legislature, three judges and a court of appeals, nine sergeants, as well as other officers," all of whom were by law exempted from the drudgery of camp duty including standing guard at night.[83]

As the privileged members constituted a majority of the company, the minority was left with camp and guard duties and soon became rebellious. Holding that the practice "smacked of favoritism and aristocracy," the colonel petitioned the company legislature for an amendment to the constitution, but was ruled out of order because the petition was not presented by one of "that august body." Nor would any of that body give up any of his privileges. An open rupture followed, and Colonel Watkins withdrew from the company, taking with him thirteen wagons and about one-third of the seventy men. Soon after the breakup, the remaining members of the original company dissolved the government of "the traveling republic" and went their separate ways. Watkins and most of his followers later fell in with a company from Dayton, Ohio, and crossed to California with them, arriving on or about September 21, 1849. It is presumed the others remained in one of the several trains moving westward and reached the gold fields about the same time.[84]

Irrespective of routes chosen or travel methods employed, Tennessee forty-niners found a society in California unlike anything they had seen before. Gold seekers were flocking in from not only the United States, but also many different parts of the world including the Orient. Mrs. John Wilson was amazed by the people she saw on the streets of San Francisco and shared her impressions in a letter home written August 15, 1850. "It is quite a curiosity to sit and look out upon the plaza and see the great variety of people and languages that are here," she wrote. "The Chinese, the Malays, the Hindoos, the Turks, the New Zealanders, the New Hollanders, the Tahitians, the Sandwich Islanders, and from every country in South America."[85] The dynamic scenario impressed Memphian William W. Gift who observed, "Such a mixed and motley crowd—such a restless, roaming, rambling, ragged multitude."[86] Mrs. Wilson and Gift beheld a mixture of races and ethnic backgrounds vastly different from the populace of Tennessee or Missouri where one principally saw only persons of European or African descent and a few Native Americans.

Those who crossed the continent in 1849 were positioned to be among the first to try mining or anything else in the magical West. They believed they had reached a land where opportunities were limited only by dreams too modest, bodies too tired, or days too short.

The first reports from California by the forty-niners reached Tennessee in time to provide added encouragement to those who planned to migrate the following year. Most of their first assessments were very positive, and they unhesitatingly shared their enthusiasm with those who might be following them.

A distinctly different Tennessee company, still on the road at the end of 1849, could have used some of the excitement and optimism shared by those newly arrived in the gold fields. It was the East Tennessee Gold Mining Company, probably the best organized and advertised of them all, but its leadership endlessly pondered routine questions even as others made their decisions and moved ahead.

CHAPTER VII

Slow Passage

T HE TRANSCONTINENTAL travels of Gen. Alexander
Outlaw Anderson's East Tennessee Gold Mining Company did little to inspire others to follow in their footsteps. Although they had
left Knoxville in the late spring of 1849, they did not reach the gold fields
until a year later, the slowest crossing identified for a Tennessee company.

Notwithstanding the slow passage, the company's travels are well doc-
umented in preserved personal letters, a diary, and letters to a Knoxville
newspaper, all informative and of unusually good literary quality. The diarist and newspaper correspondent presented pro-company, pro-Anderson
loyalist views of the experience, but personal letters to the Dr. J. G. M.
Ramsey family[1] indicate that among the men there was substantial dissent
from Anderson's day-to-day management decisions and his incredibly cautious movements.

Few, if any, of the Tennessee companies were the focus of such prolonged public attention as the East Tennessee Gold Mining Company.
Even before the company left the state, newspapers at Memphis,
Nashville, and Knoxville printed dispatches announcing that General Anderson was preparing a company for the gold fields. In fact, the mining
combine was noticed far beyond the bounds of its home state. A New York
newspaper hailed the company as made up of "all, or nearly all, intelligent
and educated young men, who—having had the choice—have preferred a
life of activity and adventure to indolent employment at home."[2]

To be certain that news of their progress was faithfully dispatched to
those left behind, Anderson appointed one of the traveling shareholders,
the Presbyterian minister Robert G. Williams, to send periodic written reports to the Knoxville *Register*. The presence of other articulate and well-

educated men in the company assured a steady flow of information to their families at home.[3]

East Tennesseans who had no direct interest in the project followed the fortunes of the mining company not only because of the gold it sought but also because of the stature of its leaders. In addition to General Anderson, there was his cousin and brother-in-law David A. Deaderick, who like him was fifty-four years old and had large landholdings and business interests in the area. Both men had attended Greeneville College, Greeneville, Tennessee,[4] and both were trustees of East Tennessee University at Knoxville[5] where Deaderick had been secretary of the board of trustees since 1838 and university treasurer since 1843. Anderson and Deaderick were accompanied by their sons James M. Anderson and John Crozier Deaderick, the latter a student at the university.[6]

From a family that was on the opposite side of the political fence and was active in competing railroad promotions as well were Dr. J. G. M. Ramsey's two sons. The elder, William Wilberforce A. Ramsey, had received an A.B. degree from East Tennessee University in 1845 and was an attorney-at-law. His brother, Francis Alexander Ramsey, had left the university classroom to join the company.[7]

There were other alumni and students from the university at Knoxville. Justin P. Garvin had been graduated in 1843, and Cyrus H. Ingles, Robert N. Barr, and John MacIntyre left their studies to join the company. Though not related to the university, three physicians were in the ranks: Dr. H. W. Peter, Dr. S. H. Flournoy, and Dr. M. L. Cozine.[8]

The company had some stay-at-home shareholders, but with the exception of N. S. Crozier and Maj. William Swann, the names of others have not been discovered. It is presumed that many of them were members of the families that had representatives going to the mines.

In preparation for the venture, the forty-niners gathered letters of introduction and recommendation necessary to obtain credit. By written instrument, Dr. Ramsey authorized his sons Wilberforce and Alexander to draw upon him for funds.[9] The Ramsey brothers also received a letter of introduction to the ranking American military officer on the West Coast, Gen. Persifor F. Smith, from Governor Neill Brown who characterized them as "young men of the first character and standing, and worthy of all confidence and regard."[10]

The company itself was well recommended. Its treasury contained cash "sufficient for all expenses," and in case of unanticipated needs,

Anderson had "letters to all the government paymasters and quartermasters on the road and in California." The men were adequately prepared both as individuals and as members of a strong, sizable organization. The company had a distinctly family flavor with a background of several marriages between members of the Anderson, Deaderick, Crozier, and Ramsey families. "Cousins" and "in-laws" were on every hand.[11]

Family members who remained at home offered assistance during the impending absences and promised to write letters regularly. They begged the gold seekers to write home at every opportunity and implored them to be on guard against everything from wild animals and belligerent Indians to the common cold. Mothers and wives were customarily preoccupied about the good health and safety of the travelers, and they gave unending advice on those subjects. One forty-niner's brother offered repeatedly to attend to the absent one's social relationships, including his courtship with a neighboring young lady.[12]

Anderson had organized the mining company as if it were a military command, and he exercised forthright control over it. He published rules and regulations to govern the behavior of his gold seekers, but no copy is known to exist. The editor of the Knoxville *Register* had seen the document and commented on the provision that dealt with keeping the Sabbath:

> An excellent regulation of the company is one relative to the observance of the Sabbath . . . that day will not be occupied in traveling or in unnecessary labor; but its hours will be devoted to appropriate religious exercises, and to rest for man and beast.[13]

In addition to a traditional observance of the Sabbath, company travel across the continent would offer many other opportunities. Learning about the land they crossed was one of these, and few gold rushers in any company were as seriously interested in learning about the West as was Wilberforce Ramsey. Letters home reflected his interest in nature, its flora and fauna, and in the culture of Native Americans and Mexicans. Taking careful notice of the geology, geography, and climate of the area, he demonstrated "an encyclopedic curiosity about the West and unusual compassion for its red and brown inhabitants." But were investigation and observation the principal reasons he joined the gold rush? Probably not, although his ambition had been loftier than "the belittling love of money."[14] Wilberforce probably joined the mining company not only because of his genuine interest in the West, but also because of the challenge of adventure, the presence of so many kin in the group, and the prospects of success in the mines that would reward him and stockholders.

Forty-seven men were the company's complement when the impressive caravan of sixteen heavily loaded horse-drawn wagons set out from Knoxville on May 4, 1849, for Independence by way of Louisville, Kentucky. Probably due to the promotional publicity generated prior to its departure, a vastly exaggerated report circulated in Kentucky that the entourage "consisted of 800 men and 100 wagons."[15]

Expecting to make the crossing to California in three months, the East Tennesseans drove their wagons from Knoxville westward through the hills and valleys of Anderson, Morgan, and Fentress Counties to Jamestown, Tennessee. There they turned northward across the state of Kentucky and reached Louisville on May 26. The truly uphill-downhill route was of sufficient difficulty to convince the rank and file that the decision to employ horses to pull the wagons was an unfortunate one. Mules would have fared much better as the leaders later recognized, but oxen would have been best for passing the western mountains.[16] The company, like others, learned by trial and error.

To protect their animals and to preserve their equipment in the best possible condition, the company shipped "thirteen wagons and their loads and two horses" from Louisville to St. Louis on the riverboat *Meteor No. 3.* Members Williams, MacIntyre, and Barr accompanied the cargo. Taking one two-horse wagon with them, the rest of the company rode out of Louisville with their horses and twelve days provisions to go by land to the same place.[17]

Hearing that cholera was rampant on riverboats plying the Missouri, General Anderson canceled his plans to send men, dray animals, and freight from St. Louis to Independence by water and instead shipped only the freight and led the men and animals overland. Before reaching Independence, he changed plans again when, on June 11, he received persistent reports that cholera was prevalent there.[18]

Anderson redirected the company to St. Joseph and that further impeded their progress, which had been beset by unanticipated delays all the way from Knoxville to St. Louis. Final preparations for the crossing detained them again, and they did not leave St. Joseph until August 6. After an unplanned halt for seven days at Fort Leavenworth, the company was three months behind schedule. If their slow progress had made it impossible for them to reach California in safety, a mother wrote unavailingly, they should return home and make an earlier start the next year.[19] Just before leaving St. Joseph, Anderson had relaxed his iron hand and asked the men to vote for their preference of a route to the gold fields. They voted unanimously to proceed along the Santa Fe Trail, the most southerly of the routes available. It was a good choice, but at that time there was virtually none other.[20]

To guide the company to Santa Fe, Anderson hired Job Skiggett, a Delaware who had traveled to California with Colonel Fremont over the same trail. The general planned to travel within protective reach of an army train of seventy-five wagons from Fort Leavenworth escorted by two companies of U.S. Dragoons and two of infantry, leaving at about the same time. Once at Santa Fe the East Tennesseans expected to choose between the Gila River route with pack mules or Cooke's Wagon Road with wagons.[21]

The first serious dissatisfaction with General Anderson's leadership had surfaced on July 14 when Frank Keller left the company to return to Tennessee. Although Keller asked for an "honorable discharge by letter from the company," General Anderson refused to issue it because the letter of resignation had "intimated" that the writer was not satisfied with the management of the company. Wilberforce Ramsey "wrote a certificate for him and got a number of signers to it." Although he risked his good standing with the general by preparing the document, Ramsey believed Keller was justified in seeking an honorable termination of his agreement with the company. Prior to Keller's resignation, there had been some "little troubles" and dissatisfaction reported in the company, and it was rumored in Knoxville that the company had broken up.[22]

While waiting at St. Joseph, the company heard repeated but unauthenticated reports of gold discoveries on the Gila River, on the south fork of the Platte River, and even closer, the Boiling Spring River, a tributary of the Arkansas. In every case the quantities were said to be abundant and the quality better than California gold. The company's correspondent hoped he and his fellows could handle the excessive riches in prospect:

> I hope we shall not become situated like the ass, between two bundles of hay, so equally drawn to each that he could go to neither. . . . If the gold is on both sides of us . . . I think we could extend our arms and grasp the whole.[23]

Before setting out, members of the East Tennessee Gold Mining Company divided their number into messes, groups of six to eight men who took their meals together. An erudite name chosen for one mess was the Adelphi. Its members included Alexander and Wilberforce Ramsey, Joseph P. and Sam B. Bailey, M. Knox, Moses McNutt, and two others not identified.[24]

Picking up the Santa Fe Trail near Fort Leavenworth on about August 10, the company made "quite an imposing display" with five wagons pulled by six-horse teams, six wagons by four-horse teams, one wagon by three horses, and one by two horses. One man expected that such a display of horses and wagons would attract Indians to visit "either for peaceable trade or rude assault."[25]

By the latter part of August, the urgent need for mules to replace their horses was apparent to all. Some of the tired animals, weakened by the hard pulling, would not be able to finish the course. When would General Anderson produce mules? He had sought without success to purchase them prior to reaching St. Joseph. Since beginning the crossing, he had traded for several and on August 24 sent the guide and four men to an Indian village nineteen miles distant to purchase additional mules, but they brought in only three.[26]

The company reached Council Grove[27] on September 1 and remained about a week repairing wagons and shoeing horses, but moved out fifteen miles to Diamond Springs on September 8. Taking them over a "series of ascending waves of land," the trail ride introduced them to the plains as nothing else could. They began to comprehend the meaning of the expression "getting up onto the plains." One of them complained, "We have been ascending for 175 miles and have not yet gotten up there."[28]

Significant quantities of game first appeared in the form of wild turkeys. From a late afternoon hunt, Wilberforce Ramsey and Sam B. Bailey brought sixteen turkey hens into camp. But the entire company was on the alert for buffalo because large herds were in the area and steaks were on the minds of all. Hunters sent from the company killed their first buffalo on September 15; the guide killed an antelope the day before. The presence of buffalo was helpful in other ways. In the absence of trees, there was need for a substitute for firewood, which was supplied by dried buffalo droppings, euphemistically called "buffalo chips."[29]

As the men of the company proceeded slowly westward, family members in East Tennessee were developing a reasonably accurate view of

California and the gold mines. It was the basis of Mrs. J. G. M. Ramsey's prophetic letter to her sons:

> All agree that it is a fine country, gold in abundance, but that few can stand the hard and constant labor of working the mines, and that it is not the miners who are making money there now, but the tavern keepers, the doctors, and traders, every other business is better than that of mining. . . . I am convinced you cannot do much at gold digging. It is stated that all companies are disbanded when they arrive in that country.[30]

On September 8, the number of the company's personnel was raised to fifty-one with the addition of five men joining for "mutual aid and comfort," but not as shareholders. At the same time the company sold two wagons, and with the successful purchase of additional mules, they had seven wagons pulled by six mules and three wagons pulled by six horses.[31]

Alert for Indian attacks, the East Tennessee company heard two alarms sounded late in the day on September 14. The signals came on separate occasions when different members of the company reported large bodies of Indians bearing down on the camp. On the second alarm when thundering hooves and a cloud of dust that obscured the animals raising it approached within the range of their rifles, the Tennesseans discovered that the interlopers were oxen from another train. They had strayed off and had been found by their owners "who were driving them in full speed." When the first reported alarm was checked out with the white drovers, it was concluded that they and their oxen had given rise to that one as well.[32]

Although there seemed to be no Indians in the area of their encampment on Walnut Creek, three hundred miles west of Fort Leavenworth, warlike tribes were ahead. Members of the company were pleased when the army train overtook them on September 15 so that, as planned, they could fall in behind the troops and travel close enough to enjoy their protection.[33]

Even without assistance from the army, Anderson's men believed they were well prepared to meet any hostile threat. Wilberforce Ramsey wrote:

> One conflict will satisfy the most formidable body of Indians that we cannot be conquered. Our body will be able to discharge more

than three hundred shots at them in one minute, and you must rec-
ollect that we are . . . Tennesseans who are well skilled in the use
of firearms. . . . We do not feel we are in much danger."[34]

On September 29 the company arrived at the crossing of the Cimar-
ron. Although their leader estimated they were about two hundred miles
from Santa Fe, the distance was nearer three hundred, and reaching it
would require four weeks instead of the two that he predicted. "We are
now in the hardest part of our journey," correspondent Williams wrote.
"The roads are quite sandy and all the teams labor hard. Several of our animals have given out so we left three or four, but I think the rest will stand
it. We are all well . . . there is not a sick man in the company."[35]

Although the army train commander Colonel Munroe[36] had agreed to
stop every seventh day in accord with the company's policy of observing
the Sabbath, he forged ahead on Sunday, October 7. To "keep under his
wing," the company reluctantly moved with him.[37]

Concerned about the impact of the hot, dry weather on their dray animals, the East Tennesseans altered their travel pattern. Instead of traveling during the hottest daylight hours, they started out each morning before
daybreak and moved five to ten miles before stopping three hours for
breakfast while the horses and mules grazed and rested. The army would
pass them during that interval, but the company would resume its march
in time to overtake the soldiers making camp later in the day.[38]

Throughout the arid part of their crossing, they saw rattlesnakes so frequently that their correspondent rarely mentioned them. They did not escape his attention completely, however, and on October 11, at the Sapello
River encampment, he reported that General Anderson killed "a very large
rattlesnake" just as they were forming the corral for the night. "It is rather
remarkable that no one has been bitten by them," Williams wrote. "They
have been in some of the tents and even in some of the beds."[39]

The men of the mining company experienced their first western snowfall on October 13, and the snow in combination with the difficulty of locating a campsite with water and wood made the day their hardest since
leaving Knoxville. The snowstorm passed as quickly as it had come, and
with moderating temperatures, the company resumed its march two days
later. Another snowfall began on October 18, and on the next day, they
came in sight of "perpetual snow" on neighboring mountain peaks. The

snows caused some to talk of taking Cooke's Wagon Road from Santa Fe to avoid the dangers of wintry weather.[40]

Snow was not their only concern, however. They were never far from Indians, and that could be dangerous to the unwary as they were reminded by the experiences of a former Knoxville family, members of a train following about two or three days behind them. Riding ahead of their company, James M. White, his wife, Ann Dunn, their young daughter Virginia, and four men were attacked by Apache at Point of Rock. The attackers killed White and the four men and took the women prisoner and held them for ransom. Later, when soldiers attempted to rescue Mrs. White, the Indians took her life by driving an arrow into her heart. They held little Virginia, but the army commander in the area believed that his troops would eventually win her freedom. He said that the Apache would not kill a little girl but "will raise it if they can." The Whites had been on their way to Santa Fe to the home of Mrs. White's father, said to be wealthy and "the most popular man" in the city.[41]

Passing through Las Vegas, Tacolate, San Miguel, and the ruins of Pecos, General Anderson and an advance committee from the East Tennessee Gold Mining Company arrived in Santa Fe on October 30. Although they had expected to find the city a complex of mud walls and adobe houses, the dirty brown sameness of it all was disappointing. Characterizing it as the "vilest place in the known world," one of the argonauts said it resembled a brick kiln with six thousand persons and ten thousand dogs. Others asked incredulously if this were indeed the town that they had crossed the wilderness to find.[42]

Prices for provisions and services were high in Santa Fe. A fellow, referred to only as Gould of Blount County, Tennessee, seemed to be profiting handsomely. On his way to the gold fields, Gould had stopped and set up a blacksmith shop in Santa Fe. His obvious success was enough to cause at least one of the company to confide to his diary, "If I had a good smith, I would put up a shop."[43]

The gold seekers had mixed opinions about Mexican "senoritas" in the villages of the Southwest. Writing for home consumption from Las Vegas, correspondent Williams regarded "some few of the females" as "tolerably good looking, but most of them are decidedly the reverse." Another member of the company confirmed, "Their women are not handsome."[44]

Jacob Stuart and Wilberforce Ramsey thought otherwise. Introduced to two "beautiful nieces" of a rich "Spanish lady" who owned much of Santa Fe, Stuart soon had stars in his eyes.

Some of them [the Spanish-American women] are exceedingly beautiful. There is a penetration and expression of countenance that is almost irresistible. . . .

I have been struck with the almost universally graceful figures and pretty faces of the senoritas. They are the most fascinating women I have ever seen . . . they wear the mantilla thrown gracefully over the head, and walk with the lightness and grace of a wood nymph.[45]

Wilberforce Ramsey reported the women to be "finely formed" and "exceedingly graceful." They had "much hair, black eyes, dark complexion," and many were "quite beautiful," he wrote. "When they show their faces in the ball room their complexion is the beautiful blending of the lily and the rose," he avowed.[46]

Beautiful women were not enough to keep the East Tennesseans together, and by the time the company camped at Galisteo, twenty-seven miles south of Santa Fe, serious trouble was brewing in the ranks. Many had lost confidence in General Anderson. Even loyal Wilberforce Ramsey wrote to his father that Anderson had made "so many false reports . . . that we put no confidence in a word he says." He would not take the risk of ridding himself of dissatisfied members because "many in the company would just as leave shoot him down as they would a robber," Ramsey declared.[47]

Most considered Anderson "disgraced beyond redemption." Wilberforce confided that he had been prepared to find Anderson "tricky and dishonest and overbearing," but was not prepared for what he saw as recurring, unnecessary, costly, dangerous delays. "When we stop for nothing, as I consider our present delay, my voice is invariably raised against it," he protested.[48]

Other letters to East Tennessee voiced the same exasperation, and there "it was expected by all except the Andersons and Deadericks, that the company would be disbanded at Santa Fe." The stockholders at home had given up "all hopes of receiving anything from them" and were surprised that the gold seekers had "adhered to the conductor so long."[49]

Notwithstanding their seething discontent with the general, the Tennesseans had to make a choice at Santa Fe. They must select a route and set a schedule for the last part of their journey. How would they go and when?

The general made the decision for them, and timing was his prime consideration. He planned to leave the area on a schedule that would take them to the gold region at the beginning of the digging season. By the first of January, he had decided to travel over Cooke's Wagon Road, having accepted the advice of frontiersman Kit Carson who was familiar with it and other possible routes. They would set out about February 1. Satisfied that the men could live more comfortably and less expensively in Albuquerque, General Anderson sent the main body there to wait until time to depart for California.[50]

While in camp at Albuquerque, the East Tennesseans caught a thief in the act of stealing some of their horses and mules. The men were understandably riled and brought the thief to trial before Maj. James Anderson. Punishment was prompt and severe. Wilberforce Ramsey explained:

> Major Anderson sentenced him to receive 100 lashes upon his naked back. I thought that twenty-five would be ample punishment. One of our party gave him the full amount which well nigh ended his existence. After he was cut down he was in a state of insensibility which frightened some of our company no little.[51]

But there was a lighter side to camp life at Albuquerque, especially for the men who liked to dance. Fandangos. The spirited Spanish-American dances took place every Saturday night, and fandangos preceded or followed marriages, religious feasts, and celebrations of almost any sort. To one of the company it seemed that fandangos in Albuquerque were held more frequently than preaching "in one of our most Christian communities." It was about the only kind of "social amusement" the Mexicans had, he said, and it brought out large numbers of young women.[52]

While his men were relaxing at Albuquerque, General Anderson set up a store in Santa Fe to dispose of the company's surplus equipment and to acquire the additional items needed to pack to California. He sold the six wagons and the ambulance with which they had reached Santa Fe and bought enough fresh mules that each mess would have twelve for packing.[53]

The East Tennesseans left the Santa Fe-Albuquerque area about February 1, 1850, after a stay of three months, "accomplishing little and spending much." By that time, Anderson had changed his choice of routes again and opted to lead the company over the route followed the year before by Col. Jack Hays. It would take them between Cooke's Wagon Road and the Gila River, which purportedly cut the distance to California by two hundred miles, a fact not lost on the men who would be making the *long walk* with their provisions and clothing packed on the backs of mules. Although

Hays's route promised a shorter trip and company funds furnished a mule for each, some of the men procured horses or mules of their own to make the march "a little more fortunate and comfortable." Only a single wagon was taken for the entire company, and it was to carry corn.[54]

Passing Socorro, "the most southern town of any importance" in the territory of New Mexico, on February 7, the company followed the Rio Grande southward for about one hundred miles. Turning away from the river at the Diego crossing, the men followed along Cooke's Wagon Road to the Two Buttes. At the Buttes, Anderson guided them onto Hays's route, which took them into Mexico.[55]

Soon after crossing the border, a group of twenty-four men broke away and proceeded on their own. They bypassed the selected evening campsite of February 26 to assert their independence. After they failed to answer signal guns fired to orient them if they were lost, the rebels sent a message by a Mexican stating only that they were going ahead in search of water. Although dissatisfied with Anderson, Wilberforce Ramsey had turned down an invitation to join the separatists. He and his brother remained with the company. Well acquainted with those who had pulled out, he said "that all the guns in Christendom could not call them to us. We should never see them again."[56] The split had come at last. Another who remained with General Anderson regarded those who left as deserters and criticized them sternly for "taking with them all the property furnished by the company." He would change his mind later.[57]

General Anderson and David A. Deaderick professed to be surprised by the defection. The latter recalled that when "near about half of our men left us, or deserted . . . we had no intimation of their purpose to leave." He was aware, however, that they had become "dissatisfied with the general management of our leader, especially with the very slow progress we had made. They went ahead of us and we saw no more of them."[58]

After the split, William G. Brownlow could not resist the temptation to express his editorial contempt for General Anderson. "The personal popularity and prudent management" of David Deaderick kept the company together "as long as circumstances would allow," Brownlow said, adding that Anderson was unfit for the leadership role he had chosen.

> Were ever the movements of a company so tardy? He would stop a company in the midst of the Rocky Mountains . . . and fit up a coach and four to show a band of savages how an English

Nobleman rides. . . . Just what any and every man might expect who knows Gen. Anderson.[59]

Reduced to seventeen members, Anderson's company bought wheat at Tucson to supply the horses and mules across an eighty-mile-wide desert that separated them from the Colorado River. With remarkably good fortune, the East Tennesseans found water each night of the crossing and reached the Pima Villages safely by March 11, 1850. Anderson purchased sufficient corn and wheat from the villagers to supply the needs of his men and animals for the remaining 283 miles to the first settlements in California. Only the Colorado River and another desert passage stood between them and the promised land.[60]

On March 22, they arrived at the Colorado and, scorning the charges proposed by a pair of ferryboat operators, one of whom was from Memphis, improvised their own ferries of hewn cottonwood and moved themselves, their animals, and baggage across. They lingered long enough to ferry about one thousand California-bound Mexicans across the Colorado at a rate less than one-half that charged by the resident ferrymen. While camped at the crossing, the company received a visit from George Ellis, a Creek who formerly lived in Tennessee near Athens. Ellis swapped two mules for the boats they had built, and he became a ferryboat operator at the popular crossing of the Colorado.[61]

Making full use of the few sources of water that obtained, the much reduced East Tennessee Gold Mining Company made its way successfully across ninety miles of desert and was within sight of Warner's Ranch by April 6. After a brief rest at Warner's, the company resumed its march and was eight miles south of Los Angeles by April 12. In a letter intended to reassure troubled stockholders at home, David A. Deaderick gave an optimistic appraisal of their prospects and concluded by saying, "We are still the East Tennessee Gold Mining Company and all are in fine health and spirits."[62]

As they made their way to Los Angeles, the members of the company decided they would begin mining on the headwaters of the San Joaquin River which was four or five weeks distant. They traveled from Los Angeles northward along the coast 362 miles to San Jose and turned eastward through Pecheco Pass across the coastal range to the San Joaquin. They crossed it at Grayson. Three miles farther they crossed the Tuolumne River and twenty-one miles later forded the Stanislaus. On May 16, they reached the mines at Sonora, the end of their journey.[63] They had left Knoxville one year and twelve days before.

The experiences of the East Tennessee Gold Mining Company demonstrated that thorough organization and strong control vested in a commander or conductor did not necessarily result in the members of the organization remaining together for a successful crossing. Few companies were able to reach the gold mines with their memberships intact, but few were as well organized as Anderson's. Flexibility, commitment, and good luck seemed to be the basic requirements for keeping emigrants on the move. The general's ponderous approach suggested he was moving a mighty army instead of fifty men; his rigid attitudes suggested there was his way and no other. Had there not been a network of family ties in the company, the organization would have disintegrated early in the passage. This account may prove that gold seekers would eventually reach the mines in spite of hesitant leadership, vainglorious pretensions, over-organized companies, internal dissension, and natural obstacles along the way. The golden magnet would ultimately pull them in.

Even as the East Tennesseans had lingered along the way, others from the state took to the trail. General Anderson's slow crossing did not dampen the enthusiasm of the scores of gold seekers who followed, many from his section of Tennessee.

CHAPTER VIII

The Thing Must Have Its Run

T HE EMIGRATION from Tennessee to California probably peaked during 1850. Although there are no records for accurate comparison, the number in 1850 seems to have increased with national totals to at least double that for 1849 before declining sharply in 1851. California fever blanketed the state and was "raging to a fearful extent" in East Tennessee, Congressman Andrew Johnson acknowledged on April 5, 1850. He received "cords of letters every mail upon the subject of California" and feared that the emigration from East Tennessee would have a tendency temporarily to check the region's prosperity. "But the thing must have its run," he conceded.[1]

Enthusiasm for going to the mines was so widely shared in 1850 that the Nashville *Daily Evening Reporter* offered to publish a weekly *"Extra"* for California news. The proposed newspaper would try to help its readers answer the question, "Which will you do—be off to California, buy a lottery ticket, or stick to your old trade?" Publication depended on the extension of "sufficient patronage," a condition that was not fulfilled.[2]

Even ministers of Protestant Christian churches were putting aside their Bibles and saddlebags to join the migration. A Nashville editor wondered whether they could restrain themselves and others from the fascination inherent in "the unholy lucre." At the very least, he warned that gold fever was epidemic and that "the very worthy characters for whom we entertain so high a respect are not free from its contagious influence."[3]

The Methodist Church press in Nashville noticed with alarm the extent of the "raging" fever. Noting that many were preparing "to leave for the gold regions," the editor acknowledged that some would succeed and others fail, but somberly warned that "many will find graves in a far distant land." Reminding them that material blessings are of a temporal nature, he recalled Jesus' counsel "to buy of me gold tried in the fire that thou mayest be rich."[4]

In the spring of 1850, gold rushers crowded Nashville's hotels. A party of seven "mountaineers" from Marion County stayed at the Nashville Inn, and hotel registers throughout the city showed "California" as the destination for a large proportion of their guests. Other companies from Smith, Bedford, and Wilson Counties were in the city to board riverboats for the first segment of their journey.[5]

Notwithstanding appearances to the contrary, emigration from the state may have been less than from "most sections of the Union," the editor of the Nashville *Daily Union* speculated. But the question of numbers[6] was less important than the quality of the 1850 Tennessee gold seekers. "The emigrants are generally of the very best class of our citizens — men of means and character as well as energy and enterprise," he declared, adding that more would be leaving the Volunteer State except for its inland location. "We are so far in the interior that the spirit of change reaches our people later than it reaches those near the seacoast or on the frontier who are constantly witnessing the departure of others in search of gold," he reasoned.[7]

Editorial speculation aside, at least 1,500 to 2,000 Tennesseans were on their way or about to set out westward during the early summer of 1850. Those who traveled overland made their approach to the prairie at the three gateway towns used the year before. But most chose to go by New Orleans, Chagres, Panama City, and San Francisco.

Travel via Fort Smith in 1850 declined sharply because of the warning of those who had been disappointed in the route the year before. One of the few who ignored the warning was John J. May, a Cumberland Presbyterian minister, dedicated to carrying on the work of his church in the West.[8]

May joined a company of twenty-five assembled from gold rushers waiting at Fort Smith for the early spring crossing, and choosing to connect to California via Salt Lake City instead of Santa Fe, they set out on April 8, 1850. At first they traveled the route established by Captain Marcy the year before. After their course intersected the Independence-Santa Fe Trail, they turned off and followed it 150 miles to the crossing of the Arkansas, and turning up the river, they reached Pueblo on June 10. Banding together with another company for mutual security, they traveled 150 miles in a northwesterly direction, crossed a range of mountains, and on July 4 crossed the North Platte River. While in camp that night, they lost thirty of their best horses and mules to raiders, presumably Indians. Notwithstanding their losses, the gold seekers again took the trail, crossed over the South Pass on July 9, paused at Fort Bridger on July 24, and arrived at Salt Lake City on July 29.[9]

Deeply suspicious of Mormons, May was "astonished" to find all that he "had previously heard of the Mormons, to be but too true, with regard to the vices and immoralities practiced by them." It was not unusual for preachers to swear and get drunk, and it was "no less strange than true, that the practice of polygamy is tolerated among them," he wrote October 24, 1850, in a letter to the editors of the *Banner of Peace and Cumberland Presbyterian Advocate* at Lebanon. He said, "Their faith is, and they reduce it to practice, that a man may have as many wives as he can maintain."

During his short stay in the city, he took comfort in finding "some good men" and making friends, but he was incensed by the Mormon Council's instructing its parishioners to charge emigrants twice the price they charged each other for provisions and other supplies. He admired two features of the Mormon city: its situation "in a beautiful valley, in full view of the Great Salt Lake" and its "beautifully laid out" building lots, "large enough for each family to have a garden spot."[10]

Soon after leaving the Mormons and proceeding along Hastings Cutoff, the company experienced an epidemic of cholera that took eight lives. One claimed by death was Return J. Meigs, son-in-law of John Ross, "the principal chief of the Cherokee Nation." Meigs, a Tennessean by birth, and several other Cherokee had joined the company as it passed near their home in the Cherokee reservation in what later became the state of Oklahoma.[11] The unfortunate Meigs was one of many Cherokee from the Indian Territory who had joined the trek for gold. Although few others are identified, several of them were probably born in Tennessee prior to the removal.[12]

May and his fellow travelers found the Humboldt to be the same impossible stream that others before them had reported. They survived the usual hardships experienced in the deserts and mountains, but their suffering was minor if compared to the siege of cholera that had so reduced their numbers. On September 20, 1850, five months and thirteen days from Fort Smith, May arrived in Nevada City, eighty miles north of Sacramento. It had been "a tedious and laborious journey."[13]

Before grass on the plains was "high enough to start out," small companies from Davidson, Sumner, Maury, and other Middle Tennessee counties gathered at St. Joseph to await a departure that was delayed because of the lateness of the season. The Tennessee Mining Company of Nashville, A. M. Rosborough, superintendent, was the group around which the other Middle Tennessee companies gathered as they set out. Although few people are identified, the Nashville *True Whig* printed periodic accounts of their collective experiences furnished by Rosborough, who had resigned as its editor to go to California. Tennessee Mining planned to extract gold from quartz and took along a steam engine to furnish power for a stamping machine.[14]

Following trails clearly marked by the passage of thousands of emigrants during the prior year, Rosborough led his small train up the Platte River valley to Fort Laramie, arriving there on June 13. The "beautiful bottoms of the Platte" were unusually dry for the season, but the rutted way was obstacle enough to encourage their decision to leave their wagons at Laramie and "pack through." The wagons were "too heavy to haul through" without risking the lives of their mules.[15]

Rosborough noted that 2,000 emigrants had passed Fort Laramie on June 16 and that the names of 32,049 men, women, and children had been entered on the fort's travel registry since January 1, 1850, more than had passed that way during the whole of 1849. Among the Tennessee companies that had registered prior to his departure from the fort, Rosborough mentioned "Backout and Bowers and Company" and "Black and Johnson," the latter of Giles County, but the former not identified.[16]

After leaving Laramie, the illnesses of A. M.'s brother, J. B. Rosborough, and Dr. W. H. Farmer delayed the company's progress for a short time, but both recovered quickly. "We have been most fortunate and blessed, not meeting with a single serious accident, and perhaps have had less sickness than any train of the same size on the route," Rosborough wrote. By bestowing much attention to their livestock, they had not lost any animals.[17]

After crossing South Pass, the train paused briefly at Pacific Springs. Rosborough estimated there were two or three hundred Tennesseans on the road within a day's travel of his train.[18]

The Tennessee Mining Company turned southwestward from Pacific Springs around the Great Salt Lake. Upon reaching the Humboldt River, the men discovered that spring floods had washed immense deposits of alkali from its banks into the channel. Although they and members of their train consumed minimum amounts of the alkaline water, other emigrants "suffered much" from drinking too much of it and "many died." Horses, mules, and oxen died by the thousands, Rosborough reported.[19]

Once beyond the arid deserts that stretched from the Humboldt Sink to the Sierra Nevada, the Tennessee company chose the Carson Trail to cross their last major obstacle. Reaching Weberville about fifty miles east of Sacramento on August 30, the company was intact: they had not lost a single man since leaving St. Joseph[20] four months and eighteen days earlier.

The Nashville and Clarksville Havilah Mining and Trading Company sent agents J. W. Mathews and J. J. Phillips from Nashville to Independence on April 23, 1850, to make arrangements for crossing the plains in advance of the arrival of the rest of the company a week later. Expecting to recover gold from quartz rock, Havilah had acquired a steam engine for power and had sent it, other equipment, and "a select assortment of drugs" by steamer around Cape Horn; George W. Seay had accompanied the shipment.[21]

Ironically, when the remaining members of the well-organized company left Nashville on April 27, they left their mules behind. Returning from Clarksville to Nashville, Dr. T. A. Thomas, superintendent of Havilah, loaded the mules on a steamboat, the *St. Paul*, that shortly before May 7 overtook his company on the Missouri River aboard *Sligo No. 2*.[22]

The men of Havilah had stopped at St. Louis on April 30, and after appearing before a magistrate to swear that they were California-bound, each had purchased a rifle from the United States arsenal, a privilege extended by the War Department. Resuming their journey by riverboat the following day, they approached Independence on May 8.[23]

Five days later they were on the road westward with eight wagons of their own and three others, one belonging to each of three small Tennessee companies traveling with them. Leaders of the three companies were H. Patterson, Thomas Wisdom, and William Walker, not to be confused with the Nashvillian of the same name who later achieved notoriety as a filibuster in Mexico and Nicaragua.[24]

The men and their eleven wagons were enmeshed in a long line with other wagons constantly in view in front and behind.[25] Soon after reaching the intersection with the St. Joseph Road near Alcove Springs, the Tennesseans considered disposing of their wagons and traveling only with packed mules. After reaching Fort Kearney, the company sold three wagons and shifted the cargo to the mules. At first the animals resisted. "A number of them cut up all manner of capers and would throw off the pack as fast as it was put on," Madison B. Moorman noted in his diary. But they finally accepted their new roles, and Havilah was on the road again on June 4.[26]

While at Fort Kearney, the company had entertained the fort's second in command at dinner. The officer was a fellow Tennessean, Maj. Sackfield Maclin of Nashville, army paymaster. Adjudged "a perfect gentleman" who was "easy and affable in manner," Maclin was "without any of that affected stiffness so common with military officers," Moorman declared.[27]

The Havilah men survived the scourge of diseases fatal to so many around them. Cholera struck Dr. Thurston, but he overcame it, Thomas was so ill he once vacated command of the train to Moorman, and William Walker, although he recovered, was so sick for a while that his case was believed hopeless. Moorman had a severe bout with measles, and no one escaped a periodic siege of diarrhea. Dr. Patterson cared for his men and, in addition, went from camp to camp doing what he could to relieve suffering. The doctor said that he believed there was a fresh grave for every mile they had traveled since leaving Fort Kearney, but was proud that there was none for any of his company.[28]

On June 24, the train reached Fort Laramie where it halted for much of the day. Most of the men wrote letters to family and friends and left them with Lieutenant Andrew Jackson Donelson, Jr., a Tennessean and great-nephew of the late President Andrew Jackson, who promised to forward them to the states "by an opportunity he knew of, much sooner than the regular mail and more certain." William Walker, still severely ill, was to remain at Laramie. His younger brother Marcus and another of their company, Thomas Pullum, stayed to care for him.[29]

Following the California Trail, Havilah passed over countryside with some breathtaking vistas. One such view was at Devil's Gate where the river passes through a narrow canyon with perpendicular walls towering about two hundred feet above. The stark walls of the canyon nestled in the shadow of the snow-clad mountain peaks inspired the company diarist. He wrote, "Notwithstanding all the difficulties of such a journey—the scarcity of provender for animals—the deep and heavy sand—the scorching sun and breaking down of wagons, the grandeur and sublimity of nature's stupendous works amply repay us."[30]

On July 20, the Havilah company entered the "city of the Great Salt Lake."[31] Although most Tennesseans neither understood nor approved of Mormon religious practices, men of the Havilah passed three days in the city, taking their meals in the private homes of citizens. Several of the Volunteer forty-niners were in the audience of five thousand to hear Mormon President Brigham Young preach on July 21. Characterizing the sermon as "affected—weak and unchaste," Moorman was unimpressed. Hearing no mention of the United States government and seeing not a single American flag in the city, he expressed his disdain: "I looked upon them as seceders and vain-glorious pretenders."[32]

Havilah's Dr. Patterson saw the Mormons in a somewhat more favorable light, "apparently enjoying themselves better than any other individuals that I have seen since I left home." Living in a valley where the soil was rich and water for irrigation was abundant, they cultivated "their lands with considerable taste, and a good profit," he said.[33]

Once away from the city where they had replenished supplies, the men agreed on July 24 to take the Hastings Cutoff, believing they might save about 300 of the 808 miles that separated them from the gold fields. Traveling the cutoff meant facing more desert with uncertain sources of water and feed for the next two to three weeks. When a water relief wagon from California met them July 31, they were so grateful that they sent money by the driver to purchase supplies for others following behind.[34]

When the Havilah men reached the end of Hastings Cutoff at its junction with the Humboldt River, they veered southward along the sandy river valley. They heard intruders firing rifles to stampede their animals at night, saw lakes of water that were only mirages, and watched their supplies dwindle. Beyond the Humboldt Sink, it was even worse. Scores of abandoned wagons and hundreds of carcasses of dead and dying horses, mules, and oxen marked the trail. The heat of the desert took its toll on humans as well. "Men were fainting for want of water under the fatigue and hardships of the miserable waste, and the amount of human suffering is indescribable," Moorman wrote.[35]

The Havilah reached Carsonville or "Hell's Hollow" on August 28. Although they estimated that they were but two hundred miles from the gold fields, the treacherous Sierra Nevada stood between them and their destination. For that last mountain crossing, Moorman, Sevier, Hart, Nichols, and Stone decided to walk, and they set out August 31. Hiking up Carson River, they successfully negotiated the stream's hazardous eight-mile canyon and reached its headwaters about September 3. A long, twisting road led them to the crest of the mountain on September 5. In the late afternoon of the next day, the footsore party arrived at Placerville on the lower western slopes, three days ahead of the main body of the company. They had reached the California gold fields, but thousands had arrived before them. The town was full of gold miners.[36]

On their way to Independence from Henry County, Tennessee, in April 1850, the brothers, William J., George W., and Perry Jackson, and their cousin John Allen Jackson assembled an informal party of ten men. The other six were Middle Tennesseans Dr. Robert Marshall, Dr. William Wright, and "a young Mr. Davis," and three Ohioans.[37]

With transportation provided by their wagon, four mules, and two horses, the Jacksons left Missouri for California on May 6. They deliberately left before the grass was high enough to support their dray animals. By bringing enough grain in their wagon to feed the horses and mules for the first twenty days of the journey, the Jacksons expected grass to be plentiful before they needed any. Depletion of their grain would reduce the wagon's cargo to about one thousand pounds, which they deemed manageable for the later and most difficult parts of their passage.[38]

After a few days on the California Trail, the Jacksons merged into a larger train with the result that camps were so large and noisy, William J. Jackson likened the din to the noise of a religious camp meeting. He complained that it made writing coherent letters almost impossible. He was aware, however, that the very large numbers provided a high level of mutual security against whatever threats might confront them.[39] One of the Jacksons noted, "The road from here back to Independence is as thick with people as any street in New Orleans."[40]

At Fort Laramie, the Jacksons cut up their wagon and made pack saddles for the six mules and two horses they then had. Leaving the three Ohioans at the fort to await the recovery of one of their number who was ill, the Tennesseans set out and soon agreed that packing was a much better way to travel than "the wagon arrangement."[41]

After crossing at the Mormon Ferry, the Jacksons decided to approach California by way of the Great Salt Lake and estimated they would be in the gold fields about August 1. They and the other three Tennesseans presumably reached California, but the time and place of arrival are not known.[42]

A Sumner County company of seventeen, organized by the brothers James O. and Tyree B. Harris and their partners, J. W. Ellis, Henry B. Day, and James Holloway, reached St. Louis with their mules and wagons on April 22 by steamboat. Although they were prepared to travel on their own responsibility, members of the company decided to sell their dray animals and wagons to Glenn and Company, a St. Louis train management firm, and to enroll as passengers with Glenn to California. For a fee of $200 per person, the firm proposed to provide transportation, board, camp guards, herders, and the services of a skilled physician during the crossing. Called "freighting through," the process seemed easy enough. Some of those who enrolled also signed to work as teamsters, often driving the mules or horses they had just sold.[43]

While waiting for the train to be assembled, Tennesseans with kin in the area visited them on their prairie farms. The Harris brothers visited their cousin Jacob Gillespie and were "well pleased" with his farm. They expressed sympathy for farmers in Tennessee and Virginia "who had to labor so hard and realize so little" while on the prairie "there is so vast a country of fertile soil inviting the hardy husbandman and promising an ample reward for all his toils." They made similar comments about the fine farms of other cousins and wrote home advising "any cramped man to sell out and come to this country." The beauty of the farms was remarkable, they said, and the land so level that "you can see for 12 or 15 miles."[44]

While Independence was receiving daily additions to its gold rush camps, members of the Harris, Ellis, Day, and Holloway company were glad to greet John B. Moore's Sumner County company of twenty-six that arrived from Hartsville by riverboat via Nashville and St. Louis. The Hartsville group had also signed an agreement to make the crossing with Glenn.[45]

Expecting to travel an average of twenty-eight miles per day, the Glenn train started across the plains on May 26. At first the travelers' spirits were high, even though they daily met returning emigrants, typically discouraged families who had turned back with their wagons and teams.

During the first few weeks on the trail, the all-male Sumner County companies were not free from the influence of women in their lives. Three married couples were traveling with them. "The women have their gab in everything to keep up a continual buzz," James O. Harris wrote, explaining that on one occasion they had "come very near" causing "an insurrection" in camp. He did not explain further.[46]

The movement of the Glenn train was intolerably slow. Restless because its pace had slowed to ten to fifteen miles per day, James Harris and eighteen others primarily from the Harris, Ellis, Day, and Holloway company left the train when it was about two hundred miles east of Salt Lake

City. They purchased eight yoke of oxen from another train and drew two good mules and their share of provisions from the Glenn combine. The provisions lasted only until they reached Salt Lake City where they replenished stocks. While they were there, the Glenn train arrived and "made a general explosion, every man for himself." The two Sumner companies, divided first by the slow, halting movement of the original train, and finally by its disintegration, were never whole again.[47]

Salt Lake City appeared to Harris to be "the size of two such as Gallatin and improving very rapidly." The houses, built of an unburnt brick "of a purplish color," were impressive as was the intricate system of open trenches that delivered water diverted from mountain streams to "every door . . . their gardens and farms." However, to obtain firewood, residents were forced to go several miles to the mountains because the valley surrounding their city was bare of trees.[48]

Harris and his associates made their way to the headwaters of the Humboldt River, traveled down its valley, trudged across the desert, and finally crossed the mountain to arrive in California about October 1, 1850. During the latter stages of their journey, Dr. Alexander and his brother from the Hartsville company had traveled with them.[49]

During the spring of 1850, nine men from the sixth civil district of Wilson County joined forces to go to the gold mines. After purchasing four mules and a wagon at Nashville, they went by riverboat to Sibley, Missouri, and, soon after, set out from Independence. The members of the company were A. J. Lyon, W. A. Mohon, D. G. Jackson, Isham Jackson, Joseph Barton, Zen Hobbs, Jim Burge, "Pus" Harris, and Carroll Haynes.[50] Accounts of their travels are missing as are details of the 1850 crossing of a Lebanon stock company headed by Col. David Cook.

William Crutsinger and a company of sixteen left Knoxville April 3, 1850, on the riverboat *Ellen White* to make the cross-country journey from Independence to California. The group was made up primarily of men from "the upper counties of East Tennessee."[51] They reached the gold fields by the middle of August 1850 where their presence was reported August 23 by J. S. Wall of Kingsport who had arrived by sea about a month before. No account of their crossing has been discovered.[52]

Individual Tennesseans often appeared at the outfitting towns to join companies already organized. B. C. Strother, William Lynch, and William C. Moore of Germantown were among the 101 members of the McPike and Strother wagon train that set out from St. Joseph in May 1850.[53]

Many who made the overland crossing were never mentioned in the newspapers, but the names of some appeared with just enough information to be tantalizing. W. L. Willis, Burwell Sneed, Henry Cox, Samuel Tilford, and "Mr. Jacobs" were reported to be aboard the steamboat *West Newton* when it left Nashville in early May 1850 for St. Louis and Independence. That brief note in the Nashville *Daily American* of May 4, 1850, is all that is known about the gold seekers, although it is presumed they were from Davidson County and they made the crossing successfully.

Young men were boarding riverboats at Chattanooga to begin their journeys westward, but the Chattanooga *Advertiser* offered few details in its passing note:

> Ho for California: The cars bring up a number of young men from Georgia nearly every trip lately, bound for California, and we notice that most of them are well armed and equipped. East Tennessee, too, is sending over a number of her enterprising sons to the gold region, who go equally well prepared to defend themselves against all aggressive attacks. They all intend to go by the overland route.[54]

Readers of the Nashville *True Whig* of May 16, 1850, learned that G. W. Wilson, M. L. Melteer, R. W. Green, a man named Roberts, and a certain Dr. Randolph, all of Nashville, had left for California by the "overland route." Tennesseans Sevier Stringfield, his wife, Elizabeth, and his sister Sarah A. Stringfield crossed the plains in 1850. Sarah afterward became the wife of A. D. Sevier, a native of Missouri and later sheriff of Humboldt County, California.[55]

Some East Tennesseans banded together to follow the arduous California Trail in 1850 with a wagon train commanded by William Wilson Hale, one of their number. Among the emigrants were Hale's wife, Delilah M., and their children Joel R., Margaret E., John M., and Levinia.[56] Overland crossings became somewhat easier after 1850 as the emigrants benefited from the experiences of their predecessors. Established routes with trails marked by usage, if not by signs, aided the passing wagon trains. But the trip was still perilous.

The Isthmus route to San Francisco was the most popular passage for Tennesseans in 1850. It offered not only year-round travel but also lower costs, and when steamboats were used in the Gulf and Pacific, the time saved was significant. The crossing required less physical effort on the part of travelers because they were aboard ship, except for the usual three days across the Isthmus with boatmen and mules. In addition, travelers did not infringe on Native American territories.

Wilson, Love and Company of Gallatin picked the Isthmus route. Leaving home on April 15, the company of seventeen men traveled to Nashville where on April 18, they took the riverboat *Countess* to Clarksville. There they went aboard "the magnificent steamer *America*" that embarked for New Orleans.[57]

Five Shelbyville men on the *America* led by Dr. Robert Frank Evans traveled with the Gallatin gold seekers to New Orleans. The doctor and M. H. Kinney, James Low, James L. Armstrong, and Dr. Rufus Caldwell had left Shelbyville on April 17. Dr. Evans proved himself a worthwhile fellow traveler when he extracted a tooth for one of the Gallatin company. At New Orleans, the men of both companies passed their time together exploring the city and nearby Lafayette, Louisiana, while waiting for separate transportation to Chagres.[58] A group of twenty East Tennesseans, also headed for the gold fields, had come on board the *America* April 21 at Paducah, Kentucky. Surviving records do not identify them, however.[59]

Securing passage on a steamship, Wilson, Love and Company left New Orleans on April 28 and arrived at Chagres May 12. There Sumner Countians William Gregory, John B. Walton, and John C. Hubbard became members of the company, apparently defecting from David Barry's Sumner Independents who had reached Chagres the same day.[60]

Barry's group[61] had left Nashville April 9 and traveled the river route to reach New Orleans where they embarked on April 16 on the brig *Florida* for Chagres. While strong head winds for two weeks slowed the passage, members of the party grew long beards and suffered from sunburn, seasickness, and boredom. Barry commented on his fellow travelers:

> We have all sorts of people on board from the gentleman down to the very lowest and most degraded of all creation. Some are always in good humor while others curse their Maker, themselves, and everything else *particularly California gold.*[62]

On board the same brig was David Saffaran's company of about twelve, although only four besides himself have been identified: Isaac Hiett, V. P. Shelton, W. H. Saffarans, and a "free boy" Governor Duke, all of Nashville.[63]

Crossing to the Pacific, the Tennessee companies arrived at Panama City about May 18. The character of the boatmen and other natives that Barry dealt with while on the Isthmus impressed him very much: "The natives . . . are entirely honest and confidential and were it not the many rascally Americans and foreigners they have to deal with, an honest man could get along without any difficulty." Wilson, Love and Company and Barry's Independents camped together near the city while awaiting passage to San Francisco.[64]

Dr. Evans and his Shelbyville colleagues had fallen behind the other two companies because they took the schooner *Charran* from New Orleans to Chagres and did not arrive there until May 24. The small company reached Panama City on May 29 where those who had arrived several days before were still waiting for transportation. On June 5 Dr. Evans's group embarked on the French sailing vessel *Cachalot*, leaving the other three Tennessee companies waiting for the steamship *New World*.[65]

Sixty-nine of the 165 passengers aboard the *Cachalot* were Tennesseans, but few of their names are known. Once under way, the miners rebelled because of the poor quality of the food, deposed the cook, and divided into messes. Proceeding on the theory that "Methodist preachers always live on the best, provided they can get it," the Shelbyville men elected George Horne, a Knox County Methodist parson attracted to the gold fields, to head their mess.[66]

Horne had led a small company of his own that reached Chagres May 25. Departing from Knoxville on May 6, they had proceeded by mail stage to Dalton, Georgia, and thence by rail to Atlanta, Augusta, and Charleston, South Carolina. They boarded the steamship *Georgia* on May 16 and cruised to Chagres with only a brief stop at Havana. During their three-day crossing of the Isthmus, the East Tennesseans were often in the company of a goodly number of other Tennesseans, many of whom seem to have become fellow passengers aboard the *Cachalot*.[67]

Eighteen Monroe County men, two of whom were slave blacks, were among those who boarded the *Cachalot*. They had left East Tennessee from Blair's Ferry on April 15 on the steamboat *Ellen White*, transferred to a flatboat at Decatur, Alabama, on April 17, and arrived at New Orleans eight days later. Fellow travelers with Dr. Evans's company on board the *Charran*, they experienced the death of one of their number while crossing the Gulf. Suffering from cholera, Houston Vincent died May 1 and was buried at sea. Other known members of the original eighteen were John

Crawford Vaughn, E. C. Harris, and James Vincent, brother of the deceased.[68]

Wilson, Love and Company and the Sumner Independents boarded the *New World* at Panama City in time to reach San Francisco on July 11, 1850. Both companies had been forced to buy their tickets from speculators at exorbitant prices because the demand far exceeded the supply.[69]

The *Cachalot* did not deliver its weary passengers to San Francisco until August 12, sixty-eight tedious days from Panama City. Its progress had been so slow that it was forced to detour by the Sandwich Islands to replenish its exhausted water supply. The ship was once becalmed for about eight days. The available food was virtually inedible even when the miners cooked it themselves, the ship "filthy and nauseous," and passenger morale was so low that the captain and crew feared that control of the ship might be taken from them.[70]

Notwithstanding the reputed conniving of ticket scalpers at Panama City that some thought included the United States consul, gold rushers flocked to the Isthmus route. G. A. Harrell, an attorney and former state legislator from Montgomery County, and Cornelius Crusman, a former Montgomery County sheriff and successful businessman, selected that course for the small companies they led from the Clarksville area. As superintendent of the Hope Mining Company, Harrell set out for California on April 6 with Dr. Joseph W. Stout, J. W. Judkins, William Stewart, William Carpenter, B. F. Thomas, Samuel L. Williamson, Lewis Sharp, and D. A. Wilkins. They reached San Francisco sixty days later. Crusman departed May 1 with company members Dr. William A. McClure, Dr. B. T. Whitney, and William Gray, and two others not affiliated: Dr. John Elder and Sidney Stephenson. They crossed successfully to California, but details of their travels are not offered.[71]

On April 28, John F. Pate, J. A. Mabry, and "companions" began their crossing from Knoxville where they took riverboats to New Orleans. Arriving in the port city on May 8, the company embarked for Chagres three days later aboard the steamship *Alabama*. Identification of Pate and Mabry's fellow travelers and details of their travel from New Orleans are not made, although it is known that they were in the California diggings at Nevada City on Deer Creek prior to October 5, 1850.[72]

The only delays of consequence along the Isthmus route usually occurred at Panama City when emigrants were waiting for ships. A Bradley County company of perhaps ten men waited fifty-eight days there in the spring of 1850 before the arrival of the ship to which they were ticketed. They reached San Francisco about July 1. The surnames of three members were reported: Grant, Bates, and Lyman.[73]

During the latter part of April, another party from Nashville set out for the Isthmus. Its members were H. B. Plummer, J. G. Shepherd, J. R. Underwood, W. W. Allen, George H. Martin, E. A. Horne, H. M. Newhall, and "Messrs. Wagner, Bailey, Brackin . . . McDonald, and Langford." When they boarded the steamer *Falcon* at New Orleans for Chagres, they were in company with Samuel Hodges and Samuel A. Davidson of Nashville and H. B. Waggoner of Whites Creek.[74] Further details of their travels are lacking.

Dr. P. W. Martin's Nashville company approached Chagres by way of New York City probably because through tickets that included sea travel on both sides of the Isthmus were more readily available there. Their plan seems to have worked well. Leaving from Nashville for New York by steamboat on May 21, the company reached Chagres on June 22. Once across the Isthmus, the travelers boarded the steamship *Oregon* on July 2 for San Francisco and, after the usual stops, steamed through the Golden Gate on July 21. They had been sixty-one days from Nashville. Members of the company, in addition to Dr. Martin and his son, were Dr. J. W. King, treasurer; R. H. Harvey; James Peacock; W. J. Childress; Thomas B. Childress; James R. McCall; and Irvin Stephenson, a slave black.[75]

Traveling from Panama City with Dr. Martin's party was native Nashvillian William Walker, educated in medicine and the law but in the months immediately prior to his departure a newspaper editor at New Orleans. Walker had steamed to Havana from New Orleans on the *Ohio* and there transferred to the *Georgia* which took him to Chagres. By June 29, he was at Panama City, and with a ticket to San Francisco purchased before he set out, he was on board the *Oregon* when it departed July 2. Planning to join a former New Orleans printer to launch a new newspaper in San Francisco, Walker discovered that his prospective partner had abandoned their plans and departed for the gold fields.[76]

Charleston was the port of departure for Chagres chosen by John T. O'Brien for four of his Knoxville company of five headed to California and quartz mining. The fifth member, Dr. William Hunt, had gone ahead and was in San Francisco before May 19, 1850. Their travel proceeded as planned until they reached Panama City where approximately two thousand gold seekers were "waiting for vessels." Two of the company, Wall and Ross, became involved in a fight between American emigrants and natives touched off by the arrest of a local man for stealing from the office of the *Panama Echo* the editor's trunk containing $600. A mob of locals took the culprit from the custody of law officers and about seventy Americans pursued the group to retake him. In the melee that followed, four Americans were killed as well as an unreported number of natives. Wall and Ross escaped harm, although the former, charged by the mob, shot one of its leaders, and Ross was saved from knife-wielding assailants by another American who seized a rifle and held off the attackers.[77]

Accepting a job as superintendent of the steerage passengers on a steamship in exchange for free passage to San Francisco and pay of $1 per day, John T. O'Brien left his three colleagues behind, but with funds enough for tickets on the next steamer. Dr. William Hunt gladly received John at San Francisco on June 23. James O'Brien, Wall, and Ross arrived on July 6.[78]

Apparently planning to follow the Isthmus route, C. K. Gillespie and six unidentified fellow Carter Countians reached Knoxville May 3, 1850, on their way to El Dorado. A Washington County company conducted by a certain Colonel Mitchell had left Charleston, South Carolina, on April 15 for Chagres. Other details of their travels are not known unless James B. Housley of Carter County, who was reported doing well in California near the end of the year, was one of Gillespie's men.[79]

The working members of the Nashville and California Mining Company, Dr. I. H. Harris, superintendent, left the city March 16 for San Francisco via the Isthmus. While waiting at Panama City for transportation, members of the company decided to divide forces for the trip. On May 1, Dr. Harris and his engineer, A. A. Adams, set out on the steamship *Oregon* and reached San Francisco nineteen days later. R. M. Ewing, the brothers B. B. and H. Brett, and their seven slave blacks, Ned, Thornton, Solomon, Moses, Henry, Elias, and Hector, left the same day on the sailing vessel *Sea Queen*. The slower vessel delivered its passengers to San Francisco on June 26. Upon their arrival Dr. Harris posted a letter to Nashville boasting that "all the company" had enjoyed "continued and uninterrupted good health" since leaving Tennessee.[80]

A Tennessee company with twenty-one members reached Chagres from New Orleans on May 21 on the steamship *Alabama*. The only known member of the entourage was Joseph Cox, seemingly from Carthage in Smith County, who wrote a brief account of their crossing to William

Bowen Campbell.[81] When they reached Panama City, they met Maj. Perrin Solomon and Maj. David Saffarans and several others from Nashville and Gallatin, including six slave blacks. Many of the group operated together when they first reached the mines as the ad hoc Nashville, Gallatin, and California Company, Cox wrote.

Solomon, Saffarans, Cox, and others unnamed embarked for San Francisco on June 5 aboard the barque *Sarah*, and the passage was far from pleasant. "We had very bad times at sea, a bad ship and [a] very drunken captain [to] say nothing about the stinking and rotten provisions," Cox declared. After seventy-five days at sea, they arrived safely in San Francisco.[82]

Aware that Panama City was crowded with Americans unable to get passage to San Francisco, McNairy Countian Joseph L. Rushing of Anderson's Store, Tennessee, waited patiently at New Orleans during the winter of 1850 until he could get a through ticket. While waiting, he declined his wife's fervent plea to abandon his journey and return home to her and their young daughter. "I set out with the intention to make something, and I do not feel willing to return without making an effort," he wrote from New Orleans.

By the middle of February, Rushing had despaired of being able to purchase a through ticket to California via the Isthmus and decided to take a southern overland route to Mazatlán and there book sea passage to California. He was en route at Brownsville, Texas, on February 26, and he reached San Francisco sometime prior to June 1.[83] Family correspondence mentions other men from McNairy County. At midyear Richard Johnson, James Dickey, and others were on their way, probably via the Isthmus, and Nip Street, William Hill, and the sheriff of Hardin County were about to leave for St. Louis and a plains crossing.[84]

A single reference to the "Union Company of Nashville" did not mention names or number, but they left New Orleans on April 10 for Chagres on the steamboat *Falcon*. Thirty other unidentified Tennesseans accompanied them to the Isthmus. In reporting the *Falcon*'s departure, a New Orleans correspondent of the Nashville *Daily American*[85] concluded that from the "numerous companies passing through this place, Tennessee is going to have a full representation in California."

After 1850, crossings from Tennessee to the gold fields, by whatever route, became somewhat routine. There were still dangers and inconveniences, but most of the time travelers received an abundance of help to see them through. Prior to 1851, Tennessee newspapers had been a prime source for information about local gold seekers. Beginning in 1851, however, parties departing for the gold fields seem to have attracted no more attention than those who might be leaving for New Orleans or St. Louis. Thereafter, the newspapers rarely published the names of west-bound emigrants, but devoted space to letters from California and interviews with the many who were returning home.

Not all obstacles had been removed from the crossing as a company of East Tennesseans led by A. G. Register and including Joseph Robertson, men named Hartman and McAll, and possibly others discovered when they set out for California about March 1, 1852. Traveling overland to Charleston, they went by ship to Havana. Giving credence to persistent reports that obtaining passage from Panama City to San Francisco was possible only after an extremely long wait, the company redirected its travels to New Orleans. They then proceeded up the Mississippi River to Independence and began their overland journey westward about May 1.[86] Traveling with two wagons, each pulled by four yoke of oxen, Register and his party arrived near Sacramento about the middle of August. He and presumably the others began working in the mines soon afterward.[87]

In 1852, former Tennessean James Bell, his wife, and his brother Andrew left from Smithland, Kentucky, for the gold fields by way of the recently opened route across Nicaragua.[88] Their final destination was Sonora, and they arrived there on November 20. Edmond Parsons, who had completed a carpenter's apprenticeship in Memphis between 1849 and 1851, chose the Isthmus of Panama route to go to California in 1852.[89]

The former Montgomery County family of Benjamin F. Hurst left Springfield, Missouri, and took up the California Trail at Independence on April 20, 1852. Riding in a wagon drawn by two yoke of oxen, Hurst, his wife, Eliza Flack, their daughter, and two sons traveled with a large train to Fiddletown, California.[90]

A third wave of the Grigsby family came overland from Independence in 1853, but death took a toll. Some of them were of the older generation, their children and nephews having made the journey in 1846 or 1850. Samuel H. Grigsby and his wife, Mary Polly Lindsay, native Giles Countians, traveled to Napa Valley, but Mary died there October 11, 1853, a week after they arrived. Lillard H. Grigsby, his wife, and others unidentified had died of "camp fever" while on the trail.[91]

J. W. Major of East Tennessee came over the California Trail in 1853 and began farming. Soon thereafter, he became superintendent of the mill at the Ferguson mine for three years before he returned to farming and ranching near Sonora.[92]

Recognizing families from his home county of Sumner, Tyree B. Harris mentioned Clint Bledsoe, Jonah Austin, William Carter, and Ed Green, with their families, as new arrivals in 1853. He said others were newly arrived, but did not name them.[93]

Dr. Harris's wife was a charming hostess to Tennesseans who visited the Harris home in Nashville, California in 1852–53. A correspondent was received warmly by the miners, but he found "the richest treat of all was meeting in this woman-forsaken country with the amiable, gifted and accomplished lady of Dr. Harris." Her conversation "caused the hours to speed by as on the lightning's wing, for the refining and all pervading influence of the gentle sex is seldom felt in this state."[94]

A rumor circulated that Mrs. Harris had come to the gold country to edit a newspaper, but when John Litton Bostick visited, he found her "engaged pretty much as ladies at home, sewing, reading, [and] attending to the chickens." The first time he dined with the Harrises, she "apologized for having a sardine box for a sugar bowl," but soon afterward "she introduced unheard of extravagances . . . such as white tablecloths, chinaware, etc.," he said.[95]

Matrimony may have been the reason Elizabeth Douglass, daughter of Dr. Elmore Douglass and his wife, Elizabeth Fulton, of Sumner County, set out for California by stage during February 1851 to visit her brother, David F. Douglass. Sometime after reaching David's home, Elizabeth was married to John A. Reed, formerly of Louisville, Kentucky.[96]

Was matrimony the object of Belle Patterson's journey across the plains to California in 1854? A sister of David Patterson, Governor Andrew Johnson's son-in-law, Belle traveled with another of her seven brothers. Sometime after reaching the Golden State, she was married to Tyler D. Heiskell, and they became longtime residents of the area.[97]

Marriage was clearly the reason Julia M. H. Hall of Nashville traveled to San Francisco in 1852. Taking the Isthmus route, Julia reached her destination aboard the *Northerner*, a steamship from Panama City. A harbor boat brought local attorney Horace P. Janes to meet her, and they were married on board the *Northerner* on April 14, 1852. The ceremony was conducted by Jesse Boring, a Methodist minister from Tennessee who was a passenger on the ship.[98]

To reach California during the years immediately following 1849 meant matrimony for very few except the multitude of miners who were married to their dreams of gold. They loved the prospect of obtaining gold, and in many cases it prompted a till-death-us-do-part commitment by them. It was not the first or the last time that Americans would embrace a dream of gold. Yet it was a very special courtship that resulted not only in the mining of many millions of dollars worth of the precious metal, but also in the marriage of the American East and West.

Notwithstanding dreams of gold, Tennessee emigrants had many first-time experiences in the crossing. They had used all the avenues westward, but a large majority of them had gone by one of two routes. Most who crossed the Isthmus saw and traveled the Gulf of Mexico and the Pacific Ocean for the first time and had their first adventures in the tropics. Passing over the California Trail had introduced Tennesseans to the prairie, the great plains, the Rocky Mountains, the deserts, and the Sierra Nevada.

Even though many of them were exhausted from their travels, the emigrants turned to the task at hand: mining for gold. It was not easy for reasons having nothing to do with gold itself. Tens of thousands of men and a few women had rushed into a vast area with no cities and few towns or villages. There was no infrastructure to supply transportation or any other public or commercial services. At first, miners improvised the services they needed. Because there were no reliable maps or charts of the gold fields, locating placers[99] or other likely gold deposits was often a matter of luck. Rumors, irresponsible reports, and intentionally misleading stories of discovery hung over every choice the miners made. But they had come to dig, and that is what they did.

A few saw opportunities in public service and participated in the creation of local and state government. Among them were several with experience in government and politics; in fact, more were experienced politicians than experienced miners. It was a phenomenon easily discernible as the development of government and mining proceeded at a brisk pace.

CHAPTER IX

The Birth of a State

T HE TURMOIL and unrest engendered by the arrival of tens of thousands of excited gold seekers in 1849 called urgently for the stabilizing hand of government. When the first prospectors arrived early in the year, there seemed to be room enough for all, and there was little cause for friction. As their number increased to more than ninety thousand, so did contentious attitudes that led to frequent outbursts of individual and group violence. Many called for law and order.[1]

Overshadowed by the arrival of the forty-niners was the broader question of how the California country, so recently acquired from Mexico, should be governed. The United States had asserted control over the territory during the early stages of the Mexican War when Pacific fleet commander Commodore John D. Sloat took possession of Monterey on July 7, 1846. He issued a conciliatory proclamation that announced American ascendancy and directed local government operations to continue as in the past. Sloat's successor in command, Commodore Robert F. Stockton, solidified United States control later in the year by sending volunteers against Mexican garrisons in the South.[2]

Instituting the practice of governing through a designated military officer on the scene, the president appointed Col. Richard B. Mason of the United States Army to be military governor on February 12, 1847. By that time the Mexican-appointed alcaldes, the next in authority and only other government officials in the short chain of command, had expanded their powers until they were virtually local dictators. Their behavior became a chronic source of trouble for Mason, and the conscientious colonel began to see the need for a duly constituted representative government in the

American tradition.[3] On February 13, Robert Sample, the editor of the California *Star*, called for a convention to draft a territorial constitution. For the rest of the year public discussion waxed and waned on the merits of that approach to organizing government.

Three notable developments during 1848 paved the way for an elected civilian government. First, the discovery of gold introduced a new instability into the area. Then on August 6, news reached California that the United States and Mexico had signed the Treaty of Guadalupe Hidalgo by which Mexico recognized California and New Mexico as territory of the United States. And finally on December 5, President Polk confirmed the existence of large deposits of gold in California and asked Congress to set up a territorial government.

Eager to have the services and protection that government could provide,[4] citizens attended mass meetings at San Jose and San Francisco in December 1848 and at Sacramento on January 6, 1849, to consider "organizing a Provisional Government for the territory of California." Those attending the rally at Sacramento elected Peter Hardeman Burnett president of the meeting. He appointed a committee to prepare and bring back within forty-eight hours a set of resolutions recommending a course of action for the people of the territory to pursue relative to self-governance.[5]

Burnett[6] had come to Sutter's Fort in December 1848, and soon after joined the government movement, invited by persons who knew something about him before he came from Oregon. "His reputation as a lawyer, jurist, politician, legislator, and authority on provisional government . . . made him an oracle in the rights of people beyond the limits of organized government," a California historian later observed. The action contemplated at the Sacramento meeting was based largely on his advice that the people "had the right to establish *de facto* government" to function until replaced by a government regularly constituted and established by the United States Congress.[7]

On January 8, 1849, the reconvened mass meeting adopted a recommendation "that the inhabitants of California should form a Provisional Government to enact laws and appoint officers" to administer them until Congress should see fit "to extend the laws of the United States" over the territory. When those present voted to instruct their delegates to oppose slavery in California "in every shape and form," they preempted the national government on that question. Most opposed not only the use of slave labor but also the presence of both slave and free blacks.[8] Indians and

Mexicans aplenty could supply the labor usually performed by slaves in the South.

Participants in the three separate meetings shared essentially the same sentiments. They united forces to call for a convention to be held at San Jose on March 5 for the purpose of "drafting and preparing a form of government to be submitted to the people for their sanction." Soon after the call was made, the promoters postponed the convention until May 1 because they wanted to give the southern districts time to elect their representatives, but also because it was believed Congress would make California a federal territory and create a government for it by that date.[9]

A citizens' meeting at Sonoma in early February 1849 elected ten delegates to represent the county at a convention to consider provisional government. Those present also voted to create a legislative assembly of twenty-five members to provide government for the county. William McCutchen and Captain John Grigsby were elected to both the convention and the assembly.[10]

Fearing that a provisional government might fall under the control of independence or separatist movements, outgoing President Polk and his successor Zachary Taylor repeatedly sent messages to California residents assuring them that they were citizens of the United States and that they enjoyed the full protection of its military forces. Nevertheless, the presidents could not conceal the truth that Congress would do nothing about government in California until it could deal with the question of slavery in new states or territories.[11] Congressional action was slowed further by the introduction of a new perspective to the slavery debate; opponents of slavery had the unusual opportunity of challenging it where it did not exist.[12]

When Congress ignored Polk's recommendation to make California a federal territory yet extended the revenue laws of the United States[13] over it, most Californians were furious. Peter Burnett immediately charged that it was "taxation without representation," pure and simple. "The principles that produced the American revolution have been forgotten," he wrote to Missouri Congressman Willard P. Hall on April 16. At least Great Britain had provided the colonies with government, he explained, but "our own Congress will give us *nothing but burthens*."[14]

There is the greatest indignation expressed here against the measure. If we have no rights left, then disregard us altogether. Leave us to ourselves, if you think we should be treated with *calm, sover-*

eign, silent and ineffable contempt. If we are citizens, give us the privileges that belong to us as such.[15]

Succeeding Colonel Mason as governor on April 13, 1849, Brig. Gen. Bennett Riley began the process of organizing civilian government for the region. He called for the election of delegates to a convention to provide for organizing either a federal territory or a state of the Union. He posted the call in San Francisco on June 9, set the election for August 1, and scheduled the convention to begin its deliberations on September 1.[16]

Five days before Riley posted the call, a native Tennessean who became the most influential political figure in California for the next decade arrived at San Francisco. William McKendree Gwin, who had waited seven weeks at Panama City before obtaining passage to San Francisco, disembarked from the steamer *Panama* with the goal of becoming one of the first two United States senators from the yet-to-be organized state of California. Before he left Washington, D.C., Gwin had told Illinois Senator Stephen A. Douglas on March 5 that he was on his way to California where, since Congress had failed to create a federal territory, he would advocate a state government. He promised with brazen and uncanny accuracy that he would return within one year and ask Douglas to present his credentials as senator from California.[17]

Gwin was a remarkable second-generation product of the Tennessee frontier. Born in 1805 in Sumner County, the son of James and Mary Gwin, the former an itinerant Methodist preacher, William was admitted to the practice of law at Gallatin in 1826. During the same year, he undertook the study of medicine at Transylvania College in Lexington, Kentucky, preparatory to entering actively into that profession in 1828. He began medical practice in Mississippi, but abandoned it in 1833 after having taken leave for six months to serve in Washington as a private secretary to President Andrew Jackson. Jackson subsequently appointed him United States marshal for the southern district of Mississippi. In 1840, Gwin won election to the House of Representatives from Mississippi, but declined to seek reelection in 1842. He moved to New Orleans in 1845 as federal commissioner to superintend construction of the customs house and was living there when he opted for political adventure in California.[18]

On June 12, Gwin and Burnett joined President Taylor's special agent, T. Butler King of Georgia, to address a San Francisco mass meeting held to promote support for organizing government. Embittered by a

Congress that would tax them but do nothing to organize representative government in the region, the audience initially displayed little enthusiasm for the undertaking. When Gwin and King insisted that the proposed convention was the result of the expressed wishes of the people of California, they won the grudging support of the crowd. Burnett, who had called the meeting to order and presented a slate of officers, was named to chair a committee of five to correspond with leaders of other districts promoting the same cause and to report to the public.[19]

Drafted by Burnett, the consensus report of the meetings contended that General Riley as military governor had no authority to set the time and place for the election of delegates to the convention, but recommended that his dates be accepted because the southern districts had already agreed to them. Otherwise conciliatory in tone, the report reflected the leaders' recognition that Riley's convention call was precisely what they wanted.[20]

During the course of the public discussions, Burnett emerged as a political leader of formidable stature. In a long, thoughtful essay printed in the *Alta California* on April 26, 1849, he analyzed President Polk's statement of December 8, 1848, about the military-alcalde or de facto government in California. The president had not ordered the people of California to accept a military governor and Mexican alcaldes, even for the short term, Burnett said. In fact, Polk had advised Californians new and old to "conform and submit for a short intervening period, before Congress would again assemble, and could legislate on the subject." As the president had only "advised" them and Congress had not yet legislated, Californians were free to provide government for themselves under the Constitution of the United States, he concluded.[21]

Burnett held traditional American reservations about the role of the military in civil affairs. He welcomed General Riley's call for the convention, but had doubts about a general officer's participation in civil government. Notwithstanding Riley's disavowal of interest in a governing role and his assurance that the military would assist government but not constitute it, Burnett was not satisfied.[22]

Further friction between the two occurred when San Francisco County organized a legislative assembly before the convention assembled. Although he doubted the wisdom of organizing this and other local government councils, Burnett agreed to accept a seat after he was elected in his absence.[23] Determined to head off the forming of unauthorized government, General Riley accused Burnett and the other members of the assembly of usurping the powers of Congress. Elected chairman of a committee to respond, Burnett icily observed that the general was wrong. Their attempt to organize local government was a matter of filling a void where no government existed, he said. Insisting that they had never intended to establish an independent national government, Burnett wrote, "To say that the people of California, ever contemplated or attempted such a thing, is to charge us with an intent to commit the highest crime known to the laws of the United States, without the shadow . . . of proof upon which to base such a grievous and most horrible accusation."[24]

Burnett's first act as a member of the San Francisco legislative assembly was to propose and win appointment of a committee to draft a proposal to the people of California imploring them to "hold a convention to form a government for the whole Territory." The proposal was prepared before General Riley published his convention call in the *Alta California* on June 14, but did not appear in the local press until a few days later. Burnett and his associates had been unaware that Riley was planning to call a convention.[25]

Gwin shared Burnett's discomfort with government administered by a military commander, and he sensed the same attitude among the citizens. "There is great dissatisfaction towards the military government and nothing prevents an outbreak but the prospect of a speedy state organization," he wrote on June 20. "The people are most indignant at the course of Congress, and will, within ninety days, have an organized state government."[26]

As August 1 approached, Gwin became a candidate to represent the San Francisco District at the convention, and Burnett announced his candidacy for a seat on the Sacramento District superior court. Both were elected. Gwin was the only native-born Tennessean among the forty-eight delegates chosen for the convention. Cave Johnson Couts was elected an alternate delegate to the convention to represent San Diego, but was not called upon to participate.[27] Although he was born in Ohio and had spent much of his life in Louisiana, another member of the convention had lived for several years in Tennessee. Elected to represent Tuolumne County, Dr. O. M. Wozencraft once practiced medicine at Nashville where he was married to Lamiza A. Ramsey, daughter of Col. William R. Ramsey. Mrs. Wozencraft and a daughter, Mary A., born to them at Nashville, accompanied her husband to California in 1849.[28]

Elected by a vote of 1,298 to 212, Burnett became the chief justice of the district court, a position that did not inhibit his public display of support for organizing state government. He seized every opportunity to speak and write on the topic.[29]

William Gwin's presence in the convention was vital to its success. Not only was he one of the best educated delegates, a protégé of the late President Andrew Jackson, and a former member of Congress, he knew how government worked, and he understood its limitations. And he was not yet personally interested in gold mines or other forms of commerce in California.

Gwin was delighted when the convention quickly opted for statehood in preference to territorial status. By so doing, it accelerated the process of achieving representative government at all levels.

Although his many interruptions in the early proceedings of the convention were criticized by some as presumptive behavior on his part, Gwin, the consummate politician, soon won the confidence of the other delegates. His high standing with the leadership of the convention was demonstrated when they appointed him chairman of the committee to draft the state constitution.[30] As a recent arrival with Washington political experience, Gwin was suspect in the eyes of enough committee members that they overruled the convention chair and elected another member to preside. Ironically, the decision freed Gwin to play an even stronger hand in the matters before them.[31]

Advising the convention to display openness and concern for individual freedoms in all its deliberations, Gwin urged respect for the rights and power of the electorate. He explained to the delegates: "Our country is like a blank sheet of paper upon which we are required to write a system of fundamental laws. Let the rights of the people be guarded in every line we write, or they will apply the sponge to our work."[32]

Ever a Jacksonian, Gwin warned against unbridled banks and loose currency, and he advocated restrictions on the legislature's powers to charter banks, to create corporations by private acts, and to create state debt. The constitution should be drawn in such a way that it would not permit the development of "a moneyed aristocracy" in the state. He was equally candid about raising revenues. "Taxation should be equal and uniform throughout the state. All property in this state shall be taxed in proportion to its value; to be ascertained as directed by law," he proposed in language included in the constitution.[33]

Although a Southerner and expected to be proslavery, Gwin took a strong position in the convention against allowing slavery in California. When he at first favored a state larger than the area proposed, critics charged he was trying to create a political subdivision that might later be cut in half for the making of one state slave, the other free. A few Southerners in California wanted slavery sanctioned, but Gwin's early interest in a larger state was no part of a Southern conspiracy to keep the prospects of slavery alive in the West. In fact, most of his fellow Southerners among the delegates voted repeatedly in favor of the smaller state.[34] Gwin had no illusions that slavery would be permitted in California, and several weeks prior to the convention, he had written to a friend in New Orleans that slavery would be voted down by a big majority.[35]

The forthright lawyer, doctor, and statesman expressed an opinion on every issue. Addressing the concerns of the Californios[36] who feared that as a minority they might lose their landholdings, Gwin explained that a primary function of representative government is to restrain the majority from trampling on the rights of the minority. As for a model constitution, he recommended the constitution of the state of Iowa, one of "the latest and the shortest." Gwin favored petitioning Congress for funds to defray the expenses of organizing the new state and passed a resolution authorizing publication of the proceedings of the convention, 1,000 copies in English and 250 in Spanish. He opposed dueling:

It is no evidence of bravery, for the greatest cowards engage in it. I say it should be discountenanced and put down . . . when you insert this provision in your constitution . . . that a man is branded when he fights a duel, he quits it. In Tennessee, where it was made a penitentiary offense, it was abandoned.[37]

On October 12, 1849, the convention adopted a constitution for the state of California and sent copies of it to General Riley to be transmitted to Congress and the White House. Both Gwin and Wozencraft voted to approve it. A surprisingly liberal document, it protected the property rights of wives, provided an elective judiciary, and prohibited slavery. Overall, it represented an impressive accomplishment by delegates working against the mounting needs of a fast-growing society of gold seekers, many of whom regarded their presence as only temporary. None had done as much as Gwin to produce a blueprint for government that would serve the needs of the new state.[38]

After the convention adjourned, political leaders maneuvered for election to the offices set forth in the constitution. Inspired by a speech made by William Van Voorhies to a San Francisco mass meeting on October 25, the Democrats of California hastily organized their party and endorsed a slate of candidates. Heading the list was the popular Peter Burnett,[39] who had announced three weeks earlier that he would run for governor as an independent candidate. He campaigned vigorously in support of the new constitution as well as for himself. On election day, November 13, the voters ratified the constitution by a vote of 12,061 to 811 and elected Burnett governor by a total of 6,783 votes to 3,220 for the runner-up. Democrats won control of both houses of the legislature. A few days later, Burnett nominated William Van Voorhies, who had been elected to the assembly, to be his secretary of state.[40]

After the inauguration of Governor Burnett in ceremonies at the state capital of San Jose on December 20, members of the legislature met to elect two United States senators. They chose John C. Fremont on the first ballot and Gwin on the third. By lot, Gwin won the full term of six years and Fremont the short term of two.[41] The state senate confirmed Voorhies as secretary of state on the next day,[42] and the legislature elected former Tennessean Richard Roman state treasurer on December 22.[43]

Former Tennesseans then held the full or long term in the United States Senate, the offices of governor, secretary of state, and state treasurer, four powerful positions in the first state west of the Rockies. David F. Douglass, representing the San Joaquin District and W. R. Bassham representing the San Jose District, both formerly of Tennessee, were two of the sixteen members of the state senate.[44] The new state's debt to another Tennessean, the recently deceased former President James K. Polk, had been acknowledged by public memorial services in August. The editor of the *Alta California* spoke for all when he wrote, "California has just cause to be indebted to the deceased, and her citizens will forever cherish the name of James K. Polk, while they enjoy the blessings promoted at his hand."[45]

Even as the California convention reported a blueprint for the government of that state, Democratic Governor William Trousdale of Tennessee urged his state's general assembly on October 22, 1849, to "adopt and forward to Congress" a protest against interference with "the rights" reserved to states in regard to the institution of slavery. Asserting that Congress had no constitutional power to act on the subject of "slavery in a territory," he warned against other acts of Congress that would "encircle the slaveholding states with free territory," prohibit slavery in the District of Columbia, and stop "the transfer of slaves from one state to another for sale." The legislature had the duty "to proclaim to our northern brethren

. . . our unalterable purpose of maintaining our rights, at all hazards and to the last extremity," he declared.[46]

In response to the governor's request, Tennessee's Whig-controlled senate and the Democratic house offered various resolutions. After extensive debate, a watered-down version of prior drafts was adopted on the final day of the session, February 11, 1850. It affirmed allegiance to the United States and declared that preservation of the Union "in its original purity, so as to secure to the several states their constitutional rights," could be achieved only "by resisting, at all hazards and to the last extremity, any and all attempts to violate the spirit and intent" of the Constitution. In his valedictory address four months prior, the Whig Governor Neill S. Brown had asserted that the federal government had no power to exclude slavery from new territories where it did not exist. Furthermore, neither the federal government nor the states had any right to interfere with slavery in states where it was practiced, he said. Insisting that the Union must be maintained, Brown nonetheless opposed federal legislation on the subject of slavery and recommended that its future be determined by local sentiment and local legislation.[47]

Among Tennesseans in the gold country, there seems to have been little concern about how their home state might be affected by the constitutional prohibition of slavery in California. Most who took public positions on the issue intended to remain in the West and were interested primarily in seeing California become a state of the Union. Few of them thought the peculiar institution had any place in their society.

The work of the California convention and further organization of the state had transpired under the threatening cloud of a Mississippi call for a convention of slaveholding states to be held in Nashville in June of 1850. Most thought the convention would defend the institution of slavery and declare the rights of slave owners to take their property into the Mexican cession lands. The latter action was expected in response to the Wilmot Proviso that, although never passed into law, had frightened the slaveholding South by proposing to prohibit slavery anywhere in the Mexican cession.[48] Although certain Southern leaders were openly discussing separation from the Union, Californians expected that their new state would be securely in the Union before the Nashville convention and thus not on its agenda.

Like Tennessee in 1796, California had suddenly organized itself into a state with encouragement but without clear authority from the national government, had elected officers, and anxiously awaited admission to the

Union. The new state dispatched its congressional delegation to Washington via the Isthmus on January 1, 1850. Slightly more than six weeks later Senators Gwin and Fremont and Congressmen Edward Gilbert and George W. Wright reached the capital.[49]

The question of accepting California into the Union brought the issue of slavery into the national spotlight as never before. Hoping to remove the question from the territorial context in which both parties in Congress had placed it, President Zachary Taylor proposed that California and New Mexico be admitted as states as soon as they were ready and with or without slavery as each chose. Instead of removing slavery from the national agenda, the president's proposal raised it to the head of the list and precipitated one of the most bitter sectional debates in United States history. Many Southerners rallied around John C. Calhoun and pledged to destroy the Union if slavery were excluded from California and New Mexico. Northern states were determined to prohibit slavery in states arising from the Mexican cession. The debate raged in Congress for seven months.[50]

As admitting the new state had become a national issue, advocacy groups formed to marshal support for the cause. Former Nashville editor John P. Heiss, who had just retired as partner and business manager of the Washington (D.C.) *Union*, received an invitation to attend the first "Ball" of the Democratic Union and California Club of New York City on April 19, 1850. The principal object of the organization was "to promote the immediate admission of California into the American Union." Their method was "to cheer on and sustain by all proper efforts the public men in the Councils of the Nation who are the avowed friends of that measure."[51] Because of the slavery issue, most such clubs were in the Northern states.

While awaiting action by Congress, Gwin responded on March 1 to an inquiry from W. M. Meredith, secretary of the treasury, that sought advice on legislation for California that would affect the treasury. He first recommended that the department should extend "the coast survey" and to execute it with maximum accuracy because existing surveys were unreliable. New surveys of bays and channels should be made carefully, noting the hydrography and topography, and new charts should be prepared and distributed to ship captains and merchants in the coastal trade, he said. Congress should construct lighthouses at critical points. Recognizing the importance of the Sacramento and San Joaquin Rivers, Gwin favored "moderate" expenditures to improve port facilities and deepen channels. He pointed out the need for "marine hospitals" at San Francisco,

Sacramento, and Stockton, "the great depots of the upper and lower mines." Given the large gold exports from California and its increasingly large import business, the government must provide every possible service to the free flow of commerce, he urged. Gwin advocated the construction of "a mint on a large scale" at San Francisco with branch mints at Sacramento and Stockton as a service to the miners. At the very least, he argued that assay offices be established in the latter two cities until such time as construction of the branch mints should be deemed proper. And to accomplish all of his suggestions, Gwin emphasized that all personnel engaged in the various activities, whether army, navy, or civilian — skilled and unskilled — "should receive an adequate compensation . . . so as to prevent desertion and vexatious delays."[52]

It was obvious to Senator Gwin from the time of his arrival in Washington that California was being held hostage to the bitter debate over slavery. Summoned to the bedside of the ill Senator John C. Calhoun, Gwin learned that the South Carolinian was opposed to the admission of California as a free state because Calhoun believed it would upset the balance of slave and free states and plunge the nation into Civil War.[53]

Equally convinced that the California question threatened the Union, Senator Henry Clay proposed a broad compromise on all slavery questions before the country that he believed would be acceptable to both South and North. Declaring that his first concern was preservation of the Union, Gwin committed to support Clay's compromise. He stood by Clay even when President Taylor summoned him to the White House and urged him and the California delegation to address Congress in behalf of immediate statehood. Clay's proposals appealed not only to Gwin but also to moderates both North and South.[54]

At a social event attended by many Southern congressmen, Gwin explained why California opposed slavery within its bounds. "In California," he said, "labor is respectable." The working miners were men of intelligence and respectability, and they were opposed to having slaves put in competition with them "side by side." His plea probably changed few votes, but it won a hearty endorsement in the eastern press.[55]

When the statehood issue reached the floor of the Senate in February 1850, Whig Senator John Bell[56] of Tennessee introduced resolutions supporting admission of California as a free state, but including provisions that a portion of Texas be cut off and made into a slave state to keep the number of free and slave states equal. He was unable to muster enough votes to pass the resolutions, but some of their contents contributed to the later favorable action for California statehood by his colleagues.[57]

The other Tennessee senator, H. L. Turney, strongly opposed the admission of California because its constitution prohibited slavery. He was so adamantly opposed that after the issue was settled, he was one of ten senators to sign a protest of the majority action.[58]

In a strong speech on the floor of the House of Representatives on April 18, Tennessee Democratic Congressman Andrew Ewing spoke in favor of "the immediate admission of California, the creation of territorial governments in Utah and New Mexico, without restrictions as to slavery, and the acknowledgment of the boundaries of Texas, with a monied compensation for her cession of a reasonable portion of her territory to the United States." Conceding for the purpose of debate that the organization of the state of California was probably attended by certain "irregularities" that he did not identify, he declared that

> the birth of States resembles the natural births—they are usually attended with difficulty and pain, but they can never be *repressed or prevented*; no human power can regenerate an individual, or replace a State in the womb of time. California has sprung, like Minerva, from the head of Jupiter, full grown and fully armed; her destiny is onward, and we may turn her aside from our confederacy, but we can never again make her our pupil.[59]

Addressing the House on June 10, Tennessee Whig Congressman M. P. Gentry placed blame for the controversy about the status of California, New Mexico, and Utah squarely on the shoulders of the Democratic party, beginning with the election of Polk and the annexation of Texas. Since that period, he had concluded that a nation of high principle would always find growth by conquest a very difficult process. Blaming extremists both North and South for injecting the slavery issue into the debate, Gentry argued that causes

> which legislation cannot change, make it impossible for slavery to obtain a permanent foothold in the territories acquired from Mexico. The character and sentiments of the people who now inhabit them, and who are likely to emigrate thither—the character of the country, its soil and climate, all conspire to make such a result impossible.

It was a reality that people North and South should accept, he said. Gentry advocated the admission of California on the president's plan that created territories of New Mexico and Utah with the slavery question to be decided by the territories at such time as they had population sufficient to apply for statehood. He concluded, however, that the quick admission of California was his first concern because he believed it would vastly reduce dangerous national tensions caused by the slavery debate.[60]

The four Californians issued a memorial to Congress calmly explaining that they and their fellow citizens sought statehood because they needed the services of local government under the Constitution of their country. They came before Congress neither as "supplicants" nor as arrogant claimants, but as free "American citizens—by treaty, by adoption and by birth." They asked only that "they be permitted to reap the common benefits, share the common ills, and promote the common welfare, as one of the United States of America."[61]

While Congress continued to debate, delegates from nine Southern states opened the Nashville convention on June 3 to lodge a united protest against the exclusion of slave owners with their slaves from the new western territories. Although there was little popular support for the convention, for the next ten days speakers paraded to the rostrum to defend Southern rights. Most claimed the Union was endangered by "the threatened aggressions of the solid North," and many advocated the creation of a "great Southern sectional party" to assure the survival of the United States. Outside critics countered that the convention was the result of a "treasonable scheme," concocted by radical Southerners from South Carolina and Mississippi, to break the Union and form a Southern confederacy.[62]

The concept of a Southern convention had received less than a lukewarm reception in Tennessee. The general assembly declined to send delegates, and the only representatives from the state were named by the defeated minority of a public mass meeting held in Nashville to elect delegates. The majority had voted against participation in the convention, but the minority held a session of its own and selected delegates.[63] Six other slaveholding states ignored the call and sent no delegates.[64]

The convention adopted thirteen resolutions, the first seven of which dealt with recognizing slave ownership in federal territories. Declaring that slaves were property, the resolutions contended that Congress had no authority to exclude from the territories "any property lawfully held in any state." As "an extreme concession," the delegates voted in favor of extending the Missouri Compromise line of 36°30' all the way to the Pacific

Ocean, an act that would have divided California, not yet a state of the Union, into a slaveholding South and a free North. Aware that Henry Clay's proposed compromise measures were at that very time before Congress, the delegates resolved that they would not anticipate the outcome nor would they speculate on "further methods of resistance should Congress act in such a way that it dishonors the Southern states."[65]

Unable to win approval for all of the series of resolutions he had originally offered, Henry Clay agreed to combine his major proposals in an "omnibus bill." It was part of a strategy by which Clay and Senator Douglas would enact each measure separately. Thus compromise forces could combine with opponents who favored individual resolutions but not all of them. The strategy was successful. The result was the Compromise of 1850 by which Congress admitted California as a free state; created the territories of New Mexico and Utah from the rest of the Mexican cession without prohibiting slavery in either; fixed the boundary of Texas; paid Texas $10,000,000 for relinquishing claims to certain lands in New Mexico; prohibited slave trading in the District of Columbia; and passed a fugitive slave act more to the liking of slaveholders than the long-standing act of 1793.[66]

By passing the "omnibus bill," the Senate voted California into the Union on August 13, 1850, as the two Tennessee senators split their vote. The House concurred on September 9, aided by the Tennessee congressmen who voted for admission seven to four. Two days later members of the congressional delegation from the newest state in the Union were sworn in and seated. On October 18, the steamship *Oregon* arrived at San Francisco bearing the news that California had been admitted as the thirty-first state of the United States of America.[67]

The voters of Tennessee wanted to give the Compromise of 1850 a chance, and Governor Trousdale concurred. He hopefully observed,

> Should this adjustment have the desired effect, it will be a matter of general joy throughout the Union. I deem it the duty of every good citizen to give this attempted adjustment a fair trial, and to endeavor by all honorable means to reconcile the disturbed elements, and to restore peace and harmony to the country.[68]

Although "sorry that Tennessee should have representatives that would vote against the admission of so noble a state," Tennessee émigré J. K. McCall described the jubilation in California:

Everyone is rejoicing; numerous flags float to the breeze, houses are illuminated, and I hear the drum and fife, followed by a noisy band of rowdies. California will do her duty, and heartily extends the hand of fellowship and *brotherhood* to her sister states of the Union.[69]

After the California senators and congressmen took their seats, the Washington *Union* paid tribute to Senator Gwin. "Never did any man better deserve his seat than Dr. Gwin," the editor declared, "by his equanimity, his patriotic devotion to the interests of the whole republic, and the large views and sagacious spirit which he brings into public councils." Gwin had been patient, indeed, and his actions justified the prediction that he was "destined to occupy a high place" in government.[70]

Tennesseans had played key roles in establishing the state of California notwithstanding the distractions of the gold rush and the tense national debate over slavery. Coming from families who had a long tradition of building ever westward, they did not hesitate to shoulder the responsibilities associated with organizing and leading the new state. They were not alone in the undertaking, but at the beginning they stood as tall as the redwoods.

Although the leadership of public officials at the highest levels is of crucial importance, most citizens interact with government in the persons of sheriffs, tax collectors, surveyors, assemblymen, mayors, county judges, and other elected officials of local government. Well aware of that, Californians next focused their attention on candidates for those offices. Tennesseans had been elected to the most celebrated political responsibilities, but what about the others? Who would step forward to fill the myriad lesser but important offices?

CHAPTER X

Political Gold

W HILE statehood for California was being debated by the Congress, several former Tennesseans moved into the front ranks of those seeking local public office. In most cases they brought with them a flair for frontier politics with its dead serious attitude about office holding. Probably the most charismatic of them all was the former Texas Ranger Col. Jack Hays, who reached San Francisco by sea from San Diego on January 25, 1850. Hays's reputation seemed always to precede him as it had in this case when the San Francisco *Alta California* predicted the day before that his arrival was imminent.

Once in the city, Hays immediately searched out J. H. and Joseph Eastland with whom he had journeyed westward from Texas to the Gila River. Their meeting was the grand reunion they had planned before parting at Tucson to follow separate routes to San Francisco.[1] Both Joseph and Hays were on their way to becoming permanent residents of California.

The Texas Ranger hardly had time to acquaint himself with the muddy streets of the city before a group of businessmen persuaded him to become a candidate for county sheriff in the approaching April 1 election. In less than a week after he stepped off the ship, Hays announced his candidacy.[2]

The *Alta California* jumped on Hays's bandwagon when his announcement appeared in its columns. In a lengthy endorsement, the editor concluded:

> To those acquainted with the singularly romantic nature of the Colonel's life and exploits for the last thirteen years—his coolness and daring under the most desperate circumstances—his many

hairbreadth escapes—his numerous fights with Mexicans and Indians, and the great energy of character for which he is distinguished, the popularity he has attained is not at all surprising.[3]

A spirited contest developed. The incumbent sheriff John E. Townes
declared his intent to seek reelection subject to being nominated by the
Whig party. J. J. Bryant, a native Kentuckian and the notoriously successful operator of a gambling house called Bryant's Exchange,
announced his candidacy and sought the nomination of the Democratic
party. Aware that the respect he had for the Whig President Zachary
Taylor, based on their military experiences in Mexico, was not pleasing to
leaders of the Democrats, Hays announced on March 13 that he was running for office as an independent.[4]

Notwithstanding that decision, the Whig party nominated Hays on
March 22. At first, he accepted the nomination, but within twenty-four
hours withdrew his acceptance and reaffirmed that he was in the contest
as an independent. The Democrats then nominated Bryant. Sheriff
Townes turned to his Whig comrades to win their blessing, but when a
mass meeting was called to ratify his nomination, it was adjourned at the
behest of Hays Whigs before agreement was reached.[5]

The campaign was a competition of personalities. Bryant tried to entice voters by offering free drinks, free lunch and, to those down on their
luck, a gold piece or two. He provided enticements not only at his
Bryant's Exchange, but also at other selected bars and gambling rooms.
He treated the public to daily band concerts from the balcony in front of
the Exchange. So confident of victory was he that he bet $10,000 on him-
self to win.[6]

Hays countered by making public appearances and leading parades
through the streets. Although he did not have personal funds comparable
to Bryant's for campaign spending, his friends contributed to a treasury
that proved more than adequate for the occasion. At one rally, "champagne
flowed like water."[7]

On election day, Bryant rushed supporters to the polls and claimed an
early lead. By midday, it was believed that Hays was ahead, but Bryant
produced a noontime spectacle on the plaza. A band, several exquisitely
decorated carriages, and a company of "gaily caparisoned mounted men"
entertained an appreciative crowd whose response caused a renewed wave
of enthusiasm for Bryant.

As the paraders left the square, Hays rode into view, alone on a splendid black horse. The crowd shouted its welcome with such enthusiasm that the spirited animal pranced and reared so that only a good rider could have kept his seat. Sensing the audience's appreciation of good horsemanship, Hays put the horse through its paces, and then rider and steed bowed to loud applause. Just as the crowd swarmed around them, Hays wheeled his mount and bolted down a side street, but even there they were cheered. It was all over for Bryant. A woman who observed the events said the outcome was determined by "the idolatrous affection in which the southern and western men" held Jack Hays.[8]

The election of Hays was more than pleasing to the Tennessee-born Whig leader Gen. John Wilson, and he wanted the Whigs to claim some of the credit for it. He wrote to a friend in Missouri, "The Whigs voted for the gallant Texas Ranger Col. Jack Hays . . . a sober, modest, honest military hero." It was a case, Wilson said, where "honest, sober military glory triumphed over whiskey, bribery, and cards."[9] A Kentucky newspaper editor noted that the defeated Bryant, who previously had amassed a large fortune, "distributed his money with great prodigality in the vain effort to secure his election."[10]

A few disappointed Bryant men discussed contesting the election because Hays had been in the state only a few weeks when elected. Such an argument was not worth the making to a local editor who observed that if Hays was deemed not properly qualified for that office, his popularity was strong enough to guarantee him any office of his choosing. Jack Hays took up the duties of sheriff of San Francisco County on April 9, 1850, and his wife and brother Bob Hays came from Texas to join him later in the year.[11]

In 1851, Hays anxiously watched the rise of a vigilante group known as the Committee of Vigilance in San Francisco, the first of several to be organized throughout the state. Former Governor Burnett attributed their appearance not to the sheriffs' failure to enforce the law, but to "the extremely deficient administration of criminal justice in California for some years." Hays could and did arrest lawbreakers and detain them when they were properly charged, but acquittal or conviction and sentencing were in the hands of the courts. At times the Committee of Vigilance conducted itself as a true friend of law enforcement, and at other times it functioned as little more than a lynch mob. Hays tried to accept the vigilantes' positive cooperation and to resist when they assumed the duties of the court and became the executioners of its justice.[12]

In a cool demonstration of high courage, Sheriff Hays removed from the custody of the vigilantes two alleged lawbreakers who had been apprehended and held by them to be hanged. On August 19, 1851, with a court order in his pocket, Hays walked into the Committee of Vigilance armed headquarters and personally led the two prisoners out and placed them in jail. Not a hand was raised against him, but two days later while Hays was attending a bullfight in a nearby town, members of the Vigilance spirited the pair out of his jail and hanged them. Although mortified by losing the prisoners, Hays won reelection in 1851 and continued in the office of sheriff until he resigned in 1853 to accept appointment by President Franklin Pierce as United States surveyor general for California.[13] In 1858, he was appointed United States surveyor general for Utah, but resigned the office a few months later to remain in California. He was an interested observer of the political scene for the rest of his life, and in 1876, he was a state delegate to the Democratic National Convention.[14]

On the same day that Hays was first elected, Ben McCulloch, born in Rutherford County, Tennessee, in 1811, was elected sheriff of Sacramento County. Like Hays, McCulloch had fought for Texas freedom, was a Mexican War hero, and was one of the first members of the Texas Rangers.[15] An opponent contested the election, but an investigation sustained McCulloch's victory, and he subscribed the oath of office soon afterward.[16]

Elected to the state senate from San Joaquin District in 1849, former Tennessean David F. Douglass was chosen to preside at a meeting of Whig legislators and a number of local citizens on February 9, 1850, at San Jose. The purpose of the meeting was to organize the Whig party in the state and make common cause against the more numerous Democrats who had held a similar strategy session a week before.[17] Later Douglass was elected one of several vice presidents in the Whig party's state organization. He bragged to the editor of the Nashville *Daily American* that the Whigs were gaining ground in California, but complained that their progress had been hampered by opposition from "Southern Democrats." He admitted that he thought Southern Whigs also were "tainted." In the local elections of that year, the Whigs gained enough voter support to win control of the legislature, however.[18]

Riding the Whig victory wave in 1850, Douglass was again elected state senator, this time from Calaveras County. Later in the year President Millard Fillmore appointed him deputy United States marshal for the northern of the two California districts.[19] When the state militia was organized, Douglass received a commission as one of the four major generals to command its four divisions. The commands, each comprised of two brigades, existed primarily on paper, and the busy public servant rarely spent time on militia matters.[20]

During the early spring of 1851, Douglass made plans to seek his party's nomination for governor at the next election. Confiding that ambition to his friend William Bowen Campbell at Nashville, he sent a list of the Whig state corresponding committee of California with the names of his supporters checked. He remarked on the coincidence that both Campbell and he would be Whig gubernatorial candidates in 1851.[21]

When Douglass wrote to Campbell, Californians were already discussing his candidacy. The San Francisco *Herald* observed a few weeks later:

> It is rumored in well informed circles that Mr. David F. Douglass . . . will be a candidate for the office of governor at the next election . . . no man in the Whig Party can so well concentrate its strength as Mr. Douglass, and a ticket having his name at its head, would under all circumstances obtain a very strong support. He is extensively known, remarkably popular, a political tactician of extraordinary shrewdness, and to electioneering he is indefatigable.[22]

Early indications of support for Douglass faded as the convention approached. He remained in the contest until May 27, the day of the convention balloting, but then, assessing his political strength as insufficient to win the nomination, he withdrew. His party fervor did not wane, however. On August 16, when the young Whigs of San Francisco held an enthusiastic meeting, they elected Douglass president for the occasion that included speeches, elections of officers, and a procession through the streets of the city. Later in the year he was reelected to the state senate from Calaveras County.[23]

In 1853, again sensing an opportunity to win the Whig nomination for governor, Douglass let his name be circulated among the faithful who were also hearing the names of his fellow former Tennesseans Henry Crabb and A. C. Russell. The Stockton *Journal* endorsed Douglass for the nomination, but by convention time all three men were out of the running. Douglass's friends put him up for lieutenant governor, and the Whigs appeared certain to nominate him. However, his chances were torpedoed on July 7 when a convention delegate charged on the floor that he had given key jobs to Democrats while he held the federal office of deputy marshal.[24]

Seven weeks before the convention, Douglass had a narrow escape when he served federal court documents on one of several residents of Colusa County who were unwilling to accept a ruling of the United States land commissioners in a disputed title case. When he began reading the court order to a certain Holliday, proprietor of a wood yard, the hearer became enraged, screamed that Douglass must die, and struck him with a heavy stick of wood from a pile that he had cut to supply steamboats like the one on which the marshal was a passenger. Douglass fended off the blow, but its force knocked him down the riverbank. Holliday retreated to his house nearby and returned with a gun, but the ship's captain persuaded him to desist from his avowed purpose. Douglass returned to San Francisco and issued warrants for five or six of the resistance ringleaders.[25]

After the breakup of the Whig party, Douglass agreed to be president of the Settlers and Miners convention in 1855, the same year he was elected assemblyman from San Joaquin County.[26] While in the assembly in 1855, he introduced a bill to divide California into three states, but the body took no action on it. It was a failed ploy to attract the support of the proslavery element to himself and his party.[27]

In 1856 and 1857, Douglass was secretary of state, appointed by Governor J. Neely Johnson.[28] During those years, he worked closely with Governor Johnson to counteract the brazen display of police authority usurped by the Vigilance Committee of 1856. He participated in talks with the army's regional commander, Gen. John Ellis Wool, by which the state sought guns to arm the militia. On one occasion he was one of a committee of five appointed by the governor to arrange for the state to borrow $25,000 "to suppress [the] existing insurrection" and bring down the Vigilance Committee.[29] In 1856, Douglass was one of three commissioners selected to contract for and superintend construction of the California state capitol.[30]

Opportunities for public service in the new state came to a few Tennesseans before they left home. Whig John Muirhead of Lebanon received presidential appointment as inspector of customs at San Francisco in 1850. He went overland from Nashville to California to take up his post. Muirhead had represented Wilson County in the state house of representatives, 1841–43, and in the senate, 1845–49. Mayor of Lebanon in 1829 and 1830, he was later an organizer of the Lebanon Woolen Mills.[31]

A political plum fell to Allen A. Hall in 1850. The former Nashville newspaper editor accepted appointment as superintendent for the erection of the Custom House and Marine Hospital at San Francisco. A loyal Whig, he had been rewarded more than most with prior lucrative appointments in the Treasury Department, the State Department, and the *Republic* in Washington, D.C., where he became an editor. Recommended by Senator John Bell of Tennessee, Hall was not acceptable to his fellow Whig, Parson Brownlow, who called him a "*humbug*," or to the Franklin, Tennessee, *Review*, a Whig newspaper that suggested the appointee would double his salary by "pickings and stealings."[32] The New York *Herald* observed laconically that he is "a lucky specimen of an editor," an example of the adage that it is better to be born lucky than rich.[33]

Whigs in Washington offered to make East Tennessean Thomas A. R. Nelson land commissioner of California in 1852, but he declined. The offer may have been inspired by friends of John Bell who wanted to keep Nelson out of the race for the United States Senate.[34] A year before, the recently widowed Nelson had refused to accept appointment as commissioner to China, although he had been confirmed by the United States Senate in April.[35]

On May 14, 1850, William M. Irwin of Nashville was elected tax collector for the city of San Francisco. He regarded it as "the best office in California" and boasted that he had rather have it than a seat in the United States Senate. Irwin had given up working in the mines when the city sought to fill the position of tax collector. John Walton, senator from El Dorado County, was appointed deputy collector for Irwin.[36]

Although he had come to California as leader of a company of miners from Clarksville, Cornelius Crusman welcomed appointment as a deputy collector for the Port of San Francisco early in 1850. He died of a fever a few months later.[37]

The political and personal presence of Gen. John Wilson in the West was registered in multiple ways during the winter of 1849 and 1850. He first broke into western public life when he and his family reached Salt Lake City from Missouri about September 1. There, in his capacity as Indian agent, he filed reports to the secretary of war in which he detailed the conditions of Indian tribes in the vicinity of Fort Bridger and of those near Salt Lake.[38]

Wilson had other duties as well. Under orders from President Taylor, he hastened to confer with Mormon leaders about the state they had organized. He learned that earlier in the year, a Mormon-controlled convention of persons living in the part of upper California east of the Sierra Nevada had adopted a state constitution and elected a bicameral legislature. The legislature, in turn, had memorialized Congress for admission to the Union as the state of Deseret, meaning land of the honeybee, and had elected a delegate to deliver the message.[39]

Meeting with Brigham Young, Heber Kimball, Willard Richards, and other Mormon leaders on September 6, Wilson unfolded the Taylor administration's plan. The president wanted to work out arrangements by which the whole of the California territory could be temporarily united under a single government so that the people of the territory could resolve the question of slavery for themselves, thus freeing Congress of that highly charged issue. The temporary union would end in 1851, and Deseret and California were to become separate states since the president expected both to have population enough for statehood by that time.[40]

At first rejecting the president's plan, Young and his colleagues reconsidered and accepted it with the provision that Wilson would accompany two representatives from Deseret to the coast and explain the proposal to the leaders there. If a convention could be called to draw a constitution formulated as the president suggested, the two representatives from Deseret and General Wilson were authorized to represent the people east of the Sierra Nevada.[41]

By December 8, 1849, when Wilson and his party reached San Francisco,[42] he learned that the state of California had been organized and was eagerly awaiting acceptance by Congress. On January 8, 1850, the Deseret representatives addressed a letter to Governor Burnett proposing the temporary plan advanced by the president with additional proposals regarding the boundaries that would separate the two states. They also asked the governor to request the legislature to call an election for delegates to a new convention to take up the question of organizing a territorial government that would give way to two states by the end of 1851.[43]

In February 1850, Governor Burnett transmitted the Mormons' proposal to the legislature with a message to each house strongly recommending that they reject it. "The two communities were too far apart," he observed, "to be combined even temporarily, and Texas and Maine might as well have been made one state as Deseret and California."[44] Agreeing with Burnett's position, the legislature took no action and let the matter die.[45] The people of California had chosen statehood by a resounding majority, and their representatives had no desire to reopen the question of state versus territory.

Remaining in San Francisco, Wilson established himself as a leader in the Whig party. In March 1850, he presided at a mass meeting called to ratify nominations for the upcoming state and local elections. Three months later he took the chair to conduct a public meeting convened to protest what he and many others regarded as unnecessarily high salaries for public officeholders in San Francisco and the tax increases proposed by the common council to fund them. A year later, Wilson was one of nine members of the Whig Central Committee for California, and he was an active participant in the party's state convention.[46]

On August 23, 1850, General Wilson was chairman of a San Francisco committee to arrange a suitable tribute to the late President Zachary Taylor. The committee included one member from each state of the Union. William M. Irwin represented Tennessee, but native Tennesseans Wilson and Jack Hays represented the states of their most recent prior residence: Missouri and Texas.[47]

Perhaps Wilson's most important service to the development of the new state was his leadership in providing relief to California-bound immigrants on the last segments of the overland crossing. Elected president of the San Francisco Immigrant Relief Association in December 1849, he raised money to purchase provisions and mules and sent them to meet trains struggling through the Sierra Nevada and beyond the mountains where deserts took such a heavy toll on humans and beasts.[48]

In 1852, Wilson was commissioner of the General Land Office, a federal agency with oversight of federal lands in California, especially as they moved to private ownership. His office set out the rules for land claims, preemption rights, and the entry of warrants.[49] But whatever office he held, he did not give up his interest in politics. When the Whig party broke up, he joined the California Temperance party and was president of its state convention in 1855.[50]

Another Tennessee Whig, Henry A. Crabb of Nashville, won election as city attorney of Stockton in 1850. That, his first venture in western politics, led to successful campaigns for the state assembly in 1852 and the senate in 1853 and 1854. In 1853, he was the reputed author of a Whig "secret circular" promoting a call for convention to consider dividing California into two or more states in at least one of which slaveholding would be legal. He was regarded as one of the ablest debaters in the senate. When elections for high-level offices occurred, his name was often prominently mentioned as a Whig candidate.[51] Crabb had begun a law practice in Vicksburg, Mississippi, about 1845, and after killing his opponent in an election duel during the campaign of 1848, he had traveled overland to California.[52]

Slow to devise policies for dealing with the Native Americans in the Far West, the national government during the autumn of 1850 selected Dr. O. M. Wozencraft to be one of three Indian commissioners for California. Loosely instructed to treat with the Indians and to negotiate reserved areas for them in exchange for their guarantee to live at peace with their neighbors, Wozencraft received notice of the appointment after he had returned to his family in New Orleans following the end of the California Constitutional Convention. Directed to rendezvous with the other commissioners at Chagres for an Isthmus crossing, the doctor, his wife, and three young children arrived promptly on November 23 and completed their crossing to San Francisco on December 27. After working as a team for several weeks, the commissioners decided to divide the state into three districts. Each man assumed responsibility for one area, and choosing by lot, Wozencraft drew the middle district that included the valleys of the Sacramento and San Joaquin Rivers.

By January 7, 1852, the commission had negotiated eighteen treaties that established reservations for most of the Indians, although white miners and settlers strongly opposed them. Despite abrasive criticism, Wozencraft worked resolutely in the Indians' behalf. A strong ally was the San Francisco *Alta California*. It was one of the few newspapers in the region that agreed Indians should have a secure place to live, free from encroachment by others. When President Fillmore sent the commissioners' treaties to the Senate for ratification, the senators rejected all of them. A newly appointed superintendent of Indian affairs for California, Edward F. Beale, dismissed the three commissioners.[53]

Former Maury Countian A. G. McCandless was chosen to represent Shasta County in the assembly of 1851 and Sutter County in 1853. He was known for his persistent efforts to enact "the Maine Liquor Law," a prohibitionist goal for California, and the religious press had high praise for him.[54] Coleman A. McDaniel won election to represent Calaveras County in the state assembly for the fifth session, 1854. Subsequently reelected, he served two additional years.[55] A Memphian, W. W. Gift, became sergeant at arms of the 1851 assembly. Known for his sense of humor, Gift chided the assemblymen of 1854 because many of them wanted to run for Congress. "Early in the session W. W. Gift entered the assembly with revolver in hand, crying out that were he to point the weapon and threaten to shoot the first one who should venture to announce himself a candidate for Congress, three-fourths of them would dodge under their desks."[56]

The indestructible leader of the East Tennessee Gold Mining Company, Alexander Outlaw Anderson, won a seat in the California state senate in 1850. He tried unsuccessfully to mount a campaign for the United States Senate in 1852 but accepted instead a seat on the state supreme court. He returned to Tennessee in 1854. His younger brother James Madison Anderson was clerk of the California assembly for the sixth (1855), seventh (1856), eleventh (1860), and twelfth (1861) sessions.[57] S. A. McMeans, a Mexican War veteran who came to the West from Dandridge, represented El Dorado County in the state assembly in 1852 and 1853. Elected state treasurer on September 7, 1853, McMeans served in that capacity until January 7, 1856. Later in the year the American party chose him to be president of its California convention.[58] W. W. Gift's son George W. Gift was McMeans's principal clerk in the treasurer's office.[59]

A native Wilson Countian, Dr. James Porter MacFarland represented Los Angeles County in the state assembly in 1853. He was elevated to the state senate for the fifth session in 1854 and the sixth in 1855.[60] Samuel W. Bell, former postmaster at Knoxville, was elected state comptroller in 1853 on the Democratic ticket. When chosen, he was serving his first term in the assembly representing Mariposa County. He left the comptroller's office to run successfully for the state senate as a Republican where he represented Santa Clara and Alameda Counties in 1857 and 1858.[61] He was a prominent participant at Republican state conventions and, in 1860, was elected a California delegate to the Republican National Convention.[62]

On May 18, 1854, the voters of San Francisco elected former Tennessee Congressman Balie Peyton city attorney, an office that he held until 1859.[63] He had arrived from Chile on November 9, 1853, where he had been United States minister for the past four years. Peyton and William Duer, former United States consul at Valparaiso who came with him, opened a law office in San Francisco. A confirmed Whig, Peyton at once assumed a leadership position in the local party.[64]

Peyton's eloquence, spiced with humor, contributed greatly to a revitalization of the Whig party, and the party carried the day in the state elections of 1855. By that time the organization in California was in the process of evolving from Whig to Know-Nothing to the American party. In the aftermath of the election, many believed that in 1856 the old party with its new emphasis on openness would be able to elect the next United States senator. Prominent among the public figures mentioned for the office were Peyton and Henry A. Crabb.[65]

Before the senatorial election, Peyton announced to his friends that he would not be a candidate, but favored the election of a Democrat. Believing that Crabb was "in no way qualified for the office" and was hostile to John Bell and himself, Peyton set out early to beat him. He wrote to Bell:

> The cause of Crabb's hostility to you as well as to myself is owing to his extreme proslavery proclivities. He went in for, he has led & supported that mischievous measure while a member of the legislature . . . was bent on forcing that issue into our platform . . . which I, being on the committee of resolutions, defeated & in a public speech denounced it as humbug. . . . He is an irascible fanatic . . . and yet as he is a young man and an old Californian . . . he is quite formidable.[66]

Peyton's defection probably cost the party the senate seat it coveted but lost. Nonetheless, in the same year, the American party named Peyton one of its four presidential electors.[67]

Another perceived breakdown in the administration of justice by the courts and widespread corruption in local government gave rise to the Vigilance Committee of 1856 and, soon after, to a counter group known as Law and Order. The former was the larger, claiming five thousand armed members or police. Law and Order opposed Vigilance's preemption of the function of law officers and the courts. In each group were many of the evildoers that both proposed to stop.[68] The Vigilance Committee might have been "the largest and best organized vigilante movement in American history," but it invited its own destruction by conducting numerous unlawful ad hoc trials and hangings.[69]

The Vigilance Committee was very convincing whenever its armed police took to the streets. On a Sunday morning in 1856 when they were marching to take two alleged killers out of jail to lynch them, a man standing on the street wondered out loud if the armed marchers would really fight. Standing nearby, W. W. Gift responded, "When you see these psalm-singing Yanks turning out with muskets on a Sunday morning instead of going to church and Sunday school with a Bible and a hymnbook under their arms, let me tell you emphatically that hell isn't half a mile away."[70]

Although their summary justice was a flagrant violation of the law, the Vigilance Committee members were generally supportive of official law enforcement. Trying to bridge the differences between the two factions, Peyton acknowledged the constructive works of the Vigilance Committee in an attempt to win from its supporters a strong commitment to respect the laws of the state and of the Union.[71] But when the hotheads continued to prevail by lynching or the threat of it, Peyton and many of its backers began to distance themselves from the committee. The governor sought arms from the federal arsenal so that he could call up the state militia to suppress the Vigilance. Peyton then joined Henry S. Foote,[72] Judge J. D. Thornton, and two others as conciliators to try to defuse the explosive situation facing the city.[73]

It remained for Tennessee-born Captain David Glasgow Farragut,[74] commander of the Mare Island Naval Yard in San Francisco Bay, to halt the Vigilance. Visited by delegations representing Law and Order, the Vigilance, and representatives of the governor, Farragut listened intently until a vocal leader of the Vigilance, J. D. Farwell, proclaimed his committee superior to city and state governments and warned that there should be no federal interference. Farragut made a strong plea for restraint and responsibility on the part of all concerned, but he left little doubt that another hanging would invite federal intervention. After three months of tumultuous existence, the Vigilance Committee disbanded its police forces in August 1856.[75]

Political responsibilities seemed to seek out former Tennesseans. In 1853, Perrin L. Solomon began serving a tenure as sheriff of Tuolumne County that ended in 1857 when he was appointed United States marshal for the northern district of California. Highly regarded in his county, Solomon enjoyed a large measure of success in dealing with the occasional instances of mob action. He intervened more than once to save prisoners about to be hanged without a trial. As a fair-minded, dedicated law enforcement officer, Solomon won the miners' respect for the law and the courts.[76]

Charles H. Randall became a deputy to Sheriff Solomon in 1853, followed Solomon to his new appointment as United States marshal in 1857, and served one year as his deputy. Later he was Tuolumne County supervisor for six years and county judge for four.[77]

Three other Sumner Countians were at various times members of the legislature. J. D. Carr of San Francisco County won a seat in the assembly of 1851. John C. Hubbard became an assemblyman representing San Francisco County in 1854.[78] Dr. John Jefferson Franklin represented Tuolumne County in the state senate in 1860–61. During the latter year, he was a delegate to the Breckinridge Democratic State Convention where he was appointed to the committee on resolutions and the committee to report an opinion on the issue of secession.[79]

Thomas M. Brown, who had crossed the plains with a team of oxen in 1849, first worked in the mines but later abandoned mining for a career in law enforcement. Klamath Countians elected him sheriff, and he held the office for thirteen years before becoming sheriff of Humboldt County for fifteen years.[80]

The office of county sheriff was popular with other Tennesseans. In 1852, M. Gray was sheriff of Yuba County; David M. Hunt, sheriff of Sacramento County; and Thomas Johnson, deputy sheriff of San Francisco County. In 1856, Clint Bledsoe was sheriff of Sonoma County. At various times, Nathaniel Jones was sheriff, administrator, and supervisor of Contra Costa County.[81]

Although Tennesseans were prominent among elected officials charged with keeping the peace, Volunteer State gold rushers participated in their share of violent personal encounters. Soon after arriving in California in late 1849, William B. Rainey of Hartsville was in an altercation that resulted in his being stabbed to death.[82] On March 6, 1850, "an exquisitely-garbed racketeer of the New York . . . type" shot and killed William Anderson in a street fight in Sonora.[83] W. H. Boose of Memphis was one of several American miners who died in a skirmish with Mexican miners at Turnersville, Calaveras County, on November 14, 1851. Austin S. Bannister died in 1853 from stab wounds inflicted by a miner who was said to have acted in self-defense.[84] Indians killed John Anderson in northern California in 1852,[85] and a gambler shot and killed William F. Newnan near Mariposa in 1854.[86]

A few Tennesseans initiated violent action against other emigrants. Robert P. Cardwell, a miner, was adjudged justified in killing a bully named Bill Ford in 1851 near Sonora. Ford had intervened in a gambling table payoff argument and attacked Cardwell. In the melee, he threw the Tennessean to the floor and bit off his lower lip. Cardwell returned to the fracas with his face bandaged and shot Ford.[87] Richard McCann shot

William Higgins when they met in a restaurant at Mokelumne Hill. The wound was not fatal, but McCann fled, fearing retaliation by his adversary's friends.[88]

John Reeves and his father, formerly of Memphis, suffered gunshot wounds when John became involved in a shooting affray near Mokelumne Hill in 1852.[89] In 1853, Edward Toby shot and killed Dr. A. B. Crane in San Francisco in a duel arranged after challenges had been exchanged during a heated discussion of the doctor's bill for services rendered Toby. Prior to their confrontation, they had been friends dating from the time they were fellow townsmen in Tennessee.[90]

Notwithstanding these and other occasions of violence, public service exerted a powerful attraction on Tennesseans. Former Secretary of State William Van Voorhies, who resigned his office in February 1853, became surveyor of the Port of San Francisco, a federal appointment, soon afterward. He remained a loyal Democrat and held responsible positions at party conventions as late as 1872.[91] Democrat Dr. E. M. Patterson was also looking for political plums. He was an applicant for the office of postmaster at Sacramento in 1853.[92] During the same year, the name of the acid-tongued Whig editor A. C. Russell was mentioned freely as a possible candidate for governor, but at convention time the party chose another.[93] Other Tennesseans became district attorneys, Tom Cox for Plumas County in 1854 and William Porter, formerly of Franklin, Tennessee, at Stockton.[94]

Some were in no hurry to enter the political arena. R. C. Haile, who attended school at Nashville and was a merchant in Sumner County from 1836 to 1839, moved from the mines near Nevada City to a farm in Napa Valley in 1850. He relocated to Suisun Valley in 1858 and purchased a farm of 540 acres there. He represented Napa and Solano Counties in the state legislature in 1868 and again in 1876.[95]

After repeated clashes between Indians and miners along the Klamath River in the northern mining country in 1853, the federal government appointed A. M. Rosborough special agent to try to restore peace. He was to open constructive communication with the several local tribes in the area where the intrusion of white settlers and miners had interfered with the fishing and hunting that sustained them. In exchange for their commitment to peace, Rosborough offered emergency food and supplies and protection against settler-miner violence. A. M. agreed with his brother J. B. Rosborough, who attributed most of the trouble to impromptu raids by whites. Spurred to action by rumors maliciously started by other miners, they had sought out and killed Indians indiscriminately. The government's long-range plan was the establishment of reserved areas for the Indians.[96]

The Indians struck back ineffectually. In 1855, a renegade chief, Red Cap, promoted an uprising against the whites among his more belligerent young men. Calling for the extermination of all of the neighboring tribes, the hotheads in the mining camps urged the formation of militia groups. But Rosborough persistently pushed for peace and on February 16, 1855, achieved a memorandum of agreement that provided for the punishment of Red Cap and the hostile Indians, the protection of all friendly Indians, and safety for the whites. Soon afterward, he resigned and was relieved by the end of March 1855.[97]

Rosborough could not rest from public service. Later in 1855, he was elected county judge for Siskiyou County and, four years later, became district judge. He made his residence in the county at Crescent City. He was a member of the Union party's state committee in 1860 and was active in Democratic politics at party conventions in 1872 and 1875.[98]

In the aftermath of the Mexican War, Benjamin Davis Wilson was acknowledged to have "aided, perhaps more than any other man in Southern California, in restoring peace and good feeling between the Americans and natives." In 1850, he was elected chief clerk of Los Angeles County, and in 1851, he became the first elected mayor of the city of Los Angeles.[99] President Fillmore appointed him Indian subagent to Superintendent E. F. Beale in 1852. In that capacity Wilson was author of the 1852 report on southern California Indians that advocated reservations for them as a humane and practical way of "guarding against raids upon ranches and settlements" and as a method of rescuing them from the prospect of extinction and advancing them "toward self-sufficiency and greater civic usefulness." He opposed the practice of punishing for unacceptable behavior and rewarding cooperation.[100]

A self-styled independent Whig, Wilson successfully sought election to the state senate for its seventh and eighth sessions in 1856 and 1857 and, later, for the eighteenth and nineteenth sessions, 1869–70 and 1871–72. During his later years, he was a founder of the city of Pasadena and a member of the city council. He was a member of the San Gabriel school board.[101]

There seemed to be no limit on public servants from Tennessee. Former Monroe Countian Tyler D. Heiskell went to the assembly to represent El Dorado County in 1856, and William M. Gwin, Jr., son of the senator, represented Calaveras County in the state senate for the eighteenth, nineteenth, and twenty-second sessions: 1869–70, 1871–72, and 1877–78.[102] Daniel Burns, brought to the West Coast by his family in 1846 when he was yet an infant, became a public figure of note. An attorney-at-law, he was elected county clerk of Yolo County in 1875 and reelected in 1877. Burns became secretary of state of California in 1880 and went to Mexico to engage in a successful mining venture in 1884. He returned in 1888 and made his home in San Francisco for the rest of his life, but spent a part of most years in Mexico attending to his business interests there. He was a leader in the state Republican party and was an unsuccessful candidate for the United States Senate in 1899.[103]

The eagerness of Tennessee-related Californians to hold public office continued long after the gold rush. For example, the second Constitutional Convention, held in 1878–79, attracted several. Among them were three representing Alameda District: William Van Voorhies, former secretary of state; and Daniel Inman and Jonathan V. Webster, farmers; Tyler D. Heiskell of the Stanislaus District; John F. McNutt, a carpenter from Yuba District; Alonzo E. Noel, a lawyer from Lake District; P. B. Tully, a lawyer from the Fourth Congressional District who in 1884 was elected to the United States Congress; and William P. Grace, a carpenter from the San Francisco District.[104]

The frequent appearance of public officeholders with Tennessee backgrounds indicated more than an affinity for government service. It meant that most of them had come to California to stay and, in many cases, to watch their children and grandchildren mature into dependable citizens, ready to assume comparable positions of responsibility in government and the private sector.

Although significant numbers of Tennesseans were becoming public officeholders, by far the greater number were in the mines or had just arrived and were paused to go. Most thought of nothing but success. With the exception of a few, those who came overland had strong, spare bodies that had become accustomed to hard work on the crossing. Even those whose strength was reduced by several weeks at sea were eager to begin mining.

CHAPTER XI

Not for the Faint of Heart

NEWS from Tennesseans and others newly arrived in the gold
fields began to reach the state during the latter part of the summer of 1849. The reports were mixed, but there was almost unanimous agreement that mining was strenuous work and was not for the faint
of heart.

The early production of gold came from laborious digging and washing of gravel and dirt. The gravel bars in streams were the first places to be
worked because the only tools needed were picks, shovels, and pans. The
process was simple. The miner filled a shallow pan with gravel and/or dirt
and dipped it repeatedly in water, shaking it all the while. The purpose was
to free the heavier gold and let it settle to the bottom. The method was slow
and minimally productive. At best, most miners could recover only enough
to pay their living expenses, but the good fortune of a few kept hope alive
for the many.

Other miners, using picks, spades, and shovels, collected gold by depositing gravel and dirt in a cradlelike device made of wood called a rocker.
One man rocked the cradle while another poured in water to wash the contents. Both looked hopefully for gold that, if present, would settle to the
bottom of the rocker. Occasionally they found lumps of the shiny metal,
but usually the harvest was in tiny flakes or "dust." The advantages of the
rocker were that it was easily portable and could be set up quickly on the
bars or placers.[1]

Nonetheless, a miner from Nashville saw himself and others using cra-
dles to work the placers as "a burlesque on humanity." He asked himself,

"Would I spend my life in such a business?" and answered, "No! I'd rather be a dog and bay the moon."[2]

Two men could set up and operate a "long tom," but typically four or five were the optimum number to maximize its efficiency. Essentially an improved rocker, enlarged, immobilized, and connected to a stream of water, the device had a bottom and sides of wood with small wooden strips called riffles tacked across the bottom. A steady flow of water, introduced at the elevated end, washed through the dirt and gravel and carried most of it out the lower extremity. Some, but not all, of the gold in the mix would be caught behind the riffles. The long tom was especially appropriate where the necessary stream flow was available at a location convenient to the diggings and when miners expected to work at that place for several days or more.[3]

The performance of the long tom was improved later by adding sections of runoff lengths or riffled sluices that provided additional time and friction to entrap gold that otherwise would have flowed out in the tailings. Sometimes the runoff was extended several hundred feet.[4]

Every known method of recovering gold was tried in the mines. The effort could be as relatively easy as using a knife to pick out particles of gold from tiny seams between stones or as difficult as diverting a large stream in order to examine its rocky bed for the elusive metal. Miners could turn the stream flow out of its bed by building dams with ditches or canals to take the water away from its usual course, or they might build flumes of wood planks to elevate the stream flow above its bed. Paddle wheels, turned by the flow of water in the flume or chute, would drive pumps for removing water from claims in holes or deep parts of the stream bed.[5]

In most other processes, water was needed to wash the diggings, and when gold was dug at a distance from stream banks, water companies came into being to build sluices to supply water. Such crude water systems made hydraulic mining possible in 1853. Water, under pressure, was focused through a nozzle on exposed tertiary gravel on hillsides to wash it into ditches below where the gold collected on the bottom. Although devastating to the land, hydraulic mining was a speedy way to wash down large tonnages. The yield of gold was comparatively low, however.

From time to time miners went underground by sinking shafts and from them opened side tunnels, a practice called "coyoting." That approach was dangerous, and not many Tennesseans used it. Some miners opened into hillsides, but the practice was not widespread.[6]

Quartz or hard rock mining, although slow and expensive, was attractive because there seemed to be an unlimited amount of quartz ore. Many expected that the thousands of rushers combing through the placers and stream beds would soon exhaust the more accessible gold deposits.

Miners attacked the hard rock formations with picks, shovels, drills, and black powder, breaking the quartz into sizes they could feed into a stamping mill. Powered by a steam engine or water wheel, the mill struck vertical, hammerlike blows to pulverize the ore into a powder. It functioned as a mechanical mortar and pestle.[7] At first many had tried using hand-operated mortars and pestles or the primitive Mexican arrastra, but the process was too slow and the yield minuscule.

When the powdered ore emerged from the stamping mills, the miners used mercury, also called quicksilver,[8] to isolate the gold particles. That process of amalgamation involved first mixing the pulverized ore with mercury and then heating the mixture. Even a small amount of heat caused the mercury to attach the gold dust, separating it from useless residue. It was necessary next to process the gold and mercury amalgam in a retort that caused the mercury to vaporize, leaving the gold free of all foreign substances. The final step captured the mercury vapor inside the retort cylinder and, by condensation, returned it to its original form.

No matter which method a miner chose, he spent long hours digging and shoveling. In most processes, he worked constantly with wet feet and often with wet clothing. He handled tons of earth and gravel every day and was continually involved in laundering it with water from cold mountain streams.

Although the miners found the work a great equalizer, their relative degree of success varied greatly. One of the first to come back from California with specimens of gold "in dust and lumps," Dr. John Jefferson Franklin reached Memphis to show them on September 25, 1849. As soon as he gathered his Sumner County family, he returned with them, bringing several slaves to work on the placers.[9] He obviously believed there was a promising future in the gold country. David F. Douglass was equally optimistic. He wrote to his partner in San Francisco that their laborers in the mines were averaging from six to eight ounces of gold per day worth from $14 to $16 per ounce. Early in 1850, Douglass sent a two-ounce lump to be displayed at a Nashville jewelry store. It was the largest nugget yet seen in the city.[10]

Others saw encouraging signs. Giving himself two years "to get rich," Thomas J. Stump, Sr., explained that mining required arduous work such as canaling to supply water for separating dirt and gravel from the targeted gold. But the large amount of money in circulation made the hard labor much more palatable. "I see more money every where here in a day that I ever saw in a year in the States," he wrote.[11] W. H. Shepard, former employee of the Nashville *Daily Union*, realized $150 from ten days in the "diggins," but was astonished that the high cost of living took much of it. Nonetheless, he said that in two years he "ought to be making more money than all the hands" in the *Union* office, "editor and publisher included."[12] Relaying reports that new discoveries were being made every few days, George H. Wyatt wrote to his hometown newspaper that he, his son, and two slaves were making about $100 per day in the mines. He spoke confidently of their future.[13]

In 1849, Nicholas Carriger of Carter County mined gold successfully at Kelsey's Diggings, and with the proceeds purchased a farm from Gen. Mariano Vallejo in Sonoma County. Carriger developed the farm into a showplace and became one of the most prominent citizens of the county.[14] Upon reaching San Francisco during the summer of 1850, Joseph L. Rushing was pleased with what he saw. He wrote to his wife in Tennessee that if she were with him, he would stay in California five or six years.[15]

John M. Barnes, formerly of Blount County, was elated at his success in the mines. Within three months, he "dug twenty-five hundred dollars" and showed it to newly arrived Tyler D. Heiskell. "Extremely poor" when he left his family behind in Oregon and came to California, he had returned to make them comfortable with the results of his diggings.[16] A Gallatin man advised that he was making $30 to $40 per day in the mines and much more when he made a good strike. Convinced that a miner could make a fortune "if he works," he nevertheless counseled against a man "leaving a comfortable home in the States" to go to California, "for the life of a miner is the roughest and most slavish that can be imagined."[17]

Some reports of success were too good to be true. A fellow Shelby Countian stated that E. Ragsdale of Memphis and an unidentified partner made more than $200,000[18] in the gold fields during 1849 and invested most of it in the best real property in San Francisco. The same source said that "S. M.," another from Memphis, had not done as well, but better than most, that is, enough to pay his way home. The reports must have confused the editor of the Memphis *Daily Eagle*, but he concluded with pleasure that citizens of his city were reaping "a fair share of the golden harvest."[19]

Stories of success in the mines traveled like wildfire among the miners, although nearly all were exaggerated and many were fabricated. Soon after the company of Harris, Ellis, Day, and Holloway reached California, they heard that the "Austin boys" of Sumner County had just started home with "eighty pounds of gold between them." A quick harvest of that size would have been rewarding indeed, but no other indications of their return with such a treasure have been discovered.[20]

A quick sampling of the placers at Merry Diggins yielded "A.T.S.," a Nashville forty-niner, about 50¢ per pan. He concluded, "From what little I have seen, I can make a fortune."[21] B. Cole of Nashville made from $15 to $50 per day when he first arrived at Long's Bar, Feather River, in September 1849, but during the winter rainy season, he made nothing. He hoped to earn enough during the next dry season to return to Tennessee about December 1, 1850, "away from this desert waste—this hospital of the world—where there is plenty of money—plenty of sickness—and plenty of wickedness and nothing else."[22]

To reap profits from mining required patience and good luck. Although "industrious and attentive to business," Angus McAlister had bad luck throughout his first two months of mining, but it did not stop him. A friend believed that Angus was "determined to make something or die in California."[23]

Thomas P. Duffy, Francis Duffy, and Ed Moore were at the Deer Creek mines on April 5, 1850, after cutting a channel "to drain the bed and bars [of an arm of the Yuba River] of about 60 feet apiece." They were expecting to make other claims along the Yuba, and when they struck a rewarding one, they would "be through with mining forever and a day." They had wintered with Maj. Richard B. Alexander, A. Ellis, William Brevard, and William Lawson. All agreed that farming was "very light work compared to mining."[24]

During the first week of April 1850, Tyler D. Heiskell and a partner made about $280 each from mining near Weaverville. Headed for the summer diggings on the Yuba River, Heiskell expected to make more: "pounds instead of dollars." Nonetheless, mining seemed to him to be "a game of chance."[25] On the Yuba during the spring of 1850, Gus M. Woodward had not yet struck it rich, but was encouraged enough to predict that, with good health, he would be able to return to Tennessee "with a handsome pile, if not a fortune."[26]

Soon after reaching California in 1850, Rutherford Countian Dr. Peter Randolph formulated a straightforward plan for success; he would search for a rich claim and, having found it, would hire Indian or Mexican laborers in the spring to dig it for him. But he could never surmount two obstacles: locating and obtaining such a claim and finding workers that he could hire to dig it.[27]

Six weeks after arriving at San Francisco, Dr. I. H. Harris and his engineer A. A. Adams had toured the mines and mountains and were ready to settle on a location for quartz mining. Although they had not yet found the quartz veins that they sought, Dr. Harris was optimistic. "Any prudent and steady man of business can make a fortune here if he will give himself time," he wrote, but "not in a year as heretofore."[28]

More than one Tennessee company arrived with plans to extract gold from quartz, but the leader of one of them, G. A. Harrell of Clarksville, had decided after six weeks of experimentation at a location on John C. Fremont's "celebrated claim" that they could expect little success with their machinery. Gold was plentiful in California, he said, "but how to get at it is the question." Mining quartz was a long-term project, he explained, adding that "those companies organized as ours, and all others coming from the states, for a limited time with a small capital" would not be able to extract gold from quartz profitably.[29] Several months would pass before Harrell could accept his own accurate assessment of quartz mining, however.

By September 1, Harris and his company discovered a rich vein of gold-bearing quartz in a mountain on the eastern bank of the Cosumnes River about fifty miles from Sacramento. Harrell's Clarksville company joined them, and the two welcomed A. M. Rosborough's Tennessee Mining Company not long after. On September 15, Rosborough reported that the quartz vein was very large, and as they excavated, it appeared to be "richer and richer."[30] Four weeks later Dr. T. A. Thomas's Havilah Company arrived and worked the unyielding diggings along the Cosumnes near Harris and Harrell while anxiously awaiting the arrival of an engine to begin serious quartz mining. Unable to find a likely quartz vein, the Havilah Company suspended its search and placed all of the company's remaining assets under Dr. Thomas's control until prospects improved. In the meantime the members of the company depended on their own resources, saving what was left of the company's capital.[31]

Nashvillians heard reassuring reports about California from Dr. Harris when he came back to the city to acquire an engine "of great power" for a stamp mill to crush quartz rock blasted from the rich vein that his company was mining. Harris left with the engine via the Isthmus route to return to the site where his men were accumulating great quantities of rock during his absence. To whet the appetites of Nashvillians, he left a specimen of gold-bearing quartz on display at the office of the Tennessee Marine and Fire Insurance Company.[32]

New arrivals who had not yet faced a wet California winter seemed to have the most sanguine views of the mines. G. S. T. Sevier believed that a lot of gold was yet to be dug at Placerville when he arrived there on September 20, 1850.[33] John O'Brien, who had been in California long enough to visit several mining sites, believed the gold supply "inexhaustible, though by no means as easily obtained as when first discovered." He insisted that "the advantages [were] superior to any in the States." The richness of the bars in the Yuba River especially impressed him.[34]

Busily engaged in throwing up dirt and gravel from dry gullies to be washed for gold after the winter rains, the recently arrived members of the Harris, Ellis, Day, and Holloway company were optimistic about their situation in the Auburn ravine at Ophir City. Making expenses while they accumulated diggings of unknown value, they estimated each would make "four or five hundred dollars or perhaps more." Tyree B. Harris wrote, "We are all perfectly contented with our lot hoping we will find our piles in time."[35] Five months later, after the winter rains had failed to materialize, the dry diggings were "almost an entire failure," and some of the company prepared to return to Sumner County. Others moved their efforts into the rivers and streams where lower stream flow, guaranteed by unusually light winter snowfall, gave promise of better results.[36]

A cloud of pessimism hung over the camp of the greatly reduced East Tennessee Gold Mining Company as General Anderson approached mining with the same hesitancy that had marked his management of the overland crossing. The first two locations he chose were a complete bust, resulting in the loss of the first six weeks of their labor. He next engaged forty-two Mexicans to assist in cutting a canal to turn the Stanislaus River, but although the laborers were ready and many of his own men were camped at the site waiting, he procrastinated four weeks for no ascertainable reason.

The final breakup of the company began about August 20 when the Ramsey brothers, Wilberforce and Francis Alexander, left. If Anderson could not get them started in the mines in three months, they saw no reason to wait further. A few days after their departure, the general canceled the canaling project when confronted with a report that neighboring companies on the river had met and agreed to allow no foreigners to work there. Although the report was baseless, Anderson accepted it at face value and "dismissed the Mexicans and abandoned the enterprise immediately."

Anderson soon buckled under pressure again. The company's claim on the Stanislaus included a small island "supposed to be rich," which could easily be worked. After he dismissed the Mexicans, his remaining miners began operations on the island. Wilberforce Ramsey detailed the subsequent events to one of the company's shareholders in Knoxville:

A gentleman who had some Sandwich Islanders working for him on the opposite side of the river sent a note over claiming the island. And the East Tenn. Gold Min. Co. with its Colt revolvers, its U.S. rifles, its unerring marksmen, with its Senator General and its "strictly military organization" yielded its last hope to an inferior force and inferior claim. Was ever conduct so contemptible?[37]

There was little in the gold recovering processes other than quartz mining to justify the continued existence of those few companies that reached California whether at full or reduced strength. The mines could best be worked by groups of two to four, and most of the gold rushers recognized that at once. "This is one truth which no miner denies," observed John R. Boyles of the Lincoln County company.[38] The result for combines such as Wilson, Love and Company, the East Tennessee Gold Mining Company, the Lincoln County company, and others was dissolution. Sometimes they broke up informally. At other times the companies held formal meetings where the members voted to disband. At yet other times they drifted apart. However dissolution was accomplished, the shareholders at home were often the last to hear of it, although any who read the daily press should have been prepared for the news.

Early in 1850, the Lincoln County company settled all accounts and disbanded.[39] Colonel Bicknell's Monroe County men had closed out their company by June 15, and the end was in sight for the Havilah Company by September 1 of the same year because its capital was nearly depleted.[40] The East Tennessee Gold Mining Company was formally dissolved on September 13, 1850, and its assets sold at auction.[41] James O. Harris's company just drifted apart.[42]

The men of a Tennessee company at the Mariposa Diggings wrote to the home stockholders on July 14, 1850, asking to be released from the original agreement. Dr. J. H. Stout, in the mines with the others of the company, said they were "all disappointed, and are satisfied that we cannot enrich ourselves nor the stockholders by any mining efforts." If released, Dr. Stout would return home, although he did not have sufficient funds to start right away. He condemned the gold promotion as "a superior humbug."[43]

Wilson, Love and Company had been one of the few companies as large as seventeen men to reach the mines with its membership intact. Arriving in San Francisco July 12, 1850, the company made its way north about 180 miles to the Yuba River, bought a $500 claim, and began mining. The project was not far along when Frank B. Wilson, one of the two managers, died. The full responsibility for the company then settled onto the shoulders of George Love, who was ill.[44]

Wilson's death may have been an omen for the compounded disappointments that followed. The claim on the Yuba did not pay expenses, and although many of the men were ill, Love withdrew the company and sent two details prospecting while the rest gathered at Sacramento. The prospectors found nothing, and with bad weather nearing, Love advised the men to seek employment for the winter. Members of the company agreed that remaining together was not a viable option. Company funds were exhausted, and every member was on his own. Although there was no formal dissolution, they regarded it as a matter of self-preservation.[45]

Only one of the original group seems to have made significantly more money than his expenses. William Patterson, who broke away from the company shortly after it reached the Yuba, probably realized the "large sums of money" attributed to the success of a mine he purchased with partners not chosen from the members of Wilson, Love and Company. Details are lacking, but his former coworkers were unanimous in their belief that he had fared well after leaving them.[46]

California gold came to Memphian Samuel B. Martin in quantity enough to sustain him for a few months and pay his way home afterward. In their first effort, he and his slave took out about $43 worth of gold in ten days of hard work, during which their living expenses were between $50 and $60. They abandoned the mines for a few weeks, but returned with two hired Mexican laborers and made about $2,500 in two months digging in "some pretty good spots." That good fortune was temporary. Martin turned to protecting his funds for living expenses and for transportation back to Tennessee early in 1850. He said he would not repeat for a large sum the experience of crossing and mining.[47]

An unattributed letter from "Reddings Diggins" written on October 1, 1849, to the miner's Nashville family disclosed that his most dedicated work had yielded only $7 per day and at that it was "all chance—all lottery." Like many others, he believed that all of the richest deposits had already been mined and that there was little hope for future success in the mines. "Every man I have seen yet," he wrote, "is dissatisfied and disappointed in the mines."[48]

After a few months in the mines, another Tennessean acknowledged that "fortunes do not lay as thick on the ground as we thought they were." Times in California were as hard as they ever were at home, and the Volunteer forty-niners were experiencing it in company with "wild and unsettled miners, the lowest of all creation from all nations . . . gathered here." If they could accumulate enough money, James Harris predicted that he and his associates in the Harris, Ellis, Day, and Holloway company would return home in the spring of 1851.[49]

B. M. Morton of Tarlton worked "a great many days" in 1850 without making "one red cent." Admitting that he had ignored his wife's advice to remain at home, he drearily concluded that "now it is too late." His work in the mines was made even more difficult by a persistent illness that had followed him across the plains.[50]

Anyone in Tennessee who was "anything like comfortably situated" should remain there, "or at least never start for the land of gold," D. J. Jackson recommended from a mining camp on the Yuba River. "I would prefer one year's comfort and ease in the states to all the gold in California," he wrote.[51] A returned Nashvillian, whose name was withheld by the newspaper that printed his comment, gave "a most distressing account of matters" in the gold fields. He had worked in the mines for six weeks and earned the barest subsistence. Considering the influx of gold hunters, he concluded with insight that "the time has gone by when individual labor at gold digging can make fortunes, but that it will require capital and heavy machinery for the purpose."[52]

Whether working the placers, digging, damming, or canaling in 1850, miners like J. S. Wall were despondent. "I have not seen a man who has come here since last spring," he said, "but is sick of his trip; many are already returning." Unable to make expenses in the mines, Wall of Kingsport bought a share in the Tennessee Damming Company for $50 and became an active participant as the company dug out a race to divert the river from its bed for a distance of about five hundred yards. It was a gamble. The investors were betting that the exposed river bed would yield worthwhile quantities of the precious dust. If it did not, Wall would turn his back on

California and return to Tennessee, if he could afford the fares. He sent word to his brother at home to remain in the states and "never come to California."[53]

As mining gold in Bear River Valley yielded Dr. R. M. Freeman only about $4.50 per day, he accepted a temporary job at $10.00 per day as manager of a quicksilver mine. Asserting that the largest amount of money in California was in the hands of gamblers and speculators, Freeman predicted stormy times ahead for the region. "Should I ever get back to Tennessee, or to a country as well supplied with the comforts of life, good-by California," he said.[54] A "shrewd, intelligent, energetic" Memphis businessman then in California warned readers of the *Daily Eagle* to stay at home. "It is worse than madness for a man to come to this country unless he brings capital with him and intends to stay at least four or five years," he wrote, terming as "all humbug this idea of making fortunes" in the "land of gold, mud and misery."[55]

Often miners expended the receipts from summer mining during the winter, leaving little or nothing to show for the entire year.[56] John S. Ross, who had lost the previous summer's earnings due to later illness, claimed that when they traveled, they "slept like hogs and lived like dogs" to reduce costs. When he wrote home on January 20, 1850, from Sacramento, he was about to set out for "fresh diggins" up the Sacramento River. He was determined "to make a raise or lose what I have like I did last fall."[57]

Mining through the spring and summer of 1850, John R. Boyles estimated that he was one of "thousands not making more than their expenses." He doubted that he would ever make a fortune, but took comfort in the belief that although "mining is dull, very dull . . . a man will never starve." He reminded himself that the number of successful miners was an extremely small percentage of the number in the field.[58]

Even those who were "generally lucky" in searching for gold often suffered illnesses that made it impossible to work for several days at a time. Two men mining on the Mokelumne River during the autumn of 1850 reported losing nearly half of their time due to sickness. The loss of work time more than offset the "rich diggins" they had just discovered.[59]

A Methodist preacher, who said that he realized about $500 for two weeks in the mines during the autumn of 1849, did not comment on the periods when he made little or nothing, but admitted he would be lucky to save enough during 1850 to pay his way back to Tennessee.[60] A Montgomery County man, declaring himself successful as a miner, was

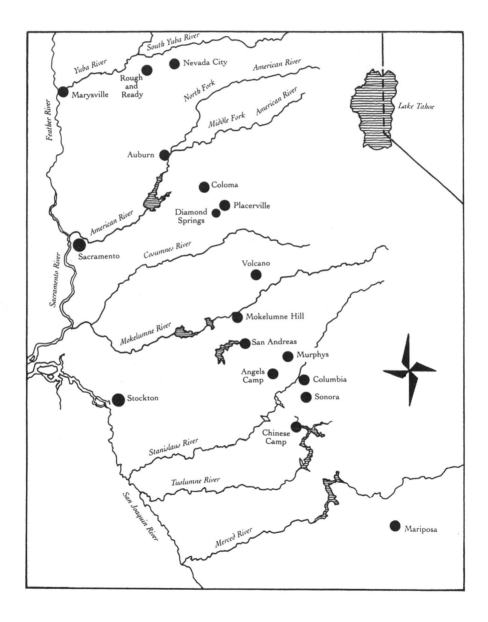

MAP 6. California Gold Country

nonetheless uncertain that he would be financially able to return home by Christmas 1850. He predicted that no more than "one out of ninety-nine" would return with a "pile" and that "many a poor fellow will never return." He advised his friends at home to stay there.[61] J. B. Mallory also warned his friends to stay at home unless they were "inured to labor of the hardest kind and blessed with strong constitutions."[62]

The large influx of immigrants from the states and foreign countries raised the question of whether there would be gold enough and space enough for all to work. Thomas Freeman feared the numbers "now flocking to the shores" would eventually "prove disastrous."[63]

Beginning early in 1849, merchants, traders, steamboat owners, and real estate speculators fabricated reports of exciting new gold discoveries to stimulate immigration to California.[64] Some newspaper editors in Tennessee who first had printed wildly exaggerated stories of success in the mines began belatedly to examine their sources more closely. On October 29, 1850, the editor of the Memphis *Daily Eagle* acknowledged that his columns fairly "sparkled" with glowing accounts of gold, yet he said, "We have not heard of a solitary instance among the many emigrants to California from this section of a 'fortune' having been made." A correspondent of another Tennessee newspaper warned from San Francisco, "Let no one put any confidence in any California paper report of gold diggings and the riches of the mines."[65] Dr. J. W. King, who returned to Nashville about November 1, 1850, condemned unethical mining promoters: "The stories of the richness of the mines are manufactured by speculators."[66]

Press reports and statements by public officials had misled many. H. Means of Memphis complained that newspapers were printing false accounts from California that led readers to believe that gold could be had for the easy taking. "Individuals cannot realize a fortune," he said, "unless it is the veriest accident in the world."[67] Employed in the Customs House in San Francisco, Dr. William Hunt of Knoxville resented the way in which public fervor for the mines had been whipped up by "extravagant accounts . . . given by the prostituted papers of this country and the letter writers in the service of the owners of steamships." He would not advise any man in the states in comfortable circumstances and out of debt to come to California.[68]

California Congressman Wright had whipped up the quartz fervor when he reached Washington, D.C., early in 1850. Among those who talked to him and heard his reports was Nashvillian J. Litton Bostick who hurried home and then to the gold country. Bostick recognized that he had been duped:

> All the exaggerated stories so ingeniously told to myself and hundreds in Washington City either originated in a disordered imagination or were the result of a vainglorious desire of attracting attention at the expense of truth . . . the impressions made by Mr. Wright's statements [about quartz] . . . are totally false.[69]

H. B. Plummer of Nashville said that his company had "prospected the quartz region" until they were "entirely satisfied that we have been most shamefully deceived and misled by representations made to us in the United States." Plummer had also tried the diggings, sometimes making nothing and at others earning barely enough to cover expenses.[70] L. Charlton, George D. Blackmore, R. Charlton, W. Wright, and Jake Tyree tried quartz mining on the Mokelumne River in 1851, but they made nothing and gave up after a few weeks.[71]

James O. Harris of Sumner County wrote home in disgust. "You may just believe that all big tales about California in newspapers are lies emphatically," he said, prompted by the speculators and merchants. "I tell you, they have lied equal to a new ash hopper." Lies notwithstanding, Harris promised to stay in California as long as he could "make grub to live on."[72]

Exaggerated reports of easily accessible gold continued into the mid-1850s. John Olinger of Greeneville, Tennessee, wrote enthusiastic letters to his hometown newspaper surely calculated to excite migration to the mines. A fellow Greene Countian in California knew that life in the mines was very different from the way Olinger had represented it. "By this exaggerated way of writing through newspapers, hundreds have been gulled into this country, who are destined to bury their bones here for the want of means to get back home," A. G. Register responded.[73]

Tennessean T. Wisdom, writing from Sacramento on September 16, 1850, tried to laugh at the promoters' exaggerations. "It is amusing to be here in the mines and know the real state of affairs and hear the glorious accounts published in the States," he wrote. "It reminds me of the stories of the 'Arabian Nights' . . . I know of nothing better to compare it to."[74]

Charlatans, schemers, and hard labor aside, all that mattered for a man in a mining camp at the beginning of the gold rush was a willingness to do his part, to be honest, fair, and candid in everything. "Clothes, money, manners, family connections, letters of introduction, never before counted for so little," according to a student of life in the mine camps. Not only were the camps a frontierlike leveler, they created "new bonds of human fellowship," especially in the relations between the two or three partners working together. They needed each other, and they needed to be able to depend on each other. Those relationships were jealously guarded by the partners and by the larger camp. The practice worked well until greater numbers of men were required by projects such as turning the channels of rivers or working deep claims.[75]

Partnerships developed in camp life inculcated a sense of confidence in others that transferred to government making and other institution building. In it was a rarely seen sense of responsible cooperation and equal sharing. Peter H. Burnett noticed it as "a practical socialism of a very interesting type."[76]

Miners often felt a shared sense of fraternity based on their living together and on the homesickness that was pervasive during their few idle moments. J. Litton Bostick of Nashville offered a nostalgic description of their hours after sundown on a typical night in midsummer 1850.

> We quit work soon after sundown, and it then takes us till dusk to finish our supper. We all then gather around our campfire; read the newspapers; discuss all the questions of the day; talk of our friends at home, and of our properties; tell what we would do with Wright[77] if we only had him out here; smoke our pipe or cigars and enjoy ourselves pretty considerably. Sometimes when we are fatigued, we stretch out our blankets and go to bed at dark, but talk till ten or eleven o'clock. At other times a meditative mood seems to come over the whole camp as we lie stretched upon the ground—not a word is spoken; not a sound disturbs the stillness of the night, except the liquid tones of the river, mingling with the sad music of the breeze as it passes through the pines, or now and then the sharp barking of a wolf from the mountainside. At such times I think of home.[78]

Nothing in camp life compensated for a lack of strong personal discipline. A Methodist preacher who had visited the mines and traveled across some of the area's fertile valleys was reluctant to advise persons to relocate there. He made an exception, however, saying, "For a sober, temperate, prudent, inflexibly religious, and steady, industrious, economical man, young or old, California is the best land on God Almighty's earth."[79] He did not hazard a guess as to how many might fit that exacting profile.

Although by 1851 numerous disappointed gold seekers had returned or were on the way to their Tennessee homes, a few others came "with their pockets well filled with the yellow dust," and almost all "with a kind of personal experience . . . their native land could not have furnished." Four Washington Countians who had left Independence on May 1, 1849, were back at home with their harvest of gold in hand by January 1851, having worked together for the entire period.[80] After thirteen months in the mines, William T. Rickman returned to Hartsville in November 1851. He had made $1,700 working the placers and $1,000 from the sale of a claim. His results were better than most.[81] Practicing medicine infrequently, Dr. Battle of Memphis seems to have devoted most of his time to working in the mines in Calaveras County. When he returned to Tennessee in 1851, he had paid all of his expenses and had in cash "a little more" than when he set out two years earlier. He said his principal achievement was the experience of traveling "8,000 miles by water, 3,300 miles on foot, and 200 on horseback."[82]

Successes sometimes soured before they could be shared at home. As the three Jackson brothers were en route home with a modest amount of gold, William died of cholera and was buried at sea in the Gulf of Mexico. George developed a fever and was put off on an island to protect the other passengers, and Perry remained with him. The pair finally reached home in Henry County, bringing $1,000 in gold to William's daughter.[83]

Two Tennesseans struck a pocket of gold near Nevada City and within a few days had extracted dust in the amount of $3,500. The experience was so intoxicating that one of the men immediately set out for home. In early August 1851, other Tennesseans working near Mariposa in "an exceedingly rich vein," blasted open a "side 'pocket'" that contained $1,400 in golden lumps.[84]

Quartz mining prospects appeared better in 1851. The Tennessee Company struck gold in the shaft it was lowering on the south side of Sandias Mountain, "and with a single breaking down of rock took out not far from $1,000." The vein was fourteen inches wide. Mining the Tennessee vein near Sonora, four workers removed about $20,000 worth of gold in a single day. Much of it was embedded in one piece of rock six feet long, one and one-half feet high, and twenty inches wide.[85] Such good news prompted Dr. Thomas to purchase a part of Dr. Harris's rich quartz vein for Havilah for $30,000. The site was about two miles above the fork of the Cosumnes River.[86] By October 1, 1851, J. K. McCall could report, "The mining and mechanical classes are prospering and merchants are in a better humor." Money was plentiful, and the year ended on a positive note.[87]

The advent of 1852 brought an "unprecedented rush" to California where the use of machinery to crush gold quartz was growing rapidly in public favor.[88] During the previous months, there had been a "wondrous change in the implements of labor," as the wooden bowl, the tin pan, the crude cradle, and the mortar and pestle gave way to the "long tom" and stamping mills powered "by water wheels and steam engines."[89] Dr. Thomas and the Havilah Company had erected a dam for water power while at the same location Dr. Harris was setting up his new, larger steam engine.[90]

The return to California of Dr. Patterson, accompanied by his family, reassured many in Tennessee who had begun to nurse doubts about making the crossing. Patterson had been in the mines for two years and regarded Havilah's early efforts as a failure, yet was going back in April 1852 for more with an apparent commitment to permanent settlement.[91] It did not escape notice that after two years in the gold country, J. K. McCall had returned to Nashville during the autumn of 1852 to visit his parents and to promote further emigration. Like Dr. Patterson, he went back to California at the conclusion of his stay.[92]

Encouraging news came to Tennessee when a forty-niner, identified as "formerly a prominent citizen" of the state, wrote to a Nashville newspaper that he was expecting to return soon "with something to spare."[93] The interest of the folks at home was periodically rekindled by reports from correspondents like "Grizzly" of the Nashville *Daily Gazette* who wrote of the flourishing mines in Calaveras County that had been presumed exhausted two years before but had since been reopened with great success. In 1852, "very rich diggings" were centered around the county seat Mokelumne Hill, one of the largest mining towns in the state.[94]

The departure of fellow gold seekers for home, often with only enough funds to pay for their transportation, was not easy for those who remained behind, whether by necessity or by choice. When, on the last day of March 1851, his partner Henry Day and "numerous others of the Sumner boys started for home," James O. Harris reflected, "It was very hard to see friends leaving . . . but I am going to be satisfied before I leave here . . . although prospects are very gloomy at present." Six months later Harris reported that most of the rest of the Sumner Countians had gone home, most with enough money to pay their way "while others had to borrow." He remained behind with five others mesmerized by the possibility of a fortune-making "strike."[95]

Disappointed that his best earnings from working Trinity River placers during the summer of 1851 had amounted to only $7 per day, James C. Cooper of Lewis County, Tennessee, expected "a chance to make something in this country yet." In a letter to his father at Newburg, Tennessee, James said that he would visit Lewis County about January 1, 1852, but planned to return to California after a month or two to reenter the mines. He hoped that some of his friends from home would accompany him.[96]

Although Drs. Harris, Thomas, and Patterson were faithful to their commitment to quartz mining, A. M. Rosborough had been somewhat skeptical from the beginning. He had entertained hopes for success, but by the early part of 1851, he left the mines.[97]

When Dr. E. M. Patterson returned with his family from Nashville to California in the spring of 1852, he found quartz mining still in the ascendancy only in the dreams of diehards who had invested time and money in it. Patterson wrote to Nashville that most of the quartz mining had been suspended or abandoned completely. Other modes were "paying tolerably well," but the doctor declared that "no person from Tennessee has procured a fortune as yet."[98]

Dr. Harris at last agreed with Nashvillian James G. Shepard, who had concluded two years prior that quartz rock mining was a "magnificent humbug." After looking for quartz veins for several weeks, Shepard declared that the statements made by Congressman Wright and others in government service in regard to quartz opportunities were "as false as hell itself."[99]

By October 1852, the Tennessee companies led by Drs. Harris and Thomas abandoned quartz operations and advertised their machinery for sale. The mining town, first called Quartzville and later Nashville because of the large number of residents from Tennessee, soon fell into decay and ruin. "Experience confirms the opinion," a correspondent observed, "that the quartz mines will not be profitably worked until labor is lower and the art of saving the gold better understood."[100]

The stamping mill sold when the Tennesseans liquidated was copied directly from others made in Tennessee and Georgia for previous attempts to extract gold from mines in the South. It was a crude device. The stamps were square in shape and the pounding heads were made of "soft iron"; the mortar and stems of the stamp were made of wood. When the new owners later put the mill in operation, it was prone to frequent breakdowns, but they remodeled it by changing to freely revolving round heads attached to iron stems. With further refinements, the mill became known as the California stamp and was thereafter reproduced for use in mining activities throughout the world.[101]

During 1852, the number of stamping mills in operation at the quartz mines began to decline until in 1854, only 34 were left. The introduction of sufficient capital to improve the mills coupled with chemical advances that separated gold from the ore more efficiently reinvigorated quartz mining and ultimately established it as the principal method for extracting gold. By 1858, there were 279 quartz mills in operation in California.[102]

Although some of the first to reach the mines made fortunes, the riches were often lost nearly as quickly as made. A Tennessean who had traveled through the mining towns in 1852, two years after a similar trip, wrote, "It is a noticeable fact that nearly all the old miners who have made large fortunes are now poor." He observed, "There are more poor, discouraged and discontented men in California than all the other states."[103]

Three years after the first emigrants reached the gold fields, a Christian minister on the scene estimated that "nine-tenths of those who come to this country are disappointed."[104] But few were as disappointed as native Tennessean Jim Rhine, a member of the Indian Bar Company, who took his life by jumping into a flume and being crushed by the water wheel it fed. Faced with losing an investment of $6,000, he had threatened previously to end his life. "Insanity, growing out of disappointments, is believed to have been the cause of the rash act," the Nashville *Daily Gazette* reported.[105]

Working the mines often called for cash investments. Miners bought and/or sold claims as when Bryson Hanna invested $1,000 in a claim in the Sacramento River[106] or when Dr. Peter Randolph "laid out" all of the money he had made the previous summer for quartz claims. He expected it to make $3,000 or $4,000 for him within the next eight months.[107] James O. and Tyree B. Harris subscribed "four thousand dollars in stock in a ditch" from Mokelumne River to the dry diggings near Diamond Springs, and Bryson Hanna and Horace Johnston took $2,000 worth. In that instance the four were to pay for their stock by labor. Built at a cost of $65,000, the ditch was designed to provide water to subscribing miners at rates that would soon return the investors' money and provide continuing income indefinitely. Tyree B. Harris was employed as the agent to "rent" the water.

James Pursley, Jacob Tyree, and William Gregory invested in a well-promoted quartz vein on the Mokelumne River in 1852.[108] To accommodate a return to Tennessee in the autumn of 1852, Dr. Randolph made plans to sell a fluming and damming claim on the south fork of Feather River as well as the quartz claim that he had obtained earlier in the same year.[109]

Some miners would do virtually anything to strike it rich, especially if the process were quick and easy. Eager to believe reports of unusually rich discoveries and to invest in them, they were easy targets for the unscrupulous. The Gold Lake humbug was an example that William Burkholder described in a letter to John Long at Clarksville: "You . . . have heard of Gold Lake here where you can load a mule in an hour with the precious metal . . . about 250 miles from this place [Sacramento] in the Sierra Nevada . . . and thousands have been induced to go there."

Assured by the promoter they would realize $14 for each pan of dirt they washed, miners gladly paid $100 each to be guided to the site. At the end of their trek, instead of "Gold Lake" they found a canyon where they were invited to begin work. Those who accepted the invitation found the work just as hard as they had experienced elsewhere and the rewards just as impecunious.[110]

During the autumn of 1850, several gullible adventurers jumped at the chance to invest in the Gold Bluff scheme advanced by the Pacific Mining Company. Investors were invited to purchase shares at $100 each in ships provisioned for three months that would presumably make large profits transporting men to and from a beach beneath a high bluff on the Pacific Coast about twenty-seven miles north of the mouth of the Trinity River, near the Oregon border. "The sands of this beach are mixed with gold to an extent almost beyond belief," the *Alta California* reported on January 15, 1851.

Asserting that the gold content of the Pacific Ocean black sand was highest "after a succession of calms," the secretary of the Pacific Mining Company predicted that each shareholder would become rich almost beyond measure. One simply scooped up gold-laden sand by the bag full. One promoter was Gen. John Wilson who declared that "thousands of men" could not exhaust the supply below the bluff on the beach "in thousands of years."[111]

Sensing fraud, Nashville *Gazette* correspondent J. K. McCall examined a package of the black sand and found not a single particle of gold. He pronounced the promotion "a monster humbug to deceive the multitude." A few days later he intoned the bursting of "the Klamath Gold bubble" describing "the auriferous bluffs as a decided 'take in.'" Nonetheless, the Pacific Mining Company promoters "made their 'piles' having disposed of a large number of $100 shares."[112]

The success of such fraudulent schemes showed that greed among the miners was rampant. Their souls panted for gold. It showed also the desperation most of them felt because they could earn only a bare existence from the mines. They had traveled far to bring back big rewards, and none wanted to go home with nothing to show for the effort.

The combination of excitement and disappointment that the miners shared contributed to their leading a seminomadic existence. They seemed always on the move as they responded to reports of better prospects at other places. Burkholder explained, "You will see ten men leaving one place for a better one and twenty from the place they start for coming to the place they left. . . . Nearly all they make is spent traveling."[113]

When a mother at La Grange, Tennessee, sent her son a newspaper clipping about a strike on Scott's River in the spring of 1852, the miner responded that he had "run after big reports for three or four years and found them to be false." He was confident that the placers he was working offered better prospects than the reported strike on Scott's River.[114]

Robert Scott Wright had committed at first to remain in the mines until he had a fortune to take home, but by April 1853, he recognized there would be no fortune. He promised to come home in the autumn even if travel expenses should require all his resources. On September 9, he was forced to make further excuses for staying in California because he had been unable to save enough money to pay his way to Tennessee. He was "no better off than" when he "first came" in 1849. In 1855, Robert, still in the mines, spoke of becoming a rancher.[115]

Disappointments in the mines were not the only worries shared by the miners. Some faced Indians turned hostile by miner intrusions into their hunting grounds and pollution of their fishing streams. Edward C. Bell of East Tennessee wrote from "Placer De Agua Fria" on March 8, 1851:

I am located in the mountains of California, one hundred miles from civilization, in a country infested by predatory bands of Indians, who are daily committing depredations within a few miles of us—cutting off small parties of miners passing from one section of the country to another.[116]

By concentrating their warriors, the several Indian tribes could mount a devastating force against the widely separated mining camps and an irresistible force against isolated ranches and rural villages. Their popu-lation, substantially in excess of the 33,539 "domesticated Indians" report-ed in the census of 1852,[117] was sufficiently large for its armed young men to pose a serious threat to present and future settlement. Even small par-ties could disrupt mining operations by making quick strikes and then retreating as quickly into the mountains they knew so well. Peaceful rela-tions were also significant to the whites because some of them employed Indians as laborers in the diggings and others hired them as ranch hands.

Recently Indians had killed a party of four miners only a few miles from Bell's camp at Agua Fria. He blamed the Indians' behavior in part on the California Indian commissioners who, in turn, were having difficulty persuading the Indians to agree among themselves on what kind of peace they would be willing to discuss with the United States government.[118]

Similar reports came from others in the northernmost mining areas. In 1852, Dr. Peter Randolph complained from his camp at Natches, Butte County, about Indians who had been "very troublesome lately." He had been one of a company of volunteers who came forward after Indians al-legedly had robbed, murdered, and mutilated more than a dozen miners. The volunteers located and chased a numerous party, shot "fifteen or twenty," and hanged four. Earlier Randolph had retained the services of a young Indian boy as interpreter and servant and promised to bring him back to Tennessee. Because the constitution of California did not allow slaves, "we substitute Indians," he said.[119]

Death stalked the mines in less dramatic ways, too. Exhaustion from the rigors of the crossing, however routed, left many miners an easy target for sickness. The two Ramsey brothers of the East Tennessee Gold Mining Company were stricken with intermittent fever at Volcano Diggings on Sutter's Creek during the autumn of 1850. The younger Francis A. sur-vived the illness, but W. Wilberforce A. Ramsey, his twenty-four-year-old brother, did not. He died on November 16.[120]

The 1849 overland crossing of Colonel Bicknell's Monroe County com-pany exacted the life of another bright, young East Tennessean. Twice on the westward journey Hugh Brown Heiskell had fought off attacks of illness of such severity that he required the nursing and close attention provided by his cousin Tyler Heiskell. But soon after the company reached Weaverville, Hugh was stricken again. Slightly more than three weeks later, the illness proved fatal. He died November 10 on Weaver Creek where he had gone with four associates to cut logs for building winter cabins.[121]

Although thousands of disappointed miners had returned to the East by the summer of 1851, many remained, their faith in the new state unshaken. One was William W. Gift who protested that opinions formed about California back home were based on the reports of miners who had come to the West with unrealistically high expectations. Residents of the states east of the Rockies, he said, were "professedly ignorant of our resources, our prospects . . . beyond their horizon, our destiny never dreamed of in their philosophy."[122]

No matter what the people back home heard, working in the mines had been a lesson in grim reality for all who tried it. In truth, expectations had been entirely too high. Many believed they had been deceived or at best misled before they left home. Some were torn between conflicting rumors of new discoveries circulated unendingly in the mines, and the rush environment was by its very panicky nature an unsettling factor for all. Almost everyone faced a monumental adjustment from the original expectation that gold was easily available everywhere to the reality that it was present in many places but obtainable only with hard work and good luck.

Tennessee miners learned the advantages of cooperative living and respect for the rights of others. Life in the camps and mines called for give-and-take as the gold seekers at first lived and worked together and made their own rules in the absence of government laws and regulations. In the end, however, they could not escape the fact that each miner's success depended principally on his own initiative and persistence.

When white miners in the North polluted the fishing streams and invaded the hunting grounds of local Indian tribes, Tennesseans were not surprised by hostile responses, but neither were more than a few moved to speak up for the natives. They saw a parallel between the situation in California and the early settlement of Tennessee when settlers regarded Indian culture as a throwback to the Stone Age and an intolerable obstacle to progress.

Most miners learned the pain of disappointment and defeat and a few the exhilaration of discovery and success. Fraudulent schemes entrapped some, but all were caught in the greater net of shining greed. Before they escaped its meshes, some had died, but it was not long before most of the rest looked anxiously to earning a livelihood outside the mines.

1. Santa Fe is shown in this drawing made about 1840. As a trail destination, it attracted many travelers but most were disappointed when they arrived to find it was a small desert town of nondescript adobe houses. Courtesy Museum of New Mexico, Neg. No. 10118

2. The practice of "panning" demonstrated here on the Mokelumne, was the most elementary method of mining.

3. Cradle rocking on the Stanislaus River illustrates a popular way to separate nuggets and flecks of gold from gravel and dirt.

4. Many gold rushers who followed the southern trails passed through Tucson, shown above about 1850 nestling beneath the protective walls of the Santa Catalina Mountains.

5. The signs of the tenant, Wells, Fargo and Company, adorn John Parrott's granite block building, erected in San Francisco after a destructive fire swept the city in 1851. It was located at the northwest corner of Montgomery and California streets. Courtesy Wells Fargo Bank, History Room, San Francisco, California.

6. In 1867 Senator William McKendree Gwin and his son, William, Jr., purchased the Paloma mine and improved it by adding a substantial water-powered hoist, a 36-stamp mill, and other improvements shown in this photograph made about 1885. Courtesy Calaveras County Historical Society, San Andreas, California.

7. Senator William McKendree Gwin

8. President James Knox Polk

9. Mazatlán Consul John Parrott

10. Governor Peter Hardeman Burnett

11. Alexander Outlaw
Anderson

12. John Jefferson
Franklin

13. Matthew Fontaine
Maury

14. John Bell

15. J. G. M. Ramsey

16. Joshua Soule

17. David Glasgow
Farragut

18. William Gannaway
Brownlow

19. Balie Peyton

20. David Barry

21. Benjamin Davis
Wilson

22. John Coffee "Jack"
Hays

23. William Walker

24. Josephus Conn Guild

25. Benjamin Franklin
Cheatham

26. O. P. Fitzgerald

27. James Harris

28. Cave Johnson Couts

29. The long tom was a reasonably efficient way to separate gold from gravel and dirt. It required more attendants than panning or rocking, however.

30. The flume shown here at Murderer's Bar was built of wood in the bed of the middle fork of the American River. Diverted into the flume, the stream turned wheels that drove pumps to remove water from deep parts of the riverbed.

31 A crude miner's cabin was raised on a hillside in Lower Rich Gulch in Calaveras County. Courtesy Calaveras County Historical Society, San Andreas, California.

32. This bracelet was made in Tennessee from gold brought from California by James O. Harris. Photo courtesy Dr. James W. Thomas; bracelet owned by Mrs. Ann Harris Anderson, Gallatin, Tennessee.

CHAPTER XII

Beyond the Mines

RELUCTANT to scrap their dreams of gold, nearly all Tennesseans had tried working in the mines. Some gave up after a few weeks, but many persisted until they returned home, whether in a few months or a few years. Those who quit the diggings and remained in California took up occupations that varied from splitting rails to ranching, buying and selling real estate, engaging in business enterprises, and practicing the professions.

Some had to find outside employment even before they entered the mines. Anyone arriving in California during the late fall and ensuing winter found that the concurrent rainy season usually made mining impossible until spring. Financially unprepared to wait a few months without income, would-be miners accepted almost any job they could find. A Campbell County attorney reached Los Angeles November 1, 1849, and worked at a sawmill for $125 per month until raging waters closed the mill. He split and cut rails long enough to decide to return to the practice of law. During the first two weeks in his chosen profession, he must have concluded that litigation was better than gold, because his fees amounted to slightly more than $1,000.[1]

Not everyone reached California in 1849 with both the willingness and the ability to improvise an income demonstrated by Benjamin F. Cheatham during his first four or five weeks at Stockton. He bragged, "Whenever a man wants anything done, I tell him that is my trade, and take the job." Working principally as a carpenter with the assistance of a slave who accompanied him, he erected two houses, installed a well pump, and built fifty feet of plank pavement within a four-week period. In between jobs, he managed to open a tavern called Hotel de Mexico and briefly to operate a general merchandise store in Stockton. He planned to go to the mines in the spring of 1850.[2]

After one week of "fruitless digging," W. W. Stovall of Dixon Springs accepted a job as a bookkeeper in a hotel.[3] Richard Woods and three other Tennesseans became blacksmiths, and James Keebler of Washington County became "engaged in an express line of stages."[4] A former Nashville wholesale grocer, Thomas P. Winston, opened a store in San Francisco.[5]

Job opportunities were varied. A Memphis forty-niner earned $10 a day for grinding coffee. Memphians Bob Wright, Bob Macon, and Willis Macon had the necessary picks and shovels when they were employed to maintain the unpaved streets of Sacramento.[6] George Blackburn made about $1,500 during a single winter season of hunting. Joe Miller and James Starkey earned a livelihood selling deer and bear meat that they obtained from successful hunts in the mountains above the mining country.[7]

Donner survivors William and Sarah Foster paused at New Helvetia on the Sacramento River in 1847,[8] but soon went on to San Francisco where they opened a furniture store. In 1848, he became a storekeeper at the mines near Foster's Bar, a productive placer on the north fork of the Yuba River where he had a large claim.[9]

Jobs outside the mines spiced the lives of many. William Gregory and Jake Tyree passed their first California winter working as carpenters. After three years in the mines, John C. Hubbard became a surveyor, aided no little by his "relation" Jack Hays, United States surveyor general for California.[10] Lycurgus Charlton, W. Wright, and J. D. Cartwright took jobs building a bridge across Bear River working for $75 per month.[11] Richard Charlton, a tanner, worked at his trade, but "Panama fever" and scurvy kept him idle for a while.[12]

During the summer of 1849, Dr. Berryman Bryant, an 1847 graduate of the Botanica Medical College of Memphis, established a hospital in Sacramento City. A native South Carolinian, Bryant had come from Memphis where he peddled springwater by the barrel, bought and sold horses, and later engaged in brick making.[13] In 1852, another Memphis physician, a certain Dr. Sullivan, conducted an infirmary at Sacramento and prospered from it. Sullivan had come to California two years before, decided that he wanted to make it his new home, returned to Shelby County, and moved his family to Sacramento.[14]

Trading real estate appealed to some of the earliest arrivals. Peter H. Burnett in 1849 promoted the sale of lots at Alviso, a proposed city of which he was a substantial owner, at the head of the bay of San Francisco. The following year, he was a partner in the development of Pacific City in Oregon.[15] The land owner and purveyor of mining supplies Charles Julian Covillaud promoted the early growth of Marysville, named for his Tennessee-born wife, Mary M. Murphy of the Donner party. The Covillauds resided on Cordua Ranch at the confluence of the Yuba and Feather Rivers.[16] After leaving federal service, Jack Hays became a prime mover in buying and selling land and town lots in Oakland and large tracts elsewhere in the state. His volume of real estate transactions was enormous and his profits comparable.[17]

Thomas Eastland speculated in land sales in the new town of Oro on Bear River in Sutter County in 1850, and during the next three years, he acquired mining claims at Indian Gulch, Chinese Camp, and elsewhere. He returned to Tennessee in 1853.[18]

Few early arrivals took up agriculture in any form. An exception was Mrs. Eli Moore of Jefferson County who earned $2,000 during her first year by raising potatoes, cabbage, and onions "with her own hands."[19] Few miners fared as well. Another who tilled the soil was Robert McCall. He stopped at San Jose and, with a partner, cultivated a vegetable garden of twenty-five acres, an occupation that he said was "certain, pleasant, and healthy."[20] Soon afterward, Robert's brother, J. K. McCall, a pharmacist, joined the partnership. Within twelve months, they had about two hundred acres irrigated and in cultivation, "one hundred in potatoes, six in onions, and fifty in wheat and barley, and the remainder in beets, cabbage, turnips, etc."[21] Operating as "McCall and Co., Dealers in all Kinds of Vegetables, Wholesale and Retail," they solicited orders from the Stockton, Sacramento, and San Francisco markets.[22] Later they became avid promoters of California's future.[23] James Madison Copeland of Polk County, who had stopped in Arkansas for fifteen months before resuming his trek to California, was a vegetable gardener selling his produce to the miners.[24]

In 1850, Louisiana Strentzel, her husband, and their children settled in the valley of the Tuolumne River near the mining camp of La Grange. They "established a ferry, hotel, and a store of general merchandise for trade with the miners [and] put up large tents or canvas houses for all needs." Two years later the Strentzels moved to a six-hundred-acre farm on the banks of the Merced River, but the floods of the first winter so damaged their land that they relocated to a valley near Benicia. There they developed extensive orchards and were the first to grow orange trees successfully at any place north of San Francisco. Their daughter Louie became the wife of the famous naturalist John Muir in 1880.[25]

The growth of population and the development of towns and cities in the 1850s had created multiple opportunities for producers of foodstuffs. With landholdings of approximately 14,000 acres located in several separate tracts in Los Angeles County, Benjamin Davis Wilson operated sheep and cattle ranches and was a pioneer in bringing horticulture and viniculture to the state. By 1874, his Shorb and Lake Vineyard estates contained 231,000 vines, approximately 6,000 fruit trees including orange, lemon, lime, and olive varieties, and several hundred walnut trees. Owner and operator of the San Gabriel Wine Company, he boasted in 1883 that his winery had the largest production capacity in the world, 1.5 million gallons annually. He was a shareholder and director in southern California's earliest railroad, oil, and telegraph companies and was an investor in several water development projects.[26]

California society was in such a state of flux that even professional men switched from one opportunity to another. Gold hunter and attorney J. Litton Bostick sold out a store that he had kept at Aurum City and was admitted to the bar in Stockton, but by June 29, 1853, he had purchased Tule Ranch nearby and was busy cutting hay and planning to build a house. His declared goal was to quit "manual labor" and to oversee operation of the ranch.[27] Tennessee physician Dr. James Porter MacFarland closed his office in Henry County to go to California in 1849 to practice medicine there. According to family tradition, he "went out to do good and did well." He not only practiced medicine, but also opened the second drugstore in Los Angeles in partnership with John D. Downey, later a governor of the state. He was an active land trader, one time owning much of the land that adjoined Los Angeles. With profits from California speculations, MacFarland purchased lands in the states of Washington, Texas, and Tennessee.[28]

Three years in the mines with little to show for the experience was enough for attorney Benjamin Butler Harris. In September 1852, he opened a law office at Mariposa.[29] Attorney J. J. Foster of Lebanon, Tennessee, brought his family to Marysville in 1854 and opened a law office there. The Nashville *Daily Gazette*'s correspondent, believing Foster immune to the gold fever, congratulated him for his serious purpose and observed, "He is one of the *few* of the profession of Coke and Blackstone who have ventured to California to pursue the practice of law."[30]

A significant number of transplanted Tennesseans were active in the trade and commerce of the new state. Thomas and Joseph Eastland established a commission house in San Francisco early in 1850,[31] and Joseph Duncan of Washington County and the three men he brought with him were "trading and carrying on a large business — making money by all their operations." On a more modest basis, Rebecca Reeve was making leather purses to hold gold dust for the miners.[32] John T. O'Brien worked in the "provision and grocery trade" in Sacramento, and R. A. Russell, who once tried unsuccessfully to bring ice from the mountains for retail distribution, operated a transportation business using horse-drawn wagons.[33] H. B. Plummer, worn out in the northern mines, wanted to return home or go down to San Francisco, get some goods, and conduct trade with the miners. Regrettably for him, he had not enough money to do either.[34] Dr. Hunt with a partner owned a riverboat that paid them well, and he and James O'Brien were prospering as traders in Nevada City during the autumn of 1850.[35]

Employed since 1851 by Donahue's Union Iron and Brass Foundry in which he had a small ownership interest, Joseph Eastland had become secretary of the San Francisco Gas Company by 1854, an experience that prepared him to be a founder of the Oakland Gas Company eleven years later. During his lifetime, he held offices and/or financial interests in hospitals, banks, savings unions, the Pacific Bell Telephone Company, a paint company, cotton mills, a wireworks, a waterworks, the North Pacific Coast Railway Company, and other rising enterprises.[36]

One of John Parrott's many commercial activities of the early 1850s was as California agent for Bogardus' Cast Iron Houses. While in New York in 1849, Parrott had ordered thirty-one prefabricated "iron houses" for shipment to San Francisco where a generous profit could be made because storehouses were in very short supply.[37] Probably his most successful venture was launched in 1855 with the establishment of Parrott and Company, a banking house in San Francisco. Under his conservative management and direction, the bank never closed for lack of funds, an enviable record for the period.[38] According to family tradition, the only secured loan that Parrott's bank ever failed to recover after default of payment was a promissory note with a large number of hams as collateral. When the bank foreclosed and seized the hams to redeem its loss, the collateral had spoiled. Thereafter, the inside saying "no more hams" was a turn-down code whenever the bank rejected a loan application.[39]

Conservative manager but willing risk taker, Parrott was a ready and successful investor. Among his extensive holdings were substantial interests in the San Francisco and Colorado River Railroad Company, the San Diego Wharf, the New Almaden Quicksilver Mine, and various real properties.[40]

In 1852 Major Wyatt, formerly of Memphis, was proprietor of Wyatt House, a hotel in Vallejo, the state capital. It was one of the largest hostelries in the city.[41] Alex H. Howard, another Memphian, conducted a mercantile business in Nevada City in 1853.[42]

The brothers James and Andrew Bell, who had lived in Tennessee fourteen years before coming to California, got a job building the courthouse at Sonora in 1852 and 1853. After that project was finished, James built and owned a flour mill on Woods Creek west of the town.[43] During the gold rush years, Mrs. C. F. Stamps kept a boardinghouse, and her husband operated a trading post.[44] Although details of their crossing are not known, the Stampses were among the first to settle and manage businesses in Nevada County.

Occupations other than mining attracted several former Tennesseans in 1854. William A. Moore was proprietor of "a large coppersmith establishment" in San Francisco, and Richard W. Green was reported to be "making money" from a venture in the same city. Ben Thomas was selling goods to miners at the mines, D. S. Woodward was a merchant in Sacramento, and Abe Shepherd and Joe Boggs sold general merchandise at Quartzburg. Burwell Sneed spent January and February in Butte County putting up ice for the Marysville market.[45]

A few divided their time between the mines and other undertakings. After five years in California, Dr. John Jefferson Franklin was on horseback almost every day trying to coax financial success from mining investments he had made in the Invincible Claim near Sonora, a claim on Hawkins Bar in Tuolumne River, and a "fluming claim at six mile bar on the Stanislaus." At the same time he was conducting a farm operation with fifty acres of grain and "some little [live] stock" on his "ranch . . . below Keeler's Ferry on the Stanislaus River." He had not yet made money enough "to settle down comfortable," but had promised himself he would never cease trying. He had decided to remain in California as a permanent settler, although most of his extended family lived in Tennessee and Texas.[46]

Some who left the mines fared no better outside. When the Wilson, Love and Company broke up, C. H. Wallace worked for a month cutting hay for a farmer who could not pay him. He next was proprietor of a public house, and that, too, was a loser. Wallace then went to the Calaveras River expecting to return to the mines, but instead accepted backing in a "trading" house on Taylor's Bar. Confronted within less than a year by another failure, he acknowledged the debt he owed his backer and paid it by working a few months as a teamster. Then free of debt, he went back to the mines where he stayed until returning to Tennessee a year later.[47]

Gambling aside, there was no faster way to lose money outside the mines than in destructive fires. Fire was a devastating force throughout the cities and towns, primarily because most of the buildings were made of wood. Soon after Christmas 1849, Cheatham witnessed the destruction of his tavern by a fire that swept through much of Stockton. Ever optimistic, he told friends he expected to recover his losses by the middle of March following. Confident that he could earn an average of $2,000 per month, a sizable sum in 1850, Cheatham promised to "either succeed or remain here," but "never come home and be a poor man in Tennessee again."[48]

Perhaps the largest loss sustained by a former Tennessean occurred in the fire that swept the San Francisco City Hospital in 1850. The loss of more than $80,000 fell "exclusively—in a pecuniary sense—on Dr. P. Smith, formerly of Nashville." Although the building and equipment were totally destroyed, all of the 150 patients safely escaped the conflagration.[49]

Dr. Peter Smith, owner-operator of the hospital, was under contract with the city of San Francisco to care for its indigent sick who constituted at any given moment a large number of the patients. Unable to pay Dr. Smith in cash, the city paid in scrip, which bore interest at the rate of 3 percent per month until redeemed by cash payments.

After the fire, Smith sought unsuccessfully to induce the city to redeem the scrip that he held in the amount of $64,431. Unable to pay his bills, the doctor turned to the courts for relief. He secured a series of judgments against the city and slowly recovered most of the debt. His recovery came at great expense to the city because commissioners of the Funded Debt regularly resisted the satisfaction of the judgments when sheriff's sales of city property were held. By advertising that the titles of the choice property would not be valid because the city did not have good titles to it, the commissioners discouraged most prospective buyers, but the few who bid bought the property for only a few cents on the dollar. In subsequent litigation, the "Peter Smith Titles," as the sheriff's sale properties were dubbed, were ruled valid in 1854.[50]

The San Francisco fire of 1851 destroyed all three of the buildings that John Parrott owned, but the resilient Tennessee native responded by erecting the "Granite Block," a three-story office structure at the northwest corner of Montgomery and California Streets. Parrott's new structure was made of granite blocks, cut, fitted, and numbered in China and transported to San Francisco by ship. It was erected by other workmen brought from China for that purpose. It was to be "the most magnificent structure in California." By 1854, Parrott's investments in local real estate made him one of the largest of San Francisco property owners.[51]

The Nashville *Gazette*'s California correspondent "Grizzly" withdrew to the high Sierra Nevada to work as a shingle maker after he lost his law books and office in the fire that raged through Sonora in June 1852. It was the fifth time that he had been burned out in California, but he reported that "among the heaviest sufferers" was John H. Ward of Nashville, whose loss amounted to "$15,000 or $20,000."[52] The family of Dr. White barely escaped with their lives when fire consumed their house in San Francisco in November 1852. Dr. White's medical library, valued at $10,000, was entirely destroyed.[53]

By May 30, 1854, Dr. T. A. Thomas had left the quartz mines and become operator of the Sewanee House in Sacramento. On July 18, fire swept a large part of Sacramento and destroyed the Sewanee House, but Dr. Thomas reopened at another location under the name Sacramento Hotel. A later conflagration consumed an unidentified business establishment belonging to Wilson Grissim, formerly of Rome, Tennessee.[54]

After completing his official duties as Indian commissioner, Dr. Wozencraft returned to his neglected medical practice. He could not abandon two public improvement projects that were churning in his mind, however. From his first days in California the doctor had been an advocate of constructing a transcontinental railroad and in 1854, he led a small party to explore and evaluate Noble's Pass through the Sierra Nevada as a possible route for the road. Although he and Senator Gwin frequently disagreed on possible routes, Wozencraft supported the concept of the coast-to-coast link until it was realized. His other project was to divert some of the waters of the Colorado River to irrigate the desert that became known years later as the Imperial Valley. He died before his dream became a reality in 1901. Engineers implemented his ambitious plan for a system of gravity-flow canals, fed by water diverted from the Colorado, and the desert bloomed.[55]

Six years of sorely limited success in the mines was enough for James O. Harris. In 1856, he and a partner bought a ranch on Russian River about forty-five miles from Petaluma. The families of his Sumner County friends Clint Bledsoe and Ed Green were living on ranches in the same area. By late summer Harris was cutting lumber for a house and stable and had arranged to have ten thousand redwood rails split to fence part of the ranch. He planned to raise cattle.[56]

A few Tennesseans with experience in journalism worked at the editorial desks of California newspapers. Two of them, William Walker and Henry Crabb, let their dreams of filibustering ultimately end their newspaper careers. At different times, Walker was an editor of the San Francisco *Herald*, the San Francisco *Commercial Advertiser*, the Sacramento *Daily Democratic State Journal*, and the San Francisco *Journal*. Crabb was copublisher of the Stockton *Journal* and first editor of its successor, the Stockton *Argus*, in 1854.[57]

A former Memphis newspaperman, Andrew Campbell Russell, had a stormy, controversial career writing for California newspapers. First he was an editor of the San Francisco *Picayune*. From 1850 to 1865, he was at various times an editor of the *Alta California*, the San Francisco *Bugle*, the new San Francisco *Daily Evening Picayune*, successor to an earlier paper of the same name, the Sacramento *Union*, the Sacramento *California Statesman*, the Marysville *California Express*, the Stockton *San Joaquin Republican*, the Stockton *Argus*, and the Los Angeles *Star*.[58]

Russell's harshly phrased editorial criticism resulted more than once in his being challenged to settle the issue on the dueling ground. When he accused J. L. Folsom of bribery in securing a Whig convention nomination of one Charles Gilbert for judge of the Superior Court, Russell received and accepted a challenge to duel. Russell and Folsom met September 10, 1851, and after an exchange of shots in which neither was injured, they settled their disagreement amicably.[59]

Rubbed raw by the San Francisco *Daily Evening Picayune*'s condemnation of his policies while governor of the state, John McDougal challenged Russell in January 1852 to meet him on the field of honor, and Russell accepted. In an exchange of fire, McDougal was unscathed, but a shot from his pistol struck Russell in the hand. Expressing regret that his connection with the San Francisco press had been "more prominent than pleasant," Russell resigned his editorial chair at the *Picayune* on March 12.[60]

A former compositor at the Memphis *Eagle* and one-time editor and proprietor of the Memphis *Commercial Journal*, Russell visited Memphis in

March 1853 to seek investors for establishing a new newspaper at San Francisco. Whether he found financial backers is not known, but he returned to California by late May.[61]

John Heckendorn was editor of the Columbia *Clipper*, established by W. W. Gift, Robert Wilson, and himself in May 1854.[62] Heckendorn and Wilson published a *Miners and Business Men's Directory for the Year Commencing January 1st, 1856*. It was "a general directory of the citizens of Tuolumne, and portions of Calaveras, Stanislaus, and San Joaquin Counties, together with the mining laws of each district, a description of the different camps, and other interesting statistical matter."[63] For a brief period, Wilson had been an editor of the Stockton *Journal*. In 1858, Heckendorn was editor-publisher of the *Big Tree Bulletin* issued at Murphy's in Calaveras County.[64] Gift compiled and published *The Settlers Guide* in 1854 while living at Benicia. He promised that it contained "all the circulars and laws relating to the pre-emption claims in California."[65]

The first editor of the California *Star*, which made its appearance January 9, 1847, published by Samuel Brannan, was Elbert P. Jones, believed to have been a former Tennessee lawyer who had immigrated to the West Coast in 1846. He remained with the *Star* until April 1847 when, after an altercation, he left the newspaper business and within the next three years became wealthy from dealing in real estate. As an editor he was criticized for his irascibility, for "a sort of uncouth felicity of thought and expression," and for a "notoriety for sharpness and low, vulgar cunning." He was accused of introducing "those petty jealousies, mean detractions, and secret hostilities" that persisted for decades between rival newspapers in California. Jones returned to "the Southern states" in 1850, but died soon after reaching home.[66]

Other former Tennesseans also worked in the newspaper business. M. D. Carr was one of several joint publishers of the *California Express* at Marysville during the early 1850s.[67] After quitting the mines, A. M. Rosborough became editor of the San Francisco *Daily Evening Picayune* during the spring of 1851.[68] Rushing to the gold fields in 1849, Charles H. Randall worked at various jobs before becoming the owner-publisher of the Sonora *Union Democrat* from 1869 to 1875. With the exception of the year 1850 when he spent the winter in Nicaragua, Randall had worked in the mines until the fall of 1853. He was in local government service for the next five years before entering the mercantile business in 1858.[69] Born in Pulaski, T. M. Yancey learned the printing trade in Mississippi, but left the South to try gold mining near Columbia. After a disappointing year in the mines, he hired on as a printer for the Columbia *Gazette* where he remained until 1876 when he entered government service.[70]

The Tennessean who probably developed the most notoriety in California was Thomas Hodges. After service in the Mexican War with Colonel Cheatham's Tennessee Volunteers, Hodges made his way to the mines. He failed at mining and gambling, and although reputed to have been a medical doctor, he turned into a highwayman. He assumed the alias Tom Bell because a petty cattle thief of that name ranged over the gold country, and he believed that the existence of two bandits of the same name in the same territory would confuse law enforcement officers.[71]

The twin aliases were not confusing enough, however, and Tennessee Tom was convicted of grand larceny and locked in the state penitentiary. Hodges may have been the Tennessean identified in the Nashville *Daily Gazette* only by the initials "T.J.H." who was being held in Sacramento in the summer of 1851. Acquitted of murder charges, he was still in custody July 8, charged with robbery. Explaining that "T.J.H.," although well-known in the city, was not a Nashvillian, the *Gazette* made the sweeping boast that he was "the only Tennessean ever charged with a criminal offense" in California.[72]

Prison deterred him only until he escaped with fellow convict Bill Gristy and rounded up a gang of "as tough characters as had ever come together in the mines." They worked individually and in small groups to rustle cattle, burglarize stores, and rob lone travelers. Anytime a person or more were present when the band performed any kind of thievery, they always mentioned that they were part of Tom Bell's gang.[73]

By 1856, Bell yearned to steal gold in large quantities. Before then, stagecoaches had safely transported millions of dollars worth of gold from mining towns to Sacramento and San Francisco for shipment to Philadelphia and New York. Challenged by the difficulty of the undertaking, Bell believed he could successfully rob a coach of the strongbox that contained its gold. He selected for his first major gold robbery the Camptonville-Marysville regular stage on its August 11 trip between the two towns.[74]

The coach rolled out on schedule. Bell planned to ambush it with six men, three on each side of the road, but a gold dealer riding a parallel road unintentionally distracted three of the gang just long enough to make them late for the attack. When Bell and two men jumped out of hiding on the coach's right, they were shocked that no one appeared on the left.

The driver, guard, and passengers exchanged shots with Bell's trio. When one of the bandits was shot, his two comrades pulled him into the bushes and abandoned the attempted robbery. The coach sped on to Marysville where it was discovered that a woman passenger was dead from a bullet and three men were wounded. The gold was safe.[75]

Bell went into hiding, but after authorities arrested his second in command, Bill Gristy, they learned about the leader's probable whereabouts. After a few weeks, a search party found him, and he surrendered without resisting. Bell admitted that he had attempted the stage robbery, and his captors made ready to hang him. They granted him enough time to write to his mother and to a woman accomplice in earlier robberies, and to make some final "rambling remarks" about his past. Moments later he was hanging from the limb of a tree, dead.[76]

Most Californians accepted with gratitude Bell's summary execution. The editor of the *Alta California* hoped the outlaw's fate would restrain others who might be tempted to follow in his footsteps:

> Will not this be a warning to our young men? Will it not restrain them from indulgence in the evil courses which have been the cause of the existence of so many amateur robbers and desperadoes in California? . . .
>
> The fate of the desperado in California is becoming a certain one . . . their careers will be as suddenly and as unexpectedly ended as that of Tom Bell.[77]

Outside the world of most Californians but at the center of public debate throughout the United States was the uncertain world of black Americans, slave or free. Notwithstanding a constitutional prohibition of slavery and early attempts to bar free blacks from the state by statute, an openness about California society made exclusion difficult.

Beginning in 1849, blacks appeared in the mining districts, although in minuscule number compared to the principal minority groups of Native Americans, Mexicans, and the newly arrived Chinese, South Americans, and Pacific Islanders. The entire black population of California in 1850 was 692 and had increased to only 2,206 by 1852. In fact, the number of slaves in California was so low and negrophobia so high that the legislature passed a law in 1852 permitting a slaveholder to reclaim and remove any black person in the state whom he had held as a slave prior to the adoption of the state constitution.[78] The low numbers were quite at odds with the breadth and intensity of the debate about allowing or prohibiting slavery in the new states and territories created from the Mexican cession. The controversy centered on the question of slavery in California, but the real issue was the future of slavery nationwide.

Blacks from Tennessee passed along the trails and were present in the gold fields, and although there is no record of their number, it was certainly of a low order. Because nearly all were slaves, few were literate enough to write letters home that might have provided information about their experiences in the gold country.

Most information about gold rush slaves is found in letters written or diaries kept by their masters and in newspapers of the period that reported departures for the West and printed progress reports both along the way and after the companies reached their destinations. Usually the mention was brief. A newspaper tally of passengers on the steamship *Alabama* from New Orleans to Chagres in 1849 listed Nashvillian "Wm. T. Yeatman and servant."[79] "Two Negro servants" was the terminology George H. Wyatt used to describe the blacks working with him and his son in the mines on November 1, 1849.[80]

As slaves were usually known by their given names, it was not surprising that the *Republican Banner and* Nashville *Whig* listed the "servants" with the Bretts of Dr. Harris's party as Ned, Thornton, Solomon, Moses, Henry, Elias, and Hector.[81] Thornton's full name, Thornton Foxhall, was printed in full on the occasion of his untimely death in 1852. Setting out from California according to arrangements made by Dr. Harris for him to return to his family in Tennessee, Foxhall started July 11 on a ten-mile walk to the nearest stage stop. About two and one-half miles short of his destination, he was robbed of $300 and shot to death. Despite the lack of clues, the members of Harris's company promised to spare no effort "to bring the guilty to punishment."[82]

Foxhall was a Methodist preacher, and his death caused "universal regret" among his fellow miners, black and white. The preacher was a man "of as consistent Christian deportment" as any man Dr. Harris had ever known. "He was a praying man, a doing Christian, and as honest a man as ever breathed," Dr. Harris said. In servitude to Harris for just over two years, the preacher had earlier been "a member of the family of the late Hardy Cryer of Sumner County."[83]

The practice of casual references, if they were mentioned at all, was a way to treat slaves as just so much baggage. Benjamin F. Cheatham referred in passing to the "Negro boys" with him, giving no names or number.[84] When E. C. Harris wrote of his Monroe County company, he put the slaves in parentheses: "Our company . . . consisted of 18 persons, (two colored)."[85] Reporting the California experiences of a former Memphis merchant, the *Daily Eagle* said that he had "carried out with him a black boy."[86] A published roster of the members of the Nashville and Clarksville Havilah Mining and Trading Company listed two slaves in company with their owners. A "Negro man John" was with J. M. McClelland, and a "Negro man Walker" was with Dr. E. M. Patterson. Mentioned also was "Ben, a Negro boy," traveling with nonmember Hugh E. Patterson.[87]

A few free blacks made the westward journey. The last sentence of an account of a Sumner County company's departure noted, "Governor Duke, a free boy, has gone along."[88] John Gryder, apparently a free black, came to California through Mexico in 1841 with Dick Gardner, "Major Burney and Major Wyeth," all from Sevier County. The white men bought and sold fine horses, and Gryder was their trainer. When the gold rush began, he hurried to the mines at Murphy's Diggins where he earned money enough to bring his mother, Caroline Gryder, to California and purchase a home for her at Marysville. After 1851, he practiced as a veterinarian at Vallejo. During the Mexican War, he had participated in the Bear Flag revolt and was recognized as a member of the exclusive Native Sons and Daughters of California. Probably free blacks, Hal Pierson and his wife came to California from Tennessee, reportedly in 1845. They settled first at Vallejo and later moved to San Francisco. A skilled mason, Pierson worked in the navy yard at Mare Island.[89]

Some slaves went to the gold fields hoping to make money enough to buy their freedom. Slave Robert Perkins, a native Tennessean, was taken to California by his Mississippi master of the same name in 1850, and by November 1851, he had worked out his freedom. When the state passed the law of 1852 that empowered slave owners to reclaim their slaves brought to California prior to adoption of the constitution, the former master claimed Robert and two others who had earned their freedom. The three went to court, but were adjudged to be their former master's property and were sent back to Mississippi under guard. It is believed that they escaped at the Isthmus and did not return to their owner.[90]

Other slaves succeeded in buying their freedom and, in a few cases, the freedom of their spouses and children. Nathaniel Nelson came to California in 1849 from Cocke County with his owner, William Russell. Nelson saved enough money from four years in the mines to purchase his, his wife's, and their children's freedom, and soon thereafter accumulated sufficient funds to bring them to California. They settled at Marysville.[91]

Tom, a Maury County slave black who was the property of planter Thomas Gilman of Mt. Pleasant, crossed to the gold fields in 1850 to earn his freedom by mining. Gilman had agreed to permit Tom to go with his blessing and with Tom's agreement to pay him for the privilege of being set free. It is not known how Tom made the journey, but he settled in Dragoon Gulch and later forwarded to his master the agreed amount for his freedom. For reasons unclear, the planter insisted that Tom pay him a second time and the former slave complied. Later the aging Gilman wrote beseeching Tom to return to Mt. Pleasant to care for him. Taking the advice of white miners, Tom ignored the pleas and remained in California until his death in 1911.[92]

Aware that former owners sometimes tried to repossess their slaves even when they had worked out their freedom, some blacks freed themselves by walking away. A Memphis slave left his owner, H. Means, in California, declared himself free, and went to work in the mines for himself. Means reported the slave to be "making a fortune" with the intention of buying his wife and children then in Mississippi. Although Means was bitter about losing the slave's services, he seems to have made no effort to return him to servitude. When Memphian James Trigg died in Marysville, California, in 1850, the "slave boy" who had accompanied him to the mines asserted his freedom in "imitation of almost every slave" brought into the state.[93]

The federal Fugitive Slave Act of 1850, passed as part of the compromise to admit California to the Union, made declaring one's own freedom a risky business. The law inflicted severe monetary penalties on anyone who assisted a slave who was out from under a master's protective wing. Under the act, a slave who declared himself free was a fugitive.

State fugitive slave laws were overridden by the federal act, but in 1855, a Tennessee slave owner, Jesse Cooper, tried to invoke the California slave law of 1852 to reclaim his former Tennessee slave, George Mitchell. Brought into California as a slave in 1849, Mitchell escaped Cooper's first efforts to return him to Tennessee when the courts held that state legislation on the subject was invalid. He was apparently beyond the reach of the federal fugitive slave act because he arrived in the state prior to its passage.[94]

The California constitution's prohibition of slavery did not completely stop the importation of slaves. Thomas W. Shearon of Nashville brought an undisclosed number of slaves to San Francisco from Tennessee in 1852 to work in the mines. He had come to California, he said, "in regard to employment of Negroes from the states," and as of a year later, January 25, 1853, "the experiment" had been successful. "In most respects" the slaves behaved "very well." Shearon said he would have no trouble at all if he could "be freed entirely from Yankee intermeddling."[95]

Hoping to reduce the cost of labor required in quartz mining, Shearon looked forward to implementing "a system of servitude" from which he predicted that "large fortunes . . . will be made." He pointed out also that "he who is fortunate enough to anticipate the adoption of a system of servitude" should secure a large number of blacks before the prices escalate. It could make him rich. Shearon ignored the California constitution.[96]

Opposing Dr. Harris's view that larger stamping mills powered by steam engines would make quartz mining profitable, Shearon proposed the use of water-powered mills operated by slave labor. Evincing little respect for Harris, he declared, "The steam mill set up by Harris crushed him and he would crush any man's fortune in a short time by his . . . want of system in all the departments of business. He does little else but talk big."[97]

Notwithstanding his contempt for the doctor, Shearon entered into a venture with Harris in quartz operations early in the next year, but by midsummer their relationship had become so strained that they did not speak to each other. Professing to want to settle the matters at issue between them, Shearon came to Dr. Harris's hotel room and asked to be admitted. When the doctor expressed his surprise at hearing Shearon's voice since they were not on speaking terms, the latter responded that his visit was a friendly one to discuss business. "Grizzly" gave an account of the confrontation to the Nashville *Daily Gazette*:

> On entering Shearon locked the door, drew a large Bowie knife, and told the Doctor he was a d____d rascal, and he was going to have satisfaction. The Doctor asked for five minutes time to prepare, as he was unarmed, and would then meet him at any time and place on equal terms; but Shearon said no, now was the time and place, and immediately struck the Doctor a blow with a heavy cane which felled him to the floor, and commenced an attack with a knife, but the Doctor's cries brought assistance before any fatal injury was done.[98]

Shearon withdrew and hid himself from W. W. Gift who, "with a double barrel gun," went out in search of him. Gift was said to be "determined to shoot Shearon down like a dog" but could not find him. Maj. E. A.

White of Lebanon, a friend of Dr. Harris who stayed at the same hotel, was absent when the attack occurred. On the next day, however, by chance White met Shearon who greeted him, "Good morning."

> The major answered, "I do not speak to a villain and assassin." Shearon said, "Do you say that to me and stand upon it?" The major replied, "Yes, here and elsewhere." Shearon then drew a revolver, holding it to the major's breast, and attempted to fire, when the major caught the pistol, turned it aside, and struck Shearon on the head with the "old knotty cane," cutting an ugly gash, causing the blood to spurt in the major's face and over his clothes. . . . Here the matter was stopped by the interference of their friends.[99]

No amount of bloodshed or slave labor or machinery then available could make quartz mining successful in 1853. Shearon's experience in the mines lasted only another six weeks. Involved in a heated argument near Coloma with A. L. Chilton of Clarksville, Tennessee, over the title of a quartz mill that both claimed to own, Shearon drew a knife and started toward his adversary to be met by a hail of pistol bullets fired at close range. He died a few moments later.[100] The pistol shots left Shearon's slaves free of their master.

The practice of leasing a slave or slaves for a stated period was pursued occasionally during the gold rush. In the summer of 1849, Edwin Winston of La Grange, Tennessee, leased "an intelligent Negro man named Giles" to a certain Mr. Palmer who was to take him to California and there supervise his work in the mines. Winston was to be paid by receiving one-half of what Giles made in California while Palmer received the other half. Absolutely failing in the southern mines where they worked, Palmer returned to Tennessee the following summer, but unable to raise enough money to pay Giles's way back, he left him behind "among strangers to shift for himself." Disappointed, Winston never expected to see him again as he was essentially a free man and could continue so "by remaining where he was, or going directly to a free state . . . without let or hindrance."[101]

Whether slave or free, Giles did not plan to remain in California. Within four months of the time that Palmer left him, he had made enough money to pay his expenses back to La Grange, and a few weeks later he landed at Memphis with money in his pockets. The Memphis *Daily Eagle* said that Giles had been "beset before leaving California, on the steamer, on the Isthmus and, in fact, throughout the entire trip by abolitionists and others who endeavored to persuade him to go on to a free state or to Canada." After delivering a large package of letters and some parcels of gold from Californians to their friends in Memphis, he made his way to La Grange and again into the service of Edwin Winston.[102]

Some master-slave relationships transcended the stereotypes and were based on mutual respect. David Barry of the Sumner Independents had held his slave John in high regard since the two had grown up on the farm playing and working together. Although it strained his budget, Barry took John with him on the long voyage from Panama City to San Francisco by steamship, paying full fare when he could have swapped his services as a waiter or steward for free passage. "The officers on the boats are generally so arbitrary and tyrannical that I preferred not placing him under their authority," Barry explained, believing that his servant friend was very much attached to him. When they embarked from Panama City, John was the only one of the Independents who had more money than when he left home.

Upon reaching San Francisco on July 11, John followed Barry and the Independents up the river to Sacramento and beyond to the north fork of the Yuba to begin mining. There he and others could do nothing to stay the course of an illness that Barry had contracted prior to leaving Panama. His master died.[103]

Put on his own responsibility by Barry's death, John was grief stricken. He left the Independents and hired out for pay. Guarding his income closely, he saved money until he had enough to pay his way home to Tennessee. He had also kept intact the $300 that was in Barry's money belt when he died.

About a year later, John returned by the Isthmus to his master's widow and five children. He brought Barry's money belt with all its contents, his watch and other small personal items, the money that he (John) had made in excess of the cost of returning, and himself, the loyal servant that he had been always.[104]

The gold rush meant new opportunities and success for Tennessee-born slave black Hiram Young. Hiram's master was plantation owner George Young who agreed to let him make enough money to buy his freedom. But by the time he had earned the necessary cash, he used it to buy his wife's freedom so that their children could be born free. When Hiram followed George Young to Missouri, a wagon shop owner, A. F. Sawyer, purchased him but agreed to make it possible for him to buy his freedom. By 1851, operating his own wagon shop at Independence, Hiram was on his way to renown for the manufacture of ox yokes, wheels, and wagons. In less than ten years, he became one of the largest wagon manufacturers in the area, producing eight or nine hundred wagons a year and thousands of yokes. Undoubtedly some of his products helped outfit some of the Tennessee companies that stopped at Independence before heading across the prairie.[105]

Beyond the mines, Tennesseans labored, ventured, speculated, risked, managed, bought, sold, built, organized, promoted, and a few earned their own freedom from slavery. Others operated hospitals and riverboats, practiced law and medicine, developed ranches, planted orchards and vineyards, organized banks, and nurtured railroad construction. They survived fires, edited and published newspapers, set up commission houses, participated in duels and, on occasion, shot it out less formally. The only identified stagecoach robber met death by hanging after his first attempt failed.

Tennesseans not only had provided key leadership to organize state government, but also had participated in virtually every phase of the growth and development of agriculture, commerce, and industry. Three score and ten years before, westward-looking pioneers, some of them ancestors of the Volunteer forty-niners, had begun the same process of building in a new land. In the golden West, however, change moved at a much faster pace.

Whenever Californians could steal a backward glance at their very recent beginnings, they saw the handiwork of two former Tennesseans: a workable state government embodying traditional American principles shaped from the gold-ignited energy explosion of 1849. The political midwifery provided by Gwin and Burnett for the state aborning was crucial to its surviving the tumultuous first years of its life. Those who looked back could see also the bloody and intrusive exploits of two other Tennesseans whose records as filibusters in Mexico and Nicaragua suggested that for the moment at least, Manifest Destiny had run its course.

CHAPTER XIII

Statesmen and Filibusters

N O TWO men had more to do with the success of the early government of the state of California than Peter Burnett and William
Gwin, although they reached California through sets of distinctly
different circumstances. Burnett had brought his family and settled in Oregon before gold was discovered. Gwin had responded to the rare political
opportunities inherent in the gold-inspired migration to the West. Neither
had crossed the continent in search of gold. Yet both were caught up in the
westward movement of their era, and both were impelled by it to be leaders in ordering the new society it created.

Two other Tennesseans reached California soon after Burnett and
Gwin, and intoxicated by the excitement of national expansion to the Pacific, they tried to create roles for themselves in further expansion. Neither
William Walker nor Henry Crabb had come to the West to dig gold, but
both responded to the discovery and came with the early flow of emigrants
from the South. Separately they dreamed of power plays in northwestern
Mexico, where later each led filibustering expeditions.

After Burnett was elected governor and the legislature was in place,
Gwin quietly cultivated the political support that would enable his election
to the United States Senate. At the same time Burnett looked to the legislature to pass laws that would build on the framework of statehood crafted
so well by the constitutional convention.

In his first annual message to the new legislature at San Jose in mid-
December 1849, Governor Burnett acknowledged that a legitimate question existed about the propriety of proceeding with "the general business
of legislation" or awaiting the action of Congress to admit the state into the

Union. Insisting that California should comply fully with the Constitution of the United States even before becoming one of them, he concluded that putting the state government into practical operation was the next logical step. He noted that both the states of Michigan and Missouri, through their general assemblies, had organized state government and passed laws while waiting to be accepted into the Union. The federal government was one of *"limited, delegated* powers," he said, and although "supreme in its appropriate sphere," it reserved certain powers to the states that, in the matter of internal social and business relations, made them "independent of the general government, of each other, and of the whole world."[1]

Presenting six major recommendations and another six of secondary priority, Burnett called first for the adoption of a civil and criminal code of law. To accomplish that end, he suggested adopting specific codes "so far as they are applicable to the conditions of the state" and so far as they do not contradict the state constitution. He recommended the definitions of crimes and misdemeanors contained in the Common Law of England; the English Law of Evidence; the English Commercial Law; the Civil Code of the State of Louisiana; and the Louisiana Code of Practice. Selections from them would provide California "the most improved and enlightened code of laws to be found in any of the states," he said.[2]

The governor called the attention of the legislature to the "grave and delicate subject of revenue." Convinced that the operating expenses of government should be paid on a current basis and that incurring debt to pay for them was unconscionable, Burnett proposed direct taxation in the forms of a capitation or poll tax and a tax on real and personal property in proportion to its value. Because the populace was so transient at that time, he proposed that tax collectors accompany the tax assessors throughout the county to assure the taxpayers did not escape their responsibility by moving from one place to another. The governor predicted that a tax on real estate would encourage land speculators and other large holders of idle land to sell portions to farmers who could be counted on to produce the foodstuffs that an increased population would require.[3]

Burnett addressed other issues. Although he complimented the constitutional convention for "wisely" prohibiting slavery in California, he advocated excluding free blacks from the state by statute. Burnett had opposed immigration of blacks into Oregon when he lived there. Declaring that he wanted to avoid "the evils . . . of mixed races," he persistently opposed a black presence in California.[4] The governor recommended holding the first local elections as soon as possible to enable government to begin operations, and in the cases of San Francisco and Sacramento, he asked the legislature to separate the courts into criminal and civil divisions to expedite the administration of justice. He proposed also that the legislators arrive at a uniform plan for the organization of towns, counties, and cities throughout the state.[5]

There were other needs of lesser urgency. The legislature should establish the punishment for crimes and misdemeanors as well as for seamen jumping ship. It should appoint an inspector of provisions at San Francisco to identify spoiled and injured goods; divide the state into counties and ascertain the number of justices of the peace; provide for registers of deeds and other keepers of public records in each county; and erect suitable public buildings.[6]

Burnett concluded his message to the legislature with a prediction and a prescription:

> Either a brilliant destiny awaits California or one of the most sordid and degraded. She will be marked by strong and decided characteristics. Much will depend on her early legislation. To confine her expenditures within due bounds—to keep the young state out of debt, and to make her punctual and just in all her engagements, are some of the *sure* and *certain* means to advance and secure her prosperity.[7]

In a brief inaugural speech on December 20, Burnett had emphasized that the future of the state would depend heavily upon the development of agriculture and commerce with capital provided from the mines. He clearly foresaw a balanced growth that took the mines into account, but achieved its success through agricultural and industrial production and commercial trade.[8]

Although earlier he had believed the costs of building a transcontinental railroad were "beyond the ability of government to pay," Governor Burnett became convinced during his first year in office that the time had come to connect "the United States to the Pacific." Like other railroad advocates, he offered specific recommendations about the location of the road. "It ought to pass through the mining region, or as near as practicable; that the markets there, the best in the world, could be open to the Western farmer and Eastern merchant," he said. "Unless this road should be made the

Eastern manufacturers will find the productions of China banishing theirs from the markets of California. This has already been the case here."[9]

He recognized the problems. "The greatest difficulty to overcome will be the want of habitable country along the line to sustain a population to defend it from the Indians, and to make repairs, etc.," he warned. "You will have to exterminate a part of the Indian tribes nearest the route, before you will be able to keep peace."[10]

When Governor Burnett went to the legislature with his second annual message on January 7, 1851, he identified needs in his first message that were still unmet. To halt the drift into debt caused primarily by lack of revenues, he again urged passage of direct tax laws but with a homestead exemption. To reduce the cost of government, he proposed a general reduction in the salaries of state officeholders and repeal of an act of the first legislature that provided for the laws to be printed in Spanish as well as English.[11]

Suggesting changes in the criminal laws of the state, he recommended adding grand larceny and robbery to the list of capital crimes until such time that "prisons and penitentiaries shall have been erected." He asked the legislature to pass laws curbing usury and to permit action against persons for criminal conduct in the interest of protecting "female virtue and chastity."[12] For the city of San Francisco, he sought the repeal of the quarantine, abolition of the Superior Court, and the creation of additional district courts.

Burnett reaffirmed his approval of the prohibition of slavery contained in the California constitution. His state had already made its decision about slavery, and he believed that the issue should be decided by each state, not by the national government. On the other hand, he maintained that "Indian troubles" were not matters for state action, but were the responsibility of the federal government, which had neglected to cultivate good relations and treat with western tribes.[13] He predicted with an appalling degree of accuracy that "a war of extermination will continue to be waged between the races until the Indian race becomes extinct" in California.[14]

Newspapers generally gave Burnett high marks for his speech. "On the whole, this message is highly interesting in regard to the condition of California, and is creditable to the head and heart of Governor Burnett," the St. Joseph *Gazette* remarked.[15] It was seen as "an important document" by the cynical Whig editor of the San Francisco *Alta California* who observed that it was not "very ill written," although of unusual length.

Reserving his right to disagree with the governor on matters of principle, the editor sarcastically complimented "the spirit which has induced his Excellency to give that attention to the interests of the state" which he had failed to do during the year just ended.[16]

Two days after delivering his message to the legislature, Peter Burnett resigned from the office of governor of California[17] to devote full time to the management of his private affairs. He was succeeded in office by the lieutenant governor John McDougal who, although a popular political figure, was incompetent. McDougal has been characterized as "a talented, charming crook, given to drink, carousals, ruffled white shirt-fronts, buff coat and pantaloons, brass-buttoned blue coats, and frequent attempts to commit suicide while in his cups."[18]

One year as governor of the newest state in the Union was enough for Peter Burnett. Specific reasons for his disenchantment with the office are not known, but the difficult combination of dealing with the "legislature of a thousand drinks"[19] and managing his sizable real estate holdings may have combined to hasten his resignation.[20]

Burnett's departure from office afforded his persistent critic, the *Alta California*, "the most unqualified satisfaction" because he had at last recognized that it "was improper to make the people pay him a very large salary simply to mind his own business." Agreeing that Burnett was a man of talent and competence, the editor regretted that he had not employed those gifts in the service of the state. "The power existed," he said, "but the will was wanting."[21]

A New York editor had an even less favorable view of Burnett before he resigned. The New York *Express* was reprinted in the Memphis *Daily Eagle* of December 6, 1850:

> The governor . . . came to Sutter's Fort, a penniless adventurer, less than two years ago. He closed in with young Sutter and laid out the town. . . . It brought him an immense fortune, which he has since spent, and now he talks of resigning.

Burnett had not spent all of his fortune; a few months later his total assets amounted to at least $393,711.[22]

Peter Burnett resumed the private practice of law, but he was a justice of the California Supreme Court in 1852, 1857, and 1858. He was a councilman for the city of Sacramento in 1853. In 1863, he was a founder of the Pacific Bank of San Francisco and was its president for the next sixteen years.[23]

Devoutly religious, Burnett adhered to the Christian faith. When he and his family reached Oregon in 1843, he was a member of the Disciples of Christ, but the next year he welcomed the West Union Baptist Church to meet in his home there. His was an ongoing search that eighteen months later led him to be received into the Catholic Church at Oregon City in June 1846. His wife, too, embraced Catholicism. In 1858, Burnett wrote a book about his religious experiences called *The Path Which Led a Protestant Lawyer to the Catholic Church*. He published it in 1859. Although his convictions were firmly held, there is no indication that they ever ameliorated his attitude toward blacks and Indians.[24] He died in 1895.

Although Governor Burnett lost his zeal for holding high-level elected public office before the end of his first term, United States Senator William Gwin had zeal aplenty. He needed it and patience as well when, three weeks after they were seated, his colleague Senator Fremont left Washington to campaign in California for reelection to his term that expired March 3, 1851. The legislature could not agree on Fremont or any other candidate and left the seat vacant until January 28, 1852, when Democrat John B. Weller was elected. For two consecutive sessions of Congress, Gwin alone represented California in the Senate.[25]

Enactment of his California land title bill in 1851 was Gwin's earliest success in the Senate. He had carried the day in spite of the opposition of the formidable Senator Thomas Hart Benton of Missouri. The bill set up a claims commission of three members and provided that the United States Supreme Court would be the final arbiter of land claims. At Gwin's insistence the Senate also passed a statute establishing a branch mint at San Francisco and, in a separate action, provided funds for a survey of the Pacific Coast.[26]

Returning home during the spring of 1851 to a resolution of thanks extended by the California legislature for his initiatives in Washington, Gwin campaigned vigorously for Democratic candidates in the upcoming races. When he recommended that a vigilance group known as the "Hounds" be sent out of the country, their exit was expedited with dispatch. He had no recommendation for dealing with the strong Committee of Vigilance in San Francisco that had been created in response to the failure of criminal court juries to punish criminals.[27]

Gwin greeted his fellow senators at the beginning of the Thirty-second Congress on December 1, 1851, by announcing that he planned to introduce a spate of California-related bills during the session. Because the House had not concurred in his earlier bill to establish a branch mint at San Francisco, he introduced the measure anew, and it was passed into law. The mint was in operation two years later. He introduced bills with key provisions that ultimately prevailed to build a telegraph line from the Mississippi River to the Pacific Coast, and to establish a navy yard and depot in the San Francisco bay area. In 1853, he pushed through a bill that appropriated $500,000 for fortifying San Francisco harbor.[28]

Success did not attend all of his legislative proposals, however. His attempts to establish monthly steamship service to Japan and China via the Sandwich Islands and to provide Mexican claim preemptions failed to pass. On December 22, at the second session of the Thirty-second Congress, he brought a consolidated bill to aid in the construction of a transcontinental railroad and telegraph line. Although it was defeated, the bill kept the railroad and communication issues alive. A railroad bill was before the Senate at virtually every session until that body finally passed a version in 1861, Gwin's last year as senator. The final bill provided northern, central, and southern routes.[29]

Gwin strongly supported the administration's plan to collect California Indians on reservations as a measure to protect both Indians and whites. In 1852 when the House of Representatives cut a budget request for that purpose from $120,000 to $20,000, Senator Gwin chaired the conference committee and expressed "mortification" at the action. "We have taken their acorns, grasshoppers, fisheries, and hunting grounds from them," he said, leaving them to "perish from cold and hunger if this government does not interpose." Should the House prevail, it would "form a dark page in our history, if it does not bring the vengeance of heaven upon us as a nation," he warned.[30] The House restored a small amount of the cut, but not nearly enough to fund the contemplated reservations.

Although he had spoken eloquently in favor of including a prohibition of dueling in the constitution of the new state, Gwin accepted a challenge from former Congressman Joseph W. McCorkle to an affair of honor. Attended by seconds, the pair met at the appointed place on June 1, 1853, armed with rifles. Both fired harmlessly into the air, and their seconds negotiated a settlement of the differences between them.[31]

Gwin was forthright in his opinions about national territorial expansion. In 1851, he had declared in favor of annexing the Sandwich Islands and the extension of continental United States territory southward. He voted against the Gadsden Purchase because he wanted to use the occasion to purchase additional land from Mexico. After delivering a speech in New York City in 1854 advocating territorial expansion, Gwin proposed a toast that showed his unbounded optimism for the future of the United States. "The City of Washington," he toasted, "may it before the close of the present century be the capital of sixty-two states instead of thirty-one."[32]

In 1854, David C. Broderick,[33] a rising political power in California, blocked Gwin's reelection and won the seat for himself. Broderick had caught Gwin unprepared by successfully maneuvering to advance the date for the election by one year, but he had won by only a single vote. On the next day, a Whig who had voted for Broderick moved to reconsider, and victory was snatched from his hands. When the legislature met in 1855 to try again to elect a senator, the members could not reach a decision, and the Senate seat held by Gwin since 1850 was vacant from March 3, 1855, to the same day in 1857.[34]

Unrelenting attacks mounted against him by newspapers owned or otherwise controlled by Broderick damaged Gwin's political standing in the state. When construction of the San Francisco mint languished for more than a year while the federally licensed assayer charged two and a half times the usual fee to miners, Broderick's henchmen claimed that Gwin was responsible for it all. The reason: they alleged the assayer was splitting fees with him. The barrage of accusations, though unproven, undercut Gwin's traditional base of support among the miners and planted doubts about his credibility in the minds of many.[35]

Gwin's widespread use of federal patronage had built a hard core of political support that opponents had difficulty in reducing. He had been at the president's side when appointments were made throughout the new state from the day it was admitted to the Union. A later critic accused Gwin of appointing so many "impecunious sons of the southern aristocracy that the San Francisco Customs House came to be known as the Virginia poor house."[36]

The Broderick press twitted Gwin for his support of national expansion. Public discussion of annexing the Sandwich Islands, a move advocated by the senator, gave the *Daily Democratic State Journal* the opportunity it wanted in the autumn of 1854. Gwin favored annexation because the state would afford him an opportunity to be elected to the United States Senate just as his California term was coming to a close, the newspaper charged. All Gwin would have to do was move to the islands, duplicating his prior move to the budding state of California.[37]

Broderick had put the political quietus on another former Tennessean in 1853. State treasurer Richard Roman wanted to have the party's nomination for governor, but Broderick's convention machinations delivered the nomination to the incumbent governor John Bigler. Sometime afterward, Roman accepted appointment as appraiser general, an office that Broderick had promised to a close supporter, but was unable to deliver.[38]

Several former Tennesseans became participants in the Gwin-Broderick contest. State senator Henry A. Crabb, state treasurer Richard Roman, surveyor of the port William Van Voorhies, Perrin L. Solomon, and Jack Hays strongly supported Gwin. William Walker, then editor of the San Francisco *Commercial Advertiser*, was a loyal lieutenant in the Broderick camp.[39]

On January 9, 1857, Broderick won election to the long-term senatorship and, with the additional power represented by his victory, determined he would name the other senator. When neither Gwin nor Milton S. Latham, the leading candidates, could muster enough votes for nomination on Saturday evening, the caucus adjourned until Monday.[40]

The caucus's indecision set the stage for Broderick and Gwin to make a face-saving deal for both. Late Saturday night, Gwin visited Broderick to acknowledge that the latter had the power to put him in or keep him out of office. In exchange for support against Latham, Gwin promised the California federal patronage to Broderick. The deal was struck. On Monday, January 12, the caucus nominated Gwin, and on the following day the legislature in joint convention reelected him to the United States Senate for a term ending March 3, 1861. In a public statement made a few days later, Gwin gave Broderick credit for his election. For many of his oldest political friends, Gwin had raised a tormenting question. Had he paid for his return to office by swapping control of patronage for votes in the party caucus? Both Broderick and Gwin insisted that they had patched up their long-standing political differences and that they would be found in the Senate cooperating in the best interests of California.[41]

Though embarrassed by Broderick's political ascendancy, Gwin watched patiently as his senatorial colleague was blocked at every turn in Washington. President Buchanan would not accord Broderick patronage opportunities, but sought Gwin's advice on the subject. Broderick faced barriers raised by Gwin's popularity with the other senators. Back in California, political developments for Broderick were even worse. Many of his supporters abandoned his camp for Gwin's. When he tried to control the

Democratic state convention, opposing forces crushed his candidate for governor by a vote of 264 to 61. The party convention elected a central committee that generally opposed him and ignored his friends "in the nominations for state offices."[42]

Broderick became more desperate as his political following turned against him. Campaigning in California for the Republican national ticket in 1859 while Gwin worked the hustings for the Democrats, Broderick became overwrought and challenged Judge David S. Terry, one of his principal political adversaries and a strong Gwin man, to a duel. When they met, Terry's single shot ripped into Broderick's lungs. He died three days later.[43]

Although death had taken his strongest and most dangerous political enemy, Gwin faced insurmountable issues in Washington. Sectional strife threatened to split the Union. As a Californian and an American, he upheld the Union of states, but as a Southerner with much property in the South, he was sympathetic to that section. He spoke to sustain the Union, yet at the same time defended what he saw as the constitutional rights of states. After Congress adjourned, he returned to California where he and the entire congressional delegation campaigned for the Breckinridge ticket in the presidential election of 1860.

But politics in California had changed radically during the prior twelve months. Californians had concluded that they could survive only as a state, "an integral and dependent part of the United States." It was the beginning of the political end for Gwin. The Breckinridge ticket lost, and the senator was attacked for his sympathy toward the South, desertion of his party, and alleged treachery to his state. When the legislature met to elect a United States senator for the term beginning January 3, 1861, Gwin's name was not even mentioned.[44]

At the end of his term, Gwin left his wife in New York and set out from Washington on March 4, 1861, to California. Later in the year when he learned that she had been falsely accused of spying for the South, he hurried back to New York. While en route, he and fellow passengers Joseph L. Brent and Calhoun Benham[45] were arrested and charged with planning to "engage in rebellion against the government." On arrival at New York on November 15, they were paroled but a few days later were arrested again and that time were confined in prison. President Lincoln ordered their release after intervention in the prisoners' behalf by George D. Prentice, editor of the Louisville *Journal* and brother-in-law of Benham.[46]

Released on the condition that he leave the United States, Gwin sent his wife and their daughter Carrie to France while he slipped behind Confederate lines, planning there to convince their other daughter Lucy and their son William to go with him to unite the family in France. After several months father and daughter ran the blockade to Bermuda, took a steamer to England, and were reunited with Mrs. Gwin and Carrie in Paris early in September. A few months later son William joined them.[47]

Contemplating new adventure with a rewarding financial component, Gwin proposed a plan to high-level French government officials to exploit the current popular interest of that country in Napoleon III's dream of a Mexican empire and the supposed mineral wealth of faraway Mexican Sonora. French troops were already in Mexico to support the Austrian archduke Maximilian, and Gwin thought that one thousand of them would be a sufficient shield to provide protection for miners that he would recruit from California, until they were numerous enough to protect themselves. In fact, if the French would commit the troops, Gwin offered to undertake the promotion and development of Sonora into a well-populated state.[48]

Gwin's proposal brought him into conferences during the summer of 1863 with Napoleon III and Maximilian, who was in Paris for part of that time. As Gwin and Napoleon III negotiated, the American's frequent visits to the Tuileries were noticed and reported in the stateside press. On the West Coast, readers of the *Alta California* noted that Gwin had been taken into the French emperor's confidence and dark things were brewing. The editor speculated that with his landholdings in Texas, Gwin might convince the emperor to "add the Lone Star State to his new Mexican empire." There was also he said, the possibility that the emperor wanted Gwin to promote a part of Mexico as a place of settlement for Confederate émigrés.[49]

Carrying a letter from Napoleon III to the ranking French officer in Mexico, Gwin arrived at Veracruz on June 28, 1864. He found jealousy and intrigue throughout French military ranks and discovered that Maximilian was cautious, uncertain, and slow to act. At the end of the year, Gwin returned to Paris, confident he could convince the emperor to pressure Maximilian and the French military to cooperate enough to make the project successful.[50]

During Gwin's absence and unknown to him, Napoleon III had decided to abandon Maximilian and quietly evacuate the French army from Mexico. Notwithstanding his true plans, the emperor signed a letter to his commander in Mexico for Gwin to deliver, suggesting that he should accommodate the senator but should not "hazard expeditions" that might endanger the security of French troops there. The emperor expressed the insincere hope that Maximilian would favor Gwin's projects.[51]

Returning to Mexico in 1865, Gwin learned upon arrival that the Confederate States had surrendered and that President Lincoln had been assassinated. Mexico City was in turmoil fearing that the American Civil War might be resumed in Mexico as Union forces followed fleeing Confederates across the border. Emperor Maximilian was out of town, but had abandoned any thought of cooperating in the Sonora venture. When United States diplomats made representations in Paris against Gwin's action in Mexico, Napoleon III distanced himself from the American and assured Washington that any Confederates seeking immigration to Mexico would be received by the Mexican government on an individual basis, unarmed, and would be dispersed throughout the country, "bound to abstain . . . from anything which might awaken the just susceptibilities of the neighboring nations." On June 28, 1865, the government newspaper in Mexico City, *El Diario del Imperio*, denied that Gwin had "any relation whatsoever" to the government. "It appears even that he is entirely unknown to members of the Administration," the editor observed. He added that the legation of the French emperor had advised the newspaper that France had no part in "the combinations which [were] being formed relative to Sonora."[52]

Abandoned by both Napoleon III and Maximilian, Gwin regretfully decided to leave Mexico and attempt to return his family and himself to the United States. Instead of going to Veracruz where mail steamers connected to Europe, Gwin and his son attempted to go to the small port of Bagdad on the Gulf at the mouth of the Rio Grande. When they were forced to abandon a sinking skiff in the river, they made their way to the nearest bank and stepped onto United States soil at Laredo, Texas. After Gwin reported his presence to the nearest military base, the commander told him that he was free to go anywhere and furnished transportation to New Orleans for him. There he reported to the military commandant, Gen. Philip Sheridan, and received assurance that he was free to travel at his own discretion. Learning of his presence from a routine report from Sheridan, the War Department ordered Gwin arrested and held in close confinement. After a few months of what seemed to him an interminable confinement, he was released, a free man.[53]

By the latter part of 1866, Gwin was in France, awaiting any change in the American political scene that would enable him to return with his family to a safe and secure life in their homeland. Early in 1868, he left his family in Paris and made his way to California where wartime hostility toward Southerners was then a thing of the past. Soon after he arrived, President Johnson issued a universal amnesty to all who had been associated in any capacity with the Confederacy. Gwin's family joined him a few months later.[54]

Looking for opportunities in mining, Gwin purchased two existing quartz mines, the Alexander and the Paloma, in Calaveras County. Assisted by his son and son-in-law, he combined the two operations into the Gwin Mining Company and soon had it returning substantial profits. At one point "the mine," as Gwin referred to his mining company, operated forty-six stamps that daily crushed eighty tons of quartz. He employed "eighty stalwart men." Although Gwin sold the company about 1894 and its new owners closed it in 1908, the Gwin Mining Company was one of the largest producers of gold in the state during the last two decades of the nineteenth century.[55]

Gwin did not again seek public office but maintained a lively interest in politics. He was elated in 1869 when his son won a seat in the state senate as a Democrat in a Republican district. In 1876, Gwin the elder was a delegate to the Democratic National Convention and returned in a similar capacity four years later. In 1884, he crossed the continent to Washington to advocate construction of a railroad across Panama proposed by "Comstock-rich Californians," and while there, he celebrated the election of Grover Cleveland, the first Democratic president since James Buchanan. Gwin traveled to the East again in 1885 in the interest of the Panama railroad. A few days before beginning his return journey to California, he was stricken ill with pneumonia. He died September 3 at his hotel in New York City.[56]

Burnett and Gwin had lived to enjoy the fruits of their later labors in the growing economy of the new state on the Pacific. Rational, deliberate hard work in public service, followed by aggressive management of their personal business interests, rewarded both men.

Neither California politics nor California gold was enough to hold the attention of William Walker and Henry Crabb who were on the way to doing what they individually could to maintain the momentum of national expansion. They watched carefully for an opportunity to inject themselves into a foreign adventure, ostensibly to benefit the United States. Walker made the first and many subsequent attempts to add territory. Crabb sought to make good on Walker's first failed expedition, but failed even more miserably than his predecessor.

Few transplanted Tennesseeans appeared in the national and international press from 1851 to 1858 as frequently as doctor-lawyer-editor-filibuster William Walker. Born in Nashville in 1824, Walker was graduated from the University of Nashville and subsequently studied medicine in Nashville and Philadelphia. After completing his studies, he spent a year in Europe before returning to the city of his birth where he decided to quit medicine and take up law. Accordingly he relocated to New Orleans, read law for two years, and began practice in 1847. A year later he forsook that career and became editor of the *Crescent*, a new newspaper in the city. Soon afterward he became one of its publishers, but late in 1849, the *Crescent* suspended publication. Walker then set his sights on California.[57]

Leaving New Orleans in the spring of 1850, he reached San Francisco on July 21. He had planned to publish a new Democratic newspaper the *Eureka* there, but found that his prospective publishing partner had deserted him for the gold fields. Thus forced to change his plans, he went to work as an editor of the San Francisco *Herald*.[58]

As editor of the *Crescent*, Walker had embraced the dream of a manifest destiny that would see the United States spread its institutions and power throughout the Western Hemisphere. That dream had encouraged his moving to California, but at the *Herald*, his primary concerns were local law and order issues. He crusaded against crime and political corruption, insisting on severe punishment for major offenses. He was one of the first to declare in print that if public officials failed to perform their duties, the citizens should take the law into their own hands. On national questions, he opposed slavery, upheld the Union, and waxed expansionist.[59]

During 1851, editor Walker was especially critical of the California courts. When he demanded to know why the courts had not punished a single murderer of the many charged, District Court Judge Levi Parsons cracked down on the *Herald*, hauled Walker into his court, and fined him $500. Invoking the constitutional guarantee of freedom of the press, the editor refused to pay the fine, and the judge promptly ordered him jailed for contempt of court.[60]

News of Walker's confinement prompted a public indignation meeting[61] attended by four thousand citizens who were prepared to set the editor free by whatever means might be required. The crowd's anger was cooled by the appearance of Walker's attorney who relayed his client's wishes: no violence and no mob action. Walker refused to be set free except by due process of law. Before the meeting was adjourned, those present voted to ask the legislature to impeach Judge Parsons.[62] A few days later the Superior Court set Walker free on a writ of habeas corpus.[63]

Walker stepped up his attacks on Parson's doubtful practices. Hoping to put a stop to the editor's inflammatory editorials, a friend of the judge, William H. Graham, provoked Walker to issue a challenge to duel. When they met, Walker received a relatively minor flesh wound in each of the two firings; Graham was unscathed.[64]

Through his editorial pen, Walker was one of those responsible in 1851 for the organization of the San Francisco Committee of Vigilance. Impatient with the justice system in the new state, he wrote editorials that suggested "the people themselves take the matter into their own hands," that "two or three . . . robbers and burglars" be lynched and hanged as an example, and finally that the citizens should organize a band of "Regulators" as the only means of providing security against criminals.[65]

Near the end of May 1851, Walker resigned from the *Herald*, moved to Marysville, and took up the practice of law.[66] He was thinking seriously about opportunities south of the border. Could he develop a role for himself in further American expansion?

After he and his law partner, Henry P. Watkins, had concocted a plan to colonize the Mexican border province of Sonora, Walker began a dangerous career that would be climaxed by his execution in 1860. He believed Sonora was ripe for United States intercession because the Mexican government could not or would not defend its scattered colonial inhabitants against Apache raids. He knew, too, that many Californians favored intervention by the United States government.[67]

Walker proposed to protect the non-Indian population by developing new colonies in the area peopled by Euro-Americans. During the summer of 1853, he traveled to Guaymas, a port town on the Gulf of California, to seek permission from Mexican officials to colonize Sonora. Unable to win their approval, he nevertheless returned to San Francisco and began to recruit for a Sonora expedition. Drawing from a plenteous supply of "excitement hunters and disappointed gold hunters . . . who would enter into almost any wild scheme," Walker quickly formed a small expeditionary force.[68] He raised funds in San Francisco for the expedition by selling bonds secured by land warrants to be perfected in Sonora.[69]

Surely among the recruits was the correspondent for the Nashville *Union and American* who wrote under the pen name "Santiago." Signing off in his letter published November 9, 1853, Santiago said that probably he would write next from a foreign land. "No doubt my correspondence hereafter will smell more of gunpowder than musk," he concluded.

When Walker was about ready to depart with men, arms, and supplies, the United States Army seized his ship. The men escaped, but when Walker slipped out of the port on October 8, 1853, on another vessel, he was accompanied by only forty-three of them with a minimum of arms, equipment, and supplies. About 230 men followed in December.[70]

Landing in lower California, Walker captured the Mexican governor. There was no military resistance. Magnifying the early success, the filibuster decreed the existence of a new republic, the Republic of Lower California, on November 3. He appointed fellow Tennessean John Jarnigan to be secretary of war. Renouncing all ties to the government of Mexico that had failed to fulfill its duties in the area, Walker explained that the republic's only real chance for security was in its freedom and independence. News of the new government was received with enthusiasm in San Francisco.[71]

In a campaign characterized by wordy proclamations but little combat, Walker pushed his dream to the waking point. Moving on Sonora, he proclaimed an end to the Republic of Lower California, made it a state, made Sonora a state and, from the two, proclaimed the creation of the new Republic of Sonora on January 18, 1854. By that time Walker's operation was becoming suspect in the eyes of many, including the editor of the *Alta California*. Adding Sonora to lower California by decree was ridiculous, the editor declared. He suggested that if Walker were going to annex territory by decree, he should just as well include the whole of Mexico.[72]

Desertions followed proclamations until the number of men was so reduced that Walker led them toward the United States border. He and thirty-three men, all who remained of his expeditionary force, crossed into California on May 8, 1854, his thirtieth birthday.[73] Charged with violating United States neutrality laws, Walker was acquitted in a jury trial a few months later. Probably reflecting public sentiment with a high degree of accuracy, the jury was more sympathetic to the workings of Manifest Destiny than it was to enforcement of the neutrality laws.[74]

Walker again took up newspaper editing in the summer of 1854, first for publisher Bryan Cole of the San Francisco *Commercial Advertiser*. He was probably drawn to Cole by the publisher's obsession with the possibilities of colonization and development in Nicaragua where he owned mines. When Cole soon afterward sold the newspaper, Walker went to the *Daily Democratic State Journal* at Sacramento.[75]

While there, Walker wrote more than one hundred editorials against Senator Gwin, "the Gwinites," and the Franklin Pierce administration. Members of the Broderick faction of the Democratic party owned the paper, and the young editor participated in its effort to destroy Gwin politically to make way for Broderick.[76]

Walker's appetite for adventure in Nicaragua increased sharply in December 1854 when, through Cole's agency, he received a land grant to be divided among three hundred new colonists who would become citizens of the country. The document had come from Francisco Castellon, leader of the revolutionary Democrats. After further contemplating the potential of the Central American country, Walker began the slow process of recruiting adventurers to go there with him.[77]

At least four Tennesseans were with Walker's army in Nicaragua. The brothers Sam D. and William C. Nichol returned to Nashville in July 1856, but Aaron Ready died of cholera in the Central American republic.[78] Disappointed in the mines since his arrival in California in 1855, David Deaderick, son of David Anderson Deaderick of the late East Tennessee Gold Mining Company, enlisted in Walker's service on December 20, 1856, at San Francisco. He went directly to Nicaragua by ship with a handful of other recruits but returned to his Knoxville home on April 15, 1857. Filibustering under the assumed name of Samuel Absalom, Deaderick afterward described his experiences in a two-part article that he wrote for the *Atlantic Monthly* entitled "The Experiences of Samuel Absalom." It was published in the magazine's issues of December 1859 and January 1860.[79]

On June 1, 1855, Walker and a nondescript army of fifty-eight men arrived by sea at Realejo, Nicaragua, near the revolutionary capital of Leon. Although his recruiting efforts had fallen far short of the three hundred that he expected to enlist, he found on arrival a significant number of men ready to join him, most of whom were deserters from the Nicaraguan army. Before long, additional groups of California adventurers overtook Walker. One hundred and twenty men came from Sacramento, and "several hundred" were expected from San Francisco. The whole expedition was gaining public favor.[80]

Walker quickly moved in to control key towns and cities. By October 13, he had captured Granada and notified the people of Nicaragua that he planned to take possession of all the towns not already under his control. He described the government he would establish as "free in its principles . . . [looking to] protection to the laboring man, security to the citizens, progress to the arts, sciences, agriculture . . . to preserve order and cause it to be preserved."[81]

Exhausted by a civil war fought over a period of several years, the government of Nicaragua capitulated to Walker. The surviving populace was ready for peace, and the intrepid filibuster had the leadership and power to provide it.[82] He had made the task easier by maintaining strict discipline among his troops throughout the conquest and by his sensitivity to the needs of the local people. A Nicaraguan newspaper editorial praised his leadership: "On every side we hear the praise of Gen. Walker. Encomiums upon the prudence, moderation, and strict sense of honor and justice which have marked his course throughout, are eloquently spoken on every hand."[83]

Although disapproving Walker's methods, the United States nonetheless recognized the Nicaraguan government that he organized. He placed Don Patricio Rivas in the presidency and kept himself in the background.[84] Even the previously hostile New York City press had kind words for him. The *Tribune* said he had shown "a great degree of political sagacity" since his triumph and "was on the highroad to renown as the founder of a new state." The *Daily Times* recognized the filibuster as a man who had "a very clear perception of his destiny" and had taken "precisely the right steps to accomplish it." The *Express* saluted Walker for establishing a government "on the California plan." It is a government, the editor observed, that is "liberal in spirit and principle, and sufficiently strong to enforce its decrees at home."[85]

Walker encouraged colonization of the country by offering citizens of the United States free land grants of 250 acres with options to purchase additional land at nominal prices, but few responded. Believing the Californians would emigrate in sizable number, he advertised job opportunities and held out exciting prospects for development of the country, especially its gold deposits.[86] On November 26, 1855, Walker wrote to Dr. John Berrien Lindsley at the University of Nashville asking for his help in sending young scientists, especially geologists and botanists, to Nicaragua.[87]

On January 29, 1856, Nicaraguan voters chose Walker to be president of their country after he had dissolved the provisional government headed by Rivas, his handpicked predecessor. The new president maneuvered adroitly to maintain peace and perpetuate his power. His first departure from Nicaragua was foretold when the Alliance of Northern Republics, assisted by Costa Rica and Great Britain, laid siege to the country. With an army of only six hundred, he held out for several months against combined forces of several times that number. Finally reduced to a hopeless condition, Walker surrendered himself and his army to representatives of the United States with the agreement that they would all be transported to the states.[88]

Former Nashville editor John P. Heiss, who became a close friend of Walker, had been employed by the secretary of state in 1856 to carry dispatches to Nicaragua. Walker soon made him a citizen of Nicaragua, and when he returned to Washington, he acted for a short time as chargé d'affaires for the Nicaraguan legation. Heiss was instrumental in winning a certain amount of press support for Walker's filibustering, but after Walker was forced out of Nicaragua, their friendship seems to have cooled markedly. There was little further contact between them.[89]

Greeted by a large, admiring crowd when he debarked at New Orleans on May 27, 1857, Walker discovered that in the eyes of many, he was a bona fide American hero. At his hometown of Nashville, he spoke to an overflowing crowd in the hall of the house of representatives in the Capitol where he declared that his evacuation of Nicaragua was merely a truce and not a final cessation of hostilities. The president summoned him to the White House, and the people of New York City turned out to honor him at a public reception. Openly acknowledging his plans to return to Central America, he organized the Central American League, a support group for Central American relations with chapters in several United States cities. Public enthusiasm for his projects slipped dramatically when his former soldiers reached New York and shared highly critical stories of him with the press.[90]

But Walker was no stranger to adversity. After a few weeks, he and an expeditionary force set out from Mobile for Nicaragua, but the United States Navy intercepted them. Charged with violating neutrality laws, Walker was acquitted by a trial jury at New Orleans. He was idolized throughout the South.[91]

In 1858, rumors told of Walker's new plan to invade Nicaragua, but when Great Britain signed a treaty with that country to protect it from filibusters, the wily adventurer changed his strategy. He would go to Honduras, join the liberals then in revolt against their government and, after establishing them in power, lead a joint assault on Nicaragua. Again about to leave from Mobile, Walker and his contingent were stopped by federal marshals. He concocted another plan by which he would travel to Cuba and there board a ship manned by his expeditionary force on its way to Honduras. Federal authorities again stepped in and would not let the ship and men leave the states. Other efforts to escape the watchful eyes of the government agents were equally unproductive until he made his way to Ruatan, an island off the coast of Honduras that Britain had just agreed to return to Honduran control. Walker claimed that he had accepted an invitation to set up an independent government there when the Union Jack was hauled down and before the Hondurans could secure the island. Word of the plan leaked to the British officials on the island, however, and they remained to turn him away. Their action left Walker with the choice of returning to the United States or invading Honduras with a force unequal to the task.[92]

Presented the difficult choice, his men voted to attack the Honduran fort on the mainland that guarded Trujillo harbor with the hope of joining the revolutionary forces then challenging the government. The small force took the fort, but their inability to contact the rebels and the impending arrival of a large Honduran army force and two British warships forced them to make a run for the interior. Pursued by the army, Walker's men fled up the river that emptied into the bay. Before they could find a safe haven, they yielded to battle wounds, disease, and fatigue. Walker surrendered his men and himself to a British naval officer whom they met on a gunboat patrolling the river.[93]

The filibustering career of William Walker was approaching its end. The British turned him over to Honduran authorities who sentenced him to die, and on September 12, 1860, a firing squad carried out the execution. Most of his public support in the United States had disappeared, but *Harper's Weekly* continued to speak well of him. The United States government should not have rejected Walker, the editor wrote. "Had William Walker been an Englishman or a Frenchman, he would never have become a 'filibuster,' but would have found ample scope for his extraordinary talents in the legitimate service of his country."[94]

Another Tennessean who had followed Walker's Sonoran expedition with keen interest was Henry A. Crabb. Frustrated by losing his seat in the California state senate in 1855 and his subsequent inability to attract Know-Nothing support in the legislature for election to the United States Senate, Crabb planned an expedition to succeed where Walker had failed. His goal: to seize and occupy Sonora. Crabb believed that his recent marriage to an attractive Sonoran woman whose large family was in exile would provide unique opportunities in that region.

Pleased by the early response of volunteer enlistments in his private army of filibusters, Crabb next focused on raising funds and procuring supplies for the campaign. While he was making those arrangements, some volunteers became impatient, and desertions reduced his army to only ninety men. But their leader did not flinch. Arranging for additional recruits to go by sea to meet the ninety he would lead overland, Crabb avoided further delays. Like his soldiers, he was ready to move out.

Early in the spring of 1857, Crabb and his small force crossed into Mexico. The element of surprise that had enabled Walker to penetrate into the interior of Sonora was not available to these later filibusters. The Mexican army expected the invasion and was prepared to block it. Unable to connect with his seaborne reinforcements, Crabb and his men walked into a devastating ambush at Caborca. On April 6, he surrendered his remaining men unconditionally. On the following morning at sunrise, Crabb and fifty-nine of his surviving fighters were executed by a firing squad. A young boy among them was permitted to return to California bearing the news.[95]

Walker and Crabb were representative of the unfulfilled dreams of many who believed that all of North America should one day be included in the United States. The addition of Texas, Oregon, the vast Mexican cession, and the Gadsden Purchase had given national expansion a dangerous momentum. Nothing encouraged filibusters more than the emergence of California with its gold and myriad other natural resources. At the beginning of their expeditions, both Walker and Crabb saw themselves setting up new Californias to become at least United States territories and at best states of the Union. The unprincipled, greedy, can't-get-enough attitude appealed much more to adventurers than to prospective settlers.

Even before Walker's first attempt to take over Sonora, many who were part of the tumultuous, fast-changing California scene called out for the sobering ministry of religion and the positive power of education. Both would have to wait for increased family emigration from the East. In the meantime, churches in Tennessee and the other states recognized the immediate need and sent missionaries.

The Catholic Church had new opportunities to expand its existing influence in the area, previously centered in several missions. Protestant churches, excluded from California when it was a part of Mexico, rushed to establish new congregations, even as they believed the state offered a well-located base for both existing and future missionary activity in the Orient.

The ministers arriving in California were not only men of the cloth but, in most cases, were staunch advocates of education and schools. Some were teachers. It was an indication that churches and schools would rise together, although at the beginning widespread vice in the cities and the large percentage of adults in the population suggested the church might be the more urgently needed.

CHAPTER XIV

Gold and the Gospel

MINISTERS and missionaries sent by Tennessee Protestant Christian churches were among the first to establish Southern Baptist, Methodist Episcopal Church South, Presbyterian, and Cumberland Presbyterian congregations in California during the gold rush era. They were invading an area in which the Catholic Church was the only institutional Christian presence. Its communicants included the few wealthy ranch owners, most of whom were of Spanish descent, but the largest number were Indian converts. Although it had been sponsored by the government of Spain long before Mexico won its independence in 1821, the Catholic Church had lost much of the power it originally held.

By granting eight million acres of mission lands to private landowners, the Mexican government had weakened Catholic ministry, conducted through a network of about twenty missions located along the coast from San Diego to San Francisco Bay. Facing such a drastic reduction in the land available for range and cultivation, the missions did not have enough work to keep their member-converts employed. As a result, thousands drifted away and ended their traditional relationship with the church. An added difficulty was the distance separating the priests from the church in the larger Mexican cities. To deliver even the most basic supplies to the missions was extremely expensive. Nevertheless, reflecting early-nineteenth-century European traditions of Catholicism, priests at the missions ministered to their local communities. Even though it had priests on the scene, the Catholic Church was almost totally unprepared for the flood of gold rushers.[1]

Recognizing the surge in population, the Catholic Church in the United States established its dominion over California Catholics in 1850 with the appointment of the first bishop to the new state: Joseph Sadoc Alemany, bishop of Monterey. Pope Pius IX appointed Alemany, who had recently completed six years with the church in Tennessee, from a short list of candidates recommended by American Catholic leaders. An especially strong recommendation was offered by Bishop Richard Pius Miles, the first bishop of Nashville with whom Alemany had worked as an assistant from 1842 to 1845 at the Nashville Cathedral of the Holy Rosary.[2]

The new bishop of Monterey had been a full-time assistant to Father Michael McLeer at St. Peter's Church in Memphis from 1845 to 1848 when he became master of novices at Saint Rose, Kentucky. In that state he served as provincial of the Province of St. Joseph until accepting the appointment to California.[3]

Born in Spain in 1814 and educated in Italy, Bishop Alemany was a member of the Dominican Order. He had come to the United States in 1840 expecting to become an assistant to Bishop Miles in what was primarily a frontier mission outreach program at Nashville. He delayed his arrival at the mission by working for nearly two years in the ministry of St. Joseph's Convent, Somerset, Kentucky, to improve his limited command of the English language.[4]

Bishop Alemany established the Diocese of Monterey that ministered to many of the forty thousand Catholics that he estimated to be in California in 1851. When the Archdiocese of San Francisco was created in 1853, he was appointed California's first archbishop. Alemany pushed his superiors in the church to hasten priests to the frontier to teach the tenets of the faith. He opened a Catholic school at Santa Clara in 1851 that a few years later became a college. He served the Catholic Church in California with distinction until 1884 when, at the age of seventy, he resigned and returned to Spain.[5]

A group of San Francisco Baptists built the first meetinghouse and organized the first Protestant congregation in California. When, in early 1850, a Tennessee preacher who had abandoned the ministry for the mines called on former Knox Countian Osgood C. Wheeler, pastor of the first Baptist Church in San Francisco, he found a "very comfortable house of worship" and a church "exerting an excellent and an extensive influence" in the city.[6]

Notwithstanding his apparent success, Wheeler candidly expressed his frustration with the miners' single-minded focus on gold. "I am trying to preach, to labor, to pray," he wrote, "and I love my work, but have never seen a harder task than to get a man to look through a lump of gold into eternity."[7]

Recognizing that both their older missionary enterprise in China and their more recent ministry in California needed every assistance possible, the Baptists of Nashville met in late April to recommend the establishment of a Baptist Publication Society in San Francisco. The plan was projected by Dr. John W. King, a medical doctor and church member, who then set out for San Francisco to assess firsthand the situation there.[8]

The Nashville daily press responded enthusiastically. Organization of the proposed publication society created an opportunity to bring light into darkness, Christianity to the heathen, one journal observed. Another saw it as "a lever that is destined to work the most wonderful revolution of any age. Asia with her 350 millions of souls as the prize!" Yet another declared that the proposed society could enable the thousands of foreigners who throng the gold fields to return to their homes bearing not only gold but also "'the pearl of great price' which has so advanced man since the times of Greece and Rome, both of whom passed into decline and oblivion without it."[9]

The opportunities for the church in California and Asia were of far greater moment than the collection of earthly riches. "It is a redeeming feature," wrote the editor of the *Tennessee Baptist*, "that whilst hundreds of thousands of our citizens are rushing to California to gather the golden harvests—that their attention is being directed to higher and nobler objects, than the mere acquisition of wealth for selfish purposes."[10]

While formulation of the publications society was under way, the Association of Baptist Churches in San Francisco advanced plans to establish a university in the city and purchased a plot of ground for that purpose located on Washington Street behind Osgood C. Wheeler's First Baptist Church. A board of eight trustees was incorporated for the project, one of whom was Wheeler. The *Alta California* recognized the plans as "praiseworthy" and recommended they be "liberally supported."[11]

A native Sumner Countian, who was one of the most controversial Baptist missionaries in the Orient, endorsed the publications society concept and joined the movement for a university in California. Issachar

Jacox Roberts, who first went to China in 1837, urged that the university plan include a professorship in the Chinese language to facilitate translations of the Bible, tracts, and other materials. Predicting that Chinese would flock to the West Coast as Europeans had to the East Coast, Roberts called for the undertaking to be carried out at once.[12]

Many Baptist leaders believed that California provided a new and open doorway to the Orient. "We sincerely believe," the editor of the *Tennessee Baptist* said, "that the God of the Bible, in answer to the prayers and efforts of the churches in behalf of China, has given our people California and Oregon, to enable us the more efficiently to prosecute the great work of evangelizing Asia and the islands of the Pacific."[13]

Roberts's command of the Chinese language plus the desire of his fellow missionaries to have him transferred from China assured him a prominent place on any list of those who might be considered to head a Chinese mission in California. The *Tennessee Baptist* was the first to recommend him, and others followed,[14] the most thoughtful of whom was Dr. King, leading Tennessee proponent of a Baptist ministry to Chinese immigrants.

The head of the Chinese mission in California should be a missionary experienced in China who speaks Chinese and is familiar with Oriental customs, King wrote. He should also edit a Chinese language newspaper for distribution in California. Those criteria established Roberts as an obvious choice for the task, but he was not interested.[15]

Agreeing that a missionary with experience in China should be chosen to head the Baptist mission activity on the West Coast, Roberts declined the position by reaffirming his commitment to the Chinese in their native land where he had worked for the previous sixteen years. Roberts probably suspected that he was about to be forced out of the Orient because the Missionary Board had "disconnected" him from his assignment in China, and the American consul at Canton had offered to arrange passage home for him and his family free of charge.[16]

William C. Buck of Nashville tried to persuade Roberts that God was calling him to come to the Chinese of California, many of whom were former residents of Canton where Roberts had labored for many years. Buck unsuccessfully urged him to reconsider.[17]

Another veteran Baptist missionary to China came as a minister to the West Coast Chinese in 1854. He found many of them were aware that the Tai-Ping Rebellion then raging in China was fueled in part by teachings from the Holy Bible as interpreted by the chieftain of the rebels, a former student of Issachar Roberts. The rebel leader printed thousands of Christian tracts and distributed them to his soldiers. Later, as the Tai-Pings threatened to overthrow the Manchu government of China, he sent for Roberts. When the Baptist missionary appeared, the rebels made him director of foreign affairs for their government that then controlled all provinces of the great country except two. He was the only non-Chinese person in the upper echelons of the Tai-Pings.[18]

The Methodist Episcopal Church South responded to the gold rush when its bishops determined in May 1849 to sponsor a mission in California. They sent two pastors from Georgia and one from Missouri; the three arrived in San Francisco on April 14, 1850.[19] Ministers of the Northern Methodist Church were already on the scene, and a meetinghouse for Methodists in San Francisco had been erected through their efforts.[20]

Tennessee Methodist preachers appeared in the West in 1850. George Horne of Knoxville had reached Nevada City, California, by October 3 where he undertook his work. Crossing by the Isthmus route, Horne preached to attentive crowds on board ship and at Panama City.[21] A Tennessee-born farmer and part-time Methodist preacher, Sevier Stringfield, crossed the plains to the gold country the same year. Stringfield first settled in Humboldt County.[22]

During the summer of 1850, Tennesseans could hear Methodist missionaries "from the churches both north and south" preach two or three times each week in a twenty-five-by-fifty-foot weatherboarded church house in San Francisco. Reporting to his Methodist preacher brother-in-law "Parson" Brownlow, Dr. William Hunt said that he attended preaching "every Sabbath" to large congregations that were "much more attentive than ever I saw them in the States."[23]

There was preaching in the open air as well, and Dr. Hunt said that he had seen "thousands listening with intense interest" while the din of construction work almost made hearing impossible. But nothing put a quietus on the "hundreds around the gambling table, whose money you could hear rattling on the table—all on Sabbath!"[24]

Convened at Lebanon in 1851, the Tennessee Conference of the Methodist Episcopal Church South appointed J. S. Malone to be a missionary to California. He landed at San Francisco on August 30 of that year and accepted assignment as pastor of the church at Sonora.[25] In 1852, the Nashville *Gazette*'s correspondent "Grizzly," who passed judgment on nearly everyone and everything, gave Malone high marks as a "very acceptable and useful minister."[26] After a *Christian Advocate*[27] for the Pacific Coast area published its first edition on January 5, 1852, Malone contributed articles written in Spanish to broaden the newspaper's outreach and readership.[28]

J. F. Blythe left the churches he pastored in and near Lexington, Tennessee, on August 2, 1851, and reached Nevada City on September 19 where a northern Methodist minister invited him to use the northern church house on Sunday nights. Accepting Colonel Bicknell's invitation to share his quarters for the winter, Blythe had been "variously engaged, traveling some, preaching . . . and begging money to erect churches." He had purchased a house suitable for church use at Nevada City and had assisted in initiating construction on houses at two other places. Notwithstanding the hardships of life about the mining camps, Blythe did not lose his sense of humor. When Bicknell confided that he had a rich quartz vein that he wished to sell in the spring and then leave the mines, Blythe proposed a partnership. In exchange for Bicknell's sharing his interest in the mineral vein, he would share his salary as a Methodist preacher with him. Bicknell's response must have included a hearty laugh.[29]

A preacher born in Overton County, Tennessee, in 1821 arrived in California about February 1, 1852, to join the missionary effort. Andrew M. Bailey had been appointed to the task by the Kentucky Conference of the Methodist Episcopal Church South on October 13, 1851.[30]

During the early spring of 1852, John Matthews, pastor of Andrew Methodist Church in Nashville, volunteered for the new mission field and left for San Francisco by way of New York on March 23. Traveling with Dr. E. M. Patterson who was returning after a visit to Nashville, he reached San Francisco on May 10. First appointed to organize a church at Shasta City 350 miles distant, Matthews accepted reassignment to Sacramento a few months later. He noticed that most Methodist church members were transfers from their eastern home congregations and that there were few converts from among the forty-niners.[31]

Hard times in the mines in 1852 prompted Matthews to write to the Nashville and Louisville *Christian Advocate*[32] asking for financial contributions to the California missionary activity. Although many Californians had been liberal givers a year ago, he explained, "Now they cannot assist because they have not the means."[33]

Early in 1852, concerned about the condition of the church on the West Coast, the Missionary Society of the Methodist Episcopal Church

South requested that Tennessee Conference Bishop Joshua Soule visit California.[34] From his Nashville office, Bishop Soule accepted the suggestion, and although his initial travel plans were delayed, he reached San Francisco via the Isthmus route on March 24, 1853.[35] Pastor A. T. Crouch, Jr., of the Memphis Conference accompanied him and later became president of the Female Institute at San Jose.[36]

The newspapers noted Soule's presence. Selecting from a somewhat irreverent San Francisco *Banner* interview, the Sacramento *Daily Democratic State Journal* observed:

> Bishop Soule—We were interested, says the *Banner* by a brief interview with this venerable servant of Christ the other day at S.F. His frame is large—very large—just large enough to support his great head, the only true measure of his great mind. In all the "Methodist Church South" his name is as a household word and the whole Christian world holds him in high esteem. We welcome him to our shores, and trust he will leave (if he leaves at all) the happy impress of his deep piety and strong faith upon all with whom he may mingle.[37]

The organizational meeting of the Pacific Annual Conference of the Methodist Episcopal Church South had been convened on April 15 of the prior year at San Francisco.[38] The conference roll listed eighteen members, three of whom were from Tennessee.[39] To prove that enlisting church members was a slow process, J. F. Blythe reported from his base at Nevada City that he had three houses of worship at four "regular preaching places" with a total membership of twenty-five.[40]

Another Tennessee preacher added his name to the rolls of the conference before it next met. In December 1852, J. R. Finley, president of Soule Female College in Murfreesboro, resigned and announced plans to join the work in California during the January following.[41]

Probably the newest member of the conference was Drury K. Bond, a native of Dickson, Tennessee, who had come to the West as a miner, but who gave up gold seeking at Sonora in favor of the Methodist ministry. He worked as a preacher until his death in 1861 at the age of thirty-eight years.[42]

Bishop Soule had planned his visit to California so that he could preside over the second Pacific Annual Conference at San Jose on April 13–20,

1853. At the age of seventy-three years, he was the senior bishop of Southern Methodism.[43] He proudly noted that the conference had grown to include thirty-eight preachers, twenty-seven churches, one college, and one newspaper.[44]

A popular figure with the California public, Soule was much in demand. He addressed the lower house of the legislature, preached at Wesley Chapel in San Francisco, preached in theaters at Marysville and Sacramento to raise money for church houses, visited and preached in the other principal towns of the state, and made a sweeping tour of the mines.[45] After nearly six months in California, he returned via the Nicaragua route and disembarked at Nashville on August 21, 1853.[46]

The bishop returned to California for his second official visit to attend the third Pacific Annual Conference in Stockton on February 15–23, 1854. Traveling with him from New Orleans was the well-known Tennessee preacher Fountain E. Pitts. Although they did not arrive until late in the evening of February 17, the bishop took the gavel on the next day and presided over the body's deliberations for the remainder of the conference. A missionary from the Holston Conference, J. L. Pendergrast of Hamilton County, had arrived in California on January 7 in time for assignment by the Pacific Conference.[47]

Bishop Soule and Pitts were back in Nashville on April 10, 1854, but after a few days of rest, the bishop was on the road again. His destination—Columbia, South Carolina—was only a few hundred miles away instead of a few thousand. But irrespective of distances, Soule had California and China on his mind. He was inspired, and he shared that inspiration with the Southern Methodists gathered at Columbia:

> [California] is the finest country I ever saw. When I have surveyed her magnificent bay, her splendid rivers, her prolific mining regions, and the relation she bears to other parts of the word, I am almost inclined to wish I were young again. I declare unto you that I am willing to go to California again. . . . I would grasp California in one hand, and China in the other.[48]

Since the Mexican War, Southern Methodist leaders shared the view of their Baptist colleagues that California was the point from which the gospel could be radiated to China and the islands of the Pacific. A Methodist bishop asked, "Who knows but that California will yet become a great missionary nursery for the church in those lands?"[49]

O. P. Fitzgerald left Tennessee Methodism to become a missionary to California in 1855 and remained there until the 1870s. He conducted much of his early ministry in and around the town of Sonora where local historians recorded that he regularly "smote the ungodly." Later he had charge successively of Methodist colleges at Vacaville and Santa Rosa and became superintendent of schools for the state of California in 1867.[50]

The only Protestant sect of the period to have had its institutional origins in Tennessee was the Cumberland Presbyterian Church, and due to its size and youth, it was not able to deliver a missionary effort in California comparable to that of the older denominations. News of the departure for California of an Arkansas minister trained at Cumberland University, Lebanon, who was "not . . . in the pursuit of gold, but on his Great Master's business," elicited editorial comment in the church's newspaper. None should be "so anxious to collect the gold which the rust doth corrupt," the editor wrote, that he failed to distribute among his fellow men "that gold which perisheth not nor ever loses its lustre."[51]

At midyear 1850, only a very few Cumberland preachers were on the West Coast. Tennessean T. A. Ish, a lay preacher, wrote home asking that an ordained minister be sent to California so that the Cumberland church could be established there.[52] From May through November 1849, Ish had preached at "unorganized Union services" in Sacramento usually held in a grove near the corner of K and Third Streets.[53] By the latter part of December, James M. Small, who had come with the Lincoln County company, was preaching twice a week, holding prayer meeting on Wednesday night, and conducting a Sunday school in an effort to draw enough members to organize a Cumberland Presbyterian Church at Napa City. He was hoping to form a presbytery with other Cumberland preachers, but he was not able to identify who they were and where they might be. At times he despaired. On November 27, 1850, he wrote the church newspaper at Lebanon that it appeared to him that "the devil, almost, has entire control of California."[54]

John J. May, a Tennessee Cumberland Presbyterian, devoted all of his energies to preaching and the supporting ministries, but tried in vain to organize a church at San Jose in the latter weeks of 1850. Moving north to Sacramento, May preached on Sunday evenings in a Methodist church and often conducted prayer meetings in family residences.[55]

Meeting April 4, 1851, with three other Cumberland ministers, Small joined them in organizing the first Cumberland Presbytery in California. At that time there were two "regularly organized" congregations, one at

Napa and one at Martinez. Small agreed to work north of the bay of San Francisco, paying special attention to Napa. The presbytery expected to organize additional congregations during the ensuing year.[56] May did not "attach" himself to the presbytery, but labored at Sonoma, hoping for assistance from the eastern states. He had decided that without aid from the established churches there, "we may as well return home where our hearts are." He begged, "*SEND US MINISTERS*, and when you send, send men of talent; otherwise we want none." Without personnel, books of standard religious works, hymnbooks, and at least token financial support, he saw no hope of competing with the Methodist, Baptist, and mainline Presbyterian churches in California. About the only help from the East that had appeared was in the form of issues of the church newspaper, the *Banner of Peace and Cumberland Presbyterian Advocate*, which had reached Cumberlands in California as early as September 15, 1851. A few months later, May had a house of worship under construction at Sonoma.[57]

A Cumberland Presbyterian preacher who came from East Tennessee to California in August 1852 went directly to the mines at Georgetown and began mining. A. G. Register had come with associates who, like him, had made the trip to gather gold. Serving the church was not his purpose at that time. He explained, "I came to this country to bear a miner's toil, that I might deliver myself from the cares of the world, and qualify myself for usefulness."[58]

After a year of mining with meager results, Register considered taking up his books and devoting himself exclusively to the ministry. From time to time he had preached with "great encouragement," and he began to think he "might effect great good" by it.[59]

In addition to mining during the autumn of 1853, he and two partners from Greene County operated a blacksmith shop near Georgetown. A year later he was surveying on weekdays, but was preaching regularly on Sundays. He remained in California, devoting most of his time to the mines, until the spring of 1857 when he returned to East Tennessee. Letters written home by Register and included in his biography make no mention of other ministers in California or of any contact with the Cumberland Presbyterian Church.[60]

The Presbyterian Church in the United States of America had ministers in California in 1849 and the following year organized the first presbytery in the new state. Three ministers convened the presbytery at Benicia and a fourth, William G. Canders of the Maury Presbytery of

Tennessee, was present as a corresponding member. The churches of Benicia and San Francisco were the two member churches. In 1852, Robert McCoy came to the California Presbytery from the Presbytery of Memphis and later became pastor of the church at Santa Clara.[61]

Although few Tennessee Presbyterian ministers were found among the pioneer leaders of that church in California, a notable exception was William Anderson Scott who came to San Francisco in 1854. Regarded then as the outstanding preacher of the city of New Orleans and one of the greatest in the South, Scott came to California in response to an invitation and pledge of support to organize a Presbyterian church in San Francisco. He and the congregation dedicated Calvary Presbyterian Church on January 14, 1855.[62]

William Anderson Scott was born in Bedford County, Tennessee, on January 30, 1813. At the age of fifteen, he became a communicant of the Cumberland Presbyterian Church, at seventeen received his license to preach, and was assigned to minister to the churches on the Carroll and Obion circuit in West Tennessee. A year later he entered Cumberland College at Princeton, Kentucky, but left to become an army chaplain at Fort Crawford, Prairie du Chien, Wisconsin. He returned to school in 1832 and was graduated from Cumberland College, Kentucky, in 1833. In 1834, he studied at Princeton Theological Seminary, Princeton, New Jersey, and a year later was ordained by the Presbytery of Louisiana. He became pastor of the church at Opelousas and teacher in an academy there.[63]

Soon after marriage to Ann Nicholson of Huntingdon, Tennessee, on January 19, 1836, Scott accepted an offer to come to Winchester to be principal of the local female academy and pastor of the Cumberland Presbyterian Church. When the trustees of Nashville Female Academy brought him to their institution as principal in 1838, he joined the Nashville Presbytery and severed his relationship with the Cumberland church.[64]

In 1839, Scott abandoned teaching and gave the pastorate his full attention. Midway in the following year, he left Nashville to become pastor of the First Presbyterian Church of Tuscaloosa, Alabama. In 1842, he answered the call of the First Presbyterian Church of New Orleans and served in its pulpit until going to California.[65]

With the outbreak of the Civil War, Scott could not suppress his sympathy for the South. Under pressure for his pro-Southern views, he left San Francisco and served churches in England and New York. But after the war, Presbyterians in San Francisco implored him to come back. In 1870, he returned to found St. John's Presbyterian Church there and continued as its pastor until his death in 1885.[66]

Scott was the author of eleven published books, editor of *The Presbyterian* for three years at New Orleans, and founder-editor of the *Pacific Expositor* in 1860. He was a leader in founding both the City College and the University Mound College in San Francisco. In 1856, he courageously declared against the Vigilance Committee.[67] Few religious leaders of the period could match his accomplishments.

Preachers who reached California during the gold rush were often the targets of criticism and sometimes ridicule. Rarely, however, did a minister of the gospel come under such bitter fire as Methodist preacher-editor Parson Brownlow leveled at Robert G. Williams, a Presbyterian preacher who crossed to the gold country as chaplain of the East Tennessee Gold Mining Company. Brownlow seriously detested Williams for several reasons. First, he was an abolitionist. In addition, he was a Presbyterian and the brother-in-law of Rector Humes, one of the owners of Brownlow's principal competition, the Knoxville *Register*. Further, Williams had supplied the *Register* with exclusive accounts of the mining company's travels across the country from Knoxville to San Francisco. When the East Tennesseans reached their destination, Williams discontinued writing for the *Register*. Brownlow railed, "Williams has disgraced himself since he has been in California by card playing, Sabbath breaking, and drinking liquor; and while he has ceased to preach and pray for the company, he has ceased to find items in the land of gold, to interest the readers of the *Register*, as a correspondent."[68]

But that was not all. Williams had filed with the company a doctor's certificate that entitled him to benefits for the certifiably sick. When he accepted the payments, he was behaving "true to the instincts of a *Yankee* of the ordinary class, as he is," Brownlow charged. "No gentleman, honest man, or Christian would have applied for this money under the circumstances."[69]

Gold seekers in 1849 found few instances of traditional Christian worship. When W. L. Jenkins arrived in Sacramento, he "rejoiced . . . to find that the people of God were accustomed to assemble regularly every Lord's Day in an open blacksmith's shop."[70] Although several church houses were in existence by midsummer 1851, worship services sometimes took the form of "a religious camp-meeting," especially where churches were yet to be built. But it was risky business. On one such occasion near San Jose, those in attendance could see "within one hundred yards of the pulpit . . . a small shanty where brandy, wines, and other liquors were sold by the glass."[71]

When John Y. Gilbert and Benjamin F. Cheatham rode out about six miles from Stockton to attend a camp meeting in September 1852, they reported "a spacious and handsomely located campground and a large and successful meeting." But best of all, they heard a "plain, sensible, old-fashioned Methodist sermon."[72]

Preaching in a crudely constructed shelter on the first night after he reached Nevada City, John J. May heard detractors just outside calling for him to "shut his mouth." On another occasion he was outraged when he saw "two drunk men come in to prayer meeting, and pretend to be much concerned about the welfare of their souls."[73]

On September 8, Madison B. Moorman found a church service under way at Hangtown in a tent about twenty by thirty feet in size. The preacher was a miner, untrained in the ministry, but zealous in his presentation. Moorman wrote in his journal, "In his embarrassed and disconnected style, he said many good things, and they were very consoling to my poor spirits, which were in a condition that needed much consolation."[74]

Churchgoers could rarely escape the appeals of worldly pleasures promoted by the gambling halls, which were far more numerous than churches. Once when J. K. McCall emerged from a San Francisco house of worship, he confronted a novel scene: "A band of musicians seated in a gaudy wagon were playing a lively air . . . [and] behind was a large transparency announcing 'This Evening GRAND COCK FIGHTS.'"[75]

Rooster fights and other distractions aside, the advent of preachers, teachers, churches, and schools suggested that California was on its way to embracing and propagating the values held by the vast majority of Americans in the older states. Men and women who remained to become permanent settlers could expect to live in circumstances much more desirable than those prevalent during the first years of the rush. But what about the thousands who came to dig a fortune and race home to bask in the glory of sudden riches? When did they return? How were they received?

CHAPTER XV

Home Again

ALTHOUGH the first forty-niners to turn their backs on California were at home again by the end of 1849, they did not come in large numbers until 1851 and afterward. Most had planned to stay only one or two years, the time they had allotted for success in the mines. Disappointed upon their arrival by the meager results miners were obtaining, they had chosen nonetheless to try the mining experience. It was almost impossible to understand, without trying it, that recovering gold was enormously difficult, required long hours of hard work, and at best brought only modest rewards to all but a very few.

Some remained in California as settlers with a majority in careers other than mining. How many? No one knows even as no one knows how many emigrated from Tennessee or how many returned home. Many settlers became prominently known throughout the state because of leadership positions they assumed in business, industry, the professions, education, religious institutions, government, and even large-scale deep shaft mining. They contributed to the growth and development of their adopted state throughout their lifetimes, and in many instances, succeeding generations continued the practice.

In Tennessee, the arrival of returning forty-niners attracted little public attention. Most returned from a failed experiment. Although few brought back enough gold or money to make a difference in their standards of living, many brought back enough souvenir gold to make a ring, bracelet, or other piece of jewelry. Dr. Fischel brought a different kind of souvenir, however. Returning through Mexico, he acquired "a strange figure—a half-length female figure carved from the tusk of an animal."

Reportedly a pre-Columbian artifact, it attracted a crowd of curiosity seekers when displayed in Gowdey's store on the public square at Nashville.[1]

Coming home without wealth was an embarrassment to many. Within family circles, however, there were warm welcomes and celebrations for the safe return of husbands, sons, brothers, and other kin. The pockets of the prodigals may have been nearly empty, but each came with a fund of stories about the crossings and their times in California. They would soon slip into old roles, but truly their lives would never be the same again.

A few found life in Tennessee too dull after living in a "growing and prosperous" state like California and/or in a dynamic young city like San Francisco. In 1853, Nashville forty-niner J. K. McCall reported his home city the same in appearance as when he left it and with few prospects for constructive change. He said that he could never be satisfied in Nashville "or even in New Orleans after living in a 'fast' city like San Francisco." A fellow Tennessean, who was then living in San Francisco, believed that few who had ever lived in California could "return to the Atlantic states and remain contented."[2]

Dr. Berryman Bryant tried to return to Tennessee after selling his hospital in November 1849, but stopped in Missouri where he remained only a few weeks before backtracking to California. In 1852, he set out again for Tennessee, but turned back by the time he had traveled only a few miles. California had a firm grip on the doctor, as it had on many others, and he remained there practicing medicine and raising livestock near San Jose until his death in 1898.[3]

Many homecomings were delayed because the miners had exhausted their funds and were waiting for a change in their luck to raise enough money to pay for their transportation. Others deferred the trip home because they were able to make living expenses and had not given up hope. They remained in the mines, believing that a rich strike might be only one season away. Some had to wait as they struggled to get their health and their funds simultaneously adequate to return home. Sicknesses contracted in the mine camps were physically debilitating and financially devastating.

Because many young men had financed their journeys to the gold fields in full or in part with loans, homecoming was a time to settle accounts. Some brought back sufficient funds to repay their backers, but others required additional time to come up with the money required. In the many instances in which parents or other family members furnished all or part of the expense money, there was a high incidence of debts forgiven.

But what about the local gold mining organizations with venture shareholders both at home and in the mines? It is not known that any of the companies returned to Tennessee and distributed dividends to stockholders. Nor is it known that any came back with accurate expense and earnings records and with their rosters intact. Although most organizations of size broke up while making the crossing or, if still together at their destination, dispersed or dissolved soon after, individual members occasionally fared well. There were just enough reports of specific forty-niners striking it rich to make investors who remained at home skeptical when miners came in empty-handed.

Stay-at-home backers and investors understandably had difficulty recognizing the real obstacles that the forty-niners faced: sickness, the weather, inflated prices, long hours at hard labor, gambling, confidence scams, and unscrupulous persons. Perhaps the greatest obstacle of all was the hurdle raised high by unrealistic expectations. Getting gold was supposed to be easy, but it was not. Wealth was said to be there for the taking, but it was not.

In most cases, their stockholders or sponsors understood the widespread failure of home-organized mining companies to come back heavily laden with treasure. From reading the daily press and letters from the miners, those at home could see that harvesting worthwhile amounts of gold was an elusive pursuit indeed. But one prominent exception was an occasion when the stay-at-home shareholders could not accept the breakup of their company in the gold fields. Consequently they sought to enforce the contract that existed between the miners and investors, calling for each of the former to work for the company in good faith until November 1, 1852, or to pay into its treasury a forfeiture of $1,000.

Upon receiving information about November 1, 1851, that their California contingent "in all probability may disband and cease to work for the company," the ten stay-at-home stockholders of Wilson, Love and Company met and drafted a resolution of protest, which they dispatched to George Love. They instructed him to share its contents with the other members in California.

Reminding the miners that they were under contract to work for the company for another twelve months, the protest acknowledged that they "would meet with occasional disappointments and difficulties," but it insisted that by perseverance they could overcome such problems. By completing their obligation, the miners could enable the company to recover the $9,000 of paid-in capital and "in all probability" a profit that would be distributed on a pro rata basis. The "Tennessee members" expected that their "friends in California" would continue to work for the company whether in the mines or outside. In fact, they made no mention of the mines, but expected the "friends" to exert themselves and "engage in things, matters, and work most profitable to the company."

A dissolution was unthinkable to those at home. "We cannot consent to the breaking up of the company and the loss of our money paid in," they declared. It was their intent that "each member of the company . . . faithfully comply" with the articles of agreement and "discharge their duties respectively."[4]

The company had dispersed before George Love received the protest, but if it had arrived earlier, it would have had no influence on their decision to break up. They survived the best way they could. When their health permitted, they worked in the mines or at whatever opportunity was promising until in groups of two or three, they began to return to Sumner County.

Shortly after November 1, 1852, the date of termination for the contract, the stay-at-home shareholders brought a lawsuit against those who "took stock in labor" instead of by cash, seeking to collect the forfeiture of $1,000 per man that was allegedly owed because they did not work in California for the contracted period. The fourteen defendants were William Patterson, Jacob A. Tyree, William Wright, William Tyree, James D. Cartwright, C. H. Wallace, William Love, Richard Charlton, George D. Blackmore, James A. Allen, Lycurgus Charlton, George Love, and F. B. Wilson and William Pryor, both deceased. At that time six of the defendants were still in California, and six had returned to Tennessee.[5]

The complainants also asked for an accounting by the individual miners. They wanted to know from each "what interest in claims, or property they have in California or . . . what amount of money or effects they brought from California, and a full disclosure made of their labors in California and what they have." The curiosity of the complainants had been piqued by reports that William Patterson had made "upwards of $10,000" in California and C. H. Wallace had returned with nearly that much.[6]

Curiosity changed to suspicion when a letter reached home written September 1, 1851, from a Sumner County miner of another company. It relayed a report that Wilson, Love and Company had found a very rich quartz vein near Sonora. The writer said that each of the ten partners involved in working it had taken out $4,000 before receiving offers of

$10,000 each for their interests.[7] Like many other gold strike reports, it was a fiction, but home shareholders wanted to believe it.

The circuit court accepted depositions from the miners who were within its reach in an attempt to discover why the company broke up, if there were earnings by individuals that should have been turned over to the company treasurer, and who and how many should pay the agreed forfeiture of $1,000. The court also allowed both sides to submit testimony from others who had been to the mines at about the same time in order to compare the profitability of their various ventures in California.

The depositions of the Wilson and Love miners made a strong case in their defense, although most were embarrassing recitals of failure. Pointing out that he had left his wife and six children at home in order to make some much needed money in the gold fields, George Love said that the failure of the company was "notorious." Not only had his coleader died soon after reaching the mines, Love had been sick much of the time. He retraced their travels as they searched unavailingly for good diggings and explained that they dispersed because it was the only way they could survive. One or two men could usually borrow enough money or secure credit enough to lay in provisions for off-season, but twelve to fifteen men could not as a group find that kind of support. Love stated that he reached home "broke down in health" with $70 to show for his entire effort in the enterprise.[8]

Lycurgus and Richard Charlton corroborated Love's statements, and the latter added that he had tried mining at Ophir, Bear River, American River, and Diamond Springs in El Dorado County and barely made expenses. He had bought a one-quarter interest in a quartz ledge for $500 and worked four months to help build a mill house, but before he received a penny from the investment of his labor, the mine collapsed into bankruptcy. Lycurgus's efforts were similarly unproductive. Each declared that he had made nothing for the company or for himself.[9]

One after another, the defendants testified to their unsuccessful efforts. William Tyree said that they all did the best they could, but did not have enough capital to stay the course. The challenges of survival preoccupied them, and they did not have time to devise a more deliberate, businesslike plan of action. In the process Tyree became ill. He was able later to come home only because a cousin had taken him in, cared for him, and eventually arranged a loan to pay for crossing to Tennessee. He said that in the gold-hunting venture he had lost his health and $1,000 cash.[10] George D. Blackmore agreed with Tyree. He had made nothing, and his time was a total loss.[11] C. H. Wallace said the report that he had made $8,000 to $10,000 in California was false, and he instead came home about $150 in debt for the experience.[12]

Many of the miners had decided to work for the company when it was organized primarily because of the respect they held for the older stay-at-home stockholders whom they generally regarded as "knowing men," Simon Elliott stated. He was so confident of their judgment that he "never thought once that it was possible that the company could make a failure," and for that reason he "did not think of requiring the home stockholders to participate in the losses." In retrospect he saw that mining with a company such as this one was "impracticable . . . [and] . . . visionary." He insisted that the dissolution of the company "was the result of necessity," and had they not done so, they would not have survived. He confidently offered "if necessary" to show that "in no instance has a company organized in the states operated successfully in that country as a company."[13]

The testimony of the defendants was upheld in depositions given by other returned miners in Sumner and Wilson Counties who were not members of Wilson, Love and Company. During four years in California, Edward A. White of Wilson County once had owned an interest in the Tennessee Mine near Sonora with Love and four others of the company, but when the operation closed and the profits were distributed, each of the Sumner Countians received about $132 for his part. White was unable to point to any other money-making by Love or any of his crew.[14] Two Sumner men who had been in the mines about the same time the company was there stated that neither had made profits. William Gregory worked at times with various members of the company, but after two years, he had made nothing.[15] After five years in the gold fields, 1850–1855, Tyree B. Harris had achieved no positive financial results. "I made nothing," he said, "[but] was a loser; did not have as much money when I returned as I started with."[16] A Hartsville home investor or sponsor who sent nine men to California in 1849 at his own expense lost about $4,000 because they failed to make a dividend while they were there.[17]

John B. Walton, who had traveled from Chagres with Wilson, Love and Company, said that he knew of no organized companies that made money. Recognizing quickly that there was little chance for profit in the frantic search for gold, he returned home eight months after he first departed, but the outing caused him to lose $1,100.[18] Another who "fell in" with the company at Chagres was John C. Hubbard whose only earning above subsistence was a $500 hit that he made in selling his shares in a quartz mine. He was rescued from impending financial disaster by his "relation" Jack Hays, who hired him as a deputy surveyor.[19]

All of the outside deponents gave members of the company credit for hard work and thoughtful effort. They agreed also that there were no viable alternatives to dissolving the company.

By the time their cause came to hearing on March 9, 1857, the complainants had decided to focus their claim on William Patterson and to discharge the other original defendants from all liability under the partnership agreement. They alleged that Patterson had traveled to the mines at the company's expense, upon arrival had refused to work and had abandoned his responsibility under the company agreement, and had purchased a mine in his own name in cooperation with others not of the company. Then and subsequently he "had made large sums of money" but had refused to account to the company in any fashion. The other defendants waived their rights to any sums recovered from Patterson, and the court decreed that the home shareholders were due recovery from Patterson of $1,000 by way of forfeiture and a portion of his earnings as might be determined.[20]

Focusing on Patterson and absolving the others closed an unhappy chapter in the lives of the members of Wilson, Love and Company. Unreasonable expectations again nearly ruined relations between neighbors, but in this case the stay-at-home shareholders were at fault. They held tightly to unjustifiable expectations and nursed dreams of golden futures long after it was common knowledge that stock companies such as theirs were ill-conceived and unproductive in the mines.

The experience of Wilson, Love and Company reflected deeply held frustrations. Two of the miners died and the others suffered exposure and illness, spent their inadequate capital, disbanded the company, and came home defeated but grateful to rejoin family circles. Josephus Conn Guild and his fellow home shareholders believed that they had provided adequate financing for the miners and a fair contract to guide their operations. Their frustration was that the men quit the company before they undertook other kinds of work on the company's behalf. They were blinded by their inability to envision the situation the miners faced in California. All of the company, whether they stayed at home or went to the mines, shared the common frustration caused by unsatisfied greed. What happened to the gold? It was a question asked of thousands of returning forty-niners in Tennessee and in every state of the Union. The gold rush experience was golden for only a few, but the California experience was an unforgettable one for all.

Notwithstanding the discouraging experiences previously shared by so many of those who were home again, the presence of Tennesseans in California had much to do with the development of the region. Those who became permanent settlers usually contributed the most, but some who returned within the first decade made vital contributions. Captain Farragut, Balie Peyton, Alexander Outlaw Anderson, Ben McCulloch, Bishop Soule, Thomas Eastland, and A. M. Rosborough were a few whose presence was short-lived, but of constructive impact. Although they did not appear on the scene in California, other Tennesseans had important roles in its early development. Matthew Fontaine Maury gave credibility to a transcontinental railroad ten years before Congress agreed to build it. President James K. Polk won the cession from Mexico, and Sam Houston wanted California in the Union.

The gold seekers came home to a state that from all outward appearances was unchanged from the time they left it, yet divisive forces were at work within its bounds. Slavery had become a sectional issue before California sought admission to the Union and forced the Compromise of 1850 that postponed a showdown on the question. Nevertheless, border states such as Tennessee and Kentucky were not prepared for the prospective division of the United States into two separate nations.

Powerful economic forces exacerbated sectional differences. The agricultural economy of the Deep South was heavily dependent on slave labor. The states of the East and Midwest had labor aplenty supplied by successive waves of European immigration and an economy sustained by industry and a growing network of railroads. To protect their perceived interests, Southern states claimed a right to withdraw or secede from the Union, and the states of the North, where the abolitionist movement was growing daily, contended that the Union was indivisible. Many Tennesseans, in their nationalistic fervor of the 1840s, had regarded Manifest Destiny and the extension of slavery as going hand in hand. When the Republican victory in the election of 1860 threatened not only that relationship but the survival of slavery where it then existed, they began to put nationalism aside and to turn to the option of separation.

The drift was toward the abyss of fratricidal war. In the antidisunionist tradition of Jackson and Polk, Tennesseans at first resisted the drift. Early in 1861, a statewide referendum recorded a solid majority in favor of remaining in the Union, but when the guns sounded in Charleston harbor, sentiment changed abruptly. On May 6 the general assembly authorized the governor to enter into a military league with the Confederate states and a month later, in a second referendum, Tennesseans voted to declare the state independent of the Union.

Many of the Volunteer forty-niners left home again to face yet another uncertain future. Most enlisted under the flag of the Confederate States, but others marched under the Stars and Stripes. There were also divided allegiances among the Tennesseans who had remained in the West, but how many, East or West, understood that by giving rise to a new state, the gold rush had been a principal cause of splitting the Union? The admission of California to statehood was the excuse for the Compromise of 1850, but there was no excuse for permitting sectional differences to grow into ir-reconcilable issues during the next decade. Leadership both North and South had failed. All that was left was the crucible of war, and its bright flame would burn for four tragic years.

APPENDIX

NOTES

BIBLIOGRAPHY

INDEX

Tennesseans in California
Prior to 1849

As young men from Tennessee and the other twenty-nine states began their various pilgrimages to the gold fields, few knew much about the others who had journeyed to California prior to the discovery at Sutter's Mill. There were probably more than one hundred Tennesseans among the two thousand[1] United States-born residents of California in 1848, and they were scattered throughout the region. Some had arrived as early as the 1830s, but probably most had come during the ten years prior to 1849.

The first Tennesseans who journeyed to California reached their destinations when the area was part of Mexico. The names of only a minority are identified, and only for a few of them are pertinent details supplied.[2] The following entries, in approximate chronological order of arrival, provide names and information about a number who reached California prior to 1849. Accounts of a few others appear in the text.

EWING YOUNG. Possibly the first Tennessean to reach California was Ewing Young, a native of Jonesborough, who led a party of trappers overland from Santa Fe to arrive during the latter part of 1829 or the early days of 1830. Born in Washington County in 1792, Young left Tennessee about 1822 and purchased a farm in Missouri, only to sell it a few months later and set out for Santa Fe. On reaching his destination, Young took up trapping and associated himself with William Wolfskill, an experienced trapper who had traveled the trail with him. He was beginning a noteworthy career as a trapper and trader.[3]

Returning to Missouri in the autumn of 1824, Young brought back merchandise to sell at Santa Fe in the spring of 1825. He was in Missouri again in the summer and back to Santa Fe in the fall. He returned to Missouri by February 1826, and by late summer had crossed to Taos. There he hired a young man to cook for his party and later took him as an apprentice trapper. He had selected Kit Carson, later famous throughout the West as a scout and guide. Young trapped extensively for the next two years, following the Salt, Gila, and Colorado Rivers nearly their entire lengths.[4]

During the latter weeks of 1829, Young led a party of approximately twenty trappers into California, making him probably the fourth American to lead an overland crossing into that future state. He took them from a point on the Colorado River below the Grand Canyon up the dry Mojave River and finally through Cajon Pass to the mission at San Gabriel. They seem to have arrived there during the last few days of 1829 or very early in 1830. They returned to Taos sometime before the end of 1830. The California journey caused at least one historian to credit Young with opening significant trade between that region and New Mexico.[5]

In the fall of 1831, the intrepid Tennessean again set out for California with a party of trappers, and they arrived at Los Angeles on February 10, 1832. After a fruitless experience hunting sea otter, Young and some of the trapping party traveled for several months over much of northern California.[6] He was again trapping in New Mexico in 1833.[7]

Probably tired of a nomadic existence, Young settled in Oregon in 1834. There he was a wheat farmer, cattleman, and lumberman, focusing his attention on the products that made the Northwest famous. He died there in 1841.[8]

LEWIS T. BURTON. Nineteen-year-old Lewis T. Burton crossed from New Mexico in 1831 where he had been a hunter. He later became a wealthy merchant and ranchero.[9]

JOSEPH REDDEFORD WALKER. Born in 1798 in the part of Tennessee that three years later became Roane County, Joseph Reddeford Walker first reached the Pacific Coast in 1833. In 1819, he had moved with his family to Missouri where, though young, he became a trapper and mountain man of note. When Captain B. L. E. Bonneville[10] gathered a party for a trapping and exploring expedition in the Rockies and beyond, he chose Walker to be his second in command. They set out from Fort Osage, Missouri, east of Independence, on May 1, 1832.[11]

After crossing the Rockies through South Pass and reaching Green River, Bonneville placed Walker in charge of about one-half of their party with instructions to trap and explore the area immediately surrounding the Great Salt Lake, country unknown to either man. Walker and his men somehow lost their bearings and several months later found themselves crossing the Sierra Nevada into California. They had missed their assignment completely.[12]

While crossing the Sierra, Walker discovered not only Yosemite Valley, but a river and a lake to each of which his name was given. Ever mindful that he was on Bonneville's payroll, Walker wasted no time as he prepared to recross the mountains during 1834 for a summer rendezvous with his boss. He acquired 315 horses to deliver to Bonneville, perhaps in lieu of the pelts they had not found and the report they could not give on the Great Salt Lake. With supplies purchased at Monterey, Walker and his men set out from the San

Joaquin valley over Greenhorn Mountain and up the South Fork valley of the Kern to "where they could look out onto the desert country to the east of the range." The vantage point was a pass known before only to a few Indians. Thereafter known as Walker's Pass, it afforded the northernmost snow-free route across the Sierra Nevada.[13]

Walker trapped and explored, principally east of the Sierras, for the next six or seven years. In February 1841, he was in southern California bartering beaver skins for horses. By that time an experienced guide, mountaineer, and Indian fighter, he returned to Fort Laramie to meet and lead the Joseph Chiles party overland by the southern route in 1843. He set out to the East again and in 1844–45 met and guided John C. Fremont's[14] party west across the continent. "Capt. Joe Walker was one of the bravest and most skillful of the mountainmen," California historian Hubert H. Bancroft said of him. "None was better acquainted than he with the geography or the native tribes of the great basin; and he was withal less boastful and pretentious than most of his class."[15]

GEORGE NIDEVER. A native East Tennessean from Sullivan County, George Nidever was a successful hunter and had ranged around the country west of the Mississippi River from a home base in Arkansas since 1820. He and a small party met Joseph Reddeford Walker at the rendezvous in the Green River valley in 1833 and crossed the Sierra Nevada in his company. Reputed to be among the few "clean-living and upright" trappers on the frontier, Nidever later settled at Santa Barbara. His chief distinction was as a hunter and marksman, although he was in demand as a guide and as a pilot for coastal ships.[16]

ISAAC GRAHAM. Captain Isaac Graham came overland to California from Tennessee in 1833. Three years later he participated in an ill-fated revolt against Mexican authority led by Juan Alvarado, a Californian seeking to establish an independent, free government for the territory. Graham settled near Santa Cruz in 1841 and erected a sawmill, probably the first in the state. He owned an extensive stand of timber nearby including a tree nineteen feet eight inches in diameter that was noticed in John C. Fremont's book on California.[17]

FRANKLIN BEDWELL. Like many of the native Tennesseans who migrated to California, Franklin Bedwell lived for a few years in Missouri before moving farther westward. He was for several years a trapper in the Rocky Mountains and in the great basin between Santa Fe and Yellowstone. He crossed into California in 1840–41 and purchased a ranch on Russian River in 1843. In 1846, he joined the Bear Flag revolt. Beginning in 1848, he worked in the mines for a two-year stint before returning to his ranch home. In 1858, he married a native Tennessean, Selina McMinn, who had come to California the year before.[18]

CAPTAIN SMITH. A certain "Captain Smith," who made up a company of volunteers from Washington County in 1838 to explore the Rockies, later settled in California. He was still in the gold country in 1854 when a Greene County man reported an unexpected meeting with him near Georgetown.[19]

WILLIAM C. MOON. William C. Moon, who came with the Workman-Rowland party through New Mexico in 1841, quarried grindstones in the Sacramento River valley in 1844–45. He went to the gold fields in 1848–49. Later he became a famous hunter and settled on a farm in Tehama County.[20]

JAMES DOAK. James Doak reached California with the Workman-Rowland party, but his time in the Far West was cut short in 1843 when he drowned while trying to swim his mule across Green River. At that time he was traveling from Los Angeles to Santa Fe with Benjamin Davis Wilson and John Rowland.[21]

DAVID FRANK McCLELLAN. The Walker-Chiles overland crossing party of 1843 brought David Frank McClellan to the West Coast. McClellan, who seemed to enjoy the vicissitudes of cross-continental travel, remained in California until early 1846 when he returned to the East with his uncle Joseph Reddeford Walker. He crossed to California again during the latter part of the same year, but made "several visits to the east until 1853" when he finally settled on a farm in Contra Costa County.[22]

THOMAS WESTLY BRADLEY. After moving to Missouri, this Tennessean crossed to California with the Walker-Chiles party in 1843. He worked for John A. Sutter and joined in the Bear Flag revolt. Bradley later lived on a ranch in Napa Valley before settling permanently in Contra Costa County in 1849.[23]

WILLIAM BALDRIDGE. Also coming to California by way of Missouri and the Walker-Chiles party of 1843, William Baldridge found work as a skilled millwright. He participated in the Bear Flag revolt. He lived on a ranch in Napa Valley until 1852 when he relocated to a ranch near Oakville.[24]

GRIGSBY-IDE PARTY. In what was one of the first major wagon crossings from Missouri, G. John Grigsby, a thirty-six-year-old native of Maryville, Tennessee, led the Grigsby-Ide[25] party to California in 1845. With him were his younger brother Franklin T. Grigsby and Tennesseans Harvey Porterfield, John York, and the latter's wife and two sons, one born en route. Most of their party was made up of families that included fifty-nine children, but identities are lacking.[26] Leaving Missouri with a train of forty wagons, Captain Grigsby led them over the plains to Fort Hall. There a caravan of sixty wagons pooled their resources with his, and members of the newly merged procession of one hundred wagons elected Grigsby wagon master for the remaining and most difficult part of the journey to California. The train reached Sutter's Fort on October 10, 1845, and split up. Grigsby and the other Tennesseans proceeded to Napa County where they settled, although Porterfield worked briefly as a carpenter in Sonoma.[27] The Grigsby brothers, York, and Porterfield participated in the Bear Flag revolt on June 14, 1846, as members of a company of thirty-three that surrounded the Sonoma garrison of Gen. Mariano G. Vallejo and arrested him. Later in the year on November 12, Captain Grigsby appeared at Monterey with thirty settlers and ninety horses ready to assist General Fremont in the South, but Fremont placed him in command of Company E of the California Regiment and then sent him back to Sonoma to maintain the rebels' position and garrison there.[28]

THOMAS MARTIN. Another Tennessean who traveled to the West Coast in 1845 was Thomas Martin, who had resided in St. Louis from 1840 to 1845 before crossing with John C. Fremont. He was in the Bear Flag episode in Company A, California Battalion, but returned to the East in 1847. He came back to California in "the expedition of 1848–49," was a horse trader in different places and, in 1853, settled at Santa Barbara.[29]

WILLIAM C. WILSON. A well-known horseman, William C. Wilson came to California from the Mexican state of Sonora in 1845. He died at San Jose in 1882.[30]

NATHANIEL G. PATTERSON. A member of the California Battalion in 1846–47, Nathaniel G. Patterson was later a miner and stable keeper at Stockton before settling at Livermore about 1850.[31]

NATHANIEL JONES. In 1846, Nathaniel Jones, his wife, and son came from their last place of residence, Missouri, to Contra Costa County.[32]

ALFRED MUSGRAVE. A member of Company E, California Battalion, in 1846, Alfred Musgrave resided in Napa.[33]

SAMUEL CROCKETT YOUNG. Born in East Tennessee, matured and married in Rutherford County, Tennessee, Samuel Crockett Young moved with his bride, Nancy Leigh, to Jackson County, Missouri, in 1831. Ready to journey to California in 1846, Young set out early in the year with his wife and at least five children[34] in a family train of eighty wagons. The large train, accompanied by a number of cattle, soon split into four smaller parties of about ten families each. Young's party reached the summit of the Sierra Nevada during a snowfall on October 16, 1846, and arrived at Sutter's Fort before the end of the month.[35] He engaged in farming in the Santa Clara valley, and at one time operated the first livery stable at San Jose.[36]

NICHOLAS CARRIGER PARTY. Leaving Round Prairie, Missouri, to go overland on April 27, 1846, Nicholas Carriger,[37] his wife, and two children, ages one and three, with a third to be born on the way, his parents, Christian and Levisa Ward Carriger, one of his sisters and her husband, and possibly others of the family made common cause with another somewhat larger California-bound family party. Of the group, Nicholas and his parents are known to have been Tennesseans because he was born to them in Carter County in 1816. It is presumed his sister, her husband, and possibly others were Tennesseans, also.[38] Once on the way west, Carriger's enlarged party banded with a much larger group under the command of Maj. Stephen Cooper making a train of fifty wagons. Together they followed what became known as the "Old Fort Kearney" road to the head of Grand Island on the Platte River. It may have been the first time that wagons had attempted that route, although after the gold rush began, thousands passed that way.[39]

While descending the western slope of the Sierra, both Nicholas's father Christian Carriger[40] and his sister-in-law died on September 26, the same evening that his wife "gave birth to a lively little girl." After burying the bodies of his loved ones near the fords of the Yuba River, Nicholas Carriger and his party went on to Sacramento and ultimately to Sonoma where he settled.[41]

BENJAMIN F. MAYFIELD. A member of Company A, the Mormon Battalion, Mayfield reached California in 1847. He was a resident of San Luis Obispo County after 1868.[42]

DONNER PARTY. Probably the most battered group of Tennesseans to arrive in 1847 was the surviving Weakley County contingent of the Donner party. They had experienced almost unimaginable suffering; half died before they reached their destination.

It had all started back in Illinois and Tennessee. Hoping for a new life in the Far West, the Springfield, Illinois, families of James F. and Margaret W. Reed and the brothers George and Jacob Donner and their wives, Tamsen and Elizabeth, set out on April 14, 1846, in a train of covered wagons to settle in California. The caravan embodied a total of thirty-one men, women, and children, but at Independence, Missouri, additional immigrants joined them including a widowed Tennessee matriarch, Lavina Jackson Murphy, her four sons, three daughters, two sons-in-law, and three grandchildren. The Murphy family was from Weakley County.[43]

Swelled to eighty-five persons by the incorporation of other smaller groups, including Tennesseans William McCutchen, his wife, and infant daughter, the party made its way across the prairies and over the Rocky Mountains. The Donners elected to take the Hastings Cutoff, which, instead of saving time, markedly slowed their pace. They did not reach the dividing ridge of the Sierra Nevada until November 3 when they were halted by a blinding snowstorm that lasted several days.

Held in the grip of deep snow and severe cold, the party exhausted its meager supplies during the ensuing six or eight weeks. They had received foodstuffs sent from Sutter's Fort on October 19 after McCutchen and another of their party had gone ahead to acquire them, but the quantities were modest, in part because McCutchen had been stricken ill at the fort and could not return with his companion.

Desperate for relief, ten men and five women set out for help on improvised snowshoes. They nearly perished for lack of food and were reduced to eating flesh from the bodies of "their dead friends who were dying every day." Eight of the men died before reaching the nearest settlement, but "all of the women got through." All three Tennessee women, Amanda McCutchen and the sisters Sarah Murphy Foster and Harriet Murphy Pike, and one of the two men, Sarah's husband William M. Foster, lived to tell the story. Lemuel B. Murphy died on the way, December 28, 1846.[44]

Upon reaching the settlements, they sent relief parties to take food and succor to those left behind in the snowy mountain heights. But help arrived too late for about one-half of the immigrants, who had died from starvation. Among the dead were the McCutchens' daughter and Weakley Countians Lavina Jackson Murphy, her son John Landrum Murphy, her grandson George Foster, and her granddaughter Catherine Pike. The other four of Lavina's family, sons William Green and Simon Peter Murphy, daughter Mary M. Murphy, and granddaughter Naomi Pike survived the dreadful camp experience. Some of the survivors had sustained life by eating from the bodies of their dead companions.[45] Sometime before the train reached the Sierra Nevada, son-in-law William Pike had died from an accidentally inflicted pistol wound.[46]

Later in the spring an eastbound traveler stopped with others of his party at the Donner camp to bury the bodily remains of the dead. The body of Mrs. Murphy was found "lying near one of the huts with her thigh cut away for food, and the saw used to dismember the body lying along side of her," the traveler reported.[47]

Harriet Murphy Pike, widowed by her husband's accidental death, was married to Michael C. Nye and lived in California and Oregon. William Green Murphy came back to Weakley County, was married, but returned to the West first to Virginia City, Nevada, and later to Marysville, California. Simon Peter Murphy returned to make his home in Weakley County. William and Sarah Foster remained in California, as did Mary Murphy who was married to Charles Julian Covillaud, a native of Cognac, France.[48]

WILLIAM F. DRANNAN. A young Tennessean was a protégé of Kit Carson along the Santa Fe Trail in the spring of 1847. Born at sea in 1832 to French immigrant parents, William F. Drannan lived with them on a farm near Nashville until 1836. During that year both parents died of cholera, leaving him and a young sister orphans. William was in the care of a plantation owner near Andrew Jackson's Hermitage for the next eleven years, but at the age of fifteen, he ran away to St. Louis, Missouri, where Kit Carson hired him to learn the life of a hunter-explorer. He worked with Carson and Fremont and, beginning in 1851, guided a number of emigrant trains from the portal cities of Missouri to California.[49]

CAVE JOHNSON COUTS. A graduate of the United States Military Academy who had participated in the Mexican War, Lieutenant Cave Johnson Couts came from Coahuila to San Diego in 1848 with Maj. Lawrence P.

Graham's First Dragoons. Couts remained in military service until 1851 and then settled at San Diego where he was county judge and, in the years afterward, became a wealthy ranchero. He was a nephew of Cave Johnson of Tennessee, postmaster general during President Polk's administration.[50]

JAMES T. WALKER. James T. Walker, nephew of the famous guide Joseph Reddeford Walker, began his overland trip in 1847, but was forced "to winter on the way" because "with true family instinct" he had sought a new route. After working as a miner in 1848 and early 1849, he journeyed to the East by sea and the Isthmus only to recross the plains and mountains to California in 1850. Seeming to enjoy the challenges of crossing, he traveled to Missouri in 1851 by way of New Mexico and in 1852 made a third overland trip to the El Dorado. In 1853, he settled in Contra Costa County.[51]

W. T. HENDERSON. W. T. Henderson arrived in San Francisco in June 1848. He is usually regarded as the slayer of the notorious bandit Joaquin Murieta in 1850.[52]

GEORGE W. GIFT. A midshipman in the United States Navy, George W. Gift first walked on California soil when his training ship, the *St. Mary*, put in at San Francisco in 1848. After leaving the navy in 1852, he returned to the West Coast.[53]

DANIEL MONROE BURNS. Probably the youngest Tennessean at Sutter's Fort when the eastern gold seekers began to arrive in 1849 was Daniel Monroe Burns, born in Paris, Tennessee, in 1845. He, an older brother Thomas M., and sister Laura A. had accompanied their parents William and Caroline Griffin Burns when they left Henry County in 1846 to lead a wagon train of settlers to Oregon. While en route, their father died of cholera. Sometime after reaching Oregon, the widowed mother married Alfred Shelby, and in February 1849, they responded to the gold discovery by relocating to Sutter's Fort. Caroline Shelby died in December, leaving her children with their stepfather, who deserted them soon afterward. Families who learned of their plight took them in and provided for them.[54]

ALBERT MILLER. Son of Judge and Mrs. Pleasant Miller of Knoxville, Captain Albert Miller came to California in 1848 with his regiment from scenes of battle in the Mexican War. A graduate of the United States Military Academy, Miller remained in the army as an infantry officer. He died at Benicia, California, in January 1853.[55]

Notes

INTRODUCTION

1. The word *blacks* is used throughout the text and notes to refer to Americans of African descent. The author chose the term because it was widely used to identify African Americans during the nineteenth century.

2. The area of the western lands including Texas, Oregon, New Mexico, and upper California was 1,193,061 square miles. *A Compilation of the Messages and Papers of the Presidents Prepared Under the Direction of the Joint Committee on Printing, of the House and Senate, Pursuant to an Act of the Fifty-second Congress of the United States*, vol. 6 (New York: Bureau of National Literature, 1897), 2484.

3. Robert E. Corlew, *Tennessee, A Short History*, 2d ed. (Knoxville: University of Tennessee Press, 1981), 270–71; David M. Potter, *The Impending Crisis 1848–1861*, comp. and ed. Don E. Fehrenbacher (New York: Harper and Row, 1976), 20–23.

4. Robert H. White, "The Volunteer State," *Tennessee Historical Quarterly* 15 (Mar. 1956): 53.

5. Potter, *The Impending Crisis 1848–1861*, 7, 13.

6. Memphis was next largest with 8,841, and the oldest major town in the state was Knoxville with a population of 2,076. J. D. B. DeBow, *The Seventh Census of the United States, 1850* (Washington D.C.: Robert Armstrong, 1853), 573–75.

7. Corlew, *Tennessee*, 200, 202–8, 227, 230–32.

8. DeBow, *The Seventh Census of the United States, 1850*, 573–75; Corlew, *Tennessee*, 216, 223.

9. Nashville *Daily Union*, December 7, 1848; Nashville *Whig*, December 7, 1848.

10. The terms *mine, mines, mine field, mine fields, gold field*, and *gold fields* are used herein to describe any place or places at which attempts were made to recover gold from the earth or streams, irrespective of the procedures and techniques employed.

11. Potter, *The Impending Crisis 1848–1861*, 17, 36.

12. Ibid., 97–103, 107–12, 114n.

CHAPTER 1

1. Robert E. Corlew, *Tennessee, A Short History*, 2d ed. (Knoxville: University of Tennessee Press, 1981), 270; Eugene Irving McCormac, *James K. Polk, A Political Biography* (Berkeley: University of California Press, 1922), 717.

2. James Wilson Marshall discovered gold on January 24, 1848, while deepening a water ditch for a sawmill he was building on the south fork of American River in partner-

ship with John Sutter. George Frederic Parsons, "The Life and Adventures of James Wilson Marshall," in *From Mexican Days to the Gold Rush*, book 1, ed. Doyce B. Nunis, Jr. (Chicago: R. R. Donnelley and Sons Co., 1993), 89–91.

3. *A Compilation of the Messages and Papers of the Presidents Prepared Under the Direction of the Joint Committee on Printing, of the House and Senate, Pursuant to an Act of the Fifty-second Congress of the United States*, vol. 6 (New York: Bureau of National Literature, 1897), 2486.

4. Ibid.   5. Ibid., 2486–87.

6. Memphis *Daily Eagle*, December 20, 1848.

7. Jonesborough *Whig and Independent Journal*, December 20, 1848.

8. Nashville *Daily Union*, December 7, 1848.

9. Athens *Post*, December 8, 1848.

10. Memphis *Daily Eagle*, December 27, 1848; January 27, 29, 30, 31, 1849; Athens *Post*, December 29, 1848.

11. Clarksville *Jeffersonian*, April 2, 1850.

12. Herschel Gower and Jack Allen, *Pen and Sword: The Life and Journals of Randal W. McGavock* (Nashville: Tennessee Historical Commission, 1959), 167.

13. J. M. Kelley to Jacob Lintz, March 29, 1849, correspondence by author, Tennessee State Library and Archives (hereinafter referred to as TSLA).

14. Memphis *Daily Eagle*, December 16, 1848.

15. Jonesborough *Whig and Independent Journal*, February 12, 1849.

16. Alexander Outlaw Anderson (1794–1869), son of the Southwest Territory Judge Joseph Anderson, was an attorney who had served in the United States Senate (1840–41) to fill the vacancy caused by resignation of Hugh Lawson White. He was a member of Gen. Andrew Jackson's army at the Battle of New Orleans, superintendent of the United States Land Office in Alabama in 1836, and government agent for removing the Native Americans from Alabama and Florida in 1838. After returning from the gold rush in 1853, he practiced law in Washington, D.C., and at Mobile and Camden, Alabama. *Biographical Directory of the United States Congress, 1774–1989*, bicentennial ed. (Washington, D.C.: U.S. Government Printing Office, 1989), 533.

17. Memphis *Daily Eagle*, February 21, 28, March 15, 19; Nashville *Daily Centre State American*, March 10, 30, April 1, 14; Jackson *Whig*, February 23; Franklin *Western Weekly Review*, January 26, February 9; and Athens *Post*, February 9, all 1849.

18. Memphis *Daily Eagle*, March 15, 1849.   19. Ibid., May 22, 1849.

20. Nashville *Daily Union*, January 27, 1849; Athens *Post*, April 27, 1849.

21. Nashville *Daily Gazette*, February 1, 1849.

22. Athens *Post*, February 16, 1849.

23. Nashville *Daily Union*, February 27, 1849; Nashville *Daily Gazette*, April 1, 15, August 4, 1849; Memphis *Daily Enquirer*, May 8, 1849; Nashville *Daily Centre State American*, March 7, 1849.

24. Clarksville *Jeffersonian*, May 14, 1850.

25. Memphis *Daily Eagle*, March 23, 1849.

26. Pulaski *Western Star*, May 31, 1849.   27. August 14, 1849.

28. Memphis *Daily Eagle*, March 15, 1849.

29. Knoxville *Register*, March 20, 1850.

30. Memphis *Daily Eagle*, December 25, 1848. 31. Ibid., January 23, 1849.

32. Ibid., May 12, 1848; January 23, 1849. Maury (1806–72) had moved with his family from Virginia to Williamson County, Tennessee, in 1811, where he lived and attended school until becoming a midshipman in the United States Navy in 1825. As a career naval officer, Maury focused on oceanography. He published his findings about ocean winds and currents with such distinction that he became known as the "Pathfinder of the Seas." He was interested in the development of a railroad from Memphis to the Pacific as part of a larger plan to provide a combination of ocean and land transport connecting South America and the eastern United States with the Orient. Dumas Malone, ed., *Dictionary of American Biography*, vol. 12 (New York: Charles Scribner's Sons, 1933), 428–31.

33. Memphis *Daily Eagle*, February 22, 24, 1849.

34. Whether in their hometowns, in cities along the way, on the trails, or on shipboard, neither citizens nor gold seekers were immune to the frequent cholera epidemics that struck at midcentury. Many died from the scourge.

35. Nashville *True Whig*, August 4, 1849.

36. Memphis *Daily Eagle*, June 9, 1849.

37. Robin C. Hale, "Gold Deposits of the Coker Creek District, Monroe County, Tennessee," *Bulletin 72*, State of Tennessee Department of Geology, Nashville, 1974, 1.

38. *West Tennessean* quoted in Franklin *Western Weekly Review*, February 16, 1849.

39. Quoted in Franklin *Western Weekly Review*, April 20, 1849. In the early 1800s, portions of the sandstone deposit had been mined and shaped into millstones. In 1848, Nashville geologist Gerard Troost recommended the sandstone as ideal for making glass. *History of Tennessee, from the Earliest Time to the Present . . .* (Nashville: Goodspeed Publishing Co., 1887), 846; Nashville *Union*, January 13, 1848.

40. Bedford *Yeoman*, May 24, 1854, quoting the Knoxville *Register*.

41. Nashville *True Whig*, July 15, 1854; Nashville *Daily Gazette*, May 3, 1854.

42. Rogersville *Times*, June 1, 1854; Nashville *True Whig*, June 7, 1854.

43. Nashville *Daily Gazette*, May 3, 1854.

44. Franklin *Western Weekly Review*, January 26, 1849.

45. Brownlow discontinued the Jonesborough newspaper on April 19 and four weeks later began publication of the Knoxville *Whig and Independent Journal*. E. Merton Coulter, *William G. Brownlow, Fighting Parson of the Southern Highlands* (Knoxville: University of Tennessee Press, 1971), 46.

46. *Banner of Peace and the Cumberland Presbyterian Advocate*, June 14, 1850.

47. March 3, 1849; March 30, 1850.

48. Reprinted in the *Presbyterian Record*.

49. Franklin *Western Weekly Review*, February 23, 1849.

50. Memphis *Daily Eagle*, February 2, 1849.

51. *Presbyterian Record*, June 2, 1849.

52. Pulaski *Western Star*, August 9, 1849. 53. Ibid., May 31, 1849.

CHAPTER 2

1. Nashville *Daily Gazette*, April 8, 1849.

2. Oscar Lewis, *Sea Routes to the Gold Fields, The Migration by Water to California in 1849–1852* (New York: Knopf, 1949), 164; John D. Unruh, Jr., *The Plains Across* (Chicago: University of Illinois Press, 1979), 402.

3. Jonesborough *Whig and Independent Journal*, January 10, 1849.

4. A few Tennesseans reached Chagres by departing on ships from New York City and/or Charleston, South Carolina, but the New Orleans connection was the most used. Nashville *Daily Gazette*, May 22, 1850; *Brownlow's* Knoxville *Whig and Independent Journal*, January 4, 1851.

5. Nashville *Daily Union*, May 30, 1849; Nashville *Daily Gazette*, August 14, 1849; Franklin *Western Weekly Review*, February 23, 1849; Memphis *Daily Eagle*, January 5, 1849.

6. Steamships offered the fastest passage. Ships under sail found navigation extremely difficult as they fought head winds all the way. To reach San Francisco, the sailing vessels had to swing far to the west until they reached a point northwest of their destination from where they could go before favorable winds southeast into the bay.

7. Nashville *Daily Gazette*, January 19, 1849; Ray A. Billington, ed., *The Gold Mines of California* (New York: Arno Press, 1973), 52.

8. Earlier, Nicaragua had signed an agreement with Vanderbilt giving him rights to construct a canal to the Pacific or, should that not be economically feasible, to operate a system of transport of his own choosing so long as it connected to both the Atlantic and the Pacific Oceans. Lewis, *Sea Routes to the Gold Fields*, 201, 209–10; Joann Levy, *They Saw the Elephant: Women in the California Gold Rush* (Hamden, Conn.: Archer Books, 1990), 101; Unruh, *The Plains Across*, 401.

9. Patricia A. Etter, "Through Mexico in '49," *Bulletin of Bibliography* 46, no. 3 (Sept. 1989): 147; Nashville *Daily Gazette*, March 30, 1849, quoting the Mexican newspaper *El Monitor*.

10. Nashville *Daily Gazette*, January 11, 1849; Athens *Post*, March 9, 1849.

11. Nashville *Daily American*, April 22, 1849; "To California Through Texas and Mexico, The Diary and Letters of Thomas B. Eastland and Joseph G. Eastland, His Son," pt. 2, *California Historical Society Quarterly* 18, no. 3 (Sept. 1939): 225–45.

12. Nashville *Daily Gazette*, March 24, 1849.

13. Jonesborough *Whig and Independent Journal*, January 17, 1849; Memphis *Eagle and Enquirer*, December 23, 1848; Nashville *Republican Banner*, January 1, 1849; Franklin *Western Weekly Review*, March 9, 1849; Paris *Gazetteer*, February 23, 1849; Memphis *Daily Eagle*, March 17, 1849.

14. Nashville *Daily Union*, January 13, 27, 1849; Pulaski *Western Star*, August 9, 1849; Memphis *Daily Eagle*, July 12, 1849.

15. Cooke's Wagon Road was the route over which Lt. Col. Philip St. George Cooke led the wagons of a Mexican War battalion of Iowa and Missouri Mormon volunteers from Santa Fe to the coast at San Diego in 1846. The road extended from Santa Fe south along

the Rio Grande to Rincon, west along the rough Sonora Road to its junction with the trail from Yanos to San Bernardino and the San Pedro River, north along the San Pedro to a point due east of Tucson, to Tucson and north to the Pima Villages on the Gila River, west along the Gila to its confluence with the Colorado, westward into California due east of San Diego, and across the Chocolate Mountains and on to San Diego. Before the Mexican War, Cooke had been an army recruiter in Tennessee for a brief period. A career officer, he returned in 1867 during Reconstruction, assigned to the Department of the Cumberland. Otis E. Young, *The West of Philip St. George Cooke, 1809–1895* (Glendale, Calif.: Arthur H. Clark, 1955), 69–70, 193–225,

16. Grant Foreman, *Marcy and the Gold Seekers* (Norman: University of Oklahoma Press, 1939), 40, opp. 402.

17. Paris *Tribune*, February 23, 1849.

18. Jonesborough *Independent Journal*, January 17, 1849; J. Orin Oliphant, ed., *On the Arkansas Route to California in 1849, The Journal of Robert B. Green of Lewisburg, Pennsylvania* (Kinsburg, Pa: Bucknell University Press, 1955), 7; Nashville *Daily Union*, January 27, 1849.

19. Hubert Howe Bancroft, *History of California, 1848–1859*, vol. 6 (1888; reprint, Santa Barbara: Wallace Hebberd, 1970), 157.

20. Ibid., 144–56.   21. Nashville *Daily Gazette*, July 21, 1849.

22. The term *Indian* or *Indians* as used in this book refers to Native Americans of the trans-Mississippi West. The term is used because it was in current usage at the mid-nineteenth century and appears in materials quoted in the text.

23. See Appendix for biographical notes on former Tennesseans not mentioned in this chapter but who are known to have been in the state prior to 1849.

24. Barbara Donohoe Jostes, *John Parrott, Consul, 1811–1884, Selected Papers of a Western Pioneer* (San Francisco: n.p., 1972), unnumbered frontispages and 146; John Parrott to William A. Leidesdorff, August 2, December 15, 1845, John Parrott Letters, Huntington Library, San Marino, Calif.

25. Jostes, *John Parrott*, 1, 53, 58, 60, 66–67.   26. Ibid., 5.

27. He estimated the white population at 15,000 "souls," "domesticated Indian population living with whites" at 4,000, and the Indian population living on the borders of the whites in detached villages, 20,000. The total was 39,000 "souls." Frank A. Knapp, Jr., "Biographical Traces of Consul John Parrott," *California Historical Society Quarterly* 34, no. 2 (June 1955): 112–21.

28. San Francisco *Alta California*, March 1, 1849.

29. Knapp, "Biographical Traces of Parrott," 121; Jostes, *John Parrott*, 72; *Alta California*, January 11, 1849.

30. Jostes, *John Parrott*, 72, 76–77; Nashville *True Whig*, June 9, 1849; *The Maury Intelligencer*, June 7, 1849.

31. Jostes, *John Parrott*, 78–79, 82–83, 87–89, 117, 181–82.

32. *Alta California*, January 11, 1849; Jostes, *John Parrott*, 94–95.

33. Hubert Howe Bancroft, *California Pioneer Register and Index, 1542–1848* (extracted

and reprinted from author's *History of California*, 7 vols., 1884–90; Baltimore: Regional Publishing Co., 1964), 124 (hereinafter cited as Bancroft, *Pioneers*); Bancroft, *History of California, 1848–1859*, 6:309n–310n.

34. The Jurupa ranch land later became the site of Riverside, California. Wilson's landholdings included much of the mid-twentieth-century sites of the cities of Pasadena and Beverly Hills. Mount Wilson, site of an important astronomical observatory in the San Bernardino chain, is named for him. Bancroft, *Pioneers*, 385; Robert Glass Cleland, *Pathfinders* (Los Angeles: Powell Publishing Co., 1929), 385–94, 396–409; *Los Angeles, A Guide to the City and Its Environs*, American Guide Series (New York: Hasting House Publishers, 1941), 202, 262, 306.

35. John Walton Caughey, "Don Benito Wilson, An Average Southern Californian," *Huntington Library Quarterly* 2, no. 3 (Apr. 1939): 285n.

36. Bancroft, *Pioneers*, 385; LeRoy R. Hafen and Ann W. Hafen, *Old Spanish Trail, Santa Fe to Los Angeles* (Glendale, Calif.: Arthur H. Clark, 1954), 203, 217, 249–50; Carlos D'Este, *Patton: A Genius for War* (New York: HarperCollins, 1995), 25–27.

37. Peter H. Burnett, *Recollections and Opinions of an Old Pioneer* (New York: D. Appleton and Co., 1880), 1, 7, 23–24, 43.

38. Nicholas Perkins Hardeman, *Wilderness Calling: The Hardeman Family in the American Westward Movement, 1750–1900* (Knoxville: University of Tennessee Press, 1977), 154–56, 160, 162, 165.

39. Ibid., 177, 179, 182, 184, 186.

40. Nashville *Daily Union*, August 24, 1848.

41. Hardeman, *Wilderness Calling*, 189, 191, 207; Bancroft, *Pioneers*, 76.

42. Hardeman, *Wilderness Calling*, 199, 202; Burnett, *Recollections and Opinions*, 288.

43. Hardeman, *Wilderness Calling*, 205; Burnett, *Recollections and Opinions*, 296.

44. Nashville *Daily Union*, January 5, 1849; Wayne Cutler, ed., *Correspondence of James K. Polk*, vol. 8, September–December, 1844 (Knoxville: University of Tennessee Press, 1993), 140 n, 144 n, 162 n, 171.

45. Commanded by Captain Cleveland Forbes, the *California* was a wooden side-wheeler of 1,057 tons launched in New York City in May 1848. It was the first steamer in service for the Pacific mail route. Sandra L. Myers, *Ho for California, Women's Overland Diaries from the Huntington Library* (San Marino: Huntington Library, 1980), 9n; Bancroft, *History of California, 1848–1859*, 6:134n.

46. Nashville *Daily Union*, January 5, 1849.

47. The vast territory had been acquired under the terms of the Treaty of Guadalupe Hidalgo between Mexico and the United States, which was signed February 2 and ratified May 30, 1848. By the treaty Mexico transferred to the United States the entire Southwest from the 42nd parallel south to the Gila and Rio Grande. The area included land that would become the states of California, New Mexico, Utah, Nevada, and Texas, the latter claimed by the United States since 1845; most of Colorado; southwestern Wyoming; most of Arizona; southwestern Kansas; and the Oklahoma panhandle. William M. Malloy, comp., *Treaties, Conventions, International Acts, Protocols, and Agreements Between the United States*

of America and Other Powers, 1776 to 1909, vol. 1 (Washington, D.C.: Government Printing Office, 1910), 1107–19.

48. Nashville *Daily Union*, January 5, 1849. 49. Ibid.

50. Ibid., October 4, 1849; Bancroft, *History of California 1848–1859*, 6:213. Prior to Voorhies's resignation, his Tennessee friend Postmaster General Cave Johnson had been relieved of his duties on March 5. *House Executive Document No. 17*, 31st Congress, 1st session, 1849–50, vol. 5, serial 573, p. 961; *Biographical Directory of the United States Congress, 1774–1989*, bicentennial ed. (Washington, D.C.: U.S. Government Printing Office, 1989), 1263–64.

CHAPTER 3

1. Oscar Lewis, *Sea Routes to the Gold Fields, The Migration by Water to California in 1849–1852* (New York: Knopf, 1949), 10–11.

2. Ibid., 193–96, 199. That kind of delay was too much for one Memphian, B. Richmond, who returned to report more than two thousand waiting, "one half of whom were penniless and many in bad health." Nashville *Daily Gazette*, May 26, 1849, quoting Memphis *Herald*.

3. Nashville *Daily Union*, January 27, 1849.

4. Ibid., June 27, 1849. 5. Ibid.

6. G. C. Crenshaw Deposition, September 4, 1855, in *Guild et al.*, vs *George Love et al.*, Sumner County Loose Court Records, Sumner County Archives (hereinafter referred to as LCR/SCA).

7. Contract, April 15, 1850; James O. Harris to Peter Bryson, May 5, 1850, Brown and Harris Papers, originals in private collection, Birmingham, Alabama, typescripts, Sumner County Archives, Gallatin.

8. The record is not clear, but "General" was apparently a complimentary title given to Anderson as organizer, strategist, and de facto commander of the company.

9. Neill S. Brown Governors Papers, 1847–49, TSLA.

10. Knoxville *Register*, June 5, 1849.

11. David Anderson Deaderick Diary, 1825–72, typescript, Special Collections, Hoskins Library, University of Tennessee, Knoxville, 86.

12. Knoxville *Register*, August 25, 1849. On August 7, 1849, membership of the company en route included forty-seven men. In addition to himself and his staff of two, they were J. B. Hatcher, ambulance driver; William King, forge driver; and three squads. First Squad — Jos. Q. Wilbur, Jacob Stuart, Jas. V. Anderson, R. H. Deaderick, J. C. Deaderick, J. C. Brown, Jos. B. Anderson, Dr. H. W. Peter, Dr. S. H. Flournoy, Dr. M. L. Cozine, and teamsters Sam. White, M. Ross, Geo. Russel, A. L. Bohrer. Second Squad — Jos. P. Bailey, Sam B. Bailey, W. W. Ramsey, F. A. Ramsey, Byron Ford, A. L. King, C. H. Ingles, N. S. Reynolds, M. W. McNutt, and teamsters J. C. Ingles, J. W. King, J. A. Anderson, Fred Kemp. Third Squad — S. G. McClellan, R. G. Williams, B. M. Knight, R. N. Barr, Jno. MacIntyre, J. P. Garvin, E. F. DeSelding, Chas. Ford, G. E. Boswell, J. Holliday, R. Coile, and teamsters F. F. Keller, A. L. Henley, M. Knox, and Henry [a slave black].

13. Knoxville *Register*, August 25, 1849.

14. Born in Banff, Scotland, Robert Farquharson (1813–69) came to the United States with his parents circa 1827 and settled in Davidson County. He moved to Fayetteville, Lincoln County, in 1830 and became a merchant, farmer, and lawyer. A Democrat, he represented Lincoln County in the 23rd and 29th General Assemblies and Lincoln and Giles in the 25th. He was in the state senate of the 30th General Assembly representing Lincoln and Franklin Counties. A major in the Mexican War, he was wounded at Cerro Gordo and returned home in 1847. After going to California in 1849, he returned to Fayetteville in 1851 where in 1854 he became clerk and master of the chancery court. During the Civil War, he was colonel of the 41st Regiment, Tennessee Infantry. Robert M. McBride and Dan M. Robison, *Biographical Directory of the Tennessee General Assembly, 1796–1861*, vol. 1 (Nashville: Tennessee State Library and Archives and the Tennessee Historical Commission, 1975), 241–43.

15. Nashville *Daily Centre State American*, March 10, 1849. No copies of the constitution and bylaws have been discovered nor have copies of the Fayetteville *Lincoln Journal*, which published them during the latter part of February 1849. See Nashville *Daily Union*, March 7, 1849.

16. The other members of the company and their previous occupations were H. K. Street, J. C. Russell, J. R. Boyles, W. W. James, and R. Patrick, clerks; J. J. Greer, J. McCartney, R. C. McEwen, J. N. Horton, T. E. Clark, W. R. Bennett, T. B. Maury, and C. A. McDaniel, farmers; John P. Homan, B. F. Ramsey, A. King, carpenters; W. A. Griffis, S. M. Jones, cabinetmakers; B. L. Commons, blacksmith; C. Mosely, machinist; C. N. Slater, harnessmaker; E. B. Reinhart, tailor; J. Pearson, schoolteacher; D. F. Wallace, printer; M. M. Marshall, Presbyterian minister; and J. M. Small, Cumberland Presbyterian minister. Nashville *Daily Union*, March 7, 1849. Three other Lincoln Countians joined the company a few days after it left Fayetteville: Jesse S. Franklin, Alfred S. Fulton, and Thomas White. Nashville *Daily Gazette*, March 18, 1849.

17. Quoted in Nashville *Daily Centre State American*, March 10, 1849.

18. Nashville *Daily Gazette*, March 18, 1849.

19. "Stories of a Forty-Niner," *Historic Maury* 13, no. 1 (Jan.–Mar. 1977): 2–1.

20. Ibid.

21. Memphis *Daily Enquirer*, March 15, 1849. Although no company records have been found, the names of the members from Tennessee were reported as E. Wilkins, John Willis, P. W. Kirkpatrick, E. Mallory, R. S. Param, J. P. Param, G. Davis, and two others listed as "Mr. Ledgerwood" and "Capt. Larke," La Grange; W. Macon, Shelby County; R. B. Macon, Hardeman County; E. Williamson, M. Williamson, Fayette County; James Ballord, Sommerville.

22. Samuel Murray Stover, *Diary of Samuel Murray Stover En Route to California, 1849* (Elizabethton, Tenn.: H. M. Folsom, 1939), 1.

23. In addition to Dr. Levy, the Trenton men were John Hogg, Anderson Davis, John Poole, William Burruss, Oscar Gilchrist, and Benton Bell Seat. The Yorkville members

were Bob McCauley, Jim Terrel, T. B. Wheeler, and two that Seat remembered only as "Lasly, and Reed." Benton Bell Seat, "Memoirs, 1849–1916," typescript courtesy of Frederick M. Culp, Gibson County Historian, Trenton, Tenn., 5.

24. Ibid.

25. Memphis *Daily Eagle*, August 21, 1849; January 16, 1850.

26. The Reeve brothers had come to East Tennessee from Medford, New Jersey, in 1821 with their father Mark, an iron manufacturer who set up forges and rolling mills in Sullivan County at Pactolus and Union Forge. Rebecca did not join the family there until 1839. Oscar Osburn Winther, ed., "From East Tennessee to California in 1849: Letters of the Reeve Family of Medford, New Jersey," *Journal of the Rutgers University Library* 11, no. 2 (June 1948): 33–34.

27. Ibid., 35–37.

28. John L. Brown to A. R. Wynne, March 7, 1849, George W. Wynne Collection, Wynne Family Papers, TSLA.

29. A perusal of the Nashville newspapers of the period yields no mention of the promotion at a time when the press was watching and reporting many departures for the El Dorado. *True Whig, Republican Banner, Daily Gazette, Daily Union, Centre State American*, January 1–September 1, 1849.

30. Nashville *Daily American*, May 17, 1850; *Republican Banner and* Nashville *Whig*, April 8, 1850.

31. Wilson, Love and Co. Agreement, March 1, 1850; bill of complaint, LCR/SCA.

32. Ibid.   33. Ibid.

34. Nashville *Daily American*, April 17, 1850. They were William Pryor, George Pearson, W. A. Winham, and John Moore.

35. The "land of Havilah, where there is gold" was within the biblical Garden of Eden. Genesis 2:10–11, *Holy Bible, Authorized King James Version* (New York: Oxford University Press, 1967).

36. Nashville *Daily American*, April 25, 1850; Irene D. Paden, ed., *The Journal of Madison Berryman Moorman, 1850–1851* (San Francisco: California Historical Society, 1948), 1.

37. Nashville *Daily American*, April 25, 1850.

38. Ibid. They were E. G. Pearl, William E. Pearl, G. S. Newsom, William G. Massey, B. F. Weakley, T. D. Fite & Co., Andrew Anderson, T. & W. Evans, Nichol & Robb, B. W. & T. Menees, Stark & Menees, J. C. Stark, John W. Hanna, David Browder, J. T. Pendleton, J. F. Petters, and B. K. Williams & Co.

39. Ibid.; The remaining "Operatives" and their ownership were William L. Robards, M. T. Conner, and E. M. Patterson, physician and druggist, four shares each; Samuel L. Phillips, J. W. Wilson, J. H. Nichol, three shares each; J. A. Springer, druggist, two shares; and four men each with one share listed as "outsider" with the expedition—D. S. Woodward, George W. Seay, N. W. Hubbard, and G. S. T. Sevier. Four additional men and "a Negro boy" were planning to accompany the expedition, "although not attached regularly" and owning no stock. They were Hugh E. Patterson and his "slave boy Ben," Moses H.

Hinkle, Jr., George A. Buchanan, and John Buffington. Although no details are given, it is probable that these five agreed to work as teamsters or guards or do whatever tasks were indicated in exchange for food and transport during the crossing (Nashville *True Whig*, April 30, 1850).

40. Nashville *True Whig*, April 30, 1850.

41. Ibid., April 23, 1850; Nashville *Daily American*, April 25, 1850.

42. Nashville *True Whig*, March 13, 1850. To travel with them "for mutual protection against the dangers and vicissitudes incident to the route," though not members of the company, were J. R. Groves, J. B. Rosborough, and another "Negro boy."

43. Ibid.

44. Bond and Hibbett Agreement, April 19, 1850, Brown and Harris Papers.

45. In addition to Moore, the two Bonds, and Hibbett, the gold seekers were Jo. Cornwell, C. Haines, Z. Z. S. Goodall, Jo Vaughan, John Dalton, A. J. Dyer, J. B. DeBow, William Britton, John Kerley, John Duncan, John Chambers, S. Andrews, J. Smothers, W. Smothers, Doug Thurmond, S. Malory, A. Duncan, S. Payne, F. G. Harris, William Allen, J. Henderson, and S. McAlister (Nashville *Daily American*, April 20, 1850).

46. *Brownlow's* Knoxville *Whig and Independent Journal*, January 22, 1853.

47. Ibid., November 16, 1850.   48. Ibid., April 6, May 4, 1850.

49. James O. Harris to Mary T. Harris, May 2, November 17, 1850; to Peter Bryson, May 5, October 8, 1850; to Green B. Harris, May 25, October 13, 1850, Brown and Harris Papers. Others of the seventeen were Bryson Hannah, James Gardner, William Toomy, and W. Britton. The letters contained references also to men named Ferguson, Toon, Tucker, Gregory, McGaughey, and two Cottons, but did not supply given names or initials. It is not clear that all were of the party of seventeen.

50. *Republican Banner and* Nashville *Whig*, April 10, 1850.

51. Crocket to Campbell, February 27, 1849, David Campbell Papers, Microfilm, TSLA. In the election of 1851, Campbell, a Whig, would become governor of Tennessee. He was a member of Congress from 1837 to 1841. Robert H. White, *Messages of the Governors of Tennessee, 1845–1857*, vol. 4 (Nashville: Tennessee Historical Commission, 1957), 402–3.

52. Andrew Johnson to David T. Patterson, April 5, 1850, Leroy P. Graf and Ralph W. Haskins, eds., *The Papers of Andrew Johnson*, vol. 1, 1822–51 (Knoxville: University of Tennessee Press, 1967), 533.

CHAPTER 4

1. Memphis *Daily Enquirer*, September 4, 1849.

2. Ibid.   3. Ibid.

4. Ibid.

5. The name of his company and/or fellow travelers are not known. He was a graduate of the University of Nashville. Nashville *True Whig*, August 8, 21, 1849.

6. Memphis *Daily Eagle*, August 21, 1849; January 16, 1850; Lucious Lucullus Battle,

"The Annals of Lucious Lucullus Battle, M.D., 1849–1851," typescript of memoir in the Memphis Room Collection of the Memphis and Shelby County Library, 81.

7. *Biographical Directory of the American Congress, 1774–1989*, bicentennial ed. (Washington, D.C.: U.S. Government Printing Office, 1989), 1927.

8. In addition to Cheatham, the company included Richard McCann, W. T. Yeatman, Woods Yeatman, L. H. Hitchcock, James York, William P. Martin, James Armstrong, Josiah H. Pitts, and five not identified. Nashville *Daily Gazette*, August 14, 22, 29, 1849.

9. Nashville *Daily Union*, April 1, 22, 1850.

10. Nashville *Daily Gazette*, August 14, 1849.

11. Nashville *Daily Union*, October 1, 1849. Family tradition is that Franklin first went to the gold country from his ranch near Washington on the Brazos, Texas. Kenneth C. Thomson notes, 1994, private collection.

12. *A History of Tuolumne County, California* (San Francisco: B. F. Alley, 1882), 418.

13. Nashville *True Whig*, April 30, 1850.

14. "To California Through Texas and Mexico, The Diary and Letters of Thomas B. Eastland and Joseph G. Eastland, His Son," pt. 1, *California Historical Society Quarterly* 18, no. 2 (June 1939): 101, 132 n, 133n.

15. Ibid., pt. 1, 101.

16. The route from San Antonio to El Paso fell between parallels of latitude 29°40' and 32° in a direction generally west northwest. Ibid., pt. 1, 123.

17. Born January 28, 1817, in Wilson County, Tennessee, Hays became a member of a surveying party in the Mississippi swamps when he was fifteen years old. Caught up in the excitement created by Texas independence, he went to the new republic and joined its army in 1836. When 75 men were enlisted as "Texas Rangers" in 1840 at San Antonio, he was appointed to command them. He distinguished himself as a Ranger both prior to and during the Mexican War and became known to all as Jack Hays. In 1848, he explored the route from San Antonio to Presidio del Norte. "To California Through Texas and Mexico," pt. 1, 131; A. B. Bender, "Opening Routes Across West Texas, 1848–1850," *Southwestern Historical Quarterly* 37, no. 2 (Oct. 1933): 119.

18. Van Horn's train was of impressive size. He had six companies of the United States Third Infantry accompanied by 275 supply wagons and 2,500 head of livestock. Bender, "Opening Routes," 123.

19. "To California Through Texas and Mexico," pt. 1, 102–3.

20. Ibid., 103.   21. Ibid., 105–6.
22. Ibid., 107.   23. Ibid., 115.
24. Ibid., 117–19.   25. Ibid., 125.
26. Ibid., 125.   27. Ibid., 120.

28. Ibid., 121, 129; "To California Through Texas and Mexico, The Diary and Letters of Thomas B. Eastland and Joseph G. Eastland, His Son," pt. 2, *California Historical Society Quarterly* 18, no. 3 (Sept. 1939): 229.

29. The party at that time included the two Eastlands, Dow, and a certain Judge

Ewing of Texas. Douglass had opted to remain with the main train. Ibid., pt. 1, 121, 129.

30. Ibid., pt. 2, 229, 231–32.   31. Ibid., 237–40.

32. Ibid., 240–41.   33. Ibid., 240–42.

34. James Kimmins Greer, *Colonel Jack Hays, Texas Frontier Leader and California Builder* (New York: E. P. Dutton, 1952), 240–41.

35. Ibid.   36. Ibid., 242–43.

37. Ibid., 245–46.   38. Ibid., 246–47.

39. Ibid., 247–48, 251–52.   40. Ibid., 248–49.

41. Jonathan Turnbull Warner had come to California in 1834. Located near Temecula in the southern part of the state, his ranch provided emigrants from the East an informal but often busy port of entry to the settlements. Kenneth L. Holmes, *Ewing Young, Master Trapper* (Portland, Oreg.: n.p., 1967), 92.

42. Greer, *Colonel Jack Hays*, 250–52.   43. Ibid., 253–54.

44. Their companions were Sidney Herring, Elbridge and Joshua Bradshaw, Dick Glenn, Cato Davis, and men listed as Thurston, Newton, Ferguson, Hereford, Campbell, and Rowe. Clarksville *Jeffersonian*, September 4, November 27, 1849; August 7, 1850.

45. Ibid., September 4, 1849.   46. Ibid., November 27, 1849.

47. Ibid., September 4, 1849.   48. Ibid., November 27, 1849.

49. Ibid.   50. Ibid.

51. Ibid.   52. Ibid., August 7, 1850.

53. Ibid., August 7, 28, 1850.   54. Ibid., November 27, 1849.

55. Louisiana Strentzel, "A Letter from California, 1849," in *Covered Wagon Women, Diaries and Letters from the Western Trails, 1840–1890*, ed. Kenneth L. Holmes, vol. 1 (Glendale, Calif.: Arthur Clark, 1983), 247.

56. Ibid., 254.   57. Ibid., 254–55.

58. Ibid., 255–56.   59. Ibid., 256–57.

60. Ibid., 257–58.   61. Ibid., 258–61, 268.

62. Benjamin Butler Harris, *The Gila Trail, The Texas Argonauts and the California Gold Rush*, ed. Richard H. Dillon (Norman: University of Oklahoma Press, 1960), 6–7.

63. Ibid., 7, 15–16, 30.   64. Ibid., 40, 43.

65. The "Tanks" were large depressions in solid rock that collected rain and melted snow in undrained reservoirs.

66. Harris, *The Gila Trail*, 48–49.   67. Ibid., p. 50.

68. Ibid., 51–52, 54, 58.   69. Ibid., 56.

70. Ibid., 62–64, 71, 73–75, 78–79.   71. Ibid., 79–80, 82, 84, 86.

72. Ibid., 88.   73. Ibid., 24, 94–99.

74. Ibid., 9, 99, 108.

75. Nashville *Daily Gazette*, April 3, 1849; Nashville *True Whig*, May 25, 1850.

76. *Alta California*, December 11, 1850; Barbara Ann Metcalf, "Oliver M. Wozencraft in California, 1849–1887"(master's thesis, University of Southern California, 1963), 8, 12.

CHAPTER 5

1. Grant Foreman, *Marcy and the Gold Seekers* (Norman: University of Oklahoma Press, 1939), 9, 14–15.

2. Ibid., 12–13, 17–19.

3. Members of the "Memphis mess" were Thomas Moran, J. D. S. Sullivan, John McKeon, M. Gaffney, C. Steeper, Joseph White, Perry White, Dr. J. H. Holmes, M. Rudolph, James H. Anthony, James Littlefield, Houston, and Williams. The four of the "Independent mess" were Dr. James L. Culler of Virginia, William Perry, Dr. Lucious Lucullus Battle, and Hamilton, his slave black, all of Memphis. Hamilton had followed American soldiers in both the Seminole War of 1836 and the Mexican War as a cook and handyman. Memphis *Daily Eagle*, March 21, 1849; Lucious Lucullus Battle, "The Annals of Lucious Lucullus Battle, M.D., 1849–1851," typescript of memoir in the Memphis Room Collection of the Memphis and Shelby County Library, 2, 13.

4. Foreman, *Marcy and the Gold Seekers*, 27.

5. Before they reached the Rocky Mountains, Captain Morgan Cook had yielded to pressure from dissident members and stepped down as company commander. Battle, "Annals of Lucious Lucullus Battle," 28.

6. Ibid., 81–84.

7. Its members were R. S. Miller, captain; W. Hubbard, T. Nixon, G. Applegate, R. Applegate, A. A. Gray, William Mann, E. Foster, G. Carpenter, S. McMiller, R. Bearley, a certain Taylor, and two slave blacks. Memphis *Daily Eagle*, March 21, 1849.

8. They were, in addition to Boardman, I. B. Gill, William H. McClain, L. J. Allan, J. R. Maltbie, Jr., Z. D. Steele, P. Clapp, and W. Feigan. Memphis *Daily Eagle*, March 21, 1849.

9. Foreman, *Marcy and the Gold Seekers*, 27.

10. "Letters of the California Gold Rush Days, 1849–1852," *Historic Maury* 13, no. 3 (July–Sept. 1977): 115; Knoxville *Register*, April 24, 1850; Nashville *Daily Union*, July 26, 1850.

11. Coleman McDaniel Diary, TSLA; Sarah N. Shouse, "None Dream But of Success, the Story of a Young Tennessean's Journey to the Gold Fields of California," *Tennessee Historical Quarterly* 36, no. 4 (winter 1977): 512–15.

12. Arkansas *State Gazette*, April 5, 1849.

13. Arkansas *State Democrat*, March 16, 1849. The presence of a large number of small companies was due in part to advertisements placed in the eastern press that were designed to attract parties of five or six men who would pool their resources to buy their supplies, a wagon, and team. Paris *Tribune*, February 23, 1849.

14. Foreman, *Marcy and the Gold Seekers*, 29, 38.

15. John R. Boyles to John T. Gordon, April 7, 1849, Eliza H. (Ball) Boyles Gordon Papers, 1823–81, Special Collections Department, William R. Perkins Library, Duke University (hereinafter cited as Duke Special Collections); Battle, "Annals of Lucious Lucullus Battle," 6.

16. McDaniel Diary.

17. Ibid.; John R. Boyles to Mrs. E. H. Boyles, April 25, 1849, Duke Special Collections.

18. McDaniel Diary.   19. Ibid.

20. Ibid.   21. Ibid.

22. Ibid.

23. John R. Boyles to Mrs. E. H. Boyles, June 18, 24, 1849, Duke Special Collections.

24. McDaniel Diary.

25. There were plenty of rattlesnakes; McDaniel killed one that had fifteen rattles. Ibid.

26. Ibid.   27. Ibid.

28. Ibid.   29. Ibid.

30. *Lincoln County, Tennessee, Pioneers* 6, no. 1, (Sept. 1976): 1.

31. "Stories of a Forty-Niner," *Historic Maury* 13, no. 1 (Jan.–Mar. 1977): 2–1, 2–2.

32. Ibid., 2–2.   33. Ibid., 2–3.

34. Ibid.; "Letters of the California Gold Rush Days," 115.

35. "Stories of a Forty-Niner," 2–5; "Letters of the California Gold Rush Days," 115.

36. Foreman, *Marcy and the Gold Seekers*, 40.

37. Lebanon *Packet* quoted in the Nashville *Daily Union*, March 7, 1849.

38. Athens *Post*, April 26, 1850.   39. Ibid.

40. Knoxville *Register*, April 24, 1850.   41. Athens *Post*, April 26, 1850.

42. Nashville *Daily Union*, July 26, 1850.   43. Ibid.

44. Ibid.   45. Ibid.

46. Foreman, *Marcy and the Gold Seekers*, 303–4; see Appendix.

47. Eugene L. Pearson, *A Pearson Family History* (n.p.: 1962), 37–38.

CHAPTER 6

1. *Weakley Remembered* 4, 43–44; Mary Murphy Covillaud to "Uncles, Aunts, and Cousins," May 25, 1847, Donner Party Letters, TSLA; Hubert Howe Bancroft, *California Pioneer Register and Index, 1542–1848* (extracted and reprinted from author's *History of California*, 7 vols., 1884–90; Baltimore: Regional Publishing Co., 1964), 230; Nashville *Whig*, September 4, 1847. For further information on the Donner Party, see Appendix.

2. Approximately 25,000 persons crossed the plains to California in 1849, most from Missouri but some from Iowa. John D. Unruh, Jr., *The Plains Across* (Chicago: University of Illinois Press, 1979), 120.

3. Samuel Murray Stover, *Diary of Samuel Murray Stover En Route to California, 1849*, (Elizabethton, Tenn.: H. M. Folsom, 1939), 1.

4. J. S. Holliday, *The World Rushed In: The California Gold Rush Experience* (New York: Simon and Schuster, 1981), 286 n; Stover, *Diary of Samuel Murray Stover*, 2–3; Hubert Howe Bancroft, *History of Utah, 1540–1887* (San Francisco: History Co., 1890), 446; *House Executive Document No. 17*, 31st Congress, 1st session, 1849–50, vol. 5, serial 573, p. 60; *Alta California*, December 15, 1849.

5. The Pioneer train was an express line of passenger and cargo wagons operating from Independence to California under the ownership of Turner and Allen of St. Louis. It had left Independence on May 9 with 125 passengers, each paying $200 for transportation and provisions. The train made use of 20 spring wagons for passengers and 18 wagons for cargo, all pulled by mules. Unruh, *The Plains Across*, 101–2.

6. Stover, *Diary of Samuel Murray Stover*, 7–8, 19.

7. Ibid., 10, 17.   8. Ibid., 7–8, 14, 15–17.

9. Ibid., 21–23.   10. Ibid., 22, 24–25, 30.

11. *Alta California*, December 15, 1849. The Donner tragedy had prompted Californians, both military and civilian, to organize relief and rescue operations on a large scale in 1849 and 1850. Unruh, *The Plains Across*, 368.

12. Stover, *Diary of Samuel Murray Stover*, 27, 29, 32.

13. Holliday, *The World Rushed In*, 225.

14. Stover, *Diary of Samuel Murray Stover*, 33–34.

15. Ibid., 33–35. Benoni Hudspeth and John J. Myers were respected leaders of emigrant trains. The former discovered Hudspeth's Cutoff, a route that left the California Trail at Soda Springs, eliminated Fort Hall from California itineraries, and shortened the trail by about ninety miles. Archer Butler Hulbert, *Forty-Niners, The Chronicle of the California Trail* (Boston: Little, Brown, 1949), 178–80.

16. Stover, *Diary of Samuel Murray Stover*, 36.   17. Ibid., 36–37.

18. Oscar Osburn Winther, ed., "From Tennessee to California in 1849: Letters of the Reeve Family of Medford, New Jersey," *Journal of the Rutgers University Library* 11, no. 2 (June 1948): 35, 37, 40–41.

19. For mutual security in their journey, the Reeve party assembled with several other small companies around a large group of Ohioans about to leave for California. About May 15, they set out. Ibid., 43–44.

20. Ibid., 46.

21. Holliday, *The World Rushed In*, 249–51.   22. Ibid., 248–66.

23. Winther, "From Tennessee to California in 1849," 47.

24. Ibid., 47.

25. The Modoc were members of one of the most warlike tribes in the West and were regarded as a serious menace to whites and to other tribes as well. A. L. Kroeber, *Handbook of the Indians of California*, Bulletin of American Ethnology #78 (Washington, D.C.: Government Printing Office, 1925), 318–20.

26. Winther, "From Tennessee to California in 1849," 44–45.

27. Ibid., 45.   28. Ibid.

29. Ibid., 47–48.   30. Ibid., 49.

31. Ibid., 49–50; Frederic A. Culmer, ed., "California Letter of John Wilson, 1850," *Missouri Historical Review* 24, no. 2 (Jan. 1930): 202.

32. Winther, "From Tennessee to California in 1849," 50–51.

33. Ibid., 35, 35 n, 42, 47.

34. In addition to Alexander, members of the company were Timothy Johnson,

Alexander Scrivener, William Bradley, J. Nicholson, William Lawson, James Crenshaw, Epaminondas Johnston, Lafayette M. DeBow, J. H. Sarver, Lt. W. C. Bradley, James H. Martin, Simpson Bennett, A. Ellis, Thomas Duffy, Isaac Bryne, T. P. Trott, William Akin, William Anthony, Jonathan White, Lewis Riddle, William Brevard, Francis Duffy, Jr., Henry Cox, J. S. Copeland, J. Burgess, Dr. Alexander Anthony, and Horace Johnston. Nashville *Daily Centre State American*, April 1, 1849.

35. Ibid.; Tom P. Duffy to Col. Francis Duffy, June 1, 1849, Duffy Papers, TSLA.

36. Duffy to Col. Francis Duffy, June 1, 1849, Duffy Papers.

37. Ibid.

38. Their original destination, Sacramento, was then 125 miles distant. Francis M. Duffy estimated later that they had traveled 600 miles from Gallatin to Independence, and another 2,208 miles from Independence to Sacramento or a total of 2,808 miles. Francis M. Duffy to a friend, November 10, 1849, Clarksville *Jeffersonian*, February 12, 1850.

39. Ibid.

40. Nashville *Daily Centre State American*, April 4, 1849. Thomas J. Stump, Jr., and his brother John T. remained on the West Coast until their deaths many years later. The senior Stump died in 1852 in California. Nell McNish Gambill, *The Kith and Kin of Capt. James Leeper and Susan Drake, His Wife, First Couple Married in Fort Nashborough, Tenn. 1780* ([Nashville]: published by author, 1946), 169, 170.

41. Nashville *Daily Union*, March 7, 1849; Louis J. Rasmussen, *California Wagon Train Lists*, vol. 1 (Colma, Calif.: San Francisco Historic Records, 1994), 10–11, 89–90. Bryant was author of *What I Saw in California*.

42. Rasmussen, *California Wagon Train Lists*, 12, 32.

43. Joshua died December 20, 1852, near Sacramento. His widow and children remained in California for the remainder of their lives. Details of their crossing have not survived. Ethel Nichols Anderson, comp., *Draper Families in America* (Nashville: Parthenon Press, 1964), 296, 300.

44. Warren County *News*, August 5, 1980.

45. They were "A. T. Michel, E. Pinkard, H. Fingan, I. Slatton, C. Blar, E. Rowen, I. Gofourth, F. Wilson, B. Buckner [and] A. Rowland." Ibid.

46. Ibid.

47. Shiloh Cumberland Presbyterian Church Minutes, p. 154, TSLA.

48. Son of the Knoxville newspaper publisher Frederick S. Heiskell, Hugh Brown Heiskell and the brothers Richard L. and Oliver P. White, sons of Thomas White of Monroe County, were alumni of East Tennessee University that later became the University of Tennessee, Knoxville. *Brownlow's* Knoxville *Whig and Independent Journal*, February 23, 1850; Neal O'Steen, "UT's Gold Rush Adventurers: The Monroe County Boys," *Tennessee Alumnus* (fall 1983): 25–26.

49. They were Albert Moss and James Brown of Montgomery County; Thomas and William Hart of Campbell County; William Wayman and son and Allen Thorpe of Sumner County; and B. Finnin "and lady," Patrick Kinney, F. Kinney, J. O'Callahan, J. O. Gordon,

Thomas Coffin, F. A. Goole, D. Miller, and William A. Boggs of Nashville. Rasmussen, *California Wagon Train Lists*, 26–27.

50. There were in addition "four black boys" in the train, but there seem to have been none with the Monroe County party. Hugh Brown Heiskell to his sister Margaret, July 1, 1849, Heiskell Family Manuscripts, TSLA; St. Joseph *Gazette*, May 18, 1849.

51. Hugh Heiskell said the entire group "got along amiably, as well as men thrown together can," but his party of nine were "*just the right sort of fellows*" getting along "as brothers." The practical effect of their closeness was that the nine had "more influence than any other party" in decisions affecting the whole group. Hugh Brown Heiskell to his sister Margaret from Fort Kearney, June 11, 1849, Heiskell Family Manuscripts.

52. Knoxville *Register*, February 16, 1850; Hugh Brown Heiskell Diary, September 8, 12, 13, 28, October 5, 1849, microfilm, TSLA; Hugh Brown Heiskell to his sister Margaret, July 1, 1849, Heiskell Family Manuscripts.

53. Hugh Brown Heiskell Diary, September 11, 1849.

54. Ibid.

55. He had come to Washington, D.C., during the latter part of May to enlist the aid of his "cousin," Mrs. James K. Polk, wife of the president, for creating the territory. He returned to Oregon to begin a career in local politics that included election to the state legislature. Leroy R. Hafen, ed., *Mountain Men and Fur Traders of the Far West* (Reprinted from *Mountain Men and Fur Trade of the Far West*, 10 vols., Glendale, Calif.: A. H. Clark, 1965–72; Lincoln: University of Nebraska Press, 1982), 363.

56. Hugh Brown Heiskell Diary, September 23, 1849.

57. *Brownlow's* Knoxville *Whig and Independent Journal*, February 23, 1850.

58. Ibid.   59. A brother of James W. Campbell of Knoxville.

60. *Brownlow's* Knoxville *Whig and Independent Journal*, February 23, 1850.

61. Ibid.

62. Ibid.; Hugh Brown Heiskell Diary, October 10, 13, 14, 1849.

63. Hugh Brown Heiskell Diary, October 16, 17, 1849.

64. Ibid., October 18, 1849.

65. Ibid., October 19, 1849; *Brownlow's* Knoxville *Whig and Independent Journal*, February 23, 1850; Knoxville *Register*, February 16, 1850.

66. Hugh Brown Heiskell Diary, October 19, 1849.

67. Ibid., October 20, 21, 1849.

68. Ibid., October 21, 1849; *Brownlow's* Knoxville *Whig and Independent Journal*, February 23, 1850.

69. Benton Bell Seat, "Memoirs, 1849–1916," typescript courtesy of Frederick M. Culp, Gibson County Historian, Trenton, Tenn., 6.

70. The Williamson County party, in addition to Dr. Freeman, included William Shepherd, J. Hale, and two others identified only as Gordon and White. Franklin *Western Weekly Review*, March 8, 1850.

71. Seat, "Memoirs," 8; Franklin *Western Weekly Review*, March 8, 1850.

72. Seat, "Memoirs," 10.   73. Ibid.

74. Franklin *Western Weekly Review*, March 8, 1850.

75. Seat, "Memoirs," 13; Franklin *Western Weekly Review*, March 8, 1850.

76. While enduring the trials along the Humboldt, White of Williamson County left the company after a "misunderstanding in camp." Franklin *Western Weekly Review*, March 8, 1850.

77. Seat, "Memoirs," 13–14; Franklin *Western Weekly Review*, March 8, 1850.

78. Seat, "Memoirs," 13–14.

79. Ibid., 14–15. Seat's account lacks dates; the only dates mentioned are April 18, 1849, when they left Trenton and June 25, 1849, when they reached the South Pass.

80. Franklin *Western Weekly Review*, March 8, 1850.

81. Ibid.

82. Watkins (1793–1891) had moved to Memphis in the 1840s to work at the Memphis Navy Yard and by the latter part of 1847 had assumed duties as purser. Joseph S. Watkins to John Y. Mason, secretary of the navy, January 14, 1848, Virginia Historical Society Collections, Richmond.

83. Alonzo Delano, *Life on the Plains and Among the Diggins Being Scenes and Adventures of an Overland Journey to California* (Auburn: Miller, Aston, and Mulligan, 1854; New York: Arno Press, 1973), 84–85.

84. Ibid., 85, 245.

85. J. Goldsborough Bruff, *Gold Rush. The Journals, Drawings, and Other Papers of J. Goldsborough Bruff, April 2, 1849–July 20, 1851*, ed. Georgia W. Read and Ruth Gaines (New York: Columbia University Press, 1949), 734.

86. Memphis *Daily Appeal*, September 30, 1851.

CHAPTER 7

1. Active in the political and commercial life of the region, Dr. Ramsey (1797–1884) lived near Knoxville. He was author of *Annals of Tennessee*, a comprehensive history of the early settlement of the state, published in 1853.

2. Memphis *Daily Eagle*, February 28, 1849; Nashville *Daily Gazette*, April 22, 1849; Knoxville *Register*, June 5, August 25, 1849; Neal O'Steen, "UT's Gold Rush Adventurers: The East Tennessee Company," *Tennessee Alumnus* (winter 1984): 23.

3. Knoxville *Register*, May 26, 1849.

4. Greeneville College was later merged with Tusculum Academy and became Tusculum College.

5. East Tennessee University had its beginning in Blount College and later became the University of Tennessee.

6. O'Steen, "UT's Gold Rush Adventurers," 22–25.

7. Ibid.   8. Ibid.

9. He gave as references for himself the names of ex-President Polk, Senator John C. Calhoun of South Carolina, Senator H. L. Turney of Tennessee, Congressman J. H. Crozier of Knoxville, Governor Neill S. Brown of Tennessee, and others. Ramsey Papers, Special Collections, Hoskins Library, University of Tennessee, Knoxville.

10. Neill S. Brown, Nashville, to Gen. Persifor F. Smith, May 5, 1849, Ramsey Papers.

11. Wilberforce Ramsey to Dr. J. G. M. Ramsey, July 14, 1849, Ramsey Papers.

12. J. Crozier Ramsey to Wilberforce Ramsey, May 7, 1849, Ramsey Papers.

13. Quoted in Nashville *Daily Gazette*, April 22, 1849.

14. William B. Hesseltine, ed., *Dr. J. G. M. Ramsey Autobiography and Letters* (Nashville: Tennessee Historical Commission, 1954), 134; Thomas J. Noel, "W. Wilberforce A. Ramsey, Esq., and the California Gold Rush," *Journal of the West* 12, no. 4 (Oct. 1973): 575.

15. Knoxville *Register*, June 9, 1849.

16. David Anderson Deaderick Diary, 1825–72, typescript, Special Collections, Hoskins Library, University of Tennessee, Knoxville, 85, 86.

17. Knoxville *Register*, June 5, 9, 12, 1849; Wilberforce Ramsey to J. Crozier Ramsey, May 30, 1849, Ramsey Papers.

18. Knoxville *Register*, June 12, July 23, 1849.

19. Mrs. M. B. C. Ramsey to Wilberforce and Alexander, May 30, 1849, Ramsey Papers.

20. Knoxville *Register*, August 8, 1849.

21. Ibid., June 9, July 23, August 8, 18, 25, September 8, 1849; David A. Deaderick Diary, 86, 87.

22. Wilberforce Ramsey to Dr. J. G. M. Ramsey, July 14, 1849, Ramsey Papers; Knoxville *Register*, June 23, August 18, 1849.

23. Knoxville *Register*, August 18, 1849.

24. Mrs. M. B. C. Ramsey to Alexander and Wilberforce, June 10, 1849, Ramsey Papers.

25. Knoxville *Register*, August 25, 1849.

26. Ibid., September 15, 22, 1849; David A. Deaderick Diary, 86.

27. Council Grove, about 125 miles west of Independence, is not to be confused with Council Bluffs, an outfitting town in southwestern Iowa.

28. Knoxville *Register*, September 22, October 27, 1849.

29. Ibid., October 17, 27, December 29, 1849.

30. Mrs. M. B. C. Ramsey to Wilberforce and Alexander Ramsey, September 2, 1849, Ramsey Papers.

31. Knoxville *Register*, October 27, 1849.

32. Ibid., November 3, 1849.   33. Ibid., October 17, 1849.

34. Wilberforce Ramsey to Dr. J. G. M. Ramsey, July 14, 1849, Ramsey Papers.

35. Knoxville *Register*, November 24, 1849.

36. Probably Col. John Munroe, a regular army officer born in Scotland who had won commendations for his military service against the Seminole in 1838–43 and in the Mexican War 1846–48. He was en route to Santa Fe to assume duties of the civil and military governor of New Mexico pending its organization as a United States territory. Charles K. Gardner, *A Dictionary of All Officers Who Have Been Commissioned, or Have Been Appointed and Served, in the Army of the United States* . . . (New York: G. P. Putnam, 1853), 333.

37. Knoxville *Register*, December 29, 1849.   38. Ibid.

39. Ibid.   40. Ibid.

41. Wilberforce Ramsey to Dr. J. G. M. Ramsey, November 3, 1849, Ramsey Papers; *Brownlow's* Knoxville *Whig and Independent Journal*, February 23, 1850.

42. Knoxville *Register*, January 5, February 20, 1850.

43. Kate White, "The Diary of a 'Forty-Niner'—Jacob Stuart," *Tennessee Historical Magazine* series 2, vol. 1, no. 4 (July 1931): 281–82.

44. Knoxville *Register*, January 5, March 7, 1850.

45. White, "The Diary of a 'Forty-Niner,'" 281–83.

46. Wilberforce Ramsey to J. Crozier Ramsey, January 18, 1850, Ramsey Papers.

47. Wilberforce Ramsey to Dr. J. G. M. Ramsey, November 3, 1849, Ramsey Papers.

48. Ibid.

49. Mrs. M. B. C. Ramsey to Wilberforce and Alexander Ramsey, July 3, 1850, Ramsey Papers.

50. Knoxville *Register*, February 20, March 7, 1850.

51. Wilberforce Ramsey to J. Crozier Ramsey, January 18, 1850, Ramsey Papers.

52. Ibid.

53. Knoxville *Register*, February 20, March 7, 1850.

54. Ibid., April 10, 1850.   55. Athens *Post*, March 7, 1851.

56. Wilberforce Ramsey to Margaret Jane Ramsey, April 15, 1850, Ramsey Papers.

57. Athens *Post*, March 7, 1851.

58. David A. Deaderick Diary, 89.

59. *Brownlow's* Knoxville *Whig and Independent Journal*, June 1, 1850.

60. Knoxville *Register*, March 11, June 25, July 3, 1850.

61. Ibid., July 3, 1850.   62. Ibid.

63. Ibid., David A. Deaderick Dairy, 91.

CHAPTER 8

1. Leroy P. Graf and Ralph W. Haskins, eds., *The Papers of Andrew Johnson*, vol. 1, 1822–51 (Knoxville: University of Tennessee Press, 1967), 533.

2. Nashville *Daily Evening Reporter* quoted in Nashville *Daily Union*, July 15, 1850.

3. Nashville *Daily Gazette*, March 30, 1850.

4. Nashville and Louisville *Christian Advocate*, April 5, 1850.

5. Nashville *Daily American*, April 12, 1850; Neal O'Steen manuscript quoting Shelbyville *Expositor*, April 24, 1850; Nashville *Daily Gazette*, April 26, 1850.

6. From reports of the agents who incompletely enumerated the white population at 171,856 for the California census of 1852, it appears that there were at least 3,000 white persons in the state at that time who were born in and emigrated from Tennessee, or were born in Tennessee but emigrated from other states, or were born in other states but emigrated from Tennessee. Not shown in these totals are those who evaded the census takers for whatever reason including fear of a capitation tax and those who had returned to

Tennessee. The author's research identifies by name at least 1,500 Tennessee-related persons in California during the period 1849–52 who were not listed in the census. It is reasonable to conclude that by the end of 1852, there were then and/or had been at least 4,500 Tennesseans in California since the inception of the gold rush and probably many more. Sacramento *Daily Democratic State Journal*, February 24, 1853; California Secretary of State, *California Census of 1852*, transcribed by the Daughters of the American Revolution, Microfilm #82, TSLA.

7. Nashville *Daily Union*, April 10, 1850.

8. *Banner of Peace and Cumberland Presbyterian Advocate*, December 27, 1850.

9. Ibid.   10. Ibid.

11. Return J. Meigs, son of Timothy and Elizabeth Meigs, was born on a farm near Charleston, Tennessee. His grandfather was Col. Return J. Meigs, a Tennessean who was Indian agent to the Cherokee from 1801 until his death in 1823. Grant Foreman, *Marcy and the Gold Seekers* (Norman: University of Oklahoma Press, 1939), 106n.

12. Ibid., 114.

13. *Banner of Peace and Cumberland Presbyterian Advocate*, December 27, 1850.

14. Nashville *True Whig*, April 13, 27, July 27, 1850.

15. Ibid., July 27, 1850.   16. Ibid.

17. Ibid., August 29, 1850.   18. Ibid.

19. Ibid., November 12, 1850.   20. Ibid.

21. Nashville *Daily Gazette*, April 23, 28, 1850; Nashville *True Whig*, April 23, 28, 1850.

22. Irene D. Paden, ed., *The Journal of Madison Berryman Moorman, 1850–51* (San Francisco: California Historical Society, 1948) 1, 6.

23. Ibid., 5–6.

24. Walker was traveling with his brother Marcus Walker, William Cowley, John McFall, and Thomas Pullum. Paden, *The Journal of Madison Berryman Moorman*, 7; Nashville *Daily American*, August 6, 1850.

25. Nashville *Daily American*, July 23, 1850.

26. Ibid.; Paden, *The Journal of Madison Berryman Moorman*, 15, 16, 17–18; *Republican Banner and* Nashville *Whig*, February 25, 1853.

27. Charles K. Gardner, *A Dictionary of All Officers, Who Have Been Commissioned, or Have Been Appointed and Served, in the Army of the United States . . .* (New York: G. P. Putnam, 1853), 301; Paden, *The Journal of Madison Berryman Moorman*, 17; *Republican Banner and* Nashville *Whig*, February 25, 1853.

28. Paden, *The Journal of Madison Berryman Moorman*, 18, 22, 23; Nashville *Daily American*, August 6, 1850.

29. Gardner, *A Dictionary of All Officers*, 152; Paden, *The Journal of Madison Berryman Moorman*, 29–30; Nashville *Daily American*, August 6, 1850; *Republican Banner and* Nashville *Whig*, February 26, 1853.

30. Paden, *The Journal of Madison Berryman Moorman*, 30–37.

31. Ibid., 41–42, 44–48.   32. Ibid., 49–51.

33. Nashville *Daily American*, January 2, 1851.

34. Paden, *The Journal of Madison Berryman Moorman*, 51, 57.

35. Ibid., *64, 66, 69, 73–74, 76.*   36. Ibid., *77–82.*

37. William J. Jackson letter to Betty, his wife, May 5, 1850, typescript courtesy Robert Winn Jackson, Paris, Tenn.

38. Ibid.   39. Ibid.

40. William J. Jackson letter to Betty, his wife, June 15, 1850, typescript.

41. Ibid.

42. The last preserved correspondence from the Henry County gold seekers was dated June 15, 1850, and was written from Salt Lake Ferry on the Platte River. Ibid.

43. Brown and Harris Papers, originals in private collection, Birmingham, Alabama, typescripts, Sumner County Archives, Gallatin.

44. Jacob Gillespie to Green B. Harris, May 25, 1850; James O. Harris to Mrs. Mary Harris, May 2, 1850, Brown and Harris Papers.

45. Nashville *Daily American*, April 20, 1850.

46. James O. Harris to Green B. Harris, May 25–28, 1850, Brown and Harris Papers.

47. James O. Harris to Green B. Harris, October 13, 1850, Brown and Harris Papers.

48. James O. Harris to Mary Harris, November 17, 1850, Brown and Harris Papers. The population of Gallatin, Tennessee, in 1850 was 1,943. *Ninth U.S. Census*, vol. 1, June 1, 1870 (Washington, D.C.: Government Printing Office, 1872).

49. James O. Harris to Green B. Harris, October 13, 1850, Brown and Harris Papers.

50. O'Steen manuscript; *Republican Banner and* Nashville *Whig*, April 10, 1850.

51. The members were Crutsinger, Joseph Powell, William Cloud, Patrick H. Vance, Thomas Titsworth, J. G. Stuart, T. W. Cawood, W. R. Anderson, William Swicegood, David Swicegood, David Wade Snapp, N. Morgan, Joseph D. Rhea, Jacob Bushong, Isaac Coakinham, H. Hicks, and J. Green. *Brownlow's* Knoxville *Whig and Independent Journal*, April 6, 1850.

52. Ibid., November 16, 1850.

53. Louis J. Rasmussen, *California Wagon Train Lists*, vol. 1 (Colma, Calif.: San Francisco Historic Records, 1994), 111–12.

54. Copied in the Nashville *Daily Centre State American*, April 16, 1850.

55. John Carr, *Pioneer Days in California, Historical and Personal Sketches* (Eureka: Times Publishing Co., 1891), 447.

56. Traveling with them were three Grigsby brothers—Achilles and his wife, Elizabeth Wilson; John Melchesadeck and wife, Margaret Hale; and Terrell Lindsay Grigsby. Elizabeth Wilson Grigsby died en route. Jonesborough *Herald and Tribune*, August 17, 1994.

57. Nashville *Daily American*, April 14, 17, 1850.

58. Nashville *Daily Centre State American*, April 14, 17, 24, 1850; Robert Frank Evans, *Notes on Land and Sea 1850* (Boston: Richard G. Badger, Gorham Press, 1922), 5–7, 16.

59. Evans, *Notes on Land and Sea 1850*, 9.

60. William Gregory Deposition, February 25, 1856; John Walton Deposition [February 25, 1856]; John C. Hubbard Deposition [February 25, 1856], Sumner County Loose Court Records, Sumner County Archives (hereinafter referred to as LCR/SCA); Nashville *Daily American*, April 17, 1850.

61. Members of the Sumner Independents were David Barry, his slave black John, Perrin L. Solomon, Robert B. Douglass, Nat. P. Turner, Charles A. Strasburg, W. L. Carr, Thomas C. Wilson, Lye Chambers, and the three who were "independent" enough to defect. Nashville *Daily American*, April 9, 1850; David Barry to sister, May 22, 1850, David Barry Papers, private collection.

62. David Barry to wife, April 16, 1850, David Barry Papers.

63. Nashville *Daily American*, April 9, 1850; David Barry to wife, April 16, 1850, David Barry Papers.

64. David Barry to wife, May 18, to sister, May 22, 1850, David Barry Papers.

65. Evans, *Notes on Land and Sea 1850*, 13, 18, 23, 45–46, 53.

66. *Brownlow's* Knoxville *Whig and Independent Journal*, January 4, 1851; Athens *Post*, July 12, 1850; Evans, *Notes on Land and Sea 1850*, 67, 87.

67. Athens *Post*, July 12, 1850; *Brownlow's* Knoxville *Whig and Independent Journal*, January 4, 1851.

68. Athens *Post*, June 28, 1850; W. B. Lenoir, *History of Sweetwater Valley* (Richmond, Va.: Presbyterian Committee of Publication, 1916), 326–28, 330.

69. David Barry to wife, June 14, July 13, 1850, David Barry Papers; Nashville *Daily American*, September 10, 1850; Evans, *Notes on Land and Sea 1850*, 45, 46.

70. Evans, *Notes on Land and Sea 1850*, 70–71, 79, 80, 83, 112; *Brownlow's* Knoxville *Whig and Independent Journal*, January 4, 1851; Oscar Lewis, *Sea Routes to the Gold Fields, The Migration by Water to California in 1849–1852* (New York: Knopf, 1949), 108–10.

71. Nashville *Daily Union*, October 21, 1850; Nashville *True Whig*, April 13, August 27, 1850; Clarksville *Jeffersonian*, May 7, 1850; W. P. Titus, *Picturesque Clarksville, Past and Present* (Clarksville, Tenn.: published by the author, 1887), 219–20.

72. Knoxville *Register*, May 22, 1850; *Brownlow's* Knoxville *Whig and Independent Journal*, November 30, 1850.

73. *Brownlow's* Knoxville *Whig and Independent Journal*, August 24, September 7, 1850.

74. Nashville *Daily American*, April 21, 1850; Nashville *Daily Gazette*, May 10, 1850.

75. Nashville *Daily Gazette*, August 6, 16, 1850; Nashville *True Whig*, May 23, 1850.

76. Alejandro Bolanos-Geyer, *William Walker, the Gray-Eyed Man of Destiny*, vol. 2 (Lake St. Louis, Mo.: n.p., 1989), 49–52; Nashville *Daily Gazette*, August 16, 1850.

77. *Brownlow's* Knoxville *Whig and Independent Journal*, June 22, 1850.

78. Ibid., August 24, 1850.   79. Ibid., May 4, December 21, 1850.

80. Nashville *Daily American*, March 17, 1850; *Republican Banner and* Nashville *Whig*, April 8, August 19, 1850.

81. Cox to Campbell, October 15, 1850, David Campbell Papers, microfilm, TSLA.

82. This appears to be the slowest passage on record for Tennessee gold seekers sailing from Panama City to the Golden Gate. Ibid.

83. Joseph L. Rushing to Mary C. Rushing, January 27, 1850; Mary C. Rushing to Joseph L. Rushing, July 18, 1850; W. T. Anderson to Joseph L. Rushing, March 25, June 18, 1850, Joseph L. Rushing Papers, TSLA.

84. J. L. Rushing to Lorane Rushing, July 22, 1850; W. T. Anderson to J. L. Rushing, March 25, June 18, 1850, Joseph L. Rushing Papers.

85. May 18, 1850.

86. A. G. Register was born in Greene County and educated at Tusculum College. He was a Cumberland Presbyterian preacher, licensed in 1850 by the Knoxville Presbytery. Mrs. G. W. Jones and Mrs. T. B. McAmis, *Life of Rev. A. G. Register, by His Daughters* (Nashville, Tenn.: Cumberland Presbyterian Publishing House, 1890), 26, 29, 34–37.

87. Ibid., 37–40.

88. Opened in June 1851, the Nicaragua route reduced the distance traveled by sea from New Orleans to San Francisco by way of Chagres and Panama City by about one thousand miles. The developers claimed that only thirty-three hours of travel time were required for crossing the Isthmus: five by road from San Juan del Sud, twelve on Lake Nicaragua, and sixteen on the river to San Juan del Norte. Although the route accommodated several thousand travelers, later political strife in the country and frequent portages on the river combined to minimize its appeal. Nashville *Daily Gazette*, July 2, 1851; *Republican Banner and* Nashville *Whig*, September 18, 1851.

89. *A History of Tuolumne County, California* (San Francisco: B. F. Alley, 1882), 347–49.

90. John Hurst, *A Little Sketch of My Life* (Clarksville, Tenn.: Sallie Hurst Peay, 1927), 5.

91. The traveling party included adults George Harrison Grigsby, George Harrison Grigsby, Jr., Jesse Foster Grigsby, Samuel Harrison Grigsby, and Benjamin Grigsby, "some with their families." Jonesborough *Herald and Tribune*, August 17, 1994.

92. *A History of Tuolumne County*, 318.

93. Tyree B. Harris to Green B. Harris, October 10, 1853, Brown and Harris Papers.

94. Nashville *Daily Gazette*, December 7, 1852.

95. John Litton Bostick to his mother, June 24, 1853, Harding P. Bostick Collection, Tennessee Historical Society, TSLA.

96. *Republican Banner and* Nashville *Whig*, February 26, 1851; Malcolm Curtis Douglass, *History, Memoirs and Genealogy of the Douglass Family* (Houston: Biggers Printing Co., 1957), 173, 188; Jay Guy Cisco, *Historic Sumner County, Tennessee* (Nashville: Folk Keelin, 1909) 210.

97. Governor Andrew Johnson had visited with Belle at Nashville just before she took a riverboat to St. Louis. Leroy P. Graf and Ralph W. Haskins, eds., *The Papers of Andrew Johnson*, vol. 2, 1852–57 (Knoxville: University of Tennessee Press, 1970), 228, 229n.

98. Louis J. Rasmussen, *San Francisco Ship Passenger Lists*, vol. 3 (Colma, Calif.: San Francisco Historic Records, 1967), 147.

99. *Placer* is a Spanish term referring to gold eroded from rock and subsequently "reduced to a loose condition that has permitted it to be transported and abraded by existing or prehistoric streams, which have finally deposited it on sandbars, in gravel banks, or

in 'potholes' in the stream beds. Such gold has long been called 'placer gold' by miners, and the deposits in which it is found are called 'placers.'" Rodman W. Paul, *Mining Frontiers of the American West, 1848–1880* (New York: Holt, Rinehart and Winston, 1963), 6.

CHAPTER 9

1. *Presbyterian Record*, February 17, 1849.

2. Hubert Howe Bancroft, *History of California, 1848–1859*, vol. 6 (1888, reprint; Santa Barbara: Wallace Hebberd, 1970), 257; William Henry Ellison, *A Self-Governing Dominion, California, 1849–1860* (Berkeley and Los Angeles: University of California Press, 1950), 4, 5.

3. Ellison, *A Self-Governing Dominion*, 10–11.

4. Those who looked beyond the ends of their noses wanted a government that could regulate and rule in the questions of land titles, a matter that would become more urgent with every passing day. There was for the miners the question of claims and claimants' rights. Whose land were they mining? Were they trespassing on government property? How could settlers obtain land grants? How could private landowners establish clear title and protect their holdings from trespassers? J. S. Holliday, *The World Rushed In: The California Gold Rush Experience* (New York: Simon and Schuster, 1981), 36.

5. *Alta California*, January 25, 1849; Peter H. Burnett, *Recollections and Opinions of an Old Pioneer* (New York: D. Appleton and Co., 1880), 296.

6. After arriving at the fort, Burnett had become counsel to Captain John A. Sutter and his agent in selling land and collecting accounts to pay off a large accumulation of debt. The discovery of gold at Sutter's Mill made it possible for Burnett to satisfy the many creditors, and by the middle of August 1849, he had paid all of Sutter's obligations. Julian Dana, *Sutter of California* (New York: Press of the Pioneers, 1934), 332–34.

7. William E. Franklin, "Peter H. Burnett and the Provisional Government Movement," *California Historical Society Quarterly* 40, no. 2 (June 1961): 124.

8. Eugene H. Berwanger, *The Frontier Against Slavery, Western Anti-Negro Prejudice and the Slavery Extension Controversy* (Urbana: University of Illinois Press, 1967), 64–65; *Alta California*, January 4, 25, June 14, 1849.

9. *Alta California*, January 25, 1849.   10. Ibid., February 15, 1849.

11. Burnett, *Recollections and Opinions of an Old Pioneer*, 316.

12. David M. Potter, *The Impending Crisis 1848–1861*, comp. and ed. Don E. Fehrenbacher (New York: Harper and Row, 1976), 49.

13. *Journal of the House of Representatives of the United States Being the Second Session of the Thirtieth Congress Begun and Held in the City of Washington December 4, 1848, in the Seventy-third Year of the Independence of the United States* (Washington, D.C.: Wendell and Benthuysen, 1848–49), 515.

14. St. Joseph *Gazette*, September 28, 1849.   15. Ibid.

16. *Alta California*, June 14, 1849; Franklin, "Burnett and the Provisional Government Movement," 130.

17. Memphis *Daily Eagle*, September 3, 1849; Ellison, *A Self-Governing Dominion*, 23.

18. Lately Thomas, *Between Two Empires, The Life Story of California's First Senator William McKendree Gwin* (Boston: Houghton Mifflin, 1969), 7–10, 18, 22.

19. Gwin and King had reached San Francisco on the same ship from Panama City. During their passage, they had not only shared their common interest in statehood for California, but surely had agreed to promote it aggressively. Ellison, *A Self-Governing Dominion*, 24; *Alta California*, June 14, 1849.

20. Franklin, "Burnett and the Provisional Government Movement," 132.

21. He might have pointed out that in his native state of Tennessee, the first settlers had organized government successively under the Watauga Association, the Cumberland Compact, and the state of Franklin when they perceived that the reasonable services of government were not being provided by the mother state of North Carolina. When that state later ceded the Tennessee country to the national government, Congress made it into a federal territory. Unable to induce Congress to expedite their progression to statehood, the settlers elected delegates to a convention where they drafted a constitution and called for the election of state officers. Then after electing a governor, senators, congressmen, and general assembly, the state of Tennessee sent its congressional delegation to Washington to seek admission to the Union. After a few weeks of debate and negotiation, Tennessee became the sixteenth state of the Union on June 1, 1796. Walter T. Durham, *Before Tennessee: The Southwest Territory, 1790–1796* (Piney Flats, Tenn.: Rocky Mount Historical Association, 1990), 8, 17–18, 209–11.

22. *Alta California*, June 14, 20, July 2, 1849.

23. Franklin, "Burnett and the Provisional Government Movement," 129.

24. *Alta California*, July 12, August 9, 1849.

25. Franklin, "Burnett and the Provisional Government Movement," 129–30; *Republican Banner and* Nashville *Whig*, October 24, 1850.

26. Memphis *Daily Eagle*, September 3, 1849.

27. *Alta California*, August 2, 1849; Henry F. Dobyns, ed., *Hepah, California! The Journal of Cave Johnson Couts, 1848–1849* (Tucson: Arizona Pioneers Historical Society, 1961), 97.

28. Colonel Ramsey crossed via the Isthmus in 1852 to visit them, but stricken ill while en route, he died in his daughter's arms on July 12, the day after he reached their home in San Francisco. *A History of Tuolumne County, California* (San Francisco: B. F. Alley, 1882), 17; Louis J. Rasmussen, *San Francisco Ship Passenger Lists*, vol. 4 (Colma, Calif.: San Francisco Historic Records, 1970), 29, 244.

29. *Alta California*, August 2, 1849; Grant Foreman, *Marcy and the Gold Seekers* (Norman: University of Oklahoma Press, 1939), 321n.

30. Charles Albro Barker, ed., *Memoirs of Elisha Oscar Crosby* (San Marino, Calif.: Huntington Library, 1945), 40, 41.

31. William Henry Ellison, ed., "Memoirs of Hon. William M. Gwin," *California Historical Society Quarterly* 19, no. 1 (1940): 7.

32. Ellison, *A Self-Governing Dominion*, 32.   33. Ibid., 32, 36.

34. Ibid., 34–36; Nashville *True Whig*, February 28, 1850.

35. Memphis *Daily Eagle*, August 14, 1849.

36. Californios were the original Spanish colonists or their descendants. Prominent among them were the large landholders of the area.

37. John Ross Browne, *Report of the Debates in the Convention of California on the Formation of the State Constitution in September and October, 1849* (Washington, D.C.: John T. Towers, 1850), 22, 24, 44, 77, 163–64, 250.

38. Ellison, *A Self-Governing Dominion*, 46; Browne, *Report of the Debates*, 77.

39. *Alta California*, November 8, 15, 1849; "Bound for the Land of Canaan, Ho! The Diary of Levi Stowell, 1849," *California Historical Society Quarterly* 28, no. 1 (Mar. 1949): 58.

40. Nicholas Perkins Hardeman, *Wilderness Calling: The Hardeman Family in the American Westward Movement, 1750–1900* (Knoxville: University of Tennessee Press, 1977), 208; *Alta California*, November 8, 15, 29, 1849; Nashville *Daily Union*, January 8, 24, 1850.

41. Ellison, *A Self-Governing Dominion*, 54–55; *Alta California*, December 29, 1849.

42. "Bound for the Land of Canaan," 68.

43. Campaigning as the Democratic party nominee, Roman was reelected by popular vote on September 3, 1851, for a term beginning January 5, 1852. He lost a bid to be lieutenant governor in the general election of 1850 and sought but failed to win his party's nomination for governor in 1851. Nashville *Daily Gazette*, September 14, 1851; *California Blue Book, 1891*, comp. E. G. Waite, secretary of state (Sacramento: State Printing Office, 1891), 244; Winfield J. Davis, *History of Political Conventions in California, 1840–1892* (Sacramento: California State Library, 1893), 5, 12.

44. Cardinal Leonidas Goodwin, *The Establishment of State Government in California, 1846–1850* (New York: Macmillan, 1914), 255.

45. August 30, 1849.

46. Robert H. White, *Messages of the Governors of Tennessee, 1845–1857*, vol. 4 (Nashville: Tennessee Historical Commission, 1957) 302–3.

47. Ibid., 265, 360–61.

48. Thelma Jennings, *The Nashville Convention: Southern Movement for Unity, 1848–1850* (Memphis: Memphis State University Press, 1980), 57; Dallas Tabor Herndon, "The Nashville Convention of 1850," *The Transactions*, no. 5 (1904), reprint no. 35, Alabama Historical Society, Montgomery, 1905, 207, 209.

49. Ellison, *A Self-Governing Dominion*, 79, 84.

50. John M. Blum, Bruce Catton, Edmund S. Morgan, Arthur M. Schlesinger, Jr., Kenneth M. Stampp, and C. Vann Woodward, *The National Experience, A History of the United States to 1877*, part 1, 2d ed. (New York: Harcourt, Brace and World, 1968), 288–90.

51. John P. Heiss Papers, 1835–72, THS, TSLA.

52. *Alta California*, April 25, 1850.

53. Ellison, *A Self-Governing Dominion*, p. 84.

54. Ibid., 85–86, 92.

55. New York *Tribune*, February 18, 1850, quoted in Nashville *True Whig*, February 18, 1850.

56. During February 1849, Bell had proposed an amendment in the Senate that called for the creation of the state of California, but neither his Whig colleagues nor the

Democrats would support it. By the ill-fated amendment, he would have extended the protection of government to the more than 100,000 persons that he expected to be in California by the end of the year. He believed Senator Stephen A. Douglas's bill, recognized as the principal California bill, would never be brought to a vote. Athens *Post*, March 2, 1849.

57. Athens *Post*, March 15, 1850; Ellison, *A Self-Governing Dominion*, 85; Joseph Howard Parks, *John Bell of Tennessee* (Baton Rouge: Louisiana State University Press, 1950), 227–29, 244–46.

58. *Republican Banner and* Nashville *Whig*, August 26, 1850.

59. *Speech of Mr. Andrew Ewing of Tennessee on the Admission of California Delivered in the House of Representatives, April 18, 1850* (Washington, D.C.: John T. Towers, 1850), 4, 10–11, 12.

60. *Speech of M. P. Gentry of Tenn., on the Admission of California, Delivered in the House of Representatives, U.S., Monday, June 10, 1850* (Washington, D.C.: Gideon and Co., 1850), 1, 6–7, 8, 10, 13.

61. *Republican Banner and* Nashville *Whig*, March 27, 1850.

62. Herndon, "The Nashville Convention of 1850," 203.

63. Nashville *True Whig*, June 18, 1850; Herndon, "The Nashville Convention of 1850," 215.

64. North Carolina, Louisiana, Delaware, Maryland, Kentucky, and Missouri sent no representation. Potter, *The Impending Crisis 1848–1861*, 104.

65. Herndon, "The Nashville Convention of 1850," 219–22.

66. Ellison, *A Self-Governing Dominion*, 93, 95; Potter, *The Impending Crisis 1848–1861*, p. 108. The Compromise of 1850 is sometimes referred to as the armistice of 1850 because it contained little real compromise but a series of balanced concessions to each side. It did not resolve the issue of slavery but deferred the crisis until the explosion in Kansas in 1855 and finally the Civil War in 1861. Potter, *The Impending Crisis, 1848–1861*, 114n.

67. Ellison, *A Self-Governing Dominion*, 97–99. Tennessee congressmen voting for admission were Whigs Albert G. Watkins, Josiah M. Anderson, Meredith P. Gentry, and Christopher H. Williams. Democrats voting in favor were Andrew Johnson, George W. Jones, and Andrew Ewing. Those who opposed were all Democrats: John H. Savage, James H. Thomas, Isham G. Harris, and Frederick P. Stanton. *Congressional Globe*, 31st Congress, 1st session, September 10, 1850 (Washington, D.C.: John C. Rives), 1772.

68. White, *Messages of the Governors of Tennessee, 1845–1857*, 401.

69. Nashville *Daily Gazette*, December 19, 1850.

70. Quoted in the Nashville *Daily Union*, September 20, 1850.

CHAPTER 10

1. James Kimmins Greer, *Colonel Jack Hays, Texas Frontier Leader and California Builder* (New York: E. P. Dutton, 1952), 255.

2. *Alta California*, February 1, 1850.   3. Ibid.

4. Greer, *Colonel Jack Hays*, 258.   5. Ibid., 259.

6. Ibid.   7. Ibid., 259, 261.

8. Ibid., 262.

9. Frederic A. Culmer, ed., "California Letter of John Wilson, 1850," *Missouri Historical Review* 24, no. 2 (Jan. 1930): 212.

10. Louisville *Courier*, reported in Clarksville *Jeffersonian*, June 4, 1850.

11. *Alta California*, April 4, 1850; Greer, *Colonel Jack Hays*, 267.

12. Mary Floyd Williams, *History of the San Francisco Committee of Vigilance of 1851. A Study of Social Control on the California Frontier in the Days of the Gold Rush* (New York: Da Capo Press, 1969), 152, 295.

13. Ibid., 295, 302, 325; Greer, *Colonel Jack Hays*, 286–90.

14. Greer, *Colonel Jack Hays*, 311; Winfield J. Davis, *History of Political Conventions in California, 1840–1892* (Sacramento: California State Library, 1893), 361.

15. Victor M. Rose, *The Life and Services of Gen. Ben McCulloch* (Philadelphia: Pictorial Bureau of the Press, 1888), 28, 122.

16. *Alta California*, September 29, 1850.

17. Nashville *Daily American*, January 29, 1850; *Alta California*, February 13, 1850.

18. Nashville *Daily American*, May 19, 1850; Nashville *Daily Gazette*, December 19, 1850.

19. Davis, *History of Political Conventions in California*, 12, 19; *Alta California*, November 22, 1850.

20. Hubert Howe Bancroft, *History of California, 1848–1859*, vol. 6 (1888, reprint; Santa Barbara: Wallace Hebberd, 1970), 319.

21. Douglass to Campbell, April 12, 1851, David Campbell Papers, microfilm, TSLA. Campbell was elected governor of Tennessee in 1851.

22. Copied in the Nashville *Daily American*, June 4, 1851.

23. *Alta California*, May 28, August 23, 1851; Davis, *History of Political Conventions in California*, 620.

24. Sacramento *Daily Democratic State Journal*, June 30, July 8, 1853.

25. Ibid., May 25, 1853.

26. Davis, *History of Political Conventions in California*, 45, 620.

27. Carl I. Wheat, ed., "California's Bantam Cock, The Journals of Charles E. DeLong, 1854–1863," *California Historical Quarterly* 10, no. 1 (Mar. 1931): 74. Division of California into separate slave and free states had been on the minds of the proslavery people from the beginning. Claiming a right to be heard because they paid three-fourths of the state's taxes and had only one-half the representation in the legislature in 1851, many southern Californians wanted slavery. The reason was economic and simple: they believed that slave labor in the mines would reduce mining costs and increase profits materially. Nashville *Daily Gazette*, November 11, 1851.

28. *California Blue Book, 1891*, comp. E. G. Waite, secretary of state (Sacramento: State Printing Office, 1891), 243.

29. Herbert L. Florcken, arr., "The Law and Order View of the San Francisco

Vigilance Committee of 1856," parts 1 and 2, *California State Historical Society Quarterly* 14, no. 4 (Dec. 1935): 356; 15, no. 1 (Mar. 1936): 78; 15, no. 2 (June 1936): 146.

30. Bancroft, *History of California, 1848–1859*, 6: 625n.

31. Franklin *Western Weekly Review*, December 20, 1850.

32. *Brownlow's* Knoxville *Whig and Independent Journal*, April 19, 1851.

33. Quoted in Nashville *Daily Union*, January 7, 1851.

34. Thomas B. Alexander, *Thomas A. R. Nelson of East Tennessee* (Nashville: Tennessee Historical Commission, 1956), 45.

35. *Alta California*, April 24, 1851.

36. Nashville *True Whig*, July 11, 1850; Sacramento *Daily Democratic State Journal*, June 2, 1853.

37. W. P. Titus, *Picturesque Clarksville, Past and Present* (Clarksville: published by the author, 1887), 220.

38. *House Executive Document No. 17*, 31st Congress, 1st session, 1849–50, vol. 5, serial 573, pp. 104–112, 182–84, 184–87.

39. Howard L. Hurwitz, *An Encyclopedic Dictionary of American History* (New York: Washington Square Press, 1970), 190; Cardinal Leonidas Goodwin, *The Establishment of State Government in California, 1846–1850* (New York: Macmillan, 1914), 160–61.

40. Hubert Howe Bancroft, *History of Utah, 1540–1887* (San Francisco: History Co., 1890), 446–47.

41. Ibid.

42. After traveling from Lassen's ranch to Sacramento City in a whaleboat they had procured at the mouth of Deer Creek, the Wilsons completed their trip to San Francisco on the steamboat *Senator*. Earlier they were "supposed to have been lost in the mountains" and, in fact, were bogged down in a three-foot snow with little to eat. The timely arrival of a rescue team, bringing food and fresh mules, enabled them to finish their crossing from the upper Pit and Feather Rivers to Lassen's. *Alta California*, December 15, 1849; St. Joseph *Gazette*, February 1, March 22, 1850.

43. Goodwin, *The Establishment of State Government in California*, 162–63.

44. Bancroft, *History of Utah*, 447.

45. Goodwin, *The Establishment of State Government in California*, 163.

46. *Alta California*, March 28, June 6, 1850; May 29, 1851.

47. Ibid., August 24, 1850.

48. Ibid., December 22, 1849; June 3, August 15, 22, 1850.

49. Sacramento *Daily Democratic State Journal*, December 29, 1853; January 2, 1854.

50. Davis, *History of Political Conventions in California*, 45.

51. Ibid., 617; *Alta California*, August 5, 1850; March 8, 1853; Nashville *Daily Gazette*, May 30, June 13, 1854; *California Blue Book, 1891*, 215.

52. Rufus Kay Wyllys, "Henry A. Crabb—A Tragedy of the Sonora Frontier," *Pacific Historical Review* 9, no. 1 (Mar. 1940): 183–84.

53. Luther A. Ingersoll, *Ingersoll's Century Annals of San Bernardino County, 1679–1704;*

prefaced with a brief history of the state of California; supplemented with an encyclopedia of local biography and embellished with views of historic subjects and portraits of many of its representative people (Los Angeles: published by the author, 1904), 686; George D. Lyman, "The Scalpel Under Three Flags," *California Historical Society Quarterly* 4, no. 2 (June 1925): 185–86; *Alta California*, July 1, September 13, 22, October 10, 1851; Nashville *Daily True Whig*, February 26, 1852; Sacramento *Daily Democratic State Journal*, April 26, 28, 1853; Barbara Ann Metcalf, "Oliver M. Wozencraft in California, 1849–1887" (master's thesis, University of Southern California, 1963), 13, 43–44, 52, 58, 101–3.

54. Sacramento *Daily Democratic State Journal*, March 5, 1853; San Francisco *Daily Evening Picayune*, March 17, 1853.

55. *California Blue Book, 1891*, 226.

56. Ibid., 264; Bancroft, *History of California, 1848–1859*, 6: 684n.

57. *California Blue Book, 1891*, 201; San Francisco *Daily Evening Picayune*, January 17, 1852.

58. *California Blue Book, 1891*, 244; Bancroft, *History of California, 1848–1859*, 6: 617; Davis, *History of Political Conventions in California*, 50.

59. Sacramento *Daily Democratic State Journal*, June 20, 1854.

60. *California Blue Book, 1891*, 206, 226.

61. Nashville *Union and American*, October 19, 1853; Nashville *Daily True Whig*, October 20, 1853.

62. Davis, *History of Political Conventions in California*, 75, 94, 97, 99, 109.

63. Peyton was a Gallatin attorney and turfman who served in Congress from 1833 to 1837. Relocating to New Orleans, he was United States attorney for eastern Louisiana in 1841, soon afterward declined President John Tyler's proffered appointment as secretary of war, and later was an aide to Gen. W. J. Worth during the Mexican War. He lived in San Francisco from 1853 to 1859, when he returned to Gallatin. He had a nationally prominent role in organizing the Constitutional Union party for the election of 1860 and was a Tennessee presidential elector on the Bell-Everett ticket. In 1866, he lost a campaign to go back to Congress, but won a term in the Tennessee state senate in 1869. *Biographical Directory of the United States Congress, 1774–1989*, bicentennial ed. (Washington, D.C.: U.S. Government Printing Office, 1989), 1639–40; Robert M. McBride and Dan M. Robison, *Biographical Directory of the Tennessee General Assembly, 1861–1901*, vol. 2 (Nashville: Tennessee State Library and Archives and Tennessee Historical Commission, 1979), 722.

64. Nashville *Daily True Whig*, December 16, 1853; *Alta California*, November 10, 1853; Dorothy H. Huggins, comp., "Continuation of the Annals of San Francisco," *California Historical Society Quarterly* 16, no. 3 (Sept. 1937): 281.

65. Sacramento *Daily Democratic State Journal*, July 27, 1854; *Republican Banner and Nashville Whig*, September 5, 1854; October 23, 1855; Peyton Hurt, "The Rise and Fall of the 'Know-Nothings' in California," *California Historical Society Quarterly* 9, no. 1 (Mar. 1930): 38–39.; 9, No. 2 (June 1930): 102–3.

66. Peyton to John Bell, February 3, 1856, John Bell Papers, TSLA.

67. Hurt, "The Rise and Fall of the 'Know-Nothings' in California," 9, no. 2, 102–3.

68. [James O'Meara], *The Vigilance Committee of 1856* (San Francisco: James H. Barry, 1887), 3, 8, 10.

69. Richard Maxwell Brown, *Strain of Violence, Historical Studies of American Violence and Vigilantism* (Oxford: Oxford University Press, 1975), 135.

70. "Sherman Was There, The Recollections of Major Edwin A. Sherman," with an introduction by Allen B. Sherman, *California Historical Society Quarterly* 24, no. 1 (Mar. 1945): 174.

71. William Henry Ellison, *A Self-Governing Dominion, California, 1849–1860* (Berkeley and Los Angeles: University of California Press, 1950), 254.

72. Foote, who represented Mississippi in the United States Senate from 1847 until elected governor in 1851, came to California in 1854. He returned to Mississippi in 1858 and about 1860 moved to Nashville. Although he had been a staunch Unionist prior to the war, he was elected to represent the Nashville district in the Confederate Congress in 1861. Nashville *Daily American*, May 21, 1880.

73. Florcken, "The Law and Order View," pt. 1, 364–65.

74. Born at Campbell's Station near Knoxville, Tennessee, David Glasgow Farragut (1801–70) went to sea at an early age. He was crew member of the naval ship *Essex* in a battle off Valparaiso, Chile, during the War of 1812. Later he fought pirates in the West Indies and took part in the war with Mexico. Loyal to the Union, he remained on duty in the United States Navy throughout the Civil War. He achieved fame as commander of the Gulf Squadron when he successively captured New Orleans, aided in the siege of Vicksburg, and captured Mobile. Congress created the rank of vice admiral for him in 1864, and two years later by special act gave him the rank of admiral. Allen Johnson and Dumas Malone, eds., *Dictionary of American Biography*, vol. 3 (New York: Charles Scribner's Sons, 1959), 286–89.

75. [O'Meara], *The Vigilance Committee of 1856*, 19, 30, 39–42, 57.

76. Edna Bryan Buckbee, *The Saga of Old Tuolumne* (New York: Press of the Pioneers, 1935), 77, 173, 221, 107–9.

77. *A History of Tuolumne County, California*, (San Francisco: B. F. Alley, 1882), 418–19.

78. *California Blue Book, 1891*, 214, 222, 264; Nashville *Daily Gazette*, September 14, 1851.

79. Davis, *History of Political Conventions in California*, 165, 172, 624.

80. John Carr, *Pioneer Days in California, Historical and Personal Sketches* (Eureka: Times Publishing Co., 1891), 424.

81. California Secretary of State, *California Census of 1852*, transcribed by the Daughters of the American Revolution, Microfilm #82, TSLA, 67, 70, 147; James O. Harris to Green B. Harris, June 30, 1856, Brown and Harris Papers, originals in private collection, Birmingham, Alabama, typescripts, Sumner County Archives, Gallatin; *California Blue Book, 1891*, 220.

82. Nashville *Daily American*, January 2, 1851.

83. Buckbee, *The Saga of Old Tuolumne*, 192.

84. San Joaquin *Republican*, November 26, 1851; December 29, 1853.

85. *Republican Banner and* Nashville *Whig*, November 8, 1852.

86. Sacramento *Daily Democratic State Journal*, March 20, 1854.

87. William Perkins, *Three Years in California . . . Journal of Life at Sonora 1849–1852*, ed. Dale L. Morgan and James R. Scobie (Berkeley: University of California Press, 1964), 247–49; Buckbee, *The Saga of Old Tuolumne*, 175.

88. Sacramento *Daily Democratic State Journal*, January 14, 1854.

89. Memphis *Daily Eagle*, March 11, 1852.

90. Nashville *Daily Gazette*, July 19, 1853.

91. Sacramento *Daily Democratic State Journal*, February 14, April 29, 1853; Davis, *History of Political Conventions in California*, 30, 55, 76, 104, 106, 111, 314.

92. *Republican Banner and* Nashville *Whig*, March 8, 1853.

93. Memphis *Eagle and Enquirer*, March 15, 1853.

94. Nashville *Daily Gazette*, June 13, 1854; J. Litton Bostick to his mother, June 29, 1853, Harding P. Bostick Collection, THS, TSLA.

95. *Solano County History*, 410–11, quoted in Bancroft, *History of California, 1848–1859*, 6: 699 n.

96. Alex. J. Rosborough, "A. M. Rosborough, Special Indian Agent," *California Historical Quarterly* 26, no. 3 (Sept. 1947): 201–2.

97. Ibid., 202–6.

98. Ibid., 207; Nashville *Daily Gazette*, March 19, 1854; Davis, *History of Political Conventions in California*, 126, 315, 350.

99. John Albert Wilson, *History of Los Angeles County, California* (Oakland: Thompson and West, 1880), 37.

100. John Walton Caughey, ed., *The Indians of Southern California in 1852, The B. D. Wilson Report and a Selection of Contemporary Comment* (San Marino: Huntington Library, 1952), xxix.

101. *California Blue Book, 1891*, 209; Carlos D'Este, *Patton: A Genius for War* (New York: HarperCollins, 1995), 27–28; Caughey, *The Indians of Southern California in 1852*, xi.

102. Davis, *History of Political Conventions in California*, 627, 629.

103. Frank T. Gilbert, *Illustrated Atlas and History of Yolo County, California* (San Francisco: De Pue and Co., 1879), 82–83; San Francisco *Chronicle*, June 1, 1927.

104. Davis, *History of Political Conventions in California*, 629, 659; *California Blue Book, 1891*, 62, 261–63.

CHAPTER 11

1. John Walton Caughey, *Gold Is the Cornerstone* (Berkeley and Los Angeles: University of California Press, 1948), 162.

2. J. L. Bostick to Nashville family, August 30, 1850, Harding P. Bostick Collection, THS, TSLA; Nashville *True Whig*, November 26, 1850.

3. The long tom had been used in the southern Appalachians as early as 1809. Caughey, *Gold Is the Cornerstone*, 164.

4. Ibid.

5. J. S. Holliday, *The World Rushed In: The California Gold Rush Experience* (New York: Simon and Schuster, 1981), 332–33.

6. Caughey, *Gold Is the Cornerstone*, 163; Rodman W. Paul, *California Gold, The Beginning of Mining in the Far West* (Cambridge: Harvard University Press, 1947), 147.

7. Caughey, *Gold Is the Cornerstone*, 251–55.

8. Quicksilver was the name then used for mercury, an element of great importance to quartz miners. *Encyclopedia Americana, International Edition*, vol. 18 (Danbury, Conn.: Grolier, 1992), 721–22.

9. Memphis *Daily Eagle*, September 26, 1849; Nashville *Daily Union*, October 1, 1849.

10. Franklin *Western Weekly Review*, August 31, 1849; Nashville *Republican Banner and True Whig*, May 16, 1850.

11. Nashville *Daily Union*, November 24, 1849.

12. Ibid., December 21, 1849.

13. Memphis *Daily Eagle*, January 16, 1850.

14. Dale L. Morgan, ed., *Overland in 1846, Diaries and Letters of the California-Oregon Trail*, vol. 1 (Georgetown, Calif.: Talisman Press, 1963), 150; see Appendix.

15. Mary C. Rushing and Lorane Rushing to Joseph L. Rushing, July 18, 1850, Joseph L. Rushing Papers, TSLA.

16. *Brownlow's* Knoxville *Whig and Independent Journal*, February 23, 1850.

17. Nashville *True Whig*, March 19, 1850.

18. Based on the increased cost of living between 1850 and 1995, the $200,000 represents about $3,554,000 in 1995 purchasing power.

19. Memphis *Daily Eagle*, March 22, 1850.

20. Tyree B. Harris to Green B. Harris, October 13, 1850, Brown and Harris Papers, originals in private collection, Birmingham, Alabama, typescripts, Sumner County Archives, Gallatin.

21. Nashville *True Whig*, May 25, 1850.

22. Nashville *Daily American*, June 28, 1850.

23. Joseph L. Rushing to Lorane Rushing, July 22, 1850, Joseph L. Rushing Papers.

24. Clarksville *Jeffersonian*, July 2, 1850.

25. Athens *Post*, July 5, 1850.

26. Nashville *Daily Gazette*, July 19, 1850.

27. Peter Randolph to John Edmondson, January 7, 1851, Edmondson Family Papers, TSLA.

28. *Republican Banner and* Nashville *Whig*, August 19, 1850.

29. Nashville *True Whig*, August 27, 1850.

30. Nashville *Daily American*, October 5, 1850; Nashville *True Whig*, November 12, 1850; Nashville *Daily Gazette*, November 6, 1850.

31. Nashville *True Whig*, November 16, 1850; Irene D. Paden, ed., *The Journal of Madison Berryman Moorman* (San Francisco: California Historical Society, 1948), 84–86, 88.

32. Nashville *Daily American*, February 19, 1851; *Republican Banner and* Nashville *Whig*, January 3, February 19, 1851.

33. *Republican Banner and* Nashville *Whig*, November 18, 1850.

34. *Brownlow's* Knoxville *Whig and Independent Journal*, November 30, 1850.

35. Tyree B. Harris to Green B. Harris, October 13, 1850, Brown and Harris Papers.

36. Tyree B. Harris to Green B. Harris, March 18, 1851, Brown and Harris Papers.

37. W. Wilberforce A. Ramsey to Maj. William Swan, August 4, 1850, Ramsey Papers, Special Collections, Hoskins Library, University of Tennessee, Knoxville.

38. John R. Boyles to Mrs. E. H. Boyles, March 17, 1850, Eliza H. (Ball) Gordon Boyles Papers 1823–81, Special Collections Department, William R. Perkins Library, Duke University.

39. Ibid.

40. Tyler D. Heiskell to Mrs. Eliza Brown Heiskell, June 15, 1850, Heiskell Family Manuscripts, TSLA; Paden, *The Journal of Madison Berryman Moorman*, 85.

41. Athens *Post*, March 7, 1851.

42. Tyree B. Harris to Green B. Harris, March 18, 1851, Brown and Harris Papers.

43. Nashville *Daily American*, September 21, 1850.

44. George Love Deposition, April 7, 1853, Loose Court Records, Sumner County Archives.

45. Ibid.; Simon Elliott Deposition, March 23, 1854; William Gregory Deposition, February 25, 1856, LCR/SCA.

46. George Love Deposition, April 7, 1853, LCR/SCA.

47. Memphis *Daily Eagle*, November 21, 1849.

48. *Republican Banner and* Nashville *Whig*, January 25, 1850.

49. James O. Harris to John Branham, December 15, 1850, Brown and Harris Papers.

50. Warren County *News*, August 5, 1980.

51. Knoxville *Register*, February 2, 1850.

52. *Republican Banner and* Nashville *Whig*, February 21, 1850.

53. *Brownlow's* Knoxville *Whig and Independent Journal*, November 16, 1850.

54. Franklin *Western Weekly Review*, March 8, 1850.

55. Memphis *Daily Eagle*, March 12, 1850.

56. Nashville *Daily Union*, March 26, 1850; James O. Harris and H. B. Day to Mrs. M. G. Harris, January 27, 1851, Brown and Harris Papers.

57. *Brownlow's* Knoxville *Whig and Independent Journal*, April 6, 1850.

58. John R. Boyles to Mrs. E. H. Boyles, May 15, July 13, August 24, 1850, Eliza H. (Ball) Gordon Boyles Papers.

59. Joseph L. Rushing to his brother, March 11, 1850, Joseph L. Rushing Papers.

60. Nashville *Daily Gazette*, March 27, 1850.

61. Clarksville *Jeffersonian*, April 30, 1850.

62. Nashville *Daily Union*, July 26, 1850.

63. James O. Harris to J. B. Harris, December 7, 1850, Brown and Harris Papers; Nashville *Daily Gazette*, July 19, 1850.

64. Nashville *Daily Union*, October 21, 1850.

65. Nashville *Daily Gazette*, November 1, 1850.

66. Nashville *Daily American*, November 6, 1850.

67. Memphis *Daily Eagle*, August 6, 1850.

68. *Brownlow's* Knoxville *Whig and Independent Journal*, August 24, 1850.

69. J. Litton Bostick to his father, August 8, 1850, Harding P. Bostick Collection.

70. Nashville *Daily Evening Reporter*, October 12, 1850.

71. William Gregory Deposition, February 25, 1856, LCR/SCA.

72. James O. Harris to Green B. Harris, January 19, 1851, Brown and Harris Papers.

73. Mrs. G. W. Jones and Mrs. T. B. McAmis, *Life of A. G. Register, by His Daughters* (Nashville, Tenn.: Cumberland Presbyterian Publishing House, 1890), 51.

74. Clarksville *Jeffersonian*, November 20, 1850.

75. Charles Howard Shinn, *Mining Camps, A Study in American Frontier Government* (New York: Knopf, 1948), 104–5.

76. Ibid., 105, 144.

77. He refers to Congressman G. W. Wright.

78. Nashville *True Whig*, November 26, 1850.

79. Nashville and Louisville *Christian Advocate*, December 6, 1850.

80. Franklin *Western Weekly Review*, February 7, 1851; Chattanooga *Advocate* copied in Nashville *Daily Union*, February 18, 1851.

81. William T. Rickman Deposition, undated, LCR/SCA.

82. Lucious Lucullus Battle, "The Annals of Lucious Lucullus Battle, M.D., 1849–1851," typescript of memoir in the Memphis Room Collection of the Memphis and Shelby County Library, 90, 102, 115, 149.

83. Nashville *Daily Gazette*, May 5, 1850.

84. Ibid., September 2, October 3, 1851.

85. *Alta California*, August 1, October 5, 1851.

86. Nashville *Daily American*, October 14, 1851.

87. Nashville *Daily Gazette*, November 15, December 21, 1851; Nashville *Daily American*, December 24, 1851.

88. *Republican Banner and* Nashville *Whig*, February 20, 1852.

89. Memphis *Daily Appeal*, February 17, 1852.

90. Nashville *Daily True Whig*, March 11, 1852.

91. Nashville *Daily American*, January 2, 1851; Nashville *Daily True Whig*, March 24, 1852.

92. Nashville *Daily Gazette*, October 14, 1852.

93. *Republican Banner and* Nashville *Whig*, November 8, 1852.

94. Nashville *Daily Gazette*, December 12, 1852.

95. James O. Harris to Green B. Harris, April 13, 1851; James O. Harris to Mrs. Rachel Harris, October 4, 1851, Brown and Harris Papers.

96. James C. Cooper to Col. R. M. Cooper, September 15, 1851, Cooper Family Papers, TSLA.

97. Neal O'Steen, "UT's Gold Rush Adventurers: The Rosborough Brothers," *Tennessee Alumnus* (summer 1983): 28–31.

98. Nashville *Daily American*, July 28, 1852.

99. Nashville *Daily Union*, October 21, 1850.

100. Edward A. White Deposition, May 4, 1856, LCR/SCA; Nashville *Daily Gazette*, December 7, 1852.

101. Paul, *California Gold*, 136–37.

102. Caughey, *Gold Is the Cornerstone*, 256, 257.

103. Nashville *Daily Gazette*, December 12, 24, 1852.

104. Nashville and Louisville *Christian Advocate*, September 30, 1852.

105. October 22, 1852.

106. James O. Harris to Green B. and Mary G. Harris, November 17, 1851, Brown and Harris Papers.

107. Peter Randolph to John Edmondson, February 7, 1852, Edmondson Family Papers.

108. James O. Harris to Green B. Harris, March 14, May 5, 1852; Tyree B. Harris to Green B. Harris, November 17, 1851, Brown and Harris Papers.

109. Peter Randolph to John Edmondson, March 9, 1852, Edmondson Family Papers.

110. Burkholder to Long, July 27, 1850, John Long Papers, Special Collections, William R. Perkins Library, Duke University, Durham.

111. *Alta California*, January 15, 1851; St. Joseph *Gazette*, March 12, 1851.

112. Nashville *Daily Gazette*, March 6, 20, 1851.

113. *Brownlow's* Knoxville *Whig and Independent Journal*, August 10, 1850; Burkholder to Long, July 27, 1850, John Long Papers.

114. Robert Scott Wright to Mary H. Wright, March 11, 1852, Wright and Green Family Papers, Southern Historical Collection, University of North Carolina, Chapel Hill.

115. Robert Scott Wright to Mary H. Wright, April 12, September 9, 1853; April 18, 1855, Wright and Green Family Papers.

116. Bell to Scotia Calpurnia Hume, Russell Hanlon Collection, McClung Historical Collection, Knoxville Public Library.

117. Sacramento *Daily Democratic State Journal*, February 24, 1853.

118. Bell to Scotia Calpurnia Hume, March 8, 1851, Russell Hanlon Collection.

119. Peter Randolph to John Edmondson, March 9, 1852, Edmondson Family Papers.

120. Obituary notice for W. Wilberforce A. Ramsey, Ramsey Papers; Thomas J. Noel, "W. Wilberforce A. Ramsey, Esq., and the California Gold Rush," *Journal of the West* 12, no. 4 (Oct. 1973): 575.

121. Tyler D. Heiskell to F. S. Heiskell, December 22, 1849, Heiskell Family Manuscripts.

122. Memphis *Daily Appeal*, September 30, 1851.

CHAPTER 12

1. Nashville *True Whig*, April 20, 1850.

2. Ibid., April 2, 1850; Memphis *Daily Eagle*, April 8, 1850; Christopher Losson, *Tennessee's Forgotten Warriors: Frank Cheatham and His Confederate Division* (Knoxville: University of Tennessee Press, 1989), 20.

3. Nashville and Louisville *Christian Advocate*, November 29, 1850.

4. *Brownlow's* Knoxville *Whig and Independent Journal*, December 21, 1850.

5. Nashville *Daily Gazette*, September 2, 1849.

6. Memphis *Daily Enquirer*, November 20, 1849.

7. *Historic Maury* 13, no. 1, (Jan.–Mar. 1977): 2–7.

8. New Helvetia was the name John Sutter had given to his fort and surrounding community. The sale of town lots that adjoined the fort created Sacramento City in 1849. Julian Dana, *Sutter of California* (New York: Press of the Pioneers, 1934), 332–33.

9. Hubert Howe Bancroft, *California Pioneer Register and Index, 1542–1848* (extracted and reprinted from author's *History of California*, 7 vols., 1884–90; Baltimore: Regional Publishing Co., 1964), 148; E. Gould Buffum, "Six Months in the Gold Mines," in *From Mexican Days to the Gold Rush*, book 2, ed. Doyce B. Nunis (Chicago: R. R. Donnelley and Sons, 1993), 235.

10. John C. Hubbard Deposition, February 25, 1856, Loose Court Records, Sumner County Archives.

11. Lycurgus Charlton Deposition, February 10, 1856, LCR/SCA.

12. Richard Charlton Deposition, December 17, 1855, LCR/SCA.

13. Sacramento *Placer Times*, August 18, 1849; Berryman Bryant, M.D., "Reminiscences of California, 1849–1852," *California Historical Society Quarterly* 11, no. 1 (Mar. 1932): 35n.

14. Robert Scott Wright to Mrs. Mary H. Wright, December 14, 1852, Wright and Green Family Papers, Southern Historical Collection, University of North Carolina, Chapel Hill.

15. *Alta California*, September 27, 1849; June 6, 1850.

16. Ibid., January 29, 1850; *Weakley Remembered*, vol. 4, 43.

17. James Kimmins Greer, *Colonel Jack Hays, Texas Frontier Leader and California Builder* (New York: E. P. Dutton, 1952), 339–42.

18. "To California Through Texas and Mexico, The Diary and Letters of Thomas B. Eastland and Joseph G. Eastland, His Son," pt. 1, *California Historical Society Quarterly* 18, no. 2 (June 1939): 100.

19. Knoxville *Register*, April 24, 1850.

20. Nashville *Daily Union*, June 4, 1850.

21. *Republican Banner and* Nashville *Whig*, August 16, 1851.

22. Nashville *Daily Gazette*, March 22, 1851.

23. Nashville *Union*, November 18, 1852; Nashville *Daily Gazette*, April 27, 1853.

24. *Studies in Polk County History*, no. 1 (1965): 10.

25. Kenneth L. Holmes, ed. and comp., *Covered Wagon Women, Diaries and Letters from the Western Trails 1840–1890*, vol. 1 (Glendale, Calif.: Arthur Clark, 1983), 247–49.

26. Carlos D'Este, *Patton: A Genius for War* (New York: HarperCollins, 1995), 28; John Walton Caughey, ed., *The Indians of Southern California in 1852, The B. D. Wilson Report and a Selection of Contemporary Comment* (San Marino: Huntington Library, 1952), xi.

27. J. Litton Bostick to his mother, June 29, 1853, Harding P. Bostick Collection, THS, TSLA.

28. Will T. Hale and Dixon L. Merritt, *A History of Tennessee and Tennesseans*, vol. 3 (Chicago: Lewis Publishing Co., 1913), 2420–21; Lonsdale Porter MacFarland, "Dr. James Porter MacFarland," typescript in possession of Alfred Towson MacFarland; Wilson County, Tenn., Records, Wills and Inventories, Book D, 505–8.

29. Benjamin Butler Harris, *The Gila Trail, The Texas Argonauts and the California Gold Rush*, ed. Richard H. Dillon (Norman: University of Oklahoma Press, 1960), 7–8.

30. Nashville *Daily Gazette*, June 13, 1854.

31. Nashville *True Whig*, May 25, 1850.

32. *Brownlow's* Knoxville *Whig and Independent Journal*, September 7, 1850.

33. Jonesborough *Railroad Journal*, October 5, 1850.

34. Nashville *Daily Evening Reporter*, October 12, 1850.

35. *Brownlow's* Knoxville *Whig and Independent Journal*, August 24, December 21, 1850.

36. "To California Through Texas and Mexico," pt. 1, 100.

37. *Alta California*, December 10, 1849.

38. Barbara Donohoe Jostes, *John Parrott, Consul, 1811–1884, Selected Papers of a Western Pioneer* (San Francisco: n.p., 1972), 128; Nashville *True Whig*, February 16, 1853.

39. Jourdan G. Myers, *A History of the Parrott, Lee, Hix, and Wilmore Families* (Deer Park, Calif.: Kinko Copy Co., 1986), 511.

40. Milton H. Shutes, "Henry Douglas Bacon, 1813–1893," *California Historical Society Quarterly* 26, no. 3 (Sept. 1947): 196; Andrew F. Rolle, "William Heath Davis and the Founding of American San Diego," *California Historical Society Quarterly* 31, no. 1 (Mar. 1952): 46 n; Jostes, *John Parrott*, 112, 146.

41. Memphis *Daily Eagle*, March 3, 1852.

42. Memphis *Eagle and Enquirer*, February 20, 1853.

43. *A History of Tuolumne County, California* (San Francisco: B. F. Alley, 1882), 348–49.

44. Joann Levy, *They Saw the Elephant: Women in the California Gold Rush* (Hamden, Conn.: Archer Books, 1990), 101.

45. Nashville *Daily Gazette*, March 19, June 13, September 29, 1854.

46. John Jefferson Franklin to John Rueben Franklin, May 11, 1854, private collection of Kenneth C. Thomson.

47. C. H. Wallace Deposition, April 9, 1853, LCR/SCA.

48. Nashville *True Whig*, April 23, 1850.

49. *Republican Banner and* Nashville *Whig*, January 4, 1851.

50. Frank Soule, John H. Gihon, and James Nisbet, *The Annals of San Francisco* (New York: D. Appleton and Co., 1854), 370–77.

51. Jostes, *John Parrott*, 102, 105–8; Nashville *Daily True Whig*, February 26, 1853; Sacramento *Daily Democratic State Journal*, October 27, 1854.

52. Nashville *Daily Gazette*, August 7, November 7, 1852.

53. Sacramento *Daily Democratic State Journal*, November 12, 1852.

54. Nashville *Daily Gazette*, August 27, 1854.

55. Barbara Ann Metcalf, "Oliver M. Wozencraft in California, 1849–1887" (Master's thesis, University of Southern California, 1963), 75–76, 81–95.

56. James O. Harris to Green B. Harris, June 30, August 10, 1856, Brown and Harris Papers, originals in private collection, Birmingham, Alabama, typescripts, Sumner County Archives, Gallatin.

57. Edward Kemble, *A History of California Newspapers, 1846–1858* (Los Gatos: Talisman Press, 1962), 101, 111, 153, 171–72; Nashville *Daily True Whig*, July 15, 1854.

58. Kemble, *A History of California Newspapers*, 96, 98, 107, 112, 116, 150, 165, 172, 177, 233.

59. *Alta California*, September 9, 11, 1851.

60. San Francisco *Daily Evening Picayune*, January 12, March 12, 1852; Memphis *Daily Eagle*, February 29, 1852.

61. Memphis *Eagle and Enquirer*, March 15, 1853.

62. Kemble, *A History of California Newspapers*, 188.

63. Columbia, Calif.: *Clipper* office, 1856.

64. Kemble, *A History of California Newspapers*, 170, 191.

65. Sacramento *Daily Democratic State Journal*, February 20, 1854.

66. Kemble, *A History of California Newspapers*, 20, 22–23, 70–71, 74, 76–77.

67. Ibid., 177.

68. Nashville *True Whig*, May 27, June 3, 1851.

69. *A History of Tuolumne County, California*, 418–19.

70. Ibid., 371–72.

71. Joseph Henry Jackson, *Anybody's Gold, The Story of California's Mining Towns* (New York: D. Appleton-Century Co., 1941), 128–29.

72. Nashville *Daily Gazette*, September 14, 16, 1851.

73. Jackson, *Anybody's Gold*, 129.

74. Ibid., 132.   75. Ibid., 132–34.

76. Ibid., 135–39.   77. Ibid., 139–40.

78. Eugene H. Berwanger, *The Frontier Against Slavery, Western Anti-Negro Prejudice and the Slavery Extension Controversy* (Urbana: University of Illinois Press, 1967), 72–73.

79. Nashville *True Whig*, September 18, 1849.

80. Memphis *Daily Eagle*, January 16, 1850.

81. April 8, 1850.

82. Nashville and Louisville *Christian Advocate*, September 30, 1852.

83. Ibid.

84. Memphis *Daily Eagle*, April 8, 1850.

85. Athens *Post*, June 28, 1850.

86. Memphis *Daily Eagle*, August 6, 1850.

87. Nashville *Daily American*, April 25, 1850.   88. Ibid., April 9, 1850.

89. Delilah L. Beasley, *The Negro Trail Blazers of California* (1919; reprint, New York: Negro Universities Press, 1969), 124, 136.

90. Ray R. Albin, "The Perkins Case: The Ordeal of Three Slaves in Gold Rush California," *California History* (The Magazine of the California Historical Society) 67, no. 4 (Dec. 1988): 216–18, 226.

91. Beasley, *The Negro Trail Blazers of California*, 71.

92. Edna Bryan Buckbee, *The Saga of Old Tuolumne* (New York: Press of the Pioneers, 1935), 308–10; W. Sherman Savage, "The Negro on the Mining Frontier," *Journal of Negro History* 30, no. 1 (Jan. 1945): 32–33, 33n.

93. Memphis *Daily Eagle*, August 6, 13, 1850.

94. *Republican Banner and* Nashville *Whig*, May 23, 1855.

95. Nashville *Daily True Whig*, December 14, 1852; Shearon to Gov. W. B. Campbell, January 25, 1853, David Campbell Papers, microfilm, TSLA.

96. Shearon to Gov. W. B. Campbell, January 25, 1853, David Campbell Papers.

97. Ibid.

98. Sacramento *Daily Democratic State Journal*, June 29, 1853; Nashville *Daily Gazette*, August 19, 1853.

99. Nashville *Daily Gazette*, August 19, 1853.

100. *Republican Banner and* Nashville *Whig*, October 4, 1853.

101. Memphis *Daily Eagle*, April 22, 1851.   102. Ibid.

103. David Barry to Priscilla Barry, July 13, 1850; Richard B. Alexander to Priscilla Barry, Mary Brown, and Thomas Barry, July 29, 1850, David Barry Papers, private collection.

104. Mrs. Rebecca Malone Harsh to the author, February 1, 1971.

105. William E. Hill, *Reading, Writing, and Riding Along the Oregon-California Trails* (Independence, Mo.: Oregon-California Trails Association, 1993), 34.

CHAPTER 13

1. *Alta California*, December 29, 1849.   2. Ibid.

3. Ibid.

4. Eugene H. Berwanger, *The Frontier Against Slavery, Western Anti-Negro Prejudice and the Slavery Extension Controversy* (Urbana: University of Illinois Press, 1967), 70–71.

5. *Alta California*, December 29, 1849.   6. Ibid.

7. Ibid.   8. Ibid.

9. Ibid., August 28, 1850.   10. Ibid.

11. St. Joseph *Gazette*, March 12, 1851.

12. Ibid.   13. Ibid.

14. Albert L. Hurtado, *Indian Survival on the California Frontier* (New Haven: Yale University Press, 1988), 135. The governor's prediction was nearly fulfilled as the Indian population declined from approximately 153,000 in 1848 to about 25,000 or 30,000 in 1860. Sherburne Friend Cook, *The Population of the California Indians 1769–1970* (Berkeley and Los Angeles: University of California Press, 1976), 199.

15. March 12, 1851.   16. January 11, 1851.

17. Ibid.

18. Julian Dana, *Sutter of California* (New York: Press of the Pioneers, 1934), 369.

19. The name was frequently used to describe the alcohol-consuming first general assembly. John Walton Caughey, *Gold Is the Cornerstone* (Berkeley and Los Angeles: University of California Press, 1948), 241.

20. New York *Express* quoted in the Memphis *Daily Eagle*, December 6, 1850.

21. *Alta California*, January 12, 1851.

22. William E. Franklin, "A Forgotten Chapter in California History: Peter H. Burnett and John A. Sutter's Fortune," *California Historical Society Quarterly* 41, no. 4 (Dec. 1962): 323.

23. Nicholas Perkins Hardeman, *Wilderness Calling: The Hardeman Family in the American Westward Movement, 1750–1900* (Knoxville: University of Tennessee Press, 1977), 213; Sacramento *Daily Democratic State Journal*, April 6, 1853.

24. William E. Franklin, "The Religious Ardor of Peter H. Burnett, California's First American Governor," *California Historical Society Quarterly* 45, no. 2 (June 1966): 125–26, 129.

25. William Henry Ellison, *A Self-Governing Dominion, California, 1849–1860* (Berkeley and Los Angeles: University of California Press, 1950), 271.

26. William Henry Ellison, ed., "Memoirs of Hon. William M. Gwin," *California Historical Society Quarterly* 19, no. 1 (1940): 157, 164–65.

27. Ibid., 166–68.   28. Ibid., 169–71, 179.

29. Ibid., 172–74, 181, 262.

30. Los Angeles *Star*, October 30, 1852.

31. James O'Meara, *Broderick and Gwin* (San Francisco: Bacon and Co., 1881), 40.

32. Ellison, "Memoirs of Hon. William M. Gwin," 178; Sacramento *Daily Democratic State Journal*, January 5, 1854.

33. A Tammany Hall-trained New York politician, Broderick had come to California in 1849 like Gwin, full of ambition for a seat in the United States Senate. Although he lacked formal education, he had made "considerable intellectual progress by developing the habit of systematic reading." His personal discipline included total abstinence from drinking alcoholic beverages, smoking, and gambling, but did not include control of his temper.

He became a member of the California state senate in 1850 and became that body's presiding officer in 1851. Soon convinced that the principal obstacle to his election to the United States Senate was Senator Gwin, he organized a faction of the Democratic party to unseat Gwin and elevate himself to the Senate. Ellison, *A Self-Governing Dominion*, 278–82.

34. O'Meara, *Broderick and Gwin*, 46, 59, 61, 73, 89, 102.

35. Lately Thomas, *Between Two Empires, the Life Story of California's First Senator William McKendree Gwin* (Boston: Houghton Mifflin, 1969), 93–94.

36. Leroy P. Graf and Ralph W. Haskins, eds., *The Papers of Andrew Johnson*, vol. 2, 1852–57 (Knoxville: University of Tennessee Press), 159n.

37. October 28, 1854.

38. O'Meara, *Broderick and Gwin*, 43, 194.

39. Ibid., 41, 43, 47–48, 51, 90, 94, 98, 194.

40. Ellison, *A Self-Governing Dominion*, 290.

41. Ibid., 292–94.

42. Ibid., 296–97.

43. Ibid., 303–306.

44. Ibid., 307–9.

45. Brent, a prominent Los Angeles Democrat, was a longtime friend of Senator Gwin. Active in the Gwin faction of the California Democratic party, Benham had been United States attorney for the district of California. Thomas, *Between Two Empires*, 186, 266.

46. Ibid., 266–68.

47. Ibid., 276–79.

48. Ibid., 293–97.

49. Ibid., 302–303.

50. Ibid., 305–6, 313–14, 326.

51. Ibid., 335–36.

52. Ibid., 337–38, 341, 344–45, 349–50.

53. Ibid., 350–52, 353–54, 366.

54. Ibid., 367–69.

55. O. Henry Mace, *Between the Rivers, A History of Early Calaveras County, California*, 2d ed. (Jackson, Calif.: Cenotto Publications, 1993), 139–40; Thomas, *Between Two Empires*, 374.

56. Thomas, *Between Two Empires*, 371, 376, 378–79.

57. Albert Z. Carr, *The World and William Walker* (New York: Harper and Row, 1963), 3, 11, 12, 14, 36, 41; Laurence Greene, *The Filibuster, The Career of William Walker* (Indianapolis: Bobbs-Merrill, 1937), 23–25.

58. Carr, *The World and William Walker*, 56; Alejandro Bolanos-Geyer, *William Walker, The Gray-Eyed Man of Destiny*, vol. 2 (Lake St. Louis, Mo.: n.p., 1989), 52, 56.

59. Carr, *The World and William Walker*, 28, 58, 59.

60. Ibid., 60; *Alta California*, March 9, 1851.

61. The Nashville *Daily True Whig* joined in the uproar. Copying an account by the Cincinnati *Commercial*'s California correspondent, the *True Whig* introduced it by noting, "Our former fellow citizen Wm. Walker, Esq. . . . has been unjustly and shamefully punished for his fearless and patriotic vindication of the freedom of speech and his condemnation of the flagrant assumptions and assertions of a reckless Judge of the District Court." April 30, 1851.

62. *Alta California*, March 10, 1851.

63. Carr, *The World and William Walker*, 60.

64. Nashville *Daily Gazette*, March 6, 1851; Carr, *The World and William Walker*, 64.

65. Bolanos-Geyer, *William Walker*, 86–87, 90.

66. Carr, *The World and William Walker*, 73.   67. Greene, *The Filibuster*, 28–29.

68. Nashville *Daily Gazette*, November 6, 1853.   69. Greene, *The Filibuster*, 34.

70. Carr, *The World and William Walker*, 79.

71. Greene, *The Filibuster*, 31–34; Nashville *Daily Gazette*, December 20, 1853. When Walker created a body of law by proclaiming the civil code of Louisiana to be in effect, many believed that he was bringing slavery in the back door. Nashville *Union and American*, February 4, 1854.

72. January 30, 1854; Greene, *The Filibuster*, 37–38.

73. Santiago may have been one of those who returned with Walker—if he ever left—because he was corresponding with the Nashville *Union and American* from Sacramento in time to be printed in their issue of September 30, 1854.

74. Greene, *The Filibuster*, 46–47; Bolanos-Geyer, *William Walker*, 294; Carr, *The World and William Walker*, 89, 96.

75. Carr, *The World and William Walker*, 93, 98.

76. Bolanos-Geyer, *William Walker*, 312, 327, 329, 341.

77. Carr, *The World and William Walker*, 98; William Walker, *The War in Nicaragua* (Mobile: S. H. Goetzel and Co., 1860), 24, 26–27.

78. *Republican Banner and* Nashville *Whig*, August 1, 1856.

79. Samuel Cole Williams, ed., "Journal of Events (1825–1873) of David Anderson Deaderick," ETHS *Publications*, no. 9 (1937): 94, 96.

80. *Republican Banner and* Nashville *Whig*, November 7, 10, 17, 1855.

81. Ibid., November 10, 17, 1855.   82. Ibid., December 5, 1855.

83. Quoted in the *Republican Banner and* Nashville *Whig*, November 17, 1855.

84. *Republican Banner and* Nashville *Whig*, December 5, 1855.

85. New York press quoted in *Republican Banner and* Nashville *Whig*, December 5, 1855.

86. *Republican Banner and* Nashville *Whig*, December 16, 1855; January 6, 1856.

87. William Walker Letters, 1845–1855, THS, TSLA.

88. Carr, *The World and William Walker*, 189, 190–95, 204–205, 216, 219.

89. "Walker-Heiss Papers, Some Diplomatic Correspondence of the Walker Regime in Nicaragua," *Tennessee Historical Magazine* 1, no. 4 (Dec. 1915): 331–32.

90. Carr, *The World and William Walker*, 225–29; New York *Herald*, July 14, 1857.

91. Carr, *The World and William Walker*, 230–31, 236, 241.

92. Ibid., 242, 252–53, 255–57, 261–62, 264.

93. Ibid., 266–70.   94. Ibid., 271, 274.

95. Rufus Kay Wyllys, "Henry A. Crabb—A Tragedy of the Sonora Frontier," *Pacific Historical Review* 9, no. 1, (Mar. 1940): 183–87, 190–91.

CHAPTER 14

1. John Walton Caughey, *Gold Is the Cornerstone* (Berkeley and Los Angeles: University of California Press, 1948), 2; J. S. Holliday, *The World Rushed In: The California Gold Rush Experience* (New York: Simon and Schuster, 1981), 27–29.

2. John Bernard McGloin, *California's First Archbishop, The Life of Joseph Sadoc Alemany, 1814–1888* (New York: Herder and Herder, 1966), 109; V. F. O'Daniel, *The Father of the Church in Tennessee, or the Life, Times, and Character of the Right Reverend Richard Pius Miles, the First Bishop of Nashville* (Washington, D.C.: Dominicana, 1926), 440.

3. McGloin, *California's First Archbishop*, 54–56.

4. Ibid., 26, 32–38, 45–46, 49; O'Daniel, *The Father of the Church in Tennessee*, 379.

5. McGloin, *California's First Archbishop*, 15; Caughey, *Gold Is the Cornerstone*, 277; O'Daniel, *The Father of the Church in Tennessee*, 441 n; Reginald M. Coffey, *The American Dominicans, A History of Saint Joseph's Province* (New York: Saint Martin De Porres Guild, 1970), 248.

6. Nashville *Daily Gazette*, March 27, 1850.

7. Knoxville *Register*, April 10, 1850.

8. *Tennessee Baptist*, May 4, 11, 1850.

9. The *Gazette, Daily American*, and *Republican Banner and* Nashville *Whig* quoted in the *Tennessee Baptist*, May 4, 1850.

10. May 11, 1850.   11. August 8, 1851.

12. *Tennessee Baptist*, November 8, 1851; Walter T. Durham, *Old Sumner, A History of Sumner County, Tennessee, From 1805 to 1861* (Gallatin: Sumner County Library Board, 1972), 466.

13. November 8, 1851.

14. *Tennessee Baptist*, April 17, 1852.   15. Ibid., May 1, 1852.

16. Ibid., July 10, 24, 1852.   17. Ibid., July 24, 1852.

18. Ibid., September 30, 1854; Yuan Chung Teng, "Reverend Issachar Jacox Roberts and the Tai Ping Rebellion," *Journal of Asian Studies* 23, no. 1 (Nov. 1963): 56, 58–61, 63–64.

19. J. C. Simmons, *The History of Southern Methodism on the Pacific Coast* (Nashville, Tenn.: Southern Methodist Publishing House, 1886), 14; Nashville *Christian Advocate*, June 21, 1850.

20. Nashville *Christian Advocate*, June 21, 1850.

21. Nashville and Louisville *Christian Advocate*, December 18, 1851; *Brownlow's* Knoxville *Whig and Independent Journal*, January 4, 1851; Athens *Post*, July 12, 1850.

22. John Carr, *Pioneer Days in California, Historical and Personal Sketches* (Eureka: Times Publishing Co., 1891), 447.

23. *Brownlow's* Knoxville *Whig and Independent Journal*, August 24, 1850.

24. Ibid., August 24, 1850.

25. Louisville and Nashville *Christian Advocate*, November 6, December 25, 1851.

26. December 24, 1852.

27. *Christian Advocate* was the name customarily used for Methodist newspapers published by a single conference or a combination of conferences.

28. Simmons, *The History of Southern Methodism on the Pacific Coast*, 48.

29. *Brownlow's* Knoxville *Whig and Independent Journal*, February 28, 1852.

30. Simmons, *The History of Southern Methodism on the Pacific Coast*, 75.

31. Louisville and Nashville *Christian Advocate*, March 25, July 1, October 14, 1852.

32. The *Advocate* was published jointly by the Tennessee and Louisville Conferences of the Methodist Episcopal Church South.

33. Nashville and Louisville *Christian Advocate*, January 13, 1853.

34. *Republican Banner and* Nashville *Whig*, April 15, 1852.

35. Sacramento *Daily Democratic State Journal*, April 7, 1853; Nashville and Louisville *Christian Advocate*, May 5, 1853.

36. Nashville and Louisville *Christian Advocate*, March 17, 1853; Simmons, *The History of Southern Methodism on the Pacific Coast*, 27.

37. April 7, 1853.

38. *Brownlow's* Knoxville *Whig and Independent Journal*, June 26, 1852.

39. Simmons, *The History of Southern Methodism on the Pacific Coast*, 55.

40. Nashville and Louisville *Christian Advocate*, April 15, 1852.

41. Nashville *Daily True Whig*, December 28, 1852.

42. Simmons, *The History of Southern Methodism on the Pacific Coast*, 124, 130, 212–13.

43. Ibid., 111.   44. Nashville *Daily Gazette*, May 12, 1853.

45. Nashville and Louisville *Christian Advocate*, May 12, May 25, June 2, July 21, 1853; Nashville *Daily True Whig*, May 25, 1853; Nashville *Union and American*, June 23, July 22, 1853; Sacramento *Daily Democratic State Journal*, July 9, 1853.

46. Nashville *Daily True Whig*, August 22, 1853; Nashville *Daily Gazette*, August 24, 1853.

47. Nashville and Louisville *Christian Advocate*, December 22, 1853; January 5, 19, April 6, 1854.

48. Ibid., April 20, 1854; Nashville *Daily True Whig*, May 29, 1854.

49. Nashville and Louisville *Christian Advocate*, June 5, 1851.

50. *California Blue Book, 1891*, comp. E. G. Waite, secretary of state (Sacramento: State Printing Office, 1891), 249; O. P. Fitzgerald, *California Sketches* (Nashville, Tenn: Southern Methodist Publishing House, 1879), 1–8; *A History of Tuolumne County, California* (San Francisco: B. F. Alley, 1882), 397.

51. Lebanon *Banner of Peace and Cumberland Presbyterian Advocate*, March 23, 1849.

52. Ibid., May 31, 1950.

53. Edward Arthur Wicher, *The Presbyterian Church in California, 1849–1927* (New York: Grafton Press, 1927), 350.

54. Lebanon *Banner of Peace and Cumberland Presbyterian Advocate*, February 7, 1851.

55. Ibid., May 23, 1851.   56. Ibid., June 6, 1851.

57. Ibid., December 12, 1851; July 30, 1852; January 21, 1853.

58. Mrs. G. W. Jones and Mrs. T. B. McAmis, *Life of Rev. A. G. Register, by His Daughters* (Nashville, Tenn.: Cumberland Presbyterian Publishing House, 1890), 34, 40, 45.

59. Ibid., 44.   60. Ibid., 40–62.

61. Wicher, *The Presbyterian Church in California*, 64, 68, 85.

62. Ibid., 89–90.

63. Clifford Merrill Drury, *William Anderson Scott, "No Ordinary Man"* (Glendale, Calif.: Arthur H. Clark, 1967), 15, 19, 24, 26, 31–32, 34, 42, 46–47.

64. Ibid., 52, 54–55, 60, 62–63.   65. Ibid., 72–74, 81–82.

66. Wicher, *The Presbyterian Church in California*, 93.   67. Ibid., 93–94, 107–109.

68. *Brownlow's* Knoxville *Whig and Independent Journal*, July 5, 1851.

69. Ibid., July 5, 1851.   70. Ibid., January 19, 1850.

71. Nashville *Daily Gazette*, August 15, 1851.

72. Nashville *Daily American*, November 7, 1852.

73. Lebanon *Banner of Peace and Cumberland Presbyterian Advocate*, December 20, 1850.

74. Irene D. Paden, ed., *The Journal of Madison Berryman Moorman, 1850–1851* (San Francisco: California Historical Society, 1948), 81–82.

75. Nashville *Daily Gazette*, September 9, 1853.

CHAPTER 15

1. *Republican Banner and* Nashville *Whig*, January 6, 1851.

2. Nashville *Daily Gazette*, July 23, 1853; Nashville *Union and American*, July 22, 1853.

3. Berryman Bryant, M.D., "Reminiscences of California, 1849–1852," *California Historical Society Quarterly* 11, no. 1 (Mar. 1932): 37, 39.

4. Preamble and Resolution, Wilson, Love and Company, November 4, 1851, Loose Court Records, Sumner County Archives.

5. B. M. Jenkins et al. vs. Wm. Patterson et al., LCR/SCA.

6. Ibid.

7. James O. Harris to James M. Bryson, September 1, 1851, Brown and Harris Papers, originals in private collection, Birmingham, Alabama, typescripts, Sumner County Archives, Gallatin.

8. George Love Deposition, April 7, 1853, LCR/SCA.

9. Richard Charlton Deposition, December 17, 1855; Lycurgus Charlton Deposition, February 10, 1856, LCR/SCA.

10. William Tyree Deposition, July 16, 1853, LCR/SCA.

11. George D. Blackmore Deposition, February 17, 1853, LCR/SCA.

12. C. H. Wallace Deposition, April 9, 1853, LCR/SCA.

13. Simon Elliott Deposition, March 23, 1854, LCR/SCA.

14. Edward A. White Deposition, March 4, 1856, LCR/SCA.

15. William Gregory Deposition, February 25, 1856, LCR/SCA.

16. Tyree B. Harris Deposition, February 25, 1856, LCR/SCA.

17. G. C. Crenshaw Deposition, September 4, 1855, LCR/SCA.

18. John B. Walton Deposition, February 25, 1856, LCR/SCA.

19. John C. Hubbard Deposition, February 25, 1856, LCR/SCA.

20. Court Order, March 9, 1857, Chancellor B. L. Ridley, LCR/SCA.

APPENDIX

1. Charles Howard Shinn, *Mining Camps, A Study in American Frontier Government* (New York: Knopf, 1948), 125.

2. Much of what is known is recorded in the work of Hubert Howe Bancroft who identifies the pioneers by state where born without mentioning their specific place of birth and/or residence within the state they left. Hubert Howe Bancroft, *California Pioneer Register and Index, 1542–1848* (extracted and reprinted from author's *History of California*, 7 vols., 1884–90; Baltimore: Regional Publishing Co., 1964).

3. LeRoy R. Hafen, ed., *Trappers of the Far West* (Reprinted from *Mountain Men and Fur Trade of the Far West*, 10 vols., Glendale, Calif.: A. H. Clark, 1965–72; Lincoln: University of Nebraska Press, 1983), 51–52.

4. Ibid., 52–58.   5. Ibid., 58–59.

6. His mother was so discouraged by his long absence from Tennessee that when she made her will in 1834, she bequeathed him only "one dollar, if he ever returns." Will of Rebecca Irwin, Washington County, Tennessee, February 20, 1834, Thomas White Collection, Reba Bayless Boyer, comp. and ed., *Monroe County, Tennessee, Records, 1820–1870*, vol. 2, (Athens, Tenn: n.p., 1970), 155.

7. Hafen, *Trappers of the Far West*, 60–63.   8. Ibid., 64, 67, 69, 72.

9. Bancroft, *Pioneers*, 78.

10. On leave from the United States Army to explore the Far West for his own purposes, Bonneville was eager to experiment as a trapper and trader while gathering "statistical information for the War Department concerning the wild countries and wild tribes he might visit in the course of his journeyings." His expenses were underwritten by an association of eastern investors interested in the fur trade. Washington Irving, *The Adventures of Captain Bonneville, U.S.A. in the Rocky Mountains and the Far West* (New York: Thomas Y. Crowell and Co., 1843), 3–5, 291–92.

11. Leroy R. Hafen, ed., *Mountain Men and Fur Traders of the Far West* (Reprinted from *Mountain Men and Fur Trade of the Far West*, 10 vols., Glendale, Calif.: A. H. Clark, 1965–72; Lincoln: University of Nebraska Press, 1982), 291–94, 298.

12. Ibid.; Irving, *The Adventures of Captain Bonneville*, 130–31, 223, 226, 233.

13. Hafen, *Mountain Men and Fur Traders*, 298–99, 309.

14. As an explorer, Fremont (1813–90) had ranged widely throughout the West during the 1840s. His explorations had introduced him to the territory north of the Great Salt Lake and led him into the vast areas that would later become the states of California, Oregon, Washington, Nevada, Idaho, and New Mexico. Howard L. Hurwitz, *An Encyclopedic Dictionary of American History* (New York: Washington Square Press, 1970), 271–72.

15. Bancroft, *Pioneers*, 373–74; LeRoy R. Hafen and Ann W. Hafen, *Old Spanish Trail, Santa Fe to Los Angeles* (Glendale, Calif.: Arthur H. Clark, 1954), 232–33, 242–43, 245; Dale L. Morgan, ed., *Overland in 1846, Diaries and Letters of the California-Oregon Trail*, vol. 1, (Georgetown, Calif.: Talisman Press, 1963), 17; William Henry Ellison, ed., *The Life and Adventures of George Nidever* (Berkeley: University of California Press, 1937), 71.

16. Bancroft, *Pioneers*, 261; Ellison, *The Life and Adventures of George Nidever*, 1–18, 32–34; Virginia Thomson, "Note on George Nidever, a Clean–Living and Up-Right Trapper," *California Historical Society Quarterly* 32, no. 3 (Sept. 1953): 263–67.

17. "Bound for the Land of Canaan, Ho! The Diary of Levi Stowell, 1849," with introduction and notes by Marco G. Thorne, *California Historical Society Quarterly* 27, no. 2 (June 1948): 164 n; no. 3 (Sept. 1948): 260.

18. Bancroft, *Pioneers*, 54.

19. Mrs. G. W. Jones and Mrs. T. B. McAmis, *Life of Rev. A. G. Register, by His Daughters* (Nashville, Tenn.: Cumberland Presbyterian Publishing House, 1890), 51–52.

20. Bancroft, *Pioneers*, 251–52.

21. Hafen and Hafen, *Old Spanish Trail*, 218n.

22. Bancroft, *Pioneers*, 47.   23. Ibid., 67.

24. Ibid., 67.

25. William B. Ide was a New Englander and a promoter of this crossing. Hubert Howe Bancroft, *History of California, 1840–1845*, vol. 4 (1888; reprint, Santa Barbara: Wallace Hebberd, 1969), 578.

26. Bancroft, *Pioneers*, 170, 290, 390; Jonesborough *Herald and Tribune*, August 17, 1994.

27. Jonesborough *Herald and Tribune*, August 17, 1994; Bancroft, *Pioneers*, 390.

28. Jonesborough *Herald and Tribune*, August 17, 1994.

29. Bancroft, *Pioneers*, 240–41.   30. Ibid., 386.

31. Ibid., 276, 391.   32. Ibid., 203.

33. Ibid., 258.

34. The five were Marshall, Leander, Jonathan, Martha, and Rufus J. Young. The number would later reach nine. San Jose *Mercury News*, October 29, 1878; April 14, 1968.

35. San Jose *Pioneer*, November 9, 1878.

36. Ibid.; San Jose *Mercury News*, May 13, 1973.

37. In 1835 Nicholas Carriger had become a member of the First Tennessee Mounted Volunteers in the Seminole War. Returning home after twelve months of military duty, he worked with his father manufacturing iron and hardware, but in 1840, he migrated to Warren County, Missouri. During the next six years he lived at three different places in Missouri and at another in Mississippi. Morgan, *Overland in 1846*, 144.

38. Ibid., 143–45.   39. Ibid., 145.

40. Christian Carriger (1779–1846) had served nine terms in the Tennessee General Assembly, eight in the house of representatives and one term in the senate. A farmer, he had held the rank of lieutenant colonel commandant, Fifth Regiment, Carter County Militia. He

moved to Missouri in the early 1840s. Robert M. McBride and Dan M. Robison, *Biographical Directory of the Tennessee General Assembly, 1796–1861*, vol. 1 (Nashville: Tennessee State Library and Archives and the Tennessee Historical Commission, 1975), 124–25.

41. Morgan, *Overland in 1846*, 147, 150.   42. Bancroft, *Pioneers*, 243.

43. Virginia Reed Murphy, "Across the Plains in the Donner Party (1846)," *The Century Magazine* 42, (July 1891): 409–11; *Weakley Remembered*, vol. 4, 43–44.

44. Bancroft, *Pioneers*, 230; Mary Murphy Covillaud to "Uncles, Aunts and Cousins," May 25, 1847, from the "California Territory," Donner Party Letters, TSLA; W. W. Waggoner, "The Donner Party and Relief Hill," *California Historical Society Quarterly* 10, no. 4 (Dec. 1931): 348.

45. Mary Murphy Covillaud to "Uncles, Aunts, and Cousins," May 25, 1847, Donner Party Letters; Bancroft, *Pioneers*, 230; San Jose *Pioneer*, November 9, 1878.

46. Ibid.; *Weakley Remembered*, vol. 4, 44; Nashville *Whig*, September 4, 1847.

47. Nashville *Whig*, September 4, 1847.

48. Bancroft, *Pioneers*, 148; *Weakley Remembered*, vol. 4, 43.

49. William F. Drannan, *Thirty-One Years on the Plains and in the Mountains* (Chicago: Rhodes and McClure Publishing Co., 1908), 17–19, 27, 82, 96.

50. Henry F. Dobyns, ed., *Hepah, California! The Journal of Cave Johnson Couts, 1848–1849* (Tucson: Arizona Pioneers Historical Society, 1961), 1–3.

51. Bancroft, *Pioneers*, 373.   52. Ibid., 110, 373, 184.

53. Ibid., 158.

54. Frank T. Gilbert, *Illustrated Atlas and History of Yolo County, California* (San Francisco: De Pue and Co., 1879), 82–83; San Francisco *Chronicle*, June 1, 1927.

55. *Daily* Nashville *American*, February 8, 1853.

Bibliography

BOOKS

Alexander, Thomas B. *Thomas A. R. Nelson of East Tennessee*. Nashville: Tennessee Historical Commission, 1956.

Anderson, Ethel Nichols, comp. *Draper Families in America*. Nashville: Parthenon Press, 1964.

Bancroft, Hubert Howe. *California Pioneer Register and Index, 1542–1848*. Extracted and reprinted from author's *History of California*, 7 vols., 1884–90; Baltimore: Regional Publishing Co., 1964.

————. *History of California*. Vol. 4, 1840–45; Vol. 6, 1848–59. 1888. Reprint, Santa Barbara: Wallace Hebberd, 1969, 1970.

————. *History of Utah, 1540–1887*. San Francisco: History Co., 1890.

Barker, Charles Albro, ed. *Memoirs of Elisha Oscar Crosby*. San Marino, Calif: Huntington Library, 1945.

Beasley, Delilah L. *The Negro Trail Blazers of California*. 1919. Reprint, New York: Negro Universities Press, 1969.

Berwanger, Eugene H. *The Frontier Against Slavery, Western Anti-Negro Prejudice and the Slavery Extension Controversy*. Urbana: University of Illinois Press, 1967.

Billington, Ray A., ed. *The Gold Mines of California*. New York: Arno Press, 1973.

Biographical Directory of the United States Congress, 1774–1989. Bicentennial ed. Washington, D.C.: U.S. Government Printing Office, 1989.

Blum, John M., Bruce Catton, Edmund S. Morgan, Arthur M. Schlesinger, Jr., Kenneth M. Stampp, and C. Vann Woodward. *The National Experience, A History of the United States to 1877*. Part 1, 2d ed. New York: Harcourt, Brace and World, 1968.

Bolanos-Geyer, Alejandro. *William Walker, the Gray-Eyed Man of Destiny*. Vol. 2. Lake St. Louis, Mo.: n.p., 1989.

Boyer, Reba Bayless, comp. and ed. *Monroe County, Tennessee, Records, 1820–1870*. Vol. 2. Athens, Tenn.: n.p., 1970.

Brown, Richard Maxwell. *Strain of Violence, Historical Studies of American Violence and Vigilantism*. Oxford: Oxford University Press, 1975.

Browne, John Ross. *Report of the Debates in the Convention of California on the Formation of the State Constitution in September and October, 1849*. Washington, D.C.: John T. Towers, 1850.

Bruff, J. Goldsborough. *Gold Rush. The Journals, Drawings, and Other Papers of J. Goldsborough*

Bruff, April 2, 1849–July 20, 1851. Ed. Georgia W. Read and Ruth Gaines. New York: Columbia University Press, 1949.

Bryant, Edwin. *What I Saw in California.* New York: D. Appleton and Co., 1848.

Buckbee, Edna Bryan. *The Saga of Old Tuolumne.* New York: Press of the Pioneers, 1935.

Buffum, E. Gould. "Six Months in the Gold Mines." In *From Mexican Days to the Gold Rush.* Book 2, ed. Doyce B. Nunis, Jr. Chicago: R. R. Donnelley and Sons, 1993.

Burnett, Peter H. *Recollections and Opinions of an Old Pioneer.* New York: D. Appleton and Co., 1880.

California Blue Book, 1891. Comp. E. G. Waite, secretary of state. Sacramento: State Printing Office, 1891.

Carr, Albert Z. *The World and William Walker.* New York: Harper and Row, 1963.

Carr, John. *Pioneer Days in California, Historical and Personal Sketches.* Eureka: Times Publishing Co., 1891.

Caughey, John Walton. *Gold Is the Cornerstone.* Berkeley and Los Angeles: University of California Press, 1948.

———, ed. *The Indians of Southern California in 1852, The B. D. Wilson Report and a Selection of Contemporary Comment.* San Marino: Huntington Library, 1952.

Cisco, Jay Guy. *Historic Sumner County, Tennessee.* Nashville: Folk Keelin, 1909.

Cleland, Robert Glass. *Pathfinders.* Los Angeles: Powell Publishing Co., 1929.

Coffey, Reginald M. *The American Dominicans, A History of Saint Joseph's Province.* New York: Saint Martin De Porres Guild, 1970.

A Compilation of the Messages and Papers of the Presidents Prepared Under the Direction of the Joint Committee on Printing, of the House and Senate, Pursuant to an Act of the Fifty-second Congress of the United States. Vol. 6. New York: Bureau of National Literature, 1897.

Congressional Globe. 31st Congress, 1st session, September 10, 1850. Washington, D.C.: John C. Rives.

Cook, Sherburne Friend. *The Population of the California Indians 1769–1970.* Berkeley and Los Angeles: University of California Press, 1976.

Corlew, Robert E. *Tennessee, A Short History.* 2d ed. Knoxville: University of Tennessee Press, 1981.

Coulter, E. Merton. *William G. Brownlow, Fighting Parson of the Southern Highlands.* Knoxville: University of Tennessee Press, 1971.

Cutler, Wayne, ed. *Correspondence of James K. Polk.* Vol. 8, September–December, 1844. Knoxville: University of Tennessee Press, 1993.

Dana, Julian. *Sutter of California.* New York: Press of the Pioneers, 1934.

Davis, Winfield J. *History of Political Conventions in California, 1840–1892.* Sacramento: California State Library, 1893.

DeBow, J. D. B. *The Seventh Census of the United States, 1850.* Washington, D.C.: Robert Armstrong, 1853.

Delano, Alonzo. *Life on the Plains and Among the Diggins Being Scenes and Adventures of an Overland Journey to California.* Auburn: Miller, Aston, and Mulligan, 1854; New York: Arno Press, 1973.

D'Este, Carlos. *Patton: A Genius for War*. New York: HarperCollins, 1995.

Dobyns, Henry F., ed. *Hepah, California! The Journal of Cave Johnson Couts, 1848–1849*. Tucson: Arizona Pioneers Historical Society, 1961.

Douglass, Malcolm Curtis. *History, Memoirs and Genealogy of the Douglass Family*. Houston: Biggers Printing Co., 1957.

Drannan, William F. *Thirty-One Years on the Plains and in the Mountains*. Chicago: Rhodes and McClure Publishing Co., 1908.

Drury, Clifford Merrill. *William Anderson Scott, "No Ordinary Man."* Glendale, Calif.: Arthur H. Clark, 1967.

Durham, Walter T. *Before Tennessee: The Southwest Territory, 1790–1796*. Piney Flats, Tenn: Rocky Mount Historical Association, 1990.

———. *Old Sumner, A History of Sumner County, Tennessee, From 1805 to 1861*. Gallatin: Sumner County Library Board, 1972.

Ellison, William Henry. *A Self-Governing Dominion, California, 1849–1860*. Berkeley and Los Angeles: University of California Press, 1950.

———, ed. *The Life and Adventures of George Nidever*. Berkeley: University of California Press, 1937.

The Encyclopedia Americana. International Edition. Vol. 18. Danbury, Conn.: Grolier, 1992.

Evans, Robert Frank. *Notes on Land and Sea 1850*. Boston: Richard G. Badger, Gorham Press, 1922.

Fitzgerald, O. P. *California Sketches*. Nashville, Tenn.: Southern Methodist Publishing House, 1879.

Foreman, Grant. *Marcy and the Gold Seekers*. Norman: University of Oklahoma Press, 1939.

Gambill, Nell McNish. *The Kith and Kin of Capt. James Leeper and Susan Drake, His Wife, First Couple Married in Fort Nashborough, Tenn. 1780*. [Nashville]: published by the author, 1946.

Gardner, Charles K. *A Dictionary of All Officers Who Have Been Commissioned, or Have Been Appointed and Served, in the Army of the United States . . . .* New York: G. P. Putnam, 1853.

Gilbert, Frank T. *Illustrated Atlas and History of Yolo County, California*. San Francisco: De Pue and Co., 1879.

Goodwin, Cardinal Leonidas. *The Establishment of State Government in California, 1846–1850*. New York: Macmillan, 1914.

Gower, Herschel, and Jack Allen. *Pen and Sword: The Life and Journals of Randal W. McGavock*. Nashville: Tennessee Historical Commission, 1959.

Graf, Leroy P., and Ralph W. Haskins, eds. *The Papers of Andrew Johnson*. Vol. 1, 1822–51; Vol. 2, 1852–57. Knoxville: University of Tennessee Press, 1967, 1970.

Greene, Laurence. *The Filibuster, The Career of William Walker*. Indianapolis: Bobbs-Merrill, 1937.

Greer, James Kimmins. *Colonel Jack Hays, Texas Frontier Leader and California Builder*. New York: E. P. Dutton, 1952.

Hafen, LeRoy R., ed. *Trappers of the Far West*. Reprinted from *Mountain Men and Fur Trade of the Far West*, 10 vols., Glendale, Calif.: A. H. Clark, 1965–72; Lincoln: University of Nebraska Press, 1983.

————, ed. *Mountain Men and Fur Traders of the Far West*. Reprinted from *Mountain Men and Fur Trade of the Far West*, 10 vols., Glendale, Calif.: A. H. Clark, 1965–72; Lincoln: University of Nebraska Press, 1982.

Hafen, LeRoy R., and Ann W. Hafen. *Old Spanish Trail, Santa Fe to Los Angeles*. Glendale, Calif.: A. H. Clark, 1954.

Hale, Will T., and Dixon L. Merritt. *A History of Tennessee and Tennesseans*. Vol. 3. Chicago: Lewis Publishing Co., 1913.

Hardeman, Nicholas Perkins. *Wilderness Calling: The Hardeman Family in the American Westward Movement, 1750–1900*. Knoxville: University of Tennessee Press, 1977.

Harris, Benjamin Butler. *The Gila Trail, The Texas Argonauts and the California Gold Rush*. Ed. Richard H. Dillon. Norman: University of Oklahoma Press, 1960.

Hesseltine, William B., ed. *Dr. J. G. M. Ramsey Autobiography and Letters*. Nashville: Tennessee Historical Commission, 1954.

Hill, William E. *Reading, Writing, and Riding Along the Oregon-California Trails*. Independence, Mo.: Oregon-California Trails Association, 1993.

History of Tennessee, from the Earliest Time to the Present. . . . Nashville: Goodspeed Publishing Co., 1887.

A History of Tuolumne County, California. San Francisco: B. F. Alley, 1882.

Holliday, J. S. *The World Rushed In: The California Gold Rush Experience*. New York: Simon and Schuster, 1981.

Holmes, Kenneth L. *Ewing Young, Master Trapper*. Portland, Oreg.: n.p., 1967.

————, ed. and comp. *Covered Wagon Women, Diaries and Letters from the Western Trails, 1840–1890*. Vol. 1. Glendale, Calif.: Arthur Clark, 1983.

Holy Bible, Authorized King James Version. New York: Oxford University Press, 1967.

House Executive Document No. 17. 31st Congress, 1st session, 1849–50. Vol. 5, serial 573.

Hulbert, Archer Butler. *Forty-Niners, The Chronicle of the California Trail*. Boston: Little, Brown, 1949.

Hurst, John. *A Little Sketch of My Life*. Clarksville, Tenn.: Sallie Hurst Peay, 1927.

Hurtado, Albert L. *Indian Survival on the California Frontier*. New Haven: Yale University Press, 1988.

Hurwitz, Howard L. *An Encyclopedic Dictionary of American History*. New York: Washington Square Press, 1970.

Ingersoll, Luther A. *Ingersoll's Century Annals of San Bernardino County, 1679–1704; prefaced with a brief history of the state of California; supplemented with an encyclopedia of local biography and embellished with views of historic subjects and portraits of many of its representative people*. Los Angeles: published by the author, 1904.

Irving, Washington. *The Adventures of Captain Bonneville, U.S.A. in the Rocky Mountains and the Far West*. New York: Thomas Y. Crowell and Co., 1843.

Jackson, Joseph Henry. *Anybody's Gold, The Story of California's Mining Towns*. New York: D. Appleton-Century Co., 1941.

Jennings, Thelma. *The Nashville Convention: Southern Movement for Unity, 1848–1850*. Memphis: Memphis State University Press, 1980.

Johnson, Allen, and Dumas Malone, eds. *Dictionary of American Biography*. Vol. 3. New York: Charles Scribner's Sons, 1959.

Jones, Mrs. G. W., and Mrs. T. B. McAmis. *Life of Rev. A. G. Register, by His Daughters*. Nashville, Tenn.: Cumberland Presbyterian Publishing House, 1890.

Jostes, Barbara Donohoe. *John Parrott, Consul, 1811–1884, Selected Papers of a Western Pioneer*. San Francisco: n.p., 1972.

Journal of the House of Representatives of the United States Being the Second Session of the Thirtieth Congress Begun and Held in the City of Washington December 4, 1848, in the Seventy-third Year of the Independence of the United States. Washington, D.C.: Wendell and Benthuysen, 1848–49.

Kemble, Edward. *A History of California Newspapers, 1846–1858*. Los Gatos: Talisman Press, 1962.

Kroeber, A. L. *Handbook of the Indians of California*. Bulletin of American Ethnology #78. Washington, D.C.: Government Printing Office, 1925.

Lenoir, W. B. *History of Sweetwater Valley*. Richmond, Va.: Presbyterian Committee of Publication, 1916.

Levy, Joann. *They Saw the Elephant: Women in the California Gold Rush*. Hamden, Conn.: Archer Books, 1990.

Lewis, Oscar. *Sea Routes to the Gold Fields, The Migration by Water to California in 1849–1852*. New York: Knopf, 1949.

Los Angeles, A Guide to the City and Its Environs. American Guide Series. New York: Hasting House Publishers, 1941.

Losson, Christopher. *Tennessee's Forgotten Warriors: Frank Cheatham and His Confederate Division*. Knoxville: University of Tennessee Press, 1989.

Mace, O. Henry. *Between the Rivers, A History of Early Calaveras County, California*. 2d ed. Jackson, Calif.: Cenotto Publications, 1993.

Malloy, William M., comp. *Treaties, Conventions, International Acts, Protocols, and Agreements Between the United States of America and Other Powers, 1776 to 1909*. Vol. 1. Washington, D.C.: Government Printing Office, 1910.

Malone, Dumas, ed. *Dictionary of American Biography*. Vol. 12. New York: Charles Scribner's Sons, 1933.

McBride, Robert M., and Dan M. Robison. *Biographical Directory of the Tennessee General Assembly*. Vol. 1, 1796–1861; Vol. 2, 1861–1901. Nashville: Tennessee State Library and Archives and the Tennessee Historical Commission, 1975, 1979.

McCormac, Eugene Irving. *James K. Polk, A Political Biography*. Berkeley: University of California Press, 1922.

McGloin, John Bernard. *California's First Archbishop, The Life of Joseph Sadoc Alemany, 1814–1888*. New York: Herder and Herder, 1966.

Miners and Business Men's Directory for the Year Commencing January 1st, 1856. Columbia, Calif.: *Clipper* office, 1856.

Morgan, Dale L., ed. *Overland in 1846, Diaries and Letters of the California-Oregon Trail.* Vol. 1. Georgetown, Calif.: Talisman Press, 1963.

Myers, Jourdan G. *A History of the Parrott, Lee, Hix, and Wilmore Families.* Deer Park, Calif.: Kinko Copy Co., 1986.

Myers, Sandra L. *Ho for California, Women's Overland Diaries from the Huntington Library.* San Marino: Huntington Library, 1980.

Ninth U.S. Census. Vol. 1, June 1, 1870. Washington, D.C.: Government Printing Office, 1872.

O'Daniel, V. F. *The Father of the Church in Tennessee, or the Life, Times, and Character of the Right Reverend Richard Pius Miles, the First Bishop of Nashville.* Washington, D.C.: Dominicana, 1926.

O'Meara, James. *Broderick and Gwin.* San Francisco: Bacon and Co., 1881.

[O'Meara, James]. *The Vigilance Committee of 1856.* San Francisco: James H. Barry, 1887.

Oliphant, J. Orin, ed. *On the Arkansas Route to California in 1849, The Journal of Robert B. Green of Lewisburg, Pennsylvania.* Kinsburg, Pa.: Bucknell University Press, 1955.

Paden, Irene D., ed. *The Journal of Madison Berryman Moorman, 1850–51.* San Francisco: California Historical Society, 1948.

Parks, Joseph Howard. *John Bell of Tennessee.* Baton Rouge: Louisiana State University Press, 1950.

Parsons, George Frederic. "The Life and Adventures of James Wilson Marshall." In *From Mexican Days to the Gold Rush.* Book 1, ed. Doyce B. Nunis, Jr. Chicago: R. R. Donnelley and Sons, 1993.

Paul, Rodman W. *California Gold, The Beginning of Mining in the Far West.* Cambridge: Harvard University Press, 1947.

———. *Mining Frontiers of the American West, 1848–1880.* New York: Holt, Rinehart and Winston, 1963.

Pearson, Eugene L. *A Pearson Family History.* N.p.: published by the author, 1962.

Perkins, William. *Three Years in California . . . Journal of Life at Sonora 1849–1852.* Ed. Dale L. Morgan and James R. Scobie. Berkeley: University of California Press, 1964.

Potter, David M. *The Impending Crisis 1848–1861.* Comp. and ed. Don E. Fehrenbacher. New York: Harper and Row, 1976.

Rasmussen, Louis J. *California Wagon Train Lists.* Vol. 1. Colma, Calif.: San Francisco Historic Records, 1994.

———. *San Francisco Ship Passenger Lists.* Vols. 3 and 4. Colma, Calif.: San Francisco Historic Records, 1967, 1970.

Rose, Victor M. *The Life and Services of Gen. Ben McCulloch.* Philadelphia: Pictorial Bureau of the Press, 1888.

Shinn, Charles Howard. *Mining Camps, A Study in American Frontier Government.* New York: Knopf, 1948.

Simmons, J. C. *The History of Southern Methodism on the Pacific Coast*. Nashville, Tenn.: Southern Methodist Publishing House, 1886.

Soule, Frank, John H. Gihon, and James Nisbet. *The Annals of San Francisco*. New York: D. Appleton and Co., 1854.

Speech of Mr. Andrew Ewing of Tennessee on the Admission of California Delivered in the House of Representatives, April 18, 1850. Washington, D.C.: John T. Towers, 1850.

Speech of M. P. Gentry of Tenn., on the Admission of California, Delivered in the House of Representatives, U.S., Monday, June 10, 1850. Washington, D.C.: Gideon and Co., 1850.

Stover, Samuel Murray. *Diary of Samuel Murray Stover En Route to California, 1849*. Elizabethton, Tenn: H. M. Folsom, 1939.

Strentzel, Louisiana. "A Letter from California, 1849." In *Covered Wagon Women, Diaries and Letters from the Western Trails, 1840–1890*, ed. Kenneth L. Holmes. Vol. 1. Glendale, Calif.: Arthur Clark, 1983.

Thomas, Lately. *Between Two Empires, The Life Story of California's First Senator William McKendree Gwin*. Boston: Houghton Mifflin, 1969.

Titus, W. P. *Picturesque Clarksville, Past and Present*. Clarksville, Tenn.: published by the author, 1887.

Unruh, John D., Jr. *The Plains Across*. Chicago: University of Illinois Press, 1979.

Walker, William. *The War in Nicaragua*. Mobile: S. H. Goetzel and Co., 1860.

White, Robert H. *Messages of the Governors of Tennessee, 1845–1857*. Vol. 4. Nashville: Tennessee Historical Commission, 1957.

Wicher, Edward Arthur. *The Presbyterian Church in California, 1849–1927*. New York: Grafton Press, 1927.

Williams, Mary Floyd. *History of the San Francisco Committee of Vigilance of 1851. A Study of Social Control on the California Frontier in the Days of the Gold Rush*. New York: Da Capo Press, 1969.

Wilson, John Albert. *History of Los Angeles County, California*. Oakland: Thompson and West, 1880.

Young, Otis E. *The West of Philip St. George Cooke, 1809–1895*. Glendale, Calif.: Arthur H. Clark, 1955.

ARTICLES

Albin, Ray R. "The Perkins Case: The Ordeal of Three Slaves in Gold Rush California." *California History* (The Magazine of the California Historical Society) 67, no. 4 (Dec. 1988).

Bender, A. B. "Opening Routes Across West Texas, 1848–1850." *Southwestern Historical Quarterly* 37, no. 2 (Oct. 1933).

"Bound for the Land of Canaan, Ho! The Diary of Levi Stowell, 1849," with introduction and notes by Marco G. Thorne. *California Historical Society Quarterly* 27, no. 2 (June 1948); no. 3 (Sept. 1948); 28, no. 1 (Mar. 1949).

Bryant, Berryman. "Reminiscences of California, 1849–1852." *California Historical Society Quarterly* 11, no. 1 (Mar. 1932).

Caughey, John Walton. "Don Benito Wilson, An Average Southern Californian." *Huntington Library Quarterly* 2, no. 3 (Apr. 1939).

Culmer, Frederic A., ed. "California Letter of John Wilson, 1850." *Missouri Historical Review* 24, no. 2 (Jan. 1930).

Ellison, William Henry, ed. "Memoirs of Hon. William M. Gwin." *California Historical Society Quarterly* 19, nos. 1–4 (1940).

Etter, Patricia A. "Through Mexico in '49." *Bulletin of Bibliography* 46, no. 3 (Sept. 1989).

Florcken, Herbert L., arr. "The Law and Order View of the San Francisco Vigilance Committee of 1856." Parts 1, 2, and 3. *California State Historical Society Quarterly* 14, no. 4 (Dec. 1935); 15, no. 1 (Mar. 1936); 15, no. 2 (June 1936).

Franklin, William E. "A Forgotten Chapter in California History: Peter H. Burnett and John A. Sutter's Fortune." *California Historical Society Quarterly* 41, no. 4 (Dec. 1962).

———. "Peter H. Burnett and the Provisional Government Movement." *California Historical Society Quarterly* 40, no. 2 (June 1961).

———. "The Religious Ardor of Peter H. Burnett, California's First American Governor." *California Historical Society Quarterly* 45, no. 2 (June 1966).

Hale, Robin C. "Gold Deposits of the Coker Creek District, Monroe County, Tennessee." *Bulletin 72*, State of Tennessee, Department of Geology, Nashville, 1974.

Herndon, Dallas Tabor. "The Nashville Convention of 1850." *The Transactions*, no. 5 (1904), reprint no. 35, Alabama Historical Society, Montgomery, 1905.

Huggins, Dorothy H., comp. "Continuation of the Annals of San Francisco." *California Historical Society Quarterly* 16, no. 1 (Mar. 1937); no. 3 (Sept. 1937).

Hurt, Peyton. "The Rise and Fall of the 'Know-Nothings' in California." *California Historical Society Quarterly* 9, no. 1 (Mar. 1930); no. 2 (June 1930).

Knapp, Frank A., Jr. "Biographical Traces of Consul John Parrott." *California Historical Society Quarterly* 34, no. 2 (June 1955).

"Letters of the California Gold Rush Days, 1849–1852." *Historic Maury* 13, no. 3 (July–Sept. 1977).

Lyman, George D. "The Scalpel Under Three Flags." *California Historical Society Quarterly* 4, no. 2 (June 1925).

Murphy, Virginia Reed. "Across the Plains in the Donner Party (1846)." *Century Magazine* 42 (July 1891).

Noel, Thomas J. "W. Wilberforce A. Ramsey, Esq., and the California Gold Rush." *Journal of the West* 12, no. 4 (Oct. 1973).

O'Steen, Neal. "UT's Gold Rush Adventurers: The East Tennessee Company." *Tennessee Alumnus* (winter 1984).

———. "UT's Gold Rush Adventurers: The Monroe County Boys." *Tennessee Alumnus* (fall 1983).

———. "UT's Gold Rush Adventurers: The Rosborough Brothers." *Tennessee Alumnus* (summer 1983).

Rolle, Andrew F. "William Heath Davis and the Founding of American San Diego." *California Historical Society Quarterly* 31, no. 1 (Mar. 1952).

Rosborough, Alex. J. "A. M. Rosborough, Special Indian Agent." *California Historical Society Quarterly* 26, no. 3 (Sept. 1947).

Savage, W. Sherman. "The Negro on the Mining Frontier." *Journal of Negro History* 30, no. 1 (Jan. 1945).

"Sherman Was There, The Recollections of Major Edwin A. Sherman." With an introduction by Allen B. Sherman. *California Historical Society Quarterly* 24, no. 1 (Mar. 1945).

Shouse, Sarah N. "None Dream But of Success, the Story of a Young Tennessean's Journey to the Gold Fields of California." *Tennessee Historical Quarterly* 36, no. 4 (winter 1977).

Shutes, Milton H. "Henry Douglas Bacon, 1813–1893." *California Historical Society Quarterly* 26, no. 3 (Sept. 1947).

"Stories of a Forty-Niner." *Historic Maury* 13, no. 1 (Jan.–Mar. 1977).

Teng, Yuan Chung. "Reverend Issachar Jacox Roberts and the Tai Ping Rebellion." *Journal of Asian Studies* 23, no. 1 (Nov. 1963).

Thomson, Virginia. "Note on George Nidever, a Clean-Living and Up-Right Trapper." *California Historical Society Quarterly* 32, no. 3 (Sept. 1953).

"To California Through Texas and Mexico, The Diary and Letters of Thomas B. Eastland and Joseph G. Eastland, His Son." Parts 1 and 2. *California Historical Society Quarterly* 18, no. 2 (June 1939); no. 3 (Sept. 1939).

Waggoner, W. W. "The Donner Party and Relief Hill." *California Historical Society Quarterly* 10, no. 4 (Dec. 1931).

"Walker-Heiss Papers, Some Diplomatic Correspondence of the Walker Regime in Nicaragua." *Tennessee Historical Magazine* 1, no. 4 (Dec. 1915).

Wheat, Carl I., ed. "California's Bantam Cock, The Journals of Charles E. DeLong, 1854–1863." *California Historical Society Quarterly* 10, no. 1 (Mar. 1931).

White, Kate. "The Diary of a 'Forty-Niner'—Jacob Stuart." *Tennessee Historical Magazine*, series 2, Vol. 1, no. 4 (July 1931).

White, Robert H. "The Volunteer State." *Tennessee Historical Quarterly* 15, no. 1 (Mar. 1956).

Williams, Samuel Cole, ed. "Journal of Events (1825–1873) of David Anderson Deaderick." ETHS *Publications*, no. 9 (1937).

Winther, Oscar Osburn, ed. "From Tennessee to California in 1849: Letters of the Reeve Family of Medford, New Jersey." *Journal of the Rutgers University Library* 11, no. 2 (June 1948).

Wyllys, Rufus Kay. "Henry A. Crabb—A Tragedy of the Sonora Frontier." *Pacific Historical Review* 9, no. 1 (Mar. 1940).

UNPUBLISHED MATERIALS

Barry, David. Papers. Private collection.

Battle, Lucious Lucullus. "The Annals of Lucious Lucullus Battle, M.D., 1849–1851."

Typescript of memoir in the Memphis Room Collection of the Memphis and Shelby County Library.

Bell, John. Papers. Tennessee State Library and Archives (TSLA), Nashville.

Bostick, Harding P. Collection. Tennessee Historical Society (THS), TSLA.

Boyles, Eliza H. (Ball) Gordon. Papers, 1823–81. Special Collections, William R. Perkins Library, Duke University, Durham.

Brown, Neill S. Governors Papers, 1847–49, TSLA.

Brown and Harris Papers. Originals in private collection, Birmingham, Alabama, typescripts, Sumner County Archives, Gallatin.

California Secretary of State, *California Census of 1852*, transcribed by the Daughters of the American Revolution. Microfilm #82, TSLA.

Campbell, David. Papers. Microfilm, TSLA; originals in Special Collections, William R. Perkins Library, Duke University, Durham.

Cooper Family Papers. TSLA.

Correspondence by author. TSLA.

Deaderick, David Anderson. Diary, 1825–72. Typescript, Special Collections, Hoskins Library, University of Tennessee, Knoxville.

Donner Party Letters. TSLA.

Duffy Papers. TSLA.

Edmondson Family Papers. TSLA.

Hanlon, Russell. Collection. McClung Historical Collection, Knoxville Public Library.

Harsh, Rebecca Malone. Letter to author, February 1, 1971.

Heiskell, Hugh Brown. Diary. Microfilm, TSLA.

Heiskell Family Manuscripts. TSLA.

Heiss, John P. Papers, 1835–72. THS, TSLA.

Jackson, William J. Letters. Typescript courtesy Robert Winn Jackson, Paris, Tenn.

Long, John. Papers. Special Collections, William R. Perkins Library, Duke University, Durham.

MacFarland, Lonsdale Porter. "Dr. James Porter MacFarland." Typescript in possession of Alfred Towson MacFarland.

McDaniel, Coleman. Diary. TSLA.

Metcalf, Barbara Ann. "Oliver M. Wozencraft in California, 1849–1887." Master's thesis, University of Southern California, 1963.

Muster Roll of Captain William M. Blackmore's Company, in the 1st Regiment (1st Brigade), of Tennessee Volunteers, commanded by Col. W. B. Campbell, called into the service of the United States by the President under the Act of Congress approved May 13, 1846, from the 31st day of October, 1846, when last mustered, to the 30th day of April, 1847, National Archives.

O'Steen, Neal. Manuscript. In possession of author, Knoxville, Tenn.

Parrott, John. Letters. Huntington Library, San Marino, Calif.

Ramsey Papers. Special Collections, Hoskins Library, University of Tennessee, Knoxville.

Rushing, Joseph L. Papers. TSLA.

Seat, Benton Bell. "Memoirs, 1849–1916." Typescript courtesy of Frederick M. Culp, Gibson County Historian, Trenton, Tenn.

Shiloh Cumberland Presbyterian Church Minutes, TSLA.

Sumner County, Tennessee, Records.

    Loose Court Records, Sumner County Archives.

Thomson, Kenneth C. Private collection.

Walker, William. Letters, 1845–55. THS, TSLA.

Watkins, Joseph S. Letter, January 14, 1848. Virginia Historical Society Collections, Richmond.

Wilson County, Tennessee, Records.

Wills and Inventories, Book D.

Wright and Green Family Papers. Southern Historical Collection, University of North Carolina, Chapel Hill.

Wynne, George W. Collection. Wynne Family Papers, TSLA.

TENNESSEE NEWSPAPERS

Athens *Post*.

Banner of Peace and Cumberland Presbyterian Advocate.

Bedford *Yeoman*.

Brownlow's Knoxville *Whig and Independent Journal*.

Clarksville *Jeffersonian*.

Franklin *Western Weekly Review*.

Jackson *Whig*.

Jonesborough *Herald and Tribune*.

Jonesborough *Independent Journal*.

Jonesborough *Railroad Journal*.

Jonesborough *Whig and Independent Journal*.

Knoxville *Register*.

Knoxville *Whig and Independent Journal*.

Lebanon *Banner of Peace and Cumberland Presbyterian Advocate*.

The Maury Intelligencer.

Memphis *Daily Appeal*.

Memphis *Daily Eagle*.

Memphis *Daily Enquirer*.

Memphis *Eagle and Enquirer*.

Nashville *Christian Advocate*.

Nashville *Daily American*.

Nashville *Daily Centre State American*.

Nashville *Daily Evening Reporter*.

Nashville *Daily Gazette*.

Nashville *Daily Union*.
Nashville and Louisville *Christian Advocate*.
Nashville *Republican Banner*.
Nashville *Republican Banner and True Whig*.
Nashville *True Whig*.
Nashville *Union*.
Nashville *Union and American*.
Nashville *Whig*.
Paris *Gazetteer*.
Paris *Tribune*.
Presbyterian Record.
Pulaski *Western Star*.
Republican Banner and Nashville *Whig*.
Rogersville *Times*.
Tennessee *Baptist*.
Warren County *News*.

OTHER NEWSPAPERS

Arkansas *State Democrat*.
Arkansas *State Gazette*.
New York *Herald*.
Los Angeles *Star*.
Sacramento *Daily Democratic State Journal*.
Sacramento *Placer Times*.
San Francisco *Alta California*.
San Francisco *Chronicle*.
San Francisco *Daily Evening Picayune*.
San Joaquin *Republican*.
San Jose *Mercury News*.
San Jose *Pioneer*.
St. Joseph *Gazette*.

TENNESSEE COUNTY HISTORICAL PERIODICALS*

Lincoln County, Tennessee, Pioneers.
Studies in Polk County History.
Weakley Remembered.

*In holdings of Tennessee State Library and Archives.

Index

Walter T. Durham, whose family has resided in Middle Tennessee since the early nineteenth century, is the author of numerous books and articles on Tennessee history. He won the Award of Merit from the American Association for State and Local History for his books *The Great Leap Westward* and *Old Sumner*. His *Before Tennessee: The Southwest Territory, 1790–1796* won the Tennessee History Book Award in 1990.

VOLUNTEER FORTY-NINERS

was composed electronically
using Cochin types, with displays in
Engravers LH Bold and Futura Light.
The book was printed on 60# Natural Smooth acid-free,
recycled paper and was Smyth sewn and cased in Roxite B-grade cloth
over 88-point binder's boards, with head bands and illustrated end leaves,
by Braun-Brumfield, Inc. The dust jacket was printed in three colors by
Vanderbilt University Printing Services.
Book and dust jacket designs are the work of Gary Gore.
Published by Vanderbilt University Press
Nashville, Tennessee 37235